EVIL JUSTICE

"You will go back to Lucel-Lor. You will find Richius Vantran. And you will steal his daughter for me."

"What? . . ."

"That's it, Simon. That's my price. Bring me the jackal's daughter."

"But, my lord, Vantran is guarded. I could never get that close to him. There's no way—"

"You underestimate yourself, my friend," laughed Biagio. "You can do it. You're my best agent, the only one who can pull it off. Get into Vantran's confidence. Find out his plans. Make him trust you. Then, when his guard is down, take the child."

"But why?" sputtered the agent. "What do you want with the girl? She's just a baby . . ."

"I want what I've always wanted," Biagio roared. "I want Vantran to suffer. I will take what is precious to him. It is justice. Nothing more."

Also by John Marco:

THE JACKAL OF NAR

THE GRAND DESIGN

BOOK TWO OF
Tyrants and Kings

JOHN MARCO

BANTAM BOOKS
NEW YORK · TORONTO · LONDON · SYDNEY · AUCKLAND

THE GRAND DESIGN

A Bantam Spectra Book / April 2000

Map by James Sinclair.

Library of Congress Cataloging-in-Publication Data
Marco, John.
The grand design / John Marco.
p. cm.—(Tyrants and kings ; bk. 2)
ISBN 0-553-38022-2
I. Title. II. Series: Marco, John. Tyrants and kings ; bk. 2.
PS3563.A63628G73 2000
813' .54—dc21 99-36358
CIP

Published simultaneously in the United States and Canada

Bantam Books are published by Bantam Books, a
division of Random House, Inc. Its trademark, consisting
of the words "Bantam Books" and the portrayal of a
rooster, is Registered in U.S. Patent and Trademark Office
and in other countries. Marca Registrada. Bantam Books,
1540 Broadway, New York, New York, 10036.

PRINTED IN THE UNITED STATES OF AMERICA

FFG 10 9 8 7 6 5 4 3 2 1

For my Grandfather

ACKNOWLEDGMENTS

The author would like to acknowledge the help and support of the following special people:

Russell Galen, Danny Baror, Anne Lesley Groell, Juliet Combes, Kristen Britain, Paul Goat Allen, Ted Xidas, Victoria Strauss, Julie Jones, and Douglas Beekman.

And as always, thanks to Deborah, for too much to mention.

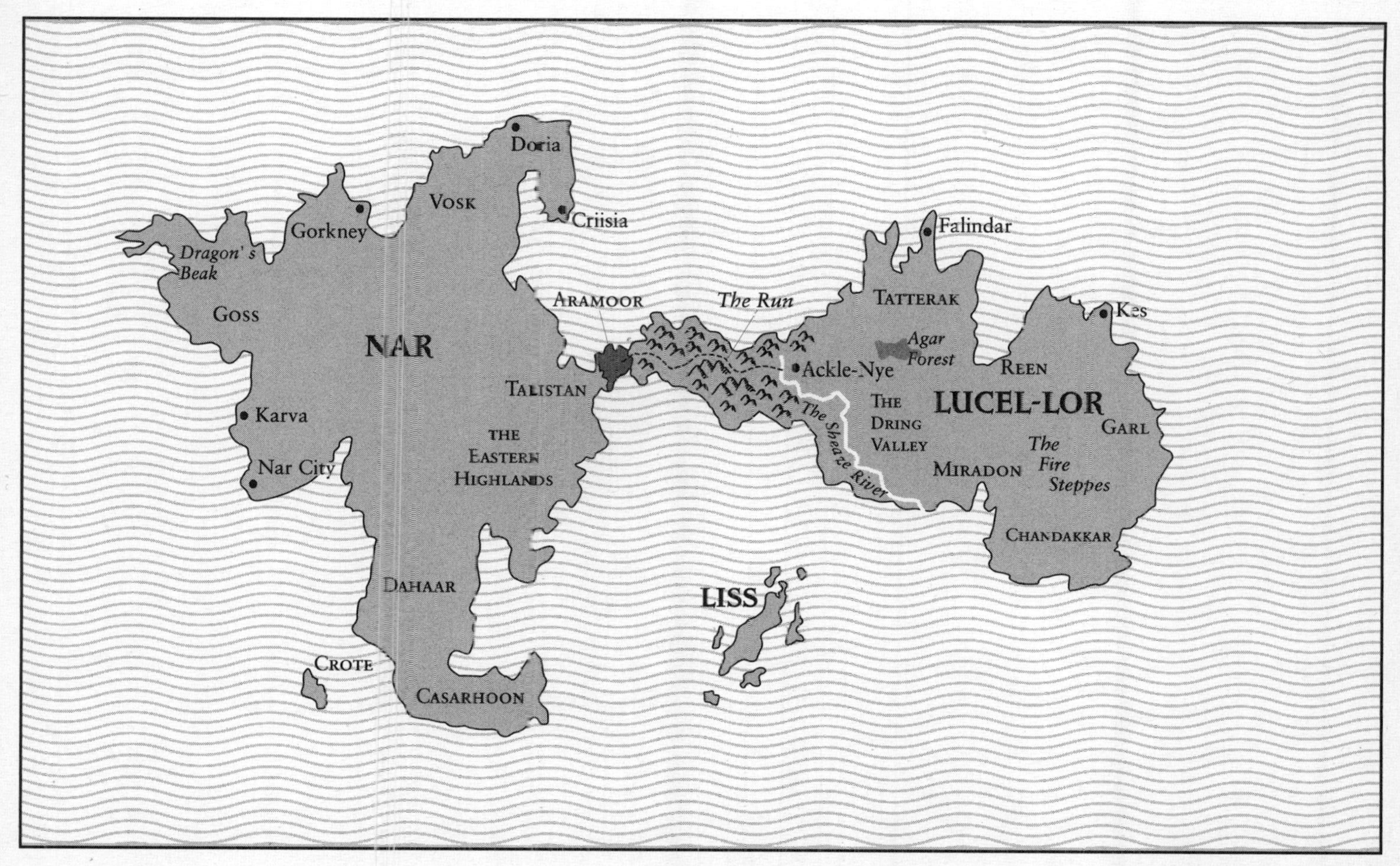

Doria
Vosk
Criisia
Gorkney
Dragon's Beak
Goss
NAR
Aramoor
The Run
Falindar
Tatterak
Kes
Agar Forest
Ackle-Nye
Reen
Talistan
Karva
The Dring Valley
LUCEL-LOR
Garl
The Eastern Highlands
Nar City
The Sheaze River
Miradon
The Fire Steppes
Chandakkar
Dahaar
LISS
Crote
Casarhoon

THE GRAND DESIGN

ONE

The Light of God

The night burned a pulsing orange.

General Vorto, supreme commander of the legions of Nar, stood on a hillside beneath the red flash of rockets, safely distant from the bombardment hammering the walls of Goth. It was a cold night with frost in the air. He could see the crystalline snow in the sky and on his eyelashes. The northern gusts blew the battle rockets up and over the city and bent the fiery plumes of flame cannons. Goth's tall walls glowed a molten amber at its weakest parts, and in the city's center small fires smoldered, the result of lucky rocket shots. Gothan archers rimmed the catwalks and battlements, raining down arrows on the thousand legionnaires encircling the city. High in the hills, rocket launchers sent off their missiles, while on the ground war wagons lumbered on their metal tracks, grinding the earth to pulp. Inside the iron tanks, teams of gunners pumped kerosene fuel into the needle-noses of flame cannons and blasted away at the unyielding stone of Goth.

The war machines of Nar were at work.

General Vorto pulled off a gauntlet and tested the wind with a finger. Southeasterly and strong, he determined. Too damn strong. A curse sprang to his lips as he pulled his metal glove back on. So far, the Walled City didn't seem to be softening from his attack, nor had the winds abated to cooperate. It had only been a few hours since he'd begun his attack but he was already growing impatient—not a good trait for a general. He ground his teeth together in frustration, and watched as the city of Goth withstood all he could throw against it.

"Resist, then," he grumbled. "Soon we will have the ram in place."

Nearby on the hillside, the gunners of a modified acid launcher awaited their general's orders. They had loaded the first cannister of Formula B hours ago, when they'd first arrived around the city. Vorto had hoped the wind might cooperate, but the breeze had picked up and so the order to fire had never come. There were five more such launchers in the hills around Goth, all primed like this one, all awaiting Vorto's order to fire. Vorto blew into his hands to warm them.

"They are strong ones," said the general to his aide, the slim and dour-faced Colonel Kye. "I've underestimated them. They have a stomach for siege, it seems. I would have thought Lokken weaker than this."

"Duke Lokken *is* weak," corrected Kye. He had a rasping voice that Vorto had to strain to understand, the result of a Triin arrow through his windpipe. "When the dawn comes he will see what's out here waiting for him, and he will surrender." The colonel smiled one of his sour smiles. "I am optimistic."

"Yes, you can afford to be," said Vorto. "I cannot." He pointed toward the city's towering walls, thick with archers ignoring the bombardment. "Look. See how many men he has? He could hold out for weeks in there. And these damned winds . . ." Vorto halted, mouthing a silent prayer. God made the winds, and he had no right to curse them. He confessed his sin, then turned his attention to the giant launcher sitting nearby. Ten cannisters of Formula B waited beside the magazine, ready for loading. The bellows that would propel the cannisters was swelled with air. It groaned with the sound of stretched leather. Vorto reached down and picked up one of the cannisters. His gunners gasped and inched away. The general held the cannister up to inspect it, turning it in the pulsing rocket light. The cylindrical container was no bigger than his head. Inside it, he could feel liquid sloshing around. There were two chambers in the cannister, one full of water, the other loaded with Formula B, the dried pellets the war labs had synthesized. Upon impact, the cannister would shatter and the components would mix. Any small breeze would do the rest.

Theoretically. Formula B had never been tested in the field. Bovadin had fled Nar before its perfection, leaving a handful of tinkerers behind to finish his work. Formula A had proved too caustic to transport, even in its dry state. But Formula B, the war labs had assured Vorto, was perfect. They had tried it on prisoners with remarkable results, and they were sure fifty cannisters of the stuff would be enough to wipe out Goth.

But the winds would have to cooperate.

Brooding, Vorto put down the cannister. Much as he wanted to, he couldn't risk detonating the formula in such stiff winds. The walls of Goth were high, certainly, but were they high enough to contain the gas? And what if one of the cannisters landed outside the walls? If there was a safe distance from the caustic fumes, no one knew its measure. Maybe Bovadin did, but the midget was in Crote now, hiding with the sodomite Biagio.

Have faith, the general reminded himself.

"If I fly with dragons, and dwell in the darkest parts of the earth," he said, "even there will Thy right hand guide me, and Thy light shine a path for me." Vorto smiled dispassionately at his colonel, who was not a religious man. "The Book of Gallion," he declared. "Chapter eleven, verse nineteen. Do you know what it means, Kye?"

Kye was unmoved. Unlike Vorto, he followed the edicts of Archbishop Herrith out of duty alone, and not of any sense of the mystic. Vorto had tried, unsuccessfully, to convince the colonel of the reality of Heaven, but Kye had remained skeptical. He was a loyal man, though, and a fine soldier, so Vorto overlooked the older man's heresy.

"They fly the flag," said Colonel Kye simply. "That's all I know."

Behind Kye, Vorto could see the city of Goth aglow in rocket fire, its stone towers tall and defiant. And at the city's heart, billowing in the winds atop Lokken's fortress, waved the Black Flag, that hated symbol of old Nar. It was a crime to fly that banner now, but Lokken and others like him flaunted Herrith's commandments. Vorto would not be satisfied until he pulled down that flag and stuffed it down Duke Lokken's lying throat himself.

Since the death of Arkus and Herrith's ascension, there was only one flag that the nations of Nar were allowed to fly. It was the same banner Vorto's men milled under now, a radiant field of gold harboring a rising sun. Herrith himself had designed the standard. And the bishop had named it wisely, and blessed it with the power to rebuke the Black Renaissance.

It was called the Light of God.

And whenever Vorto saw it, he felt a catch in his throat. Now, as they circled the enormous Walled City, his standard bearers held the Light of God high so that the glare of the rockets alighted on it like the touch of heaven and all the misguided in Goth could see it. Tonight they flew their Black Flag—tonight they displayed their loyalty to a dead Emperor and his equally dead ideals—but on the morrow if the winds were fair, the Light of God would wave above Goth forever.

"Check your azimuth," Vorto commanded the gunners. "I want no mistakes when we launch."

The gunnery chief looked at his leader questioningly. "Are we launching, sir?"

"We will be," replied Vorto. He strode over to the weapon and checked the gauges himself. It was unfamiliar work, but the crude dials and sliders were simple to understand. A small pointer along the barrel displayed the estimated distance in forty-yard increments. His gunners had set the range on maximum and pointed the barrel, high enough to scale Goth's wall and lob the cannisters into the city. Curious, Vorto regarded his gunners.

"Best guess, Chief. These winds . . . too much?"

The soldier wrinkled his nose and looked up into the night. The snow flurries were coming down in a slant. "Hard to say, sir. The cannisters are heavy, so they should fly straight. But that's a damn high wall. We'd have to call back the wagons before I'd be comfortable."

Vorto nodded. "Agreed. Be ready."

The general turned and walked to his warhorse. The powerful dapple-gray, outfitted with hammered armor, snorted unhappily as its master mounted. Vorto was an enormous man, and so required an equally enormous horse to support him. This one was from Aramoor and big in the shanks. Upon Vorto's back was strapped his axe, the only weapon he favored since the loss of two fingers. Though less precise than a sword, he had found the axe at least as devastating in battle, and its twin blades gave him a desirably frightening presence. He wore no helmet, for he liked the sounds of battle and feared no arrow. He armored himself traditionally in black, but he knew his greatest protection came from Heaven. He wore his head shaved and his cheeks smooth, and he adorned his hands with silver gauntlets polished to a mirror shine. Big in the extreme, he was not fat at all, but rather muscled the way a bull is muscled, and when he was shirtless his deltoids gave him the appearance of a wing-spanned hawk or the hood of a cobra. Save for Herrith himself, no man in the new Nar held more power than he, and no man was more feared.

Everything about Vorto was inhuman—particularly his eyes. They were a faded blue, like two lusterless gems, dim and without life. As a boy they had been brown, but the potions of the war labs had changed that. The same potions that had once made him very near immortal had done strange things to Vorto's body. Like Arkus and the rest of the dead emperor's Iron Circle, they had all become addicts, dependent on Bovadin's amazing narcotic. But since the little scientist's departure there had been no more of the drug. It was just one more secret Bovadin had taken with him to Crote, and so Vorto and the others loyal to Herrith had learned to live without it, despite the bone-crushing withdrawal. Sometimes, when it was quiet and he was alone,

Vorto still had cravings, but with God's help he had tamed his demons. Others had not been so lucky. Some of the foppish Naren lords had been unable to withstand the pain and had perished. A few had even flung themselves out of Nar's towers rather than endure another moment of agony.

But Vorto was more stout-hearted than those weaklings. He had overcome the drug and Biagio's schemes for the throne, and he considered that his proudest struggle. Now he and Herrith were rid of this tribulation, mostly, and ready to destroy the rest of Biagio's designs. There was wise work to be done in Nar these days. Men like Lokken still held on to the ideals of the Black Renaissance, Arkus' godless disease. The Black Flag still flew in at least four other nations, and those who didn't fly the symbol of the past often refused to fly the flag of the future. Very few had come willingly to the Light of God. Archbishop Herrith could count only a handful of the Naren nations as true allies. But he had Vorto behind him, and Vorto had all the legions of Nar. In time, Lokken and everyone like him would heel.

God's will, thought Vorto as he spied the city. *God's will that they should die this way. Like cows on the killing floor.*

In the days of Arkus and the Black Renaissance, Vorto had trod the world like a prince. He had maimed and slaughtered for the emperor's false ideals, and had bargained away his soul for soft beds and lewd company. But he was not that man anymore. He had heard the call of the Lord and had been cleansed. Herrith and God had saved him.

Vorto had no remorse. The Black Renaissance was a cancer, and the only way to deal with it was to eradicate it utterly. Ideas were powerful, hard to kill. To leave a trace of them was to invite death. Those who were called to do Heaven's work needed to be iron-willed and, sometimes, iron-stomached. There would be a stench from Goth for months, and the buzzards would feast, but Duke Lokken would be dead. Biagio would have one less ally on Naren soil to threaten the throne, and the Light of God would fly above the city, a symbol of God and his mercy.

Vorto spurred on his horse and guided it down the slope. When this was over, he would sleep well. Colonel Kye mounted his own horse and followed his superior down the hillside, sidling up to Vorto and shooting him a suspect stare.

"We're going to launch?" he asked. "When?"

"When I say so, Kye."

"But the winds . . ."

"I've come a long way to bring justice to Duke Lokken and his rebels," snapped Vorto. "I won't leave defeated."

Kye grimaced. "Begging the general's pardon, but I think you just want to try the formula."

Vorto shrugged. Kye was almost a friend, and sometimes overly familiar. "It's God's will," he said simply. "When the other nations see what's happened here, they will think twice about siding with Biagio. They all have armies, Kye. Vosk, Dragon's Beak, Doria. We can't be everywhere. Biagio knows this. And the memory of Arkus is strong." He gave his second a mordant glare. "We must be at least as strong."

"General," said Kye evenly. "We have enough men to take the city."

"I intend to take the city and more, Kye. Now get that damned ram into position. It's time we knocked on Lokken's door."

Inside his castle of stone and cedar, Duke Lokken of Goth kept the lights out. The rockets were imprecise and hardly a threat to his fortress at all, but his family was in this room and Lokken was a superstitious man. One stray battle rocket, one lucky shot, and a fire might start that would consume them all. Around his private chambers high in the western tower, there were guards aplenty to hold back Vorto's legions, but they could do nothing against the onslaught of flame cannons and rockets. Lokken stood by a window, brooding over his falling city, his face awash in the glare. In his chambers were his wife and two daughters. His eldest and only son was outside somewhere, probably on the wall.

A rocket slammed into the courtyard below, rattling the tower. In the hills around the city, the duke could see the distant flares of launchers as they sent their missiles screaming skyward. His daughters were crying. The bombardment had hardly dented his wall, but it had already turned the brains of his people to mush. Even Lokken was starting to fracture.

The room was dark. Lokken felt a shiver of cold and the unmistakable shoulder-tapping of remorse. Overhead, the Black Flag of Nar still flew above his castle, along with Lion's Blood, Goth's own standard. In a fit of outrage, Lokken had ordered that detestable banner of Herrith's shredded. He had sent the flag's remains to the bishop in Nar City. But now, looking down at the legions, he wondered if his valor had merely been bravado, and he regretted the ugly death he had invited for his family.

Arkus had not been a perfect emperor. He had been a tyrant, and Biagio was probably no better. But he had been *Lokken's* tyrant, and he had understood the importance of a nation's pride. Never once had Arkus asked any country of the Empire to lower their own flag, nor did he ever insist that they fly the Black Flag. Lokken had complied with Arkus for years, and for years the old man had left Goth alone, content with the yearly taxes Lokken sent to Nar City. But this Herrith was a demon.

Lokken missed Arkus. He missed the old ideals of the Black Renaissance, of peace through strength and world domination. And when the old man had finally died, Lokken knew with whom to side.

"Kill me if you can," whispered the duke. "I will never fly your flag."

"Uncle?"

At the sound of the voice Lokken turned from the window. There in the darkness was little Lorla, her face full of dread. She had dressed for travel, as ordered. In her tiny hands she clutched a leather bag full of food, hopefully enough to get her to safety. Her brilliant green eyes looked up at Lokken with profound sadness.

"I'm ready, Uncle," she said. Her eight-year-old's face tried to smile, but there was no joy in the expression. Lokken dropped down to a knee and took her hand. It was small and soft, belying the truth of her nature. Not surprisingly, Lorla hadn't shed a single tear throughout the entire bombardment. Lokken was proud of her.

"I wish I could take you to Duke Enli myself," he said. "But you'll be safe with Daevn. He knows the way better than any of my men. He'll get you past the legions."

Lorla looked dubious. "I've seen them through my window. There may be too many to pass. And they won't hesitate to kill me."

Lokken smiled. "Then you mustn't get caught, right?" He ran his hand through her splendid hair. She had been his ward for almost a year now, ever since Nar fell to Herrith. Biagio had asked Lokken to keep the child safe, and though Lokken had thought it a hardship at the time, he had adored every moment he'd spent with Lorla. Blood might have separated them, but she still felt every bit his daughter.

"Lorla," began the duke solemnly. "I don't know what's going to happen to you, even if you do reach Dragon's Beak. Biagio hasn't told me anything more about you, and I've never met Duke Enli. But it's important that you get there. It's important to Nar. You know that, don't you?"

"I know what I am, Uncle. Whatever the Master has planned for me, I'm ready."

The Master. Lokken still hated that term. Since coming to Goth, Lorla never referred to Biagio as anything but the Master. He supposed it was Roshann programming. Very thorough. Lorla knew what she was, but that was all. In a sense she was a freak, a growing woman frozen in the body of an eight-year-old. She didn't know what Biagio had planned for her, and her incubation in the labs had made her trust the count implicitly. Lokken pitied the girl.

"You've meant a lot to me," he said. "I'm proud to have been part of this. I wish I could have known you better."

Lorla's gaze dropped. "I wish you could have told me more. Maybe someday."

Lokken's grin was crooked. They both knew there wouldn't be a someday. Not for Lokken, and not for the family that had cared for Lorla this past year. Like Biagio's Roshann, Vorto's legions were thorough. Given time, there would be very little left of Goth. But Goth wouldn't perish entirely. If Lorla made it to Dragon's Beak, Herrith and Vorto would hear from the Walled City again. Perhaps Biagio was a madman, but he was brilliant. Whatever the Count of Crote had planned, Lokken had confidence. Just like Goth, the Black Renaissance would not go quietly.

Lorla walked past Duke Lokken toward the window. Standing on her tiptoes, she regarded the battle raging outside. Her eyes scanned the hills and circling war wagons, the legionnaires armed with flame cannons and maces. This was the gauntlet she had to cross, with only her diminutive size and the cloak of darkness to hide her.

"I should go now," she declared. "The snow will slow them."

Lokken nodded grimly. "There's a pony waiting for you. Daevn is in the courtyard. He'll take you to the hidden gate. Remember, wait 'til the rockets die down, then head for the first hill with the apple trees. It's rugged there, and . . ."

"I know the way," Lorla interrupted. She was getting agitated. Too much talk. So Lokken said no more.

For an hour, Vorto watched his siege machines circle the city. Then the ram was ready. Vorto rode down to inspect it, surrounded by an armored entourage of legionnaires. The ram was enormous, the largest the war labs had ever constructed. Twenty greegans had dragged the war machine to Goth. Its wheels were as tall as a man, and a hundred wooden handles poked from its side like the legs of a centipede. Its head was of granite, fastened to the stout oak shaft with bands of riveted iron, and along its top length were loops of rope to keep the men from being dragged beneath its crushing wheels. As he brought his mount up alongside the weapon, Vorto wondered if it was up to the task. Goth's walls were legendary, and the city gate was reinforced with spikes and lengths of petrified timber. The Walled City had stood for generations, shrugging off countless wars. Some said it was impregnable.

But then, nothing was impregnable to God or Nar. Vorto reined in his bucking horse and turned to Kye. The colonel's helmet was covered with a sheen of snow.

"Bring up two platoons of cannoneers. Have them concentrate fire on the walls around the gate. We have to keep the archers back. And stop the rocket barrage. I don't want those damn things landing near the ram. When the gate comes down, we'll swarm. Is your infantry ready, Kye?"

"They've been ready, sir."

"Then keep the cavalry back until I give the order. We need a clear passage for the charge. I don't want them bunching up near the gate; Lokken will be expecting that. And he'll probably have some surprises for us."

Kye grimaced. "Sir, if we're going to use the gas anyway . . ."

"I want Lokken, Kye. I have a surprise for him. Off with you now. Do as I say."

Kye dismissed himself with a shrug, then rode off to gather the flame cannoneers his lord had requested. Vorto watched him go. Once again, impatience was gnawing at him. The snow was deepening, and the cessation of rocket fire would bring back the darkness. Beneath his metal gauntlets his fingertips were blue. Goth could hold out for weeks, and winter was coming fast. Hunger and cold would soon eat away at his legion's morale, and he couldn't risk that.

It took only moments before Kye had the cannoneers arranged. As ordered, he had them flank the ram's path to the gate. A steady stream of fire belched from the nozzles of the cannons, pushing back the archers defending the city's entrance. The wooden catwalks along the wall burst into flames under the barrage. Gothan archers drew back to safer positions. Vorto heard their desperate cries for reinforcements. They had seen the ram.

Vorto pulled his double-sided axe from his back and thundered down the hillside. Behind him followed his standard bearers, holding high the Light of God. The sight of the golden flag attracted the attention of some of the archers on the wall. Vorto laughed and shook his fist at them.

"I'm here!" he taunted. "Put one through my heart!"

But he was still too distant and the archers knew it, so instead they pumped their arrows at the ram and the legionnaires taking up position alongside it. Vorto shouted orders at the hundred-man team. Above the ram's pulling stations was a hood of metal, a deflector against the rain of missiles. Each soldier in turn tethered himself to the ram, dropping loops of rope around his waist. Vorto moved in a little closer, until he was with Colonel Kye again. The platoons of cannons fired at the wall, pressing back the wave of Gothans. Fingers of flame splashed against the monolithic wall. Overhead the rockets had ceased. A dull darkness pressed down on the world.

The walls of Goth loomed fifty feet tall. The gates themselves stood a proud twenty. General Vorto quickly calculated the required force. Five passes; maybe more. But that would take time, and the cannons wouldn't hold forever. Already longbowmen had scored some lucky hits against his men. From the torches in a nearby tower, Vorto could see the shadows of more Gothans taking up position. His men would have to hurry.

"Kye," he said very calmly. "Now."

Colonel Kye raised his saber. "Ram!" he directed.

A grunt of exertion filled the air. Very slowly, the massive wheels of the ram began grinding forward. Lieutenants near the ram cursed orders, urging on their men. The weapon picked up speed as it rolled toward Goth's gate. Vorto licked his wind-chapped lips. The ram groaned as it accelerated. A panicked shout went up from the Gothans. Flame cannons detonated, spilling against the wall. Faster and faster went the ram. Larger and larger loomed the gates. Vorto grit his teeth. . . .

Louder than a crack of thunder, the ram smashed against the wooden gate. All the world seemed to shudder. Archers along the wall tumbled backward with the impact, and for one moment the cannoneers stopped their endless fire, astonished by the sound. Vorto peered expectantly through the murkiness. As the light grew again, he saw the damaged gate. Impossibly, a hairline fissure was snaking its way through the petrified wood.

"God in Heaven!" Vorto laughed. A cheer went up from the legionnaires gathered around the ram. They were two hundred strong now, called from their circling of the city to storm falling Goth. Men on horseback shook their swords in victory. Even Colonel Kye broke into an unreserved smile.

"Again!" ordered Vorto. Already the ram was being pushed back into position. Again the night flashed with cannon fire. A new rain of arrows poured down upon the soldiers, catching some in their backs. Kye directed a squad of handhelds toward the new threat. The two-man teams hurried up to the wall and hosed it down with streams of fire. Though small and lacking the range of their bigger brothers, the handheld cannons threw their fire high into the night, scorching the tower of the Gothan archers and halting their barrage.

Once more the ram inched forward. Vorto heard the agonized shouts of the men as their muscles strained with effort. The ram accelerated slowly, then faster and faster still. Another concussion shook the ground as the ram battered the wooden portal. This time the fissure became a groaning rent. Vorto hurried his charger nearer the gate. Through the crack he could almost see the city. Several poles of timber still held the doorway fast, but these had bowed and would never withstand another blow. Kye shouted orders to his men. The ram started backward for one last assault. Vorto pranced triumphantly in the cannon-light, laughing and praising Heaven for his coming victory. The Light of God waved above his head.

"Time's up, Lokken," caroled Vorto gleefully. He spared one last look into the hills where the launchers were waiting, and a little pang of anticipation ran through him.

• • •

Lorla reached the hidden gate just as the snow began falling in earnest. Her pony was exhausted from the hard, fast ride through the city. Daevn, her guide and guardian, was slick with sleet and sweat. He was a tall man and a fast talker, and Lorla watched anxiously as he spoke to the Gothan soldiers at the gate, and shouted up to the men pacing the wall. Except for the soldiers, Goth was locked up tight. The rockets had stopped falling now, and darkness crept over the city. Lorla fidgeted as she listened to the far off pounding at the main gate. The sound reminded her of a drum.

Daevn returned, mounting his horse as he waited for the portal to slide open. It was far smaller than the main gate, more like a door really, and made up of the same dull gray as the rest of the wall. Lorla tried to peer through as it opened. Beyond it she could see only darkness and snow.

"What's that sound?" she asked nervously.

"Battering ram," Daevn explained. "They've started to break through. Lucky for us, too. The rest of the Naren soldiers are gathering near the main gate." He smiled at her wickedly. "We just might make it."

Lorla hardly knew Daevn at all, and wasn't sure he understood what she truly was. But she tried to smile, because she would need the brute's goodwill, and when the hidden gate creaked open she ushered her pony closer to it.

"It's clear, I think," said one of the soldiers. He looked up to the catwalk where another Gothan silently gave them the go-ahead. "Hurry now. Stay to the shadows, but don't linger."

Daevn nodded. "Ready, girl?"

"I'm ready," Lorla lied.

Daevn took the lead, trotting his horse outside the wall. At once the darkness swallowed him. Lorla steeled herself before urging her pony outside. The beast seemed to sense her trepidation and moved with leaden legs. Lorla heard another concussion from the far side of the city, and fear sped her on. Daevn impatiently waved her forward. Outside the wall, everything was silent. The din of battle was oddly quieter here. Lorla spared a sad look backward as the hidden gate drew slowly closed. Remarkably, it seemed to disappear.

"Come on," Daevn ordered. He began speeding for the hills. It would be thick there and dark. Dressed in black, Lorla and Daevn quickly became part of the shadows. Fast and silent, they rode toward the looming unknown of Dragon's Beak.

• • •

Duke Lokken stepped out onto the balcony of his tower and brooded over his falling city. Reports were coming in faster than he could comprehend them, and his private chambers were flooded with aides. Vorto's legions had broken through the gate and were swarming into the city. The glow of flame cannons told the duke how near they were. Larius, his Counselor-at-Arms, was tugging at his shirtsleeve like a little boy, begging for guidance or any semblance of life. But Duke Lokken was a million miles away. His eyes had glazed over with dreadful visions, and his thoughts had slowed to a crawl. His boy Jevin was on the main gate. Dead by now, surely. And in another hour or so his daughters would join him—but not before they lost their virtue to the marauders. Very quickly, Goth was becoming a Naren ruin.

"Larius," the duke said quietly. "Take my wife and daughters to the throne room. Wait with them there. I will be down presently. Just a few moments alone . . ."

"No," cried his wife. Kareena rushed up to him and took his hand. Throughout the siege she had been resolute, but now the dam of her emotions was crumbling. "I won't be away from you."

Lokken smiled forlornly. "Kareena, do this for me. I want to watch the city. Alone."

"We will stay with you," his wife offered. "Send the others away, but not us. Please, the girls—"

"Will have their father with them in minutes," Lokken said. "Go to the throne room. Wait for me there. And have the guards wait outside." He turned to his counselor. "Larius, you hear? I want no soldiers in the chamber. You alone will stay with them, understood?"

"I understand, my Duke."

Lokken took his wife's face in his hands and pulled it close, his voice a whisper. "I have to be strong, Kareena, and there's not much time. Just let me have my moment of weakness, will you?"

Kareena's lips shuddered. Without a word she slipped from the duke's embrace, gathered her daughters, and led them out of the chamber. Larius was silent too. The old warrior gave his duke a sad smile before leaving the balcony and ordering the others out of the chamber.

Alone, Duke Lokken of Goth cast his eyes out over his burning city. Goth the fair. Goth the strong. Built by slaves, mortared with blood, it had been the only home the duke had ever known. Tears trickled down his cheeks. Soon Vorto would come for him, and by then he wanted to be purged of tears. He would face the butcher of Nar with the same contempt that had made him shred Herrith's hateful flag. This day, even as Goth collapsed, he would give his enemies no satisfaction.

• • •

On a thousand armored feet and breathing flame, Vorto's imperial legions rolled through the city of Goth. Above them rose the granite towers thick with archers, and the streets were barricaded with human flesh—Lokken's wild, sword-wielding defenders. Naren cavalry pushed through the narrow avenues, slicing down Gothan infantry with their sabers while flame cannons cut them a blazing path. Overhead the dawn was breaking red and harsh. Men were barking like dogs, ordering advances and retreats, and the screams of the burning echoed down the stone corridors.

Fighting street to street, Vorto's legions had nearly made their way to Lokken's castle. Now the fortress could be clearly seen, tall and impressive in the snowy dawn, its two flags wet with ice in the chilling wind. General Vorto rode his horse through the carnage, an expression of victory on his face. Not far away, Colonel Kye was leading the cavalry assault on the main thoroughfare, ignoring the flood of arrows from the granite towers. Vorto followed him, his massive axe cutting through Gothan infantry, buckling helmets and crushing heads. Gore splashed his armored legs and the flanks of his horse. Detonating flame cannons rocked the avenue. A horde of Gothan defenders rode toward them furiously, trying to trap them against the foot soldiers. Screaming, Vorto turned to charge them.

"Follow me!" he bellowed. Twenty heavy-horsemen heard the cry and galloped off after him. A quick-thinking cannoneer turned his weapon against the coming Gothans, burning down a third of them in a fireball. The heat from the blast struck Vorto in the face, singeing his eyebrows, but he rode on heedlessly. When the bloom of fire had dissipated he collided with the Gothan horsemen. At once he felt a sword glance off his armored shoulder. Vorto brought his axe up and then down, shearing off the offending arm. He whirled to catch another horsemen, too near to avoid the flashing hatchet. And then his men were with him, crashing against the horsemen of Goth. Lost in the blinding melee, Vorto crooned his terrible battle chant and swung his weapon, slamming through flesh and armor and dousing himself in blood.

When the melee was nearly over, Vorto pulled his horse out of the crowd and followed Colonel Kye's brigade down the street toward the fortress. Kye had cut a path wide enough for the greegans, and the war wagons were lumbering forward, heedless of the Gothan archers. Unstoppable, bristling with swords and bright with cannon fire, the column moved slowly toward the waiting fortress. Ahead of them, the Gothans were retreating for the castle, regrouping for one last battle. Vorto could see the structure plainly now. A three-tiered masterpiece of rock and wood, it reminded the general of a bulldog, its power born from a squat and determined stance. Vorto hurried his mount up to the center of his army, shouldering past the thickness of men and horseflesh. Colonel Kye gave him a sinister grin.

"The fortress, General?" he asked.

Vorto nodded. "They'll make their stand there, no doubt. Take up positions to the east and west, four platoons each with cannons. The rest of us will ride up to Lokken's door."

Kye looked around suspiciously. "Quiet," he remarked.

Vorto surveyed their surroundings. It *was* quiet. They had met only pathetic resistance from the populace, and now the streets were fairly deserted. Soon the formula would do the rest. Unnerved by the silence, Vorto and his legionnaires fanned out toward the waiting fortress.

The Gothan regulars scurried down the streets in retreat, taking up positions near Lokken's hideout. The archers ceased firing. Vorto's column moved deliberately through the deserted avenues. The general's eyes moved over the streets and towers, waiting for an assassin's arrow that never came. In the distance around the fortress he heard the shouts of men. An eerie pall blanketed Goth. People in their houses peered nervously from windows. Vorto's brow furrowed. . . .

Then he saw the flash. It was more brilliant than the sun. Breathtaken, Vorto reined in his horse as the rockets climbed skyward over the fortress, hung high above, then burst into a cascade of fireworks. For one beautiful moment, the sky over Lokken's home was the only thing in the world, alive with light meant for one defiant purpose—to illuminate the flags of Goth. Vorto's face did an impossible contortion at the sight of it. There was the Black Flag, lit with all the grace of Heaven, an impudent beacon in a darkness of snow. One last spit from the disloyal duke.

"Lokken," seethed Vorto, "you will burn in Hell for this." The general crossed himself and closed his eyes in prayer, begging God to be unmerciful. His simmering rage boiled over. "Fly your flag?" he hissed. "Your black and faithless flag?"

It was all he could manage not to scream.

"Hurry now," he roared at his men. "I want this bastard found!"

The Naren legion double-timed it through the streets. The war wagons rumbled forward as quickly as the mammoth greegans could pull, and the cavalry horses snorted. Vorto fought his way to the front of his column. The flame cannons had stopped now, but Vorto could see platoons of them taking up positions near the fortress, balancing their needle-nosed weapons unsteadily in makeshift cradles. Colonel Kye brought his horse up alongside his superior's. The soldier sniffed at the sight of the fortress.

"It's as if they have no defenses at all," he laughed. "Maybe you were right, sir. Maybe we should just knock!"

They were in a large courtyard of stone. A garrison of Gothans stood before them, armed and sullen, flanked by the remains of their cavalry. The men of the Walled City made no pretense at defense. They simply waited. Vorto leaned over to whisper in Kye's ear.

"Kye," he said softly. "What is this?"

Colonel Kye shrugged, clearly puzzled by the mob. "I don't know. Surrender?"

Vorto put up a hand to halt his column. The order echoed down the line. Almost in unison the armored snake came to a stop. Vorto looked around uneasily. A trap was his first instinct, but he saw nothing to indicate aggression, not even the smallest movement. He eyed the Gothan soldiers standing guard around the fortress. They hadn't lowered their swords, yet the archers made no attempt to notch new shafts.

"Now I'm curious," quipped Vorto.

"You there!" called Kye across the courtyard. "Is this surrender?"

Still the Gothans said nothing. They were fifty yards away at least, and Vorto wondered if they had heard the question over the wind.

"My God," grumbled Vorto. "They surrender as poorly as they fight."

And then the spiked gate of Lokken's castle began drawing upward. The Gothan guardians parted like waves, revealing the murky insides of the keep. Vorto and Kye both strained to see past the gathering snow. A small figure emerged from the darkness. Thinking it was the duke, Vorto's heart leapt with excitement. But then he saw the crimson uniform of the Gothan military and knew the man wasn't Lokken. This soldier was old, far older than the duke, and slightly stooped. He walked past the guardians of the fortress without regard, heading straight for Vorto and his army.

"What's this?" asked Vorto. He drew himself erect, then handed his battle axe to Kye. "Who are you?" he demanded of the soldier. "And what business have you with me?"

Without ceremony, the soldier stopped mere feet from the general of Nar.

"You are Vorto?" he asked pointedly.

"Old man, I asked you a question," warned Vorto. "Do you speak for Lokken?"

"I speak for the duke, yes," replied the soldier. "I am Larius, Counselor-at-Arms for the Walled City. You are Vorto, are you not?"

Vorto smiled. "I am your master and lord high executioner, dog. Servant of Heaven and Archbishop Herrith." The general glared down hard. "Where is your duke?"

"The duke awaits you in his throne room," said Larius. "I am to take you there."

"A personal invitation? Oh, how gracious. I accept, Gothan. Take me to the pig."

Colonel Kye cleared his throat. "General . . ."

"Be fearless, Kye," said Vorto. "We are in God's hands. Counselor, lead on. Kye, you come with me."

Larius of Goth made a disdainful face but said nothing more. He turned his back on the legions and headed again for the fortress gates. Vorto followed, as did Kye, with the ten soldiers that shadowed the general everywhere in tow. When they reached the gates, Vorto and his entourage dismounted, handing their horses off to the Naren infantry. The soldiers of Goth eyed them balefully. Vorto watched Larius disappear into the fortress. Inside, the great hall was lit with torches and lined with perfectly positioned soldiers, all in uniforms of bright crimson. They had their swords drawn and held erect at their sides, so that they looked more like toys than things of flesh. Vorto hesitated at the threshold.

Larius paused to regard him.

"Come, General," ordered the soldier impatiently. "They won't hurt you. They have their orders."

Vorto stepped unflinchingly into the hall, spurred on by the insult. Colonel Kye was equally deliberate. At the far end of the hall was a set of open doors. Larius led the intruders through the hall, and when he reached the doors he stepped aside.

"The duke," he said.

Vorto stepped into the room. At the other end of the expansive chamber he saw Lokken, sitting upon his modest throne. At his right hand was the austerely beautiful Kareena. Her eyes flashed when she glimpsed the general. At the feet of the duchess were two small girls, Lokken's daughters, looking stricken and confused. The duke himself seemed surprisingly composed. There were no guardians in the chamber, no soldiers of any kind. Only Lokken and his brood. Vorto strode noisily into the chamber, his armor dripping Gothan blood. When he came to the small dais he paused, choked up saliva, and spit the wad in Lokken's tranquil face. With perfect composure, Duke Lokken wiped the spittle away.

"So," grated Vorto. "This is where the king sits, eh?"

Lokken said nothing.

"Oh, you treacherous thing. You are abhorrent in the eyes of God! How is it you dare defy the will of Heaven?"

Still the duke was silent.

"Say something, you arrogant maggot!"

But it was Kareena who responded. She lunged at Vorto, screaming, her nails raking his face. Vorto hissed and caught her arm, twisting it and driving her to her knees. His other hand slapped her face, splitting her lip.

"No!" cried Lokken, leaping from his throne. He grabbed his wife and drew her into his arms.

"Control your woman, Lokken," warned Vorto, "or I will take her back with me and teach her manners myself."

"Don't you touch her!" Lokken seethed. He rose to his feet and faced the towering general. "You're here for me, butcher. Me alone."

Suddenly Vorto understood. "Is that why you surrender? To spare your family, dog?"

Lokken grimaced. "Yes. Spare them, and no one else dies today. I can kill you now just with a word, Vorto. But I won't. Not if you agree to spare my kin."

"It is for Heaven to judge, not I."

"Spare them," Lokken begged, "and you can walk out of here alive. With your men."

Vorto's eyes narrowed. "Threats from a traitor. How horrible to hear."

"I'm no traitor," said Lokken. "I am loyal to our emperor and his memory. You're the usurper, Vorto. You and your bishop. Call it what you will, but I fly the flag of Nar."

"Oh, yes," crooned Vorto. "The flag. You're keen on flags, aren't you, Lokken?" Vorto turned to his waiting men. "Take him," he ordered. "The females, too."

At once his waiting legionnaires seized the royal family of Goth, dragging them after Vorto who was exiting the chamber.

"Not my family!" the duke cried as the men took hold of him. "God, not them!"

"God doesn't hear *you*," said Vorto over his shoulder.

"Not them, please!"

"Not them," agreed Vorto. Outside the chamber he found the worried Larius again. The man looked about to faint. "Counselor, your master has something to tell you."

"Duke Lokken?" gasped Larius.

"Tell him, Lokken. About our agreement . . ."

Lokken looked relieved. He tried shrugging off the grasp of the soldiers, but they wouldn't yield. All the Gothan guardians watched their duke, their jaws slack. Duchess Kareena was in tears, as were her two children.

"Safe passage," said Lokken at last. "For all of them. If they let my family live, all of you will let them go. Promise me, Larius."

"My Duke . . ."

"Promise me!"

"Promise him," urged Vorto. "Or they *all* die right now. And even if you kill us, my legion will burn Goth to the ground."

"My Duke, it's your death. . . ." Larius begged. "Don't make me do this."

Duke Lokken finally shook off his captors. When they tried to seize him again, Vorto put up a hand to stop them. He let the duke go to his man and clasp his hands firmly on the soldier's shoulders.

"I die," said the duke. "You hear me? I die. And no one else after me. Now promise me, my friend. Safe passage for these Naren beasts. It's my last order. Will you carry it out?"

Larius' expression collapsed. "I will, my Duke. My . . . friend."

"No archers, no cavalry," pressed Vorto. "Nothing 'til we reach the gate, old man. Is that understood?"

"Aye," said Larius. "I hear you, Naren."

"Good for you." Vorto smiled sharply. "Then, to the tower. I want to see these flags of yours up close, Lokken. Take us there. Now."

Once again the soldiers tried to take hold of him, and once again the duke shrugged them off.

"I won't drag you if there's no need," said Vorto. "Or your bitches. Let's go."

Lokken took hold of his young wife's hand. "My love," he choked. "I'm so sorry I did this to you." He went down to his knees to his crying daughters, who looked to Vorto like twins of no more than four. The children didn't seem to know what was happening. He kissed them both on the forehead, wiped away their confused tears, then stood to face his executioner.

"I'm ready."

"Take us to your flags," Vorto ordered. "Your family can watch you die, or they can wait here. I don't care which."

Kareena would not let go of her husband. "I want to be with you," she pleaded.

"No." The duke's voice was icy. He spared her one last kiss—one last, long look—then went down the corridor. Vorto and his men followed. Larius tried to follow too, but Kye kicked at him.

"Just the duke," snarled the colonel.

With a bravado that impressed Vorto, Duke Lokken never wavered. He led them directly to a spiral staircase within a tower of gray granite, a dark place lit with sconces which sent up an oily smoke. As they disappeared into the spire, Duchess Kareena uttered a wailing, agonized sob. But Lokken remained as unbending as steel. Without a word he guided the Narens up the stairs. When he came to the top of the tower he pushed open the door and let an icy breeze blow in.

They were atop the tallest spire in the city, with all of Goth burning at their feet. Vorto stepped out onto the roof. In the center was the flagpole that had caused them all such grief. And at the top of the pole, hideously aglow in the coming dawn, were the two offending flags of Goth. The old flag of Nar made Vorto shudder with disgust. He stared at it for a long moment, then bowed his head and prayed.

"Dear God, Lord of all things, give me strength to destroy this travesty. God of mercy and light, be with us, Your servants."

No one else prayed with Vorto, but all except Lokken inclined their heads. When he was done praying, Vorto sighed and looked at the duke.

"I give you one chance to redeem yourself, Lokken. Here and now, will you renounce the Black Renaissance? Will you accept Heaven as your salvation? Your lord Biagio is a sodomite and a devil. He lies with men and defies the church of Nar. For your soul, Lokken, renounce him and his works."

Lokken stared at Vorto, and then the duke was laughing, shaking his head in disbelief.

"Mad," he declared. "You are truly mad. Oh, I pity you, Vorto. I pity all of Nar. You're under a spell, can't you see? You've fallen for a myth."

"God and Hell are no myths," said Vorto. "Save yourself from the eternal burning. Renounce Biagio so your soul may rest."

The duke was resolute. "If there is a Hell, then I would gladly burn there. Better that than to grovel to Herrith's church."

It was the answer Vorto expected. "So be it." He went to the flag pole, undid the knots, and quickly lowered the flags. Lion's Blood came down first, and this the general crumpled into a ball and threw off the ledge. Taken by the wind, the crimson standard of Goth drifted out of sight. Vorto went back to the pole and cut down the Black Flag. It was the most unremarkable standard in the Empire, nothing more than a field of black fabric, but it held generations of evil in its stitching.

"Bind him," the general ordered. At once his soldiers cut off lengths of rope and tethered the duke's wrists behind his back. As they worked Vorto mumbled over the Black Flag, praying in High Naren to exorcise its unholy powers. Then he grabbed hold of the flag and tore it in two. Lokken watched the destruction, unmoved. Vorto stuffed the two halves in the duke's lapel.

"You want to fly your flags, Duke? You want to defy Heaven? Then fly your damnable flags!"

Colonel Kye pushed the bound Lokken toward the flag pole. Two more soldiers made a noose of the rope and looped it around Lokken's neck. They gave it a quick jerk to tighten it, bringing the duke to his toes.

"No regrets, Lokken?" taunted Vorto. "None at all? There's still time, demon. But the clock is ticking fast away. Tick tock, tick tock . . ."

"Damn you and your bishop both, butcher. I will see you in your Hell!"

"Yes, yes," agreed Vorto. With a wave of his hand he ordered the legionnaires to tighten the rope. Lokken's pale eyes protruded from their sockets and his tongue darted out for air. He held his breath halfway to the top before letting out a belching cry. His feet kicked the rest of the way, and when at last he reached the top, Duke Lokken of Goth was dead. Vorto looked up at him, satisfied. Now all the Walled City could see his folly.

"God have mercy on you," said the general quietly. But it was no less than the heretic deserved. Someday, Vorto pledged, he would do the same to Biagio, and then at last Nar would be free of its dynasty of tyrants.

Weary to the bone, General Vorto turned to his loyal colonel. "Kye, come. There is still work to do."

Vorto left the rooftop first, eager to be gone from the dead duke's bulging gaze.

General Vorto quietly led his legion out of the Walled City. True to his promise, Larius called back the archers from the towers and the tattered remains of Gothan infantry. Their city was in flames anyway, and all hands were needed to stem the growing fires. General Vorto rode resolutely past the astonished faces of the civilians, enduring muttered insults and the tearful, spiteful looks of children. The sun was higher now, bright and burning away the earth's snowy sheen. And the wind had fled with the night. As he reached the city gates, Vorto looked to Heaven for guidance. Beyond the staggered clouds he saw the gray-blue sky. God was speaking to him, as He had been for months now. On the dying breeze he heard the Lord's breath. Vorto nodded, understanding.

When he was safely clear of the city, Vorto called over Colonel Kye. His second trotted closer, then closer still when he heard Vorto whispering.

"Kye, it's time. Get the men away from the city. But leave the ram. Keep it near the gates to block it."

"The ram?" Colonel Kye looked over his shoulder to where the giant weapon waited, still blocking a good portion of the ruined portal. On either side of it men and horses squeezed through. "We're leaving it behind?"

"We're leaving it exactly where it is. Gather the lieutenants. Have them ride for the launchers and tell the gunners to make ready."

Colonel Kye seemed stricken. "General . . ."

"It is the will of God, Kye. This place reeks of evil. It must be cleansed."

"General, you promised Lokken you'd spare them. His family . . ."

"His family bears the same taint he did," said Vorto firmly. "And so does all of Goth. We came here to stop the Renaissance, to stomp it out like a fire. I won't leave the job half done."

Kye's expression hardened. "Sir, may I speak freely?"

"You always do," snapped Vorto.

"Sir, this is genocide. It's murder."

"Murder?" Vorto flared. "Who said anything about murder? This is salvation, Colonel, make no mistake. The Black Renaissance is a tumor. If you had a disease in your flesh, would you not carve it out? This is what we're doing here. We're saving Nar. Stop being a dullard, Kye. See the truth for once!"

Silenced by his general's implicit threat, Kye merely looked away, toward the hills around the city where the deadly launchers awaited their orders.

"Wait until we're clear," said Vorto. "Then send up the signal rocket."

Kye nodded sullenly and trotted off, but Vorto called after him.

"Kye . . ."

The colonel turned to face Vorto. "General?"

"It's not easy to do the work of Heaven, Kye. Not for me, not for anyone. Pray for strength. He will provide."

"Yes, General," replied Kye dully.

The colonel rode away.

Duchess Kareena of Goth, newly widowed, stood on the rooftop of the fortress tower, watching her dead husband pendulate in the breeze. The tightness of rope about his throat had turned his face a curious purple, making it scarcely recognizable, even to the woman who had borne him three children. The tower roof was cold. Except for a few stray flurries, the snow had stopped falling. Larius drew his dagger and began cutting his dead master down. Good Larius, the only person in the world Kareena could bear to be with for this gruesome task. Downstairs her daughters were weeping, inconsolable. Her only boy was probably dead, a casualty lying blood-soaked on the wall. Kareena trembled. Somehow, she had tamed her tears, but a terrible fog had descended, drawing out the time of things. She was in her twenty-ninth year and had never thought she could love this much-older man, but now that he was gone she wondered what life there could possibly be without him.

Around the city, Vorto's army had retreated as promised, a fact that astounded Kareena. She hadn't expected the butcher to be good to his word. As morning flooded the valley, she could see them riding away, satisfied to have murdered her husband. The duchess stifled a sob and went to the flag pole, helping Larius draw Lokken down. His body had gone cold. Kareena cradled him and lowered him to the ground, cursing as she fought to free the noose.

"Oh, God," she moaned. "My husband . . ."

Lokken's eyes were wide. Unseeing, they stared at her. Larius put a hand over them and closed the lids. The old soldier knelt, kissed his master's forehead, then backed away, leaving his mistress to grieve. Kareena held Lokken's head to her bosom and rocked him. Was she leader of Goth now? she wondered. Would Vorto return for more vengeance? Kareena stroked her husband's head, brushing strands of hair from his lifeless, distorted face. Larius walked over to the edge of the rooftop and looked out over the city. Wet snow blanketed the horizon, punctuated with fire and smoke. Far below, Kareena heard the wails of her people, the aimless, bewildered cries of children and their mothers. Soldiers moved through the avenues, fighting back the fires with blankets and bucket brigades. Kareena closed her eyes and mouthed a prayer—not to the new God of Nar but to the old, when God was mild. Before the death of Arkus, she had loved the church. She had even made a pilgrimage to Nar City to see the great Cathedral of the Martyrs and to hear the words of Herrith. But in the ruins of the old Empire, something had gone horribly awry.

A sound in the distance halted Kareena's prayers. A popping in the hillside, followed by another and another still. Kareena craned her neck to see. The sound was all around her suddenly. Panicked, she laid Lokken down and hastened to Larius' side. The counselor was scanning the horizon.

"Larius? What is it? What's that sound?"

"My lady, I don't know. Cannons?"

"Cannons? Oh, no, that can't be."

"I don't see flashes," agreed Larius. "But the sound—"

Overhead an object whistled past. Larius grabbed his mistress and pulled her to the ground. Kareena screamed as another missile hissed, slamming into the tower wall. There was a sound like exploding steam. The far-off popping in the hills intensified. Kareena pulled free of Larius and ran to the stone railing.

"What is it?" she screamed. She put her hands to her ears to banish the sound. "Larius, what . . . ?"

All around Goth, green smoke exploded, its emerald fingers crawling through the streets. The strange bombardment had the city looking skyward. Men screamed, tearing at their eyes as the relentless vapor engulfed them. On the wind came the sweet smell of something evil. Kareena sniffed at the air, too late to know the poison she was breathing. Fire climbed into her nostrils, burning out the membranes. Her throat constricted and a flood of tears rushed from her eyes. She staggered from the wall, reeling backward into Larius. Desperately she grabbed for him. The old man's eyes were filled with blood. Horrified, unable to breathe or scream, Duchess Kareena looked down at her stained dress and realized that her tears were crimson.

TWO

The Golden Count

He was called the Mind Bender.

The name had been given to him by his former master, Arkus of Nar, and Savros bore it proudly, and referred to himself as such even in the presence of good imperial ladies. He handled his tools as a painter would a brush, delicately and with the flair of genius. Some said he was mad, but all agreed that he was peerless in his work, one of Nar's rare artisans. Soldiers envied his deftness with a knife, and women fainted when he told his dark tales. He had known his true vocation since his boyhood.

Simon watched the Mind Bender work, aghast at the love he had for his craft. His spidery fingers crawled over his victim's flesh, his arsenal of narrow scalpels twirling between his digits like sharp batons. Simon knew he was watching a master, and despite the howls of the thing hanging in chains from the ceiling, it was wholly fascinating to witness.

"It's so easy," whispered the torturer. His tongue darted out to lick the man's ear. "So easy to die . . ."

The voice was honey, sickly sweet and cloying. It rose from the Mind Bender's throat like a song, teasing the man and compelling him to talk. But the man was almost past coherence. Only Triin gibberish trickled from his lips now, but Savros the Mind Bender wasn't finished. He produced another blade from his white vest and made his victim behold it, turning it slowly in the dungeon's feeble light so the flicker of the torch glowed orange on its edge. Simon stood motionless in the corner of the cell, awaiting the prisoner's end.

Like all Triin, this one was perfectly white. Savros had been delighted when he'd seen him. For him the white skin was a canvas to be stretched out with chains. Promptly he had set to work, using his knives to carve out screaming figures on the man's naked back. There were almost twenty of them now, forming a twisting, living mural. Blood dripped relentlessly onto the floor, and little bits of Triin flesh clung to the Mind Bender's boots. But Savros seemed not to notice them at all, and Simon wondered as he watched the spectacle if this was what Hell was like.

"Beautiful," remarked the torturer as he regarded his prized scalpel. He put it up to the Triin's gray eyeball, now hazed with fatigue and pain. "There is a smith in the Black City who works for days to make just one of these for me. He is the finest blade-maker in Nar." Savros tested the edge with his fingertip and grinned. "Oooh; sharp."

Savros no longer bothered speaking Triin. His victim was past comprehension, and he knew it. But this was the best part. Disgusted, Simon fought to keep focused. He was Roshann, and if he looked away Biagio would surely hear about it. So he steeled himself and watched while Savros caressed a tear-stained cheek with the thin blade and crooned his song, and the Triin man in chains trembled against the coming death.

"Just do it," Simon growled, his patience snapping. Savros turned his laughing eyes to the dark corner where Simon was lurking. A ripe web sack filled with newborn arachnids clung defiantly to the ceiling overhead, but Simon didn't stir from his spot.

"Shhh," urged Savros, putting a slender finger to his lips. The air was thick and smelled of treacle; too close for Simon's liking. The Mind Bender's voice rang in his brain. He had been hearing it for hours and his feet ached from standing. Outside in the real world, the sun was probably up. If he could have, Simon would have run from the place and vomited, but there was dirty business still to do.

"If you have your information, kill him," ordered Simon. "He's still a man. Treat him like one."

Savros seemed shocked. "You brought him here for me," he reminded Simon. "Now let me do my work."

"Your work is done, Mind Bender. Get yourself a goat from the farm if you need something to butcher. He was a Triin warrior. Leave him some honor."

"Why so squeamish?" taunted Savros. The thin blade rolled between his fingertips. "Don't they teach interrogation in the Roshann?"

Simon stepped out of the shadows. In the center of the cell was a small table set with the Mind Bender's implements, a curious collection of metal objects with points and pincers, all arranged neatly on a silver tray. Beside the gruesome platter stood a pitcher of rose water. It was a strange habit of Savros' to dapple his victim's lips with the cool liquid and make them agonize for more. Simon pushed the torturer aside and lifted the pitcher to the Triin's mouth, pouring the water over his lips and tongue. The man let out a thankful whimper.

"What are you doing?" asked Savros.

Simon ignored him, lifting another blade from the table even as he continued to pour. This one was less beautiful than the others. It was wide and heavy, with a toothy edge like a butcher's saw. Simon grasped it tightly, leaning forward so that his lips almost brushed the captive's ear.

"Good death, warrior," he said simply, then plunged the jagged blade into the Triin's heart. There was a quick rattle from the prisoner's throat. The hands spasmed into fists, shaking the manacles and the long, stout chains. The eyes widened, focused on Simon for a moment, then swiftly dimmed. Simon put down the pitcher, then the knife, and calmly stared at Savros. The Mind Bender's jaw dropped.

"You've killed him," Savros sputtered.

"You're like a cat playing with a bird," said Simon sharply. "I won't watch such nonsense."

"I wasn't done with him!" Savros wailed. He rushed over to the limp body and searched for a pulse. "I'm going to tell Biagio about this!"

"I'll tell him myself. Now what did he say? I heard you mention Vantran. Is he in Falindar?"

Savros wasn't listening. He ran his long fingers over his victim's back, admiring his artwork and feeling the waning heat of the corpse on his face. Simon shifted impatiently. In the days when Savros served the emperor he had been one of Arkus' favorites, a member of his privileged "Iron Circle." Now he was in exile like the rest of Biagio's loyalists, stuck here on Crote. None of them liked being here, but Savros seemed to be faring the worst. The Mind Bender had spent his entire life in the Black City plying his dark trade. He was accustomed to the belching smokestacks of war labs and the dankness of dungeons; the clean ocean air of the island seemed to depress him. But Biagio still cared for him, and that meant he had sway with the count. Simon knew not to push him too far.

"Savros," urged Simon. "What did he say? Is Vantran in Falindar?"

"He was so beautiful," replied Savros absently. "I want another."

"Vantran—"

"Yes, yes!" flared the torturer. Savros released the dead man and turned toward the table, pulling bloodied implements out of his vest and placing them on the silver tray with a petulant frown. "It's as you suspected, *spy*." He spit out the word like a curse. "Vantran is in Falindar with his wife."

"What else?" pressed Simon.

"Oh, learn the damned language! Or weren't you listening?"

Simon bristled but said nothing. Of all the people who had fled with Biagio to Crote, only Savros understood the clicking language of the Triin. It was, he had explained once, "necessary to know the tongue of his subjects." And Savros had a genius for language Simon could only marvel at. This had been Simon's first mission to Lucel-Lor, and he hoped his last. He had tried to learn at least a few Triin phrases, but Savros was a poor teacher and Simon an unwilling student. The animosity between them had only grown from there.

Simon regarded Savros carefully, watching him turn a white towel red with the gore from his hands. He caught a glimmer in the Mind Bender's preternatural eyes, a spark of something hiding in the blazing blue irises. There was something more.

"What else?" said Simon. "There is something, I can tell."

"Can you?" taunted Savros. "You are Roshann, Simon Darquis. You are supposed to be observant. What have I learned? Can you guess?"

"Stop fooling," ordered Simon.

Savros surrendered with an evil smile. "There is a child," he said with satisfaction. "Vantran has a daughter."

Simon's heart sank. "A daughter? How old?"

"Very young; a baby really. Maybe a year. Maybe older, I don't know. But she lives with them in the citadel." Savros put down the soiled cloth. "Looks like you'll be going back, eh?"

Simon grimaced. That was the last thing he wanted.

"Vantran still expects something," Savros added. "You should tell the Master that. Tell him to stop bothering with this vendetta and get us off this bloody island."

I will, thought Simon darkly. He took a final look at the dead man dangling from the ceiling. The lifeless eyes were open and staring at him blankly. An invisible breeze made the corpse sway and the chains rattle. Simon felt unclean. It had been a long and miserable journey back from Lucel-Lor, and this warrior had borne his indignity proudly. Trussed up like a pig in the ship's stinking cargo hold, he had hardly said a word or eaten a crumb. Simon looked at the man's emaciated body, ruined by the Mind Bender's insane artwork. Only Savros had been able to break the Triin's iron will, and he had done it in mere hours.

"What was his name?" asked Simon quietly.

Savros looked at him incredulously. "What?"

"His name. What was it?"

"I taught you that phrase," Savros reminded him. "Didn't you ask him yourself?"

Simon shook his head. He hadn't wanted to know the man's name before.

"Hakan," said Savros. The torturer sighed. "What a waste. He could have lived so much longer."

"Hakan," Simon repeated. Then he glanced at Savros and said with venom, "I'm glad I killed him."

Without another word Simon hurried out of the cell. He slipped through the iron gate separating the dungeon from the rest of the catacombs and passed by the count's wine cellars, where a thousand barrels of priceless vintages slumbered and sweetened the air. Most were from Biagio's own vineyards, a nectar sought after throughout the Empire. The count had an army of servants tending his grapes, and here in the cellars collared slaves toiled with the heavy barrels and tasted the wines for their perfection. The slaves did not acknowledge Simon as he passed them. They knew he was a favorite of the count's, but he was not a Naren lord. He was Roshann, and that meant he was Biagio's servant, hardly different from themselves.

Past the wine cellars was a monolithic staircase of carved granite, its steps worn smooth by centuries of traffic. Simon ascended quickly, anxious for some fresh air. He pushed open the door at the top of the steps and was soon in the servants' section at the back of the count's sprawling home. It was indeed morning. Fine strands of sunlight splashed through the crystal windows and onto the red tile floor. Simon could hear the rattle of iron pots in the nearby kitchen as the slaves set to work on breakfast. He went to a window and glanced outside. The count's mansion was set on a hill, and from here Simon could see the rolling vineyards to the west and the sparkling ocean far in the distance. He drew a breath of the sweet air and closed his eyes. The Triin's dead face still haunted him. Worse, he was exhausted. He longed for sleep—or even to pull off his boots and rest his blistered feet—but he knew his master was waiting for him. The thought made Simon shudder. He had only spoken to the count briefly when they had arrived the night before, then had followed Savros into the dungeon.

Biagio had been correct about the Mind Bender's thoroughness.

"God," hissed Simon, closing his eyes. He still smelled of blood. Eris would smell it too. A little moan passed his lips. She would be worried about him. But she would have to wait, just a little while longer.

A kitchen girl passed by him. Simon grabbed hold of her elbow, startling her. "The count," he said. "Where is he?"

"The Master?" the girl stammered. There was a basket of eggs in her hands that she barely managed to hold still. "In the baths, I think, sir."

He let her go with an apologetic smile, realizing what a sight he must be with the spray of blood staining his tunic. They were still not used to their guests from the Black City, these servants of the count, and though Simon had lived in the mansion on and off for years, he was still treated like an outsider.

He proceeded through the mansion and out a covered walkway of red brick trimmed with flowers and magnificent statues. The pungent scents of the gardens wafted over him. He brushed at the wrinkles in his clothes self-consciously. Biagio abhorred untidyness. And in this part of the castle, even the slaves were better dressed than Simon. This was the east wing, the count's own sanctuary, where very few people were welcome. Simon doubted that Savros or the other Naren lords had even been invited here. So as he approached the white building—an artisan's dream of stone and gold—Simon instinctively slowed his pace, quieting his footfalls. In Biagio's garden, only the birds were allowed to speak. Already, industrious gardeners had begun their morning work, shaping giant rose bushes and plucking out weeds. A thrush nesting in a peach tree whistled disapprovingly when it sighted Simon. Simon glared back at it, wishing for a rock.

The walkway ended near a bronze arch crowned with thorny vines. Here a giant eunuch with a spiked halberd guarded the way. The soldier stepped aside when he noticed Simon, and Simon passed under the arch and into a narrow courtyard. Skirting the courtyard, he headed for the baths. In moments he saw the cedar door to the steam house, its tiny window dappled with condensation. The tubular chimney spouted moist smoke into the morning. A pair of lavender slippers had been left at the foot of the door. A single matching robe hung from a wooden peg.

Good, thought Simon as he approached. *He's alone.*

He knocked gently. The wood felt warm under his knuckles. After a brief silence, he heard his master's yawning reply.

"Come," commanded Biagio's velvet voice. Simon cracked open the door. A rush of steam struck his face. Another man might have been shocked by the temperature, but Simon knew his master's affectations and had expected the scalding. He blinked against the perfumed vapor, peering into the steam house. The room was dark, lit only by the glow of a brazier used to heat the rocks. In the corner of the room, stretched out like a lounging cat, sat Count Renato Biagio, naked save for a modest towel draped over his groin. Sweat glistened on his golden skin, and his amber hair hung long and wet around his shoulders. His impossibly blue eyes snapped open when he heard Simon enter, and a welcoming smile played across his beautiful face.

"Hello, my friend," said Biagio. The voice was alien, inhuman, with the timbre of an expensive instrument. Simon heard it over the hiss of steam, a hypnotic melody bidding him forward. Even after all these years, that voice sometimes made him tremble.

"Good morning, Master," replied Simon. "Am I disturbing you?"

"You never disturb me, Simon," said Biagio. "Come in. Let me see you."

"I'm sorry, Master. I'm filthy. I'll come back when I have dressed for you."

Biagio seemed to love this. "Let me see you," he said again. "Open the door."

Reluctantly, Simon opened the door and stepped into the heated chamber. All at once the steam engulfed him. Biagio's blue eyes widened.

"Indeed! You've gotten too close to the Mind Bender, I see. You look hideous, Simon."

"Forgive me, Master. I was anxious to give you news. I will return shortly."

He turned to go, but Biagio stopped him.

"Nonsense," said the count. "This is a bath, after all. Strip off those things and join me." He patted the place on the bench beside him. "Here."

Simon stifled a curse. He could already feel Biagio's hungry eyes tracing him. "I couldn't, my lord. I would only offend you."

"Stop playing the tart, Simon," said the count. "I insist you join me. Now undress. There's a towel behind you."

There was indeed another towel. Simon removed his clothes and lunged for the scrap of cloth, wrapping it tightly around his waist. The steam was unbearable. Simon felt its heat bite into his skin. He watched as Biagio lifted the dipper from the bowl and poured more liquid over the burning rocks. A plume of watery smoke gushed from the stones. Biagio sighed and closed his eyes, drawing in a breath. Like all of Arkus' former associates, the count had a disdain for cold. It was an odd side-effect of the drug they used to sustain themselves. Even in the longest days of summer, Biagio's skin was winter cold. The same alchemy that had turned his eyes blue had converted his blood to ice water. It had also made him immortal, or very near. Simon supposed the count was at least fifty, but he looked no more than half that age. Here in the baths, with his body fully exposed, Biagio seemed a mythical creature. He was not a big man, but his muscles were hard and corded and flexed fluidly beneath his skin. The count was proud of his body and liked to show it off, especially to Simon.

Simon sat down beside his master, the hot wood of the bench scalding his backside. He shifted his towel so that Biagio would see as little of him as possible. Biagio opened a single eye and smiled at him, slipping a frigid hand over Simon's.

"I'm glad you're home, my friend," said the count. "I've missed you."

"It is good to be back," replied Simon. Already the heat was working on him, making his eyelids droop. "Crote was never such a beautiful sight. When we saw it from the ship I thought I'd weep. You know how little I like the water."

"And Lucel-Lor? How was that foul place?"

"Distant," joked Simon. "And different. They are a strange breed, Master. You should have seen the one I brought back for Savros. His skin was like milk. His hair, too. They are more than just fair. They are . . . freakish."

"He is dead now, the one you captured?"

Simon nodded. "I killed him myself. Savros has a disgusting way about him. I couldn't watch him any longer. But the Triin had given up all he had. I made sure of that before I killed him."

Biagio laughed. "Our Mind Bender is so like a child. He was looking forward to working on a Triin. I'll take a look at this creature before he is disposed of. I want to see one for myself. Arkus was always enamored with them, and now Vantran has chosen to make his life with them. I would like to know what the fuss is about." The count's face clouded with concern. "I have heard they are very beautiful. Is that so?"

"Beautiful, Master? To other Triin, I suppose. I didn't see many of them. When I knew this one was from Falindar, I took him and left."

"You were right to, of course," said the count, easing back against the wall. "It's been a while, but I'm sure Vantran still expects something from me. It was lucky you weren't seen. You've done very well, my friend. As always. Now, what news?"

Simon steeled himself. "As suspected, Vantran is in the citadel at Falindar. He lives with his wife, a Triin."

"Yes," whispered Biagio. Everyone knew Vantran had betrayed the Empire for a woman. "The wife. Good . . ."

"This warrior was one of those guarding the citadel. He wore the same indigo blue as the others from the region. Savros says there are many more like him in Falindar, probably guarding Vantran."

"The Jackal is a hero to them, no doubt," spat Biagio. "That boy is bewitching. What else?"

For the smallest moment Simon meant to lie, but that would have been unthinkable. He was one of Biagio's Roshann, a Crotan word meaning "the Order." He was elite, and that meant he owed his master everything. Especially the truth.

"There is a child," Simon blurted. "A girl. She's Vantran's."

Biagio gasped. "A child? The Jackal has a daughter?"

"If the Triin can be believed, he does. She lives with him in the citadel. But I think she is rarely seen. Perhaps Vantran *does* still fear you. This Triin seemed to know what I was doing there. I could see it in his eyes when I captured him."

Biagio laughed and clapped his hands together. "Wonderful! A child! I couldn't ask for better! To take her . . . now that would be pain, wouldn't it, Simon? That would be beautiful."

It was the suggestion Simon had expected. "Only if she could be gotten to, Master, and I don't think that's likely. If she is in the citadel, she is sure to be heavily guarded. Better that we simply assassinate Vantran. If he goes out for a hunt or—"

"No," said Biagio sharply. "That is not pain, Simon. That is not loss. When Vantran betrayed Arkus, he sentenced him to death. And he took Arkus away from *me*. I loved Arkus. I will never be the same, and neither will Nar." The count looked away with disgust. "You disappoint me."

"Forgive me," said Simon softly, hurrying his hand onto Biagio's. "I know how you grieve, Master. The emperor's death still stings us all. I merely thought to suggest a revenge that is possible. To take his daughter or his wife is—"

"The only revenge fitting," said the count. "He must suffer as I have suffered. I will take from him what is most precious, just as he took Arkus from me." Biagio squeezed Simon's hand hard. "Understand me, my friend, I beg you. I am alone here but for you. These others don't know me. They follow me out of ambition alone. But I must have your devotion, Simon."

"Always, Master," said Simon. "You know you have my loyalty. The Roshann will always be with you."

And it was true. Even as Simon doubted his fealty, there were others in Biagio's secret society scattered throughout the fractured Empire. Biagio had formed them from the dust of Crote's farms, used them to overthrow his father and later to serve the emperor. No matter what became of Biagio or his designs on the throne, the Roshann would always be his. He was their founder, their god, and their guiding light. Biagio was the Roshann, and his agents adored him.

"It does no good to dwell on Arkus' death, Master," consoled Simon. "Think on other things. We need you. Nar needs you. Only you can make the Empire whole again."

Biagio gave a chuckle. "No one can fill the Iron Throne like Arkus did. But I will try if I can."

"Soon?" probed Simon.

"Time is a luxury we have that our enemies do not, my friend. We have Nicabar's fleet to protect us, and all the wealth of this island. Herrith and his cronies cannot touch us here. And we have the drug." Biagio's face became sardonic. "I wonder how Herrith is feeling these days. By now his withdrawal should be quite unbearable. Bovadin thinks it might ultimately kill him."

"Fine," said Simon, wiping the sweat from his brow. "That would make a quick end to our exile."

"But not as sweet as the end I have planned for him," countered Biagio. "Trust me, my friend. The usurpers have some surprises coming to them. Let them suffer without the drug and wonder what we've cooked up for them. Herrith always said suffering is good for the soul."

They both laughed, imagining the portly bishop starving for the life-sustaining potion. Since Biagio and his loyalists had fled to Crote, there had been no one left in Nar who could synthesize the drug. Herrith might have the throne, but Biagio had Bovadin, and the little scientist had always been tight-lipped about the formula. More importantly, the count had Admiral Nicabar. The commander of the Black Fleet had made their exile possible. His dreadnoughts had abandoned Nar and Archbishop Herrith, and even now the admiral's floating war machines could be seen bobbing darkly on the horizon, patrolling the waters around Biagio's island. Crote had become their adopted home, and the count had been more than gracious. They all lived like kings here, sharing Biagio's wines and fine foods and being attended to by his servants. In their homesickness they had even dubbed the tiny island "Little Nar."

"I have been away a long time, Master," said Simon. "What other news from the Black City? Does Herrith sit on the throne now?"

"Not alone. It is as I suspected. He has co-opted Vorto to act in his stead. The general pretends to be emperor now, though he doesn't dare call himself thus."

Simon raised a worried eyebrow. "Then there is no chance of the army joining us?"

"There was never that chance. Vorto is too ambitious to let the throne go. And we never cared for each other, even when Arkus was alive. He knows the only way to seize power is to side with Herrith." Biagio sneered. "Our bloody bishop is a clever man. It is land versus sea now."

"Then we must be sure of Nicabar's loyalty, Master. If we lose his navy, we are doomed."

Biagio seemed shocked. "Simon, you surprise me! Danar is canny, but he has never been traitorous. He is my friend, as you are. I won't have you speaking against him."

"It's my duty to look out for you, Master," explained Simon. "I will watch him, not because I doubt you, but because I care for you. We'll need his navy if we're to have any chance at all against Vorto's legions."

"Oh, Simon," laughed the count. "You are my mother hen. Do you think I've not been busy while you were gone? There are wheels in motion." He made a circular gesture with his finger. "Vantran is not the only one I have designs for. Herrith and Vorto will soon see what it means to trifle with Count Biagio."

A grin split Biagio's face, and Simon felt suddenly foolish. Of course his master had been hard at work. How could he have doubted it? It was a cerebral work, and difficult to penetrate, but it was clever and cruel. It was why men pledged themselves to him, why Simon had become a Roshann agent himself. Biagio was brilliant. Not like the scientist Bovadin or the demented Savros. Biagio had been born with a genius for secrets. Arkus himself had seen it, and had made the count his closest counselor. In the days of the old Empire, Biagio's Roshann, his "Order," were more feared even than Vorto's military. His was an invisible army, a legion of ghosts.

Simon settled back, letting the hot air loosen his muscles. It felt good to be out of the dungeon, and even better to be free of the ship. He had spent most of the voyage below-deck, trying to keep his stomach from thundering up his throat. And all the while he had daydreamed of the Triin in shackles in the hold, and wondered why he had participated in such a thing. These days, it wasn't enough to tell himself he was Roshann. For some reason, he seemed to be developing a conscience.

"May I ask you something, Master?" he ventured.

"Of course."

"We saw no Lissen ships on the entire journey home. I was wondering what has become of them. Do you know?"

Biagio glanced at Simon. "I think you already know the answer to that, my friend."

"So they've begun their attacks?"

"Nicabar has told me they have been hitting Naren shipping lanes for some time now. While you were gone they raided Doria."

Simon was astonished. "So close to the Black City? What's Nicabar done about it?"

"Nothing," said Biagio icily. "You know this, Simon. Don't look at me with such villainy. You must trust me. It is all part of my plan."

"Nar will not be able to defend itself from them, Master. Not without a navy."

"I know this."

"Yet you do nothing?"

Biagio's blue eyes flared a warning. "I won't explain myself, not even to you. It wasn't I who stole the Empire, remember? Our people have Herrith to blame for the Lissen attacks."

"But the Black Fleet can stop them, my lord. We're talking about innocents. . . ."

"That's enough," said Biagio, putting up a hand. "Really, Simon, sometimes I think I indulge you far too much. You have upset me now. My bath is ruined."

Simon lowered his eyes. "I'm sorry, Master."

Biagio continued to pout but said nothing until Simon got up to leave. Then, "Where are you going?" asked the count sharply.

"I thought it best to leave you now."

"Are you going to see *her*?"

There was so much jealousy in the question Simon could only shrug. "If I may, Master."

Biagio looked away. "I don't care."

Simon hovered near the door. "My lord, if you don't wish it . . ."

"You have been very rude to me today, Simon. Yes, yes, go to your woman. But remember who it is that makes this relationship possible. It is by my grace that you may consort with her. You are Roshann, Simon. You are supposed to be devoted to me only. I tolerate this infatuation only because I care so much for you. Don't abuse me."

"Yes, my lord," said Simon sheepishly.

"Oh, just go," bid Biagio, waving him away. "But be around tomorrow. *I* want to spend some time with you too."

Simon headed for the door, but Biagio called after him yet again. This time the count's tone was softer.

"Simon," began Biagio. There was real concern in his eyes. "This is difficult for you, I know. But I ask for your trust. I know what I am doing."

"I have no doubt, Master."

"In a few days I will know more. We will all sup then together, and I will try to explain things to you all. Wait until then before you judge me too harshly."

"As you say," replied Simon with a bow. He backed out of the chamber, leaving his master encased in the scalding steam.

Simon waited until mid-morning to see Eris. She would be worried about him, but he wanted to bathe properly and discard his soiled shirt. Because he was Biagio's favorite, the closets in his chambers bulged with fine clothes to choose from, and he selected a light shirt of red Crotan silk. He shaved his beard, combed his hair, and did his best to pick the dried blood from beneath his fingernails. While he dressed servants brought him a breakfast of milk and biscuits which he promptly devoured, and when he was sure his master had left the baths and started in on his day's work, he returned to the east wing of the mansion. There he found Eris alone in the music room, absently stretching against the exercise bar. Her green eyes seemed to stare into nothingness as she warmed up her muscles. Simon paused in the doorway to watch her. She looked sad, and that made him wistful. He wished he had plucked some flowers from the garden for her. Stealthily he slipped over to the piano and depressed a key. Eris looked up, startled by the note, and beamed when she noticed him.

"Hello, sweetling," he said softly.

"Simon!" Eris freed her leg from the bar and darted over to him, wrapping her arms around him and burying her head in his chest. Simon groaned and kissed her dark hair, loving its lilac scent.

"I'm sorry, my love," he whispered. "I couldn't see you earlier. I arrived last night, but—"

She hushed him with a kiss. Simon stole another, and when they were done he looked at her hungrily.

"Oh, I've missed you," he said. "How are you? Has he been treating you well?"

The girl laughed. "Of course. Why wouldn't he? I'm his prize."

"You're my prize," Simon purred, lifting her off her feet and twirling around the room. Eris squealed with delight. "You see? I can dance too!" Simon sang, spinning across the tiled floor. He came to rest on the piano bench, setting the little dancer upon his lap as he nibbled at her neck. Eris giggled some more, then tossed back her head and groaned. It had been endless weeks since they had touched each other, and neither of them could stem the tide.

"Not here," cautioned Eris. "Not now."

"Tonight, then," Simon insisted. "When he goes to sleep."

"Yes, tonight," she agreed. "Oh, my love, I was so worried. . . ."

"Do not be," said Simon. He cupped her face in his hands and stared into her eyes. "Look at me. I told you I'd come back, didn't I? And here I am."

"Yes," she said breathlessly, wrapping him in her arms. "Don't leave me again."

He grimaced. "You know I can't promise that. Don't make me lie to you."

"I know," said Eris. "But you're back now, and there's nowhere for any of us to go, not until the Master moves against Nar. And that may be months yet." She sighed dreamily. "Months together . . ."

"Or less," interjected Simon. He didn't want to shatter the moment, but she had to know the truth. "I don't know what Biagio has planned for Herrith, or even Vantran. He may need me for something."

"Not yet," begged Eris. "Not so soon. You've just returned. Tell him to wait."

Simon laughed. "Oh, yes, he'd love to hear that. Sorry, Master, but your slave doesn't want me to go. You can put off all your plans, can't you? You can? Wonderful!"

"Plans?" scoffed Eris. "Does the Master have plans? You wouldn't think so from the way everyone is acting."

"Then they don't know him," said Simon. "The Master always has a strategy. And I think he's going to tell us about it, in a few days. At least that's what he told me."

Eris traced her finger over his lips. "Mmm; then that gives you time to talk to him about us, doesn't it?"

"I can't. He's already angry with me. I can't ask him for anything now."

Eris uncoiled her arms from his neck. "Simon, you promised. . . ."

"I know, but it's different now. He's too obsessed with Vantran. I think he wants me to go back to Lucel-Lor."

"No," Eris shrieked. "You said you would ask him when you returned. He already knows about us anyway. He won't refuse you this. Not you. I've seen him with you, Simon. He can refuse you nothing. He's in love with you. . . ."

"Stop," Simon warned, putting up his hands. "Don't say it. I know what the Master is. But I am Roshann, Eris. No Roshann agent has ever married before."

"He will make an exception for you," said Eris evenly. "I'm sure he will."

Simon wasn't sure at all. He loved Eris; he had ever since Biagio had purchased her and brought her back to Crote, but he had taken an oath to the Master long ago. He was already married to the Roshann. He was bound to the Order for life, and such exceptions simply weren't made. More, they were never requested. He had promised Eris he would ask Biagio to bend the rules and stretch their strange friendship, but now that he was back under the count's dark wing his enthusiasm had chilled. Biagio was too enamored to share him with a woman.

Simon fingered the golden collar around the girl's slender neck. Except for that unwanted piece of jewelry, she hardly looked like a slave at all. Her skin smelled of expensive oils and perfumes, not the coals of the kitchens. She was Biagio's pampered pet, his prize dancer, and he had paid a royal ransom for her. He adored her—not in the way Simon did, but as a collector would adore any fine piece. There were portraits and statues aplenty in Biagio's rambling mansion, all of them priceless. But

Eris was his greatest possession. She was perhaps the finest performer in the Empire, a prodigy not unlike Biagio himself. When Biagio looked at her, Simon knew, he was seeing some of Heaven.

"I will speak to him," said Simon sullenly.

"When?" Eris pressed. "After he sends you away again?"

"*If* he sends me away again," Simon corrected. "I don't know what he has planned yet. It may be he has nothing for me. I'm very popular around here, it seems. You both like to keep me close."

It wasn't a joke, so Eris didn't laugh. She watched as Simon rose from the piano bench and went to a window. Outside, larks were singing. It had been hot when Simon left for Lucel-Lor, but now the island was cooling, hinting at a seasonal change. That's all Crote ever did—hint at autumn. Simon wanted to escape outside, to lie with Eris under an oak and stare at the clouds like children. He wanted to be away, to stop being Biagio's top man. He wanted to be normal.

"I'm changing," he muttered. Eris slipped up beside him and took his hand, but Simon stayed focused on the panorama through the window.

"You're tired, my love," offered Eris. "Rest now. Come to me tonight if you wish. Or do not, and just sleep."

Simon chuckled. "You're not hearing me. I'm changing, Eris. I'm not sure I belong here anymore. The Master is different these days. All he thinks of is revenge. That drug has driven him mad. And we are all caught up in his insanity."

"Do not say such things," Eris cautioned. "Someone may hear you."

"It doesn't matter. Everyone knows that Biagio has gone mad. Do you know he had me kidnap a man from Lucel-Lor? I brought him back with me. Savros spent the night torturing him to find out where Vantran is."

Eris blanched. "What happened to him?"

"I killed him," said Simon. "I had to. Savros was playing with him. It was sickening. I had to stop it."

"You were merciful to him," said Eris softly. "You see? You are a good man, my love."

"A good man?" scoffed Simon. "I am Roshann. There are no good men in the Roshann. And if I am good, then I don't belong here."

She took his hand, and there was endless forgiveness in her sea-green eyes. "You do what you must, as do I. We are his. To defy him is death."

Simon feigned acquiescence. "You're right," he said, hoping to end the conversation. "I was ill on the ship. It has unbalanced me." He kissed her hand. "I'm sorry to greet you like this. I promise you, I'll be a different man tonight."

"Do not come if you don't wish to," she said gently. "Or if you think it will upset the Master. I'll understand."

"I will be there," said Simon. He let his hand slide gently out of hers. "Look for me at midnight, near the garden wall. Now, get to your practice. Biagio wouldn't want me keeping you from work."

They spared each other a final kiss before Simon left the music room, his heart thundering with anticipation.

THREE

Richius Vantran

Richius Vantran drew back on the reins of his gelding and brought the beast to a halt near a grove of berry bushes. Here in the hills around Falindar the breeze was stiff, and if not for the wind he might never have noticed the bloodied swatch of cloth skewered like a flag onto the gnarled branch. He spotted it from atop his saddle, took a wary look around, then dismounted.

It was tranquil save for the buzz of the wind; the animals of the hills had fallen into a disquieting hush. Not far away, Lucyler and Karlaz were following him, stealthily scanning the land, but somehow Richius knew their search had finally ended.

The sun was bright on the mountains. Richius shaded his eyes and turned the tapering cloth in the light to examine it. It appeared to have been torn from a well-worn shirt, like the sturdy kind the farmers wore. It wasn't indigo so it wasn't Hakan's, but it wasn't weathered either, and the dried blood still had color. Triin blood, he supposed, unless the farmer had been doing some slaughtering of his own. Richius looked around. Not far above, the rocky hill disappeared into what looked like a cave. He craned his neck to see, but the entrance was dark and hidden behind an avalanche of stones. The horse, seeming to read his mind, gave an unhappy snort.

"Don't worry, boy," said Richius to his mount, going over to the beast and scratching its ear. "We're not going in there."

The gelding dropped its head, letting Richius tickle its neck. A horse was a rare commodity in this part of Lucel-Lor, and this one seemed to appreciate its station. The land was rugged here, and most of those who had owned horses had eaten them during the lean days of the war. This one was a Naren beast, given to Richius by an old comrade. It had an impeccable gait and an easy manner that reminded him of home.

"Richius?" Lucyler and Karlaz were coming up the hill on foot, their white Triin faces shining in the sun. Richius hurried over to them.

"Quiet," he cautioned. "I've found something."

He handed the shred of cloth to Lucyler. The Triin's gray eyes narrowed as he inspected it. Lucyler nodded knowingly and passed the tatter to Karlaz, who sniffed it and grunted.

"Where did you find this?" Lucyler asked.

Richius gestured to the bushes. "There, near the rocks. It was in a branch." Together they walked to the bushes where Richius showed them the spiky twig that had impaled the cloth. It was a stout bush with thorny appendages reaching out in all directions, but there were no other fragments of cloth. Several more branches had been snapped away and lay strewn on the rocky ground. Karlaz ran his hand over the top of the bush, examined the dirt, and grunted again.

"Tasson," whispered the lion-master knowingly. It was the name of the beast they were hunting, a Triin word meaning "gold." Just as Richius had dubbed his sturdy horse Lightning, the lion riders always named their enormous cats. Karlaz knelt down and put his face to the earth, drawing a breath. Then he dug a finger into the dirt and tasted the soil. Seemingly satisfied, he looked up at Lucyler and nodded.

"What was that?" Richius asked. Then, in the Triin's own tongue, he said, "Karlaz? What is it?"

"Urine," Lucyler explained. "The cats always mark where they have been. Karlaz can taste it. He thinks it is very near."

Richius pointed toward the cave's maw. "Up there," he guessed.

Karlaz seemed to agree. The trio reached for their weapons. Both Triin undid the jiiktars from their backs while Richius freed his giant sword Jessicane. Lucyler chuckled when he saw the monstrous blade.

"A good weapon for slaughtering lions," he remarked. "Not much else."

Richius drew an unsteady breath and wrapped his hands around the sword's hilt. He was under six feet tall, and the sword stood almost as high as a man. It had been made decades ago for his father, and even after months of practice with it the huge blade could still exhaust him.

"This is not Hakan's," said Lucyler glumly, tucking the soiled cloth into his own shirt. Hakan had been missing now for weeks, and while some assumed that Karlaz's rogue lion had devoured him, the lion had only escaped a few days ago. They all hoped the warrior would return to the citadel with some bizarre story of having fallen into a well or being injured in the mountains, but as the weeks passed each story seemed equally absurd.

The rogue lion, however, had already killed two people. One was its rider, who had probably been more shocked than anyone by his mount's sudden madness. The other was a farmer from a nearby village. Richius hadn't known either man, but he had seen the incredible damage done to the lion rider's body. A single swipe of the beast's paw had decapitated him. The farmer hadn't been as lucky. His children claimed he was still screaming when the cat dragged him into the forest.

Richius didn't expect to find Hakan in the lion's lair. He didn't think he had fallen into a well, either. Hakan was a Triin warrior, one of Falindar's best, intimately familiar with all of Lucel-Lor's dangers. Some said the lion had found him, some said snow leopards, but Richius suspected a more sinister creature had gotten to his friend, a monster with golden hair and blue eyes and an insatiable appetite for cruelty.

"We're not going to find him here, Lucyler," said Richius.

"He was out hunting," Lucyler reminded Richius sharply. "He might have come along here on his way back to the citadel."

"It's been too long, Lucyler. No one goes out hunting for two weeks. Even if—"

"Eeashay!" Karlaz snapped, silencing them. The leader of the lion people crouched down, motioning them to do the same. Richius realized what the man had planned.

"No," he hissed. "Are you mad? We can't go in there after it!"

Lucyler looked at Richius sternly. "We have to. The thing is a killer."

"But not in *there*," argued Richius. "It'll have us trapped."

"Karlaz thinks it might be sleeping. It is the best time."

Richius shook his head. "No way. Now that we've found it we should get help. It's going to take more than the three of us to kill it."

"Karlaz will kill it," said Lucyler. "We just have to protect him."

Richius closed his eyes and mumbled a prayer. The sight of the decapitated lion rider sprang into his mind, making his stomach pitch. Karlaz was certainly a capable fighter, but even he was no match for one of his lions. Though he was twice the size of Richius, the lion was three times the size of him. Worse, this one was mad. It would not recognize its master when it saw him, and it would not hesitate to attack.

But he also knew Lucyler was right. The thing had already killed two men, and would kill again if not stopped. They had tracked it for two days and now they had it trapped. Richius felt the weight of Jessicane in his fists. The old blade hadn't been bloodied in over a year. He hoped it would only be the cat's blood that stained it this time.

Karlaz went first, shimmying up the rocky incline toward the mouth of the cave, his big body scraping against the stone. Next was Lucyler, as silent as the cat itself as he picked his way up the slope. Richius was the last and the clumsiest, trying vainly to keep his sword from banging against the rocks and announcing their arrival. When they had all slithered up the cliff face, they paused at the opening of the cave and peered inside. Darkness shrouded the inner chamber, but they could nonetheless see that it was vast and moist and filled with ledges and dentate stalactites. Not far inside, where the sunlight surrendered to the endless rock, they saw the unmistakable outline of a human torso. There were no legs to the thing, just two bony stumps encased in ragged flesh. The face was gone. Karlaz had once explained this odd practice of rogue lions. For some inexplicable reason, the dead eyes of their victims enraged them, so they always went for the face first.

"I think we've found it," Richius quipped.

He stood up and peered farther into the blackness, but could see nothing more than the ruined corpse and the endless gloom of the twisting cavern. Karlaz proceeded into the cave, his twin-bladed jiiktar held out before him. Lucyler and Richius followed, quickly engulfed in the cavern's dripping darkness. Already vermin had set to work on the farmer's body. Maggots swam in the cavities of its nose and eyes, and Richius could hear the squeaking of well-fed rats. Karlaz cursed.

"The lion is farther in," said Lucyler. "Be ready."

It was advice Richius didn't need. All his senses were alert, picking up each tiny sound in the cavern. They stalked farther into the darkness, until the mouth of the cave became a far-off circle of brightness and they could barely see their feet beneath them. For Richius progress was slow and treacherous, but the two Triin moved with inhuman accuracy, picking their way instinctively over the terrain. Richius tried to focus on them, to use their white skin and hair as beacons. They were in a vast chamber of blue-gray rock where the air was dense and the stones rose from the earth like grotesque statues. Pockets of blackness honeycombed the walls where narrow tunnels twisted into nothingness, and the roof perspired a viscous green water that echoed as it splashed into pools a hundred feet below.

But they found no lion.

"Where is it?" asked Richius. "I can't see anything."

He was getting nervous now. He could barely see the entrance to the cave, and the heat of the place made him sweat. Lucyler was licking his lips and scanning the chamber, while Karlaz had his eyes closed tight and was sniffing the dank air. When at last his eyes opened, the lionmaster seemed confused. He growled something Richius barely heard.

"He does not know where the lion is," Lucyler whispered. "The air is too thick. He cannot smell him."

"We should go then," said Richius. "We aren't safe."

Lucyler shook his head. "No. We have to find him. You stay here, Richius. You will not be able to see if you go any further. Karlaz and I will start searching the tunnels."

"What? Just the two of you? Forget it. I'm coming with you."

"No," insisted Lucyler. "You would be blind in there. Stay here."

Richius started to protest but Lucyler and Karlaz quickly disappeared into a large tunnel, leaving him alone in the echoing chamber. He let Jessicane's tip droop to the floor. In Aramoor, he had been a king, albeit briefly. But here he was just a pink-skinned human, an outsider with none of the physical prowess of his Triin hosts. He loved Lucyler like a brother, but at times like this he resented him.

Richius busied himself with searching the chamber. It was true what Lucyler had said; he was nearly blind. But he picked his way along carefully, watching the shadows and the ledges overhead, listening for the throaty notes of the lion's breath. Somewhere in the darkness a frog or a snake splashed through a filthy pool, and he could hear the whistle of the wind as it skirted through the hills. Yet still he could find no trace of the monster, and he wondered suddenly if the lion was stalking him instead. Uneasily he looked up. There was nothing on the ledges. He started off toward the tunnel where Lucyler and Karlaz were, then heard a panicked whinny from outside.

Lightning!

"Lucyler!" Richius screamed, dashing for the mouth of the cave. "I've found it!"

Rocks and dust flew from his feet as he scrambled back through the darkness. He had Jessicane raised as the sunlight splashed across his face. Below the cliff edge, he heard the horse's manic cry, and peered down to see the beast stalking his steed, trapping it between two ridges. The thing's hind legs were taut with coiled muscles, its body poised to pounce.

"No!" Richius screamed, flinging himself from the cliff. The lion glanced upward and widened its yellow eyes. A paw came up a moment too late as Jessicane fell. The paw split open and Richius hit the ground, rolling away from the enraged creature as it bellowed in pain.

"Run!" Richius screamed, but Lightning wouldn't move. He merely stood in mute terror, watching the combatants. The lion opened its mouth and roared, baring its pointed fangs. Richius hurried to his feet and raised his sword, waiting for the beast to jump. The lion lowered its head. Richius took a step back. Giant haunches poised to spring. Jessicane trembled. . . .

And then a whoop came from above, followed by a blur of muscled flesh. Karlaz was in the air. He slammed into the monster's side, driving his jiiktar into flesh. The lion pitched in agony and batted the man away, its eyes alight with hatred. It sprang for Karlaz, and the lion-master met the charge, colliding with the creature and wrapping his sinewy arms around its neck.

Dumbfounded, Richius could barely move. Lucyler slid down the ledge and hurried toward the melee. Richius hurried after him, sword in hand. But the beast was a blur, thrashing wildly as it fought to toss Karlaz from its back. Unable to get a clean blow, Richius and Lucyler circled, jabbing at the beast. Karlaz had lost his weapon. The creature roared and fought to dislodge the man, but Karlaz's iron limbs were wrapped implacably around its throat. Blood sluiced from the lion's back and its ruined paw, and its eyes bulged from the pressure around its windpipe. But still it fought and at last threw Karlaz from its back, dashing him against the rocky ridge of the cave.

Lucyler raced forward. The Triin moved with impossible grace, slicing his razor-thin jiiktar into the beast's hindquarters. The lion spun and thrashed, but Lucyler struck again, this time slicing its throat. The lion gasped. Its yellow eyes dimmed. Then Karlaz was on his feet again, jiiktar in hand. He raised his weapon and plunged it into the lion's brain. A fountain of blood sprayed from the skull. The beast collapsed at his feet.

Karlaz dropped his weapon to the dirt. He knelt down beside the dead lion, put his bloodied face against its body, and kissed its hide. Then, with Richius and Lucyler watching, the lion-master of Chandakkar hung his head and wept.

Richius and Lucyler returned to Falindar without Karlaz. The lion rider stayed in the forest to bury the creature and take its teeth for a necklace for his son. It was an odd custom, but Richius respected it, so he left Karlaz alone to grieve. He liked the lion riders. He liked their simple ways and purity. For years they had been outcasts from the rest of the Triin, a nomadic tribe from faroff Chandakkar who wanted nothing more than to be left alone. Nar's invasion had changed all that, and now the lion people were Lucel-Lor's benefactors. They stood watch over the Saccenne Run, the only land route into Lucel-Lor.

Like all the Triin warlords, Karlaz had come to Falindar to meet with Lucyler. Lucyler was master of the citadel now. Kronin, the former warlord of the region, had no heir, and the people knew and respected Lucyler. Lucyler had accepted the position reluctantly, and said on numerous occasions that he had only one reason for taking it—peace.

And Lucel-Lor *was* at peace now. The revolution that had brought the warlords together had held even after the Narens were defeated. Lucyler took no credit for this, but Richius knew his Triin friend was proud of the accomplishment. He had worked tirelessly to keep the tenuous alliance from tattering, and even the warlords appreciated his efforts. From time to time they came to the citadel to meet with Lucyler, to discuss whatever difficulties they were having. Lucyler, they knew, could refuse no one.

But Karlaz hadn't come to the citadel to beg a favor. The man who had served Lucyler most asked the least from him, and so he had been invited to Falindar because he had never seen the spectacular place and because Lucyler simply wanted to show him some small measure of appreciation. There wasn't much in the citadel these days, but it was still a breathtaking sight and its servants could provide a fine meal. Lucyler had ordered that Karlaz be treated like a king, a reward for the sacrifices his people were making to keep Lucel-Lor safe.

The first few days had been wonderfully good. Then the lion went rogue. Karlaz couldn't explain it any more than to say it happened sometimes to older beasts. There was a fragile link between lion and rider and on very rare occasions it was severed—either by disease or some feline senility. Richius grieved for Karlaz. He had come to love the cats that kept them safe from Nar, and he could not erase the memory of Karlaz's profound sorrow. He and Lucyler rode back to Lucel-Lor under a pall, neither of them speaking.

Falindar was beautiful. They rode up the long, wide path leading to the citadel and looked at its perfectly turned spires shining brightly in the sun. In the distance the surf pounded, filling the air with brine, and a flock of gulls passed overhead, winging their way to the ocean. On the grounds of the castle they could see the milling of servants. Blue-jacketed guardians stood watch in the towers, their milky hair long around their shoulders.

Richius ached to see his wife and daughter again. Dyana would be worried about him. She always worried, and he loved her for it. He turned to Lucyler who was trotting along silently beside him. The Triin's face was long and distant.

"I'm going," he told his friend. "I'll see you tonight, maybe?"

Lucyler shrugged. "Maybe. I have things to do."

"All right," said Richius. He started to go, then abruptly stopped himself. Lucyler glanced at him questioningly.

"What?"

"I'm very sorry," said Richius. "I know you didn't want this."

Lucyler smiled awkwardly. "You are right," he said, gesturing toward the citadel. "I wanted none of this."

"I meant Karlaz," Richius corrected. "And Hakan. But it's not your fault. Remember that, all right?"

Lucyler spied the citadel. "Sometimes this is all too much for me. And we still do not know where Hakan is. Gods, what will I tell his wife?"

"I'll go with you," offered Richius. "Come. We'll do it now."

"No," said Lucyler. He straightened up in the saddle. "I have to do this myself. If I am going to be master of these people, I have to act like it."

"What are you going to say?"

"That he is still missing," replied Lucyler. "What else can I say?"

Richius grimaced. "You know what I think."

"I know," said Lucyler darkly. "And I do not believe it. It has been over a year, Richius. I think you fear ghosts."

"Lucyler—"

"No," snapped the Triin. "Stop it now. Stop it and get on with your life."

It was Lucyler who sped off this time, hastening toward the waiting citadel. Richius bit back a curse, but did not pursue his friend. Instead, he lingered until Lucyler vanished into the citadel. These had been difficult days for Lucyler, and they had changed him. He had never been jovial, but now the pressures of his unwanted position had evaporated what little good humor he had. Richius missed his old friend. He missed the man Lucyler had been. In Aramoor, Richius had known how crushing the responsibilities of kingship could be. It was the one thing about his usurped homeland he didn't miss.

When he was certain he would not encounter Lucyler in the courtyard, Richius made his own way up the winding road toward the citadel. There he saw Tresh, Dyana's friend and nurse, sitting under an immense oak tree, a pile of knitting in her lap. She was an older woman of at least forty, but her eyes were bright and youthful. Lost in her needlework, she did not see Richius ride up to her until the shadow of his horse crossed her face.

"Richius!" she said with relief. "You are home!"

Like many of the Triin in Falindar, Tresh spoke the Naren tongue fluently. She was a holdover from the days when Lucel-Lor had believed the words of Nar's manipulative emperor, when Narens and Triin had crossed into each other's lands under the guise of friendship. The former ruler of the citadel had made all his servants learn the Naren tongue, supposedly to make his Naren guests feel welcome. Whatever the reason, Richius was grateful for the dead Triin's insight. He spoke the Triin tongue well these days, but not perfectly. He got off his horse and smiled down at Tresh, who put her knitting aside and patted the ground next to her.

"You look tired," she remarked. "Sit. Rest."

"I can't, Tresh," said Richius. "I'm looking for Dyana. Do you know where she is?"

"She is with the child. They are playing." Tresh grimaced. "Behind the north tower."

Richius blanched. "Outside? Tresh!"

"I know," said the nurse miserably. "But she would not listen to me, Richius. She never does. I told her you would be angry. . . ."

"Look after my horse," Richius snapped. He raced toward the north tower. A few friends waved and called to him, but he ignored them as he crossed the courtyard and soon found himself near the back of the citadel.

Here the north tower rose out of the earth, dwarfed only by the endless sea beyond it. It was a secluded part of the castle, and Dyana liked to come here and think while their daughter played. Sometimes she would sit Shani on her lap and they would watch the ocean together, and Dyana would relate long stories. This happy recollection did nothing to soften Richius' mood, however. Even when he saw them his rage did not diminish. They were walking along the cliff, Shani's little hand in her mother's as she toddled shakily alongside. The warm breeze stirred Dyana's hair, making her look beautiful. Richius bit his lip. He did not want to love her just now. He wanted to be angry.

"Dyana," he called out. Dyana lifted her face and peered through the sunshine. She waved back happily when she recognized him, pulling the little girl's hand and making her laugh. They met halfway to the cliff, and Richius bent down and picked up his daughter and held her close.

"Richius," said Dyana innocently. "When did you get home?"

"Just now," replied Richius stiffly. She offered him a kiss but he turned away, storming off with his daughter toward the citadel. Behind him he heard his wife sigh.

"Richius, please . . ."

"I don't want to talk, Dyana," he said as he walked.

"Did you find the lion?"

"Yes."

Dyana hurried up to him and seized his sleeve. "Tell me," she insisted. "Are you all right?"

"Everyone's fine," said Richius. Shani had her hands on his face and was tracing his nose with her tiny fingers. She giggled when her father put her on his shoulders.

"Why are you angry?" Dyana asked.

At last Richius stopped and faced her. "You know why," he said. "Lord almighty, Dyana, what were you thinking? Don't you hear anything I say? It's dangerous out here."

"It is not," said Dyana. She touched his arm again but he shrugged her off.

"Don't," he warned.

"You are angry," replied Dyana, "but for no good reason. We were safe out here, Richius. Look . . ." She pointed up to the tower where a pair of Falindar's blue-garbed warriors paced a watch. "They would see any trouble before it got to us. There is nothing here. There is nothing anywhere."

Exasperated, Richius started back to the castle. "Don't argue about this anymore, Dyana. When I'm not around, you stay in the citadel. Understand? Don't go outside again without me. Especially not with Shani."

This time Dyana hurried to block his path. "I will not be a prisoner in my own home, Richius. Not anymore. It has been over a year. Nothing is going to happen to us."

"You just don't get it, do you? You don't know what he's like. A year is nothing to him. He's the head of the Roshann, Dyana. If you were a Naren you'd know what that means." He shook his head. "But you're not Naren. None of you are. Just me. So why won't any of you listen to me, damn it?"

"Easy," urged Dyana. She brought up a hand to caress his cheek, and this time he did not pull away. "You look tired."

She hefted Shani from his back and set her down. Shani teetered but did not fall. Richius smiled. He hadn't wanted to come home like this. All through the ride back he had dreamed of seeing them, and now he had shattered the moment with his rage.

"Oh, lord, you're right," he groaned, dropping to the ground. "I am tired." He reached up and pulled his wife down next to him. Her hand felt small and insubstantial in his own. "Sit with me, and let me tell you what a bastard I am."

Dyana chuckled. "An ogre," she agreed. But then her face became serious and she rested her head against his shoulder. "I am glad you are home. I was worried about you." She hesitated before asking the expected question. "What happened?"

"We found it, near a cave," said Richius. "It's dead. Karlaz killed it."

"Good."

"It got a farmer this morning near the river bed. We found him in the cave. He was dead, too."

Dyana curled closer to him. "My love . . ."

"No, I'm all right." Richius was watching Shani toddle around them, picking up sticks and tasting them. He had already given up trying to break her of this habit. Now he simply watched out for what she ate. "Karlaz stayed behind to bury it. You should have seen him, Dyana. I swear he was heartbroken. I remembered losing a horse when I came home to Aramoor after the first war. My father had already died, and I was lost and afraid. But my father had given me Thunder, and he meant everything to me."

"What happened?" asked Dyana.

"We went out riding one morning. It had snowed the night before and we were going through the forest when a pack of wolves attacked." Richius' voice trailed off. "They killed Thunder. They dragged him out from under me and killed him."

"Richius . . ."

"That horse meant everything to me," Richius continued. "He was one of my best friends. That's how it was for Karlaz, I think. Like losing a friend." He tightened his arm around Dyana; she smelled of the sea. "We have both lost a lot, Dyana," he said. "I don't want to lose any more. I don't want anything to happen to you. Can you understand that?"

"Of course."

"I'm sorry I was angry, but if anything ever happened . . ."

She hushed him. "We are fine. We are all safe here, Richius. Nothing can happen to us."

"You're wrong," said Richius. "Biagio is not a man. He is a devil, and he's still powerful, no matter what we hear. In Nar, everyone fears him. And his Roshann."

"He is nothing now, my love," said Dyana. "He is broken, an outcast."

"If only," chuckled Richius. "No, not him. He'll never give up the throne that easily. And his agents will always be loyal to him. In Nar there's an expression—'the Roshann is everywhere.' It's said that Arkus had Biagio place a Roshann agent in every Naren court, to keep an eye on them and make them afraid. They *are* everywhere, and they can reach us even here."

"Richius, it has been too long. And if he is fighting for the throne, why would he bother with us? I think you worry too much. I doubt we are so important to him."

"But Arkus was important to him. He loved the old man, and he blames me for his death. I was sent here to find magic to save Arkus. Biagio will never forgive me for betraying that trust."

"He is too busy with that bishop," insisted Dyana. "It is the bishop, yes?"

Richius shrugged. "I don't know," he said bitterly. "God, we're so blind here! I've heard nothing since the Lissens left to fight Nar."

The mere mention of Liss made Dyana stiffen. "Let us not speak of them," she implored. "Please. Not today."

"Not today? And not tomorrow? Then when?"

Dyana closed her eyes. "Never."

"Dyana . . ."

"Please, Richius. I cannot bear it. I know you want to join them, but I hope they never come back for you."

Her love was unendurable. He put his lips to her forehead and deposited a gentle kiss, caressing her shoulders and trying to comfort her.

Liss was a subject that always drove them apart, and the recent rumors that the island kingdom had at last begun its assault on Nar had made Dyana even more skittish. She called them pirates now, much the way Biagio had. She hated them, forgetting all they had done for Lucel-Lor in its struggle against the Empire. Dyana had stopped seeing them as allies. To her, they were warmongers who only wanted to take her husband away.

"It's been a long time, Dyana," Richius said. "Longer even than I'd hoped. I told you I would have to go eventually."

"Eventually," she said. "It sounded so distant then."

But it was how it had to be. For Richius, there was no alternative. He had tried and failed to convince her, and knew now that he never would. It changed nothing. His heart still yearned for vengeance—for his trampled homeland, and for Sabrina, who still came to him sometimes in dreams, screaming. They had murdered her, his first wife, simply out of hatred for him. Biagio had ordered it. Arkus was dead, as was Blackwood Gayle. But the golden man of Nar still lived. And while he existed, they could never be safe.

"You are not happy here," Dyana said. "I have tried. I thought Shani and I would be enough. I thought time would help you. But you do not want peace."

It was a miserable thing to say, but Richius recognized the truth of it. "I'm sorry," he said gently. "It is just the way of things."

"No," countered Dyana. "Things are the way you make them. If Prakna comes back for you and you go, it is *your* decision. Do not call it fate, Richius. You want this vengeance. You are letting it destroy you . . . and us."

"What would you have me do?" he flared. "Let Aramoor stay under Nar's heel forever? Live like a coward while the Lissens do my fighting? I am the king of Aramoor."

Very slowly, Dyana released herself from his embrace. "There is no more Aramoor. It is part of Talistan now. And you can never change that. Liss cannot help you get it back."

"But they fight," argued Richius. "They stand up for their honor."

"They fight only for revenge," said Dyana. "Nar no longer threatens them, so why must they attack? Because their hearts are full of poison, as is yours. They go to avenge the deaths of loved ones, yet they can never make them live again. And if you join them you leave me and Shani behind, to be alone." She looked away. "It makes me wonder when you say you love us."

This brought Richius to his feet. "Never doubt that. I gave up everything to be with you. I love you, Dyana. Shani, too. More than anything."

"Except revenge." She got up, dusted the dirt from her dress, and went over to where Shani was fixedly examining a cricket. "We will go inside now," she told her husband over her shoulder. "We will lock ourselves in the bedchamber for you."

There was so much ice in her voice, Richius could only let them leave. When they were gone he turned his attention to the ocean. Somewhere, the navy of Liss was under sail, their schooners armed and eager to exact their toll on the Black Empire. Maybe Prakna was on one of those ships. And maybe the Lissen commander was thinking about the Jackal of Nar.

FOUR

The Iron Circle

There were portents enough, Biagio supposed. He simply hadn't heeded them.

Biagio's Roshann—his "Order"—had warned him for months before the emperor's death. Blinded by his mission to save Arkus from old age, Biagio hadn't seen Herrith's rise until it was too late. Even before the emperor had slipped into dementia, Herrith had been laying plans with Vorto and convincing Naren noblemen to join him. Sure that Arkus could never die, Biagio had let the bishop play his dangerous game. For this he blamed himself, and no one else. Nar had fallen into the hands of a zealot, and the Black Renaissance was being erased.

Biagio liked being home again. He adored Crote almost as much as Nar City. Since overthrowing his father, he had spent precious little time on his island, and this forced exile from Nar had made him see the place differently. He valued it more, as his father had, and even the olives and grapes seemed sweeter somehow. The winds off the sea were warm and good for his condition, and the recent weeks of sunshine had returned his skin to its natural bronze. More, the tranquility of Crote had eased his knotted mind.

It had given him time to think.

Count Renato Biagio moved with feline grace through the marble corridors of his villa, his heels clicking loudly on the ornately tiled floor. The sculpted eyes of masterpieces watched him pass, a dozen priceless sentinels purchased or looted from around the Empire. At the end of the corridor was a staircase twisting down into darkness. Biagio was in that part of his mansion forbidden to guests, a wing that was his alone and more splendid than any other. Except for the slaves and servants who occasionally disturbed him, only one other person now shared this space with the count.

Biagio took the stairs two at a time, his mood buoyant. Torchlight quickly enveloped him. The chirping of birds fell away in the distance. Near the bottom of the stairs were a pair of tiny shoes, discarded haphazardly in the corner. Biagio could hear the sounds of tinkering up ahead. He took the last step softly and peered through the smoky light. The hallway opened into a cavernous workroom lined with tall bookcases and shelves stuffed with curiosities. The floor was littered with tools and bits of junk: spools of rope; metal fasteners; a small, dirty anvil. The torches on the wall tossed up flames and shadows, giving the place a sense of gloom, and the ceiling was high and stained with soot. In the center of the room stood a stout oak table, and on the table was a bizarre apparatus, a vaguely cylindrical thing of metal and hoses, almost organic in complexity. Its shiny tubes hung limply off the tabletop, and its domed head bore a spring-loaded lever that looked to Biagio like a door handle.

Crouched beneath the table was Bovadin, his eyes gazing up through a cutout in the wood. The scientist's naked toes balanced a long, sawtoothed cutting tool, while his small hands worked on the hoses burgeoning from his creation. He squinted in frustration as he peered up into the center of the apparatus, both hands working to stuff in metal hoses. When he heard Biagio arrive, he let out a frustrated curse and barked, "What is it?"

Biagio took a wary step forward. He didn't like bothering the scientist, especially during such important work. The room was cool and the count rubbed his hands together.

"I need to speak to you," said Biagio.

"Now?"

"Yes."

Bovadin sighed. The foot with the cutting tool started sawing away at a length of hose. Biagio watched, fascinated at the freakish precision. It was like watching an ape work.

"Well?" pressed Bovadin sourly.

"I have news," said Biagio, striding toward Bovadin. When he reached the table he studied the bizarre machine, running his hands over its smooth surface. With its appendage-like hoses, it seemed like a silver octopus. "It's good news," Biagio continued as he examined the thing. "You'll be happy."

Bovadin's squeaky voice rang from beneath the table. "Happy? Does that mean we can all go home?"

"Your fuel is here. Nicabar just arrived."

There was no more tinkering under the table. Biagio smiled and dropped down to see Bovadin's face. The scientist stared at him in relief.

"Did he get it all?" asked Bovadin. "Three shipments, like I asked?"

"Three shipments," agreed the count. "Just like you asked."

Bovadin beamed. "Oh, thank Heaven."

"Thank *me*," Biagio corrected. "And Nicabar. He could have blown up his whole damn ship carrying that cargo so far south for you. He didn't run into any Lissens, though. I suppose that's some good fortune."

Bovadin nodded. "Your duke in Dragon's Beak has done well, Renato. I'm sorry I doubted you."

Biagio's smile widened. "I'm often underestimated. Duke Enli has strings just like any other man. I just needed to pull the right ones. I knew he still had the fuel you needed. I remember when your war labs agreed to his order."

"So do I," said the scientist. "But I would have thought it long gone by now. Even so far north the fuel breaks down, becomes dangerous. Duke Enli was taking a chance keeping it so long."

"Duke Enli's kept every weapon ever shipped to him, my friend. Fear of his brother, I suppose. I knew he'd still have the fuel. I just needed Nicabar to persuade him."

"He hasn't unloaded it yet, has he? I should be there for that."

"Be as close as you like," said Biagio, grinning. "I will be nowhere near you at the time."

The count rose to study the device again, marveling at its intricacy. The little genius had outdone himself this time. The thing was heavy and the table bowed slightly under its weight. Loaded with fuel, it would certainly be heavier yet. And such unstable fuel; how would he keep it cool?

"How does it work?" asked Biagio. "Show me."

"Renato, I'm busy right now."

"What are these hoses for?"

"Later."

"Take a break, little man," insisted the count. "I want an explanation of this thing. It intrigues me."

Bovadin groaned but rose, brushing his knees of dust and metal filings. Once again playing the monkey, he climbed onto the table and stood over his invention, proudly walking around it. He was not much taller than the device and the scene was oddly comical, but Biagio had vast respect for Bovadin. The little scientist had created the war labs; he had invented the flame cannon and the acid launcher and, most importantly, he had created the drug that kept them all from aging.

"Explain it to me," Biagio said. "How does it work?"

"Oooh, now that's a secret, my friend. And I don't really think you could grasp it."

"Don't patronize me, midget. Tell me."

Bovadin laughed gleefully, and his filthy face split with a grin. "It's simple really. Beautifully simple. I'm very proud of this, Renato. Very proud . . ."

"I'm glad for you," said Biagio dryly. "But will it work?"

"Oh, it will work," promised Bovadin. "I plan to test it. That's why I wanted three crates of fuel. It will be working flawlessly by the time it's delivered." Bovadin looked at the count skeptically. "*If* it's delivered as you say."

"It will be," replied Biagio. "Don't worry. I've already made those arrangements with Duke Enli. It's all coming together as planned."

"I'll make a deal with you, Renato. I'll explain how the device works if you explain to me what's going on. I'm getting tired of your little island. I want to go home to Nar. Soon."

"Soon enough, my friend. The wheels are in motion. More than that I can't explain to you now."

"When, then?"

"Tonight," said Biagio. "Now that Nicabar has returned I can tell you a bit more. We will all sup together tonight. I will explain myself."

Bovadin seemed surprised by this. "Oh? Has Nicabar brought news from the Empire?"

"Some news, yes," said Biagio, trying to evade the inquiry. He didn't like having his plans questioned, especially by someone with a mind as keen as Bovadin's. "Enough news for me to act on, at least. Now . . ." The count pointed a finger at the device. "Tell me about this machine of yours."

"As I said, it's simple." Bovadin pulled on the lever at the thing's domed top and opened it like a hatch. Two iron hinges groaned. "This is where the fuel goes. It loads like an ordinary flame cannon. Same basic idea. But the fuel doesn't just stay in the fuel chamber like a cannon. It's dispersed throughout the device by its own pressure. That pressure keeps the fuel moving through the hoses."

"Uh-huh," replied Biagio. Already he was regretting his inquiry. "Go on."

The scientist fingered a little mechanism in the middle of the thing, a thin metal rod protruding from the device. "This is the starter," he explained. "It will be set for a delay of one hour. Once this lever is moved from side to side, the countdown will begin."

"It needs to be set easily, Bovadin," the count reminded him. "That starter piece can't be hidden."

"It won't be. Not if you deliver it as you said you would. The starter rod will be attached to the archangel. The angel has a large wing-span, remember? It will hide the lever behind it. When the angel is moved, the device will start."

Biagio chuckled at the midget's ingenuity. He remembered the marble archangel over the gates of Herrith's cathedral. Bovadin had built the device exactly to plan. Now it was up to Biagio to see its delivery. The count had spent long weeks devising the perfect means of getting the device to Herrith. Biagio was pleased with himself. The angel would be innocuous and wouldn't arouse Herrith's suspicions. And it would be easy enough for Lorla to set.

"What about the fuel?" asked Biagio. "How will you keep it cool?"

"The hoses," Bovadin explained. "The fuel will run through them constantly, getting contact with the outside air." He pointed out the tiny vanes in each hose. "See here? I designed the hoses myself. Strong, and the vanes increase air flow. The fuel will stabilize once I get it inside. But it shouldn't be jostled, either. You know that, right?"

"I know that," said Biagio. The scientist had reminded him a hundred times. He, in turn, would remind everyone else. There were a great many people involved in this scheme. The device would pass through untested hands before reaching Herrith. For Bovadin's sake, Biagio tried not to look worried. The inventor had enough on his mind.

"I'm impressed," said Biagio finally. "You've done a fine job, my friend. I only wish I could be there to see it used."

"When we take back Nar, you'll get to see the crater it leaves," joked Bovadin. His blue eyes sparkled. "It will be like the sunrise, Renato."

"Mmm, sounds perfect." Biagio closed his eyes, imagining the sun's scalding heat. If everything went properly, Herrith *would* see the device at work. And when he did, it would crush his very soul. "Remember—Herrith mustn't be killed. I want him alive."

"Don't worry. Herrith should be out of the cathedral by then, giving Absolution."

"If he's not, my plan will fail. . . ."

"Stop fretting," directed Bovadin. His smile sharpened. "Everything will work. I just need to test it."

"Let me know when you're going to test this thing," Biagio said. "I want to be alerted of any danger."

"There's no danger. The device can't really work unless it's filled with fuel. The tests will only use a little, just to see how it works. Test for leaks, that sort of thing."

It was all too technical for Biagio, who waved the remarks away. "Even so, I want to know. My whole life is in this place now. I don't want it going up in smoke. And don't test it alone. I'll get you some assistants. I don't like you tinkering away down here by yourself. You look terrible. You need more sun."

"Assistants?" scoffed Bovadin. "Kidnap some of my workers from the war labs if you want to get me help, Renato. I don't need help from your olive pickers. I spend so much time down here because I've got work to do. I'm the one making the drug, remember, and trying to finish this damn machine. Savros and Nicabar—"

"Enough," snapped Biagio. "Everyone is busy, my friend. Tempers rise. I understand that." He let his voice take on its honey-sweet tone. "Now, you will be at dinner tonight. And dress for it for once. Put some shoes on. I want a civilized evening."

"Renato—"

"I'm tired too, Bovadin. I want to go back to Nar. And I don't want to bicker. Get some rest. Sleep. I will see you tonight."

Simon spent the bulk of the day sleeping. Still exhausted from his long trip and the night in Savros' dungeon, he found his bed an impossible enticement, and slept deeply and soundly until the sun slipped below the horizon. He hardly dreamed at all, but when he did the faces he saw in his mind were white and frightened. Hakan, the Triin he had captured, came briefly to haunt him. He asked questions in his arcane tongue, begging to know why Simon had abducted him, why he had delivered him to the madman with the knives. As Simon awoke he recalled the dream, and was suddenly glad it was time to get up. He crossed his chamber and went to the window. The carpet was cool on his bare feet. Outside in the distance he saw moonlight on water and the ubiquitous profile of the Black Fleet. Another ship had joined them. Bigger than the rest. Darker, too. Simon recognized the *Fearless* at once. Nicabar's flagship. The admiral was back from Dragon's Beak. Simon smiled to himself. His master would be in a good mood tonight, maybe good enough to grant favors.

"After dinner," Simon reminded himself gently. "Take it easy . . ."

Eris would be so pleased, and he loved her too dearly not to ask this of the Master. Simon knew of no other Roshann agent who had married, except when it was convenient for a role, but he knew he was more than just an agent to Biagio. In some strange way the two men were friends. And Simon was no slave. He was a free man who had served the count long and loyally, and free men had the right to ask for rewards. Though Biagio's aristocratic blood kept them from ever being equals, Simon knew he had a special place in his master's heart. Tonight he would exploit it.

Hurriedly he cleaned his face and hands. The splash of water revived him. Biagio would be expecting him soon, so he combed his hair, giving himself a cursory check in the mirror. The Master was looking forward to the evening, and Simon wanted to look his best. If Biagio were at all disappointed in him, his favor might be declined. When he was satisfied with his appearance, Simon went to his closets and selected a fine shirt and trousers. He completed the outfit with a broad leather belt and a shiny, supple pair of thigh-high boots. Simon grinned at his reflection, then left his rooms to find Biagio.

The mansion was characteristically quiet. As he moved through the halls, Simon could hear the muffled sounds of servants in the distance and the delicate smells wafting from the kitchens. His stomach grumbled slightly, reminding him of his appetite. Crote had the finest food and chefs in the Empire, that's what all Crotans thought. Simon's own mother had been an extraordinary cook, though she was not native to the island. He missed her whenever he was hungry. Sometimes he missed Crote too much to ever leave again, and if they never returned to Nar, Simon wouldn't object. Nar was cold and tall, whereas Crote was warm and flat, a good place for a man to settle. Eris would love it here, Simon was sure. So far she had only known the gilded cage of Biagio's mansion, but if just once he could take her to the markets or walk with her along the shore, she would fall for his magnificent island.

Simon crossed the hallways to the count's private wing, passing the avenue of sculptures and the walls hung with tapestries. A vast window looked out over the grounds, flooding the corridor with purple moonlight. Here in the Master's wing, the air was sweet and smelled of lilacs. Open windows funnelled in the briny scent of sea water. When he was a boy, Simon would look up at this white palace on the hill and imagine the wealth of the man inside. The vision had fueled the young boy's dreams, had drawn him to Biagio's glamour. He had been poor then, hungry for gold and the power it could buy. And all the while as he grew to manhood, the white palace on the hill taunted him with its magnificence. Now, years later, Simon still felt a rush when he walked its halls.

When at last he came to Biagio's private chambers, he found the double doors open. Simon peered inside. Biagio was seated on a red leather chair near the window, his back to the door, slowly draining a glass of sherry. The count's golden hair glinted in the reflected moonbeams. Before Simon could knock, Biagio spoke.

"I've been sitting here, thinking," said the count softly.

Simon hesitated. Was that an invitation? Carefully he inched into the chamber, drawing closer to his master. Biagio's breathing was languid, as if he were drunk or very close to sleeping.

"Master?" probed Simon. "Are you all right?"

"Oh, I'm quite all right, dear Simon. Just relaxing. It's beautiful here, isn't it?"

Simon stopped a pace behind Biagio's chair. "Yes, very beautiful. I've been thinking that myself, lately."

"I wish I could spend more time here. I've been away too long, neglected things. . . ."

"The call of duty," replied Simon lightly. "Nar has needed you."

"Yes." Biagio put down his sherry. The jeweled hand beckoned Simon closer. As Simon approached Biagio looked up at him, his preternatural eyes glowing a furious blue. "I want you to stay close to me tonight. And I don't want you to say anything. Just be near."

Simon shrugged. He was always near his master. "Of course. You don't have to worry about that, my lord."

"The others are growing restless. And Nicabar has brought news with him from Nar. I'm worried how they might react. Stay close. Remind them of my strength. Things are going forward, but the others can't always see that. I need them to trust me. Or I need them to fear me. I don't care which."

"My lord, I will be with you. Always."

Biagio smiled warmly, one of his wild, insane smiles. He put up a hand for Simon to take. "You're my finest friend," he said. "Come. Let's go to dinner."

Simon took the count's hand and lifted him from the chair. Though loose clothing gave him a delicate look, Simon knew his lord was far from frail. The drugs he took to keep him vital had other side-effects. Besides the color of his eyes, Biagio was among the strongest men Simon knew, possessed of an almost super-human vigor. No one could run farther or longer without becoming winded, and no one could lift more weight above his head. Still, the count liked being pampered, and very rarely bragged about his strength. He ate sparingly and only of the freshest foods, and the wines he chose were always from his own, well-controlled vineyards. In old Nar, Biagio had enjoyed a reputation as a fop, but no one ever called him that to his face.

The head of the Roshann had dressed for dinner. His sable-trimmed cape made a peculiar rustling sound as he rose from the chair, and his luxurious hair hung loosely around his shoulders. Nearly all of his digits boasted a shiny bauble, and his teeth gleamed when he smiled, giving him the uneasy appearance of a prowling wolf. The count inspected Simon. A grin of approval graced his face.

"Ready?" Simon asked.

Biagio nodded. "Let's go."

As always, Count Biagio took the lead, exiting the chamber with a graceful stride that made his cape billow out behind him. Simon kept back the customary pace, close enough to hear his master yet far enough back not to overshadow him. Not that overshadowing Biagio was possible. The count shined like a beacon.

They crossed the corridors quickly, leaving Biagio's personal wing behind and entering the main living area of the villa, where the count's

Naren guests were quartered. This part of the mansion was only slightly less garish than Biagio's own. A pair of gilded glass doors hung wide at the entrance, bidding Biagio and Simon forward. Over the huge, octagonal table was a chandelier of blue and white crystal that glinted hypnotically in the candlelight. Biagio slowed a little before entering, and a practiced, theatrical smile appeared on his face. The servants in the dining room paused when they saw him. The men seated around the table looked in his direction. Simon dropped back a step and let Biagio make his entrance.

"Good evening, my friends," crooned the count. He opened his arms to the gathered Narens. "It's good to see you. Thank you all for coming."

Each of the Naren nobles greeted their host, their uniformly blue eyes watching him coolly. Simon quickly sized up the group. At the far end of the table was Savros. The Mind Bender rose from his seat and beamed. Next to the torturer sat the diminutive Bovadin. Too fascinated with his plate of appetizers, the scientist remained seated. Biagio seemed not to notice the snub. He was pumping the hands of another man, a giant in the uniform of the Naren navy. Nicabar, Admiral of the Black Fleet, embraced Biagio with a good-natured laugh.

"Renato," said Nicabar. "You look well."

Nicabar's chest was a rainbow of ribbons and medals he had earned in countless campaigns. Biagio seemed to disappear in his embrace. Simon watched Nicabar carefully, studying the hard face for any trace of insincerity. The count and the admiral had known each other many years. Biagio counted Nicabar among his closest friends. Together they had left Nar to Herrith and had orchestrated the secession of the Black Fleet. They had even convinced Bovadin and Savros to join them. They were, in Simon's estimation, an odd and dangerous team.

"I'm so glad you're back, my friend," said Biagio. The count placed a kiss on Nicabar's cheek. "And undamaged."

"Good to be back," said Nicabar, "though sailing the Empire's oceans was a pleasure. I miss them, Renato."

This got Bovadin's attention. "We all miss them," he said peevishly.

"Please, sit," Biagio bid Nicabar, ignoring Bovadin's jibe. The count took the admiral's arm and led him back to his seat. Simon followed, and when Nicabar was seated he pulled out his master's chair for Biagio to sit. Only when they were all seated did Simon take his own chair, the one at Biagio's right hand.

"Let's have wine," suggested Biagio. A clap of his hands brought servants from the shadows, collared men and women expertly balancing silver platters and flagons of Crote's fragrant vintages. As usual, Simon was served last. He waited for them all to take a sip before tasting the wine himself. It was typically excellent, and he watched the strange gathering as he sipped. From his position across the table, the midget Bovadin seemed hardly more than a disembodied head. Savros was chatting aimlessly with him. Nicabar was silent as stone. Of the four, only Biagio was married, to a woman he had left behind in Nar City. Countess Elliann hadn't shared her husband's lust for power, and had disappointed him by siding with Herrith. Now no one knew exactly where she was, and Simon doubted Biagio even cared. Nicabar was fond of saying he was married to the sea, and Savros was far too bizarre for any woman. Bovadin had the excuse of his affliction to ward off wedding bands. To Simon, the little man belonged in a grotesquery anyway. But not the golden count. He was handsome in an androgynous sort of way, and Elliann had never minded the way he bedded both women and men. Like him, she was of noble birth, and equally fickle in matters of the bedroom. What she hadn't liked—what had appalled her about her husband—was his desire to continue the Black Renaissance. Elliann wasn't a warrior. She was a pampered she-wolf who wanted only perfumed sheets and the good things of her birthright. She belonged in Nar. Not surprisingly, Biagio had let her stay.

The others had actually given up very little. Herrith knew how close they were to Biagio, and would never have let them live. Even Nicabar, Naren hero though he was, had stood beside the Count of Crote far too long to be safe from the bishop's assassins. And Simon knew how he and Vorto hated each other. It was that old rivalry, the legions against the navy, and neither would surrender or bow to the other. When Arkus died and Herrith stole the throne, Nicabar had simply ordered his Black Fleet out of Naren waters. It had left the Empire easy prey to the marauding Lissens. Part of Biagio's "grand design," Simon supposed. There were still some nations loyal to Biagio, but they were few and probably dwindling. Since returning from Lucel-Lor, Biagio had only dropped tantalizing hints of their situation. Tonight, Simon hoped, they would all have some answers.

Biagio raised up his crystal goblet. "My friends, let me speak," he said. He shot a glare at Savros to silence the torturer. "I want to say thank you. I want you to know again how much I appreciate your patience and loyalty."

They all raised their glasses. Even Bovadin, who snickered slightly, agreed to the toast. But when the drinking was done, the midget was the first to open his mouth.

"What news from Nar, Admiral?" he asked pointedly. "Renato says you've learned things."

Nicabar started to speak but Biagio raised a quieting hand. "I'll tell you all the news from Nar myself," he said. "Danar has brought news, it's true, but I want you all to understand me first. I know you're growing impatient. I know you all want to return home to Nar. But there are things in the works, things I can't tell you about."

"Hopefully things that will get us home," said Bovadin sourly. "I've built the device for you, Renato. I've kept making the drug. I want to know everything that's going on. I insist."

"The *device*," said Biagio calmly, "is not a subject I care to talk about tonight."

Device. Simon tucked the word in the back of his brain. He had known Bovadin was working on something, but had yet to learn what. The count continued.

"I called us together because of some news Danar's heard from Dragon's Beak, and because I want to assure you all that I'm in control. Things are going according to my plans. I want you to believe that." Biagio looked troubled suddenly. "Still, what Danar's heard may make you doubt that."

"The Lissens?" asked Savros.

Danar Nicabar shook his head. "No, not just the Lissens."

"Herrith," Bovadin guessed.

Biagio took a contemplative pull from his glass, then leaned back in his chair. "Yes, Herrith. I'm afraid the news from Nar isn't good these days. Herrith has been making . . . trouble."

"Trouble?" said Bovadin. "What does that mean? Renato, stop fooling. What's going on?"

"Genocide," said Biagio. There was no more humor in his expression. "What does your mighty brain tell you about that, Bovadin?"

Bovadin laughed. "He's wiping out the loyalists. We all knew that would happen. That's why we came here."

Biagio sighed. "Does the term Formula B mean anything to you?"

Bovadin stopped laughing. His insectoid face went ashen. Biagio leaned forward and hissed, "Yes, your experiment seems to work, my friend. Too bloody well."

"It was used?" demanded Bovadin.

"Two weeks ago," answered Nicabar. "In Goth. Vorto had Lokken's forces surrounded. They surrendered, because they had no choice. Vorto went in, killed Lokken, then gassed the city." Nicabar looked down into his glass. "Only a few survivors. All blind."

Bovadin was dumbfounded. "I can't believe it," he said. "They got it to work. It's incredible."

"Incredible?" spat Biagio. "Is that your word for it, Bovadin? You left a lot behind for them to build on, didn't you? You promised me they would never get Formula B stable."

"I . . . I don't know what happened," sputtered the scientist. "There aren't many people in the war labs with the knowledge to continue the work. I thought for sure it would be too dangerous for them to go on without me."

"Herrith must have changed their minds," said Savros. The Mind Bender's brow furrowed. "I wonder how."

"It doesn't matter," said Nicabar. "He's got the formula. First Goth. Then what? Vosk? Or Dragon's Beak?"

Biagio drummed his thin fingers on the table. "Apparently Herrith takes his mandate from Heaven seriously. My people in Nar City say he's determined to wipe out the Renaissance. Completely. He won't rest until there's nothing left of it. Or us."

"Then we have to move quickly," said Bovadin. "Now."

"We are moving," said Biagio. "Don't doubt that. As I've said, there are plans in the works to stop this madness. But it's going to take time. You all have to be patient."

"We have been patient," flared Bovadin. "Renato, in a few months there may be nothing for us to go back to. We have to act. We have the navy, and the device is almost ready. I say we strike back."

"Is that the best you can think of, Bovadin? How can we strike back? True, we have the navy. And yes, some of the nations are still on our side. But Vorto controls the land, not us. His legions are loyal to him, and to Herrith. We can't win with force. Not that way." Biagio tapped his skull with a finger. "We have to use our brains. Thankfully, I have been."

Challenged, the tiny genius got out of his chair. To Simon he seemed no taller. "Really?" said Bovadin. "And what have you come up with? I for one am tired of your riddles, Renato. I followed you because you said you would win this struggle. But I don't see you winning. I see you hiding."

Biagio's smile was terrible. "You followed me because if you didn't, you'd be dead now. Sit down, my friend. You're making a spectacle of yourself."

There was just enough steel in the voice to make Bovadin obey. He returned to his chair, brooding.

"We won't get anywhere by arguing," Biagio went on. "And after all, there's no need for it. My plan is simple. I have agents poised to help us, and allies sympathetic to our cause. Duke Enli of Dragon's Beak has given us the fuel we needed for your device, yes, Bovadin? He is still on our side. And there are others."

"What others?" asked Savros. The Mind Bender had been studying the argument with detached fascination while he ate, his tongue scooping oysters from their shells.

"Others who I'm sure will come through for us," Biagio replied evasively. "Others whom I trust."

"The girl?" asked Bovadin.

"Yes," said Biagio.

"What girl?" pressed Savros.

"Oh, my dear Mind Bender, you would have loved this one." Biagio chuckled and brought a dainty hand to his mouth. "A truly beautiful thing. Too young for you, I think, but smashing."

"Renato?" said Danar. "What girl?"

"A very special girl, my friend. Someone Herrith won't be able to resist. He has a fondness for children, you remember. I think this one will steal his heart."

Baffled, Admiral Nicabar lowered his drink. "Explain yourself. Who is this child?"

Count Biagio steepled his hands. Everyone hung on his words, even Simon. Bovadin, however, seemed less interested, as if he already knew the story.

"A long while ago," Biagio began, "when Arkus was still alive, Bovadin and I set up an experiment of sorts. An experiment regarding the drug. An experiment with children."

Bovadin began to squirm.

"It was a secret project of the war labs," the count continued. "We wanted to know if the drug could stop the aging process entirely. Bovadin thought the drug might work better on children."

"Their metabolisms are different," Bovadin jumped in. "I found that the way they process the drugs isn't the same as adults, probably because their bodies are still developing."

"We were able to arrest body development," said Biagio. "Rather successfully, with one child in particular."

Nicabar was plainly shocked. "My God. How many of these freaks are there?"

"Just one, now," replied the count. "We had to abandon the experiment when we fled Nar. But we saved one. A very special girl. One that I knew I could use against Herrith when the time came."

"Abandon?" asked Savros. "I don't understand. What happened to the other children?"

Bovadin looked away. The truth was sickeningly obvious.

"There was no choice," said Biagio. "We couldn't risk being discovered, especially by Herrith. Only the girl was spared." The Crotan looked around the table warily. "And don't accuse us of crimes, my friends. The experiment had a noble purpose. We were trying to save Arkus, and perhaps save ourselves. We're all still getting older, no matter how slowly. And if not for this girl, we wouldn't have a weapon against Herrith."

"Where's the child now?" asked Nicabar.

"Duke Enli is taking care of her. And that's all I will tell you."

"Enli mentioned none of this to me," said the admiral. "God, you keep such secrets, my friend. Don't you trust anyone?"

Biagio looked hurt. "Dear Danar, I trust you all. In fact, I have something very special to entrust to you. Another mission. To Nar City, this time."

"Nar City?" laughed Nicabar. "A love note for Herrith?"

"Not a love note, no. But it is for Herrith."

The admiral frowned. "Renato . . . ?"

"I want you to take the *Fearless* and some of your dreadnoughts to the Black City. I have a message for the bishop I want you to deliver personally."

"What message?"

"A letter, asking Herrith to sit down and talk peace with me."

Now they were all astonished. Even Simon's jaw slackened. Biagio looked about the room, grinning like a madman.

"This isn't a joke, my friends. You should say something."

"I don't know what to say," sputtered Nicabar.

"Is this your plan?" asked Bovadin incredulously. "To surrender?"

"Don't be ridiculous," said Biagio. He beckoned a servant over to refill his glass, then rolled the goblet between his palms. "It's just part of my grand design, you see. Herrith will never accept. He will eventually, but not right away. Gradually we will pressure him to come here. But first he'll think we're weakening. And that's all I want for now. The girl and the Lissens will do the rest for me."

"But why me?" asked Nicabar. "Why can't one of your agents deliver this message?"

"Because they can't sail the flagship," said Biagio. "And it's two messages, really. One is for Herrith. The other is for the Lissens. I want them to see the *Fearless*. I want them to think it's out of Crotan waters."

Exasperated, Nicabar shook his head. "Renato, you're not making sense. Why would you want the Lissens to think Crote's unguarded? The Black Fleet is probably the only thing keeping them away from here. Besides, I thought you wanted them to attack the Empire."

"I do," said Biagio. "Trust me, Danar. The Lissens have been attacking Nar, and I say let them continue. But let them also think we here are unprotected. Let them think we've come to the aid of the Empire. It's all part of the plan."

"Oh, yes," muttered Bovadin. "The 'grand design.' Sounds like nonsense to me. What are you trying to do, get us all killed? If the Black Fleet leaves, the Lissens will swarm over Crote. You know that, Renato. They blame you as much as anyone for the war."

Biagio put up his hands. "Enough. Danar, you will do this thing for me. You will leave in a few days. But you are not to engage the Lissens or sink their ships. Do you understand that?"

Confused, Nicabar nodded glumly.

"Say it."

"I understand."

Biagio smiled. "Good. Now . . ." He picked up a fork and plunged it into an oyster. "Let's eat."

Evenings on Crote were always warm. Winter was coming, but not to this island. The trade winds off the ocean drew in the southerly air, keeping away the frost and making the flowers bloom throughout the year. In the damp of spring, lovers walking through the ancient avenues could hear the calls of night birds and the exotic music of insects. But it was cooler now, slightly, and the creatures of the island slumbered. Along the beach meandering past Biagio's villa, Simon heard only the tranquil rhythm of the ocean. His master Biagio walked a few paces in front of him, the gentle surf lapping at his boots. They were both full of oysters and stuffed duck, and the heaviness in their guts had made them quiet. It was very late now. Even the moon had started to dip. A train of clouds crossed its path, turning the ocean black. Simon felt his eyelids drooping. He had hoped to go to Eris tonight, but the dinner had taken longer than he'd hoped, and Biagio had wanted his company.

For over an hour they had walked along the beach, barely speaking a word to each other. The Master seemed troubled. Occasionally he dipped his jeweled hand into the sand, retrieving a shell or stone, then pitching it into the water, but mostly he just walked, slowly, aimlessly, making Simon wonder what plots he was hatching in his mind.

"Simon?" the count called over his shoulder.

"Yes, my lord?"

"I'm getting tired, but I don't want to go back yet. You know what that's like?"

Simon shrugged. He had no idea what Biagio meant. "Yes, I think so."

"It's a nice night, isn't it?"

More nonsense. "Yes, very nice."

"Come closer," bade Biagio. "Walk with me."

Simon did as requested. Together they strode along the beach and let the water soak their boots, while Biagio kept his eyes on the horizon. The silhouettes of Nicabar's Black Fleet bobbed in the blackness. To the east where the land hooked around, Simon could see the lights of Galamier, the town where he'd grown up and where he'd first learned to pick pockets. Galamier was very dim tonight and glowed a hazy orange. Simon's eyes lingered there, and Biagio's melancholy was suddenly contagious.

"I think they doubt me," said Biagio.

Simon grimaced. "It's a lot to ask of them. They don't know you as I do."

"Yes," Biagio agreed. "But I have plans, you see. Great plans for Herrith and that dog, Vorto. I can't just kill them as Bovadin suggests; that would solve nothing. Herrith would be dead and we would still be stuck on Crote. One of our enemies would rise to the throne. We must destroy them all."

"Of course you're right," said Simon.

"I have many enemies in Nar these days."

"And many friends, my lord."

Biagio chuckled. "That number is dwindling, dear Simon. Lokken's death proves that." The count's expression hardened. "And there will be Talistan to deal with, too. They will not accept me as emperor. Tassis Gayle is like Herrith. He thinks I am not 'man enough' to be emperor!"

"They are both fools, Master."

"Yes." Biagio kicked at the sand with his boot. "Duke Lokken was a good man. Loyal. He knew what the Black Renaissance was about, what Arkus was trying to achieve. He died a hero. I won't forget him."

"He'll be avenged, my lord."

"Oh, indeed," said Biagio. He turned to Simon and clasped his cold hands on his shoulders. "Look at me, Simon."

Simon looked. Biagio's eyes were impossibly bright. "Yes?"

"Whatever else you hear from the others, whatever you may think of my plan, I promise you it will work. I don't just intend to kill Herrith. I plan to destroy him—and all his sycophants. When we return to power, there will not be anyone else to contend with. Not Herrith and his sick church, not Vorto and his legions, not anyone. My grand design will take care of them all, Simon. All of our enemies."

"I believe you, my lord," said Simon. "I truly do."

"But you worry. You think I'm letting the Lissens attack Nar out of spite. It's not spite, Simon. It's part of my plan. Can you understand that?"

Simon smiled. "I don't have your gift for such things. But if you say it's so, then I believe it. Without question."

Biagio's expression melted. "Thank you, my friend."

Simon felt his courage cresting. His mouth dried up as he fought to form the words. Biagio started back off toward the villa.

Now, Simon screamed at himself. *Do it now!*

"My lord?" he said weakly.

"Uhmm?"

"May I ask a favor?"

"Of course."

Simon hurried to catch up. He stayed one pace behind the count as he framed the request. What he was asking bordered on impossible, but he and Biagio were friends. Almost.

"Simon," said Biagio. "Stop dallying and ask your question."

Simon wet his lips. "It's about Eris, my lord."

The count's pace slowed perceptibly. "Oh?"

"You see, I am very fond of her."

"Yes, I know," said Biagio. The old, familiar jealousy crept into his tone.

"My lord, what I want to ask is . . . difficult." Simon stopped walking and lowered his eyes. Biagio stopped, too. The count stared at his servant curiously.

"You started this," Biagio warned. "Finish it. Go on and ask your question."

Simon straightened and stared directly into Biagio's eyes. "I love Eris, my lord. I've loved her since you purchased her. I want to be with her. I want her for my wife."

Simon waited for the rage, but it never came. Biagio's expression was serene for a moment, and then a different emotion overcame him, one not of anger but of sadness. For a moment Simon thought his lord might weep. Biagio looked away.

"This seems sudden," said the Crotan. "I'm . . ." His voice trailed off with a shrug. "Surprised."

"I know it's asking a lot, my lord. It's not tradition, I know. But I do love her." Simon bowed his head, then fell to one knee in the sand. He took Biagio's cold hand and kissed it. "My lord, I beg this of you. Let me have Eris. I've served you loyally. I always will. You are my greatest passion."

Biagio scoffed. "Not as great as the dancer, though. Get up, Simon. You're embarrassing yourself."

Simon rose but kept his head bowed. Biagio turned his back to him. For a long moment the count stared off into the horizon, hardly breathing as the breeze stirred his golden hair. The ocean came and retreated, and Biagio just stood there like one of the statues in his mansion, cold and unapproachable.

"Simon, I will do this thing for you," said the count at last. "Because I care for you. Do you know that? Do you know how much I care for you?"

Simon knew. "I do, my lord."

"Eris is my prize, my property. There is no other dancer like her in the Empire. But I give her to *you*, Simon. I break with the traditions of the Roshann, for *you*."

"Thank you, my lord. You are truly great. . . ."

Biagio turned to face him. "But in return, you will do something for me."

"Anything," agreed Simon quickly. "Ask me anything, my lord. I will do it willingly."

"You will go back to Lucel-Lor. You will find Richius Vantran. And you will steal his daughter for me."

"What . . . ?"

"That's it, Simon. That's my price for the woman. Bring me the Jackal's daughter."

"But my lord, Vantran is guarded. I could never get that close to him. There's no way—"

"You underestimate yourself, my friend," laughed Biagio. "You can do it. You're my best agent, the only one who can pull it off. Get into Vantran's confidence. Find out his plans. Make him trust you. Then, when his guard is down, take the child."

"But why?" sputtered Simon. "What do you want with the girl? She's just a baby. . . ."

"I want what I've always wanted," Biagio roared. "I want Vantran to suffer! He took Arkus from me. Now I will take what is precious to him. It is justice, Simon. Nothing more."

Simon fought to control himself. It was madness, not justice, but he couldn't say so. Not now. Eris was almost his. They could marry. Biagio had agreed.

"My lord, even if I could get into his confidence and steal the baby, how could I possibly get back here with her? We're a long way from Lucel-Lor."

"A ship of the Black Fleet will take you to Lucel-Lor. While you're there, it will stay behind to patrol Triin waters. It will be there when you need it to return."

You've got this all planned, don't you? thought Simon bitterly. *The master puppeteer at work.*

"My lord," said Simon cautiously. "Think again on this, please. Your vengeance against Vantran is clouding your mind. There are other things to worry about. Herrith and Vorto—"

"Are being dealt with," snapped the count. "But Vantran has gone on too long without tasting my wrath. It's time for him to suffer. Time for him to pay for what he's done." Biagio stepped closer to Simon, until their noses almost touched. "He killed Arkus, Simon. He betrayed Arkus and the emperor died because of it. And all for a god-damned woman. Now I will take what has come from their cursed union. In the name of Arkus, I will take it!"

Simon stood very still.

"You will do this for me," Biagio continued. "And in return I will give you the dancer. That is our bargain. Do you accept it?"

"Yes," said Simon sadly. It was the only word he could manage, for his voice had abandoned him.

"You will leave in a few days," said Biagio. "I will look after Eris for you."

And with that the golden count turned from his servant and strode away.

FIVE

The Conscience of a King

The citadel of Falindar stood on a cliff overhanging the ocean, erupting from the rocky earth. In all the vastness of Lucel-Lor there existed no other structure as high or as splendid, nor any with such a pedigree. It had stood for centuries on its perch, weathering wars and the occasional hurricane, housing the royal family of Lucel-Lor—that long lineage of Triin noblemen that had called themselves Daegog. The Daegogs had ruled Lucel-Lor from Falindar, showering themselves in wealth and taxes, and had watched apathetically as the warlords of their land methodically carved up the nation and claimed territories of their own. In the era of the warlords, the last of the Daegogs had merely been figureheads, rulers in name only, until finally there were no more of their greedy clan. There were only the warlords and their squabbles.

But Falindar remained. Like the memory of the Daegog, the citadel was permanent, and in these days of peace, the warlords looked to Falindar for strength and guidance and asked favors of the man who now called the place home. The new master of Falindar had taken the job reluctantly. The death of the old master had made any other choice impossible.

Richius Vantran knew the sad chronicle of Falindar. He knew the warlords personally and had fought with them against Nar, had watched Triin comrades die at the hands of his Empire. Lucyler, Falindar's new master, was his closest friend, and the two had become like brothers. Yet still, long months after the war, Richius was no closer to understanding the Triin. In Aramoor, his homeland, he had been a king. A poor one, he believed, but a king nonetheless. He had not been an oddity because of his pink skin. There had been servants and responsibilities to occupy him, and the days were quickened by demands. He had despised the kingship the death of his father had thrust on him, but it had defined his life. It had given him purpose.

All men need a purpose. Richius' father had told him that, and it haunted him. But in Falindar, the days dragged and the nights were unbearable. Richius had become little more than another of the castle's ornaments. He was still Kalak, the Jackal, and a hero to the Triin, but they seemed not to notice or need him anymore. In the months since Lucel-Lor's victory over Nar, Richius had rested and gained weight. He had watched the growth of his daughter, and had speculated about the goings-on back in the Empire, but he was isolated. Lucyler busied himself with the famines and the reconstruction of the Dring Valley—and the other territories scarred by the war—and he rarely had time for his Naren friend. Richius watched Lucyler with envy, remembering fondly what it was like to be busy. He helped when he could, loading carts full of grain and patrolling the grounds around Falindar, but he was nagged constantly by the feeling that he was simply in the way.

He spent most of his days with Shani, idling the hours away. Shani was leading a pampered life. She was Kalak's daughter and so wanted for nothing, and Richius wondered sometimes what type of woman this would make her. Her face had some of his features, and that marked her as something more or less than Triin, but she could never go to Nar and discover the other half of her heritage. Aramoor was now firmly in the hands of the Empire. Unless he could create a miracle, she would never see the place her father considered home. Biagio had seen to that. Even exiled, the golden count had influence. Aramoor was ruled by Talistan now, just as it had been before the little nation had broken free. A new governor had been appointed to replace Blackwood Gayle—the iron-fisted Elrad Leth. Richius didn't know Leth well, but he knew his reputation. Aramoor was suffering under him, certainly.

Today was a day like any other in Falindar. Dyana had spent the morning playing with Shani and trying to teach the girl her first Triin phrases. Shani could barely gurgle, but Dyana was convinced she knew the word *mother*. Feeling melancholy, Richius had gone off riding. Before leaving he had made Dyana promise that she and Shani would not leave the grounds of the citadel. Reluctantly, his wife agreed.

So Richius rode for an hour and more under the cool afternoon sun, losing himself in the colorful show of Lucel-Lor's autumn. He rode until he reached the forest far to the east of Falindar, an ancient grove of tangled trees with bark like stone and black branches. Here is where he had left Karlaz to weep, when the lion-master had slain his rogue mount. Karlaz had not returned to the citadel. Instead he had remained in the woods.

And perhaps it was this that drove Richius to the forest. Lonely but not truly wanting to be alone, Richius steered his steed into the heart of the forest, past the village where the rogue lion had attacked, and finally to the range of mountains where he and Lucyler had left Karlaz behind.

Richius had barely arrived at the mountain lair when he heard Karlaz's unmistakable voice, singing. It was a low, droning chant, strangely joyous, and Richius followed it, hoping not to disturb the warlord. He tracked the voice to a clearing by a shallow lake, where Karlaz, his hair wet and matted with filth, knelt in the mud and cupped water in his hands, letting it dribble over his face as he sang. Richius reined in his horse a safe distance from the warlord, observing the odd ritual from the safety of the trees. Karlaz continued with his song through three more handfuls of water. When he was done, he laid his palms down on the soft ground, stooped, and kissed the earth. Then he raised his head. He did not turn, but instead sniffed the air like an animal.

"Kalak?" he guessed.

Richius grimaced. "Yes," he replied in Triin. He formed his words with effort, speaking slowly as he made the Triin language. "I am sorry, Karlaz. I did not mean to disturb you."

"You are not disturbing me. My prayer is done." Then the warlord chuckled. "But if the Gods heard me, I know not."

"Gods hear very little, I've learned," said Richius. He understood most of what the warlord was saying, filling in the rest with his imagination. "I can leave if you want."

"Kalak, you have come a very long way. To find me?"

"Yes."

"Why?"

Richius dismounted. Still Karlaz did not turn to face him. "Because I need to speak with someone," said Richius. "Because I am troubled."

"And you chose me?" This intrigued the warlord enough so that he turned his head. There was a curious smile on his face. "I am not the village wise-woman. Why me?"

"I am not sure," said Richius with a shrug. "Maybe because I have no one else who would listen. Or understand. I am—"

"Troubled. Yes, so you have said. Come." Karlaz patted the wet ground next to him. "Sit with me."

Richius grimaced. "In the mud?"

Again the warlord beckoned Richius forward. "I have been watching you, Kalak. You live among us, but you are not Triin yet. I will teach you something. Come."

Reluctantly, Richius picked his way over the rocky ground toward

Karlaz. At the warlord's insistence he knelt down beside him. Immediately his knees disappeared with a sucking sound, the water soaking through his trousers to the skin.

"Now what?"

"Shhh," Karlaz directed. "This will calm your mind. But you must be quiet. You of Nar, you are never quiet enough. You cannot hear the silence." Karlaz made a cup of his hands again. "Do this," he said. "Yes, that is good. Now . . ." He dipped his hands into the water until his hands filled, watching as Richius did the same. But when Karlaz dropped the cold water over his face and chest, Richius balked.

"Karlaz, I am not very religious. I do not want to pray."

"Shhh," said Karlaz. "This is not prayer. No. This is for you, not the Gods. When we do this thing, *we* are the center of the world."

It was all cryptic nonsense, but Richius did as the warlord asked, raising his hands to his face and letting the water slowly dribble out. Not surprisingly, he felt no different, but he dipped his hands in the water again and repeated the process three more times along with Karlaz. Richius stole a glance at the lion rider, whose eyes were closed in contemplation.

"What are we doing?" he whispered.

"We are becoming part of the earth," said Karlaz. "Part of the soil, part of the water. Part of the sky if you look at it. Look at the sky, Kalak. Keep your eyes open and look."

Richius looked. He poured the water over his face, straining not to blink, and watched the blueness of the heavens blur in the waterfall. He felt giddy suddenly and he laughed.

"Good!" Karlaz encouraged. "You see? You are part of the earth now. Part of nature. Now sing with me."

Again Karlaz began to chant, elbowing Richius to join him. Richius joined in, shyly at first, then stronger as the mood swept him. It was still nonsense, but he loved it. He loved being part of nature, and he imagined the water washing him clean, carrying away his sins and his past. He chanted with the warlord for long minutes, and when Karlaz stopped singing Richius went on alone, louder until the birds flew from the trees and his song wasn't a chant suddenly but a pained, cathartic cry. . . .

Richius let all the frustration blow out of him, and when he was done he opened his eyes and glanced at Karlaz, horrified. The lion-master stared at him.

"Troubled," murmured Karlaz.

Richius was breathing hard. "Yes. Oh, yes . . ."

He had no other words. He was a prisoner of his memories. Aramoor flashed before him, perfect and green, and the shattering sight of Sabrina's head in a box, staring. A gift from Biagio. He had never truly loved her but he loved her now, and he feared suddenly that she would never be silent, that her screams would echo endlessly. He brought his hands to his face and covered his eyes, willing the images away, but they remained, just as they had always remained.

"Karlaz," he said shakily. "I am alone here. I am like you. A stranger in Falindar."

The warlord took Richius' chin in his hand and pulled him closer. "You are not alone, Kalak. Hear me? Kalak can never be alone here. You have a wife, and a daughter. I have seen them with you." He smiled, and the expression was surprisingly gentle. "Kalak is not alone."

"Dyana," Richius nodded. "Yes, she is wonderful. I love her, but she does not understand. She does not know what I am going through."

The warlord's grin broadened. "Always men talk about the wife that does not understand. Triin men are the same. They should listen to their wives more. The females know more than we think."

Richius nodded, somewhat ruefully. "Yes. But I have tried to speak to her, and she will not hear me. She does not want to listen to what I have to tell her. To her, it is just bad news."

The warlord's eyes narrowed to scrutinize him. "I have been watching you, Kalak. I have seen you at work, and I have heard the way the others talk about you. I know that you were married before; that Dyana is not your first wife. The guards, they talk. They say that you are unhappy here, and that your heart is full of vengeance. And you walk alone at night, in the courtyard. I have seen you."

It was all true, so Richius didn't deny it. Those nighttime walks had been his only means to exorcise the demons that always came to him in sleep. But suddenly the warlord's perception made him uneasy. He got up from the ground, brushing the mud from his knees and wiping his filthy hands on his trousers. Karlaz looked up at him, but did not rise.

"I have disturbed you," said Richius. "I am sorry. I will go now."

He turned to go, making it halfway to his horse before Karlaz called after him.

"Now Kalak runs," said the warlord. "And he still has no answers."

Richius turned. "Karlaz, I . . ."

"Yes?"

"Talking about this is hard for me."

Still Karlaz stared at him. "If you go, you will only be frustrated. And then you will tell your wife that you are frustrated, and you will both be angry. You came to talk. So talk. I will listen."

It was an odd invitation, but of all the Triin warlords Richius had known, only Karlaz had seemed like kindred. Perhaps it was why the other warlords had always shunned him; he was nothing like them at all. Richius lingered between his horse and the stream, contemplating what to say. He could think of no tangible reason for coming to Karlaz.

He just wanted a companion. Amazingly, Karlaz seemed to read his mind. The man rose from his knees and strode over to him.

"Lucyler is a good man," he said. "I trust him. But he is busy these days with great matters. The other warlords, they look to him for answers to their silly feuds. They eat up his time with nonsense. He has no time for you. And this discourages you."

Richius laughed. Perhaps Karlaz was a magician. "Yes," he admitted. "That is right, I think. I feel alone here. I am not Triin, and I am out of place. And . . ." He stopped himself, wondering if he should go further. The warlord cocked his head inquisitively.

"And?"

"I have dreams," said Richius. "Bad dreams. Of home. Of my first wife, Sabrina. It is all inside me, in here, crying to get out. I do not belong here. Since the war with Nar ended, I have done nothing for my people in Aramoor. They think I have betrayed them, and they are right. Sabrina died because of me." He looked away, horrified at what he was admitting. "I am cursed, Karlaz. Everyone who trusts me dies, but I always live. That is my curse—to live while everyone else dies."

Karlaz's brow wrinkled. "Narens are superstitious. Curses and portents—they are nonsense. It does you ill to speak so. I know of your wife, Kalak, the cruel thing they did to her. Your vengeance must be great. It is right to feel your anger. It is what a man should feel."

"It screams at me, Karlaz. Sometimes it is all I think about. I need to be doing something for Aramoor, something to avenge what they did to Sabrina."

"But you have avenged her," said Karlaz. "I have heard the story of the man with the metal face, the one called Gayle. You battled and killed him. She *is* avenged, Kalak. You cannot slay a man twice."

"Would that I could," spat Richius. He would love to have that pleasure again. Often he remembered his sword cutting through Gayle's skull and the look of astonishment on the baron's face. But Blackwood Gayle had only been a pawn, a puppet on Biagio's strings. Gayle was dead but Biagio lived on, and had yet to answer for his crimes.

"There is another man," Richius explained. "The one who ordered her death. I know you do not know much about Nar, but this one is a devil. He is a Naren nobleman. He was the emperor's closest advisor before the old man died. His name is Biagio."

Karlaz tried to wrap his tongue around the name. "Beeagyo," he managed to say. "A bad man?"

"Oh, worse than bad. Evil. Do Triin believe in Hell? Because he is from Hell, I swear it. He ordered my homeland overrun, and he gave it to Talistan to rule."

Karlaz folded his arms over his chest. "Where is this Beeagyo?" he growled. "In the Empire?"

"I am not sure," said Richius with a shrug. "The news I hear from Nar is not very reliable or recent, but I have heard he is in exile. After the emperor died, there was chaos in Nar. Biagio had to flee, probably to his island. There is a bishop in power now, a holy man you might call him. Not a friend of Biagio's. But not a friend of mine, either." He sighed. "I cannot really explain this to you. It is something you have to see to believe, but Nar is run by evil men. Not just bad or cruel, but truly evil. Their souls are black, you see? Black like death. They have to be stopped."

The warlord looked at him suspiciously. "By you?"

"Maybe," said Richius. "Why not?"

"One man alone against an empire. That sounds like a fool's crusade, Kalak. And you are an outlaw in Nar, yes? Show your face, and you are dead. Your wife is widowed, your daughter fatherless. That is not being a hero."

"But I would not be alone. I would go with the Lissens. I would join in their fight."

"The Lissens have left our waters. They do not come to Lucel-Lor anymore."

"But they might be back. Their commander told me so. He said I could join them if I wanted."

"And what did you say?" asked Karlaz, looking like he already knew the answer.

"I told him that I would help if I was needed. Can you understand that, Karlaz? You helped the other Triin to fight Nar because they invaded your land. You were willing to die. Should I not be at least as brave as that?"

"It is different, Kalak."

"Why?" asked Richius hotly. "Why is defending Aramoor any different from defending your village?"

"It *is* different," repeated the warlord firmly, "and I will not argue this with you." Then he sighed and his face became mournful. "You have much to think on, Kalak. You should talk to the sky."

For a moment Richius thought that his Triin had failed him. Talk to the sky? "What does that mean?"

"In Chandakkar, when a man is troubled, he talks to the sky. He goes away from all others, like I have been doing here. I have had things to think on. I have been talking to the sky."

And to the mud and water and trees, thought Richius wryly. "Karlaz, I am not understanding you. You want me to go away? Leave Falindar?"

"For a time, yes. Talk to the sky. Listen to what it tells you." The big man poked his finger into Richius' chest. "Listen to what *this* tells you. Your heart, Kalak. Your heart."

. . .

Dyana Vantran was barely twenty years old, but she had seen a lot in her brief lifetime. The daughter of wealthy Triin parents, she had been bred as an aristocrat, had learned the tongue of the Naren Empire, and had been married to a man who slew her father. She had been a refugee, a prostitute, a symbol of derision, and the object of more than one man's madness. She had survived two devastating wars. Yet in all the roles she had played, she was only happy in her current incarnation—the wife of Richius and the mother of their small daughter, Shani. She was satisfied in Falindar, and despite her best attempts to understand her husband's moods, she could not understand why Richius wasn't.

Dyana remembered empty stomachs, and her bitter past made her grateful for the bounty of Falindar. No one in the citadel ever hungered—especially not Shani—and they were sheltered here from the violent whims of the warlords. Lucyler had done an admirable job as Falindar's master, and because of his friendship with Richius, he had made sure they wanted for nothing. And they enjoyed the respect of the people in the region; Richius was a hero here. But he never saw it that way, and it irritated Dyana. In the last few months he had grown distant and moody, his eyes always drifting toward the sea, where Dyana knew he searched for Lissen ships. He was still a good father and attentive to their child, but something had changed. She had fallen in love with a man with boyish charm, and she missed his eagerness, his innocence. He was somehow diminished. These days, Richius was quiet. He shared precious little with her, leaving her to wonder what went on in his head. When they had first married, she could read his expressions easily, but no longer. He had erected a wall around himself that even she couldn't scale. They made love in perfect silence.

That night, Dyana was asleep when Richius finally returned to the citadel. It was very late, and she had gone to bed alone, as had become her custom. Shani was in a nearby room, also sleeping. Dyana heard the door to her bed chamber open. She cracked one eye to glimpse Richius in the threshold, moving furtively in the moonlight. He peered at her through the darkness, checking to see if he had awoken her. Dyana didn't move. She listened as Richius stripped off his clothes, then washed quietly from the basin by the window. After pulling on a nightshirt, he very carefully slid into bed next to her.

"I was worried," said Dyana.

There was a long pause before she heard Richius sigh.

"I'm sorry," he offered.

"It is late." She stole a glance out the window. The moon was dim. "Almost morning. Where have you been?"

"Out. Thinking."

"Thinking? You have been gone all day." When he did not answer she rolled over to touch his shoulder. He seemed reluctant to face her. "Richius," she whispered. "Tell me what is wrong."

"Nothing that you can help, Dyana. Go back to sleep. I'm sorry I woke you."

"I cannot sleep. Not now." She gave his shoulder a shake. "Please . . ."

At last he rolled over to look at her, his face grim and exhausted. He stank of the fields.

"I know you are unhappy here," Dyana said. "I know you want revenge. But I cannot let you, Richius."

Richius' voice was barely a whisper. "Dyana, I love you. And I love Shani. You're everything to me. So why am I so restless?"

"Bad memories," she said. She stroked his head, hoping to soothe those burning recollections. "War does this to a man. It will pass. I know you cannot believe that now, but it will. You need time to heal."

"Every night I think of going back to Nar," he said. "Back to Aramoor. I've abandoned them all, Dyana. I let them die. And I hear them screaming at me, accusing me. Even Sabrina."

Sabrina. Dyana glanced away. She had never told Richius how she shared his guilt over her death, though she had never even met the girl. But he had abandoned Sabrina and Nar for her, and for that his wife had been murdered. Dyana's hand trembled a little and she pulled it from his brow.

"Sabrina is dead," she said coldly. "You cannot bring her back."

Richius stared at her. "I know that. But there are crimes to answer for. Someone has to pay."

"Someone is paying, my love," said Dyana. "You."

"Dyana . . ."

"No," snapped Dyana. "Stop and listen to me. Sabrina is dead. And Aramoor is gone. You live here now, Richius. You live among the Triin because you cannot go home again. This is all there is for you." She looked away. "I am all there is for you."

A lumbering guilt assailed her. She had said it. And it had felt good. But now, in its aftermath, came a terrible silence. Richius was staring at her. She could feel his eyes through the blackness. He resented her and she knew it.

"You came back here for me," she said glumly. "But that was your choice, Richius. I never asked you to. You thought it would make you happy, but nothing makes you happy. And now you blame me for your misery."

Richius sat up. "I don't," he insisted. "Don't say that."

"You do. I see it when you look at me. You want to go off and fight Nar with the Lissens, but you do not care what will happen to us. And you do not see the danger, because you are blind with hate. Nar is pulling itself to pieces, and you want to be part of that."

"Aramoor is my land, Dyana. I'm the king."

"You are not," said Dyana. "Not anymore. And no matter what you do to Nar, even if you kill your Count Biagio, you will never get Aramoor back." Her shoulders slumped. "Why do you make me be so cruel? Why do I have to tell you this, when it should be so plain to you?"

Richius' bravado melted away. "I just want to do what's right," he said weakly. "But I don't know what that is."

Dyana shrugged. "Nor do I. But I want you to be whole. I want my husband back."

Gentle as a breeze, he slipped an arm around her. Dyana shuddered at the touch. He put her head down against him and stroked her white hair, and she was like a child in his embrace, frail and adored. She didn't want him to see her cry. She wanted to be strong for him.

"The Triin have an expression," he said. "Talking to the sky. That's what I have to do, I think."

"What?"

"I have to talk to the sky. You don't know that expression?"

"Where did you hear that?"

"From Karlaz. He says it's what Triin men do when they're troubled. They go off and be with nature for a time. They look for answers."

"In Chandakkar, maybe. I have never heard that before." She pulled herself free of him. "Is that what you want to do? Leave Falindar?"

"Yes," he said.

"Alone?"

"It wouldn't be much good if I weren't alone, Dyana. I need to think. I need to get away from here for a little while. I have a lot inside I need to sort out. Is that all right?"

"I cannot stop you."

He tried to smile. "You're angry."

"Yes," said Dyana. "You are always telling me what danger I am in, and now you say you want to leave. What about Biagio? Are you not worried about him?"

"Lucyler will look after you," said Richius. "And if you do as I say, stay inside while I'm gone, nothing will happen to you." He gave her an imploring look. "Please, don't fight me on this. Let me go with a clear conscience. I'll be back to you."

Dyana sighed. She didn't need him to swear it. She knew how much he loved her and Shani.

"How long will you be gone for?" she asked.

"I don't know. A week or so, I suppose. Not much longer."

"Where will you go?"

"I don't know that either, really. I thought of going to Chandakkar with Karlaz. He's leaving Falindar soon. But he said I should be alone. . . ." Richius laughed. "It's probably all some spiritual nonsense. But I want to try. I just want to—"

"Be alone. Yes, I know." Dyana went back to him and curled against him. It was warm in his embrace, wonderfully safe. It always had been. "Go," she said to him. "Go and talk to the sky. See what it has to say."

"Ah, now you mock me. . . ."

"I do not," she said. "People are very different, Richius. Some find their way in the company of family. Others need to be alone. You are one of those. You always have been, I think."

SIX

The Twin Dukes

Lorla didn't know her last name.

She didn't know if she had siblings, and she didn't know who her parents were or why they had given her into the care of the labs. She had vague memories of them, and that was all. Her mother, whom she could only recall with the opaque quality of a dream, had been a short woman and not very attractive. Her father had been stout, with dark hair. More than that she simply couldn't recall, and it bothered her sometimes—usually when she was feeling lonely, which of late had been happening to her more and more. On the road to Dragon's Beak, it seemed her fractured memories were all she had.

An ever-darkening sky had dogged them for days. Daevn, her tight-lipped guide, had kept their pace brisk to out-distance the storm, but a cold rain had fallen on them anyway, and Lorla blew onto her hands often to keep them from freezing. She had fled Goth with a wool cloak and a fat pair of mittens, but they were travelling north and winter was coming. Soon it would be too cold to go on, and Lorla craved hot food and a warm place to sleep. They had not bedded in any of the villages they'd passed. She supposed her mission was too grave to risk being seen by anyone, so she had stayed to the forests while Daevn bartered for provisions, and together they had camped each night beneath the starless sky, keeping their fires small so as not to attract attention. Lorla was tired of the tiny fires. She wanted a blaze.

Trying to keep the wind from her face, Lorla pulled the hood of her cloak around her mouth and nose. She hated the cold. She had been warned by her teachers that her body was delicate, and particularly susceptible to the winter. She wondered if Daevn was not aware of the temperature, or if her strange body had simply conjured up the frost of its own imagining.

The pony she had named Phantom was warm, and Lorla clung to it, crouching low against its neck. Phantom was a good companion, and Lorla hoped she could keep the beast when they got to Dragon's Beak. In the lab she had been allowed precious little, but Lokken had been good to her, treating her like one of his own daughters. But the duke was dead now, certainly. Duchess Kareena, too. They had heard no news of Goth, not even in the villages where Daevn had stopped. At least that's what Daevn had claimed. Lorla's eyes narrowed on Daevn. He had been suspiciously quiet since coming from the last village. Lorla thought to question him, then stopped herself. Daevn had been given orders to escort her, nothing more, and had made no effort to comfort her or even speak to her. She supposed this was best for her mission.

Whatever her mission was.

I will get to Dragon's Beak and be warm there, she told herself. *And the duke there will take care of me. Lokken said he would.*

She wondered if Duke Enli was anything like Lokken, and if Dragon's Beak was anything like Goth. She had adored Goth. The Walled City had been a wondrous place to spend a year, like being on holiday. So much better than the war labs and the atrocious women who had raised her. But it had all been for a purpose, Lorla knew. She was something very special. In the labs they were fond of the word *destiny.* Lorla had destiny, they had told her, and the memory made the girl sit up straighter in her saddle. Whatever the Master had planned for her, she would not disappoint him.

Even so, her mind wandered. In Goth there had been other children for companionship, and though she had been much their elder mentally, she missed them. She wondered if Dragon's Beak had children. Perhaps a boy her own age . . .

Lorla stopped daydreaming, admonishing herself for the thought. Her own age. What was that, really? She could count up the years easily enough, but that didn't seem to make sense, not when she looked down at her stunted body.

Stop it! she ordered herself. She needed to focus, the way they had taught her to. The cold was getting to her; they had warned her it might. She struggled out of her fantasy and blew into her hands. She wanted to stop and build a fire, but it was early in the afternoon and a long road awaited them. Daevn had said they might reach Dragon's Beak by nightfall.

"Hot tea," she murmured. "Hot with honey. And bread." She laughed.

Might as well throw that on the table. She imagined a feast spread out before her, in a dining room of warm wood with a fire blazing in a hearth. Lorla sighed softly, enjoying the game. Despite her years, she still had a child's imagination, though she was aware of the awakenings of her mind and body, at this age where most girls had their blood cycles. Lorla's body was too underdeveloped to bleed like a woman's, but it had its own curiosities. The words from the labs came back to her again—she was something very special.

To Lorla's dismay, they did not reach Dragon's Beak that night. The sun had disappeared behind a swathe of clouds, quickening the arrival of night, so at dusk they found a place at the roadside to break. Daevn used his hatchet to clear a place for them in the brush, then let the horses trample down the tall, dead grass. He lit a fire—a big one, at Lorla's insistence—and made them a meal of bread and dried sausages, a delicacy he had acquired in the last town. Because they would soon be in Dragon's Beak, they did not pick at their rations but instead ate their fill, and Lorla slept soundly until morning.

A dreadful gale blew from the north as they set out. The sun glowed without warmth, impossibly pallid on the gray horizon. Lorla clung close to Phantom's neck, gleaning what comfort she could from the animal. The road soon became desolate. This far north, winter had already stripped the trees naked so that they seemed burnt and barren. A little sense of dread grew in Lorla. No one had told her about Dragon's Beak, but the mystical name had conjured up a different image in her mind, and she didn't like the reality. Lokken had told her only that Dragon's Beak was very far north and often full of snow, and that it was shaped like a dragon's long snout protruding into the sea. It was a single kingdom ruled by two dukes, the twins Enli and Eneas. Each duke had a castle of their own. Duke Enli's was on the dragon's lower jaw. His brother's was on the upper. Lorla had pictured fairy-tale spires and stained glass, but the dreariness around her reminded her more of spider webs and decay.

They rode on for an hour more, until at last Lorla could smell the sea. The road ahead forked. Daevn stopped his horse. The road was thick with trees and both directions looked equally unappealing. He looked over his shoulder at Lorla.

"Dragon's Beak," he said.

Lorla grimaced. "Which way?"

"Either way. We're taking the south fork, to Enli. The north fork leads to Eneas."

Lorla had a thousand questions. "Do you know Enli, Daevn? What is he like?"

Daevn was typically unhelpful. "I have never met the duke," he said. "I have never been to Dragon's Beak."

"It's quiet here," said Lorla. She looked ahead and saw only a canopy of dead branches closing over the road. "Where is everyone?"

"Smart enough to get in from the cold. Now stop talking so we can do the same."

Without waiting for her, Daevn sped his horse down the road. Phantom kept pace, and soon they were on their way to Enli. The trees grew tall, reaching high into the sky, a tangled home for wide-eyed mammals and enormous, black-feathered grackles. Lorla stared skyward, marveling at the maze of branches above her head. The wind had abated some, slowed by the thickness of trees, and brown leaves tumbled toward them, dry and dead and held aloft by the breeze's breath. The air was brackish, moist with sea water. Lorla licked her lips and tasted salt. When the canopy thinned to reveal the sky, she saw a great blanket of storm clouds waiting.

"Daevn?" she asked nervously. "How far are we from the castle?"

Daevn shrugged. "Dunno."

"It's going to rain. Hard."

A moment later the sky exploded with rain. The road quickly filled with water, turning to mud beneath the horses' hooves. Lorla peered through the downpour for Daevn.

"Come on," he shouted. "It can't be much farther."

Lorla shivered beneath her garments, already soaked through. The fingers in her mittens had turned to icicles. Phantom moved sure-footed through the storm, following Daevn's horse. A flash of lightning cracked the sky, followed by a rumbling detonation of thunder. Lorla closed her eyes and wished the storm away, but only got another bolt of lightning for her troubles. She hurried Phantom to Daevn's side.

"Should we stop?" she asked.

The big man shook his head. "It won't last." He glanced at her through the rain and smiled. "Don't worry. It's only thunder."

"I'm not afraid," she lied, not wanting him to think her a coward. "I'm just wet. And cold, and tired of this ride. Find the castle, Daevn."

Daevn bowed sarcastically at her. "Oh, yes, my lady. What do you think I'm trying to do?"

They rode on in silence, sloshing down the narrow lane, until at last the rain slackened.

"There," Daevn declared. "Look."

Lorla followed Daevn's finger toward the horizon. Atop a hill and shrouded in mist was a castle of red stone. Lorla peered through the rain. It was tall and dark and it frightened her, and she knew from her melancholy feeling that the dismal sight was Enli's home. The Duke of Dragon's Beak did not dwell in the fairy-tale house she had imagined, but rather in a dreary nightmare of cold brick and dark windows, a single, monolithic tower jutting from the earth. Even against the beauty of the sea it was a cruel vision, as if it meant to mock the ocean with its own vast ugliness. Lorla bit her lower lip, then noticed the flag flying atop the castle.

"Daevn, look. He flies the Light of God. Do you see?"

Daevn was circumspect. "I see it," he said. Clearly he had expected the Black Flag to be waving in Dragon's Beak. "But I trust Lokken even now, girl. If this is where he wants you, then it's no mistake."

"But—"

"Trust him, Lorla," he said. Then he laughed and added, "You'll be warm again soon. And tonight I might sleep with a real woman!"

The insult struck Lorla like an icy slap. A *real* woman? What did that mean? She scowled at the soldier but he seemed not to take her meaning. Instead Daevn rode off, his horse trotting through the mud toward the castle on the hill. When he noticed Lorla wasn't following, he turned around and waved to her.

"Coming? Or do you want to drown out here?"

"Drown," she mumbled. Suddenly anything seemed better than the castle. But she was frozen and exhausted, and that made her snap the reins. Phantom jumped forward at her command. The little pony seemed as eager as Daevn to be out of the damp. The road widened some as they approached, and they passed by small houses and storefronts, all quiet and shuttered. A few candles burned dimly in the windows. Lorla felt invisible eyes staring at her, but each time she turned to face them they had vanished.

When they reached the hill, she noticed the pine trees lining the roadway, great guardians that loomed over them and cast crooked shadows in the feeble light. Beneath them the gray gravel of the path crunched under the steady pressure of horses' hooves, and the rain was cold and steady. Lorla glimpsed the castle gates through the mist. They were high up on the hill now, with the fitful ocean far below. Two sentries stood at the entrance, their bodies encased in ugly black armor, their faces hidden behind reptilian helmets. In their fists were bladed halberds. Lorla looked up at the towering castle. There was a distinct list to the structure, as if it were waiting to topple. Gargoyles perched on the high ledges, spouting rain water, and a bloom of rubbery lichens grew from the mortar, turning the red brick yellow. The riveted wooden gates were closed up tight. Both guardians fixed their stern gazes at the riders. Daevn rode forward, his hand raised in friendship.

"We are from Goth," he called to the men. "I am Daevn of the Walled City, here to see your duke."

The sentries nodded. "Dismount," one of them ordered. He stepped forward while his brother opened the gate. Daevn got down from his horse, bidding Lorla to do the same. The guardian took the reins of his mount and stared at Lorla, who wasn't sure yet if she trusted him.

"Come on, Lorla," urged Daevn. "Get down so we can go inside."

Lorla got down from Phantom's back and handed the pony over to the armored man, who looked at her questioningly. She hurried to Daevn's side. The other guardian had opened the gates, letting loose a flood of orange torchlight. It was all the encouragement Lorla needed. She entered and found herself in a huge chamber of gray stone, where armored men strutted with sidearms and laughed amongst themselves. A few women moved through the halls in the distance. When they noticed Lorla they paused to regard her, apparently struck to have a child in their midst.

"Wait here," ordered the guardian. "I will tell Duke Enli you've arrived."

"He's expecting us, I think," said Daevn. He looked around the vast chamber. "We could use a place to sit and rest."

"The duke will be down quickly, I'm sure," said the soldier. "He'll see to your needs himself. Just wait here."

Daevn and Lorla watched the soldier go, stung by his gruffness but grateful to be out of the rain. Lorla gravitated toward one of the giant torches on the wall, reaching high to warm her hands. She pulled off her drenched mittens and massaged her fingers. Her joints were stiff, her fingertips blue. She felt cold water drip from her hair and trickle down her neck, and hoped that the duke could get her fresh clothes. She slid her soiled cloak off her small shoulders and felt its surprising, waterlogged weight. Daevn was nearby, talking to the soldiers. They were peculiar-looking men, she decided, but she liked their fancy helmets. Forged into the likenesses of dragon heads, each bore engravings like scales and two obsidian gems for eyes. Their armor was spiked and black, like the legionnaires of Nar, but bulkier and more noisy. Lorla watched them clank around, fascinated by the sound.

"Lorla?"

Lorla jumped when she heard her name. Coming down the hallway was a tall, thin man with dirty hair and a wide smile. He wasn't dressed like a soldier but instead wore a warm cape of wolf's fur around his shoulders. He headed toward her, one hand outstretched. Daevn stepped between them.

"Are you the duke?" he asked rudely.

The man grinned at Daevn but did not answer. He craned to look over Daevn's shoulder at Lorla. "Lorla, yes?" he asked. "How are you, child?"

"Fine, sir," said Lorla. She looked him up and down. He had a nice face. Daevn cleared his throat noisily. The man regarded him.

"Yes, the bodyguard. Welcome, both of you."

"The name's Daevn," said Daevn coldly. "From Goth. Are you Duke Enli?"

"No, I'm not," said the man. "My name is Faren. I'm one of the duke's servants. I've come to collect you both. The duke is very pleased you're here. He would like to see you both at once."

"Can we have something to drink?" asked Lorla anxiously. "Some hot tea?"

"What are all the soldiers for?" asked Daevn. "Is there some trouble?"

Faren walked past Daevn, ignoring him. He bent down to one knee to be at Lorla's level. "Tea we have aplenty, dear Lorla. And fresh milk, too. I can have the maids bring you some if you want."

Lorla tried not to cringe. Milk was for babies. "Just the tea, please," she said. "If you don't mind."

"Whatever you want," said Faren. His smile was impossibly broad. "Come. Let's get you out of those wet things and into something warm." He put out his hand for Lorla. When she didn't take it, his smile dimmed.

"Where is the duke?" asked Daevn.

"I will take you to him. This way, please."

Lorla shot Daevn a questioning glance, but the big man only shrugged. They followed Faren out of the great chamber, past kitchens filled with fine odors. Another grand hall greeted them, this one with many doors of dull oak. One of the doors was open. Through the entrance Lorla saw the dancing shadows of a burning fire. The smell of crackling alder drew her forward. Faren stopped at the threshold, bidding Lorla to enter.

"This is the duke's sitting room. Please go in. The duke will be joining you very soon."

Lorla walked inside, drawn like an insect to the blazing hearth. It was the most comfortable room she'd ever seen, with bookcases full of manuscripts and big, cushy chairs of worn leather. The room smelled of age and expensive tobacco. On one of the small tables a pipe rested, its bowl full of ashes. But the most dominant feature of all was the portrait over the hearth, a huge oil painting of two young men, each the mirror image of the other. They were on horseback, both dressed in resplendent armor, their heads naked and their swords dangling at their sides. It was a magnificent painting.

"Wait here please, Lorla," said Faren. "The duke will be here shortly. Meanwhile I'll have a maid bring you that tea you wanted, and some biscuits, eh?"

"Thank you," said Lorla.

"I'd like some tea too," said Daevn sourly. "If it's not too much trouble."

Faren said, "Actually, Sir Daevn, the duke would like to speak to you alone first. If you would follow me, please?"

"Daevn?" asked Lorla, alarmed.

"It's all right, girl," said Daevn. "Stay here; I'll be back with the duke. Enjoy your tea and biscuits." Daevn looked at Faren. "You got some clothes for the girl? She's soaked to the bone."

"Of course," said Faren. "Lorla, make yourself at home. I'll get you some dry clothes."

Lorla said a soft good-bye, then turned her attention to the marvelous room. There were trinkets on the tables, some old rings with clouded gems, and dozens of dusty books, enough to occupy a hundred years. Lorla loved to read. She had gone through all the books and manuscripts in the labs—at least the ones she had been allowed to read—and she had devoured Lokken's library. She wondered if Duke Enli would let her read his books, or if he'd be stingy and keep them to himself. On one of the large chairs she found a small scarlet blanket. When she touched it the fabric sang of warmth. It was supple, like the leather of the chair, and Lorla put it to her face, burying her nose and sniffing it. The blanket held all the perfumes of the room. Shivering, Lorla stripped off her drenched clothes and dropped them to the floor. Quickly she jumped into the chair, and her small body seemed to vanish in its embrace. The leather cushion creaked as she sank into it. She covered herself with the blanket and surveyed the room from her new vantage. Once again the painting over the hearth seized her attention. Lorla stared at it for a long time. She liked the horses, but she wasn't sure about the men.

Soon a maid arrived and set down a teakettle on the table next to Lorla. Noticing the pile of wet clothes on the floor, the woman assured Lorla she would bring some dry garments. Cheerily she poured Lorla a cup of tea and placed it in her small hands, then waved a plate of sweet-smelling biscuits beneath her nose. Lorla chose the biggest one and put it in her mouth, holding it between her teeth as she warmed her hands on the teacup. The maid left with a smile, leaving Lorla once again to puzzle over the portrait. She was getting warm quickly, and it felt good. A drowsy mood fell over her, making her eyelids droop. She watched the portrait as her eyes fell closed. . . .

"You like that picture?" boomed a voice.

Lorla snapped awake, so suddenly the cup in her hands jostled tea over the rim. She looked down at the stained blanket sheepishly, then up at the man in the threshold. It wasn't Faren, but a much broader man, big through the shoulders, with jet hair and a shiny black beard. He had a stern face and eyes that smoldered when he stared. Now he stared at Lorla.

"I'm sorry," Lorla offered. She set down the cup and jumped out of the chair, keeping the blanket wrapped about her naked body. Suddenly she was embarrassed. "I ruined the blanket."

"It's just a blanket," said the man. He stepped into the chamber and closed the door behind him. All at once a strange silence enveloped them. Lorla inspected the man.

"Who are you?" she asked.

"I am Duke Enli, Master of Red Tower." He tried to smile but managed only a crooked grin. "Your host. For now."

Duke Enli came closer, looking over Lorla. His beard glowed in the hearth's orange light and the many rings on his fingers twinkled. Like Faren, he wore a cape to shield him from the cold, a long garment trimmed in crimson and fastened around his throat with a golden broach—a shiny, fanged dragon's head. The duke had big hands that he spread toward Lorla in welcome.

"Little Lorla," he said. "I'm glad you made it safely. I've been waiting for you. And this weather had me concerned."

Lorla nodded. "It was cold."

"Cold?" laughed the duke. "This is not cold, girl. To me, this is like summer. But yes, you look wretched. Faren has ordered clothes for you, and there's a warm bed waiting."

"Thank you, sir."

The duke looked down at her, his eyes glinting with curiosity. "How old are you?" he asked. "Seven? Eight?"

"Almost sixteen," said Lorla indignantly. The duke's eyes widened.

"Sixteen? God almighty, you don't look a day over eight. I swear, not a day." He dropped down to inspect her more closely, running one of his big fingers over her cheek as if she were a house pet. "Remarkable," he chuckled. "Truly remarkable."

"Duke Enli, where is Daevn?" asked Lorla.

"Ah, well . . ." Enli retracted his finger and attempted another smile. "Daevn is resting now, Lorla. I actually wanted to speak to you alone."

"Alone? But Faren said—"

"I know," interrupted the duke. He gestured toward the chair. "Sit down, Lorla."

Lorla did as the duke asked, keeping a cautious eye on him. He was quiet for a long time, contemplative, and sighed as he took his pipe from the table. He stuck it between his teeth and took a seat in one of the other chairs. As he chewed on his pipe he watched her, fascinated. Lorla could read his incredulity.

Something special, she told herself.

"I don't want you to worry about Daevn," said Enli finally. "He brought you here, and for that I'm grateful. But his business is done; I'll be sending him away."

Lorla grimaced. "Duke Enli, I'm not sure I trust you."

Enli laughed. "Great God, you don't talk like an eight-year-old, do you? You're as suspicious as your master." He took the pipe out of his mouth and pointed it at her. "I see now why Biagio wants you. You're a beauty, aren't you? And smart."

"Thank you," replied Lorla dryly. She wasn't sure it was a compliment.

"What about your eyes? Why aren't they blue?"

"I don't know," said Lorla. "Should they be?"

"How much do you know about yourself, girl? How much have they told you?"

The question vexed Lorla. She didn't really have memories, just fractured bits. Ghosts mostly, and feelings.

"I am sixteen and I look eight," she said. "I get cold even when it's warm. I remember Duke Lokken perfectly. I liked it in Goth. More than that, I can't speak of. The labs were a secret place."

Enli's smile was evil. "Oh, yes. I've heard about Bovadin's war labs. And your parents? What were they like?"

"I don't know. I don't remember. Is this important?"

"No, I don't suppose it is," said Enli. "What *is* important is what you and I are about to do, little Lorla. What we're going to do will shape the destiny of the Empire forever." He leaned forward in his chair and his voice dipped to a conspiratorial whisper. "How does that make you feel?"

"All right," replied Lorla. She didn't feel anything, and wondered why. She wanted to please the Master. That was all. "I'm here to do the Master's bidding," she said. "I was told you would help me. You will explain it to me, won't you?"

"Oh, yes," said the duke. "Tell me something, Lorla. Have you ever met Biagio?"

"No, sir."

"And yet he is your master? You don't doubt that?"

"No, sir," said Lorla, surprised by the question. "He is the Master."

"Yes," Enli sighed. "Of course." He seemed to withdraw into himself. "You're perfect," he murmured. "Purely perfect . . ."

"Duke Enli, will I be able to read these books? I mean, may I?"

"If you wish," said Enli. "You will be staying here for a little while. You should make yourself at home. I have things to do before I take you to Nar."

"Nar? I'm going to Nar?"

"Not right away. There are things I need to work out first. It will be a few weeks yet. But yes, you will be going to Nar with me."

Lorla leaned back in her chair, astounded at the news. She hadn't seen the Black City in over a year, not since leaving the lab to go live with Lokken. And she had never actually experienced Nar. There had been few windows in the labs. Windows were for the older people, the workers. Lorla's mind raced. What great things did the Master want from her?

"I haven't been to Nar in a long time," she said dreamily. "Not since going to Goth. I will like this."

Duke Enli scowled. "It will be difficult, Lorla. What Biagio wants of you is no trifle. You must be absolutely dedicated. Do you understand that?"

"Of course I do," Lorla shot back. "I know what I am, Duke Enli. I'm something very special."

"You certainly are," said Enli. "I saw you looking at the painting when I came in. Do you know who those two men are?"

"Yes," replied Lorla. She looked again at the portrait, searching for a resemblance. "Which one is you?"

"On the left. Not that it really matters. My brother is still my perfect twin, even today." Enli's lips twisted in disgust as he examined the portrait. "Eneas has a scar on his cheek. Look closely, you'll see it. That's the only difference between us. That and the Renaissance."

"Your brother lives in a castle too; that's what Duke Lokken told me. Is it red, like this one?"

"No," said Enli. "Eneas lives in the Gray Tower, just across the channel. You can see it from some of the other rooms. We rule the forks of Dragon's Beak separately. We always have, really, even when Arkus was alive." The duke looked at Lorla sharply. "You know who Arkus is, don't you?"

It was a silly question. Lorla cleared her throat dramatically. "Arkus of Nar, Arkus the Great. Arkus, founder of the Black Renaissance. The Beast of Goss, the Plague of Criisia. The Conqueror—"

"All right," Enli barked, putting his hands to his ears. "I meant no insult, girl. Just wondering who—or what—I'm dealing with in you. But you must get a lot of that, eh? People underestimating you?"

"I suppose," said Lorla. "I'm not what I seem." She looked again at the painting. "How old are you there, you and your brother?"

"Twenty," said Enli. "I remember because our mother had that picture commissioned for her birthday. She wanted something of us together." The duke sighed. "We didn't hate each other then."

"You hate your brother?" asked Lorla. "Really?"

"Hell, yes," said Enli. "For a girl who knows so much you astound me with ignorance. Everyone in Nar knows about the twin dukes of Dragon's Beak."

Lorla frowned. "I don't."

"Well, I'm not going to explain it to you. It's a private matter, and it has no bearing on your mission with Herrith." Enli stopped himself. "Herrith, the bishop. You know of him, don't you?"

Lorla nodded. "The bishop is why the Master sent me to Goth," she answered. "When Emperor Arkus died, I had to flee the labs. The Master sent me to Duke Lokken for protection. But he flew the flag of old Nar and was killed." Lorla regarded Enli sharply. "He didn't fly the Light of God. Like you do."

"The Light of God is an abomination," said the duke. "And I don't fly it out of loyalty. It is all part of something greater, Lorla."

"What?"

"I will tell you. Soon. And you will have your revenge against the bishop for chasing you from Nar. You more than any of us will have a hand in Herrith's comeuppance. Believe what I tell you and do as I say, and you will make your master very proud. But you have to be patient, all right? I have business with my brother first."

"Your brother?" Lorla asked, puzzled. "But Duke Lokken said you would help me. Your business with your brother; will it interfere with the Master's plans for me?"

"Not even a wee bit," the duke assured her. "For you see, the plans are really one and the same." Enli got out of his chair and went over to Lorla. Kneeling down beside her, he took her hand and looked into her eyes. "Lorla, you have to trust me. What we're going to do together will be the marvel of the Empire. And when your master returns to Nar, we will both be rewarded. The Master might make you a queen! Would you like that, Lorla?"

He was talking to her like a little child, and it irked her. Still, she rolled the idea over in her mind. Being a queen might be wonderful. Maybe it would make her desirable to men, even. And maybe she could have a family of her own.

"A queen," she sighed. "Yes, if the Master lets me, I would like that."

Enli squeezed her hand and smiled. "Then you shall have it, little Lorla. You and I, we shall take back the Empire for Biagio. You and I will resurrect the Black Renaissance, and not even Herrith's foul God will stop us."

Daevn waited in the castle's library for nearly an hour, assured by Faren that the duke was "on his way." He rested on one of the library's soft chairs and enjoyed a meal of hot soup and freshly baked bread, and flirted with the maid who had brought it. His request for dry clothes went unheeded, although he was assured by Faren that the maids were trying to find him something suitable. To Daevn, suitable would have been anything dry. It didn't even have to be clean. But they had set a fire for him in the library and that felt good, and he gorged himself on the soup and bread while he waited for Enli.

After almost an hour had passed, Faren came back into the chamber. The man spread his hands apologetically. "I'm so sorry," he offered. "But Duke Enli is feeling very poorly tonight. A bad fish from the kitchen, perhaps. He won't be able to see you now. In the morning maybe."

Daevn dropped his spoon into the empty soup bowl. "Where's Lorla?"

"I assure you the girl is unharmed," said the ever-smiling man. "She has been given a room of her own. I think she's already asleep. I've made arrangements for you to have a room next to hers. You can see her if you like."

Daevn picked up what was left of the bread and got to his feet. "Show her to me," he said, trying and failing to sound polite. It wouldn't do to upset his hosts too much. With Goth destroyed, he had nowhere else to go. "And Faren, those clothes?"

"Waiting for you in your bedchamber," said Faren. He stood aside and gestured toward the threshold. "If you care to go . . . ?"

"Now, yes," said Daevn. He walked past the servant toward the door, and was almost out of the room when he felt the sharp tug at his throat. Daevn's hands shot to his neck. He was being dragged backward. A wire, or a rope . . . Faren was grunting, pulling him off his feet. Daevn tried to scream and couldn't. His throat muscles strained, gasping, but the wire was there, cutting into his flesh, making the smallest gulp of air impossible. He fought to dig his fingers under the garrote, but Faren was thrashing like a shark, dragging and pulling, making the wire dig deeper until it cut the flesh.

"You're a strong one, eh?" growled Faren. "Like reeling in a big fish!"

Daevn gulped for breath. Faren pulled harder still. Daevn's knees buckled.

"No one must ever know this thing we do!"

Daevn heard the words without understanding. And then there was oblivion. He felt the distant sensation of the wire slicing his windpipe. Remarkably, it was hardly painful at all. . . .

SEVEN

The Prince of Liss

On the oceans of Nar, the days were short and the nights were long. Here in the north of the world, autumn had all but perished, and the white caps on the water grew taller as winter crawled closer. The Black Empire, that vast and criminal place, spread out in an endless sprawl on the horizon, but for the sailors of Liss the sight of so much land was far from comforting. They had put to sea months ago, leaving behind the ruins of their homeland and their sad wives, and had only their bright memories to comfort them in the cold quarters of the schooners. It was a bold and heartless mission, and many of them, barely boys, were untested. But battle was making men of them.

Fleet Commander Prakna had a single porthole in his cabin. It was a cramped room in the forecastle, and the round pane of glass was hardly the size of his head. But for Prakna, the porthole was a looking glass into another world. On quiet nights like this, when the lateness of the hour had hushed the sailors on deck, Prakna would stare out his window at the hazy glow of Nar, and wonder about its inhabitants. After ten years of war, he still found his enemies inscrutable. He would lose himself in the sight, lulled by the constant rocking of his ship, and recall his memories. And sometimes he would dream; of food and fresh fruit, of the warmth of the Hundred Isles, of the friendship of his wife and their lost lovemaking.

Prakna was weary. Like pirates he and his fleet patrolled the coasts of Nar, a great wolf-pack sharpening their teeth on imperial shipping. Prakna had been making good on his pledge to bring his enemy to its knees. Without the Black Fleet to protect them, the shores of Nar were his for the raiding. But only the shores, for the land was still dominated by Nar's army. In time, Prakna hoped, the strife inside the Empire would crack it in two, but until then they would sail the Naren waters and take what they wished, and make the Narens pay for what they had done.

Tonight was like any other for the fleet commander. His ship, the *Prince of Liss,* drifted lazily over the ocean. His tiny cabin was cold. A single candle burned in a hurricane glass on his desk. Above his head, the shallow ceiling creaked with the slow motion of the vessel, and a salty spray had opaqued his window. The blankets on Prakna's bunk were disheveled, the symptoms of another restless night, and Prakna sat at his desk, his pale face lit by candlelight, waiting for another dawn. A sheet of yellow paper lay on the desk in front of him. Prakna stared at it. Quite possibly, the letter would never reach its intended recipient. Yet Prakna had written it anyway. When he wrote, it was like she was here with him. He looked it over, then dipped his pen in the ink well to continue.

I will come back when I can. The Narens are not so strong without their navy, and I don't believe the Black Fleet will abandon them forever. Nar is still their home. And I know the pull of home, my love. When we have lured the fleet away from Crote, I will come back.

Prakna frowned at the last line. Bold promise. But one he wanted desperately to keep. J'lari would be needing him. Since the deaths of their sons, she had become like a ghost. He thought of writing about the Narens he'd killed, the vengeance he had taken, but then thought better of it. J'lari didn't like war. She had begged him to stay home. But he was the fleet commander, and there was no way the armada could sail without him. So he had left her. Long months ago.

When I return I will have gifts for you. I have a ring and other jewelry I've taken from the Naren women. You should see the women here, my love. They are not at all like the fine-boned girls of Liss. They are all big here and hard. The sight of them makes me miss you even more. And when they see us, they are horrified. They wonder why their navy won't protect them, and they scream at the sight of our ships.

Prakna loved their screams. He loved the terror the sight of his armada engendered in the Narens.

We have taken few losses. We are strong, so do not worry about me.

A lie, but Prakna wrote it anyway. Each time they raided a town their numbers diminished. They were not soldiers, his men of Liss. They were sailors. It was why they needed Vantran.

My love, I miss you. I miss our sons. If you knew the truth of my heart, you would not wonder why I do this thing. Men are different from the wives they leave behind, and I cannot help this vengeance that moves me. Tell the women of this ship's crew that their husbands do not fight for themselves, but for the honor of Liss.

Liss the raped. That's what they were calling his homeland now. The Hundred Isles had been ravaged by the Narens and their decade-long blockade, but she had never surrendered or lost her honor. She had stared down the dragon of Nar, defying the Black Empire and its voracious ruler, Arkus. For ten years Liss had hung on, alone, while the rest of the world watched the butchery, too afraid to challenge their imperial masters. Except for the Triin of Lucel-Lor, only Liss had out-lived Arkus. And now that Arkus was dead and his Empire in chaos, Liss was ready to rise from its ashes.

Sweet wife, I hope you're sleeping well tonight. I hope it's warm in Liss and that the morning sun will be fair. And remember my promise. You will see me again.

He signed it very simply, *Prakna*.

The fleet commander stared at his writing, returning the pen to the ink well. This letter would join the others in his drawer until a ship could be spared to return to Liss. That was happening less frequently now. They were very far north, and Prakna wanted them well prepared for the Black Fleet's return. For months they had been raiding the Naren coasts, hoping to lure Nicabar's dreadnoughts out of Crote's harbors. They had made some impressive gains, sunk over thirty merchant vessels. Eventually, Prakna knew, Nicabar would have to respond. He had never met the admiral but he knew his mind. He knew the captain of the *Fearless* could never live with such disgrace.

"We will take Crote," he whispered. "We will. . . ."

It was the perfect base, ideally situated to attack the Black City. If they could take it, they could turn the tide of the war forever. But first they had to lure away the *Fearless*.

Prakna pushed the letter aside and leaned back in his chair. The *Fearless*. His one great nemesis. Not even the *Prince of Liss* was a match for that marvel. The flagship of the Black Fleet was like nothing he had ever seen—a floating fortress, indomitable. Unsinkable, they said. Prakna wondered. Nicabar and his ship had been the bane of the Lissen navy. A secret weapon meant to destroy them, the *Fearless* had been the cornerstone of the Naren blockade. She was slower than her sister dreadnoughts, but that was like saying a mountain was slow. She had a hull of spiked steel and twin long-range flame cannons, and she had sunk every schooner sent against her.

Like the *Fire Bird*.

Off the island of Meer, the *Fire Bird* had met the *Fearless*. A lucky shot from a cannon and she had burned, sinking in minutes. Some of the crew had made it to shore. But the waters of Meer were warm, good for sharks. Prakna closed his eyes. He had never wanted both his sons to serve on the same vessel. The news had come to him a week later. J'lari had been a ghost ever since. Silent. She and Prakna didn't make love anymore. To her, it seemed a waste. She was too old to bear him more sons. And Prakna had changed, too. The death of his boys had murdered his conscience, and he knew it. So he had been the one to whisper vengeful musings in the ear of his queen. He had rebuilt the navy and formed the armada. And when the word came to sail, he had been eager. There was nothing left for Prakna now but the honor of Liss.

Bleary-eyed with fatigue, Prakna laid his head down on the desk. He felt the rhythmic swaying of the vessel through the rafters, heard the hard slap of water against the hull as the *Prince of Liss* cut through the waves. His eyelids drooped as sleep took him. He hoped he wouldn't dream. . . .

A knock at the cabin door awakened him. Prakna's eyes slowly opened. Not more than an hour could have passed. The room remained dark. The candle still burned in its protective glass.

"Yes?" he said wearily.

The little door creaked open and Marus peered inside. Prakna's first officer smiled apologetically when he noticed his commander's head on the desk. "Prakna?"

The commander lifted his head and waved his friend inside. "Come in, Marus," he croaked. "I wasn't sleeping."

"You were," Marus corrected. "I'm sorry to disturb you."

"What is it?"

"A ship. Twenty degrees off port, running parallel to us."

"What kind of ship?"

"Too far to tell," said the officer. "But I thought you should know."

It was standard practice with Marus, and Prakna appreciated it. Marus was a fine officer—the kind of man a captain needed at his side. They had served together for years, and had known each other since their teens. When the time had come to pilot the *Prince*, Marus had been Prakna's first choice. And there was more to their kinship than just time. Marus had lost a boy, too.

"Go topside and wait for me," said Prakna. He looked around the room for his boots. "I'll be up."

Marus left the room and closed the door. Prakna located his boots beneath his bunk and slipped them on his feet. Outside the window he saw only darkness, but he knew that dawn was on their heels. He wondered what the light would bring. Another Naren ship. Merchant, almost certainly. Their course was bringing them near Doria again, a main seaport of the Empire. They had already raided Doria once, and the success of the campaign had sent a shockwave through the local shipping concerns. Prakna had ordered his patrol to keep near the city, waiting for the inevitable return of the merchant vessels. The fleet commander smiled to himself, pleased with his tactic.

He pulled on his coat, blew into the hurricane glass to extinguish the candle, and left his chamber. Out in the empty gangway he found the little ladder leading above deck. He ran up the ladder and pushed open the hatch, then stepped out onto the forecastle. A biting wind struck his face. Around him, the ocean roared. On the forecastle deck he located Marus. With him were two crewmen, both ensigns, both staring out into the darkness. Marus had a spyglass pressed to one eye. A single oil lantern flickered in the breeze. The *Prince of Liss* pitched violently as a swale slammed against her hull. Prakna joined the group, squinting as he scanned the distance portside. As the *Prince* rose on a wave, he glimpsed something far away. Cabin lights, he guessed. Marus handed him the spyglass.

"Too dark to see much," said the officer. "Not a warship, though. No escorts. She sails alone."

Prakna brought up the spyglass. The horizon was black and it took a moment to spot the vessel, but he caught a hazy glimmer. Big. Slow. But not a warship. Prakna's heart sank a notch. He hadn't really expected to see *her* here, but he was disappointed anyway. He collapsed the spyglass and handed it back to Marus.

"Signal the other ships," he said. "We'll pursue until it's light. Then we'll see what we're dealing with."

"Aye, sir," replied Marus, who immediately started barking orders to the men. The deck snapped alive with activity. Amidships the seamen cranked levers to trim the sails, while signalmen flashed messages with flags to the other vessels of the patrol. The *Prince of Liss* lurched to port as the pilot spun the wheel, turning the rudder in pursuit. She was in the lead, with a dozen of her wolf pups following. Prakna glanced to starboard. The first slivers of sunlight struggled over the horizon, lighting the Naren Empire. He had charted a course back to Doria, and he could see the landscape of the Dorian territories, infinitesimally small in the distance. To port was the blackness of the ocean, endless and deep. They were tacking north by northwest, into the wind. The heading had slowed them, but Prakna knew his schooner could run down whatever was out there. Nothing in the Black Fleet could outrun his schooners. During their long war with Liss the Narens had tested countless ship designs, yet still their vaunted war labs had been unable to develop a fast-enough keel. It was the one tactical advantage the Lissen navy had over their well-armed adversaries.

The *Prince of Liss* and the rest of her patrol pursued the unknown vessel for another hour, until the light grew. Prakna and his officers stood on the forecastle deck at the ship's prow, leaning over the railings as the sun illuminated their prey. The fleet commander had his eye fixed to the spyglass again. He could see the vessel clearly now. She was a big bastard, with wide mastheads and her sails full of air as she tacked to catch the wind. From her center mast flew the flag of Nar, the new one called the Light of God. Beneath that was the triangular standard of Doria, a yellow field bearing a single sword. Clearly, this was no warship. Amidships she was fat and multidecked, with huge cargo holds. Prakna closed the spyglass and made his deduction.

"Slaver," he said distastefully. "Probably sailing out of Bisenna."

Marus nodded. "Slaves. Poor wretches. Should we break off pursuit?"

"Pursue and overtake."

"Sir?"

"Those are my orders, Marus."

"Yes, sir. The *Vindicator* and the *Gray Lady* are closest."

"Have them approach port and starboard. We'll lead."

"Aye, sir," said Marus, then went off to carry out his commander's orders.

Prakna held tight to the rails as the *Prince of Liss* leapt forward, its razor-shaped keel slicing through the ocean. The *Vindicator* and *Gray Lady* broke free of the patrol and joined her, their steel-covered prows ready to ram. The fat slaver ship had obviously seen them and was maneuvering sloppily to evade. Marus shouted orders at the crew as the *Prince* ran headlong after the fleeing vessel. The sea-serpent flags of Liss tore at the masts as the schooners devoured the ocean. Sailors ran about the deck, drenched in spray, pulling ropes and trimming sails. The *Prince*'s massive spritsail groaned and swelled with air. Off the port bow the *Vindicator* lurched ahead, while her smaller cousin, the *Gray Lady*, churned up the waves.

"They see us," Prakna shouted to Marus.

Marus looked distressed. "Aye, sir. That they do."

"No sentiment, Marus," Prakna called back. "They're not just slaves—they're Narens!"

It wasn't a slaver ship that Prakna desired, but for a time it would slake his lust. Even now, with the Empire wasting, Nar still dealt in slaves. It sickened Prakna. All Narens sickened him. In the conquered land of Bisenna, the Naren nobles harvested slaves like grain. Prakna had heard the tales. Some of his own countrymen had been enslaved, taken away to the Black City to toil in the filthy foundries of the war labs. To Prakna, it was a fate worse than death.

The *Prince of Liss* maneuvered closer to the fleeing slaver. Prakna could see the men on her deck now, wide-eyed with fear at the sight of the marauders. To the slaver's port side the *Vindicator* was narrowing the gap, its steel prow ready to ram. The *Prince of Liss* drew nearer. The

Gray Lady tacked to the slaver's starboard. Prakna shouted to Marus, ordering the *Prince* ahead of their quarry. The schooner lurched as the captain spun the wheel. Abaft the forecastle, Prakna's sailors readied their cutlasses and clung to the railings.

Today we are pirates, thought Prakna. *Like the Narens always say.*

But they deserved nothing better, not even these wretches from Bisenna. To Prakna, they were simply Narens. They were of that hedonistic, evil race that enslaved their own and raped others. If he could, he would have burned them all alive.

Obviously outmatched, it didn't take long for the Naren slaver to fly its white. The big ship slowed as its sails slackened. Naren sailors were waving on its deck, signaling their surrender. Prakna was very still. The *Prince of Liss* churned forward. The *Vindicator* and *Gray Lady* swept wide, maneuvering to ram. Over the roaring surf Prakna could hear the muffled cries of the Naren sailors. He took a long breath, and for the smallest second reconsidered.

Then he gave the order.

"Signal the *Vindicator*," he shouted to Marus. "Ram her."

Marus nodded grimly. Along the deck the order was passed. The signalmen flashed their colored flags. A quick reply followed from the *Vindicator*. The schooner changed course by mere degrees, pointing her shining steel prow at the hull of her prey. Like a giant shark the vessel swam forward, ever faster as her sails took up the wind. The men on deck braced themselves. *Gray Lady* broke away, paralleling the lumbering slaver, while the *Prince of Liss* took up position in front of her. The captain of the Naren vessel was screaming, frantically waving off the *Vindicator*. Prakna shook his fist.

"Now!"

Vindicator's prow slammed the helpless slaver. The crack and groan of wood shuddered as the slaver's hull imploded. Screams went up from her deck and cargo holds. *Vindicator* bobbed upward as her prow tore through planking, rising like a rhino horn to open the fatal wound. The *Prince of Liss* circled in front of the crippled slaver, her crew silent.

"Look at that," muttered Marus.

The Naren ship trembled as the ocean poured into her, drowning her lower decks and holds. Naren sailors abandoned the doomed vessel as she listed starboard. The *Gray Lady* bore down on the sailors as they bobbed aimlessly in the water, shocked and panicked. Prakna watched as the *Gray Lady*'s keel flattened the sailors. The *Vindicator* ripped free of the ruined hull, pulling out a gory mess of wood and pitch as she fought to change direction before the wreck could drag her down.

Prakna crossed his arms over his chest, satisfied. The *Prince of Liss* slowed as it circled the Naren ship. The big slaver was listing badly, sucking in water. She groaned and shook as the ocean consumed her, pulling her relentlessly down. A medley of shouts rang from her decks as the men raced to abandon her, throwing themselves over her broken railings.

The flooded cargo holds were silent.

Vindicator had broken free and was slowly sailing away from her victim. *Gray Lady* circled around for another pass. Wild-eyed Narens swam in all directions, desperate to escape the hunting schooners. Some swam toward shore, foolishly attempting the impossible distance. Others merely floated there, astonished, as the keels of the warships smashed in their skulls.

In a few short moments, the Naren vessel was gone. Prakna's jaw clenched. She was a god-cursed slaver. She deserved to go down—with her crew and cargo. The fleet commander watched the bubbling ocean until all that was left of the ship was froth and even that vanished away. He turned away from the railing and found himself looking at Marus. The first officer's expression was grave.

"She carried slaves," Prakna mumbled, more to himself than to Marus. "To work in the war labs. To build ships . . ."

"Yes, sir."

Prakna swallowed. "Return to patrol," he said softly. "I'll be back in my cabin."

"Aye, sir." Marus let his commander walk away. But Prakna took only a few steps before Marus called after him.

"Prakna?"

Prakna stopped to face his friend. "Yes?"

"Next time," said Marus, "it will be the *Fearless*."

EIGHT

Dark-Heart

On board the *Intimidator*, Simon Darquis whiled away the hours topside. Around him, the everyday tedium of sea-life went on oblivious to his presence. He was the special passenger of Count Renato Biagio, and that was all any of the crew needed to know about their strange shipmate. Simon did what he could to stay out of their way, but he needed to be out in the sun, to let its weak rays redden his skin and let the wind chafe his face. Because his stomach couldn't stand the endless rocking of the ocean, he found the self-imposed starvation easy; everything that went down his gullet came right back up anyway. It had been three agonizing weeks since they had set out from Crote, and Simon hadn't downed a decent meal since. Always thin, Simon was now gaunt, precisely the look required for fooling the Jackal. He had hung his disguise—the uniform of a Naren legionnaire—from one of the mastheads, and he occasionally bundled it in a net and trolled it overboard. Like his own flesh, the uniform needed to be well weathered if he were to look his part. He had a pair of standard-issue boots in his cabin too, the soles so worn that his toes almost touched the earth. Simon had come up with the ruse himself, and Biagio had approved it.

Simon didn't know the Jackal of Nar and bore him no grudges. In an odd way he even admired Vantran. He had thrown the Empire into chaos, had abandoned his kingship in Aramoor, and had forged the Triin into an army capable of defeating Vorto's legions. And all for the love of a woman. Had circumstances been vastly different, Simon imagined, they might have even been friends. But Simon was Roshann, and Biagio's vengeance was unstoppable.

He hadn't explained his mission to Eris. She could never understand it anyway, and if she knew the truth it might have ended her love instantly. Despite her proximity to Biagio, the innocent girl knew very little about the Roshann's business. And it wasn't exactly a bargain he had struck with Biagio. Whether or not he married the dancer, Biagio expected this of him. Eris was merely a prize for years of good service. She was also the Master's way of showing his unique affection for Simon. Simon knew this and shuddered at it. But he had been honest with Biagio. He loved Eris, and would do anything to marry her—even steal a child. Truthfully, he knew the child would never leave Crote alive. If she left the island at all, it would be in pieces. Biagio was fond of sending people heads.

His lord was a monster; Simon knew that now. As he watched the waves go by from the deck, he realized that he served a madman, someone whose mind had been devoured by drugs. Biagio hadn't always been this way, and Simon mourned his memory. In the early days of the Roshann, when Biagio was young and Simon but a boy, the count had been a hero to the people of Crote. He had brought the island into the folds of the Empire, had fed the peasants with endless shipments of supplies from the mainland, and had given Crote something it desperately desired—respect. With Biagio at the emperor's right hand, it was no longer fashionable to call Crotans olive pickers or drunks. They were the people of the Roshann, feared and dangerous. And for that one great gift the people of the island adored Count Biagio, and would forgive him anything.

Even insanity.

It was a cold day on the deck of the *Intimidator*. The cruiser cut through the churning waters effortlessly, her sails full of air. Simon stood at her stern and watched the cruiser's wake. She was a fine ship, newer than most in the fleet. Not as grand as the *Fearless*, of course, but far better suited to their secretive task. They had rounded the cape of Lucel-Lor and were heading for Falindar. Captain N'Dek wanted no mistakes, so he kept his vessel far from shore. In these waters, N'Dek had told Simon, there were giant sea serpents and squids capable of dragging even the *Fearless* beneath the waves. N'Dek was a vicious man, prone to alarming lies, but Simon kept one suspicious eye on the deep anyway. For a man raised on an island, he detested the sea.

Soon they would be in Lucel-Lor. Simon relished the thought of solid ground beneath him, but the idea of his mission frightened him. It was impossible, after all, and he really didn't expect to succeed. Vantran would be suspicious of everything. He had outlived the emperor, he had slain the Baron Blackwood Gayle, and, most incredibly, he had outwitted Biagio. It seemed impossible to Simon that such a quick-witted man would let a stranger steal his daughter. But there was one thing Simon was sure Richius Vantran suffered from. He was Naren. And that meant he was alone in Lucel-Lor. With no one of his kind to talk to, he would certainly be desperate for a fellow countryman. It was a gamble, Simon knew, but it was a good one. He would play on Vantran's sympathies, work his way into his graces. Vantran would get used to having a friend. Then, like a cobra, Simon would strike.

I am without morals, thought Simon. *God help me.*

It was why he was good at being Roshann, why Biagio had come to lean on him. Simon's last name was no accident of fate. He had chosen the designation *Darquis* carefully. In the tongue of Vosk, where his mother had been born, the word meant "dark-heart." To Simon, it seemed the perfect tag for a man without conscience.

No, Simon corrected himself. Not without conscience. Not completely. He felt remorse for this mission, just enough to make him human, and that pleased him. If he were a religious man he would have prayed for forgiveness, but the new God of Nar was deaf to Crotans. So he remained silent and merely watched the warship's wake, marveling at its size. The wind whipped his bearded face and sucked the moisture from his lips. Over his shoulder the sun was descending, heralding night's return, and the men on board called to each other and busied themselves with work. Simon thought of Eris, of her sharp face and perfect breasts. She had the legs of a goddess, long and slender, and Simon felt desire rise up in him until he was awash in his own loneliness. Soon he would take the Jackal's daughter and he would be free of this longing forever. He and Eris would wed. Simon closed his eyes and smiled, then heard the footfalls on the deck behind him.

"See any serpents?" asked N'Dek. The captain shouldered up to Simon and stuck an elbow in his ribs. "Good place to vomit, eh, Darquis?" jibed the captain. "Perhaps we should move your bunk up here."

Simon laughed. Despite the man's sardonic personality, Simon liked him. He was witty and strange, and had a reputation among his crew as a hard but fair captain.

"Don't stand too close to me, N'Dek. I might empty myself on your pretty uniform."

"If you emptied anything it would be water only," said the captain. "You should eat more. A strong wind and you'll go overboard."

"I can't eat," said Simon. "Not the swill your galley serves. I've tried, and all it does is come back up."

"It's not the food," said N'Dek, pointing a sharp finger into Simon's shoulder. "It's you. You're a weakling, Darquis. Like all land fighters." The captain cackled, baiting his hook, but Simon didn't rise to it.

"You're right," said Simon calmly. "That's why the legions are still in Nar, and the Black Fleet is sailing around safe little Crote. A pity Vorto's men can't all be as strong as you, N'Dek."

N'Dek's expression soured. "I should pitch you over the rail for that, Darquis. But then, Biagio might be angry if I killed his favorite spy."

There was a curious stress on the word *favorite* that made Simon squirm a little. "What's it like to be the count's messenger boy, N'Dek? Good job?"

"I am not a messenger boy," hissed N'Dek.

"Biagio should get himself some pigeons to deliver his messages. They'd certainly be faster than this wreck."

"Darquis, you astonish me. I'm the captain of this vessel. I could leave you stranded with your new Triin friends. How would you like that, eh? Marooned with the gogs? I'll just tell the count you were lost, or that you never came back. That would be a shame, wouldn't it? If you were lost?"

"Not so big a pity, N'Dek. At least I wouldn't have to endure this trip again."

N'Dek laughed. "Not much longer, spy. I've taken new bearings. According to my rutters, we should be reaching the citadel in the next two days."

"Two days? Are you sure?"

"If the winds hold, yes. We'll stop before Falindar, of course. Don't want to be seen."

"The watchtower," Simon reminded him. "Leave me at the tower."

N'Dek nodded impatiently. "Yes, yes . . ."

"You can't overshoot, N'Dek," said Simon. "The citadel is too damn high. If we get too close we might be seen."

"You presume a great deal," smoldered the captain. "I don't need your help to chart a course. Stick to your poisons and daggers, Roshann."

Simon accepted the warning. N'Dek was a playful man, but could only be pushed so far. Like all of Nicabar's captains, this one had a sore spot for Roshann agents, an umbrage he hid very poorly. N'Dek didn't like hiding in Crote. He wanted to be back in Nar, aiming his guns at Vorto's legions and the Lissens swarming the Empire's coasts. He endured the disgrace of cargo voyages because Admiral Nicabar ordered him to, but he bore a heavy resentment toward the Count of Crote and all his Roshann agents.

"You've been out here all day," said N'Dek at last. "Go below and get some rest. You'll need it for what's ahead."

It wasn't worth arguing, so Simon didn't. He was exhausted, weak from lack of food and the constant rising of his stomach. The air was better topside, but he heard his bunk calling. He nodded and turned from the captain, making his way toward the gang ladder. He had almost reached it when he heard N'Dek's snipe.

"Oh, Darquis, I almost forgot. We're having octopus tonight. Care to dine at my table?"

"Burn in Hell, N'Dek."

Simon spent the next day in his cabin, resting, wondering how near they were to Falindar. At around sundown, a little nervous flutter started growing in his stomach. He was always nervous before a mission, and he always appreciated the anxiousness. It kept him sharp. But this was different. As he lay in bed and watched the sunlight fade, he thought of Eris and their future, and he hoped it would be a life without regrets. His parents had loved each other, and when his father had died his mother had wept in agony, and told him how she hadn't regretted one moment of their lives together. Now, as he lay in bed, ill with seasickness, his mother's face kept coming to him, and he thought of Eris on the island with the mad Biagio, and of Savros who loved pain, and the little midget with the clever mind.

And Simon was afraid.

That night he hardly slept at all. When morning finally came he greeted it like an old friend. If the winds were fair, they would reach their destination that day. He dressed quickly and found his appetite returning. Up on deck N'Dek and his officers were pacing amidships. The sails were half-masted. The *Intimidator* moved slowly through the waters, like some great shark stalking prey. Simon hurried over to the captain, who flashed him an apprehensive smile.

"Good morning, Darquis. Look over my shoulder."

Simon paused, doing as N'Dek asked. It was a foggy morning and visibility was poor, but Simon saw the shape of land in the distance, unmistakable even in the mist. He took a deep breath and looked at N'Dek.

"That it?"

"Yes," nodded the captain. "According to my rutters. Any of this look familiar to you?"

Simon shook his head. He couldn't see the watchtower, and he wondered at the accuracy of N'Dek's charts. Though he had been here before, he was no expert on Triin terrain.

"I can't see anything from here," he said. "Can you get me closer?"

"We're piloting in. Get your gear together, Darquis. If this fog holds you can row ashore without being seen."

"Agreed," said Simon, returning to his cabin. Again that feeling of fear pecked at him, and he shook his head to be rid of it. He didn't really have gear, just his ragged disguise, and as he slid into it he made sure not to put any more tears in the threadbare fabric. He found his shabby boots beneath his bunk and slid these on too, and then completed his ensemble with the only weapon he would allow himself—a legionnaire's dagger. This he tucked into his belt. There was a mirror in the cabin and he inspected himself in it. His appearance made him smile. Weeks of sea-sickness had made him suitably gaunt, and his skin was chapped and weathered. His hair was filthy too, matted to his head by the accumulation of ocean salt.

"You can do this," he whispered to his reflection. "You must. For Eris."

For Eris. He drew a breath, held it, then left the cabin. The *Intimidator* was closer to shore now. Simon could barely see the scratchy outline of the Triin coast. This region of Lucel-Lor was called Tatterak. It was where Falindar stood. There had been a warlord here once, a Triin named Kronin, but he had been killed in the Naren invasion. According to the Triin Hakan, a man named Lucyler was Falindar's new master. Simon recited these facts like a mantra, searching for anything useful. If he truly had spent a year wandering Lucel-Lor, he would have known these things and more. One mistake, and Vantran would know the truth.

The cruiser sailed ever closer to land. When it was near enough to row ashore, N'Dek ordered the anchors lowered. The great weights dropped into the ocean with a splash, dragging down rattling chains. Simon waited at the railing for N'Dek's orders. The captain's face was unusually serious as he stepped up to Simon.

"You ready?"

Simon nodded. He still couldn't see the tower through the fog, but the light was increasing, threatening the haze. He would have to disembark quickly.

"I'll have two men row you ashore. Find the tower as soon as you can. You'll be given a signal lantern and some flint. Hide them well. You'll need them to signal us. We'll be waiting out here for you in forty days."

"Forty days," Simon echoed. "All right."

N'Dek looked at him hard. "Forty days precisely, Darquis. Don't make any mistakes. I'm already uncomfortable in Triin waters alone. If there are still Lissens around—"

"There are no Lissens."

"If there are Lissens," continued N'Dek ruthlessly, "they will chase us out of here and you'll be on your own. If you miss the date, we sail home to Crote without you. Do you understand that?"

"I understand," said Simon. "Thanks."

"Don't blame me for this rotten task," said the captain. "I don't envy you, it's true. But I've got my own crew to worry about."

"And your own skin. Yes, I know. Don't apologize, N'Dek. I meant what I said. Thanks for taking me this far." Then he jabbed a finger into the man's chest and added, "Just be here when I get back."

Surprisingly, N'Dek returned the grin. "I'll be here in forty days. You have my word." The captain put his hand out for Simon. "Luck to you, spy."

Simon took the hand and shook it. "And to you," he said, then left to find the waiting rowboat. The little craft was dangling from the side of the *Intimidator*, ready to be lowered into the water. In it were two sailors, one of whom held a sack of provisions. Simon stepped gingerly into the rowboat, almost slipping as it swayed beneath him. When he was safely aboard, one of the sailors ordered the boat lowered, and it slowly began its descent. Simon watched N'Dek as the rowboat hit the water. The sailors took up the oars and began rowing toward the foggy shore, leaving behind the looming warship. In a short moment the *Intimidator* was shimmering in fog. Simon looked toward shore. There he saw the harsh terrain of Lucel-Lor coming into focus.

"God," he muttered. "I had hoped never to see this place again."

The sailors rowed without comment. Simon's eyes darted suspiciously around the rocky inlet, but all he saw were birds and a swarm of mosquitoes. Then out of the mist the watchtower grew. It was just as he'd left it, ancient and leaning, a dilapidated spire from the old days of the warlords, rising out of the craggy earth. Simon pointed at it.

"There," he whispered, directing the sailors. The little vessel turned and headed for the tower, and in a moment slid onto the gravelly shore. The two sailors pulled in the oars and waited for Simon to depart. Simon took up his sack of provisions, spared a last glance at the ocean where the unseen *Intimidator* was anchored, then stepped from the rowboat. At once the cold ocean soaked into his worn-out boots.

"Tell your captain not to miss his rendezvous," he said. "I'll be back here in forty days."

One of the sailors nodded. "Just use the signal lantern. We'll come for you."

You'd better, thought Simon bitterly. He pushed the little rowboat back out to sea and watched the sailors fade into the mist, then turned and waded toward the shore. Lucel-Lor, tall and forbidding, rose up before him, shriveling his bravado. This was an ancient world, strange beyond imagining, and the people here were unlike any race in the Empire. Some said they were sorcerers, but Simon wasn't superstitious. He knew only that they were a mystery, a race that Arkus of Nar had tried to understand and failed. Simon moved quickly toward the brush, hiding himself in a grove of trees, then made his way to the abandoned tower. He had found it on his first mission to Lucel-Lor and it had made the perfect hideout. Too far from any villages, the tower never got visitors, not even curious children. It had a haunted quality to it, the kind of place seen in nightmares. It had no door but its stairs were sound, and Simon could climb to its top and see for miles.

About the tower was a clearing. Simon reached it quickly, then surveyed the tower from his hiding place in the trees. He saw no one; heard nothing. He sniffed the air for campfires and smelled only the ocean. Satisfied, he moved stealthily out of the trees and crossed the twenty yards to the tower, dashing across its threshold. Once inside, Simon stopped. Blackness enveloped him. He could hear the wind outside and the throbbing of his heart. The sack in his hand quavered. Something was wrong. Simon cursed himself.

Easy, you damn fool. There's nothing here.

His eyes adjusted to the light. Whoever had abandoned the place had left only stale air behind. There had been war in this region when the tower was built. There were towers like this one all throughout Lucel-Lor—great perches where watchmen could spy on the movements of their enemies. Lucel-Lor had endured a long and violent history, not unlike the history of Nar. They were a cruel people too, sometimes. Simon gave a nervous laugh. The similarities were striking.

He laid the sack down on the brick floor and began rummaging through it. The lantern and flint were there, as promised, along with a water skin and some dried meat and bread. Hardly enough to subsist on, but then Simon wasn't supposed to look like he'd been eating from ample supplies. He removed the lantern from the sack, struck the flint repeatedly to make it spark, then set the precious oil in the lantern aflame. The wick caught quickly and the fire died down, leaving a warm glow. Simon took up the sack, held the lantern out before him, and began making his way up the narrow stairway. Once he had left behind the entry chamber, all was dark but for the steady glow of his lamp. Along the walls were iron sconces and torch holders, now rusted away, and the mortar between the bricks had dissolved to dust. As he walked, Simon dragged his hand along the wall, feeling the imperfect stone.

When at last he reached the top of the spire, he was in a round chamber full of shattered windows. A fierce wind blew in from the ocean, chilling him. He dropped his sack on the ground and shielded the gentle flame inside the lantern with his hand. Lucel-Lor, vast and impenetrable, was at his feet. He went over to one of the windows and looked outside. Morning sunlight poured over the earth and the sea to the north. To the south was rocky earth, patched with autumn forests and the ever-rising slopes of small mountains. Simon felt a rush of insignificance.

Here at the top of the world, he realized again how small he was, and how fleeting time could be. Someday the ocean would reclaim the land it had forfeited to men, and this proud tower would tumble, forgotten.

Still shaky from his ordeal on the *Intimidator*, Simon decided to rest. Vantran would wait, and he needed to stop his head from swimming. He opened the glass of the lantern and blew out the small flame, not needing it up here in the sunlight. Simon leaned out of the broken window and let the warming rays strike his face. Beneath him, the world was solid again.

He went from the window and put his lantern back in the burlap sack. Pulling out the crusty bread, he ate some sparingly, so as not to get sick. Then he settled back against one of the filthy walls and went over his impossible plan. The citadel of Falindar was miles away, a full day's hike. That would give him time to get more grimy, to pick up some of the land's odors. This afternoon, when the sun was high and warmer, he would leave the tower. He would make his way to Falindar and Richius Vantran, and he would begin his elaborate charade.

He would take the Jackal's daughter, he resolved. He *would*. And if Herrith was right and there truly was a Hell, he would burn for it.

That afternoon, Simon left the tower and began his trek toward Falindar. The sun that had looked so promising earlier had failed to materialize into anything more than a hazy orange ball, and within a few hours Simon was shivering. His feet ached too—the result of shoddy boots—and he knew that blisters were boiling up on his skin. But these were small annoyances. He was free of the confines of the ship, out in the air again, and he was grateful for the feeble sun and the fresh breeze. Tatterak was different from the other Triin territories. It was colder here, starker, and the trees were enormous. Simon moved slowly but with purpose, aware of every sound. He was in a valley between two hillsides, a green place thick with yellow flowers and blown leaves. The tall grass felt good against his thighs, and as he walked he brushed the tops of it with his palms. A school-boy smile played across his lips. This was a pristine land, not at all like Nar City with its smokestacks and choked avenues. It was as if the Triin had forgotten this place, or had left it fallow.

By late afternoon Simon had made it through most of the valley. He had almost reached its end when the smell of something dangerous alerted him. Simon stood as still as a cat, and quickly determined the source of the smell.

"Fire," he whispered.

Nearby? He cocked his head to listen, heard the breeze and the chirping of birds. Up ahead was another line of trees—big pines a mile deep.

Guessing the smell was coming from the forest, he approached it warily. Then he caught the first sight of smoke. White and thin. And close by. A campfire, certainly. Simon steadied himself. He would go around, he decided, and avoid whoever was here. But when he turned to go he saw a man with an arm full of firewood.

Simon froze.

The man dropped the firewood and stood gaping at him. Not Triin. Simon didn't move.

Not bloody Triin!

"Who the hell are you?" barked the man. He was shorter than Simon but broader in the shoulders, dark-haired, and as he spoke he surged forward, one arm reaching for his blade. Simon put up his hands, his mind groping for his pretext—the one he'd rehearsed so long.

"Don't you move!" the man roared. He had his broadsword drawn and held it out in both hands. Simon raised his hands higher above his hands.

"Easy," he urged. "Take it easy. . . ."

The man was dressed like a Triin, but was unmistakably Naren. Simon stopped moving backward and let the stranger approach.

"I'm unarmed," he said loudly. "Just a dagger, in my belt. A dagger, all right?"

"Don't you move," repeated the man. He had the tip of his sword at Simon's throat now. "Or I swear to God I'll cut your miserable throat!"

"I'm not moving," said Simon. "Not a hair."

The man looked him up and down, then his hand flashed out and grabbed hold of Simon's collar. He dragged Simon to his knees, then flung him down. Simon's chest hit the ground with a painful thud. The man put his foot on his neck and leaned.

"Stop!" Simon gasped.

"Shut up!" snapped the stranger. He bent down and fixed his knee into Simon's back, pressing down hard and putting the edge of his sword to Simon's throat. With his other hand he grabbed a fistful of hair and jerked back Simon's head.

"Who the hell are you? Tell me quick or I'll break your neck."

Simon calmed himself, retreating into his training. "My name is Simon," he said calmly.

"Simon what?"

"Simon Darquis. From Vosk."

"Liar!" flared the man. He slammed Simon's face into the ground. At once Simon felt blood gushing from his nose. He cried out and the man jerked his head back up. "Tell me the truth, you Naren pig! What are you doing here?"

"I . . . I'm a deserter," Simon stammered. "From the Naren legions. Like you?"

This caused another outburst from the stranger. "Now you listen to me, you dirty little weasel. I'm no deserter. And you're not either, are you? *Are you?*"

Simon could hardly breathe. "I am," he gasped. But inside he laughed. He couldn't believe his good fortune. "I swear it. My name is Simon Darquis. I'm a lieutenant."

"With whom? What regiment?"

"They're gone. I told you. . . ."

"With the Naren legions?"

"Yes!"

"I'll snap your neck if you move," whispered the man. "Now you tell me everything. Why are you here? Who sent you?"

"No one sent me," Simon managed to croak. "God! You're killing me!"

Enraged, the man Simon supposed was Vantran violently rolled Simon onto his back and put the tip of his sword under his chin.

"I'll run you through if you don't tell me what I want to know," he growled. His eyes were wild, like a rabid dog's. Simon was breathing hard. Suddenly he wasn't sure if he could convince Vantran.

"I swear to God I'm no one," he gasped. "Please, I swear it. I'm just a deserter. I left my regiment behind. A year ago. More, maybe. I don't know . . ."

"Then what are you doing here?" barked Vantran. "Why did you desert?"

Simon shrugged as though he was too afraid to answer. "To be free. To get away. I wandered here. That's all. . . ."

There was a softening in Vantran's face. Simon relaxed a little. It was working.

"I meant no harm," he added. "I swear it. If this is your land—"

"Quiet," snapped Vantran.

"Let me go," Simon begged. "I'll leave; go back the way I came. Please . . ."

"I said be quiet!" Vantran pulled the blade away, but only slightly. "Tell me the truth," he ordered again. This time his voice was almost desperate.

"What can I tell you?" Simon cried. "I'm a deserter. I'm Simon Darquis!"

"If you're lying I'll find out about it, Simon Darquis. I will, and then you'll be sorry." Vantran didn't move his boot from Simon's chest. "Did Biagio send you?"

Inside, Simon's smile widened. "What the hell are you talking about?"

"This is a game, I know it is. All right then, don't tell me." He took the blade from Simon's neck. "You'll come back with me," he declared. "Or I'll cut you down. Do you understand?"

"Back with you? Where?"

"Stop with your questions," said Vantran. He rose to his feet, careful to keep the sword near his prisoner. "Get up."

Simon got up very slowly. Vantran reached over and pulled the dagger from his belt, sticking it in his own. He gestured toward the trees where his campfire burned.

"That way," he ordered. "Move."

"Why? Where are we going?"

"Just move." Vantran seemed nervous. Simon struggled to keep his glee in check. The bleeding of his nose made it easy to look helpless. He walked toward the trees and the smell of smoke, Vantran's sharp blade at his back. There was a distinct tremor in the young man's voice. Good. Vantran would be easy to keep unbalanced. And that wildness in his eyes—he was restless.

"Where are you taking me?" Simon asked again. "Tell me."

"Why should I?"

"Your camp is nearby. I smelled it. That's why I was coming this way. I am hungry."

"And you're going to get a lot hungrier, my friend."

They walked on until at last they reached Vantran's campsite. It was a pleasant place, well worn, as if Vantran had spent some time there. Next to the campfire was a blanket and some utensils, and there was a horse tethered to one of the pine trees—a strapping, tawny creature that turned its eyes on them as they approached. Simon moved close to the fire. The heat felt good against his skin.

"Sit," ordered Vantran.

Simon did as directed. Vantran remained standing, staring down at him. The sun was sinking quickly. Vantran's face was lit with worry, and he didn't speak for a very long time, but instead simply watched his captive. Simon returned the stare, mustering up all his contempt. He ran a sleeve over his nose and found that the wound was worse than he'd thought. Pain shot through his face and a dull throbbing hammered his ears.

"You broke my nose, you bloody bastard."

Vantran sighed. He rested the sword point on the ground and leaned on its pommel. "Do you know who I am?"

Simon nodded. "I think I do. You're Vantran, aren't you?"

"You answered that quickly."

"Who else would you be?" Simon's eyes surveyed the young man. "Look at you, all dressed up like a Triin. I guessed who you were when I saw you."

"I bet you did. After all, you were looking for me, weren't you?"

"Vantran, I'll tell you something. All this time in Lucel-Lor has made you crazy. I can see it in your eyes. Now I don't know who the hell you think I am, and I don't really give a damn. I just want to be on my way. Would that be all right with you?"

"Stray from that spot, and I'll cut your head off. Do you understand?"

"Piss on you."

Vantran scowled. "You lousy assassin. Don't you lie to me. I know who you are. Biagio sent you!"

"Biagio!" Simon railed, half laughing. "Like I said. You're insane."

"Yes, insane. And you're just some poor wandering deserter, who just can't stand the thought of going back home to Nar, right? You expect me to believe that?"

"Believe whatever you want," said Simon. "I really don't care. Frankly, I'm enjoying your fire."

"You're from Vosk?"

"That's right."

"A lieutenant?"

Simon nodded. "I was with the regiment sent to help Blackwood Gayle find you."

The mere mention of Gayle made Vantran twitch. Simon watched him, reading his expression, and for the smallest instant he pitied the man. What Blackwood Gayle had done to Vantran was legendary. Amazingly, Vantran lowered his sword, almost dropping it from his fingers. He slid down onto the ground in front of Simon, his shoulders slumped, his eyes dim and clouded.

"I don't know what to believe. Are you who you claim? Maybe. If you're not, then I'm dead already, aren't I? If you're an assassin, then Biagio knows where I am."

Simon scoffed. "Do I look like an assassin?"

"I've seen the count's handiwork. I know how clever he can be."

"Clever enough to turn starving deserters into killers, then?" Simon jabbed a finger at himself. "Look at me. I'm a rag. All the grain fields from here to Ackle-Nye were burned. I've been living in bloody caves, eating anything I can catch or pull off a tree. You think I'm one of that bastard's pampered Roshann? I should live so long!"

Vantran gazed into the sky, considering the sinking sun. "I have to take you back with me to Falindar, but it's getting dark. We'll stay here tonight and leave in the morning."

"Falindar?" croaked Simon. "Oh, no. I'm not going to that god-cursed place."

"You're going. You're my prisoner now."

"In hell," spat Simon. "What if I say no?"

Vantran shrugged. "I'll just drag you there."

Simon grimaced. "I'm hungry."

"Sorry."

"Are you just going to let me starve?"

The young man looked at Simon. The harshness in his face began to ebb. "No, I suppose not."

The sun dropped behind the mountains; night blanketed the valley. Richius Vantran sat stretched out on the ground near his fire, his face awash in dancing firelight. On the ground near him was a plateful of half-eaten game bird. Simon watched the young man pensively. They had shared a meal together in utter silence. Simon had devoured his portion instantly. Now he felt full and satisfied. More, he was surprised at how quickly he was wearing Vantran down. The fool had even untied his hands so he could eat. When the meal was over he had tied them again, but the simple act of trust told Simon he was already winning.

It was late now, and the gray day had given up to a clear night with a bright moon. The cold fingers of autumn crept up to the campsite, held at bay by the glowing fire, and the trees in the valley moved with the stirrings of night creatures. Richius Vantran ate his supper slowly, pensively, occasionally raising his eyes to look across the campfire to where Simon was sitting. It was necessary, Vantran had explained. He didn't trust his prisoner, especially in the dark, and wouldn't have been able to sleep any other way. Simon had protested but only just enough to look convincing. Too weak in appearance to fight Vantran, he had let the young man bind him again after eating. Simon tried vainly to get comfortable against a tree trunk, his booted feet outstretched toward the warming fire. His wrists ached and his head swam. His nose still throbbed but the bleeding had stopped and Vantran had taken the care to wash some of it away with a damp cloth. The gesture had made Simon wonder about the man. How old was he now? Nearly twenty-seven? Not so young anymore, yet he sometimes acted like a boy. Simon liked his muddled innocence. He watched Vantran through the flickering fire, his brown eyes full of questions. Simon was safe now; he knew it. Vantran was no killer. And the way he had wiped Simon's face had betrayed a dangerous sympathy. Already his skepticism was eroding.

"I'm still hungry," Simon said finally. "You gonna eat all that bird?"

"You've had your share," said Vantran.

"I'll need more food if you're going to march me to Falindar. I might collapse on the way."

"It's not that far."

"I won't be able to make it, I tell you. Let me share your horse."

"Tell you what—you tell me who you really are and I'll think about it."

"What's wrong with you, you bloody fool? I've told you everything. You're just not listening."

Richius Vantran yawned and stretched his arms into the air. "I'm too tired for this. In the morning we'll talk more."

"That's it?" Simon railed. "You're just going to leave me tied up all night? I'm a legionnaire of Nar, damn it! I want some respect!"

"A legionnaire? Oh, yes, sir!" Vantran wrapped his arms around his knees and grinned. "You have the nerve of a bull, my friend. Legionnaire, indeed. Even if you were one, you're a deserter. A traitor."

"Oh, yes," said Simon. "And you'd be an expert on spotting traitors, wouldn't you, Jackal?"

The smile vanished from Vantran's face. "Don't call me that."

"Why not? That's what they were calling you in Nar. You know that, don't you? Frankly, I think it suits you."

"I'm Richius Vantran, King of Aramoor. Call me king or Vantran or anything else, but don't call me Jackal. I won't allow it."

"King," scoffed Simon. "There is no Aramoor, Vantran. Not anymore. How much do you know about the Empire anyway? Blackwood Gayle's family took over your country. It's a province of Talistan now."

"I know that."

"What do they call you here?" Simon asked. "Do they call you king?"

"No," the young man admitted. "They don't."

"No. Because you're not a king. Even the Triin know that, Jackal. They call you Kalak here, don't they? That's their word for you, isn't it?"

"You are an obnoxious creature," Vantran declared. "Be quiet and let me sleep."

"What are you doing out here?" Simon pressed. "Why are you alone?"

Vantran rolled his eyes. "Lord, you talk too much."

"Do you live in Falindar?"

"I live with my wife."

Simon smiled wickedly. "Yes, your wife. You left your kingdom for her, didn't you? We all knew the story. Blackwood Gayle told us what you'd done. She must be something, eh?"

"Fellow, I'm going to tell you this one more time. I don't want you talking anymore tonight, all right? And I don't want you ever speaking about my wife. I don't trust you, and I'm not going to tell you a blessed thing. So save your breath and go to sleep."

Simon leaned in closer. "Who do you think I am? Really now, tell me? You think I was sent to kill you?"

He watched Vantran grimace at the question.

"I have enemies," said the man. "You might be one of them. I don't know. But I can't take any chances."

"Biagio sent us all here to find you, to bring you back alive. That was part of our mission. We were supposed to find magic to save the emperor, but Gayle and Biagio wanted you captured. I admit that. But that was a long time ago, Vantran. And as far as I know, I'm the only Naren left in Lucel-Lor besides you." Simon offered a gentle smile. "You've been hiding for a year now, I can see that. You're unbalanced, fearful. I can see it in your eyes."

"Are you a mystic too?" asked Vantran sarcastically.

"I don't need mysticism to see you're afraid. Maybe you should be, I don't know. But not of me. I swear this to you, Vantran. I'm just a deserter."

Vantran looked at him skeptically. "That's impossible. Legionnaires are loyal."

"So are kings," chided Simon. "Yet here you are."

There was a contemplative silence. Vantran's hard eyes softened with understanding, and Simon watched him coolly, reading his weakening defenses. The young man buried his chin in his knees and stared into the fire, and suddenly he was miles away. When he spoke it was out of a fugue, his tone emotionless.

"So why did you desert, then?" he asked softly. "What happened to you?"

"Nar happened to me, Vantran. Nar and its misery. I never belonged in uniform. I joined because I had nowhere else to go, and I needed to eat. But when they sent me here, I realized I didn't belong with them."

"That's not an answer." The young man was still distant, staring blankly into the flames. "What made you leave?"

Simon looked into the fire too, recalling his pretense. He had expected these questions. "Ackle-Nye," he said softly. "Do you know what happened there?"

Vantran merely nodded.

"It was butchery, plain and simple. When we came through the mountain pass, the Triin there tried to defend themselves against us, but they had nothing. We burned the city to the ground. We killed everything. I . . ." Simon paused theatrically, choking on fake emotion. "I murdered children. Little ones no taller than my knee. I was ordered to do it but that didn't make me feel better about it. And when we were done we lit the whole place on fire."

"The burning city," Vantran echoed. It was what Ackle-Nye was called that night of the massacre. It was said the flames of the city could be seen across the world.

"That's right. They were beggars and refugees and old women, and we killed them. I will never be the same again, Vantran. So don't you lecture me about being a traitor. What I did took courage. I can never go back to the Empire. I'm stuck here."

Vantran turned his eyes on Simon. "You made your choice," he said. "Live with it."

"I have been living with it," said Simon. Then he cocked his head inquisitively and asked, "What about you?"

As expected, Vantran balked at the question. "I've been just fine," he said. "Not that it's any of your business."

"You live in Falindar?"

"Yes."

"With the warlord?"

"There is no warlord in Tatterak anymore. Not since the old one died."

"Then who are you taking me to see?" Simon asked. "Why am I your prisoner?"

"Because you can't be trusted. I don't know if what you've told me is the truth, or if this is all some elaborate lie of Biagio's. Either way, I want to keep an eye on you, Simon Darquis. That means you have to come back with me to the citadel. You will speak to the master there, Lucyler. We'll both decide what to do with you."

"Triin justice?" flared Simon. "That's your idea of fair? They'll slit my throat just for being Naren!"

"Maybe," said Vantran casually. "Maybe not." He smiled faintly at Simon. "I want to believe you, I really do. But I can't. If you were hunted like me, you would understand that."

"Rubbish," sneered Simon. "You're not hunted any more than I am. It's all in your imagination. You're living in fear of nothing, and now you want to drag me into your illusion. That's all this is—one man's fantasy. I pity you, Vantran."

The young man's face hardened. "Pity yourself," he said. "Because if I find out you're lying, nothing on earth will save you from me."

Then Richius Vantran rose and stalked off into the darkness, leaving Simon alone by the fire. Simon watched him go, watched the night and his own black mood swallow him, and knew with certainty that his mission would succeed.

NINE

The Cathedral of the Martyrs

In the center of Nar City, near the shining Black Palace across the river Kiel, the great Cathedral of the Martyrs rose above the polluted avenues, its metal steeple reaching for heaven over the constant smoke of the war labs. Ancient gargoyles stalked its ledges, their stone eyes fixed on the metropolis around them, and windows of stained glass cast colorful shadows, bathing the streets in rainbows. A century of rainstorms had rubbed the limestone smooth and turned the copper green, and when the sun was bright the cathedral glimmered like a star through the haze of the capital. Ten thousand slaves had labored ten years to construct it, and even in the current chaos of Nar she was an ambition, a destination for pilgrims from around the Empire. Each holy day the square around her filled with believers eager to hear the word of God and to gain absolution for their wicked lives.

Archbishop Herrith understood the importance of the cathedral. It was more dear to him than scripture, more dear even than his life. He believed that God truly dwelled within its walls and vaunted steeple. It was where, he presumed, God lived on earth. He was nearly fifty now, and had spent the majority of his years in this holy place, walking its halls and greeting the faithful. It was where Naren nobles took wives, where Richius Vantran, the Jackal of Nar, had been made king, and where, Herrith hoped, the Lord would take him when he died. In its many tabernacles Herrith had seen many things—miracles certainly, like the weeping God-Mother and the bleeding chalice, and these things were precious to him too. They gave him strength. And in these dark days, Herrith needed strength. He needed God to speak to him in a clear voice, without being muddled by interpreters and priests. Herrith spent long hours in prayer now, fasting and begging Heaven to hear him, and wrestling with the things God the Father had told him to do.

On this day, like any other, Herrith saw to the functioning of his majestic cathedral. He had acolytes to oversee and an army of cowled priests, and a thousand tedious details nagging for his attention. He was worn from the war in Goth and his ongoing feud with the traitor Biagio, and he longed for some solitude, to be merely a priest again, a servant of the Almighty. He had spent the morning with General Vorto listening to details of the soldier's campaigns, and his head ached from Vorto's voice. Herrith moved through the cathedral's gilded hallways, hoping no one would see him. It was Seventh Day, the day the cathedral opened its private chambers for confession. This, the most intimate of sacraments, had been taken from Herrith by the pressures of his lofty office, but on rare occasion he participated in it and heard the sins of his flock. Today the archbishop needed to hear confession. He needed to know there were others in the world who sinned.

Herrith pulled his white silk cowl closer around his face as he walked like a whisper down the golden corridors. Father Todos, his assistant, was waiting for him in one of the confession chambers. A very special confessor was with him, hidden from sight in the booth. But Todos had thought he'd recognized the voice, and so had summoned his master to hear the confession himself. It was a private confession, the confessor had explained, and so he had come to the private chambers. Naren nobles and men of high rank were allowed the privilege, leaving the less fortunate of the flock to crowd into the main tabernacle and wait for acolytes to hear their sins. Herrith had always thought it an odd separation, but he had allowed it because it had been the will of Arkus. In the wake of the emperor's death, the archbishop had thought it best to leave the private chambers available. He needed the goodwill of the nobles. Too many of them had already sided with Biagio. Goth had been the latest, and worst, of the secessionists, and Herrith prayed mightily for no more fractures in his weak coalition. God's hand was vengeful, he had learned, and the pain of it was destroying him.

Across the great hall where the painter Darago worked tirelessly on his latest masterpiece, the private confession chambers stood apart from the public tabernacles. Herrith moved cautiously through the hall, careful not to disturb the artist's tools. Because it was Seventh Day, Darago wasn't working, but his implements—his brushes and knives and pots of colors—all remained behind. As he walked through the hall, Herrith glanced up at the ceiling he had commissioned. Soon Darago would be finished and the great hall would be open once again to the public. They would see the work of the master-painter, and they would know with certainty that God existed. For without divine inspiration, no man could paint like Darago. His ceiling was like staring into Heaven itself.

Herrith's gaze lingered on the ceiling for a long time. He craned his neck to survey the fresco, some of which was draped with cloth to hide it from curious eyes. There were panels even the archbishop hadn't seen yet, for Darago was an intensely private man, moody like all artists, and though Herrith regularly pestered him about his progress, Darago kept his secrets locked away, constantly promising Herrith that he would be pleased with the results. Herrith was already pleased. The ceiling was the masterpiece he had imagined. It was the perfect gift for God.

God had delivered Nar to him. God had killed the immortal Arkus and had banished the demon Biagio. God's was the glory, and Herrith wanted to repay his heavenly Father. He had commissioned the ceiling years ago, well before the first cracks in the Iron Circle, but it seemed fitting to him that Darago was finishing now, when Herrith's hold on Nar was becoming final. It was all divine, the bishop decided, part of a design more vast than them all. The Black Renaissance that had relegated the Lord to nothing more than a means of controlling Nar had been almost entirely vanquished, and God had spoken to General Vorto and brought him into the fold. God was good and powerful. God wanted the Black Renaissance dead. And Herrith, who had dedicated his life to the service of Heaven, was not about to disappoint his Lord.

He slipped through the hall to a secondary chamber guarded by a consecrated statue. Saint Carlarian the Confessor watched him enter with marble eyes. When he was inside the chamber Herrith lowered his cowl and looked around. The room was empty. He had expected Todos to be waiting for him. The bishop crossed the room and peered through the door leading to the confession chambers. Father Todos was outside one of them. His eyes were closed in prayer.

"Todos?" asked the bishop.

The priest's eyes snapped open. He put a finger to his lips to quiet his master. Then he pointed into the confession booth.

"In there," he mouthed silently.

"Who?"

Todos went over to his master and whispered a single word. "Kye."

Herrith frowned. He didn't need Kye backing away from their grim work. Without his leadership, the legions might splinter.

"I thought you should know," said Todos apologetically. "I'm almost certain it's him. The voice . . ."

Herrith nodded. Kye's voice was unmistakable—a low-pitched rattle, the result of a Triin arrow through his neck. It took an experienced ear to understand him now.

"You did the right thing," said Herrith gently. "Thank you."

"He's been waiting," said Todos. "But I'm not sure you should hear his confession, Your Holiness. He will recognize your voice."

"Let him. He will be talking to God, not me. Go now, my friend. You've done well."

"Thank you, Your Holiness."

Herrith watched his assistant leave. He loved his old friend dearly, but wanted no witnesses to what was about to happen. Kye was an unbeliever, and he needed to be convinced. And although Herrith knew he had a placid reputation, God demanded things of him these days, things that often changed his personality. It wouldn't do for his underlings to hear him rage.

Take care, he reminded himself as he walked into the booth and closed the door behind him. *You need this one.*

Like he needed Vorto and all his soldiers. They were the only thing keeping together the fragile coalition of Naren nations. Fear of the legions had kept Biagio's loyalists in check. Fear was the fist of God. Without the army to prop up his church, Herrith knew, Biagio and his hateful Renaissance would triumph.

In the small chamber was a comfortable stool for the attending priest. Herrith took a seat and looked at the mesh screen separating him from the man on the other side. He barely made out Kye's shadow as the colonel sat opposite him, patiently waiting. The bishop said a silent prayer, crossed himself, and softly bade his penitent to speak.

"Go ahead, my child."

There was a long delay as the man on the other side of the screen adjusted himself.

"Yes, Father," he croaked. "I'm here because I think I've sinned."

Herrith closed his eyes. The voice was obviously Kye's. "How long has it been since your last confession, my son?"

"I've never had confession, Father. This is my first time."

"I see. Don't be frightened, then. I will help you."

Herrith knew Kye was listening intently, trying to decipher the voice on the other side of the booth. There was a long pause before the colonel spoke again.

"I don't know where to begin," he said shakily. "Perhaps I should go."

He knows it's me, thought Herrith. *Fine.*

"Don't leave. God doesn't care if you know the rituals. He only cares that you speak from your heart. Can you do that for Him?"

More silence. And then, "Yes. Yes, I can."

"Good, my son. We are listening, God and I. Tell us your sins. What troubles you so to bring you here?"

"I have never been a believer," said Kye's disembodied voice. "But I need God now. I need to know if I'm damned for what I've done."

"What have you done?"

"So much," moaned the colonel. "So bloody much . . ."

"Tell me," urged Herrith. "Tell God."

There was a sigh from the other side of the chamber. Colonel Kye's shadow lifted a hand to its head and rubbed. His breathing was erratic, unstable. It quavered as though he was about to weep. Archbishop Herrith said nothing, letting the colonel compose himself.

"I've killed so many people," said Kye. "Your Holiness, there is blood on me. So much blood . . ."

"You know who I am," said the bishop. "Does that not frighten you, Kye?"

"Yes, it does," admitted the colonel. "But you should know what we've been doing for you. You should know the blood we've spilled. It is like a river, Holiness."

Herrith began to tremble too, not with rage but with remorse. He had already heard the reports from Goth. Formula B had worked better than promised. And he had given that order himself. If there was blood on Kye's hands, then Herrith was drenched in it, too.

"The horror," Kye went on, his voice breaking. "God have mercy on me for what I've done." His shoulders slumped and he began to gasp, until at last the sobs overcame him and the booth rang with his anguish. "Tell me there's a God," he begged. "Absolve me, Holiness."

"There is a God more powerful than you or I, Colonel Kye. A God whose plan might seem harsh to us both, but who makes demands on us sometimes. You are pure in His eyes, Colonel. You are one of *His* soldiers, not Vorto's. Trust in Him. You are doing His work."

Even as he said it, Herrith wondered. Kye seemed to take no solace in the words. His sobs went on and on, until Herrith could hardly understand the babbling of his raspy voice. Kye was mumbling about children and screams, and something about mothers dying. Goth, the city of death, where nothing lived or could live anymore.

"It is God's will," said the bishop, trying to comfort Kye. "They are in His hands now. Death is a doorway. You know that, don't you? The righteous of Goth are with Him now."

"Oh, no," moaned Kye. "How can children be righteous? How can I do such evil work? I am damned! Forever damned . . ."

The Archbishop of Nar seethed. "Listen to me," he thundered. "God's work is not evil. It is a cleansing of this vile world. Goth stood with the devil Biagio. They flew the Black Flag, in defiance of the Lord.

You are on the righteous side, Kye, make no mistake. We are ridding the world of cancer."

Kye fought to calm himself, clearing his throat of phlegm. "I'm just a man," he said. "I'm not a priest, I'm not a God. I know nothing of Heaven. I can't be asked to do its work."

"You listen to me," insisted Herrith. "God is more real than you or I, and He knows your heart, Kye of Nar. He knows if it's pure. You fear the damnation of Hell for doing His work, but you don't see the glory of what you're doing."

"I see only slaughter," agreed Kye, "and dead faces in my dreams."

"But what you see is only earth," pressed Herrith. "It is the nothingness of this existence. There is another life after this one, Kye. And those who do the work of the Lord exalt in their next lives; those who do not will suffer the endless fire. You will not go to Hell for destroying Goth's children. You will go to Heaven for saving them!"

Kye was silent. He leaned his head back against the wall and stared up at the ceiling, and would not speak a word or utter the smallest sound. The sobs had left him. He was suddenly a shell, unmoving, and Herrith watched his silhouette mournfully, and all the colonel's dark regrets became his own.

"It is in the holy book, my child," said Herrith softly. He heard his words and knew he was talking to himself. "Serve the Lord and be rewarded. We defy Him at our peril."

"I do not defy Him," said Kye. "I question Him."

This time Herrith was without an answer. He considered the soldier's words carefully, groping for a response, but of late he had questioned Heaven, too. Herrith had found solace in scripture, but only a little. Like Kye, he grieved. But God's word was plain. Biagio *was* a sodomite and sinner. He lay with men. And the Black Renaissance he prescribed spoke of the emperor as the highest power, a heresy the bishop had let thrive for too long.

"It is unwise to question the Lord," said Herrith finally. "If you ignore the portents, Kye, you do so at your peril."

Kye's voice was a whisper. "Is it so clear to you?" he asked. "If you had been at Goth, it would be different, I think. I have never seen anything so terrible, Holiness, and I have seen a great deal. Your Formula B cannot be of God. I swear, it must be of the devil."

"It is the inspiration of faithful men that created the formula," said the bishop. "It can only be of God."

"That's a lie," snapped Kye. "I know Bovadin made the formula first. The war labs only perfected it."

"But God is perfection. And the formula does His work." Herrith put his face to the screen. "Oh, sweet Kye. I feel your agony. Do not think I am as heartless as that. I am God's servant on earth, after all. I care for children here in the cathedral, and I know it all seems impossible to you. But we are not always to question the will of our Father. The Black Renaissance is a terrible thing, and it runs through our land like a wound. We must burn it out of our flesh because there is no other way."

"Children, Holiness," said Kye. "Without skin. Without eyes." He put his hands to his head. "And they won't stop screaming at me. They won't stop. Make them stop, Holiness. Take them away from me. . . ."

Herrith knew that he could not. He had heard the same screams in his own head and no amount of prayer could silence them. They were relentless, these children of Goth. In death they were louder than in life.

"They are like dark angels," said Herrith. "Ignore them and they will be powerless over you. Rebuke them, Kye. You do the work of God. You need not answer to these phantoms."

Kye seemed to nod slightly. "Then I am absolved?" he asked.

"There is nothing to absolve you of. Go with God, Colonel. Rejoice in the work you do. And look to Vorto for guidance. He will help you understand."

Vorto was a butcher and Herrith knew it. But his name had a magical effect on the legionnaires who served with him. The general was legendary. And Kye, who was certainly less than a legend, admired Vorto. He could gain strength from him. Vorto could be an example to them all. "Do you understand what I have told you, my son?"

"I think I do," rasped Kye. "And God help me, I will try."

"God asks only your love," said the bishop. "Love him, and He will help you. You will see that. And you'll see also that what we're doing is not a lie but the greatest truth Nar has ever known. I promise you, Colonel. I swear it to Heaven."

Kye rose unsteadily to his feet. He put his face to the screen and stared through it at Herrith. "You have a law about this place," he said. "I know you do. Everything I've said to you is secret, isn't it? My men must never know of this conversation. Nor General Vorto. That is so, yes?"

"Yes," said Herrith. "That is so."

"And you will never convey this talk to anyone, not by lips or by pen?"

"Of course not," said Herrith, mildly annoyed.

"Swear it, Your Holiness."

"What?"

"Swear that you will never speak of our conversation today with anyone. Swear it to Heaven right now."

Herrith raised his hand to the screen and said, "As you have said, so do I swear."

Satisfied, Kye turned and quit the chamber, leaving Herrith in the dimness. The archbishop closed his eyes and leaned back against the wall, and all the misery he had heard in Kye's voice came washing over him. A red, unstoppable torrent of blood, and he had been the one to unleash it. The war labs had perfected Formula B under his orders, and Vorto and Kye had launched it against Goth because he had told them to. He wondered bleakly if what he heard really was the voice of God, or just the subtle whispers of his own vengeful mind. He put a hand to his forehead, striving to drive away the evil thoughts.

So many children. The duke's own daughters. The Duchess Kareena. How innocent were they? he wondered. He remembered Kareena's glowing face, how young she was and how she had pilgrimaged to Nar to see the great cathedral. He had spoken to her then, and her only confession was that she had waited too long to see God's house. She had knelt and kissed his ring and he had adored her, for she had perfect beauty, the kind of grace that comes from Heaven.

And now he had murdered her.

All of Goth was a wasteland; that's what Vorto had said. And the reports from people like Kye echoed that truth. The horrible formula loosed by the war labs had worked more perfectly than anyone had foreseen. But it seemed to Herrith that his general suffered none of the guilt of his underlings. Vorto had come back to Nar City wearing a smile. Now Herrith wept, and he could not erase that smile from his mind or the evil images portrayed by Kye. There was an orphanage not far from the cathedral, a place that Herrith had built himself and sustained with church monies. He adored children. But children became adults, didn't they? And didn't their parents sometimes poison them beyond repair? The Black Renaissance had been like that; an artful knife slipping through the ribs of God's people. Herrith had prayed mightily for its end, and all God had given him was Formula B. No peace, just this awful weapon. So it had been a sign. Bovadin himself had been unable to perfect the formula of his own creation. But the war labs had done it without him, and that was truly astonishing. That, Herrith had decided, was a miracle.

How hard it was now to live with that deduction. Herrith buried his hands in his face. God was real, and sometimes he gave men burdens. But Herrith knew they were never more than the man could handle, so he focused his mind on Heaven and his Father, and cried out in silent desperation.

Holy Father, help me. Help me bear this thing I do. I do it for you, Lord. You get the power and the glory. Forever and ever. I beg You, fortify me for this bloody work. Make me strong and wise. Turn my hand to gentleness as soon as You are able.

He crossed himself and fought down his sobs, and when he opened his eyes he was still alone in the confessional, and the world was deathly quiet. This happened to him sometimes now. Since stopping the drug, he lost control more often than seemly. The drug had checked his emotions, just as it had checked the progress of his aging. Without it, keeping himself together was a constant, tumultuous battle.

"Biagio," he growled. That bastard was to blame for all of this. The golden count went on taking the drug and spitting in God's face. He claimed to love Nar but he was a lying sodomite, orchestrating the Empire's destruction from his island lair. Herrith trembled at the thought of his ageless foe. Biagio had always been Arkus' favorite. Together the two of them had made religion meaningless. They had used it as a tool of control but had never truly believed. And God had finally tired of them both. Arkus the immortal had died. Biagio the devil was banished. Herrith took a steadying breath, composing his fractured emotions.

"Wise work to do," he reminded himself. He wiped his tearing eyes with his silk sleeve. "No time for nonsense. God is watching me, always. I can't fail Him. I—"

"Your Holiness?"

Herrith bit down on his lip. Todos? Frantically he wiped the remaining tears from his face and tried to look natural. Todos was right outside. The priest knocked lightly on the door.

"Your Holiness? Are you in there?"

"What is it?" Herrith snapped.

"Your Holiness, please. I must speak to you urgently. Something's happened."

Todos sounded suitably scared. Herrith cursed under his breath. "Heaven and Hell, Todos, I'm busy! What do you want?"

"Please, Holiness. You have to come. It's the *Fearless*!"

It was like hearing that God had returned. "What?" sputtered Herrith, rising from his stool and pulling open the door. Todos seemed not to notice his master's appearance. "What did you just say?"

"It's the *Fearless*, Holiness. In the harbor! And she's not alone. There are four other ships with her, very close. What should we do?"

Herrith was stunned. What was Nicabar doing in the Black City? Was this an invasion? He had to tell Vorto, prepare the troops. Lord, it was unthinkable!

"What's he doing?" Herrith asked.

Todos shrugged nervously. "I don't know, Holiness. The ships just appeared. I came and got you as soon as I heard."

"And there are five ships you say? That's all?"

"I think so, yes. Holiness, I'm not sure. But we have to do something."

Herrith grit his teeth. "We do indeed, Todos. We have to find out what that bloody bastard is doing here!"

• • •

Admiral Danar Nicabar stood on the deck of his warship and watched the harbor as the little boat rowed toward him. Next to the *Fearless*, her four smaller sisters stood at anchor, their guns trained on the city. The Cathedral of the Martyrs, that tall and terrible structure, loomed high, its silvery-green steeple reflecting sunlight. Nicabar had ordered the flame cannons turned toward the cathedral. Even the long-range guns of the *Fearless* were too far away to reach the church, but the admiral had known that the threat of firing would get Herrith's attention. He had in his vest the letter from Biagio, waxed closed with the count's own seal. It had been a long and blessedly boring voyage from Crote, and Nicabar was pleased to see his home port again. Little had changed. The labs still choked up plumes of noxious smoke. Nar City's broad avenues had filled with curious onlookers, all pointing at the returning fleet. Noble men and ladies shouldered up to beggars on the docks to better see the *Fearless*. Vorto's legionnaires had gathered too, a whole garrison of them. Vorto himself was nowhere to be seen, an unexpected pleasantry. Nicabar had always despised the general.

The dreadnoughts *Notorious* and *Black City* bobbed alongside the *Fearless*. Behind them in the harbor were two light cruisers, the *Iron Duke*, captained by Nicabar's long-time friend Dane, and a smaller warship, the quick sailing *Relentless*. Both cruisers slowly patrolled the harbor, ready for any unexpected surprises. Nicabar had no idea how close the Lissens might be to Nar City, and he didn't want to be caught unaware. Though the guns of the *Fearless* could outmatch any Lissen schooner, there were only two dreadnoughts.

The little rowboat drew closer. Nicabar could see its passenger now. As requested, his sailors had brought back Father Todos, Herrith's aide. The admiral smiled, surprised that Herrith had agreed to the exchange. He didn't think the bishop trusted him so much, but it was the only logical exchange. Herrith wasn't about to step aboard the *Fearless*, and if they were to talk, Nicabar needed to feel safe. He knew Herrith and Todos were like brothers. The Holy Father would never willingly let anything happen to Todos. Nicabar breathed a sigh of relief. The mere sight of Todos told him there would be no tricks.

"It's him," said the admiral confidently. Lieutenant Garii nodded. The lieutenant held a small metal box, plain and unadorned, barely the size of a man's hand. A gift for the Archbishop of Nar. "Have him come aboard, Garii," ordered Nicabar. "I want him to feel welcome. Give him whatever he needs—food, drink, anything. Understood?"

"Aye, sir," said the lieutenant. The young man called out to the sailors in the rowboat to come alongside. A rope ladder was lowered amidships. The sailors in the rowboat waved and shouldered the little craft up to the warship. Father Todos looked at the hulking *Fearless*, his jaw set. Nicabar stared down at him, grinning. Todos was a decent man. He believed in his church and that made him an enemy, but in the days of Arkus they had almost been friends. The admiral had no desire to hurt this gentle man, and hoped Herrith had planned no betrayals. If he did and Nicabar was captured or killed, Todos would die.

The sailors in the rowboat helped the priest shimmy up the rope ladder. Nicabar went to greet him. Halfway up, the Father noticed his host and stopped.

"Come ahead, Father," boomed Nicabar. "Nothing will happen to you, not by my doing."

Father Todos grimaced but continued up the ladder anyway. Admiral Nicabar extended out a hand, which the priest reluctantly accepted, and pulled him aboard. The sailors in the rowboat remained behind, waiting for the admiral. Father Todos cleared his throat nervously and stared at Nicabar, trying to look brave.

"I'm here, as requested," said Todos. "God protect me."

Nicabar chuckled. "You have *my* protection, priest," he said. "Nothing will happen to you, so long as nothing happens to me." He looked out over the docks to where Vorto's garrisons were pompously arranged. "Safe passage through those legionnaires, to the cathedral and back again. That's the deal, right?"

"Yes," said Todos. "The archbishop will be waiting for you. Have your talk with him quickly. Take care of your devilish business and return to your ship. I won't leave until you come back."

"I'd say not," laughed Nicabar. "It's a long swim." The admiral turned to Garii and took the metal box from him. Todos noticed it, eyeing the thing suspiciously.

"What is that?" he asked.

"A gift for your bishop," replied Nicabar. "From Count Biagio."

Todos made a disgusted face. "He won't accept it. It's an insult. How dare that demon try to buy the bishop's pardon!"

"There's food and wine aboard, Father. Lieutenant Garii will see to your needs. Be comfortable. I will return when I can."

"What news do you bring the bishop, heretic?" asked Todos. "Has your twisted count come to his senses?"

Nicabar bristled but tried to ignore the insult. He backed down onto the rope ladder, tucking the metal box under his armpit. "You'll know when you get back to the cathedral, Todos. Enjoy my ship's hospitality."

"Admiral?" said Todos.

Nicabar stopped and looked at the priest. "What?"

Todos crossed the air in front of him. "Go with God."

"Yes," said Nicabar dryly. "As you say." Then he dropped down below the railings and out of Todos' sight, lowering himself on the rope ladder until he reached the rowboat. The sailors on board fumbled to help him but he shook off their hands. They heaved away from the *Fearless* and sat down, taking up their oars and rowing toward shore, but Nicabar remained standing, ever defiant as he faced the legionnaires gathered to greet him. He was resplendent in his perfect uniform of black and gold, and the ribbons and medals on his chest gleamed in the sunlight. In his vest pocket was the note to Herrith, while in his hands he held the little silver box, the gift Biagio had ordered him to present to the bishop. Nicabar smiled, wondering how Herrith would react to the present. It would be unexpected, certainly.

Almost at shore, the rowboat skidded toward a dock lined thickly with waiting soldiers. The heavily armed men did not bow or show any deference to Nicabar as he stared at them. They merely waited, stone-faced, while their brothers behind them held back the curious push of spectators who had gathered to gape at the returning admiral. Danar Nicabar smirked at the crowd and the helmeted soldiers, but his cocky smile vanished when he noticed the carriage waiting for him. It was a large conveyance, one of the dead emperor's own, trimmed in jewels and pulled by four white stallions. And near the carriage, looking down from his great black warhorse, was General Vorto, battle axe strapped across his back. It had been nearly a year since Nicabar had seen the general, and Vorto's ugly features hadn't softened a bit. More huge than ever in his brawny armor, Vorto still seemed like one of Nar's statues—cold and sterile and completely immovable. The general trotted his charger toward the dock as the rowboat slid into a slip. Admiral Nicabar waited for his sailors to cleat the boat before he stepped onto the dock. Vorto was waiting for him, watching mischievously, but he did not dismount from his snorting beast.

"Welcome home, Danar," boomed the general. There was a mocking quality to the voice. "It's so wonderful to see you again."

"I would say the same, but I would be lying," said Nicabar. He didn't bow to the general or show any of the usual niceties. Not dismounting for him was clearly an insult, and Nicabar had no intention of showing the butcher any respect. "I've come bearing a message for His Holiness, Vorto. I have nothing to discuss with *you*."

"Our discussion can wait then, seaman. But I promise you—we will talk again. Get in the carriage. I will take you to the cathedral."

Nicabar looked around at the swelling crowd. "You and your bishop have cast quite a spell on these people. I suppose I should congratulate you. But it won't last. That's *my* promise to you." The admiral gestured to his flagship anchored in the harbor. "Take a good look at my vessels.

If anything happens to me, they have orders to open fire. They'll blast a whole in Nar City so big even you could walk through it."

"God forgive your blasphemy, Danar. Truly, I pity you. Get in the carriage. Just for today you have my word—you will be unharmed."

Vorto's word was meaningless, but Nicabar got into the carriage anyway. It was empty, and the plush velvet seats were unbelievably comfortable. Nicabar sat down and leaned out the window. A few bold Narens in the crowd waved to him and he waved back, suddenly delighted with the strange homecoming. He had missed Nar. Life at sea was only bearable when you had a home to return to, and he had none. Losing the Black City was like losing a beautiful woman. She was unforgettable.

Vorto barked orders at his columns to depart, and the carriage lurched forward, bearing Nicabar away from the docks and through the avenues of Nar City. Colossal skyscrapers rose up quickly around him, burying him in their shadows. Haze and fire obscured the sky as the towering smokestacks vomited up clouds. In the distance, Nicabar saw the towers of the Black Palace, former home of Arkus, and the giant mausoleum on its great lawn, built by Biagio to remember his beloved emperor. Sunlight played on the river Kiel, that wide, polluted waterway, and as the carriage crossed the iron bridge Nicabar gazed across the river through his open window, seeing all the splendor of sprawling Nar feeding from the Kiel's banks. The Cathedral of the Martyrs rose into view, blocking out the sun behind its girdered steeple. The carriage rolled over the bridge and was swallowed by the church's shadow. At the head of the column, General Vorto guided the procession through the Avenue of the Holy, toward the great open gates of Herrith's home. A thousand people had gathered around the cathedral to catch a glimpse of the admiral, and Nicabar's heart sank at the sight of them. He was one of them, and not at all like the languid Crotans he was forced to live among. At that moment, he would have given anything to end the stalemate.

But this was a war of ideals, he reminded himself, and his resolve strengthened as the garish cathedral loomed. It was both glorious and terrible, and the fanatic at its core was two-hearted, with one made of gold and the other of iron. Herrith was Nar's perfect master, inscrutable and capable of the most far-reaching atrocities even as he fed the city's starving children. Arkus of Nar had been a butcher too, but what Herrith had done to Goth had made the emperor's worst massacres seem pale. The tales coming out of the Walled City had made even Biagio's blood run cold. Nicabar detested Herrith almost as much as Vorto himself. Vorto he hated because the general was stupid. Like a good dog he followed Herrith's edicts blindly.

General Vorto stopped the march just outside the cathedral's doors.

The portals of oak hung open, but Nicabar could see nothing inside the church's secretive folds. A group of acolytes waited, their faces obscured in white cowls. The priests seemed to float there, bodiless. Nicabar got out of the carriage, still clutching the metal box. At last Vorto got down off his horse. The general came up to Nicabar and scowled.

"This is a holy place, Admiral," he said. "I would ask that you show it some respect. If you don't, I will pull your head off your shoulders with my bare hands. Do you understand?"

Nicabar gave Vorto his best stone face. "You are still the same brute, aren't you, Vorto? I would advise you strongly not to threaten me again. The *Fearless* hasn't fired her cannons in a while. We could use the practice."

Vorto chuckled. "God would strike you down before you fired a shot. He protects this place. It is free of your villainy."

"I would like to test that theory, General. And I will at the smallest opportunity. Now take me to Herrith and stop babbling. I'm already sick from the sight of you."

Vorto turned from Nicabar and strode toward the cathedral and its waiting priests. Nicabar followed, as did two of the general's bodyguards, both fully armored and bearing drawn swords. The general bowed deeply to the ghostlike priests, who did not speak a word but simply led them into the cavernous cathedral. The vaulted ceiling rose up above them in a magnificent arc, gold-leafed and detailed with the finest manmade minutiae. There were angels and demons, white-bearded images of God and bare-breasted reliefs of His Mother. Bright lamps lit the ceiling and the frescoed walls, and the altar far in front of them burned with incense and a chalice filled with flaming liquid, the symbol of eternal life for Herrith and his believers. The expansive chamber was empty, and as they walked their footfalls echoed loudly off the walls and statues, and the sounds of the crowd outside died off behind them as they reached the altar. Vorto and his men all fell to a knee before the altar, as did the legionnaires. But despite the general's earlier threat, Nicabar remained standing. When they had finished their short prayer, the priests led them out of the chamber into a corridor and then to an endless flight of stairs that seemed to ascend into Heaven itself. The legionnaires stayed behind.

This was a private area. Only the highest ranking soldiers were allowed here, and only then by invitation. The stairs went up in a ceaseless spiral, but after long minutes of climbing they finally ended, spilling them into another hallway. This one was lined with stained glass—a marvelous wall of transparent colors depicting scenes from the holy book. Nicabar could barely see through the glass but he could tell they were very high. His fingers tingled a little with the cold draft.

They came at last to a door at the end of the hall. The priests entered without knocking. Vorto said nothing, waiting patiently for the acolytes to return. At last they did reappear, opening the door wide for the general and Nicabar. Nicabar peered around Vorto's enormous girth and saw inside the chamber. It was another big room and flooded with sunlight. An immense window made up the entire far wall, showing off the expanse of the Black City. And at the window, staring blithely through the clear glass, was Archbishop Herrith, his hands clasped casually behind his back. The priests left the room and disappeared back down the hall. Nicabar waited. Vorto wasn't moving.

"Enter, my friends," said Herrith at last. His voice was pure, like the sunlight he bathed in. It seemed to Nicabar that the bishop had lost some weight, no doubt a result of the drug withdrawal. He snickered to himself, pleased with the image of Herrith's mortality. His eyes would be dim now, like Vorto's. General Vorto finally moved into the chamber. Nicabar followed him. He had never been in this chamber and he marveled at the huge window, tall as a tree and wide as a river. From here he could see all of eastern Nar City and the ocean beyond, with his small armada bobbing in the harbor. Vorto went to the bishop and dropped to his knees. Without turning from the window Herrith listlessly put out his hand. Vorto seized it and kissed it.

"Your Holiness," said the giant softly. "I've brought him for you."

"Yes, thank you, my friend. I noticed." Herrith turned his head and rewarded Vorto with a smile. "Arise, General. Admiral Nicabar . . ."

Nicabar didn't bow or crack the smallest smile. He simply walked into the center of the room, saying, "I have a message for you, Herrith, from Count Biagio. I would like to give it to you and be on my way."

Herrith smiled serenely. "Danar, it's been so long. Please, let's not talk like enemies." He gestured to a table at the far end of the room, a sunny spot complete with plates of breakfast foods and cups of steaming beverages. "I've arranged a meal for us. I would like to sit with you awhile."

"I'm not hungry," said Nicabar.

"Pity," said Herrith, going to the table and sitting down. "I am. Please . . ." He gestured to one of the chairs. "If you don't sit with me I will take it as an offense, old friend. And we have so much to talk about."

"We have very little to talk about, Herrith. I have a message, and that is all."

"Sit down, you blasphemous fool," seethed Vorto, barely containing his rage. "I warn you, Nicabar . . ."

"I don't take well to warnings, Vorto," said Nicabar coolly. "And I don't care to speak long with either of you. Herrith, will you accept my message or not?"

Herrith was folding a napkin onto his lap. "Yes, yes. Of course I will, Danar. But there's time enough to eat, surely? I can't believe you're not weary from your voyage." He picked up a pastry from the table and popped it into his mouth, sighing with satisfaction. "Oh, now, that is *good*. Really, Danar, you should have something."

"Very well," agreed Nicabar, already tired of the argument. He sat down at the table across from Herrith and laid down his silver box. The bauble immediately caught the bishop's attention.

"What's that?" asked Herrith through a mouth full of pastry.

"This is a gift," replied Nicabar. He slid the box across the table to Herrith. "From Count Biagio."

"A gift? Is this your message?"

"No." Nicabar slipped his hand into his uniform and pulled out the letter Biagio had given him. "This is my message, sealed with the Count's own seal. You'll recognize it, I'm sure. That other thing is merely a gift, as I've said."

Herrith picked up the box and shook it like a child, a wide smile on his face. "What is it?" he asked, listening to it rattle.

"Holiness, please," said Vorto. He held out his hands for the box. "Give it to me. I will open it for you."

"You will not!" laughed Herrith. "It's mine."

"It may be a trick, Holiness. Something dangerous from the Crotan devil. Please, let me open it for you."

Herrith's eyes narrowed on Nicabar. "Is it a trick, Danar?"

"No trick," said the admiral. "Just a present. And perfectly safe, I promise."

"Hmm, just the same . . ." Herrith handed the box over to Vorto. "I think you should open it, my friend. The devil is the father of lies, after all. Be careful, though."

Stupidly brave, Vorto opened the box quickly and peered at its contents. Nicabar watched the general closely, gratified by the look of terrible awe on his face.

"Mother of God," he whispered.

"What is it?" pressed Herrith.

Vorto turned his blazing eyes on Nicabar. "You sinful snake," he seethed. "I should kill you for this!"

"Enough!" thundered Herrith. "Vorto, what's in the box? Give it to me, I insist!"

"Holiness . . ."

Herrith snatched the box from Vorto's hands and looked inside. He, too, was awed by its contents. But the bishop didn't anger. He simply stared at it longingly. It was a vial of Bovadin's life-lengthening drug, perfectly blue in its clear glass container, shining and desirable and worth a fortune. Herrith took the vial from the box and turned it in the sunlight, his hand trembling as he inspected it.

"Heaven help us," he said. "What have you brought me, Danar? Damnation in a bottle?"

"You know what it is, Bishop," said Nicabar carefully. "And it's not from me. It's from Biagio. Personally, I would never have given it to you, but the count insisted."

"Of course he did!" raged Vorto. "That black-hearted beast. He wants to see us all dependent on his fiendish brew again. Damn him to Hell!"

Herrith held up a calming hand. "Be easy, my friend." He continued admiring the beautiful liquid with his dull, dead eyes. Once Herrith's eyes had blazed a brilliant blue, but they were flat now, desolate, less than alive. A familiar fire grew in them as they looked upon the drug. "Ah, Danar," sighed the bishop. "Should I curse you or praise you for bringing me this? You and Biagio are devils, to be sure."

"That's a goodly supply, Herrith," said Nicabar. "Enough to bring you back to how you were. Bovadin mixed it strong for you, so it would last. But it has to be administered slowly. If not, you'll die."

"He won't be using it," snapped Vorto. "You may take your poison back with you, dog."

Herrith put the vial back in the box and closed the lid. But he did not return the gift to Nicabar. Instead he kept it near him, guarding it with a firm hand. "Sit down, Vorto," he said softly. "We are arguing too much. I didn't want it to be this way." He picked up the letter but did not open it. Instead he handed it to Vorto. "Read this for me," he directed. "Out loud, so we all can hear."

Vorto took a chair next to his master and opened the letter, breaking the wax seal. He looked it over suspiciously for a moment, then started to read. " 'My dear Bishop,' " he began. " 'I hope this letter finds you well. I hope, too, that you are taking good care of the city and the Empire. These are dark days for us all, and I will not lie to you and say that I do not miss the Black City. I do, with all my heart.' " Vorto stopped to sneer at this. "Heart," he scoffed. "What heart?"

"Go on, please, General," ordered Herrith. The bishop kept his eyes on Nicabar as he listened.

" 'We are not so different, you and I,' " Vorto continued. " 'Our past has made us enemies, but our future holds promise if we work together. There are things I can offer you, and would give you gladly. Bovadin's drug is merely one of these. None of us need die, dear Herrith.' "

Herrith interrupted Vorto with a chuckle. "He's a long-winded one, isn't he?"

Nicabar said nothing.

"Go on," said Herrith. "Let's see if he ever says anything useful."

Vorto continued reading. " 'I propose a meeting between all the Naren lords, to take place here on my island of Crote. It is the only safe place where I know I will not be harmed. We can discuss our differences amicably, and make a new beginning. I urge you to consider this offer carefully. We can rule Nar together, as Arkus would have wanted. The drug can be yours again. Nar can be strong.' " Vorto looked up from the paper. "That's it," he declared. He tossed the letter onto the table before him. "You've got an audacious master, Nicabar. How dare he think he can buy us off with promises of peace? And a meeting in Crote? Is he serious?"

Nicabar did not address Vorto, only Herrith. "I am to wait for your response and then return to Crote with your answer," he said. "I will wait aboard my ship in the harbor. Get me your answer by the morrow."

"There's no need to wait," said Herrith simply. "I already have my answer." Herrith reached across the table and picked up the letter, crumpling it into a ball and bouncing it over to Nicabar. "The answer is no."

Nicabar smirked. "As I thought. Biagio is too good to you, Herrith. I told him not to bother offering you peace, but he insisted. Apparently he thinks you have a brain somewhere in that thick skull. I do not."

"If and when I decide to talk peace with that hellspawn, *I* will say when and where. These are not his terms to dictate. I'm no warrior, but it's the victor who makes terms, isn't it?"

"You will not be victorious, Herrith," said Nicabar calmly. "You don't have the means. The nations of Nar will never follow you, because they simply don't believe your fairy tales. And now you have Liss to deal with." The admiral winked sardonically. "And I know what a handful they can be."

The mere mention of Liss erased all pleasantness from the bishop's face. "It is your fault what happens with Liss, Danar. They raid our coasts and you do nothing. They sink our ships and you do nothing. You say you are an Admiral of Nar? I think you are laughable. If you were truly the hero some say, you would be defending Nar."

"But I am, Holiness," said Nicabar. "I'm defending it from you."

"Blasphemer," rumbled Vorto. The general rose from his chair, toppling it over. "Show some respect in this house of God, or I swear I will kill you!"

"Sit down, Vorto," directed Nicabar. "You're very tiresome. Bishop, as I've already explained to this primate, anything that happens to me will be revisited on the Black City a hundred fold. The *Fearless* has her guns trained on the cathedral. She might be able to reach it, or she might not. Either way, the city burns. So I would be very careful what you or your dog soldier say to me, because I am sick of being threatened."

Herrith considered the implication, searching the tone for a bluff. When he found none he gestured for Vorto to sit. Reluctantly, the general retrieved his toppled chair and took his place beside the bishop. Herrith drummed his pudgy fingers on the silver box.

"What shall I do?" he mused aloud. "I had hoped our talk would be beneficial, Danar. Shame on me, but I had actually hoped you had come to your senses and seen the truth about your count. It's been so many years that you have been friends with him. Can't you see the truth yet?"

"*The* truth?" asked Nicabar. "Or *your* truth?"

"They are the same, Danar," warned the bishop. "My truth is the honesty of God, the bread of angels. Biagio is a sodomite, a sinner. Even his marriage was an abomination. He lies with men. You know this, yet you defend him? A full-blooded man like yourself?"

"Aye, I know the truth of him," said Nicabar. "And truly, I don't care. Neither did Arkus. It may be a sin in your eyes and in the vision of your mythical God, but not in mine. He is a friend. And a far better one than you ever were, Herrith."

"A warning, Danar," said the bishop. "Biagio's time is past. The Black Renaissance died with Arkus. And its small remnants are being dealt with."

"Yes," hissed Nicabar. "Like Goth."

Herrith's face hardened. "Like Goth," he echoed. "It is God's will."

An icy hand seized Nicabar's heart. Something was horribly wrong with Herrith. Perhaps the drug had rotted his mind like it had Biagio's, or maybe it was the awful withdrawal. Either way, it seemed an impossible task to talk rationally with this man who believed his own genocidal messages.

"Very well," said Nicabar, rising from his chair. "Then our business is concluded."

The bishop spread out his hands. "It seems so. Please give the count my answer, Danar. And tell him that I will pray for the repose of his soul."

"I'm sure he'll appreciate that," quipped Nicabar. "And shall I thank him for the gift? Or will I be taking that back with me as well?"

Vorto's eyes shifted to the box, then to Herrith, then back again. The bishop's hand curled over the gift greedily.

"I think I should hold on to this," he said. "And after all, it's a gift. Thank Biagio for his thoughtfulness."

Vorto blanched. "Holiness . . ."

"Shut up," growled Herrith. "Danar, thank you for coming to see me. You may not believe this, but it was a pleasure. The general will escort you back to your ship now. Safe journey, old friend."

Nicabar left the chamber without saying good-bye, trailed by the dumbfounded Vorto. As he left, he stole a glance over his shoulder to see Herrith caressing the box.

TEN

The Assassin's Promise

After a morning of travel, Richius and Simon returned to Falindar. The spires of the citadel were a welcome sight to the men, who were both exhausted from each other's company. Seeing that his odd companion was hardly in shape to make the trip, Richius had let Simon share his gelding's back, and they had each walked while the other enjoyed the comfort of the horse. It had been the only choice left to Richius. Simon seemed near collapse. And Richius, well rested from a year in Falindar, had welcomed the exercise. So while Simon rode, Richius walked and considered things.

Out in the wilderness, he hadn't found the answers he was searching for. Despite Karlaz's advice, his talk with the sky had been a one-sided conversation. And although he was eager to see Falindar again, part of him dreaded confronting Dyana. She would be expecting some change in him, and would be disappointed.

Simon had proved a pleasant enough travelling companion. Inquisitive but thoughtful, he often fell into the same contemplative silences as Richius, and only occasionally did they get on each other's nerves. Because Simon couldn't travel tethered, Richius had undone his bindings. Simon had repaid the favor by doing nothing threatening. He explained to Richius that he really had nowhere to go anyway, and though he feared the citadel's violent reputation, the promise of a roof and warm food spurred him on. Richius almost liked the deserter; if that's what Simon truly was. After a full day together, Richius still wasn't sure about the Naren, and his doubts troubled him. He knew Biagio's capabilities. Every Naren had heard the stories. The Roshann were everywhere. Ruthless and subtle, Biagio's secret society permeated every strata of imperial life. They were like the air. Invisible. Inescapable.

And so it was that when they arrived at the citadel, Richius at once took the awestruck Simon to see Lucyler. As master of Falindar, it would be Lucyler's decision to cast judgment on the stranger, to determine whether he was a spy or if the citadel's hospitality should be extended to him. But Lucyler was preoccupied upon their return. The warlord Ishia had come from his mountain keep to seek counsel from Lucyler, and Lucyler was locked in his meeting chambers with strict orders not to be disturbed. Given the opportunity to see his wife and child, Richius went to his own chambers. Simon was relegated to a guarded room, left there to wait. He said good-bye to Richius with a worried smile, and Richius couldn't help but try to ease his fears.

"If you're telling the truth, nothing will happen to you," he promised as he shut the door. A Triin warrior had been stationed outside the room. Meals, clothing, and a bath were ordered for Simon, and Richius went off to see Dyana. His wife was pleased to see him, though there was still tension between them. Little Shani gave him a hug that made things better, but not completely. Richius and Dyana slept together that night, but still with that strange wall separating them, and in the morning Richius went off to see Lucyler. His Triin friend had risen early. Ishia, warlord of Kes, had ridden out of the citadel, and the warriors of Falindar were buzzing about him. Richius listened, troubled by the talk. Ishia's ongoing feud with the warlord Praxtin-Tar hadn't calmed very much in these peaceful days. If there was trouble in Kes, Lucyler would almost certainly be dragged into it.

Richius went to Lucyler's chambers, a group of rooms on Falindar's ground floor. Once they had been the offices of Tharn, the citadel's former master. Lucyler hadn't done much to the chambers. Tharn's many books still collected dust on shelves, and piles of Naren manuscripts lay huddled in the corners. The only personal touch Lucyler had added was a ceremonial jiiktar. He had placed the weapon on the wall, and when the sunlight came through the windows its twin blades gleamed. Richius arrived at Lucyler's rooms expecting to find them empty. Instead he found a Triin warrior at the threshold, the same one he had left with Simon the night before. The door to Lucyler's room was open. Richius peered inside and found to his great dismay that the master of Falindar was not alone.

Simon was with him.

The two were talking amicably. Richius stood in the doorway, dumbfounded. Simon's broken nose was dressed with a clean white bandage.

It made him seem comical and unthreatening. As ordered, he had been given new clothing—traditional Triin garb, completely inappropriate. Lucyler looked up at Richius and flashed a smile.

"Richius, greetings. I expected you."

"Did you?" said Richius. "How nice."

"Sit," said Lucyler, waving him toward a chair. Richius shot Simon a barbed glare. The Naren merely grinned.

"Lucyler, how did he get in here?" Richius asked.

"I sent for him. I would have sent for you, too, but I knew you would be on your way. Do not look at me like that."

"Like what?"

"Like I have betrayed you. I wanted to see this Naren for myself, without you around to make up my mind for me. Please, sit down."

Reluctantly, Richius pulled up one of the room's wooden chairs and sat down next to Simon. The Naren gave him a ragged smile.

"Good morning," he said innocently. "Sleep well?"

"Stop," Richius warned. "Just stop right now. Don't start with your games." He looked at Lucyler caustically. "This was supposed to be an interrogation, Lucyler. Why didn't you tell me you were meeting with him?"

Lucyler raised his eyebrows. "An interrogation? Richius, I am not the Daegog. What would you have me do? Put him in the catacombs?"

"Maybe," Richius said. "A few days down there might loosen his tongue. Lord, Lucyler, why didn't you talk to me first? I have things to tell you."

"I am sure you do. No offense, old friend, but you see too many phantoms."

Richius struggled to control himself. For months Lucyler had been accusing him of paranoia, and he didn't want to play the part, not in front of Simon. But Lucyler had never been to Nar. He didn't know the genesis of Richius' fears.

"Lucyler, listen to me, please," he said, trying to stay calm. "I don't know who this man is. He might be what he claims, or he might not. But I brought him here because I didn't want him running free in Lucel-Lor. If he is one of Biagio's men, he's dangerous."

The Triin seemed insulted. "I have no intention of being foolish. I brought him here so I could talk to him. Alone. But you are right, I think. I cannot tell who he is. Maybe he is telling the truth, or maybe—"

"I am telling the truth," Simon insisted, exasperated. "What's with you bloody people? Look at me!"

"I have looked, Simon Darquis," said Lucyler. "I have looked and listened. But I still do not trust you. To be truthful, the only Naren I trust is in this room, and it is not you. I know what your Empire is capable of, their deceit. And Richius has told me about Biagio's grudge. You may simply be one of his dogs."

Simon shook his head, laughing mirthlessly. "You're all insane. Truly, you are. If I wanted to kill Vantran he'd be dead by now. Lord, the fool breaks my nose, then lets me ride his bloody horse! You think it would take a Roshann agent to assassinate him? A baby could do it with a sharp toy!"

"I let you ride because you looked so damned feeble," said Richius. "And because I wanted to get you here sometime before spring. Don't mistake our talks for trust, Simon. I don't trust you, and neither does Lucyler." He looked to his friend for support. "Right, Lucyler?"

The Triin shrugged. "You think I know? You are the Naren, Richius. You tell me. I have talked with him for nearly an hour. What he tells me sounds possible at least." Lucyler turned to Simon. "You are a deserter, yes?"

"Oh, for God's sake . . ."

"Answer me," ordered the Triin.

"Yes, for the last bloody time, I'm a god-damned deserter."

"And how did you get here?"

Simon rolled his eyes. "From the south."

"And who saw you?"

"A lot of people saw me," said Simon. "Don't be stupid, I couldn't hide forever. I needed food, water. But I didn't talk to anyone, not if I could help it. I don't speak the language, now do I?"

"Where did you get food?"

"I stole it when I could. Hunted some." Simon turned to Richius. "You still have my dagger? I want it back."

"You'll get it back when I'm ready to give it to you," said Richius.

"The south, you say?" pressed Lucyler. "South where?"

"How the hell should I know? I came through Dring with the rest of Gayle's men. After that I left them. This isn't my land, Triin. I don't have any maps. I just walked. I wandered for a year, and then I ran into Vantran. Now here I am."

Richius listened, searching for a gaff and finding none. It was all as Simon had already claimed, flawlessly unchanged. Despite the cautious inner voice warning him otherwise, he began to believe the Naren's tale. Or maybe he simply wanted to believe. He missed the company of Narens. The long ride back with Simon had proved that to him. Simon was one of his own kind. Being with him was something like being back in Aramoor. . . .

Richius scolded himself suddenly, angry for such thoughts. Simon might still be a danger—not only to him but to Dyana and Shani. Biagio was just evil enough to plan something so elaborate. But then Richius found himself looking at Simon and his emaciated face. Maybe he was merely what he claimed. . . .

"Simon," he said carefully. "I want to believe you. I think you know that. But I just can't. Not yet."

Simon shrugged. "Jackal, I don't really care what you believe. If you want to think I'm some demon or ghost, go ahead. But I won't be held prisoner here." He glared suddenly at Lucyler. "You hear me? I'm a legionnaire of Nar. So if you're going to kill me, do it now and get it over with, because I'm tired of being threatened. But I won't be thrown into some stinking cage."

"First of all," bristled Lucyler, "you do not give orders here. I do. I am Lucyler of Falindar, master of this citadel. That makes me *your* master. I could kill you in an instant, Simon Darquis, do not doubt that. And I will if you give me cause. So do not tempt me."

Simon seethed. "So I'm your prisoner then? For what crime?" He pointed at Richius accusingly. "Because he sees ghosts?"

Lucyler's eyes flicked to Richius. "You brought him here, Richius. What do you want me to do with him?"

"I don't know," admitted Richius. It seemed an impossible decision. He wondered why he had even bothered dragging the Naren to Falindar. With his broken nose and pale complexion, Simon looked no more a threat than a child or some crippled beggar. And when he looked at Richius with his bewildered eyes, Richius thought he glimpsed something innocent there, something confused and afraid. If this was an act, it went beyond clever.

"I've done nothing, Jackal," said Simon. "Not to you or anyone else. I just want to be left alone. That's why I deserted, to be free. I won't be thrown in some Triin dungeon. I'd die first."

"You don't listen very well, do you?" said Richius. "I'm not the Jackal. Call me Kalak if you have to, that's my Triin name. Or call me Richius or Vantran. But if you call me Jackal one more time . . ."

"What? You'll have one of your Triin followers murder me? Yes, I've seen the way they bow and scrape around you, Jackal. No wonder you deserted. You're like a bloody king here."

Richius laughed. "You see, Lucyler? We should shackle him up just for talking so much."

"I do not care what you decide," said Lucyler sternly. "I am leaving this in your hands, Richius. Simon, until then you are confined to your rooms. You are not to move out of them, do you understand? There will be a warrior guarding you. Step out of your chamber, and he will kill you. I promise that."

Richius wasn't satisfied. "That's it? That's all you're going to say?"

"Yes," snapped Lucyler. "Lorris and Pris, you brought him here,

Richius. He did not follow you home like some stray cat. He is your problem, not mine." The Triin frowned. "I have enough of my own problems to deal with."

"Well then?" pressed Simon. "What do you say, Vantran? What will you do with me?"

Richius got out of his chair, glaring at Lucyler. "Come on," he said to Simon. "Obviously coming to the master of Falindar was a bad idea. I'll take you back to your room."

"Am I free?" asked Simon, unwilling to leave the chamber.

"Not yet," said Richius. He moved toward the door. The warrior positioned outside the room stepped inside to escort Simon. Simon blanched at the sight of him.

"Master Lucyler," he urged. "Please help me. I'm not a criminal. I swear it."

"Then you should not have deserted," said Lucyler. "I leave this with Richius." He looked up at his old friend. "Richius, stay please. Simon, you go with the warrior." Lucyler spoke in quick Triin to the warrior, who nodded and grabbed hold of Simon's sleeve, dragging him from the room.

"God damn it, Vantran," spat Simon. He shrugged off the warrior's grip and stood firm in the doorway. "Let me go!"

The warrior regained Simon's sleeve and pulled him roughly out of the room. All the while Simon glared at Richius, until at last he had disappeared down the hallway. He was a wildcat, this Simon Darquis, and Richius liked him. He smiled in spite of himself as he listened to Simon's lingering curses.

"Close the door, Richius," said Lucyler softly.

Richius did as his friend asked, then hovered over him, refusing to sit. Lucyler's face was drawn and haggard, like a father who's spent too much time with bickering children. "Please," he said, "sit down."

Richius glared at him.

"No? You will not sit? Fine, you stubborn fool. Then just stand there and listen to me. I am very tired, Richius. You think I do nothing all day, but you are wrong. And then you bring this Naren to me and ask for justice. What should I do? You want me to kill him for you?"

"Of course not," scoffed Richius. "But I could have used a little more support, Lucyler."

"I have given you support!" Lucyler railed. "Ever since you came here with Dyana. And all you do is complain. You sulk like a child because you feel out of place."

"Are you a mind-reader now, Lucyler?"

"I do not have to be. What you are thinking is obvious. But that is not my fault or Dyana's, and it is not right for you to blame us."

"I don't," said Richius.

"You do. I see it in your eyes. And now this Simon Darquis, what should I do with him? He is *your* problem, Richius. I resent you trying to make him mine."

"All right, I'm sorry," said Richius. "But I didn't know what I should do."

Lucyler shrugged. "You broke his nose. Maybe that is enough."

They both laughed, and Richius pulled up a chair, sitting close to his Triin friend. These were rare moments now, when they could both get together and laugh, and Richius wanted to savor it. In these days of politics and power, getting a laugh from Lucyler was like getting a golden coin.

"What's the matter, Lucyler?" Richius asked. "Something's wrong, I can tell."

"How was your trip?" Lucyler countered, evading the question. "Did you find your answers?"

"No," Richius sighed. "I was about to come home anyway when I found Simon. Really, I don't know why I went. To think, I suppose."

"And what did you discover?"

"Lucyler, why are you asking me this? I'm all right."

"You are not," said Lucyler. "Do not lie to me, Richius. You are troubled and it is obvious. But I do not think I can help you. Whatever you need can only come from inside."

Richius grinned. It sounded like more of Karlaz's supernatural nonsense. "You're avoiding the subject," he said playfully. "Tell me what happened with Ishia."

"Oh, that one," groaned Lucyler. The master of Falindar leaned back in his chair and stared at the ceiling. "He says Praxtin-Tar is massing troops west of Kes. Over two hundred warriors, maybe more."

"Ishia sees ghosts the way I do," joked Richius. "And he's always insulting Praxtin-Tar. Do you believe him?"

"Believe him? I have to. I am lord of Tatterak now." Lucyler closed his eyes. "He wants me to go and talk to Praxtin-Tar, to mediate a new truce between them. He thinks that by seeing me and the flag of Falindar, Praxtin-Tar will know he cannot invade Kes. Not without a fight."

"Will you go?"

"Yes," said Lucyler. "I have no choice." He opened his eyes and looked at Richius sadly. "I have worked too hard keeping the peace to let it crumble. And I am weary, my friend. All this is too much for me sometimes."

Richius nodded. "I know, Lucyler."

"Do you? I wonder. You want me to use my armies to get Aramoor back for you, but I cannot. You want me to help the Lissens against Nar, but I cannot do that either. What do you really think of me, Richius? Do you hate what I have become?"

"Not at all," said Richius. "God, don't ever say that. You're like my brother, Lucyler. I'll always support you. And those other things; don't explain yourself. What I want wouldn't help Lucel-Lor, and that's where your loyalty has to lie; I know that."

Lucyler smiled feebly. "This is hard for you, living here with us. I am sorry for that. I did not want you to be unhappy here."

"Stop," Richius insisted. "I'm not unhappy."

"You have something else to worry about now," said Lucyler. "I was not joking about this Naren being your responsibility, Richius. You must decide what is to be done with him."

"But I don't know what to do with him," said Richius. "Maybe I shouldn't have brought him here, but I didn't think I had a choice. If he is who he claims, he needs our help. I can't explain this, Lucyler, but I was actually glad to see him." Richius grimaced. "I must be losing my mind."

"And what if he is not what he claims? What if he really is one of Biagio's assassins?"

It was an impossible question. Richius steepled his fingers, considering the possibility. "Then I am dead, I suppose. But wouldn't I have been dead already? I mean, what Simon said makes sense, doesn't it? He could have killed me a hundred times by now if he wanted to. And his story seems to hold together. It's believable, at least."

Lucyler frowned. "But do legionnaires desert?"

"Maybe," said Richius. "Do kings?"

"So? Is that your decision, then? You will let him go?"

"I didn't say that," Richius corrected. "I don't know."

"All right," said Lucyler, failing to hide his disappointment. "Then maybe when I return Simon Darquis will still be here. And maybe he will not."

"Maybe."

"This is bad business, decisions. I do not want to go to Kes. I do not want any more war in Lucel-Lor either. But I have to do what is right," Lucyler looked away. "And so do you."

"What if I don't know what's right?" Richius asked. "What then?"

"Then you make the best decision you can, and live with the consequences." Lucyler smiled. "Richius, let me tell you something. As a friend. May I?"

"All right."

"You have a life here in Lucel-Lor. But you do not see it, because you are always looking over your shoulder. Someday, you will have to stop looking backward and start looking in front of you again. And you must do it before you ruin yourself."

Richius was silent. Then he asked, "When are you leaving for Kes?"

"The day after tomorrow. Ishia needs me quickly. I told him I would come."

Richius nodded grimly. "I have to go," he said. "I have something to do."

"Are you going to talk to Simon?"

Richius was almost out the door. "Sort of," he called over his shoulder, then left the room. He walked quickly to the room where Simon was being held. It was in the castle's eastern wing, a dreary place that had long ago been stripped of valuables to pay for the war against Nar. The halls were narrow here and darker than the castle's other corridors. It was where the Daegog's servants had lived, that former ruler of Lucel-Lor that had once called Falindar home. Richius found Simon's room easily. It was the only one guarded. The warrior at the door looked bored, but he brightened a bit when he noticed Richius.

"Greetings, Kalak," he said in Triin. "You wish to speak with the Naren?"

"Yes," said Richius. "I want to take him somewhere. Is that all right?"

The warrior laughed. "He is your prisoner, Kalak. You may do with him as you like." The Triin opened the door and stepped aside for Richius to enter. "Shall I come with you?" he asked.

"No," said Richius. He peered inside the spartan room. Simon was laid out on the bed, his eyes closed. But when he heard Richius' voice he raised his head. "Wait here," Richius said to the guard, then walked inside without closing the door. Simon swung his feet over the edge of the bed.

"What do you want?" he asked pointedly.

"I want to talk to you," said Richius. "I want to show you something."

"What?"

"Come with me," said Richius. "Please."

"Vantran . . ."

"Simon, please. Do me this favor all right? It's important."

He didn't wait for Simon to rise, but instead left the chamber and proceeded down the hallway. As he'd hoped, Simon followed, albeit suspiciously. The Naren swiveled his head and surveyed the corridor, looking for a trap, but when he realized there was none he hurried up to Richius' side.

"Where are you taking me?" he asked.

"Outside. Like I said, I want to show you something."

The hallway spilled them into another just like it, then into Falindar's great entrance chamber—the high-ceilinged marvel that greeted all the citadel's visitors. The gates to the castle were open, as they always were on fair days, and autumn sunlight poured in. Richius led them outside, considering his plan. It had come to him in a flash of desperate inspiration, and now that he was outside he fretted over its soundness. Every morning Dyana walked with Shani. If it was warm outside like it was today, they would sit in the courtyard and play together, and Dyana would read from one of Tharn's books. If Richius' hunch was right, they would be outside right about now.

"Vantran," probed Simon. "What is all this?"

Richius put up a hand. "Don't talk. You'll see in a moment."

Simon grumbled but said no more, letting Richius lead him out into the courtyard. As always, there was the ubiquitous milling of warriors and workers, of horses being shoed and lovers whispering in shadows. Richius went to the edge of the courtyard where it was green and the land fell off down the hillside. Among the trees he found Dyana, sitting with Shani against a rock. His wife had a book in her hands. Richius slowed his pace so that Simon could see where they were headed. The Naren whistled as he caught sight of Dyana.

"Who is that?" he asked, mesmerized.

Richius didn't answer. He walked up to Dyana and his daughter and pointed at them both. Dyana looked up, startled.

"Richius?" she asked. She noticed Simon and her expression grew curious. "Who is this? What is wrong?"

"Simon," said Richius desperately, "this is my wife, Dyana. And that little girl is Shani. That's our daughter. I want you to look at them."

"Richius, what are you doing?" Dyana asked.

"That's my family, Simon," Richius went on. "That's why I'm here—why I left Nar and why I stayed behind when the war was over. Look at them. Are they not beautiful?"

"Yes," Simon whispered. "Yes, they are."

"They're everything to me," Richius said, his voice breaking. "I love them. Do you know what that means? I love them, Simon."

"What do you want me to say?" asked Simon. He seemed desperate to leave. "Yes, they're your family. I understand. Why are you showing them to me?"

"Because I have no choice but to trust you, and I don't want to. I want you to see what you would be destroying if you harm them. Look!"

Dyana became indignant. "Richius, what is going on? What are you talking about?"

"This is the Naren I told you about last night, Dyana," said Richius. "He's the one I think might be here to kill me. Or you, or Shani. I want him to see you both. I want him to see why I betrayed Arkus and Biagio. Are you looking, Simon?"

"Yes," said Simon soberly. His shoulders slumped and all the cockiness had gone out of him. He offered Dyana a thin smile. "They are beautiful. You are lucky."

"Yes." Richius reached down and offered out his hand to Dyana, who took it hesitantly while she spied Simon. "Biagio knows how much I love this woman. He might also know about Shani; I'm not sure. Whoever you are, Simon Darquis, I need your word. Lucyler is going away in two days, and he won't make a decision about you. He wants me to decide your fate, and I can't do that. I don't know who you are."

"Richius?" said Dyana. "What are you saying?"

"Look at them, Simon," said Richius. "Remember their faces. Then give me your promise you won't harm them. Are you looking?"

Simon's voice was a whisper. "Yes. I'm looking."

"Promise me, then. Please."

"Would you believe me if I gave it?" asked Simon softly.

"I would have to," replied Richius. "I don't have a choice. I can't keep you as prisoner, and you have nowhere else to go. If you leave Falindar you'll starve or freeze to death in the winter. Just give me your promise. I'm begging you."

Simon's haunted eyes moved over Dyana and Shani. To Richius he seemed distant, as though his mind was skipping back over the years of his life, blowing the dust off his past.

"You have my word," he said. "Nothing will happen to them by my hand. I swear it."

"Again," Richius insisted. "Swear it again, before God."

Simon crossed himself. "Before God, I swear it."

And then Simon smiled at Dyana, a sincere expression that lit his solemn face. Then he turned and left the tiny family, disappearing back into the courtyard. Richius watched him go. Dyana was tugging at his hand, insistently dragging him down next to her. He dropped listlessly to the ground as he stared after the departing Simon.

"Richius?" Dyana pressed. "What is going on?"

"I don't really know," said Richius gently. He still did not look at her. "But don't worry. We'll be safe, I think."

ELEVEN

Enli's Angel

During the endless nights of autumn, the Red Tower of Dragon's Beak was a solitary place. The ocean breezes pounded mercilessly against the castle's degenerating bricks, making the evening candles flicker. The warm smell of the kitchens and the hearths drew crowds of soldiers and servant boys eager to stay warm. This far north, the sun sank quickly. And Red Tower was too big for a person the size of Lorla. At night she slept alone, far from the chambers of Duke Enli, in a haunted corridor of squeaky doors and formidable drafts. Hidden under her thick blankets, Lorla would listen to the dark music of Dragon's Beak, and would wonder about the timeless castle.

Since coming to Red Tower with Daevn, she had seen precious little of her host. The lord of the castle was always preoccupied. At first Lorla had not minded the solitude, because she was tired from her long journey and she had all of the tower to explore. She had almost full run of the place, and she exploited the duke's good intentions, forming polite friendships with the kitchen staff and the stable boys and getting to know her new home. The Red Tower was nothing like Duke Lokken's castle at Goth. That one was bright and predictable. She had adored the Walled City, but Enli's tower was a treasure trove, a maze of windy tunnels and twisting halls, of giant windows stained like rainbows and endless doors to forgotten chambers. There were artifacts of old wars, rusty weapons and mementos stacked high in cellars, dusty closets full of clothing and moths, and balconies engulfed in vines, with thorns as big as thumbs and crimson flowers that seemed oblivious to the cold. And there were books, enough to last Lorla a lifetime—yellowed tomes ripe with the scent of old leather and full of faded writings. Lorla had collected her favorites and had stacked them beside her bed. Some were in High Naren, and because she had learned a smattering of that dead language back in the labs, she was able to practice the tongue again, something she hadn't done for months.

Lorla was looking forward to her trip to Nar City, where she hoped to visit the labs again, but Enli hadn't spoken of her mission, and Lorla had not asked. She had learned not to be too inquisitive. That was one of her most important lessons, and her teachers had been adamant on the point. The Master had plans for her. That was all she needed to know. And the Master had entrusted Enli with her mission. She would not question the duke, for she knew he had her best interests at heart. But she missed Enli. She missed his voice and the direct way he spoke to her. The others in Red Tower weren't like him. They were all polite and pleasant, but Lorla sensed an avoidance in them, an almost fearful quality that made her wonder about her appearance or mannerisms. At mealtimes she would eat alone in a small chamber off the kitchens. The other children of the castle, and there was surprisingly few, ate together or with their parents, but not so with Lorla. Lady Preen brought her meals to her, and never sat down to share the food. Lorla ate her bread and soup staring out a window, with only the startling view to ease her loneliness. Lady Preen was a plump and pleasant house servant, a cook and cleaner mostly, but she was not a friend to Lorla, nor were the soldiers who constantly drilled in the courtyard or the stable boys who groomed their horses, and the children of Red Tower were pensive like their parents, always quiet when Lorla was around. They did not shun her precisely, for they always offered her a kind word, but never once did they spare her any more than the most basic courtesy. By Lorla's reckoning it had been at least two weeks since she'd arrived at the castle, and the magic of the place was wearing off. She wanted to see Enli.

But Enli was almost never seen, and when Lorla did catch a glimpse of him he was with his soldiers. Curiously, the number of men in the castle seemed to grow almost daily. Now when Lorla looked down into the courtyard she counted more of the soldiers with their fancy dragon helmets. More horses, too. So many, in fact, that Duke Enli had no time for her. So far he had come to her only once. She had been in bed, reading, and he had sat down on the edge of her mattress and had spoken kindly to her, stroking her hair the way she thought her mother might have, and had apologized for his absence.

It was necessary, he had explained to her.

As he had told her when she had arrived in Dragon's Beak, he had business with his brother. That first, then they would go to Nar City.

Duke Enli had kissed her good-night. The memory of the touch burned in Lorla.

On the first afternoon of her third week in Dragon's Beak, Lorla decided to go looking for the duke. It was a typically gray day, and she had made the decision over another lonely meal in the little room off the kitchen. Lady Preen had told her that the duke would be leaving soon, and when Lorla had asked her why, the house servant had simply shrugged as though she didn't know. More precisely, Lorla was sure, Lady Preen had dropped a secret, and was a very poor liar. So Lorla finished her food and left, telling Lady Preen she was going to her room to read. But Lorla didn't take the hallway back to her chamber. Instead she skirted off in the opposite direction, to the north side of the castle where Duke Enli's personal chambers were. Lorla had never been in this part of Red Tower before; Enli had politely forbidden her. She felt nervousness in her stomach as she moved quietly down the deserted corridor, but Enli was kind. He wouldn't be mad at her.

Much to her surprise, Lorla found that the north side of the castle was much the same as the rest of the place, although slightly colder and quieter. The familiar sounds of castle life fell off behind her as she made her way down the halls, all lit with oil lamps that stained the ceiling black with soot. The walls were faded brick, and family memorabilia lined the way, old swords and suits of armor guarding closed doors, each baring the furious reptilian crest of Dragon's Beak. Lorla moved silently, suddenly frightened. She thought to try one of the doorknobs, then hesitated. She didn't want to startle Duke Enli or get him angry. But she didn't want to turn around, either. That strange loneliness pushed her on, deeper into the forbidden halls. She glanced behind her uncertainly and was relieved to find no one there. She felt tiny, ridiculously out of place, as though the house were made for giants. The doors loomed up, taunting her to try them. Lorla reached out for one cold doorknob and gave it a wary turn . . .

. . . and found the room exquisite.

She stood in the threshold, wide-eyed and thunderstruck. Before her was a magnificent chamber, with a high ceiling like a cathedral and walls lined with endless bookcases, all stuffed full of manuscripts. Light flooded in from two tall windows, setting the mahogany shelves aglow, and a monstrous hearth blazed against the western wall, crackling comfortably and filling the room with heat. Above the hearth was another of the duke's curious artworks, this one of a golden-haired woman, her green eyes looking down serenely on Lorla. Near the window were two big chairs, more enormous than Lorla had ever seen. Soft and lulling, they beckoned Lorla to rest on them, to pull a book from the shelves and lose herself in their leather embrace. In the center of the room, near a table and some neglected teacups, was a pedestal cage housing a sable-feathered raven that squawked when it noticed Lorla. Yet despite the bird and the blazing hearth and the dirty teacups, the room seemed empty. Lorla stepped unsteadily into the chamber, leaving the door open behind her. The raven watched her, its beady eyes tracking her every move.

"Hello?" called Lorla softly. "Is anyone here?"

To her great relief, no one answered. The library was indeed empty. Again she chanced another step. The raven gave a disapproving caw. Lorla put a finger to her lips.

"Shhh," she ordered. "Be quiet. I'm not going to hurt you. I just want to look around."

Her eyes scanned the towering bookcases. There was a ladder for reaching the highest shelves. Up and up they went, touching the ceiling. Lorla spun around to see them all, an astounded smile on her face. Enli had said nothing of *this*. There were already books aplenty to occupy her in the other rooms, but this was spectacular. She laughed, unafraid of who might hear her, and the raven joined her, cackling.

"How lovely!" she exclaimed.

As she spun she caught a glimpse of the portrait, watching her.

"And you, lady. Who are you?" she asked the painting. The woman's face was bright like the sun. Her long, golden locks fell on her shoulders and emerald dress, and her ruby-painted lips seemed to move with smiling animation. Her green eyes were lashed long and sensually, and they watched Lorla without judgment. Lorla walked up to the portrait, craning her neck to see it better.

"You're very beautiful," Lorla whispered. A forlornness washed over her. "Who are you?"

She wished the portrait could answer and ease her solitude. But the painting was only a painting. The raven rustled its feathers noisily. Lorla turned from the portrait and went to the bird, studying it. Its black eyes turned on her, full of mirth.

"Who are you?" it said in its startling bird-voice. Lorla jumped back, delighted.

"You can talk?" she asked. "That's wonderful!"

"Wonderful. Wonderful. Who are you?"

Lorla laughed and clapped her hands. "Oooh, you're so beautiful, bird. What's your name?"

"Wonderful. Wonderful."

"Yes, yes," said Lorla. She tried to talk slowly so that it might understand. "What is your name?"

This time the bird only cawed, stretching out its wings with a bored yawn.

"My name's Lorla," she said, pointing to herself. "Looorlaa. Can you say that?"

The bird said nothing.

"All right then, don't talk. I don't care." She turned around and pretended to ignore it. A second later it spoke again.

"Lorla."

"Yes!" cried Lorla.

"Angel! Angel!" cawed the raven. It shuffled back and forth on its perch impatiently. "Wonderful."

Lorla brightened. "Angel? Is that your name?"

"Lorla. Wonderful."

"No, no, not me. Is that your name? Angel?"

"Angel," the raven echoed. "Angel."

Lorla put her face to the cage and smiled at the bird. "Well, hello then, Angel. I'm pleased to meet you. I'm new here. Did Duke Enli tell you about me?"

The bird said nothing.

"I'm Lorla, from Goth. Well, from Nar City. That's where I was born, I think. But I moved to Goth to live with Duke Lokken. Now I live here in Dragon's Beak. But not for long. Duke Enli is taking me back to Nar City soon. Angel, have you ever been to Nar City?"

"No, he hasn't," said a voice. Lorla jumped. In the doorway was a young woman, fresh-faced and lovely. "He hasn't been anywhere but Dragon's Beak," she said, stepping into the room. "He was born here. Like me."

"Who are you?" Lorla asked.

"I should ask, rather, who you are, don't you think? But I already know who you are . . . Lorla."

She was stunning. Worse, she was exactly the woman pictured in the portrait. Lorla stared at her, oddly terrified.

"I'm sorry," she stammered. "I shouldn't have come here."

"That's right, you shouldn't have. Didn't anyone tell you this part of the castle was forbidden?"

"I was just looking around," Lorla explained.

The young woman undid the latch on the raven's cage and put her hand inside, offering the bird a finger. The raven jumped on and she pulled it out of it cage, whistling gently to it. Lorla watched, fascinated. The bird was perfectly tame and cocked its tiny head for the woman to scratch it.

"My sweet one," she purred happily. "Did Lorla frighten you?"

"I didn't," said Lorla indignantly. "I didn't even touch him."

"Lorla," cawed the raven. "Wonderful."

The woman smiled. "Cackle likes you, I think." She reached out her hand and touched Lorla's shoulder. The bird hopped on. Lorla giggled excitedly.

"Oooh," she cooed, feeling its scratching talons through her dress.

The sensation wasn't painful, just strange. The raven began nibbling on Lorla's hair.

"Cackle?" said Lorla. "Is that his name?"

"Yes," replied the woman. "We call him that because of his laugh. Have you heard it?"

Lorla nodded, carefully so not to disturb the bird. "I think so. But I thought his name was Angel. He told me so."

"Oh, no," said the woman. "That's not his name. That's just something he says sometimes, when people look at the painting." She gestured to the magnificent portrait above the hearth. "*That* is Angel."

"That's you," said Lorla. "Isn't it?"

"No. My name is Nina. That's my mother. Her name was Angel."

"She's very beautiful," Lorla said. "And you look just like her."

Nina reached up toward the painting, then withdrew her hand. "It's my father's favorite painting. He has so many of them, but only this one of her." Nina turned to Lorla and frowned. "You shouldn't be in here. Duke Enli wouldn't approve. This is his private library."

"Yes, I'm sorry," said Lorla. She turned her shoulder toward Nina, offering her the raven. "Could you? . . ."

With an outstretched finger Nina summoned the bird, who leapt from Lorla's shoulder back to its mistress. Nina stroked its head, looking at Lorla for an explanation.

"I shouldn't have come here, I know," offered Lorla. "But I was looking for Duke Enli. I have to speak to him. Do you know where he is?"

The woman grinned. "Do you know who I am, Lorla?"

"I don't think so," said Lorla. "Should I?"

"Duke Enli didn't mention me?"

Lorla grimaced, perplexed by the odd question. Duke Enli hadn't really mentioned anything. If he had, Lorla might not have come here, looking for answers. "You're Nina," she said simply. "That's all I know."

"Lorla, I'm Duke Enli's daughter. I live here with him. Didn't anyone tell you that?"

"His daughter?" asked Lorla, embarrassed. "Lady Nina, no one tells me anything. I'm too little to get much interest here. I'm very sorry." She made a poor effort at curtsying. "I'm pleased to meet you." She looked up from her bow nervously. The duke's daughter was smiling.

"You have an honest face," said the woman. "I think I can trust you. But you shouldn't take lightly what my father orders. He's a very private man. He doesn't like having people in this part of Red Tower. Hardly any of his servants are allowed in here. If he told you not to come, you should have listened."

"But I needed to see him," Lorla argued. "I need to talk to him. Lady

Preen says he's going away soon. And he's supposed to be taking me to Nar City. I want to know what's happening."

Nina's face dimmed a little. She put Cackle back in his cage, then went to sit in one of the chairs by the window. She sighed and stared at Lorla pensively, as though thinking very hard. Finally she stretched out a hand.

"Lorla, come here," she said gently. "I think we should talk a little. Like girlfriends, all right?"

"Yes," said Lorla. "Yes, I'd like that." She went and sat beside Nina, jumping into one of the chairs. Like all the duke's furnishings, this one swallowed her. "What do you want to talk about, Lady Nina? You can tell me anything. I'm good with secrets. They taught me about secrets in Nar, how to keep them and all. I won't tell anyone."

Nina's expression was haunted. "Yes, I believe that," she drawled. "Tell me something. Do you know why you're here?"

Lorla shrugged. "Your father the duke is taking me to Nar City. I have work to do there for my master, Count Biagio."

"What kind of work?"

"I don't know," answered Lorla honestly. She didn't like sounding ignorant, but she thought it best not to lie. "Your father hasn't told me yet. That's also why I'm looking for him. I've been here a good while now."

"How old are you?"

It was the same tiresome question everyone asked. Lorla answered, bracing herself for the reaction. "I'm sixteen."

Nina's eyes went wide. "Sixteen? But that's impossible. I mean, look at you. . . ."

"I'm sixteen, Lady Nina. I'm sure of that."

The lady arched a brow. "Yes. Yes, of course you are. I meant no offense, Lorla. But when my father told me you were here, he wouldn't tell me why. I thought you might know. I'm sorry."

The apology wasn't necessary; Lorla rarely took offense. "I know that I'm different, Lady Nina," she said. "Please don't act uncomfortable around me. The others here do, and I don't like it." She leaned forward in the chair. "You're very pretty. Like your mother. I wish I were like you."

Nina chuckled. "But you are pretty, Lorla. You're very pretty."

"No," said Lorla darkly. "I'm pretty like a little girl is pretty. I can never be like you. You're . . ." Lorla searched for the word. "Full."

Nina blanched. "Full?"

"You're full grown, up top. And taller than me. I don't know if I'll ever be taller. But I'm special. You see? I'm very special. That's what they say about me in Nar City."

The duke's daughter put up her hands, unwilling to listen further. "Lorla, stop. I shouldn't have asked you anything. I'm sorry. Let's not talk of this anymore." Nina tried a crooked smile. "No one here talks to you, you say?"

"I think they're all afraid of me. But I don't know why."

"Oh, I don't believe that," said Nina gently. "They probably just know my father brought you here, and don't want to say anything wrong to you. My father can be very strict. The servants are afraid of *him*, not you."

"Afraid of him? But he's so nice. And he talks to me, because he knows what I am. That's why I wanted to see him. Can you tell me where he is?"

"You can't see him, Lorla. Not today. Lady Preen was right. My father *is* going away for a little while. Not too long, but he's very busy. He won't be able to speak to you."

"But it's important," said Lorla earnestly. The big chair tried to hold her back as she leaned forward imploringly. "Can't you tell him that for me? Or can your mother?"

"Lorla, don't ever say that again," ordered Nina. "My mother is dead. You must never speak of her in front of my father. Do you understand that?"

"Yes," said Lorla, confused. "All right." She glanced up at the portrait of the beautiful Angel, her eyes darting between Nina and the painting. They were so much alike it disturbed her. "I won't mention her to your father. I promise. And I'm sorry for you, Lady Nina."

"That painting is all we really have of my mother. My father cherishes it. That's why he keeps it in here, to himself. He loved her very much."

"What happened to her?" Lorla asked. "Can you tell me?"

"That's a long story. And I'm not sure it's suited to someone so young."

"But I'm not so young, remember? I'm sixteen. Almost a full woman like you. How old are you? Seventeen maybe?"

"Eighteen. And you should mind your manners. It's not polite to ask a woman her age."

Frustrated, Lorla folded her arms. "If I had a mother, I'd talk about her," she said. "I wouldn't hide her from people. And she's such a pretty woman. She should be in the main dining hall or someplace better than this. It's not right to lock her away in here."

Nina chuckled. "My, you don't talk like an eight-year-old, that's for sure!"

Lorla grinned. "I'm surprised your father didn't warn you."

"Oh, but he did. Well, sort of. He told me you were smarter than you look." Nina sighed. "I'll tell you about my mother if you want. It's not such a great secret. Lots of people know the story of Dragon's Beak. But you can't tell my father I told you. He wouldn't want me telling this story, not to you."

"Why not?"

"Because I think he has plans for you. I'm not supposed to know because I'm his daughter and he protects me from things, or at least tries to. But there's a lot going on in the Empire these days, and my father is part of it. You're part of it too, I'd wager."

Lorla couldn't help but be intrigued. "Part of what?" she asked eagerly. "Something important?"

"You'll find out in time, when my father is ready to tell you. But I want your promise, Lorla. You musn't say anything to my father about what I tell you."

"I won't." Lorla leaned forward, anticipating the story. "Promise."

Nina glanced around the room suspiciously. Lorla loved the intimacy of it. "Have you heard about my Uncle Eneas?"

"He lives in the Gray Tower," said Lorla, remembering what Enli had told her. "He's your father's twin."

"That's right. And you know how similar they are, just like in that painting in my father's study. You've seen that, yes?"

Lorla nodded. "I've seen it. I don't like it."

"Nor do I." Nina laughed. "My Uncle Eneas doesn't come around here very much: In fact, I haven't seen him for years. He and my father don't speak anymore. Not since they killed my mother."

Astonished, Lorla fell back in her chair. "Killed her? You said your father loved her."

"Oh, he loved her. Loved her to death. She was a lovely woman, and she had many suitors, or at least that's what I've heard. Lady Preen was here in those days. She tells me things. But my father wasn't the only man who loved Angel. So did Eneas, his brother. They fought over her hand for many months, and it drove them apart."

"How?" Lorla asked.

"Uncle Eneas was jealous of my father. He never forgave him for marrying my mother. He accused him of stealing her away from him."

"Did he? Steal her, I mean?"

"I don't know, really. But I doubt it. My father is a good man, Lorla. Dangerous sometimes, but honorable. You'll learn that when you get to know him better."

"*If* I do," sulked Lorla. Without Lokken and Kareena around to attend her, she craved the attention of adults, anyone who knew her true nature. "But tell me more," she said. "What happened to your mother?"

"As I said, Uncle Eneas thought my father stole Angel from him. So one night he came to Red Tower to steal her back. He and some of his men snuck in and tried to take my mother away. They almost made it, too." Nina's face went ashen. "But only almost."

"Tell me."

"There was a fight. When they got her outside the tower, my mother screamed. No one really knows how, but she managed to shout for my father. My father's guards heard her and pursued Eneas and his men into the night. They were on horses and riding fast. It was very late and dark. My father ran out of the castle after them, but . . ." Nina's voice trailed away.

Lorla waited a polite amount of time before speaking. "But what?" she asked. "What happened?"

"My mother fell from the horse," said Nina blankly. "Broke her neck. Lady Preen says that my father found his brother bent over Angel, weeping. She was dead and all Eneas' men had gone back to Gray Tower, but Eneas had stayed to confront my father. They carried her back here together. She's still buried on the north side of the castle, overlooking the sea." Nina made a pale glance at Lorla. "I was so young then. Barely six years old."

Lorla bit her lip, wanting to comfort her new friend and not knowing how. Nina's pretty face had lost its glow. Lorla slid out of her chair and went over to Nina, offering her a weak smile and an uninvited touch.

"That's very sad," she said softly. "I'm sorry for you. And for your father."

Nina took Lorla's hand and squeezed it warmly. "That's dear," said Nina. She patted the space next to her on the big chair. "Here, sit with me, Lorla. You can comfort me, all right? Lord, I'm such a silly fool. It's been so long, and I never really even knew her!"

"But that's what it's like," said Lorla. She got into the chair and pressed against Nina's warm body. "For me it is. I think of my mother. My father, too. But I don't remember them much. I don't really remember anything. I just remember leaving Nar City and—"

She stopped herself. Nina was staring at her again.

"So what happened then?" Lorla asked, anxiously shifting subjects. "Did your father fight with his brother?"

"No," said Nina. "They never fought. But every year on the anniversary of Angel's death, Eneas would come here to Red Tower and beg my father to forgive him for what he did. And every year my father shunned him. Finally Uncle Eneas stopped coming around. He used to give me gifts when he came, to try and make up for what he had done. Like that was possible! Wretched man."

"But he doesn't come here anymore?"

"It's been years. Five at least." Nina pointed with her chin toward the raven in its cage. "Cackle was my last gift from Eneas. After that I never saw him anymore. He and my father haven't spoken since."

The story was profoundly sad, and for some strange reason Lorla wanted to weep. But she did not. She was resolute, just as they had taught her to be. Special girls like Lorla needed to be strong. So instead of telling Nina how she really felt, she said the only thing that came to her lips.

"Cackle was a gift? That's strange."

Nina laughed. "Yes, I suppose it is. But Eneas raises ravens. It's a pastime of his. He's very good at it, I've heard."

"Raises them? What for?"

"To defend his castle. My father says that Eneas has trained his birds to fight like falcons. Eneas calls them his 'army of the air.' They're all over Gray Tower, guarding it from invasion."

"I don't believe that," Lorla laughed. "It's impossible."

"It's true. My father told me so. Everyone knows about it. Except you, of course. You don't know much about Dragon's Beak, do you?"

"No," Lorla had to admit. "But it's a good story. And I like birds. I wish I could see Eneas' tower."

"You'll have to make do with Cackle, I'm afraid. Besides, I'd bet Cackle is smarter than any of Eneas' other ravens. Father has spent a lot of time with him, training him. Cackle likes Father better than he does me, I think." Nina turned to smile at the bird in its cage. "Don't you, my darling? You love Father, don't you?"

The bird said nothing, but Nina's smile didn't dim.

"Cackle's been a good friend," she said. She looked at Lorla. "I know how lonely Red Tower can be, Lorla." She squeezed Lorla's hand again. "Are you lonely?"

The pointed question made Lorla grimace. "Yes," she admitted. "A little."

"Well, it doesn't have to be so bad for you. You'll be going to Nar City eventually, and until then you and I can be friends. All right?"

"I would like that," said Lorla. "Very much."

"Good. Then you can start by calling me Nina. *Just* Nina. Friends don't use titles. And I won't call you princess, all right?"

Lorla laughed. "Fine . . . Nina."

"And you'll be patient? You won't go looking for my father anymore?"

That question was more difficult. Lorla needed Enli desperately, to find out what arcane work he and Master Biagio had planned for her. But Nina was watching her, waiting for an answer, and Lorla didn't want to jeopardize her new friendship.

"All right," she agreed. "I won't go looking for Duke Enli anymore. But can I stay here for a while? Look at some of these books?"

"Is that all you want? To read?"

"For now," replied Lorla evasively.

Nina gestured to the bookcases crammed full with manuscripts. "Pick one."

It was all the encouragement Lorla needed. She leapt from the chair and headed for the closest bookcase, climbing the shelves like a monkey, the only advantage to her embarrassing body.

TWELVE

The Raven Master

Gray Tower stood on the north fork of the dragon's tongue, alone and frigid on an outcropping of rock. Like its brother, Enli's Red Tower, Gray Tower was a stoic place. It weathered storms without a blink and ate the salty lashings of the ocean. It was, like its red brother, built to separate its lord from the people he governed, to keep him high and far away from the peasant stock that toiled in his fields. Duke Eneas loved his Gray Tower. He loved the view from its high perches, and its grounds filled with oak trees, and its tall iron gates, always guarded by his raven-faced soldiers—those men of the fork who pledged themselves to his defense and wore the black armor. They were loyal and devoted to their eccentric master, and Eneas treated them handsomely for their service. All of the north fork were contented. And Gray Tower was well protected, not only by the guards in their metal garb, but by Duke Eneas' greatest accomplishment, a force he had literally grown himself.

His army of the air.

It was an affectation, really. Eneas knew this but liked the ring of it. Five hundred ravens. They were the terror of the populace. All of Dragon's Beak knew about the army of the air, and none dared come to the tower unannounced lest they wished their eyes pecked out. Duke Eneas slept well in Gray Tower, safeguarded from his brother's harmful intents and any foolhardy invaders. His army of the air protected him. They were his children and they did his bidding, for he was their God and mother, and Eneas needed only to flex a finger or whistle or turn his head to make them understand. It was a gift he had enjoyed since boyhood, one that Enli had envied and feared, and in these years of solitude from his brother, Eneas appreciated his dominion over the ravens. Five hundred pairs of eyes watched over him. In Gray Tower, Eneas could rest.

He had not always feared his brother. Once, the siblings had been the best of friends. They had shared every secret, and had grown to love and respect each other. Their mother had been sainted, a precious jewel of a woman whom they'd both adored, and they had wept together at her passing and at the death of their father, crying in each other's arms, unashamed of their tears. In the early days of Arkus they had both been loyal to the emperor and his Black Renaissance, and they had flown the Black Flag proudly, divided by the channel of water but always together in spirit. They had separate castles but not separate lives, and they wrote to each other often. They spoke of governing the nation their father had bequeathed them and they quibbled over where to find the best wines. Like soldiers together in a crusade, they were closer than blood.

But that was long ago, before Angel had come between them.

Like most evenings in Dragon's Beak, this one was pensively quiet. The sun was slipping down and painting the sky crimson. A determined breeze chilled the grounds around Gray Tower, pulling at the tree branches and the cloaks of the guardians pacing through the courtyard. Ravens cawed and waddled along the bricks, pecking at the seeds lodged between the cobblestones, ruffling their feathers in deference to the cold. Near the far end of the courtyard a fire blazed in a pit as wide as a man, its flames warming the ravens gathered around it. Beside the pit was a three-tiered shelter, open mostly to the elements but breaking the winds that blew in from the sea, protecting and warming the duke's precious birds. Like the ravens, the fire was tended constantly. Duke Eneas spared no expense for his army of the air, and paid his handlers well to endure the cold with the birds. Just now the shelter was sparse of ravens, but Eneas knew they would gather when the sun disappeared, and would sleep near the warm glow of the fire, protected from the worst winds. They were hearty birds, and because they were pampered and adored they never strayed far from the tower.

As he did every night before retiring, Duke Eneas walked the grounds of Gray Tower, his bearded face hidden from the cold by a thick wool cloak. On his shoulder was his ubiquitous companion, Black, his lead raven and closest friend. Eneas spoke softly to Black as he walked, telling the bird about his backaches and the other ailments of growing older, and generally expending energy on nonsense. As always, Black listened. He was a fine bird, worthy of his status, and all the other ravens followed him, for they knew that Black was favored. To mark his status, Black wore a thin silver chain around his neck, just tight enough to keep it from coming off in flight. A small medallion dangled from the chain bearing the crest of Dragon's Beak. Black was clever and a good companion, and Eneas often abused the bird's silence. When he was sad, as he was tonight, Eneas would talk without end.

"Winter's coming," Eneas murmured. They had rounded the front of the sprawling yard and were heading toward the fire pit and shelter. Black didn't stay outside with the other birds, though. He slept beside Eneas' bed and ate his meals with the duke. For Eneas, Black had replaced Enli as his brother.

When he heard his master's comment, the raven ruffled his feathers. "Cold," clipped the bird. Eneas realized he did not really know what the word meant. He had just heard Eneas use the term often enough. Eneas put his gloved hands together and blew into them.

"Aye, cold," he agreed. He paused in the courtyard to look at the sun and study its descent. He didn't like winter anymore. His body rebelled against the cold. And he wondered as he shivered if Enli suffered as he did, or if his twin had better escaped the ravages of time. Angel had died in the winter, and whenever the unwelcome season came Eneas relived those horrible days and martyred himself over his beloved's death. That day, everything had died. He stared at the sun and saw Angel's face in it.

"Cold," Black said again. "Cold."

Duke Eneas gave a wan smile. "Indeed it is, my friend. Let's get inside."

Together they went to the main doors of Gray Tower, passing a pair of raven-helmeted guards who opened the wooden portals for them without a word. Inside, Gray Tower was warm. Black flew from Eneas' shoulder and darted down the hallway to perch on the mantel of a fireplace. It was very near mealtime, and Eneas could smell food being prepared. His stomach rumbled at the odor. Tonight he would eat and retire early, and pray to God that he didn't dream. Of late, dreams came to him even while awake. He had taken to writing them down in his journal, and had been comparing them. He wasn't at all surprised by their unified theme of loneliness.

Winter was a very lonely time in Dragon's Beak.

Eneas walked past the mantel where Black was sitting, pausing to warm his hands. He pulled off his gloves and spread his long fingers, enjoying the warmth. Black closed his ebony eyes as if thinking. It was a strange magic the two shared. Eneas had been gifted with this power since his youth. Their father had shown a smattering of it, and their mother could read the minds of cats, but only Eneas was truly a master of the trick. Only he could peer into the primeval brains of birds and know what they were thinking. He knew now that Black was more hungry than tired, a fact others would miss from the bird's sleepy countenance. Eneas knew when his birds were sick or afraid or vengeful, or when they needed exercise or attention. He was a magician of sorts, and though his ability had frightened Enli, he himself had never been afraid of it. He adored his gift just as he adored his ravens. In these bleak seasons, the ravens were his only true companions. He shared secrets with them, the sort of things he used to share with Enli. He told them his thoughts and his memories, and regaled them often with tales about Angel and the one he called his daughter.

"Hungry, my friend?" he asked Black. The duke stroked an index finger over the raven's plumage. What passed for a smile crossed Black's corvine face. He hopped onto Eneas's shoulder, then playfully nibbled the duke's ear. More than hungry, the nibble meant. Famished.

"We'll eat now," said the duke. He turned his back on the fire and escorted Black down the hallway, toward the kitchens and their waiting meals.

On the south fork of Dragon's Beak, Duke Enli waited. And watched. He watched the sun go down, watched the eastern half of the world plunge into darkness, and watched the darkness spread across the earth until the channel separating him from his brother across the sea became black and the wind picked up. On the far side of Dragon's Beak, he could barely see Gray Tower on its precipice of rock. The water was rising and sea foam licked at Enli's boots. He was cold and his men were cold, and the little boat that would convey them all across the channel seemed dubiously small. The moon lit the land with strands of light; moonbeams danced on the white caps. Enli opened the door of his lantern and extinguished the flame. His men did the same. There were six of them in all, including Enli and not including Cackle, who perched patiently on Enli's shoulder. The men gathered around the boat waited for Enli to speak, but he did not.

He trusted these men. He knew they were skilled and would do their best for him. Yet still Enli fretted over the coming melee. They had doffed their dragon armor for ease of motion, and all had some minor experience with clandestine work. Unlike the mercenaries he was buying with Biagio's fortune, Enli trusted these men. They were loyal to more than just coins. They had been with him for years, and he had hand-picked them for tonight's work. Already the mercenary forces were rolling out of Red Tower, taking up positions outside Eneas' fork. If all went well tonight, Enli would order them against Gray Tower. But there was one problem, one almost insurmountable obstacle. And it had taken Biagio's keen mind to devise a solution. Now, with Cackle on his shoulder, the plan had seemed too obvious. But that was Biagio's gift. The count was cunning. He could see things no other man could, and that was why Arkus had chosen him to head the Roshann. Some said the scientist Bovadin had the biggest brain in the Empire, but Enli knew that wasn't so. Biagio—he was the mastermind. Enli smiled. He fished a nutmeat from his pocket and fed it to Cackle, who devoured it greedily. The raven clacked for another and Enli obliged. Tonight Cackle was more important than any of the others gathered here on shore. Only Cackle could subdue the army of the air. Eneas had guardians and a happy populace to protect him, but he also had his dreaded ravens, and a more bloodthirsty army existed nowhere else in Nar. There was something evil about Eneas' ravens, something that made strong men wither. But tonight, if Biagio's grand design proved correct, the army of the air would be theirs.

"You're a good boy," Enli crooned to his pet. "Do well for me tonight, all right?"

"Good boy," Cackle echoed. "Good boy."

They waited another hour, not speaking, until at last Enli felt comfortable with the darkness and ordered them all into the long boat. Each man had a short sword and a crossbow that he stowed beneath the seats, and the two with the strongest backs took up positions near the oars. Cackle flew into the boat before Enli, staking out the seat nearest the bow. The duke stepped into the vessel as the last two men shoved them off. The boat slipped out onto the cold sea. Above them, Red Tower glowed with candlelight and torches, and Enli steeled himself as he slowly drifted away from his home, studying its windows for Nina's silhouette. He did not see her, but he hadn't really expected to. She knew only that he planned to avenge himself on his brother, and that all the soldiers who had lately invaded their home would soon be gone to invade Gray Tower. Nina was a sensible girl. It was why Enli was convinced she had grown from his seed, and not Eneas'. She had given him no trouble at all about his plans to conquer the north fork. But that was because he had lied to her. He had promised her that her Uncle Eneas would be spared. Enli knew that if his daughter ever found out what he was really doing tonight, she would hate him forever.

The notion made the duke close his eyes. He sat down on the bench next to Cackle and banished the image of Red Tower from his mind. There was work to do, he scolded himself. No time for sentiment. The rowers grunted as they fought against the wind and tide, hastening the boat toward the ever-looming shadow of Gray Tower. The moon disappeared behind a cloud, deadening the world. Cackle cawed angrily and bit at Enli's hand, demanding attention. The duke put out a finger for Cackle to hop onto and lifted the bird to his shoulder, where the raven rested, contented for the moment. Enli's soldiers looked about, murmuring darkly. They fidgeted with their weapons but their movements never rose above a whisper. It took nearly another full hour to make the channel crossing, and when at last Gray Tower rose on the rocky cliff above them, Enli raised his hand to stop the rowers.

"Easy," he directed. "Go slow."

He didn't want to be seen, not by the tower's guards or by any of the beastly ravens. The duke set his jaw and peered through the blackness. Lights flickered in the tower. It was early still and the moon had re-emerged. Carefully, stealthily, the little boat let the tide pull it toward shore. Enli felt the touch of dread. It had been a long time since he'd seen Eneas. Curiously, he wondered if his brother had changed much. A flood of memories crashed into his brain, momentarily shattering his resolve. He had loved his brother once. But then he remembered Angel and Eneas' wicked claims about Nina, and the old ire rose up in him. Tonight, he would have the revenge denied him for so long. And Biagio's fortune would be put to good use as the mercenaries fought for the north fork.

The little boat drifted toward shore. The men aboard stopped murmuring. They retrieved their swords and crossbows and made ready. The oarsmen steered ashore, directed by the whispering Enli. *To the east side,* the duke counseled. *Slowly, slowly.* There were rocks and trees on the east side to hide them, and the main road was there. If his ruse was going to work, it had to be perfect. The rowboat skidded ashore and Enli's soldiers scurried out, cloaked by darkness and the outcroppings of rocks. Gray Tower hovered nearby, just over the stony hills. Enli waited for the boat to be well grounded before trudging out. Together his men hauled the boat onto the land and dragged it toward the rocks, where they wedged it beneath a granite shelf covered with moss. The duke took the time to study Cackle. The raven seemed unconcerned.

"Go to the road, like I told you," Enli told his men. "Wait for me there. I won't be long."

"You should come with us," said Faren, one of Enli's most trusted confidants. "Let the bird go from the road. I don't want to lose sight of you."

"Just go," said Enli, untouched by the sentiment. He wasn't in the mood to have his orders questioned, and just now he wanted to be alone on the shores of the north fork. It had been too many years since his boots had trod this side of the dragon's tongue. And in less than an hour his brother might be dead. For the moment, at least, Enli needed solitude. "I will be there directly," he promised Faren. "Now go."

The soldiers departed reluctantly, shimmying up the rocks and disappearing. Enli watched them leave, and when he was sure they were well away he pulled the note from his pocket. It had been folded thrice into a tight little package, light enough for Cackle to convey to Eneas' window. He set the bird onto the rock shelf, then took the string from his pocket, using it to fasten the note to Cackle's leg. The bird shifted a bit but did not bite at the string the way he had previously, a small favor for which Enli was enormously grateful. He had rehearsed this a dozen times with the clever bird. He was sure Cackle could do it. He tied the knot securing the note and stepped away from the raven, inspecting his work. Cackle's black eyes twinkled.

"All right now," said Enli. "You know what to do. It's all up to you."

The bird seemed to yawn, but he stretched his wings and cast his master a sober look.

"Angel," cawed the bird. "Angel."

Enli's smile was sardonic. "That's right. For Angel. Now fly, little beauty. Fly for my revenge!"

With a giant hop the raven leapt from the rock and gathered the air beneath his wings, going up and up against the wind, determined to deliver his master's message. Enli watched as Cackle darted toward Gray Tower and the large balcony overlooking the western sea, the one with the tower's only marble gargoyles.

Just as he had been trained to do.

Duke Eneas had eaten a hearty meal with his men and Black and had retired to his chambers early. In Gray Tower, when winter came, there was very little to do, and men of nobility in the northern lands generally occupied themselves with books and journals to fill the long hours. Because his mother had taught him a love of reading, Eneas often took to his bed early in the dark months, curling into his sheets with a cup of honey tea while Black watched over him from an open cage hanging not too near the fire. This evening, a bit of undigested stew had soured Eneas' stomach, and so the duke had neglected the tea and instead taken only the book with him to bed, and even this gave his stomach little solace. As was his routine, though, he finished several pages before setting the book aside in favor of sleep. The hallway outside his bedchamber was customarily quiet, for the folk of Gray Tower knew their lord's penchant for silence, and so tiptoed past his rooms so as not to disturb his studies or slumber. The breezes off the ocean beat against the old glass of his balcony doors, and outside Eneas could hear the whistle of wind through stone and the groaning of the gargoyles perched on the ledge. His was the only balcony in the tower decorated with the grotesques, a gift from the renowned Darago to celebrate his fortieth birthday. At first he had thought the gargoyles a pair of monstrosities, but Darago was an artisan whose works graced the Black Palace and the Cathedral of the Martyrs and countless other landmarks throughout the Empire. The emperor had commissioned the sculptures himself. To spurn a gift from Darago would have been the height of bad taste, and

Eneas had grown oddly attached to the gargoyles over the years. They were like his ravens now—a permanent fixture of Gray Tower.

It did not take long for sleep to capture Eneas. The book he had been reading lay on the night table beside him, under the glow of a single candle. The lulling music of the wind helped calm the duke's stomach, and very soon Eneas was asleep. He was dreaming of something he couldn't quite recall when an intrusive tapping dragged him back to the world. His eyes fluttered open, and for a moment the sound was gone. The wind? He looked to Black who had also awakened and was staring at the doors. The duke's own eyes shifted toward the glass. Outside on the balcony, its beak pressed against the pane, was another raven. Curious and groggy, Eneas watched, and a familiarity dawned in his mind. The strange raven tapped again at the glass, insistent. Eneas frowned.

"What the hell is this?" he muttered. He flung his naked feet over the bedside and spied the balcony for others, but all he could see was the lone bird. Black flew from his cage to land on the duke's shoulder. Eneas stroked his friend for strength. The visitation had unnerved him and he didn't know why. The raven beyond the glass was big, as big as Black himself, and with the same intelligent expression. The duke eased toward the glass doors, then noticed the object around the raven's leg. A note? He reached out to open the door, but Black screeched in his ear, stopping him.

"Quiet!" Eneas commanded, frightened by the bird's scream. "There's nothing to worry about, you jealous beast. It's just a bird."

With Black still protesting, he turned the handle and opened the glass door. At once the strange raven hopped inside, clicking and cawing for the duke's attention. Black's talons dug angrily into Eneas' shoulder, a warning not to be ignored. Eneas stepped away from the raven, pondering it.

"What do we have here, my friend?" he asked Black. His raven made an unusual hissing sound, and its ruddy little tongue clicked at the intruder. Eneas nodded.

"Curious, indeed. You don't trust him."

But the raven who had awakened them would not be silenced. It hopped around the duke's feet, looking up at him, its wings fluttering wildly. Eneas had never seen such obstinance in a bird. Not even Black could be so forceful. He squatted down. The bird was oddly familiar to him, and the little note tethered to its leg simply begged to be read. Despite Black's repeated warnings, Eneas reached out and plucked at the string, carefully loosening it. The raven stopped fidgeting as he worked, allowing the note to be freed. After a few delicate moments the tightly folded package dropped from the bird's leg. Eneas sat back on the floor and regarded the bird.

"You look familiar to me," he mused, his eyes narrowing. "But then, I see so many birds. Who are you?"

The raven stopped moving. It simply stared at the duke with its black eyes. Eneas stretched out his mind and buried himself in the creature, tapping into its primordial brain. His memory flared with sudden recognition. A rush of excitement and fear blew over him.

"Cackle," he gasped. "It *is* you!"

The raven bobbed its head in assent.

"My God . . ."

It was unthinkable. Unimaginable. Cackle. His daughter. But to make the trip across the sound! Why? In his shock, it took a moment for the duke to remember the note. Nervously he unfolded the paper. Still on the floor, his legs bent beneath him, he studied the perfect penmanship. It was brief. The duke's heart leapt as he read.

Dear Father,

Father!

Please help. I am outside the castle near the main road. Your brother is pursuing me. I know who I am now. Please come.

It was signed very simply, *Nina.*

Eneas couldn't stop his heart from thundering. A million questions raced through his mind, muddled by a million memories. His breath came in hurried, bewildered gasps. Nina! Here, at Gray Tower. Outside now, and waiting for him. He turned to look at Black perched on his shoulder.

"My daughter," he said to the bird. "She's here!"

"No!" Black barked at him. "No!"

Eneas ignored his friend. No one else could have sent Cackle to him. Cackle had been a gift to the girl; they would have bonded by now. And Enli was too foolish to ever control the creature. It *had* to be his daughter. He stared at the note, wondering what to do.

"She's too afraid to come to the tower," he surmised. No one came to Gray Tower for fear of the ravens. But she was probably alone and frightened. He had to hurry to her. He had to bring soldiers and warn the guardians that Enli was coming. Eneas put his hand to his mouth. If Enli was coming, they were all in grave danger. And how had Nina learned the truth of her birth? The duke rocked back and forth like an anxious child, unable to think clearly. Black was staring at him angrily, and Cackle's gaze was mad with panic. The duke's eyes shifted between the birds, not knowing which to believe. If it truly was Nina, she needed him. Now. And perhaps Black was merely jealous. . . .

Eneas dipped down and scooped up Cackle, looking at the bird intently. "Can you take me to Nina?" he asked the raven pointedly. "Take me to your mistress?"

"Yes-yes," cawed the bird. "Nina. Yes-yes."

"All right then. Take me."

The duke rose and went to the door, practically kicking it open. He bellowed down the empty corridor for his guards. *Enli is coming,* he screamed at them. *Awaken the army of the air! Warn the guardians and ready my horse to ride! My brother is coming. My daughter is here!*

Just outside the shadow of the tower, near the roadside amongst the overgrown trees, Duke Enli sat spying the path and listening for the approach of his quarry. Faren and Yory, two of his crossbowmen, lay on the knoll beside him, their weapons trained on the road. On the other side of the road were L'rou and Devon, also invisible, while Jace and Sen were just behind them. His brother wouldn't come alone, Enli knew, but he wouldn't come with a whole brigade, either. His mass of men would remain at the tower, to guard against a coming attack. And Enli would have the element of surprise. It was dark on the road and that gave them good cover. Enli could barely see Faren and Yory, and they were merely feet away. The others had blended in perfectly. The duke was cold but exhilarated, and the thought of his coming revenge warmed his soul. Soon, very soon, he would end the charade he'd been living since Angel's death. Nina would never hear the lies of her uncle, her so-called father. The thought of Eneas' claims tightened Enli's jaw.

Angel was no whore, but Eneas had made her sound like one, soiling her memory. He had vowed to kill his brother for the crime. Tonight, finally, he would make good on that pledge, and in the process help to restore Biagio and the Black Renaissance.

"Remember," Enli whispered to Faren. "If there are too many of them, just let them pass. They'll eventually split up and start looking for Nina. When they do, we'll kill Eneas."

"And how many is too many?" asked Faren anxiously. He was a brave soldier, but his master's plan had unnerved him.

"Ten, twelve maybe," said the duke. "No more than a dozen. Don't worry. It won't be that many. I know Eneas. I know how foolishly trusting he can be."

His brother would never be able to resist the note, not if he believed it had truly come from Nina. And believe it he would, for in their youth Enli had always been the clumsy one with animals. Enli was sure his brother thought him incapable of controlling Cackle. Overconfidence. It was just one more of Eneas' flaws.

The mercenaries purchased by Biagio had taken up position just outside the north fork, barely within Enli's border. When the order came, they would sweep in and start what promised to be a protracted battle for Gray Tower. It would have been an unthinkable folly were it not for Biagio's plan. The army of the air could have protected the tower indefinitely. Coupled with the might of Eneas' guardians, the ravens made the castle impregnable. An entire legion of Vorto's best soldiers might have had trouble sacking Gray Tower.

But not after tonight.

"Don't let the bird get away," Enli reminded Faren and Yory. "Kill it. Or capture it. But don't let it escape."

"What if it's not with him?" Faren asked.

"It will be. He goes nowhere without it. Let the bird be your first target if you like. Just make sure to kill it. Understand?"

Faren grunted angrily. "It's going to be hard in this darkness, my lord. We'll do our best."

"Do better than that," Enli hissed.

Yory swallowed hard and nodded, returning his attention to the empty road. Enli took up his own crossbow, stretched out on his stomach, and propped the weapon up on his elbows, closing one eye for accuracy. This chance would never come again. His heart boomed in his temples, and his breath was shallow and edgy. Unlike the others, he was only a fair shot with a crossbow, so he quickly decided to go for a bigger target than the raven. He would plant the bolt in the first soldier to show his face. At this range the weapons would easily penetrate the chain mail. Enli licked his wind-dried lips.

Good-night, dear brother. Say hello to Father for me.

A sound in the distance startled him. They all cocked their heads to listen. Faren put a finger to his lips to caution quiet. A horse. No. More than one. Coming closer. The duke lowered himself back into the dirt, disappearing among the tree limbs. Slowly, purposefully, he lifted his crossbow and snapped closed an eye, focusing on the black and narrow path.

Duke Eneas wasn't in the mood to quibble. He was on a mission and in a hurry, and the calls to slow his horse fell on deaf ears. He had not bothered to draw his sword or wear his raven-helm, for he wanted Nina to recognize him and not be afraid. His men, however, were far more cautious. Each of the eight wore a helmet and mail, and each had their swords at the ready, a single torch held by a young squire brightening their way. The ravens had been awakened and were patrolling the grounds, ready for any attack from sea or land, and the guardians of the castle were on alert, armed and prepared should Enli's forces charge.

Duke Eneas rode at the head of his column, frantic to find his daughter before Enli could recapture her. The road before him was black and featureless, and the wind pulled his red hair out behind him like a comet's tail. Black waited dutifully on his shoulder, cawing curses at the other raven leading the way. Cackle was hopping swiftly down the road, half walking, half flying as he led the soldiers.

"Keep your eyes open," the duke called over his shoulder. "I don't know where she is, or if Enli's men have gotten her. Be sharp, lads."

They were all sharp. They were Gray Tower's best, and Eneas trusted them to protect him and find his daughter. And when they did, when they were together again as they should have been for eighteen years, he would take Nina back to the tower and launch his army of the air against his brother and have an end to the decades of madness. Nina would be his at last. Just as Angel would have wanted.

In the road up ahead, Cackle chittered at them to hurry. Eneas watched the bird and watched the knolls and trees around him, frightened of an ambush but frightened more of not finding his daughter. He didn't know how long ago the note had been sent. Had Cackle found him quickly, or had all this happened hours ago? Was Nina already back in Enli's clutches? The thought made the duke's insides pitch. To lose her now after being so close was unthinkable.

"Hurry," he called to his men, his voice echoing over the wind. "We've got to find her!"

Cackle cawed some more. Black's talons dug into Eneas' chain mail. The duke's horse snorted out a plume of steam, and the narrow roadway closed in on them. The trees overhead bent in the breeze. Eneas heard the horses' hooves and the insistent breathing of his men behind him. And then a peculiar sound reached the duke, whistling past his ears. Then another and another more. Cackle flew up into the air. Eneas reined in his horse and watched the raven flee. He heard a scream behind him, then felt a burning in his shoulder. Black squawked and struggled skyward. Eneas turned just in time to see his beloved bird impaled.

"What the hell . . . ?"

The duke's shoulder burst with pain. There was an arrow in it, almost clean through. He grabbed at his shoulder in agony, nearly falling from his horse. The world around him erupted in chaos. His men were screaming. He turned to see one topple to the ground as a bolt pierced his helmet. The swordsmen were rushing toward the duke to protect him. Eneas watched them struggle toward him through the rain of arrows. The boy with the torch fell as a missile punctured his neck. He gurgled out a cry and fell to his knees, wheezing blood as he gasped for air. Near him on the ground was Black, a huddled mass of mangled feathers, his breast turned inside-out. Eneas whirled in his saddle and drew his sword, cursing at the darkness.

"Enli!" he screamed. "You murderer! Face me!"

His answer was another arrow, this one slamming into his ribs. The duke cursed and doubled over. He swayed in his saddle, trying to stay aloft, but another bolt hammered into his horse's forehead, felling the beast. Eneas dropped his sword as he toppled, the breath shooting out of him with the force of the fall. His swordsmen were in a frenzy. They scanned the blackness for their enemies even as the marksmen in the trees peppered them with arrows. Duke Eneas clutched at the earth, pulling himself to the side of the road and shouting at his men to cover themselves. He had almost made it to the shoulder when he saw the trees come alive. A band of wraiths brandishing rapiers swarmed over his unsuspecting guards, cutting them down. Eneas struggled to his feet. Unarmed, he staggered toward his men with both fists barreled.

"Enli!" he roared. "Here I am! Come to me!"

A meaty arm wrapped itself around Eneas' throat and a dagger pricked his neck.

"Right here, brother dear."

Eneas froze. The dagger beneath his chin drew a bead of blood.

"Enli," he rasped. "You bastard . . ."

The melee went on. His men went down; one, then another and one more. Enli's assassins cut through the night. Eneas choked on emotion and his own blood, which was now filling his throat from a punctured lung.

"Where is she?" the duke demanded, barely able to breathe. "What have you done with Nina?"

"Nina?" said the voice in his ear. The arm around him fell away, letting Eneas drop to his knees. Eneas looked up, gasping and clutching his chest. In the light of the dying torch he glimpsed his twin, staring disdainfully down on him. From out of the sky a raven swooped, settling on Enli's shoulder.

"You treacherous little monster," Eneas seethed, addressing both the bird and its master. Behind him his men groaned and died. He heard the hacking of heavy swords dispatching the living and the pleas of the young light-bearer, begging to be spared. And then he heard nothing at all. Eneas glared at his brother as the assassins gathered to flank him. Enli's face was wild and mad, not at all like Eneas remembered it. His dark eyes smoldered as he looked down, happily victorious, and the bird on his shoulder smiled a peculiar, avian grin. Eneas knew he had only moments left. He could barely keep himself up, and every breath he drew sent new pain plunging through him.

"My daughter," he gasped. "Where is she?"

"*My* daughter is safe at home, dear brother," said Enli. "Where she belongs."

Eneas gargled out a laugh. "She knows the truth though, doesn't she? She knows?"

"She knows none of your lies! She knows that I'm her father." Enli's eyes narrowed. "And now she will never hear your lies, Eneas, because now you will die."

"Then kill me," said Eneas. He raised his head and spread out his hands for Enli to strike him down. "Go on and murder me. Have that on your conscience too. Kill me like you killed Angel!"

Enli struck his brother hard across the face. "Liar!" he roared. "I loved her. I love her still. And you took her from me."

Eneas laughed. Angel had never loved Enli. She had seen him for the madman he was, and had tried to flee from him. And Eneas had killed her for it.

"Live your lie, brother," said Eneas softly. "Kill me. Send me to my Angel. We'll be together if you do."

His brother shook with rage. The dagger in his fist quavered.

"Damn you!" Enli cried. "Damn you for making me do this!"

"I die, brother," Eneas taunted. "Hurry now. Take your vengeance before I go."

"You stole her from me!"

"Kill me, you wretched coward."

Enli screamed, high and horrible. Eneas watched his brother's breakdown, and all the hate in him evaporated. He kept his arms outstretched even as the dagger plummeted down.

Duke Enli stood over his brother's dead body for a small eternity. The night had fallen quiet again and the light from the torch had been smothered by the dirt. It was very cold and the duke shivered, warmed only by the tears streaking his face. He was aware of his men staring at him, of Faren's incredulous gaze and Devon's slack jaw, yet he couldn't bring himself to stir, not even to clean the dagger of Eneas' blood. He was a murderer now. He felt it as surely as he felt the wind. Blindly, he stared at his brother crumpled at his feet. He poked at Eneas with the toe of his boot and was oddly disappointed when his brother didn't respond.

"Duke Enli?" probed Faren. "My lord, we have to hurry."

"Yes," whispered Enli absently. "Yes, hurry."

"The bird's dead, my lord. Your plan . . ."

"Yes," said Enli again. "My plan . . ."

The raven Cackle was still on his shoulder. Enli took an unsteady breath and gestured toward his dead brother.

"Undress him," he ordered. "Quickly."

The duke started undoing his own clothing, slowly working the buttons of his shirt. His men fell upon Eneas' body, unceremoniously pulling away his garments. Yory, who had been silent through the entire fight, stalked over to the dead raven in the roadway and scooped the thing up, bringing it over to Enli. The silver chain still clung around its broken neck. Enli sighed with relief.

"Take the chain off," he directed. "Don't break it."

Very carefully Yory undid the chain from around the dead bird's neck, nearly pulling off the raven's head as he stretched the neck for slack. When he had freed the tiny chain he handed it gingerly to his master. Enli, now shirtless, took the necklace to Cackle.

"Easy now," the duke ordered as he slipped the ornament over the raven's head. "Just take it easy. I'm not going to hurt you."

Remarkably, Cackle twisted his head to accommodate the chain, and it slid quickly over his glossy feathers. Enli checked the chain to be sure it wouldn't slip off in flight. Satisfied, he lifted Cackle in his hand and smiled at the bird.

"You're a wonderful little beast," he said softly. "Go now, my friend. Bring back your brothers and sisters."

The duke hoisted his hand into the air and Cackle took flight, disappearing once more into the darkness. Enli watched him soar.

"My lord!" Faren scolded. "Dress now! You'll catch your death."

It was unspeakably cold, but Enli hadn't really noticed it until Faren reminded him. His soldiers handed him Eneas' shirt and mail, and Enli dressed in a fevered hurry, all the while looking at his dead, naked brother in the roadway, his body pricked with arrows and sliced open with a dagger wound. Eneas' clothes were warm and bloody. Enli could smell his brother's scent on them. One by one he fitted himself with the dead man's accoutrements, finishing off by buckling the sword belt around his waist. When he was done, he gestured disgustedly at Eneas' body.

"Take it away. And be quick. The ravens musn't see him."

Yory and Jace did as their duke directed, dragging Eneas unceremoniously into the woods. They would take him far away, far enough so that the ravens wouldn't smell his familiar odor or catch a glimpse of their former master. If they did, Enli knew, they might turn on him. These were intelligent monsters, hardly ravens at all anymore. They were creations. Like Lorla born in the war labs, they had become more than nature ever intended. The trick now was to control them. Faren and the others took up positions around Enli, nervously watching the sky. None of them knew if this elaborate scheme would work, or how long it would take if it did. Back in Gray Tower, Eneas' men were no doubt awaiting the return of their master. If Eneas didn't return soon, they would come looking for him, and in greater numbers. Enli shuddered a little. He didn't want to die here on the north fork.

Together they waited, then waited some more, until long minutes slipped by and Yory and Jace returned from the forest, slick with Eneas' blood. They looked puzzled by the absence of the birds but said nothing, merely joining their comrades in looking eastward. A cloud crossed the moon, blanketing them in darkness. Enli's heart sank. They might not come, he realized. But at least he had killed Eneas.

"Holy Mother . . ." drawled Faren. The soldier pointed at the moon. "Look at that!"

Enli looked skyward. Across the distance came a vaporous, black hand, a massive swarm of ravens, their beaks and feathers glistening in the moonlight. Enli's men fell back in terror, crossing themselves and muttering prayers to stay the evil horde. But Enli stood his ground, a smile spliting his face. He opened up his arms as if to embrace the heavens, and summoned the army of the air to him.

THIRTEEN

Against the Fearless

The *Prince of Liss* sailed full-winded against the white caps, her masts groaning as she tacked north by northwest along the coast of Nar. On the orders of her commander, she had left the rest of her escort behind, and was now just two days south of Nar City. Her escort ships, *Vindicator*, *Battle Axe*, and the others, waited for her off the coast of Casarhoon, one of the Empire's more southerly regions, to pirate what supplies they could from the ill-armed ships that sailed there. The *Prince of Liss* had gone north alone.

Fleet Commander Prakna waited in his quarters, worrying over charts as his flagship sailed again into the cold. *Gray Lady* had been gone for over a week, far longer than her patrol should have required, and Prakna was worried. On their long trek south they had seen almost no Naren ships, but the ocean was vast and any ships, even dreadnoughts, might have evaded them. They had sailed into southern waters to enjoy some sun, and Prakna himself had ordered *Gray Lady* back north to scout out the sea traffic around the Naren capital. That had been eight days ago. Captain Haggi was a careful sailor, and Prakna trusted him. Haggi was also a friend, and Prakna had wondered about the prudence of sending him north unescorted. But there had been no signs of trouble, and Haggi had agreed to the patrol willingly. Prakna brooded as he absently studied his charts and rutters. *Gray Lady* was a fine ship, but she was no match for imperial dreadnoughts.

This cat-and-mouse game they were playing with Nar had wearied Prakna. It was dangerous, and Prakna realized that their recent successes had made him cocky. As far as he knew, the Black Fleet still stood at anchor around Crote, protecting Biagio, and that meant easy sailing for the schooners of Liss. After sinking the slaver some weeks ago, Prakna had turned his attention south and launched a raid on the port town of Karva. He hadn't lost a single man in the conflict, an astounding accomplishment, and from there they had sailed on to Dahaar, where a convoy of merchant vessels were bringing their cargo to Nar City. These, too, had gone down under the rams of his ships. And all for the sake of luring the Black Fleet away from Crote. Now, as Prakna contemplated the fate of *Gray Lady*, he wondered if his plan had succeeded.

It was growing cold again but the afternoon was bright. Prakna worked to the sunlight streaming through his tiny window. On deck, Marus and the others were keeping watch for their missing comrades. The roof above Prakna's head creaked with the familiar sounds of shipboard life. Despite the foolhardiness of his plan to go after *Gray Lady* alone, his men had agreed to it willingly. Long days at sea had made them lean and irritable, but they were still the best crew Prakna had ever commanded, and they were loyal to a fault. If there was trouble up north, Prakna didn't want his entire fleet embroiled in it. Better that they should stay hidden around Casarhoon. Prakna was confident he could outrun any dreadnoughts they might encounter, provided he sighted them before they sighted the *Prince*. *Gray Lady* might not have been so lucky. It was one of the great tricks of warring against the dreadnoughts. Their long-range flame cannons could burn down a schooner's riggings with a single, well-placed shot. But they were ungainly beasts, these ships of Nar, not at all like the fleet-footed schooners of Liss. And Haggi was an accomplished captain. If he had encountered dreadnoughts, he would have known what to do.

Or so Prakna hoped.

Too fast, mused Prakna. Haggi always went too fast. If he had blundered into a dreadnought's path, he might not have had enough time to change course, to out-maneuver the ponderous devils. And all it would take was one lucky shot.

The fleet commander scolded himself for his lack of faith and shoved his charts aside, burying his tired eyes in his hands. Like the rest of his crew, he hadn't slept much the past two days. Sailing the coast required attention. They weren't in deep waters anymore, and anyone might see them. They needed to be alert, a razor's edge. But Prakna didn't feel very much like a razor. He felt dull, easily distracted. He heard a call from the deck above that hardly stirred him, but then it grew louder. Curious, Prakna lifted his head. Someone was racing down the gangway toward his quarters. There was a thundering at the door and Captain Marus poked his head in, not waiting to be invited.

"Prakna, it's the *Lady*," he said anxiously. His face was drawn with worry. "We've sighted her!"

Prakna sprang from his chair and headed for the door. "Where? Is she alone?"

"Not alone," said Marus. "Dreadnoughts."

"Damn it! How many?"

"Three, I think. They're far away yet; I couldn't tell. They're pursuing."

The two men climbed the gang ladder and emerged onto the deck. Prakna's lieutenants were shouting orders to the men. Cannoneers made ready on the guns, packing powder and loading grapeshot. Up in the crow's nest the lookouts were pointing north, dead ahead. Prakna buttoned up his jacket and looked past the prow. He could see the *Gray Lady* in the distance, pitching on the sea. A pack of dreadnoughts were steaming after her, their masts full of wind as they tried to flank the schooner and catch her in their gunnery range. Just behind *Gray Lady* was another ship, this one smaller than the dreadnoughts. Probably a cruiser. She was dogging the Lissen vessel, tacking parallel to her, keeping her toward shore. And behind them all, looming large against the horizon, was the giant of the pack, a black behemoth with square-rigging and a prow as big as a hillside. Prakna's jaw fell open at the sight of her.

"Oh, lord," he whispered. "The *Fearless* . . ."

"Prakna?" asked Marus. "Your orders?"

"Stay on course," said Prakna. "Get me closer. Shift all the cannons to the starboard side. We'll cover *Gray Lady*'s escape. Go, man. Quickly."

"Aye, sir," said Marus, snapping into action. He grabbed hold of a young ensign and started toward the cannons. The *Prince of Liss* had only four of the weapons, but they could easily be moved about on the upper deck of a ship, and that made them perfect for the schooners. Yet, because they weren't permanently secured to the deck, they were dangerous weapons to use. They were also small, with a much shorter range than the guns of the dreadnoughts. But when loaded with grapeshot they could pull down the rigging of a ship, crippling her. Marus and a group of sailors started hoisting the port cannons to the right-hand side of the *Prince*, fitting the barrels into the makeshift cradles. The guns were spaced far enough apart so that a concussion from one wouldn't send a spark flying to another. The cannoneers lit their fuse poles, readying to fire. They were far out of range still, but it wouldn't take long for the *Prince* to make up the distance.

Prakna went to the prow of his vessel, peering out over the sea. He was elated, even in his dread. The sight of the *Fearless* had buoyed his mood, causing an evil smile to stretch across his face. They had actually succeeded in luring the big bastard away from Crote, and he could scarcely believe the luck of it. But *Gray Lady* was in trouble. Lieutenant Vax rushed up to him with a spyglass, handing it to him. Vax was a young man, tall and lean. He was a good sailor but the appearance of the dreadnoughts had turned his face ashen.

"*Gray Lady*'s been hit," he said unsteadily. "Look."

Prakna put the spyglass to his eye. He could see *Gray Lady* sailing desperately toward them, her armored sides marked by cannon fire. Her stunsail had been torn to tatters and her front yards and rigging were ruined, pulled apart and blackened to ashes. She was limping, only barely quicker than the dreadnoughts now. The cruiser pursuing her was fast on her stern, still maneuvering to get alongside for a shot. Behind the cruiser were the two smaller dreadnoughts, sailing wide apart like a net, while the enormous *Fearless* kept its distance, unable to match even the damaged *Lady*'s speed. Prakna lowered the spyglass, collapsing it with a sigh. Doubtlessly the dreadnoughts had already seen the *Prince*. But they were too far away to be much of a threat. It was the cruiser Prakna was worried about.

"The cruiser's maneuvering to overtake *Gray Lady*," he told Vax. "Probably been trying for days. We're going to shake 'em loose. Full sails, Lieutenant. Bring us along starboard."

"Between them?" asked Vax incredulously.

"Right between them. We're going to cut them off. Make haste, boy. Do it now."

Vax nodded and passed the order down the line. The *Prince* lurched left, slicing to port as she pointed her prow between *Gray Lady* and the cruiser. If the *Prince* were quick enough, and Prakna knew she was, he could get in between them and open fire with the starboard cannons before the dreadnoughts got much closer.

"Let's make some noise, lads!" cried Prakna to his crew. "I want those bastards to know we're here!"

Admiral Danar Nicabar stood on the forecastle of the *Fearless*, laughing in disbelief. Two days out of Nar, and he had not only ensnared the Lissen schooner, but now another fish had entered his net, and this one was a prize indeed. The admiral rubbed his hands together, anticipating the coming battle. He had only seen the *Prince of Liss* once before, and only from a distance, but its flag and keel design were unmistakable. For two days Nicabar's ships had pursued the fleeing schooner, sure that it would lead them to others of its ilk. They had damaged her only slightly when they could have easily burned her to pieces, but Nicabar had held back the order to sink the Lissen vessel. Biagio wanted the Lissens to see the Black Fleet. And Nicabar, never one to question his count, had planned to let the schooner escape him. But not anymore. Now Prakna himself had seen the *Fearless* in Naren waters, and that meant Nicabar could quench his lust on the wounded, fleeing schooner.

"You're a brave and clever fool, Prakna," said Nicabar softly, studying the logistics playing out in front of him.

Prakna was moving in between the schooner and the *Relentless*. If he had cannons on the *Prince*, he would have shifted them starboard to fire on *Relentless*' rigging. Nicabar hoped Captain Carce had figured this out. Did Carce even recognize the *Prince*? Nicabar's brow furrowed with worry. The cruiser *Relentless* was quick, but not quick enough. The admiral looked to the right, toward the dreadnought *Notorious*. She was hanging back from the *Relentless* and flanking her. Prakna's course would take him straight toward *Notorious*.

"Captain Blasco," said Nicabar calmly. His second-in-command was at his shoulder, waiting for instructions. "Change course. Give me ten degrees starboard, toward *Notorious*. Let's make things more interesting for Prakna."

"Aye, sir," said Blasco, grinning. "Should we prime the flame cannons?"

Nicabar took a long time considering the question. He didn't want to sink the *Prince* or damage her too badly. She was to be their pawn, after all. She would tell the others about the Black Fleet. And Biagio would be proven correct—again. The admiral's smile grew. Maybe Herrith was right about Biagio. Maybe he was a devil.

"Yes," decided Nicabar at last. "Yes, prime the cannons. I want to bloody Prakna's nose a bit."

The *Prince of Liss* swept over the waves, devouring the distance between herself and *Gray Lady*. Prakna could see his sister ship clearer now, tacking wildly as she tried to out-maneuver the cruiser. Normally, the fast ships of Liss could out-pace Naren cruisers, but *Gray Lady*'s condition prevented her from gathering enough wind to escape. The two combatants seemed evenly matched now, neither any quicker than the other, and since she was out of range from her prey, the cruiser had stopped firing. *Gray Lady* had no doubt seen the *Prince* coming to her aid and had tried to keep as straight a course as possible so that the flagship could get between them. On the *Prince*'s starboard side, the four cannons had been readied, and the cannoneers watched as they approached the cruiser, ready to fire. The cruiser hadn't slowed, and no orders had flashed from the *Fearless*. But the big dreadnought had changed course to intercept the *Prince*, and Prakna fretted a little over his plan. They were already heading toward one of the smaller dreadnoughts, and Prakna had gambled that his vessel's superior maneuverability would keep them safe. But now the *Fearless* was bearing down on them too. It was either change course and let the *Gray Lady* die, or take their chances against the two dreadnoughts. Prakna cursed under his breath, just loud enough for Marus to hear him.

"Shall we change course?" asked the captain anxiously.

Prakna shook his head. "No. Not an inch."

"Sir, the *Fearless*—"

"I see her, Marus."

Marus said no more. He was not a coward, and Prakna knew his officer would do as ordered. So the *Prince* held its course, and in mere minutes was only leagues away from the two vessels. *Gray Lady* pulled hard to port to close the distance between her and the *Prince*. A giant wave slammed into the *Prince*'s prow, pitching her up like a surfacing whale. The pursuing cruiser stayed on course, perpendicular to the *Prince* as if to ram her. Prakna's four starboard cannons were almost in range, ready to shred the cruiser's rigging. Up in the far distance, the dreadnought on the left of the diamond formation had changed course to intercept the *Prince of Liss*, and the *Fearless* was grinding relentlessly toward them, her masts straining as the northern winds filled her sails.

"Get us closer," Prakna shouted to his pilot. "Closer!"

The short-range cannons needed to be close to be effective. The fuse poles of the cannons fizzled and popped eagerly, waiting for the chance to light the powder and launch the grapeshot. Prakna glanced over his shoulder toward the third dreadnought. She had changed course, too, and was eating up the distance to the damaged *Gray Lady*. The fleet commander's heart sank at the sight of the dreadnought. At her angle she would be able to reach *Gray Lady* and fire her flame cannons before Prakna could take out the cruiser. Prakna grit his teeth.

"Ready . . ." he shouted to the cannoneers.

The *Gray Lady* slipped behind them.

"Ready . . ."

The Naren cruiser was just ahead, nearly in range.

"Ready . . ."

The *Lady* was safe. The cruiser aimed amidships to the *Prince*, barely a league from ramming and refusing to change course. Prakna balled up a fist and screamed the order.

"Fire!"

All around him the deck erupted. One by one the cannons detonated, rocking the schooner. Red lightning shot from their muzzles as they expelled their barrels full of shot and shrapnel. The deck of the *Prince* filled with white smoke. Prakna squinted to see through the haze and watched as the cruiser's rigging suffered the barrage, wailing in torture as the hot metal of the cannons ravaged it. The cruiser churned onward, damaged but still on course. Prakna shouted to his pilot to steer hard to port to avoid the collision. The Lissen flagship bent to its new course, nearly pitching the sailors overboard as she groaned with effort. The cannoneers hurried to reload for another barrage, but the *Prince* was already past the cruiser and out of range. The cruiser skidded by, missing the *Prince* by mere yards, and as she passed, Prakna caught a glimpse of her ruined rigging, now in flames and coming apart at the yards. A victorious cheer went up from his men, but Prakna barely heard it. The *Fearless* and the other dreadnought were bearing down on them. Behind them, *Gray Lady*, who had so narrowly escaped the cruiser, was now being stalked by the third dreadnought.

The signalmen along the deck of the *Fearless* passed their admiral's orders to the other ships of the escort. To the *Notorious* they sent the order not to fire on the *Prince of Liss*. But their signal to the *Black City* was far more dire.

Sink the damaged schooner.

Admiral Nicabar had remained on the prow of his flagship and had watched as Prakna maneuvered the *Prince* between the *Relentless* and the fleeing Lissen schooner. He had even laughed when *Relentless*' rigging had been ruined, cursing Carce's stupidity at trying to ram the *Prince*. The *Relentless* was driving without sails now, and would have to limp back to Crote. But Prakna's bold move had come at a price. Now he was looking down the throat of both the *Fearless* and *Notorious*, passing between them in much the same way he had the two other ships. This time, however, *Notorious* was angled guns forward, and the *Fearless* herself was positioning to fire.

"Ten degrees left rudder," Nicabar called to his captain, who relayed the order to the pilot. At once the giant warship lurched left, positioning her starboard side toward the *Prince of Liss*. On the gun deck below, the starboard flame cannons hissed to life. The *Fearless* had a battery of six flame cannons on both the port and starboard sides, and any one of them could easily reach Prakna's vessel. One shot could put down a vessel's rigging, setting it aflame. Nicabar knew he needed to be cautious. He didn't want to cripple the *Prince of Liss*. He just wanted to teach his old enemy a lesson.

In just a few moments the *Fearless* was in position. The upper deck shook with the mechanical movement of the cannons on the gun deck below. While the flame cannons cranked into position, the *Notorious* made a bold turn to sail parallel to the *Prince*. The two dreadnoughts sailed a southeast heading. The *Prince* was heading northwest, directly between the two of them, but in the opposite direction. It looked like a foolish move, Nicabar knew, but it would give Prakna a much needed escape.

"He'll think me an idiot for this," sneered Nicabar. "I promise you, Prakna. I'll kill you another day." He turned to call over his shoulder. "Blasco, get ready to fire. And signal *Black City* again! What the hell are they waiting for?"

The *Prince of Liss* was at full speed. The wind cut into Prakna's face. A terrible exhilaration went through him as he watched the big silhouette of the *Fearless* grow ever larger. To port was the smaller dreadnought, its flame cannons bearing down on them, just out of range. To starboard loomed the *Fearless*, her own guns certainly in range but holding their fire. Prakna wondered why. Both dreadnoughts would be sailing past the *Prince*, and Prakna was dead in their crossfire, ready to be pommelled with fire. His mind skipped over the possibilities. His own starboard cannons were ready to fire again, but they were no match for the heavy armor of Nicabar's flagship, and so Prakna didn't bother giving the order to fire. The shots would have simply bounced off the *Fearless*' hull. He had no cannons to use against the smaller dreadnought to port but it wouldn't have mattered either. Like her big sister, the dreadnought was dressed to withstand such small attacks. Only a full-speed ramming could sink one of Nar's warships. Prakna took a deep breath of cold air and made his decision.

"Marus," he said quickly. "Left full rudder. Turn us against the small one."

"Left full rudder, aye, sir," shouted Marus. He called the order down to the pilot. At once the *Prince* moved to port, turning her shining metal ram toward the hull of the smaller dreadnought. A giant concussion ripped open the air. Prakna turned to look at the *Fearless*, afraid she had opened fire. But it wasn't the flagship that was firing. It was the third dreadnought, the one stalking *Gray Lady*. Far in the distance, the dreadnought's flame cannons exploded to life, sending streams of fire against *Gray Lady*'s already damaged hull. The guns sang out in unison, obscuring the dreadnought behind a wall of flame and black smoke, and in a moment the *Gray Lady* was engulfed in fire. The flames caught the wind and spread across her deck and rigging.

Prakna watched, horrified. The dreadnought's flame cannons detonated again. And again they blasted *Gray Lady*, scorching her hull and blowing apart her yardarms, until she was only a flaming hulk drifting across the ocean. The men on board the *Prince of Liss* fell mute.

"Attention, lads!" Prakna screamed at them. "Look alive!"

The sound of their commander's voice snapped the sailors from their stupor. Each of them braced for the ramming. The dreadnought was perpendicular to them now, growing ever closer but still refusing to fire. The *Fearless* opened fire instead.

To Prakna, it was the like end of the world. Only once before had he heard the Naren flagship's cannons, and then it had been from a great distance. This time, he was the target. The sky overhead ripped open with an orange blast, burning down the tops of his masts and incinerating the men in the crow's nest. Louder than an earthquake came the wave, searing off the flag and slicing through the high rigging. Another blast ripped past them to starboard and another one to port, and all at once the air turned rancid with the smell of burning kerosene. Prakna's eyes flooded with tears and the skin beneath his uniform cooked in the heat. The *Prince* roiled forward, toward the smaller dreadnought. The blasts from the *Fearless* dissipated, and Prakna knew suddenly why he was still alive. The *Fearless* couldn't fire directly at them for fear of striking her sister.

"Stay on course!" Prakna shouted to his crew. The other dreadnought was still not firing on them, probably for fear of striking the Naren flagship. The *Prince of Liss*, the top of her masts smoldering, churned toward her prey, her giant ram extended. Quickly the dreadnought changed course, steering hard away from the advancing schooner. Prakna cursed and shook his fist at them, but the dreadnought was just fast enough to avoid the *Prince*'s ram, scraping away from her. Behind the *Prince*, the *Fearless* was still sailing away in the opposite direction, almost out of gun angle and not maneuvering to re-acquire. The small dreadnought followed her big sister away from the *Prince*. Prakna gripped the railing, his knuckles white, his mind racing. Miraculously, they had escaped, and with enough sail intact to carry them away. Slowly, ponderously, the *Fearless* tried to turn its starboard guns against the *Prince*, but the schooner was already pulling away from them. The crewmen cheered at their escape, howling at the Naren vessels as they skirted away. But the burning hulk of the distant *Gray Lady* tempered their mirth. Already the three dreadnoughts were converging on her, and the little cruiser with the ruined rigging had managed to turn back toward the *Fearless*. *Gray Lady* burned in the center of them, helpless.

"Prakna?" asked Marus carefully. "Should we change course to help her?"

"Help her?" said Prakna gravely. "How? She's dead, Marus. Stay on course. Get us the hell out of here."

Dead. Haggi and the rest of them. As the *Prince* churned away from the melee, her flags torn away and two of her crewmen burned to husks, Prakna fell into a miserable silence. He watched in revulsion as the *Fearless* and her escort vessels closed the noose around *Gray Lady*'s neck. The Naren flagship turned cannon-side to the schooner. All along her burning decks, the men of the *Gray Lady* jumped overboard, abandoning their attempts to tame the flames engulfing their ship. With a thunderous boom, the *Fearless*' guns opened fire on the schooner, annihilating her.

She just blew apart. She was there and then she wasn't, and all that was left of the small schooner was a burning slick on the ocean and a collection of flotsam. The men of the *Prince* stared in disbelief. Prakna stared too, and was completely unable to speak—not even to Marus who was looking at him for support.

"Prakna?" asked the captain. "What now?"

Prakna held up a hand to silence his friend. Haggi had been a good man. A family man, like Prakna himself. When they returned to Liss, Prakna knew, he would have to tell Haggi's young wife that her husband was dead. But he wouldn't tell her that he had been destroyed so casually, or that his ship had simply evaporated. His memory deserved better than that.

"Sir," Marus pressed. "What course? Should we turn to warn the others?"

"We go south," declared Prakna. "We'll warn the others if we see them. If not we sail for Lucel-Lor, as fast as we can." The fleet commander smiled sadly at his captain. "She's out of Crote, Marus. Now we have to find Vantran."

FOURTEEN

The Ancient Oak

Richius Vantran was accustomed to the forest. He had grown up in Aramoor, a small nation famous for horses and huge, brooding fir trees. He had spent a lifetime in the woods, travelling with his kingly father and fishing along lakesides, and hunting when the deer were in season. Richius always welcomed the chance to be outside among the trees, to taste sweet air and expel the foul castle breath from his lungs. Like all Aramoorians, he was as much a woodsman as he was a soldier and, also as other Aramoorians, he vastly preferred the first profession. To be with nature and think on small things was what Richius liked best. And to be on horseback was the most sublime of all.

In Lucel-Lor, just as back home, the coming winter meant the need for firewood. The citadel of Falindar lay far to the north, and the ocean winds could be fierce. There were many hearths to fill in the grand palace, many hands and feet to warm. And the Triin of the citadel, more warriors than woodsmen, had gladly granted the responsibility to Richius. It had been days since Lucyler had left for Kes, and the castle on the hill was quieter than usual. Richius had idled the hours away with his wife and daughter, enjoying their company, yet still with his mind adrift. He worried about Lucyler. He worried about Simon. But most of all he worried about Aramoor and the armies of Talistan trampling his homeland. He needed to get home. He needed to know what was happening in Aramoor and with Biagio. Even with Dyana and

Shani and all the friends and warriors of Falindar around him, he was alone on an island, adrift and deaf, and he hated it.

And so it did not surprise Richius at all when he willingly agreed to help provide firewood for the citadel. It did not surprise Dyana either, who was glad to have her brooding husband occupied. What surprised them both, however, was Richius' choice of assistant. Chopping down trees and lugging back logs was heavy work and couldn't be done alone, and so Richius had selected Simon to help him. Richius liked Simon. He had made this startling admission to himself just hours after meeting the odd fellow. And Simon had been the perfect guest since. He was never underfoot and kept his promise to stay far away from Dyana and the baby. Instead of skulking the halls, Simon spent the bulk of his time in his chambers, alone, eating everything the kitchen would bring him. He and Richius spoke on occasion, and Simon's temperament had become somewhat less waspish. Most surprisingly of all, the Naren had been grateful for Richius' suggestion.

"It would be good to get out of the castle," Simon had told him. "For both of us."

So the next morning, Richius and Simon set out from Falindar, the oddest-looking pair the palace had ever seen. They were dressed in traditional Triin garb—not the blue jackets of warriors but the plain clothing of ordinary workers. Richius had left his prize sword behind, trading it for a toothy axe, a twin of which was carried by Simon. Lightning, Richius' mount, led the way down the long and winding hillside road, and Simon trotted along behind on a powerfully built gelding. Behind were a pair of mules, brawny gray beasts strong enough to haul the wagon they would soon be filling with logs. The wagon would hold two good-sized trees, a full day's labor, at least.

It was a good morning, clear of clouds. Richius' breath trailed out in puffs of steam. On the horizon, the rocky mountains of Tatterak loomed with austere permanence, and at their base was the emerald hue of the forest.

Richius relished the ride ahead. They kept their pace light and easy, not wanting to exhaust the mules, and before long they were in the confines of the forest. A narrow road wound through the woods, reaching toward Dring and the southern regions of Lucel-Lor. The path was empty today and quiet, and the birds that hadn't migrated to warmer climes chirped and whistled in the trees. The path was full of fallen leaves, collecting in pockets along the roadside where the wind had mindlessly shunted them.

Richius and Simon hardly spoke as they rode. Simon kept to the rear and attended the mules, who plodded along without complaint or interest in their surroundings. When they were well into the forest, Richius at last turned to speak to his companion.

"Beautiful, isn't it?" he asked. "The forest, I mean. Like home, sort of."

"It's very nice," said Simon dryly. "Cold, but nice."

"Oh, this isn't cold, Simon. It's going to get a lot colder before long."

"Then we'd better stop sightseeing and get our wood, shouldn't we?" The Naren looked around with an unseasoned eye. "This looks like as good a place as any to start chopping some trees."

Richius shook his head. "No. A little farther. Let's explore the forest a bit more. Personally, I'm glad to be away from the citadel. The longer we're gone the better. And we're not going to get it all done in a day."

Simon raised a questioning eyebrow. "You don't think much of the place, do you, Vantran? I can tell."

"That's because it's not really home. Not my home, anyway. And not Dyana's either. I don't think any of us belong in Falindar. Not even Lucyler." Richius shrugged, resigned to his fate. "But it looks like we're stuck with it. Come on. Not much farther."

Simon agreed, not caring where they found their firewood. He followed Richius apathetically, like some sort of older brother, and trotted along without speaking as Richius spied the forest. But Richius felt Simon's eyes on his back, always watching. It was an uncomplicated stare, without malice, and Richius had given up trying to decipher it. Since bringing Simon to Falindar, he had decided to accept Simon's story—mainly because Simon hadn't given him cause to doubt it—and the older Naren's strange ways were becoming predictable. It had been a long time since Richius had lived among his own kind; he had almost forgotten how pensive they could be.

They travelled for another mile and more, until at last the elms and birch trees thinned and fell away, and they were in a grove of oak trees. The giants of the forest reached high into the autumn sky, dominating the world with their height and their stout, rugged trunks. Richius smiled when he saw them. This was why he had ridden so deep.

"Here," he declared proudly. He reined his horse to a stop and dropped down to the ground, surveying their surroundings. The place was serene, like a dream. He unstrapped his axe from the saddle and turned his smile on Simon. "This is it. We'll find what we want here."

Simon slid nonchalantly off his own horse, plainly unimpressed. He took hold of his axe and strolled over to Richius. "Which one?" he asked.

"I don't know," said Richius. "Pick one."

"You're the woodsman, Vantran. They all look the same to me." He blew into his hands to emphasize his discomfort. "Frankly, I don't give a damn which one we cut down. As long as it keeps us warm."

"You'll get warm enough swinging that axe," Richius assured him. "Come on, your choice. But not too near the road. I don't want to block it." After tying off the horses and mules, Richius walked off the road and into the forest a little, bidding Simon to follow. The older man laughed a bit and shook his head, obviously amused with Richius' enthusiasm but polite enough not to insult him. Richius held his tongue, determined to get Simon involved. He wanted—he *needed*—a friend of his own bloodline, and Simon was the closest thing he had. Like it or not, Simon was going to pick a tree for them.

"That's a good one," Richius suggested, pointing out a hardy-looking oak not too close to other trees. "Enough distance to swing our axes. Big, too. What do you think?"

"Fine," agreed Simon quickly. "Whatever."

"Come on, Simon. Put some heart into it. What do you think? Really, I mean."

Simon looked at Richius squarely. "I think it's a tree. I think if we cut it into pieces it will burn. That's good enough for me."

Richius tried not to look hurt. Simon caught the little furrowing of his brow and sighed.

"I'm just not a woodsman, all right? I mean, hell, I only agreed to help you to get away from the castle for a while, breathe some clean air. So now we're out here, right? Let's just chop the thing down and be done with it."

"Fine," said Richius. He hefted up his axe and went toward the oak. Simon followed quietly after him. The dead leaves crunched beneath their boots, emphasizing the cool silence between them. Richius lifted his axe and made to strike, but Simon abruptly stopped him.

"Wait," said Simon. "Wait." He looked at the oak disdainfully, shaking his head. "Not this one. It's too . . ."

"What?"

Simon scoffed. "Too small. Yes, too small. This thing wouldn't keep us warm for a week."

"Too small? This tree is plenty big. Come on, Simon, quit playing games."

"It's too small, I tell you." Simon buried his axe head in the ground and folded his arms over his chest. "I won't chop this one. I want to pick one of my own."

"Lord almighty . . ."

"You said I could," snapped Simon. He retrieved his axe and tramped off deeper into the forest.

"How big do you want it?" Richius called after Simon.

"Big!" Simon laughed over his shoulder. "As big as Falindar. Bigger!"

"Oh, yes? And who's going to cut it down? You and I? Alone?"

"I'm not as feeble as you think I am, Vantran. I'll show you how to cut down a tree!"

Richius laughed, caught up in the folly. Behind them, Lightning and the other animals had disappeared from view but Richius gave little heed. For the first time in months, he was actually enjoying himself. Simon stopped at several trees, looking each of them up and down before dismissing them with feigned disgust.

"Bring me a giant!" he called dramatically, wringing his axe in both hands. And then suddenly Simon stopped walking, and his eyes lifted toward the heavens. Before them, blocking out the sun and the sky beyond, was the widest, tallest, greatest oak tree ever, a behemoth that made all the others in the forest shrink like dwarves. Older than the mountains, older it seemed than earth herself, the ancient oak stood before them, a perfect specimen of untouched time.

"That one," Simon whispered, thunderstruck.

"That one?" asked Richius incredulously. "Are you insane? We can't chop that thing down alone. It would take the two of us all day. Lord, it's bigger around the middle than Aramoor."

Simon was resolute. "That one," he said again. "Oh, yes. No doubt about it. That's the bastard I want."

"Simon, be reasonable. We've only got one wagon."

"We can come back for the rest," argued Simon. He did not take his eyes from the tree or raise his voice an octave. He was entranced. And something more. An unhealthy spark played in his eyes. Now when he wrung the axe handle he did so slowly, absently, studying the quarry before him. Richius let out a loud, exasperated breath.

"It's too old," he said. "I don't think we should cut it down. Look how beautiful it is. It's probably been here for centuries."

Simon nodded darkly. "Yes. Centuries."

"We should let it be, show it some respect."

"No. I won't. It *is* too old. Too damn old." He pointed his axe at it accusingly. "Look at it. It should have been dead decades ago, but it's a cheat. It's stealing life it has no right to anymore, like some piggish Naren lord."

Richius felt profoundly sad. "I think it's very beautiful," he said. "I don't want to chop it down."

"Beautiful?" chuckled Simon. "On the surface, maybe. But not deep down beneath the skin. No. It's lived too bloody long to be anything but a graceless pig. You said I could pick the tree. Well I pick this old wretch. Help if you want. Or don't. Whatever."

And without another word Simon swung his axe against the ancient oak, slamming the blade into its bark and slicing a deep wound. He took another blow and then another, and soon the chips were flying out of the enormous trunk, little dents in a suit of armor ten feet wide. Richius watched Simon work, wondering at the hatred that had so suddenly engulfed him. Simon kept swinging his axe without pause. Finally, inexplicably, Richius took up position on the other side of the great tree trunk and began hacking away at it. Simon stopped. His eyes lifted to look at Richius, and a smile crossed his lips. He waited for Richius to complete his swing before swinging his own axe again, and within two strokes they had the rhythm—Richius then Simon then Richius then Simon, and slowly, very slowly, they chipped away at the ancient oak.

It was a monumental task. Within minutes Richius' forehead beaded with sweat. Simon was already breathing hard. But they shared encouraging glances as they fought against the stubborn bark and stony flesh, grunting as they pushed their muscles to the maximum. They worked for an hour or more, and when they had finally cleaved a deep crevice in the trunk, Simon held up a hand in surrender.

"God, I'm tired," he wheezed, laughing. He leaned against his axe, his face and shirt doused with sweat. They had only dug a fraction into the massive tree, and had many more hours of work ahead of them.

"You're sure this was a good idea?" quipped Richius. He, too, was exhausted.

Simon nodded angrily. "Very sure. Water." He pointed weakly toward the roadway in the distance. "We should have brought some water."

"I'll get it," said Richius. He dropped his axe and made his way back to where they had left their horses. The water skins they had brought with them were fat and cool. Richius retrieved them, along with the food they had brought along. He was more than just thirsty. The hard work had famished him. And there was still so much more to do. First they had to fell the big tree, then start chopping it, then drag the pieces into the wagon. Richius cursed a little under his breath, berating himself for letting Simon choose the tree. But then he remembered the Naren's determined glare and the violent way he swung his axe, and he decided that he was glad Simon had chosen the tree. Whatever anger he was feeling was being directed straight through his axe and into the old oak, and it was like they were truly countrymen, maybe even friends.

Richius hurried back with the water and food. He found Simon back at work, hacking at the tree trunk. He waved to the older man to stop, holding up the water skin. Simon dropped his axe gratefully and took the water, drinking down a healthy swig and wiping his mouth on his sleeve.

"That's good," he sighed. "Thanks. What's that? Food?"

"My wife packed some for us. Hungry?"

"Always." Simon grinned. He cast a look at the tree. "But we've got a lot of work to do. Maybe we should wait."

Richius sat down cross-legged on the ground and began rummaging through the pack. "You can wait if you like. I'll just sit here and watch you work. All right?"

"Not hardly," said Simon, dropping his axe. He craned his neck to peek inside the pack. "What've you got in there?"

Richius started pulling food out of the package. Two rounds of flat-bread, some vegetables, some dried meat, fruit shaped like apples. It was all Triin food, but Richius had long since grown accustomed to it, and Simon, who would seemingly eat anything, sat down greedily in front of the feast. He snatched up one of the fruits and took a deep bite of it, sighing with satisfaction at the taste.

"What is this?" he asked. "It's good."

"The Triin call that a *shibo*," said Richius. "A love fruit. It comes from a tree that grows not far from here. They harvest them in the autumn like apples."

Simon pulled his dagger out of his belt and began slicing off pieces of the fruit. He offered one of the slices to Richius. This was the time of year for the shibo. Richius tore off a hunk of the Triin bread and gave it to Simon. The Naren put it up to his nose and took a whiff. His nostrils were still swollen, but he could smell it.

"Lord, it's bloody good to see food again," he said. "And so much of it. I don't know why you're not contented here, Vantran. A man could do worse for himself."

"I suppose," Richius shrugged. "But life is more than food, you know. Sometimes a man needs different things besides a solid roof and full stomach." He raised his eyes to examine Simon's reaction. "Don't you think?"

"A man needs precious little," said Simon. "You're royalty. You don't know what it's like to have nothing. I do. And when I eat good bread, I think I taste more than you do. You're used to having everything handed to you, aren't you? No insult, really. It's just the truth. Am I right?"

"You're wrong. When I fought in the Dring Valley we had nothing, not even provisions from the Empire. And I never wanted to be made a king, either. That happened when my father died and I had no say in it. And no one gave me Dyana or Shani. I had to fight to get them back. My exile from Nar is the price I paid. I lost Aramoor in the bargain. So don't go thinking I have so much, Simon, because I don't. Not anymore."

Simon was unimpressed. Deliberately, he cut another section of fruit with his dagger, sliding it off the blade and onto his tongue. There was a sly smile on his face as he chewed. "You want to trade sad stories, Jackal? I don't recommend it. You'd lose."

"Maybe. But I don't want you getting ideas about me. Whatever you learned about me in Nar or from Blackwood Gayle is false. I'm not some spoiled brat-prince. I fought hard here in Lucel-Lor. I saw my share of horrors. And I lost friends. Don't make me defend their memories, Simon. *You'd* lose."

Simon held up a hand in mock surrender. "All right. Like I said, no offense. But you go moping around the castle like the weight of the world is on your shoulders."

"You have no idea," said Richius softly.

"Maybe not. Why don't you tell me?"

"No thanks. It's a bit personal."

"We might be together a long time," said Simon. "I've already told you some things about me, why I deserted. It's your turn now."

"It's not a game we're playing, Simon. I don't have to tell you anything."

Simon grinned. "You know what I see when I look at you, Vantran?"

"What?"

Simon leaned back, making himself comfortable. "You're really tired of living with the Triin. I can tell. You want to be back in Nar, with your own kind. And you can't stop wondering what's going on back in Aramoor, can you? I know because I have the same kind of thoughts. I wonder what's going on in the Empire too, especially back in Doria. But I left it behind. You haven't. You won't."

"I can't," Richius corrected. "You're not the king of Doria, Simon. You didn't leave folks behind to get slaughtered."

The most probing light came on in Simon's eyes. "Did you?"

It was a horrible question. Richius turned from it, staring at the ground and his half-eaten bread.

"Yes," he whispered. "I left my wife behind. You already know that. Blackwood Gayle killed her. Gayle and Biagio." He closed his eyes and her face came into his mind. "Her name was Sabrina."

"She was very beautiful," said Simon. "All of us who served with Gayle had heard that. It was barbaric what he did to her. I'm very sorry for you."

"Gayle did the killing. Now he's dead. And by my hand, thank God. But not that other devil, Biagio. He was the one who gave the order. He and Arkus both handed Aramoor over to Talistan." Richius looked up at Simon and found that the older man was staring at him, his face full of sorrow. "And I can't live with that. That's what you see when you look at me, Simon. It's not sadness. It's revenge."

"Like I said, I'm sorry for you," said Simon. Oddly, he glanced at the tree. "Revenge is a horrible thing. It consumes men. And it will consume you if you let it."

"It already has," said Richius. "I can think of nothing else but going after Biagio. And then Aramoor. I've vowed to free it someday, to make it my own again."

Simon let out a mocking chuckle. "That's a big boast, boy. You should be careful what you vow. Make them small so you won't die with them still on your head."

"I will do it," said Richius seriously. "I know it sounds impossible, but I will. Someday." He shrugged. "Somehow."

"You'll go to your grave with that one," Simon promised. "You don't know what you're trying to fight. You ever been to Nar?"

"I was made king there," said Richius. "I met the emperor."

"Did you? Well then you should have the common sense to figure out what you're up against. Nar isn't just an army or a nation. Nar isn't even the legions. It's a way of life. That's what the Black Renaissance is, Vantran. It's like a living thing. And no one can stop it. Especially not you." Simon's face grew dark. "One man just can't make that kind of difference."

"They brainwash you legionnaires. They make you think you're nothing without them. But you're wrong. One man *can* make a difference. I've proven that already. And I'm going to keep being a thorn in the Empire's side, and I'm going to free Aramoor someday. You just watch me."

"One man is like a dead leaf against Nar, Vantran. You're just too young and naive to see that. Maybe someday you'll understand."

It was a lost argument, Richius knew, so he merely tore off another piece of bread and stuffed it in his mouth, washing it down with a gulp from the water skin. He noticed then that Simon had stopped eating. The Naren stared pensively at the tree, at the giant gash in the oak's trunk, and his eyes were distant, as if he were looking through the thing to something invisible beyond.

"Simon?" Richius asked. "Eat."

Simon got up. He walked over to where he had left his axe and retrieved the tool, glancing between its sharp head and the exposed belly of the tree.

"You go ahead and eat," he said. "I've got a tree to chop down."

FIFTEEN

The Orphan

They were called the hills of Locwala, and they were splendid. Tall and green, lush and quiet, they were legendary throughout the Empire, not only for their verdancy and their peaceful music, but also because they hid the greatest city ever constructed. It was not possible to reach the capital of the Empire without first crossing the hills of Locwala, unless you were a sea traveller and could pay the exorbitant sums to hire a ship. All others who made the pilgrimage to Nar City—the Black City—did so by crossing Locwala. And they did so at their peril, for no one could see the hills without being changed forever.

The hills of Locwala were paradise. They were what the artists and laureates of Nar called its most splendid place, an oasis of nature left untouched by the metal city just beyond. In the hills of Locwala, one could barely detect the acrid stench of the capital or hear the drone of the foundries as they smelted copper and iron. It was a perfect place, unpolluted, made so by decree of Nar's last emperor, the one who called himself "Arkus the Great." He was an emperor with a fondness for roses and a voracious appetite for beauty, and though he had loved the mechanical behemoth he had built on the shores of the Dhoon Sea, he had been a pragmatic man, too, and knew that the Naren nobles who dwelt in the Black City would grow tired of the towers and the beggars in the streets and would long for a place of clean air and tall trees. The hills of Locwala had been untouched for generations, and to cut down one of its trees or improperly dispose of something on its roads was still a crime, punishable by death. Even Archbishop Herrith, de facto ruler of Nar in the wake of Arkus' death, upheld those laws. It was said that Herrith considered Locwala a sacred place, a place that God Himself had told Arkus to set aside, and no one in the Black City, faithful or loyalist, had a mind to question the decree. Locwala belonged to them all, and they were content just to know it existed.

Lorla reached out from the back of her pony and snatched a dried leaf from a branch. She knew all about the rules of Locwala, but didn't think a single leaf would matter. It was a dead leaf, anyway, like all the leaves this time of year, and it crackled in her hand, providing little entertainment. Locwala was beautiful, but she had been riding through it for a full day now and had grown tired of the hills and tree-lined avenues. Phantom, the pony she had ridden out of Goth, trotted quietly beneath her, following the caravan. Ahead of them, Enli sat sternly atop his black warhorse. He had grown very distant in the last weeks, and Lorla wasn't sure about him anymore. He was still kind to her in his own brusque way, but he hardly spoke at all anymore. Since leaving Dragon's Beak, Enli had changed. He was agitated now, distant and snappish with his men, the ones with the crossbows who stayed very close to him.

Lorla missed Dragon's Beak. She missed Nina and all the books and having a room of her own to sleep in. She missed exploring Red Tower and her brief friendship with the duke's daughter, but most of all she missed having some place—any place—to call home. It had been a long ride from Dragon's Beak. Enli had paid for inns and beds when they were available, and they had been well fed, but even the good roads to Nar were treacherous and tedious, and not at all restful for such a small girl. And that's exactly how Lorla saw herself these days—a small girl. Despite her nearly adult years, she was a child really, just a pawn in the game the Master was playing. Enli had already told her what to say and do when they reached Nar, and he had scolded her when she asked if she could see the war labs again.

"You are not to mention the war labs," he had insisted. "Forget what you know about them. You are Lorla Lon now, from Dragon's Beak. An orphan. Remember the Master, Lorla. He is depending on you."

They were all depending on her now, and it was like a great weight crushing her. Even Nina was depending on her. The duke's daughter had kissed her good-bye and hugged her, but not before warning her that she had to succeed. There was war in Dragon's Beak now. And the Master was counting on her.

The Master. Always the Master.

Lorla had never met Count Renato Biagio, but she had never had a truer father. It was his voice she heard when she wondered about herself, his decrees that rang in her head like church bells. She had been taught in the war labs that Biagio was the source of all knowledge and goodness, and that he loved her very much. It surprised Lorla that she loved Biagio as well. Or at least she supposed it was love she felt. Truly, she didn't know precisely what love felt like. But when she thought of the Master she felt fear and a kind of gratitude at having been made special according to his orders, and that was love, surely.

Duke Enli had only told her snippets about what was happening in Dragon's Beak, but Lorla had been able to guess the rest. It was a simple matter to put things together, and Nina's evasiveness had helped Lorla to fill the gaps. The duke hated his brother. The duke had soldiers all over his castle and grounds. And now they were travelling to Nar to ask the bishop's aid and to beg soldiers from the Black City. Whatever elaborate plan the Master had set into motion, Lorla knew Dragon's Beak would never be the same. The two forks were at war now. She had even overheard some of Enli's own men saying that Eneas was dead. She wondered if Enli felt sorry for his brother. But Enli was tight-lipped. He had given her Biagio's orders, and had volunteered no further information.

Lorla's expression soured as she rode. Enli's back was turned toward her, the way it always was now. She had tried to be a good houseguest, yet he had spurned her. It hurt her to wonder what he really thought of her. Still, she did not speak or try to get the duke's attention. That had always been a useless ploy. Duke Enli was lost in his own grim world. Even his men couldn't speak to him. He seemed remarkably sad.

Alone with only her pony for company, Lorla rode behind the rest of the column, studying the trees. Soon they would be in Nar City. It had been many, many months since she had left her room in the war labs to live in Goth. Lorla craned her neck to try and peer over the hills, but she could not even sense the first inkling of Nar's skyline.

Still, knowing it was there kept her going. She was eager to be off the road, and Duke Enli had told her that Herrith would pamper her. He was not going to be able to resist her, he had promised. The claim had made her uneasy. Was she so beautiful? Or had Biagio's servants in the labs created her especially for Herrith? Lorla trembled a little, afraid for herself. Herrith was said to be an insatiable monster. She wondered how young girls figured in his appetites.

At the end of the day, when the sun began to dip and the air grew cool, Duke Enli spoke the first words he had in hours, bringing his small caravan to a halt. It would be dark soon. Time to make camp. The duke helped his soldiers unload the provisions from the backs of the horses while others made a fire not far from the road, spying a clearing in which they could spend the night. Lorla, who was accustomed to the routine now, undid her own bed roll and laid it by the fire, then went into the forest to help gather sticks to keep the flame alive. Faren, the duke's aide, made them dinner and told off-color jokes as they ate. Faren was a simple man, and Lorla liked him. He was also dangerous and handsome and even a bit arrogant. But he was kind to her and generous with water and food, enough so that Lorla trusted sleeping near him. She never slept near the duke, for Enli kept to himself even at sleep time, never getting too near the others. That night the duke ate his supper alone, taking his tin plate with him and sitting under a dark and brooding tree, absently listening to the laughter of his men. Lorla stole glances at him as she ate, feeling sorry for him. How quickly he had lost the mirthful glint in his eyes that had been there when they'd met. Now his eyes were dead. He was dropping weight, too, hardly touching his food. And in the morning he was always the first to rise, glad to be free of his restless slumber. His men dared not whisper behind his back, but Lorla knew they sensed the change in him.

After eating, the men stayed around the fire and talked. Lorla remained with them, listening without speaking, wondering about the Black City and her new home with Herrith. Enli strolled off by himself and was missing for an hour before he returned. His face was ashen in the firelight. Lorla looked up at him through the smoke.

"Lorla," he said softly. "Come here."

Lorla did as the duke asked, getting up and wiping the dirt from her clothes. Faren and the others watched her go, then quickly resumed their conversation. The duke stretched out his hand for Lorla. It was big and cold and she took it warily.

"Walk with me," he said, pulling her away from the light. Lorla tried to smile but couldn't. They went to a dark place in a grove of birch trees. Enli paused and looked skyward toward the bloodred moon. His red beard and red lips glowed with lunar fire. He squeezed Lorla's hand tightly.

"Tomorrow we will reach the city," he said. "I will be giving you over to Herrith and we won't see each other anymore."

Lorla nodded. "I know."

"It's a very important thing you're doing. You must not forget that."

"I won't forget."

The duke smiled down at her. "I know you won't. It's true, everything I had heard about you. You are a very remarkable girl, Lorla. And now you're going to do a very remarkable thing. You may not understand everything the Master asks of you, but it's a great task you've been given. History will be made by what you do these next few weeks."

The weight of the statement weakened Lorla's knees. "I will do my best, Duke Enli. Thank you."

"You know what to do, then?"

"Yes," said Lorla. They had gone over it a dozen times. She was

Lorla Lon, an orphan from the war in Dragon's Beak. Duke Eneas had attacked them. Her parents had been killed by Eneas' men. And now she needed Herrith's help to survive. He would, if Enli's estimation was correct, be unable to resist her.

"How long until your birthday?" he drilled her.

"Two weeks."

"And the name of the street with the toymaker?"

"High Street," she answered. "On a corner near a candle shop."

Enli sighed. "Good." He let go of her hand slowly, letting it fall away, and stared up at the sky. "All you have to do is play your part," he continued. "Herrith will love you. Biagio is right. He knows the bishop better than any of us, and he has spies. Earn Herrith's confidence. Get him to take you to the toymaker. Biagio will do the rest."

"I will," Lorla promised.

"I believe you," said the duke. "Truly." He sighed again, and this time it was loud, almost painful to hear. He dropped to one knee in the dirt and took hold of Lorla's shoulders. His giant hands ensnared her like a python, but his touch was soft and gentle. "I want to tell you something," he said. "And I want you to listen carefully. It's something you deserve to hear."

Lorla braced herself. "Yes, Duke Enli?"

"I want you to hear the truth," said the duke. "My truth. I want you to listen. Will you do that for me?"

"Of course," said Lorla. "You can tell me anything. I'm good with secrets."

"Yes, you are. Then listen well, because it will serve you. You need to know I killed my brother."

"I had guessed that," Lorla said. "You had reason, I'm sure."

"I had good reason," said Enli. "Or I thought I did. But what matters now is that Eneas is dead, and that I am fighting for Dragon's Beak. Biagio is helping me. But I won't be able to win this war if you don't help me, Lorla. If you fail, I'll lose Dragon's Beak and the war there will go on. Many people will die. Do you understand that?"

"No," Lorla answered honestly. "I don't understand anything. I never have. I just do what I'm told." She looked down to avoid the duke's eyes. "And I hate it. I hate being this thing I am. I hate being used by you and the Master. I'm . . ."

She stopped herself. How could she tell the duke she was lonely? He would laugh at her.

"What, Lorla?" asked the duke. "Tell me."

Lorla looked up at him. "Duke Enli, I will do what I am asked to do, because I want what is best for you and the Master. And because I can't do anything else. Something inside me stops me even from thinking of it." She felt emotion rising in her, tears threatening to burst. "I will go to Herrith and make him love me. If that's what the Master wants, I'll do it for him."

"Lorla, I promise you, this is more than something Biagio wants. And it's more than something I want. The Empire is depending on you."

Lorla nodded, hoping she wouldn't cry. "Yes. I know all this."

"Oh, child . . ."

"I am not a child!" she flared, yanking herself away from him. "I'm sixteen. Almost a woman."

"A woman in a child's body," the duke corrected. "You've been bred for this moment. It's like they told you in the war labs—you're something special." He reached out to stroke her fine hair. It was all the contact Lorla needed to start the tears flowing. "Don't forget that," sighed the duke. "Don't forget your mission or who you are. The Master needs you. Nar needs you."

"It's a lot," Lorla sniffled. "Maybe too much."

"Small shoulders, but strong," the duke joked with a smile. "I know you can do it."

"I'm afraid."

"That's all right," said Enli. His voice became a whisper. "To tell you the truth, I get frightened, too. It doesn't make us less brave, though. We do what we must." He brushed a strand of hair from her forehead. Lorla closed her eyes and took a deep, shaking breath. All the faces came flooding over her; Duke Lokken's gentle smile and the lips of his wife, Kareena. She thought of Goth, destroyed by Herrith, and of her new friend Nina, whom she missed like a long-gone sister. She wanted them all to be proud of her, even the ghosts.

"I will do what you and the Master have asked of me," she resolved. "I won't disappoint you, Duke Enli."

"I know you won't. I have great faith in you, as does your master." Duke Enli replaced his hands on her shoulders, firmly now so she couldn't pull away. "I haven't been a very good host to you. I'm sorry for that. You deserved better. But there are so many matters that plague me." He smiled weakly. "I will miss you, Lorla."

"You will?"

Enli nodded. "I'm not such an evil man, am I? Please tell me I'm not."

"You're not," laughed Lorla. "You do the Master's work. How can you be evil?"

Enli's face turned gray. His hands dropped from Lorla's shoulder, stopping to dangle deathly still at his sides. "Of course," he said blackly. "The Master's work . . ."

And then the night enveloped them as a cloud crossed the moon. "Herrith is a devil," said Enli as he contemplated the sky. "Remember that. No matter how kindly he acts toward you, remember what he is. That advice is the only protection I can give you."

"I will remember it," said Lorla. "Thank you."

She watched the duke pensively, and he did not seem to mind her stare or even notice it. He was lost in the stars above. Tomorrow they would go to Nar and she would meet this strange bishop at last, and if she could she would corrupt him and steal his heart away. But that was hours away yet, and the night and moon had conspired to attenuate time so that her mission seemed a lifetime away. Tonight, she would sleep and remember what she could of her old life. And in the morning, she would die and be reborn.

In the Cathedral of the Martyrs, in a high tower overlooking the city streets, Archbishop Herrith lay in his bed, unmoving, his eyes locked on the ceiling. Morning sunlight streamed through the big window, warming his satin sheets. A holy book lay open on his chest, unread, rising and falling slowly with the rhythm of his breathing. The archbishop gasped, straining to bring air into his lungs. At his bedside stood a tall and twisted apparatus of silver metal, a rack holding an upside-down bottle of blue liquid. From the bottle came a hose that snaked away from the rack toward the bed. The hose terminated in a shiny needle. The needle terminated in Herrith's arm.

The bishop kept very still as the liquid dripped into his vein. Occasionally he flexed his fist to coax it along. His eyes burned as if scalding water was flowing over them. His body felt torn, cleaved down the center as the potent mixture moved through his vessels. But even in his pain the Archbishop of Nar did not cry out. It was a glorious agony, easily endurable. And it was, very slowly, returning him to life.

Biagio's devilish gift had not been poison as Herrith had feared. It was what Nicabar had promised, a very potent distillation of Bovadin's drug. At Nicabar's warning Herrith had mixed the solution himself, diluting it with water into manageable dosages. It would be a weekly ritual now. Like it had been before he'd conquered the habit. But it was so delicious to be vital again. Herrith closed his eyes, hating himself. Biagio was a clever devil. In all the years they had served together under Arkus, Biagio had never once spoken openly against Herrith, even as the bishop whispered curses in the emperor's ear. But the hatred between the two of them had grown into a mighty thing. Herrith had thought he had gained the upper hand. Now, as he sat in his bed sampling the count's malevolent gift, he wasn't so certain.

But he had time. Time to think. And plan. The little bottle Nicabar had delivered wasn't a third empty yet. He could get more. Biagio was eager to talk. He would bargain with the beast, Herrith told himself. By the time the vial was empty, he would have more. If Biagio ever wanted to be part of Nar again, he would give up more of the precious drug.

"You're not the only one that's clever," Herrith hissed. "I can play, too."

It was a vast and dangerous game for Herrith. He wasn't a tactician or spy. But Herrith had lived a long time in the Black City and he knew the pulse of the place. He wasn't entirely without influence of his own. The bishop's lips twisted into a slight smile. The drug burned inside him. Yet he endured it, loving it, feeling the potion work its magic on his joints and teeth and muscles, tightening and strengthening them, making him young again and halting the march of time. Already his eyes had regained their brightness. When he looked in a mirror now he saw two azure gems staring back at him.

I'm strong, the bishop told himself. *Strong enough, and getting stronger.*

He would not lose Nar to Biagio. Not now, after all he had been through.

Slowly the drug dripped into the tube, making the long voyage to his bloodstream. Herrith opened his eyes to stare at the vial. It was almost empty. He shuddered, trying to control himself. Treatments like these could be insufferable, and he had only just recently started them again. His cravings were gone now and his appetite had returned with a vengeance. He could clear a table like an athlete and have room left for dessert. In old Nar, he had been famous for his girth, but the withdrawal had slimmed him. He was older now and not pretty, not like Biagio, but it was strength he needed to conquer the Black Renaissance, not beauty. Strength was flowing into him. Wicked vitality, created in a bottle by Bovadin.

Outside his window the sun was rising. Soon his skin would turn to ice again and he would yearn for sunlight like a flower. Along with the changing of his eyes his flesh would freeze and no man or woman would be able to endure his touch. Not that it mattered. It was the one great sacrifice he had made for Heaven, never to lie with another person. He was a man of yearnings, yet he was a powerhouse at keeping them chained, and though the pretty painted ladies of Nar quickened his pulse, he had a gift for squashing his desires. He did the work of the Lord. He cared for children in his orphanage and spread the Word. He didn't need the comfort of flesh, so weak and fleeting. In his youth, before he had heard the call of Heaven, he had prowled the city for women, sating his appetite with slave girls and whores, but God had rescued him from that. His body was clean now, undiseased. As was his mind.

Mostly.

He still thought of Goth, especially when the burn of the treatments was its deepest. And God still taunted him with half-answers. He thought of Kye, too, and the colonel's enormous grief, crushing him like an anvil. God's ways were meant to be a mystery. And the clues from Heaven had been so clear. Herrith knew with his heart that the work he did was necessary. But his conscience still screamed at him, so loudly sometimes that even the embrace of the narcotic could not silence it.

Almost done, he mused, watching the remains of the pale potion drain from the bottle. It would be another week or so before he needed another treatment. Bovadin had indeed mixed the drug strong. Herrith flexed his fingers. They seemed thicker than they had just days ago, more muscular.

A knock at the door startled Herrith out of his daydream. He held his breath, angered at the interruption. He was still in his bed clothes and always left strict orders not to be disturbed. If it was Vorto . . .

"What?" Herrith bellowed at the door. Very slowly the portal pushed open. Father Todos peeked his head into the bedchamber apologetically, trying to avert his eyes from the gruesome sight on the bed.

"Forgive me, Holiness," he stammered. "But . . . there are visitors."

"Visitors? So?"

"From Dragon's Beak, Holiness. Duke Enli. He says he must speak to you at once. He insisted—"

"Look at me, you fool! I'm in no condition for this!"

Todos stepped into the room and closed the door behind him. Herrith was astonished at his gall. The priest kept his head bowed as he explained himself.

"I'm sorry, Holiness, but Duke Enli is very insistent. He begs an audience with you immediately. There is war in his land."

The word *war* made Herrith sit up. "What do you mean?" he asked. "What war?"

Todos shrugged. "Holiness, I don't know. The duke says he will speak only to you. But it's very urgent."

Herrith sat back on his soft pillows, forcing himself to relax. War in Dragon's Beak had been brewing for years. That it should erupt now, when the Empire was in chaos, was hardly a surprise. And Enli and his brother had both been thorns in the emperor's side. Herrith always knew something catastrophic would happen between them.

"Whatever it is can wait until I'm done," he said. With his free hand he shooed Todos away. "Go and tell the duke I'm indisposed. I will see him as soon as I am able."

The priest frowned nervously. "How soon might that be? So that I may tell the duke, I mean."

"You are worse than a mother, Todos! Give me a few moments, please!"

"Yes, Holiness, forgive me. I will tell the duke to wait for you."

"Get out!"

The priest scurried from the room, closing the door behind him. Herrith laid in his bed and cursed.

It took Herrith less than half an hour to finish his treatment and regain his strength. By the close of the hour, he was fully dressed and ready to greet the Duke of Dragon's Beak. Father Todos met Herrith outside his chambers, telling the bishop that the duke was waiting for him down on the main floor of the cathedral, in one of the church's many offices. Todos eyed Herrith bleakly as he spoke, plainly astonished at the change in him. Herrith smiled and apologized to his friend. He felt invigorated, strangely buoyant. The remarkable drug had once again worked its mysteries on him.

Todos accompanied the bishop down the spire to the office where the duke was waiting. It was an elaborate room, bigger than necessary, with a typically oversized window and tiny sculptures of holy things arranged on shelves and bookcases. There was a desk in the office that Herrith hardly used and an assortment of austere chairs. The treacly smell of leather wafted from the office as Todos opened the door. The duke was standing anxiously in the center of the room, looking tired and haggard. He had no soldiers with him but he was not alone. Beside him, sitting with her legs dangling from the chair, was a bright-faced girl. Both of them turned their eyes on Herrith as he entered the office.

"Duke Enli," said Father Todos. "Archbishop Herrith."

Duke Enli went to his knees before the bishop, bowed his head deeply, then took Herrith's hand and placed a reverent kiss on his ring.

"Your Grace," he said softly. "Thank you for honoring me with your presence. I am your servant."

Herrith heard the words as if from a distance. His eyes were on the exquisite girl in the chair. She smiled at him but did not move from her seat.

"Rise, Duke Enli," said the bishop. "And sit. Please . . ." He gestured to one of the chairs near the desk. "You look exhausted."

"I am, Holiness," the duke admitted. He took a chair and seemed to fall into it. "Thank you."

"Todos, have you offered our guests anything to eat or drink?"

"Yes, Your Grace," said the priest.

"The Father has been very gracious, Holiness," explained the duke. "But I'm afraid my mind isn't on food. It's very urgent that I speak with you."

"And I am here, Duke," said the bishop. He went to his own chair behind the ornate desk, a giant seat of red velvet that looked more like a throne. "Todos, please leave us. I think the duke might be more comfortable speaking in private."

Ever compliant, Todos left. In his wake the duke took a deep breath and spread his hands out in surrender.

"Your Holiness, I beg your forgiveness for this intrusion. But I simply didn't know where else to turn. We've travelled all the way from Dragon's Beak to plead your help."

"I am listening, dear friend," said Herrith. "You have always been a loyal lord. You may ask anything of me. But first . . ." Herrith turned his attention toward the girl. "Please tell me who this beautiful child is."

"Her name is Lorla," said Enli. "Lorla Lon. She's from Dragon's Beak, the south fork. Her parents were killed in the attack."

"Attack?" asked Herrith.

"It's why I've come, Holiness. Dragon's Beak is at war with itself. My brother Eneas has attacked my southern fork. He flies the Black Flag." The duke turned a sad smile on the girl. "Lorla was orphaned in the fighting. I brought her here to you because I hoped you would help her. I know how generous you are to orphans. I thought you might help me find a place for her."

She was lovely, with platinum hair cut in bangs and bright eyes to rival Herrith's own, and the bishop took pains to smile at her carefully, not too boldly, not too weakly.

"Hello, Lorla," he said softly, as if speaking to a bird he didn't want to frighten. She smiled back at him, wonderfully shy.

"Hello, Your Holiness," she said, inclining her head.

"Are you well?" he asked. "You look tired."

"I am tired," said the girl. "Very." A look of sadness crossed her face. "And afraid."

"There's nothing for you to be afraid of here, I promise. No one is going to hurt you. This is the house of God. All are safe here."

"Don't be afraid, Lorla," echoed the duke. "His Holiness is a great and good man. He'll help you." Enli turned to the bishop. "Won't you, Your Grace?"

"Of course I will," beamed Herrith. "You're very pretty, Lorla. You remind me of an angel. And your eyes. They're almost as bright as my own!"

Lorla smiled demurely. "Thank you, Holiness."

The bishop leaned forward in his chair. "How old are you, child? Do you know?"

"I am eight," replied the girl. "Almost nine."

"That's a wonderful age," said Herrith. "We have many children in the orphanage your age. You can meet some of them if you like, make some new friends. Would you like that?"

Lorla glanced at Enli for support. The duke gave her a comforting nod.

"You can talk to the bishop, Lorla," said Enli. "I promise, he won't hurt you."

The girl considered the statement with care. She looked exhausted, confused. "I would like that, I suppose. I just want to have a place to stay."

"There's a place here for you, child, do not worry," Herrith promised. "We can take care of you. Are you hungry? We have food." He patted his burgeoning stomach merrily. "Plenty of it."

"I would like that," said Lorla. "If it's all right with Duke Enli." Again she looked at Enli. "Would that be all right, my lord? May I have something to eat?"

"Certainly," said Enli. "Don't wait for me. You go and eat."

"You'll find Father Todos out in the hall," said Herrith. "Tell him that you're hungry and want to rest. He'll find a room for you."

Lorla hopped out of the chair and went to the door. "I will," she said happily. Herrith's heart ached to see her, so starved and desperate-looking. War was most terrible on the children. The Black Renaissance had taught him that. The many wars of the Renaissance had orphaned thousands. It was why Herrith had started his orphanage. The bishop watched the child go, his eyes lingering on her as she closed the door.

"That's a remarkable child," he whispered, not really wanting Enli to hear him.

"Oh, yes," said the duke. "She's been through so much, yet she didn't complain the whole way here, not once. You do have a place for her, don't you, Holiness? I don't want to impose. I just thought—"

"Don't fret over the girl," said Herrith. "We'll find a place for her. But now tell me, Duke Enli, what is this bad news? War with your brother?"

"Aye, bad news indeed," said Enli. He put a hand to his forehead and rubbed, working the kinks out of his face. "It's black, Holiness. Dragon's Beak is divided, like I always feared. Eneas, my brother . . ."

"He attacked you?" coaxed the bishop.

Enli nodded. "He's sided with Biagio. He flies the Black Flag now. My own men have seen it over his castle. We were attacked without warning." The duke balled his hands into fists. "God curse me, I should have seen this coming. I knew when Arkus died Eneas would try something like this. Yet I did nothing!"

"Be easy," crooned Herrith. "And tell me everything that happened. When did your brother attack?"

"Oh, it must be weeks now. I don't even know what's going on back home. When we left, the battle was at a stalemate. Eneas' troops had gained some territory on the south fork, but my own men had kept them back. I don't know how long they'll last, though. The army of the air is voracious, Holiness. They keep us from fighting back." The duke's face grew earnest. "I'm afraid, Your Grace."

Herrith rose from his chair and walked around the desk. Enli's pain was like a magnet drawing him closer. He gazed down at the duke, trying to look resolute.

"Do not be frightened, my son. You fly the Light of God in Dragon's Beak, yes?"

"Yes, Holiness. Of course."

"Then God will protect you. Have faith."

"Holiness, I need more than faith. I need your help."

Enli started to rise, but Herrith held up a hand, stopping him. "Sit, Duke Enli. You need rest. Tell me what you want of me."

"We need troops in Dragon's Beak, Holiness. To fight back my brother. We need the legions to come and help us. Like in Goth."

Herrith froze. "Goth? What do you know of Goth?"

"I know that you crushed the Black Renaissance there," said Enli, blanching. "I'm sorry, Holiness. I thought it was common knowledge. I meant no disrespect. . . ."

"There is none taken, my son," said Herrith. He hadn't expected news of Goth to have travelled so quickly. "It's true. We did subdue the Renaissance in Goth. A horrible price, but necessary."

"Yes," said Enli. "And you can help me do the same. Please, I beg you. Send General Vorto and his men back to Dragon's Beak with me. If Eneas sees them he might even surrender. But it must be done quickly, before we lose the southern fork."

Herrith leaned back against his desk, thinking on what Enli had said. It was a bold request. Dragon's Beak was very far, and not particularly important. It would take weeks for Vorto to march a legion there. Worse, winter was coming—not the best time of year to fight a war. The bishop mulled the request over. Enli watched him. He was a good man, this duke. Despite his reputation as an independent thinker, he had been loyal to Arkus and the old Empire, and when the old man had died he had refused to side with Biagio, choosing the Light of God instead. A man of high ideals. Very rare these days.

"What you ask is difficult," said Herrith. "If Vorto gets to Dragon's Beak and finds that Eneas has already taken over, it could be another massacre. I don't mind telling you that I don't crave another one of those on my conscience."

"But we on the south fork are loyal," the duke implored. "We're faithful to you and the new order. Holiness, you can't let Dragon's Beak fall to the Black Renaissance. I don't ask this for myself, but for Nar. Dragon's Beak is only the beginning. Where will it end?"

Where indeed? wondered Herrith grimly. Enli was dramatic, but correct. Biagio could never be allowed to regain a foothold in Nar. It was why Herrith had ordered Goth destroyed, why he had let Formula B escape the war labs. God was testing him, he decided. He would not fail.

"I will consider what you've told me, Duke Enli. Be at ease. God will direct me to the proper action. And I will confer with General Vorto. He is the military man, after all. Much will depend on what he says."

"With respect, Holiness, there isn't time for this. We've got to—"

"There is always time for prayer, Duke Enli. We must make time for God." Herrith stretched out his hand for the duke. Enli took it, but didn't hide his disappointment. Reluctantly, he let Herrith help him out of the chair, flinching a little at the frigid touch. "Go and find Father Todos. He will give you food and drink and a place to sleep. Have you brought men with you?"

"Yes, Holiness. The Father has already seen to their needs."

"Good, then. Don't be afraid, my son. God will guide us toward the right decision."

Enli bowed deeply and left the chamber. The door closed quietly behind him, leaving Herrith alone.

Biagio.

Truly, he was hell-spawn. Even from Crote he weaved his little webs, hoping to ensnare the Empire and drag it back into darkness. It was up to men like Herrith to bring light to the world. Herrith crossed the room and went to the window, looking down over the city. The sun had climbed higher and was pouring through the glass, warming his frigid skin. He could see with awesome clarity now, picking up every fleck of dust floating above the city, every wisp of smoke from the foundries. Across the river, the abandoned Black Palace stood on its hilltop, dwarfing the landscape beneath it. Inside its empty chambers stood the iron throne, vacant seat of the dead emperor. The thought of Biagio on that throne made Herrith's insides twist.

"Never," he hissed. "Not while there is breath in me."

And then his thoughts shifted to the little girl, Lorla. She was a precious jewel, almost crushed by the weight of war. Herrith's hard expression softened. Poor thing. Sometimes the world was unimaginably cruel.

Lorla stood alone in the room, sipping on a glass of fruit juice and staring out over the enormous city. She was very high up, higher by far than she had ever been in the Red Tower, and the great expanse of Nar made her feel like a bird floating across the world. Father Todos had brought her here to rest and take some food. There was a bed in the chamber, soft and comfortable, with clean white sheets and plush pillows that swallowed Lorla's head when she tested them. The gigantic breakfast that Father Todos had fetched for her sat half-eaten on a tray near the bed. It was more than enough for two, and Lorla had eaten her fill. Outside the thick glass, Nar was entrancing. She hadn't remembered it being so vast or frightening, but then she had only seen glimpses of it through the tiny, dingy windows of the war labs. Now, high in the cathedral, she could see it all, and she knew why it was called "Nar the Magnificent." She felt weightless, bodiless, as if she were not tethered to the earth at all.

Faren and the others were nowhere to be seen, but Lorla wasn't worried about them. She knew she wouldn't be seeing them anymore. Her new life was here in Nar. Nina, Duke Enli, her memories of Goth; they would all have to be forgotten. She was Lorla Lon, now. An orphan. Lorla smiled to herself. She could play that part easily. What was she but an orphan, anyway? She had no mother or father. The only parent she knew remotely was Biagio, and he was more like a ghost or a fairy tale, no more tangible than air. She supposed she might see Duke Enli again before he left, but even that didn't concern her. It was time to cut those ties. Time to become something truly different.

Lorla Lon had a mother named Nefri and a father named Po, she told herself. *She is eight years old going on nine. Her birthday is in two weeks. She wants a doll's house for her birthday, one that looks just like the cathedral. There's a toymaker on High Street that can make her one. And if she doesn't get it, she will cry.*

The game made Lorla grin. Why was she so good at it? She had learned a lot in the labs, more than she had realized, and it surprised her. It would surprise Herrith, too. Lorla frowned, a bit ashamed of herself. Other children learned it was wrong to lie. She knew that because she had seen mothers in Goth with their children, scolding them. But no one ever scolded Lorla. Was it because she was perfect?

Or just something special?

There was a gentle knock on the door. Lorla looked around sheepishly. "Hello?" she called.

The door creaked open and Archbishop Herrith appeared, smiling at her. "Lorla?" he asked cheerfully. "May I come in?"

"Yes," said Lorla. She thought of getting up to greet him, but didn't. The bishop slipped through the door and came in to stand over her, inspecting her breakfast tray.

"Well, you certainly were hungry," he joked. "Was everything all right?"

"Yes, sir," she replied. "Very good, Your Holiness."

The bishop smiled. "You'll like it here, I think. It's safe. I want you to believe that. Nothing is going to happen to you. We've got a whole army to protect you."

"I'm not afraid, Holiness," said Lorla. She returned his smile as warmly as she could. "Not anymore." She looked around. "This is a nice room. Are the rooms in the orphanage like this one?"

Herrith grimaced. "No, not really. But they're clean and we have good people to look after the children. They do God's work. We have many children to look after. Too many, I'm sad to say. There's been a lot of war in the Empire."

"Where is the orphanage? Can I see it from the window?"

"No, I don't think so," said the bishop. "It's on the other side of the cathedral. But I don't want you to think about the orphanage, Lorla." He walked around the table and sat down beside her on the bed, leaving barely an inch between them. "You like this room, eh?"

"Oh, yes," Lorla answered honestly. She had never seen a view so grand. "It's very nice."

"I'm glad," said Herrith. He picked up a piece of fruit and rolled it around in his hand. "You can stay here if you like. You don't have to go to the orphanage. I'm not sure that would be right for you."

"Stay here? In this room?"

"It's up to you, of course. My orphanage is nice too, and there are others your age there. But then you wouldn't have this lovely view or a private place to sleep."

Lorla felt afraid but tried not to look it. Herrith certainly moved quickly. She studied his tone, but to her surprise detected nothing but sincerity. The bishop was looking at her, his blue eyes sparkling. Her mind raced for an answer. Instead she asked a question.

"Why? I mean, why give this to me, Holiness?"

Archbishop Herrith put the apple back down on the table. Lorla could tell he was deciding how best to answer. Finally he shrugged and let out a pensive sigh.

"Lorla, I'm going to tell you something that might surprise you. I'm a very lonely old man. I've given my life to God. Do you know what that means?"

"Not really," she replied.

"Priests aren't allowed to marry or take a woman. That means they can have no families of their own, save the church. We can't have children." Herrith seemed embarrassed by this confession. "I love the church very much. I love Nar. But I get lonely sometimes. I suppose that's why I started the orphanage, so that I could be around children. I've always wanted a daughter or son of my own. I . . ."

He stopped himself, suddenly flushing. "Oh, but I'm frightening you. Forgive me." He rose from the bed and went to the door. "Stay here as long as you like. Spend the night and get some rest. In the morning we can talk, or Father Todos can take you to the orphanage."

Lorla knew she had to stop him. "Wait, please . . ."

He paused in the threshold. "Yes?"

"I . . . I don't want to be alone. I'm afraid. Would you stay with me awhile?"

Even as she spoke she was ashamed of herself, and the expression on the old man's face made her hate herself all the more. Herrith's eyes leapt with inner glee at her invitation.

"We can be lonely together," he said with a smile. "If you would like."

"I would like that," said Lorla. Amazingly, she meant it. She jumped off the bed and went to him. *This is a man of guile and great deceit,* she tried to remind herself. He was the Master's enemy, and the Master always knew best. Still, he was kind to her—the sort of kindness a father might have shown—and Lorla could barely help herself from responding to his gentle voice.

"Show me more of this place," she implored. "Would you?"

"Oh, child, I would love to," beamed the bishop. "This is a magical place. It's my home." He snapped his fingers excitedly. "Yes! I will show you something wonderful!" He put out his hand for her. "Come, there's something very special for you to see."

Lorla took his hand without hesitation. It was as large as Duke Enli's, but softer, almost cottony. It was also unbearably cold. Lorla gasped and pulled away.

"I'm sorry," said the bishop. He looked down at his hand disgustedly. "It's nothing. Just some treatments I take for some ailments. Forgive me." He opened the door. "Please . . ."

Together they stepped out into the splendid corridor. Lorla let the bishop lead her through the painted hall, all gilded with gold and utterly magnificent. The ceilings were high and frescoed, and everywhere angels watched them, staring down with marble eyes. Tall sconces of silver hung on the walls, and the polished floor beneath them echoed every footfall, bouncing them off the high ceilings like a concert hall. Lorla struggled to see every fabulous nuance, determined to miss nothing. In all her life, she had never seen anything to compare to this holy place.

"Where are we going?" she asked.

"You'll see. Trust me. It's something beautiful."

Everything in the place was beautiful. As they hurried down the hall Lorla kept her eyes on the windows and their fabulous stained-glass depictions. The sun was coming through them, dazzling, its rays setting the colored glass on fire. At the end of the hall they came to a staircase that spiraled endlessly downward. Herrith took the stairs like a man half his age, almost running in anticipation. Lorla wanted to laugh at the sight of him. She raced after him, keeping pace, until at last they reached the bottom of the staircase. Herrith finally stopped and looked at her.

"Shhh," he directed, putting a finger to his lips. "We're almost there."

"Where?" Lorla whispered.

"Almost there," Herrith teased. "Yes, yes . . ."

The bishop turned and strode down the hallway. Lorla followed. It was a quiet part of the great cathedral, and though she could hear voices far away, there was no one else in the hall. The corridor was wide and graceful, with a rounded ceiling trimmed with delicate plaster work. Up ahead was an archway leading to a dim chamber. As they approached it, Herrith's gait slowed.

"The great hall," he whispered. "This is what I want to show you."

They crossed under the arch and entered the great hall. Throughout the chamber, pots of paint and soiled brushes littered the floor, and canvas had been laid on the marble tiles, adorned with colorful footprints. The great hall was a fountain of light, fed by banks of stained-glass windows that tossed radiant sunshine into the chamber. Lorla looked around, baffled by it all. But when she glanced at the bishop for guidance, he merely grinned and pointed at the ceiling.

"Look up," he said softly.

Lorla looked. What she saw astonished her. Above her was a masterwork, a rolling fresco of color, meticulously painted into the plaster of the ceiling a hundred feet up. There were scaffolds and ladders along the walls, reaching up to touch the top, and all along the roof danced painted cherubs with wide cheeks and red-tongued devils, maidens and heroes and beautiful gods, all entwined in an endless waltz that looked to Lorla like the canvas of Heaven. She gasped, unable to speak for the beauty of it. It was alive, unimaginably bright, and the sight of it took her breath away.

"What is it?" asked Lorla. "It's beautiful."

"The book of Creation," whispered Herrith. "All told in paintings." He directed her view toward a panel on the north side. "See? That's the betrayal of Adan. And that one is the murder of Kian. Do you recognize them?"

"No," said Lorla. "But they are beautiful. Oh, so beautiful . . ."

"I will teach you these things, Lorla," said Herrith softly. "A child should know about the holy book. It's all up there, the whole story." His face split with a proud smile. "The artist Darago has worked years on this. Now it's almost done. When it is I will open this hall to the people again, and everyone will see the glory of God." He knelt down beside her. "This is my greatest gift to Nar. And I wanted you to see it, Lorla. This ceiling, this whole place, means more to me than just about anything. It's the house of God, and it's my home. It can be your home, too, if you want."

So awed was Lorla by all she had seen, she could hardly bring herself to answer. Herrith's face was soft and imploring, and try as she might to turn away, she could not.

"What will happen to me here?" she asked. "What will I do?"

"Whatever you wish," said Herrith. "You will be schooled and learn things, and grow to be a fine woman. Nar is changing. Soon, I hope, this will be a great city for you to live in. I will make it great. For you and all the children." His hands hovered just above her, wanting to embrace her but not daring to touch. "I can't replace the family you lost, but I can treat you well, and I can teach you things. You can be happy here, Lorla. With me."

Lorla nodded, unsure of what to say. With all her heart she wanted to accept his offer, and the desire startled her. This was a grand place, and this man was not what she'd expected. Suddenly she was afraid. A sickness grew in her stomach.

Just the breakfast, she told herself. *You ate too much.*

"If I stay here, that room will be mine?"

Herrith glowed. "Yes. And so much more. I have all of Nar to show you, child." He stared at her, waiting and hoping for an answer. At last, Lorla's defenses collapsed.

"I would like that," she said. "I don't want to be an orphan anymore."

SIXTEEN

The Device

Count Renato Biagio stood on his private beach and watched his men at work, his polished boots soiled with sand. It was a warm day, like most in Crote, and the breeze off the ocean stirred the count's silken shirt and made his hair fall into his eyes. Beside him stood Admiral Danar Nicabar, looking tired and agitated. Thirty feet away, a handful of his men were struggling with a huge wooden crate, fighting to fit it into the boat that would ferry the parcel to the warship anchored in the distance. Bovadin directed them, shouting at them to be careful. It was the day Nicabar had dreaded—the day that they loaded the device. Biagio smiled sunnily, hardly concerned at all. Bovadin had built the device with all the necessary tolerances. Despite the twisted worry on the scientist's face, Biagio knew Bovadin was confident about his creation. It would not detonate until its time, Biagio was certain. The count folded his arms over his chest, satisfied. His exile on Crote had grown long in the tooth lately, and he was grateful to see this day's arrival.

"You're afraid, Danar," said Biagio. "Don't be. Bovadin knows what he's doing."

Nicabar snorted. "It's loaded with fuel, Renato."

"Bovadin has taken precautions. Trust, my friend, trust . . ."

"Look there," snapped Nicabar, pointing at his men. They had nearly dropped one side of the crate. Bovadin was screaming at them. "Lord, almighty. Maybe we should back up a bit."

Biagio laughed prettily. "Dear Danar, if that thing was such a threat I wouldn't have let Bovadin build it in my home, now would I? The dangerous part is done." Then he grinned maliciously, adding, "At least for us. It's Herrith's problem now."

"Darago's almost done with his painting. Have I told you?"

Biagio nodded. Nicabar's memory wasn't always sharp, an unfortunate and unpredictable effect of the drug. "Yes."

"Herrith's very proud of it. I saw part of it when I went to the cathedral."

When he turned down my peace plan, thought Biagio. Herrith was a perfect fool. "A shame, really," he remarked casually. "For Nar, I mean. Darago is a great artisan. But alas, these are the prices we pay."

Out on the banks, Bovadin was jumping into the boat, guiding the ungainly crate. The boat hardly moved with his diminutive weight, but when the first half of the crate creaked aboard, the vessel dipped noticeably. Bovadin gave a nervous grimace, obviously afraid for himself. Biagio's smile finally vanished. Was the boat big enough?

"Danar . . . ?"

"Don't worry," chirped the admiral. "She'll hold it."

"She'd better. Bovadin counted on blowing himself to bits, not drowning. I don't think the little monkey can swim."

Nicabar didn't laugh. He merely stood there, stone-faced, watching as his men struggled with the crate. Biagio stole a glance at the admiral, noting his anxiety. It was good to have him back. He was glad Nicabar wasn't delivering the device to Nar personally. Since Simon had left for Lucel-Lor, there had been precious little company for him. Bovadin was always busy with his tinkering, and Savros the Mind Bender was the quiet sort, keeping to himself. Of all of them, Biagio counted only Nicabar among his friends. And friends were a scarce commodity these days. It was the sad truth about being the head of a secret organization—no one trusted him. In Nar, when Arkus was alive, there had always been people around—gilded women and ambitious princes ready to bargain—but they had all been treacherous and never really interested in friendship. But not so Danar Nicabar. He was one of those rare specimens; a man of high ideals. Perhaps it was some military code that made him righteous, or perhaps a noble upbringing. Either way, Biagio trusted him. He cared for Nicabar as almost none other.

Except for Simon.

It had been many days since Simon's departure for Lucel-Lor, and many more lay ahead until his return. The mansion was dreadfully quiet without him. Biagio had tried to pass the time with plans of revenge, and with training his protégée, Eris, but always Simon's handsome face strong-armed its way back into his brain. The count's good mood evaporated. He missed Simon more than he wanted to. Worse, it was something like the loss he felt over Arkus, something in his heart that ached. It was not something he could explain or talk away with Nicabar, though, and so the count forced the memory down, concentrating on the scene before him.

Almost time, Herrith, he mused. *Tick-tock, tick-tock . . .*

He wondered what Herrith's reaction would be. The bishop cherished his cathedral, like Biagio cherished Crote. But prices had to be paid.

"It'll take about three days for the *Sea Shadow* to reach Casarhoon," said Nicabar. "From there another three to Nar City."

"Make sure Thot gets it on a speedy ship," said Biagio. He didn't want the delivery delayed by switching ships, but he knew it was necessary. Every eye in the Black City would see the *Sea Shadow* coming; they needed a merchant ship to deliver the device. Biagio was glad Bovadin was going along.

"Captain Thot knows what he's doing," said Nicabar curtly.

"Of course, Danar. I meant no insult. But the device has to get there on time. This is all planned out perfectly. A tiny slip, and my grand design falls apart. I won't have that."

"There will be no slips," promised Nicabar. "Trust *me* for once. Thot and the *Sea Shadow* will get the device there on time. And I have no doubt Bovadin will be yelling at him the entire trip, making sure he's quick."

As if he'd heard his name, Bovadin lifted his head toward shore, staring at the admiral. The scientist gave the crate a glance and, satisfied it was safely aboard, jumped out of the boat and waded ashore, his bare feet breaking the surf as he stomped toward them. His little features seemed less distressed now, almost relieved. He strode up to Biagio and Nicabar and sighed, pointing a thumb over his shoulder.

"We're taking it aboard *Sea Shadow* now," he said.

Biagio smiled down at Bovadin. "Good journey, my friend. Enjoy Nar. I almost envy you."

"If this goes right you'll get back there soon enough," said the scientist. "And to tell you the truth, I wish I was staying. I don't much like the thought of being on rough seas with that thing."

"You built it," snapped Nicabar. "Don't tell me it's not shipworthy. That's my vessel out there."

"I didn't say that. But there are risks. If anything goes wrong, if there's a leak in one of the hoses—"

"You said you tested the damn thing!"

"I did! But there are always risks." Bovadin looked to Biagio for support. "Tell him, Renato."

Biagio merely yawned. "I suppose. The important thing is that it's on its way. But be smart, Bovadin. Don't rush it. Let Thot do his job and steer the ship. If he says the seas are too rough, you let him go around or wait it out. Do you understand?"

"You said I had to get it there on time, Renato," argued Bovadin. "Let me do my job. I'll find this toymaker and get him the device. You just make sure your little girl doesn't forget her birthday."

Threats didn't rest well with Biagio, but he let it pass. Bovadin had done fine work. He deserved a little slack. "Just be careful," said the count. "That's all I ask."

"I will. And I'll see you both back in Nar." What passed for a smile flitted over Bovadin's face. "Good luck."

"To you, too, my friend," said Biagio, striking out his hand. Bovadin took it and gave a weak shake, then turned and departed for the rowboat, all weighed down with the crate and sailors. Biagio watched the scientist go, relieved. He hadn't really expected a mishap, but then Bovadin had never built anything like the device before. And though he had made elaborate drawings and performed his inscrutable tests, even Bovadin couldn't swear to the thing's stability. It was a dangerous creation, maybe the greatest weapon ever produced, and Biagio didn't really want it on his island. Soon, if all went according to plan, Crote would be in dire trouble anyway; the count saw no need to hasten his homeland's demise. He watched Bovadin shuffle into the rowboat. The vessel shoved off, bearing the crate out to where the *Sea Shadow* waited. Onboard the big ship he could see the anxious faces of sailors, fearful of their cargo.

"Let's go inside," said Biagio. "There is nothing else to see here."

"I'll wait," replied Nicabar. "I want to be sure."

"Suit yourself, my friend. But don't be too long. I want to talk to you about Dragon's Beak."

Nicabar looked over. "What about it?"

"You'll need to be leaving soon. We should discuss it."

"I know the way, Renato."

"This is no joke," said Biagio sternly. "If Vorto goes to Dragon's Beak as Enli asks, he's going to need you there to help him. My mercenaries won't be able to stand alone against the legions. I promised Enli you'd be there."

"I'll be there," pledged Nicabar. "I wouldn't miss it. And the army of the air?"

"I don't know yet," Biagio said honestly. News from Dragon's Beak was always scarce. "All the more reason for you to get there on time. If Enli doesn't have control of the ravens, he may need a quick escape from Vorto. You'll have to help him with that."

Nicabar shook his head. "I'm not going to Dragon's Beak just to pull his ass out of the fire, Renato. I'm going there to decapitate Vorto."

"Oh, let's hope so," said Biagio with an evil grin. "That'll be just about the time for me to send another message to Herrith. You'll deliver that for me, won't you, my friend?"

The admiral took the count's meaning. "With pleasure, my friend."

That night, Count Biagio slept restlessly on his expensive sheets, sick with anticipation. The device Bovadin had built dominated his dreams. He saw the great Cathedral of the Martyrs and the little toymaker's shop on the corner of High Street, that busy thoroughfare where well-to-do Narens shopped and sated greedy whims. And in his dreams Lorla came to visit him, her eyes shining unnaturally green. In the dream she spoke to him, but when Biagio awoke he could not recall her words. It was well past midnight when he awakened. The moonlight through his window was pale, tinting everything an eerie silver. Lorla's face winked out of existence as his eyes opened. Startled, Biagio swung his naked feet over the bedside and rubbed his forehead. The world was perfectly quiet. He had gone to bed alone tonight, as he had most nights recently, and the slaves he usually awoke to were gone. He glanced out the window to the fruit tree in the garden and saw a crow looking back at him, smiling crookedly. Biagio sneered at the thing, reminded of Eneas' ravens. There was too much in his mind tonight, too many grinding thoughts. He was weary, so tired he couldn't sleep. On his bedside table was a crystal goblet of half-consumed brandy. He reached for it, but in his daze knocked it over, spilling it.

"Damn it!" he growled. The brandy splashed onto the expensive carpet. The count watched it stain, helpless.

I'm tired, he reminded himself. *So bloody tired.*

It hadn't always been this way. When he was in Nar and at the height of his power, he had been razor-sharp. He and Arkus had tread the world like gods, and he had been the emperor's closest friend—the only one of the Iron Circle who had truly been like a son to the elderly ruler. Now he was an outcast, forced to scheme every minute. The effort was dulling him. Even Bovadin's drug wasn't keeping him vital. Biagio was exhausted.

Ignoring his ruined carpet, he went to the window and opened it, taking a deep gulp of air. He could smell brine on the breeze. Music came from the far-off surf. The crow on the fruit tree leapt at his intrusion, flying off. Biagio cursed after it. If it ever came back, he promised the bird, he would have it for lunch. The sight of the fleeing bird cheered him a little. Crote was his. And it always would be, no matter what happened to it. He would get it back from the Lissens after it fell. When Nar was his, so too would be the world.

As happened too often these days, he thought again of Simon. He wondered if Simon knew his true feelings. Simon was Crotan, after all, and Crotans often experimented. But Simon wasn't like that. He was more like Herrith, really. Hardly pious, but unwilling to try things. The count's shoulders slumped. He didn't like fawning over lovers. He felt like a schoolboy, dazed and impotent. Elliann, his wife, had always thought him cold, even during their most savage lovemaking. Elliann could bed a tiger and come out alive. She was truly a wild animal, and she had been exciting during the first years of their marriage. But like Naren lords are apt to do, they had both grown quietly tired of each other, and neither of them had quarrelled when the other took different lovers. Biagio still liked his wife and bore her no ill. War and rebellion wasn't what she was bred for, and she had sniffed at the thought of it. And because she had thought Herrith would win their struggle, she had sided with him. Biagio had let her go, willingly. He stared out into the darkness, imagining her somewhere in the Black City, probably asleep by now with a suitor in her sheets. A little smile crossed his face. Perhaps he would send for her when he returned to Nar.

Biagio glanced back at his bed, so cold and sterile. His was an excellent chamber, large and immaculate, with priceless heirlooms dotting the walls and shelves. But he gleaned no comfort from these things, and the urge to leave his rooms became overwhelming. In the great music room was a piano, and when he was troubled he would go to the piano and thunder out a song and lose himself. It was odd therapy but it worked for him, and so he pulled off his night clothes and chose some simple garments from his many closets, dressing hurriedly. Sliding his feet into a pair of slippers, he went out into the deserted hallway of his wing, where the only sound he heard was the faint sizzling of flames from the oil sconces along the wall. His shadow leapt across the floor, large and ominous, and as he walked his slippers squeaked. There were no guardians to disturb him, no servants around to grovel. Biagio walked in a trance to his music room, eager to bang on the piano keys. But when he reached the chamber he found the door half open and a light glowing inside.

Curious, the count slowed. Eris, his treasured slave, was alone in the room, gliding across the floor in a silent, expressive dance. Biagio held his breath. She was lovely. She moved with the grace of a dove, her long legs twirling her effortlessly through pirouettes, her arms stretching heavenward, as if imploring God to hear her. Her face was aglow in the light of a single candle, flush with sweat and shadows. And her wide eyes seemed to cry as she danced, sadly, purposefully, oblivious to all the world in her melancholy.

Count Biagio watched, utterly enthralled. She was his greatest prize.

When she danced for him the angels wept with jealousy. He knew as he watched her why Simon's heart was hers. As a woman she was perfection. As a dancer, she was a goddess. No man could resist her. Especially not poor Simon.

When she was done with her dance, Eris crumpled to the floor, bowing her head into her lap and lying there, motionless. Biagio thought he heard her whimper. Very gently he pushed open the door. Still she did not hear him.

"You were wonderful," he whispered. "Thank you."

Eris looked up, mortified. "Master!" she cried, springing to her feet and lowering her eyes. "Forgive me, I . . . I was practicing. I didn't know you were here."

"Don't apologize," said Biagio, floating into the room. He put his cold hand to her chin, lifting her face and looking into her eyes. "It was a pleasure for me."

Eris looked embarrassed, but didn't pull away. "I am glad," she managed. "I was just practicing."

"You were not," Biagio corrected. With his frozen thumb he brushed a tear from her cheek. "I have never seen you weep when practicing. What tears are these?"

"Nothing, Master. The piece I was dancing is emotional, that's all."

"What was the piece? I did not recognize it."

He watched her face twitch as she decided to confess. "Only something of my own imagining. I was restless tonight. There are things occupying me." She struggled to smile. "But unimportant things, my lord. Truly not worth bothering with."

Enjoying her fear, Biagio dropped his fingers to her neck and the golden collar she wore. His fingernail picked at it.

"I would curse the day you could not tell the truth to me, dear Eris," he said. "Why don't you explain this to me? I, too, was sleepless tonight. I thought I might play some music. You were an unexpected surprise."

"Forgive me, Master," begged the girl. Her age showed when she spoke, so small was her voice. "I will go now, if you like."

"No, I would not like that." The count let go of her collar. He turned and went to his piano, sitting himself down on its crushed velvet bench. Eris stood uncertainly in the center of the room. His eyes washed over her, drinking in her loveliness. "This is not a good night for me, Eris. There are things on my mind, too. It might help me to hear your own troubles, to put mine aside for a while. Tell me, please. What is obsessing you?"

"Oh, Master, it's truly nothing. I would never burden you with such trivia."

"I insist." Biagio gestured to the floor at his feet. "Come. Sit here by me."

Eris complied. He was a tall man, and when she sat he towered over her. But he was in a gentle mood tonight, and he had suspicions why the girl might be troubled. Their troubles might be twins. Eris looked up at him, and her sad expression made him reach out and stroke her dark hair.

"Be at ease, girl," he said. "I only want to talk to you. Or more truly, to hear you. This is about your lover, isn't it?"

"Master . . ."

"Stop. I know all about it, remember? I gave you to Simon, after all."

"Yes, Master. Thank you. I don't know how to repay that."

"You repay me every time you dance, child. And when we get back to Nar and you dance for them in the Black City, that will be a triumph and all debts will be paid." Biagio felt a rush of exhilaration. "The three of us will return to Nar together. It will be glorious."

"I would like that," said Eris. "To dance in the Black Palace for all the lords of Nar. I've dreamt of it since I was young."

"You will dance for them, Eris, and it will be a conquest. The lords of Nar will swoon at your feet. Your name will be famous throughout the Empire. I promise you that."

"And we will marry? Simon and I?"

The count's heart sank. "If that's what you wish. I stand by my word to Simon Darquis, girl. You are his, just as soon as he does this thing for me. When he returns, you may marry. That soon, if it's what you want."

"I do, Master. Very much. He is dear to me. And I to him." She stopped abruptly, realizing what she was saying. "But many things are dear to him, of course. Serving you is dear to him. It's all he talks of."

"I'm sure," said the count dryly. Eris lied very poorly. "And how dear are you to Simon? I wonder. You've been given a great gift, child. Performers in the Empire would willingly sell their souls for your talent. Which do you love more?"

Eris crinkled her nose. "Master?"

"If you had to choose, which would it be?"

"But I could never choose," said the girl. "They are both part of me. I love Simon dearly. But dance is what I am. I would be nothing if I couldn't dance. I would be dead."

Dead. Biagio lingered on the word. He knew what it was like to feel so close to something. It was how he felt about Nar, even about his dead emperor. Only now, a full year later, was he starting to recover from Arkus' death. Surprisingly, he was glad for Eris. Her life had direction, something too many Narens lacked these days.

"You are a great prize to me, Eris," he said. "But I give you to Simon because he is also dear to me. He has served me very well, for years now. When he returns, you will be his. He may free you if he wishes, but I ask only that you come to Nar with me and perform. And you will do that, yes?"

"Oh, yes, Master," said the girl. "Happily."

"And Simon will come with you, and the three of us will live together in the Black City. Perhaps together in the Black Palace, eh?"

Eris didn't smile at the notion. "If you wish, Master."

Biagio sighed. He was tired and making foolish statements. Simon had no interest in him, and that was the truth of it. Simon was in love with this fragile thing on the floor, with its green eyes and soft breasts and its mortality. When they did return to Nar—if they did—Simon and Eris would go off and have a family of their own, and Biagio would be alone in the Black Palace, without a wife or emperor to comfort him.

Carefully, Biagio reached out again for the girl and stroked her raven hair, loving the feel of it between his fingers. Eris bowed her head submissively. Biagio sensed the fear in her but ignored it. Much as he craved her, he would not take her to his bed. He was a man of his word, and he had promised her to another.

She belonged to Simon now.

SEVENTEEN

A Call to Arms

Sharp as a razor, the *Prince of Liss* sliced through the waters of northern Lucel-Lor. Three weeks out of Nar, she had rounded the cape of Kes and was charging full-winded toward the isthmus of Tatterak. It was midday and the visibility from the warship's deck afforded a perfect view of the horizon. The crew of the *Prince* gathered on the prow, their curious eyes fixed on their destination. For days they had hugged the coast of Tatterak, navigating the cold and unfamiliar waters. They were weary and homesick and a little afraid, but the sight of the citadel put joy back in their hearts.

Fleet Commander Prakna looked up at Falindar and felt his world diminish. He had seen many things in his life, had been many places, but nothing had prepared him for this. The mountain castle dominated the landscape, climbing in a shining arc toward Heaven, its white spires agleam, as if adorned with shattered diamonds. At its zenith the citadel was a stepladder for angels, at its base a sprawling metropolis of stables, gardens and grounds, all cut defiantly into the side of a mountain. Prakna felt a rush of exhilaration. They had made it.

"It's amazing," said Marus. "You were right."

"Unforgettable," said Prakna. The fleet commander had only seen the citadel once before, and then only from a distance on a cloudy day, but it still had been awesome.

"We should send up a signal," suggested Marus. "Let them know we're coming."

Prakna laughed. "Don't you think they see us from up there?"

"It's not that. It's been a long time since a Lissen ship has been in their waters. We shouldn't be furtive."

"We're one ship, Marus. And they'll recognize our colors as friendly." As he spoke he pointed to the Lissen flag snapping above their heads. "We're not so easy to forget, either."

Satisfied, Marus settled down. They were piloting the *Prince* directly toward the citadel, preparing to anchor offshore. Prakna himself would row ashore to meet Vantran and the other one, the new lord of the castle. Prakna struggled to remember the name. Lucyler? But Vantran would remember him, certainly. As if reading his commander's mind, Marus floated a question.

"What if Vantran isn't here? What then?"

"He's here," replied Prakna. "Where else would he be?"

"It's a big land, Prakna. He could be anywhere."

Prakna didn't answer, because he had no answer. All he had was hope. If Vantran wasn't in Falindar, they had wasted the trip.

"You talk too much, old friend," Prakna told Marus.

"Maybe," admitted Marus wryly. "But even if he is here, how are you going to convince him to come with us? You haven't explained *that* to me, either."

"You are full of questions today."

"Yes, I am. Why aren't you?"

"I'm not worried," said Prakna. "Convincing the Jackal to fight against Nar is like convincing water to flow. No need to even try. "

"That was a long time ago," said Marus. The officer nodded toward the citadel. "Living in such a grand place might change a man's mind about things."

Prakna turned to his friend. "Really? Do you think living in a palace would change your mind about avenging Liss, Marus?"

"Of course not."

Prakna said no more. He turned and watched the citadel grow closer. Vantran *would* join them, he was sure of it. It was the same need that had driven them all against Nar, made them leave their families and homes, turned them into pirates. Vantran was no different. Like all of them, he knew about loss. It had glowed in his eyes like fire when they'd met. And a fire like that didn't just extinguish itself. Prakna knew that from experience. So did Marus.

"I would like to meet this Vantran myself," said Marus. "I hope he comes aboard. I could tell my wife I've met him."

"You'll have bragging rights to that, don't worry," Prakna assured him. "When he hears what we're offering, he won't turn us away."

• • •

Richius Vantran stood on shore, staring at the Lissen schooner in the distance. He had been in his chambers with Dyana and Shani when he'd heard the news of the ship's arrival, and had raced to his window to catch a glimpse of the vessel.

She was unmistakable.

In the absence of Lucyler, Deemis was in charge of the citadel. Deemis had been one of Kronin's men, and Lucyler trusted him implicitly. It was Deemis that had brought Richius the news of the ship, guessing correctly that Richius would want to accompany them to greet the vessel. Without waiting for Dyana, Richius had followed Deemis down the mountain road to the shore. After finding a nurse to look after Shani, Dyana had joined them. Now she stood beside her husband, pale-faced and silent as she watched the schooner in the distance. Deemis and his warriors stood proudly in front of them, their jiiktars strapped to their backs. A little boat was dispatched from the schooner, rowing toward them with three men inside. Richius fought to still his anticipation. He couldn't see the vessel's occupants, but he was sure he knew one of them already.

Prakna.

It seemed now that the Lissen commander had indeed lived up to his pledge. Prakna had promised Richius he would return to Lucel-Lor if he ever needed help. Richius bit his lip. His eyes flicked to his wife. Dyana was mute with worry. Very gently he slipped his hand over hers, giving it a reassuring squeeze.

She pulled away. "This is a nightmare," she whispered.

Richius attempted a smile. "Perhaps it's nothing," he offered, then realized how stupid that sounded.

"What's going on here?" asked a voice from behind them. Simon sauntered up and shielded his eyes with his hand. "Lissens?"

"Yes," said Richius.

"Here for Richius," added Dyana sourly.

"We don't know that."

"For you, Richius?" asked Simon, astonished. "Looks like you were right. They did come back for you."

"Simon, please . . ."

Seeing Dyana's expression, the Naren grimaced. "I'm sorry. That was thoughtless."

The careless statement made Richius bristle. Over the past few weeks, Simon had grown almost too comfortable with them both—even Dyana. Though the two of them rarely spoke, Simon no longer shunned her or tried to avoid her when she walked down the hall. Until now, Richius had been glad about that.

Simon flashed Richius an apologetic grin, backing up a step. The wind ruffled his hair, blowing it into his eyes. Dyana shivered a little and wrapped her arms around her shoulders. Deemis and his men stood stone-faced, oblivious to the cold, looking regal on the shore, their long, white hair pulled back by the breeze. Counting Deemis, there were five of them. Not the welcome Prakna anticipated, Richius imagined. He hoped the sight of the warriors wouldn't startle the commander. More than likely, Prakna was expecting Lucyler.

The Lissen rowboat was almost to shore. A tall man stood up in its center and folded his arms across his chest. His head bobbed a little as he tried to make out the figures on the beach. Richius squinted for a better look, recalling his memories of Prakna. He recognized the thin face and the light, short-cropped hair cut in bangs across his forehead. He wore a well-worn uniform of deep blue that gleamed with golden buttons and bore no sidearm from his belt. As he drew closer the man raised a hand in greeting. Richius returned the gesture. Deemis and his warriors did not.

"Is that him?" Dyana asked.

"I think so," Richius replied. It was hard to tell in the sunlight, and all Lissens sort of looked the same to him, like all Triin once had. Dyana groaned hopelessly.

"Tall," Simon remarked. "I've never seen a Lissen before. They sort of look like Triin."

In fact, they were remarkably similar, a trait that never went unnoticed by an outsider. Like their Triin brethren, the people of the Hundred Isles were delicate and fair, with reedy limbs and long bones and almond eyes that made them seem otherworldly. They were a handsome race, too, strangely compelling to behold. As he watched them approach, Richius suddenly understood Arkus' long fascination with them.

"King Vantran?" called the man as the boat skidded onto the beach. "Is that you?"

"It's me," replied Richius uncertainly. He stepped out of the group to greet the visitors. "Prakna?"

"Yes, boy!" said the Lissen excitedly. He didn't wait for his men to rack the oars, but instead jumped out of the rowboat and splashed ashore. There was a giant, relieved smile on his face. The Lissen commander walked up the beach, paying no heed to Deemis and his warriors, and reached out for Richius' hand, shaking it vigorously. "God help me, I'm glad to see you. I feared you might not be here."

"Prakna, hello," stammered Richius, unsure what to say. "It's good to see you too, I guess. But I must say I'm confused. What's this about?"

Prakna's grin was inscrutable. "We'll talk, Vantran. I'll explain it all to you. But first . . ." The fleet commander turned to Dyana and, his face full of reverence, dropped to one knee in the sand. "You're Dyana, aren't you?" he asked. "Vantran's wife?"

"Yes," said Dyana, flabbergasted. She glanced at Richius for an answer, but her husband only shrugged. "Yes, that is me. Greetings, Prakna."

The Lissen kept his head bowed as he spoke. "I am honored to meet you at last, Lady. You are spoken of in Liss with great regard."

"Am I?"

"Indeed, you and your husband both. He is the Jackal of Nar, after all. A hero. And you are his woman." Prakna straightened and flashed a beautiful smile. But when he saw Simon standing behind Richius, his pleasantness vanished. "Who is this?" he asked pointedly.

Richius stood aside so Simon could step forward. "This is Simon Darquis, Prakna."

"A Naren?"

"A friend of mine," Richius corrected. "From Nar, yes. He's a deserter from the legions of the Black City."

Simon inclined his head to the Lissen. "Commander . . ."

An icy pall fell over Prakna. He studied every inch of Simon, even his swollen nose. "A deserter from the legions? I didn't think there was such a thing. How long has he been here with you, Vantran?"

"A few weeks," said Richius. "A bit more maybe." He didn't like the Lissen's probing and so volunteered nothing. "He's not a threat if that's what you're worried about, Prakna. I had those doubts myself at first. Be at ease."

"Forgive me, but it's not easy for me to relax around Naren butchers." As he spoke the commander stared directly at Simon, refusing to flinch. "No offense, Simon Darquis."

There was a long silence before Simon spoke, and when he did his voice was sweet like candy. "I am not offended at all, Lissen. I know what the Empire is like, and what they did to Liss. It's why I deserted."

"You can never know what they did to Liss," said Prakna gravely. "Please don't say that to me again."

"Prakna, this is Deemis," interrupted Richius, hoping to change the subject. "He's one of the protectors of the citadel."

Deemis' granite facade cracked with an offered smile. The fleet commander of Liss returned the grin tenfold, bowing deeply to the Triin and his warriors.

"An honor," he said. "Forgive me, I speak no Triin. Tell him for me, please, Lady Dyana. Tell him I am honored to meet him and be on his shores again."

Dyana quickly translated, and each of the warriors softened in turn, lowering their guard just a little. In the rowboat, the men who had ferried Prakna ashore were dragging the vessel onto the sand. They were garbed similarly to their superior, with fancy uniforms that had gone threadbare. Prakna waved them both over to him.

"These are two of my crew," he said. "They've been on the *Prince* with me for months now, patrolling Nar's coast."

"Yes," said Richius. "I'd heard stories that Lissens were raiding the Naren coasts. It's true, then?"

"More than just true," said Prakna. "Successful. I have a lot to tell you, King Vantran. If you'd permit me, I would like to accompany you back to the citadel, tell you why I'm here. And see your lord Lucyler, too, if he would allow it."

"I'm sorry, Prakna, but that's not possible," said Richius. He explained how Lucyler had been called away to Kes, to quell some growing animosity between two of the Triin warlords. Prakna shook his head miserably at the news.

"This Lucyler has his hands full," he said sadly. "I don't envy him. Tharn's been dead little more than a year, and already the Triin warlords are at each other's throats again." He glanced at the five Triin warriors, then added softly. "May God end war forever, everywhere."

"Yes," added Dyana. "May He do that. And quickly, too."

Her meaning wasn't lost on Prakna. "Dyana Vantran, I know you don't want me here. I ask only that you don't judge me too quickly. The business I have with your husband is grave indeed."

"I have been through wars before, sir," said Dyana. "I know what they are about."

Prakna smiled deferentially. "I won't argue with you, lady. I'm no lover of battles myself." He turned to Richius. "If we can speak, then, King Vantran?"

"Inside," Richius offered. "Your men, too. If you're hungry and tired . . ."

"Anything you can offer my men would be appreciated, thank you. But I prefer to speak to you alone."

Dyana raised an eyebrow. "I would like to hear this myself. I think it concerns me."

"Forgive me, Lady," said Prakna. "But the things I have to discuss are between me and your husband."

"Dyana, please," said Richius, offering her a smile. "Let me talk with Prakna alone, all right?"

Dyana's face tightened, and she bit back a protest.

"Prakna," Richius continued, "I'll have some servants bring us in some food. I'm sure you could use some."

"That would be very fine," said the commander. Then he glanced over at Simon, hinting at Richius. "When you say alone, I hope you mean without this one."

"Who, Simon?" asked Richius. "No, he won't be with us."

"Good," said Prakna with relief.

Richius asked Simon, "You don't mind, do you?"

"No, not at all," replied Simon. He turned a slick smile against the Lissen. "It was a pleasure meeting you, Fleet Commander. I wish you good luck with whatever you have planned."

Without waiting for a response Simon turned and stalked up the beach toward the mountain and the citadel. Richius watched him go, feeling sorry for him.

"Prakna," said Richius, "I wish you would watch your tone around Simon. I have very few friends, so I guard them jealousy. The next time you see Simon, please be more courteous."

Frowning, the commander said, "Because he is your friend, I will try. Now, we have much to talk about. And it's very urgent."

"Let's get to it, then," said Richius, leading the men up the beach.

Dyana lingered in the hallway outside the meeting chamber, far enough from the door so that Richius and Prakna would not hear her. Of course, she couldn't hear them either, and that vexed her. They had only been inside the chamber for a few minutes, but she was already riddled with anxiety. At Richius' request, Deemis and his warriors had taken Prakna's sailors to another part of the citadel to rest and take food. Richius had also asked Dyana to accompany them. She had agreed, reluctantly, but halfway there she had turned around, drawn inexorably back to the chamber where Richius was meeting the Lissen commander. Like an abandoned child she waited at the end of the hall, trying to listen and hearing nothing. But she couldn't pull herself away. She was full of dread, unable to think about anything but her husband.

"Dyana?"

Startled, Dyana turned to see who had called. To her surprise she saw Simon around the corner, a twisted smile on his face. The Naren seemed disturbed, too. Dyana waved him closer.

"What are you doing here?" she asked.

"Looking for you," he answered. "I thought I might find you here. I was . . ." He shrugged. "Well, concerned."

"He is going to take my husband away," said Dyana miserably.

"Maybe he won't go."

"He will go," said Dyana. "It is all he thinks about. You know that by now. Richius is just like those Lissens. Obsessed."

Simon shuffled closer. "He loves you," he said.

Dyana looked at him. What did the Naren know of love?

"How do you know that?" she asked.

"I see it. Everyone does. You might be underestimating him. I'm not so sure he'll be able to leave you."

Dyana leaned back against the wall. "I wish that were so. I know he loves me, but there is one thing about Richius—he never forgives. Or forgets. If this fellow Prakna offers him revenge, he will take it. And I will not be able to stop him."

"He's not happy here, I know," Simon admitted. "But what really can this Lissen want with him? Richius is not a sailor."

Dyana shrugged. "I do not know." She looked at Simon and was glad suddenly that he was with her. Just now, she needed to confide in someone, anyone. Even Simon. At times, the Naren surprised her by being thoughtful. He was a mystery, certainly, but one that was slowly unraveling. "Simon, are you happy here?" she asked. "Do you miss being home?"

The Naren frowned. "Why are you asking that?"

"You are a Naren, like Richius. I have never been to Nar. Is it so much better than living here in Falindar?"

"That's an impossible question," said Simon. "But home is always better than a strange place, I suppose. Especially if you have someone there that loves you."

This intrigued Dyana. "Do you have someone at home that loves you? A woman, I mean?"

"I haven't been home in a long time," said Simon sadly.

"But did you? Did you leave someone behind when you deserted?"

Simon was stoic. His eyes almost closed as he answered. "Something like that."

"I am sorry," said Dyana. "I should not have asked that. Forgive me."

"There's nothing to forgive. I made the choice I had to make."

"Deserting?"

He nodded grimly. "Yes, I guess that's what it's called."

Dyana felt ashamed. She hardly knew this man, and yet she was forcing him open like a book. But something made her keep talking, something sad and hidden in Simon's eyes. He wasn't all he claimed to be, she knew that now. He had obviously seen many horrors. Like Richius. Both of them were damaged by war. It had made them impenetrable.

"I am here, you know. If you want to talk, I mean. Richius, too. We can be your friends. If you let us."

"You're very kind," said Simon. His expression dimmed a little. "You've already done a great deal for me. Thank you." Then he laughed, adding, "I thought I was a dead man when your husband found me!"

"Richius can be suspicious," Dyana admitted. "But he likes you. I can tell. It is a good thing he found you, too. Especially with winter coming."

"Aye, but I would have found shelter for myself. There are enough abandoned buildings from the wars. I would have stayed in one of those."

Dyana frowned. "Abandoned? Where?"

Simon paused. "Well, yes. From the war. I saw them on my way here. A tower." He glanced distractedly at the closed door down the hall. "You know, I think we should go. They might hear us and think we're eavesdropping."

"They would be right," said Dyana sourly. "Lorris and Pris, I wish I knew what they were talking about."

Fleet Commander Prakna put his goblet down on the table and sighed. For the first five minutes they had hardly spoken at all while Prakna fed himself on the bounty of Falindar. His need to talk "urgently" had miraculously disappeared when he'd seen fresh fruit. Richius knew what hunger was like, but when at last Prakna had stopped eating long enough to look up, he seized the opportunity.

"So, Commander," said Richius. "What's this about?"

"Did you expect me?" asked Prakna, avoiding Richius' question. "I told you I'd come back if I needed you. Did you think I would?"

"I had wondered. I'm out of touch here in Falindar."

"But you hoped I would, didn't you?" probed the Lissen. He leaned forward across the table. "You wouldn't have met my ship if you didn't."

"Prakna, I don't mean to seem rude, but I could really use some answers," said Richius. "Tell me why you're here."

"Why? For you, of course. We need your help."

"Who's we?"

"Liss," said the commander. He shoved his plate of food aside as if it were suddenly annoying him. "All those who owe Nar a debt, you might say. I'm going to be truthful with you, Vantran. You want revenge as much as I do. I saw it in your eyes when we first met, and I'm looking right at it again now. I'm offering you that chance."

"More," said Richius, waving over an explanation. He didn't like Prakna's circular conversation. "Start at the beginning. What's going on with Liss? I've heard that you've been attacking Naren shipping, but that's all I know."

"I have an armada of over fifty ships patrolling the coasts of the Empire," said Prakna. "Mostly schooners like the *Prince*."

"Prince?"

"My flagship, anchored offshore. And we've done a lot more than just sink a few Naren ships. So far the count is at least twenty-five. We've raided some coastal towns, too. Doria, even." Prakna's face lit with satisfaction. "For the first time those Naren pigs know what it's like to be invaded."

Richius was astonished. "Doria? How? The Black Fleet—"

"Stop," bade Prakna, holding up a hand. "You're in need of a history lesson, aren't you?"

"I guess so," Richius admitted. "As I said, news travels slowly here."

"Let me educate you, then," said Prakna. He explained to Richius how Nar had fallen into turmoil after Arkus' death, and how the two factions of the Empire, Biagio's and Herrith's, were at odds. Richius knew that much already. What he didn't know was that the Black Fleet had sided completely with Biagio and were protecting him on his home island of Crote. Prakna went on to tell how the Black Renaissance was almost extinguished in Nar, and how Herrith had the imperial legions in his control. The Naren navy, he explained, had been staying away from the Empire.

"We had the run of Naren waters," Prakna said. "And we pressed the advantage. But not just because we wanted to hurt Nar. We had a more important mission—to lure the *Fearless* and the rest of the fleet back to Nar."

Richius was thoroughly confused. "The *Fearless*? That's Nicabar's ship, isn't it? Why would you want him coming after you? I've seen Naren dreadnoughts. They're a handful, I'm sure."

"Two handfuls," said Prakna. "But you're not listening. The point wasn't to lure them back to Nar, exactly. The point was to lure them away from Crote. And we've done that finally. I myself came across the *Fearless* two weeks ago. She and at least two other dreadnoughts are out of Crotan waters. They're no longer protecting Biagio."

Richius shrugged. "So?"

"So we finally have the chance we've been looking for," said Prakna. He put his hands on the table and steepled his fingers contemplatively, thinking very hard before he spoke. At last he looked straight at Richius and said, "King Vantran, Liss is planning an invasion of Crote."

It took a moment for the words to register. When they did, Richius could only gasp. "What?"

"Crote is a strategic weak point for Nar. If Liss could gain control of Crote, our navy would be in easy striking distance from the mainland. We could set up supply lines, run blockades of merchant shipping—"

"Are you insane?" Richius blurted out. "Invade Crote? Biagio—"

"Would never know what hit him!" growled the commander. "With the Black Fleet gone, he has no one there to protect him. My schooners could sweep in there and let loose an invasion force long before he could ever summon help. And Crote has only a very small army, mostly guarding Biagio in his mansion."

"And just where are you going to get this 'invasion force'? I may not be very informed, but I know Liss was devastated during its war with

Nar. You don't have an army. You're a bunch of sailors! I'm surprised you have enough ships left to harass the Empire."

"We've been rebuilding," said Prakna proudly. "But you're right. We're not land fighters. Never have been. That's why we need you."

Richius couldn't help but laugh. He had almost seen it coming. "Oh, yes. I'm the answer to your troubles, eh? What do you want me to do? Train an army for you?"

"And lead the invasion," said the commander with all seriousness. "We have more volunteers to go against Nar than you can imagine. Men *and* women. All ages, too. You could—"

"No, Prakna," said Richius. He stood up and shook his head. "I think you've got the wrong idea about me. I'm no leader."

"With respect, *you're* wrong," countered Prakna. "I know all about you, Vantran. You were the one who beat back the Narens in the battle of Dring. And you led your own company for Aramoor. You're a horse soldier. Good with a sword, I'd bet, too."

"Not very."

"Good enough to defeat Blackwood Gayle," said Prakna. "And that's good enough for me. I wouldn't have come all this way if I didn't think you could help us. Liss needs you. We need someone with your gift for strategy, your experience in land fighting." His face was earnest, imploring. "King Vantran, you're our only hope."

It was like hearing a prayer, and Richius couldn't ignore it. He dragged his chair over to Prakna's side of the table and sat down face-to-face with the Lissen.

"Prakna," he said softly. "This whole trip of yours was a waste. I thought you were coming here to ask if I wanted to join you, not lead you. I'm no leader, despite what you've heard. Maybe when you get back home you can tell your people to stop worshiping me like some kind of hero. I had a lot of help defeating the Narens. Triin help. And most of them died doing it. You should think about that."

Prakna's voice was icy. "I have thought about it. Don't lecture me about death, boy. I've drowned in a decade of it. But now is our chance to get even. Don't you see that? I know what Biagio did to your wife. He gave the order for her execution. You can't sit there and tell me you don't yearn for revenge."

"Enough," hissed Richius. He held up a warning finger. "That far, no further. My wife is none of your concern. And get out of my mind! You don't know what I'm feeling."

"Wrong again. I lost two boys in the war against Nar. When Nar invaded they were hardly in their teens. But they ran off to defend their home just as soon as they were old enough. And now they're both dead. You want to trade one wife for two sons? I think it's at least equal, don't you?"

There was so much pain in Prakna's voice Richius could barely stand it. "I'm sorry for you," he said. "I didn't know. But it doesn't change anything, Prakna. I can't help you, or lead this invasion. I don't know how to make an army out of fishermen."

"But you do," said Prakna. "You led your own people, right? What is Aramoor but a land of farmers and horse breeders? Some fishermen, too, I'd wager. We're not so different from your own folk. Let us help you take your revenge on Nar. And let's do it now, while they're weak."

Admittedly, it was tempting. Prakna was a very persuasive speaker. More, Richius knew the plan had at least some chance at success. Crote was small, hardly protected at all. And Prakna was right about its strategic position. So close to the mainland, Liss could indeed strike against Nar. But these things were ancillary. Prakna was dangling a far greater prize in front of Richius.

Biagio.

"What makes you think the Black Fleet won't go back to Crote?" he asked. "Biagio isn't used to being unprotected."

"Not all of our ships will be involved in the invasion. Just enough to carry the troops and supplies we'll need. The rest of my armada will continue to occupy Nicabar's fleet around the mainland." The Lissen sat back smugly. "We'll make sure the Black Fleet stays put, don't worry."

"Don't be so sure. Biagio has his fingers in everything. If he so much as suspects an invasion, your plan is doomed."

Prakna waved the remark away. "Biagio is completely isolated. He's clever, I admit, but we're clever, too. He won't suspect anything."

"And what do you plan on doing with him once you take the island?"

"That's up to you," promised the Lissen. "That's part of my bargain. I take the island. You take Biagio. He's yours. You can snuff him out like a candle. That would be justice, wouldn't it?"

"I'm not a murderer, Prakna. I'm better than that."

"Nonsense," said Prakna. "None of us are any better than the next. You're not so different from me, Vantran. We may be from different sides of the world, but we're both the same now. Life has made us brothers. And you know that, don't you? You can't hide from it. It's all over your face. You may not be a butcher like Biagio, but you can kill him. If I handed him to you, you'd slice his throat." Prakna leaned in and whispered, "Wouldn't you?"

Richius stood up, unable or unwilling to answer, he wasn't sure which. "You may stay in Falindar as long as you like," he told Prakna. "Have your men come ashore for fresh food and drink. There's lodging here for all of them."

"Vantran," cautioned the Lissen. "I need an answer." He struck out a hand for Richius to take. "Are you with us?"

"Prakna . . ."

"Don't make this all be a waste of my time," Prakna begged. "We can't do it without you. We don't have the knowledge."

Richius sighed. "When are you leaving? I'll give you an answer then."

"You're thinking of your wife, I know. I left my wife behind, too. Her name is J'lari. I love her very much. It changes nothing." Prakna kept his hand out-stretched. "Liss needs you. Please . . ."

"We might both be fools, my friend," Richius whispered gravely.

Then he clasped Prakna's hand.

All was silent. Out in the garden the world had grown cold, and Simon shivered in the moonlight. Two eyes blinked at him from a treetop, the curious gaze of a night bird, and the garden statues, half-eaten with lichens, listened deafly to the breeze. Simon cocked his head, surveying his surroundings. Except for his anxious breathing, he heard nothing. Overhead, the towers of Falindar glowed with candlelight. It was late, and most of the citadel had retired. A moment ago two Triin guardians had paced through the garden, giving him a puzzled stare. Simon nodded at them, and the small gesture was enough to send them on their way. Thanks to Vantran, he was trusted now.

Simon stuck his hand in his coat pocket and pulled out a piece of paper, neatly folded into a tiny square. Unfolding it, he inspected the numbers one through forty he had scribbled on the paper. All but five of them had been struck through, denoting the passing of the days. Simon looked up to consider the moon. There were still many hours until dawn, but he pulled his piece of black chalk from his pocket anyway and drew a line through day number thirty-six. In four days the *Intimidator* would be offshore, waiting for him. He had that much time to steal Shani. Simon muttered a curse. He had done a remarkable job of earning Vantran's confidence. Normally he would have been proud of himself. This time, however, he felt hollow and sick. Vantran and his wife had treated him like a friend, a turn of events even he hadn't foreseen, one that made the despicable act of stealing their child all the more difficult. He liked Richius. He liked Dyana, too. And he knew the young woman would be heartbroken by the loss of her daughter. Simon folded the paper again and returned it to his pocket.

Biagio, he seethed. *May God damn you eternally for making me do this.*

There was no choice, Simon told himself; there never had been. Despite the kindness of the Vantrans, he had never wavered in his commitment to his mission. This was about Eris. If he didn't return with the child as he'd promised, her life would be forfeit. It wasn't just that Biagio would forbid them to marry. He would kill her. Worse, he would hand her over to the monstrous Savros, who would ritualistically disembowel her. That was Biagio's way.

He hated Biagio now. The feeling had stunned him, because he had loved his master once. He was Roshann, and that meant unwavering loyalty. But Biagio had changed over the years, corrupted by the drug and thoughts of immortal power. There was a time when even Biagio would have spared a little girl, but no longer. Now he cut off heads without regard, and turned whole families over to the war labs for experiments. He was a monster, like Savros and the rest of them. And Simon was trapped. Simon knew he could only obey.

"You'll have the baby, Biagio," he whispered to the wind. "And that is all."

When he was done with this mission and Eris was his, Simon would take her away from Crote. They would not go to the Black City with Biagio. They would leave him and go underground, someplace where the Count of Crote would never find them, and they would live together as normal people and Simon would forget the blood he had spilled.

If he could.

He wasn't at all certain about that anymore. He knew he would see Dyana's face for the rest of his life. And Richius would haunt him, too. The Jackal would come after him. He would forgo his vendetta against Biagio and dedicate his every breath to finding the man who had kidnapped his daughter. And he would fail. Like Biagio would fail. Simon was the Roshann. The years had taught him tricks.

"I'm sorry," he whispered sadly, staring at the moon. "It's just the way it has to be."

He would have wept if he were more of a man, but Roshann conditioning had erased that part of him, too. The lump in his throat was contention enough. He wondered what Eris would think of him if she ever learned the truth. She already knew the sort of work he did for the count, but he was certain she could never understand this. Most likely, the baby would be murdered. Simon hoped it didn't wind up in the Mind Bender's hands. He put a hand to his forehead to banish the image.

Quickly! he shouted in his mind. *Make it quick, you bastard. She's only a child.*

In the end, though, Biagio's whim would determine how much the child suffered. If he felt magnanimous, the baby might die swiftly. If not, she might linger for months. Simon fell back against the brick wall of the garden and slowly melted to the ground. He sat there for long minutes, finding it impossible to move.

Four more days.

A boot scraped the pavement on the other side of the garden. Simon snapped out of his stupor and looked left. Past a nest of ferns a figure was approaching.

"Simon?" It was Richius.

Simon sat very still, hoping to pass unnoticed. But Richius rounded the ferns and saw him sitting on the ground with his arms wrapped around his knees. The young man stopped a few yards away.

"Simon? Are you all right?"

"I'm fine."

Richius chanced a step closer. "What are you doing out here?"

"Good question. What are you doing?"

"Looking for you. The guards told me they had seen you out here." Richius looked around for something interesting, then, seeing nothing, looked back at Simon. "Why are you sitting here in the cold?"

"I like the cold," said Simon. "And my privacy."

Richius refused to take the hint. "Is something wrong?"

"No."

"Tell me."

"What do you want, Richius?" Simon spat. All his anger at Biagio foamed over. "Can't you see I'm busy?"

"I can see you're brooding," said Richius. "That's all. I was hoping I could talk to you. I've been looking for you for an hour."

"Well, you found me." Simon patted the cold bricks beside him. "Sit down."

To Simon's surprise, Richius didn't hesitate to slide down next to him. Simon stole a glance at the younger man, sizing him up. Richius was studying the moon.

"You've got something on your mind," Simon declared. "Spit it out."

"All right," said Richius. "I'm going to Liss with Prakna."

Simon nodded. "I thought you would. Have you told your wife?"

"I have. She's angry."

"And what has the Lissen promised you? A chance to fight for Aramoor? Some Naren heads?"

"Oh, much more than that. He's promised me Biagio."

Dumbfounded, Simon could only blink. What the hell was Prakna planning?

"Biagio?" he blurted. "How?"

"By invading Biagio's island," Richius explained. "Says he's been decoying the Black Fleet away from Crote. Apparently Nicabar's ships have been lurking around Crote, protecting Biagio. But all the Lissen raids on the mainland have finally lured the Naren dreadnoughts back to imperial waters. Prakna plans to invade just as soon as he has an army ready."

Good God almighty! Simon looked away, trying hard not to betray his shock, but he was staggered by the news. An invasion of Crote? And Biagio didn't know? There would be hundreds killed. More, maybe. Maybe Eris.

"What does he want you for?" asked Simon. "To help him fight?"

"Sort of. He wants me to lead his army. Train them, too." Richius laughed bitterly. "He thinks he needs me. The Lissens are sailors, not soldiers. They need someone experienced to lead them."

"And you're the best they could get?" exclaimed Simon. "Good luck to them."

"I've led men before, Simon. I think I can do the job. Besides . . ." He rubbed his hands together. "It's my chance to get that bastard Biagio. If we capture him, I can do what I want with him. Prakna said so."

The old training rose up in Simon like a wave. He thought of pulling his dagger and ramming it through Vantran's ribs. He thought of smashing his smug head against the wall until it cracked. Like the old days. But he just sat there and did nothing, reminding himself of his role and mission.

"You're a damned fool," Simon said finally. "You're starting down a path you won't ever come back from."

"I have to do this, Simon. I have a responsibility to Aramoor, and to Sabrina. It's—"

"Stop fooling yourself, Richius. This isn't about Aramoor, and it isn't about your first wife, either. This is about revenge."

"So what if it is?" rumbled Richius, getting to his feet. He glared down at Simon, his eyes wild. "I thought at least you would understand! You know what Nar is like. Is it so wrong to want revenge?" He jammed a thumb into his chest. "I want revenge, Simon. And God damn it all, I'm going to have it!"

Simon smiled mercilessly. "Good for you. Is that why you wanted to see me? To tell me about your heroic quest?"

"No," said Richius. "I have a favor to ask. I want you to look after Dyana and Shani while I'm gone. Be Dyana's friend for me. She's alone here, especially with Lucyler gone. But she likes you, I think. You can protect her. Will you do that?"

Simon refused to think about it. "No, I won't," he said flatly. "Your wife and daughter are *your* responsibility, Richius. Don't try to push them off on me."

Even as he said it, Simon felt nauseated. But he had already broken one promise to Richius, that day when he had met Dyana and the baby in the field. He had sworn not to harm them, and that pledge was going to be broken in four more days. He wasn't about to leave Lucel-Lor with another shattered oath on his conscience.

"Simon, I'm asking you as a friend," said Richius. "Look after them for me, just for a while; until I return."

"And what if you don't come back, Richius? What am I supposed to do with them?"

"Simon, what is this?" asked Richius. He knelt down on the hard ground of the garden. "Why are you so angry with me? I thought you of all people would understand."

"Wrong." Simon looked away, unable to stand Vantran's earnest face. Yet he knew it wasn't hatred he felt. It was shame. "Don't make your problems mine. I've got a plateful of my own."

"Please," Richius cajoled. "I'm leaving with Prakna the day after tomorrow. Say you'll change your mind by then. Don't make me leave worrying about them. Without Lucyler—"

"I said no! Are you deaf? I'm not going to look after them. I'm not going to give you my blessing, and I'm not going to say everything is all right. So make this stupid decision without me!"

Richius was stunned. Very slowly he got to his feet. He lingered over Simon for a moment, then turned and stalked away. But before he was gone he paused near the ferns and cast one last look in Simon's direction.

"I don't know what I did to make you so mad, Simon," he said softly, "but I thought we were friends."

He was gone as quickly as he'd come, swallowed up by the darkness. Simon buried his head in his arms and closed his eyes.

"You want to know why I'm mad, you fool?" he whispered. "Because when you're gone and I take the baby, Dyana will have nothing."

EIGHTEEN

Men-at-Arms

Duke Enli sat back into the cushions of the coach, highly satisfied with himself. Barely three days had passed since he'd come to Nar's capital, and already Vorto's army was readying itself. At the duke's urging, the Archbishop of Nar had wasted no time in preparing for the coming battle in Dragon's Beak. That night he had summoned Vorto to the cathedral and together the three of them had laid plans. General Vorto had been vocal and displeased, but had acquiesced to Herrith's demands. And despite his opposition to the long trek, Vorto had moved with amazing speed. Through the windows of his coach Enli glanced at the driver who had brought him the news. He was a small man in service to the general, and had come unannounced to Enli's room in the cathedral.

"General Vorto wants you," he had said. "Quickly."

Now it was just past dawn. Enli rubbed fatigue from his eyes. He had thought of sending the driver away, but he thought it best not to antagonize the general. Vorto was the key to their entire plan. Enli wanted his trust. Alone in the comfortable carriage, Enli pondered their destination. They had crossed the bridge over the river Kiel and were heading toward the Black Palace, the vacated seat of Naren power. Enli put his cheek against the glass to see better. In the Black City, the palace was called "the onyx jewel," and now Enli knew why. It was an awesome structure. Not beautiful the way the cathedral was, but chilling and strangely stunning. The sun was coming up behind it, setting it aflame. Compared to his own Red Tower, the palace was massive, fit for giants.

His driver had neglected to tell him where they were going, so Enli had guessed. Vorto, he supposed, had taken up residence in the palace.

Balls of iron, thought the duke.

Outside the window, the breaking dawn tossed shadows through the streets. The smell of the polluted river and the smoke of the war labs wafted through the glass, stinging Enli's nose. An umber sky lit their way as sunlight struggled in the haze. The Black City was awakening. Already vendors and merchants pushed through the avenues, dragging their wares to the market. A slave trader and his convoy shuffled past, and a band of beggars stretched in an alleyway between two houses, roused by the light. They would breakfast on rats, and if they were lucky pick a few pockets, for this was life in Nar for the poor. But higher up, in the towers and tall spires, the Naren lords awoke in splendor in perfumed beds, their skin soft and oiled, their minds cloudy with narcotics. Weary from a night of lovemaking, they would go to the window and check the weather, and not think twice of the toil in the streets. Enli's eyes narrowed as his gaze drifted upward. Biagio was one of those lords. And the count didn't give a damn about the destitute or the depraved. He only wanted Nar.

The carriage driver steered them through a broad street and ascended the palace road. The Black Palace had only one approach, a wide avenue trimmed with golden lamps and marble bricks that wound snakelike up to the impressive castle. But though Enli had expected to find the road deserted, it was not. A caravan of soldiers was walking toward the castle, while another was coming down. Men wearing the insignia of the Naren legions walked and rode on horseback and dragged packs and animals up and down the way, and the street quickly choked with activity. Enli rapped hard on the carriage wall with his boot, bidding the driver to hurry. But the driver kept his slow ascent up the mountain road, leaving the duke to puzzle. Aggravated, Enli pressed his nose up against the glass to study the throng of soldiers. There was purpose in their movement, and Enli realized at once that this was the force Vorto had arrayed for him.

His heart sank.

So many men. He had asked for a division without really knowing what the number meant to Vorto. It was Biagio's plan to get as many legionnaires out of the city as possible, but now the success of the count's design became apparent. Enli's eyes widened. Vorto had taken his plea for help with all seriousness. Quickly Enli tabulated the figures. He had the army of the air back at home, and Biagio's mercenaries, all waiting for him in Dragon's Beak. He also had Nicabar's Black Fleet, if the admiral was on his way as Biagio had promised. But were they all enough? This really *was* a division, and the sight of it withered Enli's confidence.

The coach picked its way through the swarm of soldiers, finally stopping at the apex of the hill, just outside the sprawling parade grounds at the base of the Black Palace. Enli waited inside, awed by the sight before him. Hundreds of men, garbed in metal and heavy coats, toiled in the new-day sun, stuffing backpacks and shoeing horses, sharpening steel and loading carts. Horned greegans, the huge, armor-plated beasts used to pull war wagons, honked and snorted as trainers brushed their scaly hides and fixed their mouths with bridles. Horsemen trotted by, dwarfing the scurrying infantrymen in their high-topped boots. In the center of the grounds stood a gang of officers, chatting among themselves and shouting directions to their men. Bare-chested slaves heaved their shoulders against the nearly immovable weight of steel wagons, pushing them into position while their brethren hooked up the flame cannons. Acid launchers waited atop wheeled frames, their baglike bellows slack. Cannisters of munitions stood beside them, filled with the corrosive agents that could eat through human flesh.

"Too many," Enli whispered nervously. "Too bloody many."

Before he had left for Nar City, there had been four hundred mercenaries in his army, plus the two hundred men of his own brigade. That meant they would be outnumbered by the legion, and certainly outgunned. If Nicabar and the heavy guns of the *Fearless* failed to make it to Dragon's Beak, they would be routed. He gave a low curse, hating himself for making such a convincing case to Herrith. He had begged the bishop for the troops, and now bitterly recalled that old adage—Be careful what you wish for.

The coach driver got down from his bench and came around to open Enli's door. A rushing stench of horse manure blasted Enli in the face. He got out and stepped into the trampled earth of the parade ground, swallowed by a cacophony of noise.

"Where's Vorto?" he asked the driver. The slow-witted man pointed a bony finger at the officers in the center of the throng. Enli squinted to see past the press of bodies and detected the giant general among his men. Vorto's shaved head stood taller than the rest. He was busying himself with a pair of officers, one of whom Enli had met two days before, the dour-faced Colonel Kye. Vorto was gesturing to a flat-bedded wagon, while a crew of engineers hoisted rocket launchers into the conveyance and strapped them down securely. Beside the wagon stood a dozen metal cannisters, oddly shaped and bigger than those of the acid launchers. Seeing that his driver wouldn't lead him farther, Enli shouldered into the crowd and approached General Vorto. The bald giant caught a glimpse of him as he neared and a sardonic smile split his face.

"Duke Enli," he bellowed, waving the duke over. "Come and see what I've done for you."

Enli didn't bother to greet the general or his underlings. "Are these your men?" he asked. "The ones dispatched to Dragon's Beak?"

"Enough for you, I hope?" said Vorto. "We've been preparing throughout the night for the trip. With luck we'll be ready to deploy on the morrow."

"This is quite an army you've arranged," said the duke, looking around. "How many are there?"

"A division," said Vorto. "What you asked for."

"And how many is that, precisely?"

Vorto and a young officer chortled. Colonel Kye remained quiet.

"A division is three units. Does that help you at all, Duke?"

Enli sighed, too tired to play the game. "They look like enough. And if they're as good as you claim, we should win the day."

"We will win the day. *In* a day," Vorto prophesied. "Against that undisciplined rabble of Dragon's Beak, it will be over in an hour. Look . . ." The general gestured toward the crowd. "More men and materials than I took with me to Goth. We have war wagons, acid launchers, supplies for the trip, everything." Vorto reached out and patted Enli's cheek. "Don't worry, sweet fellow. We'll get your country back for you."

The taunting gesture raised Enli's hackles, but he checked his anger, saying, "This is wonderful, Vorto. You've done a very good job. Dragon's Beak will thank you."

Vorto's enormous chest puffed out. "I want some pretty maids when we're done with our work, Enli. Let Dragon's Beak's daughters show me their thanks!"

More laughing from the young lieutenant. More dark silence from Kye. A stray horse trotted by, then voided itself near their boots. Enli turned his nose away. Vorto's round face reddened.

"I'll see to it," said Kye quickly. He took hold of the horse's reins and led the beast away in search of its master. Vorto watched him go, keeping his eyes on the colonel's back. Enli noted Vorto's sourness.

"A good man," said Vorto, "but no faith." He turned to Enli and jabbed a finger into the duke's chest. "You must have faith, Duke Enli. Do you?"

"Faith in what?"

"Faith in God almighty," thundered Vorto. He took his finger out of Enli's chest and pointed it at the flag flying in the center of the company. The Light of God, that ubiquitous symbol seen everywhere in Nar, fluttered in the wind. "That's what we're fighting for, Enli. Make no mistake. If our hearts are pure, God will deliver victory."

Enli smiled thinly. "I welcome any help the Lord might offer. But don't get overconfident. This won't be the walk in a rose garden you're imagining. It's already winter in Dragon's Beak. My brother has many troops of his own. And he has his army of the air."

"Bah! I have heard of your brother's trained birds. You make too much of them, I think."

"You wouldn't say that if you'd ever seen them," observed Enli. A tremor of anticipation overcame him. "Or fought against them. They're not just ravens, not like you're used to. These are bloody beasts, big as your head. Bigger, even. They feast on eyeballs and drink blood, like a bunch of bloody vampires."

The lieutenant standing next to Vorto blanched at the description. "How big?" he queried. He held his hands a foot apart. "Like this?"

"Bigger," said Enli. "Not like your head, boy. Like the general's."

Vorto frowned. "That's all brain."

"Whatever. These ravens will eat that too, if you let them." Enli grinned at the young soldier. "Take a helmet with you, lad."

"General?" squeaked the soldier.

"He's trying to scare you, Vale. You just keep your wits about you. We'll swat those damnable birds right out of the sky." He turned on Enli and laughed. "Bloody birds. The day I'm afraid of a bird I'll hang myself."

The duke shrugged. "That day may be sooner than you think. But we'll worry about that then, eh?"

"General . . . ?"

"Shut up, Vale. Enli, I'm looking forward to dealing with those butcher birds. This legion wears the armor of Heaven." Vorto folded his meaty arms across his chest. "We have some surprises of our own for your bastard brother."

"Such as?"

With his chin, the general pointed toward the flatbed of rocket launchers. "That."

Enli shook his head. "It won't work. It's already winter up north. Too much wind for rockets."

"Not rockets, Duke Enli." Vorto leaned in with a conspiratorial smile. "Something better."

Enli's eyes flicked toward the cannisters. "What's in those? Acid?"

Vorto put his arm around the duke and led him toward the wagon. The engineers worked a little quicker as their leader approached. Enli squirmed at the general's touch but did not pull away.

"This is something very special," whispered the general. "Something not even the army of the air will be able to escape from. A present from the war labs."

The cannisters were the size of a helmet, polished metal containers smooth to Enli's touch. He ran his hand over one and felt its cool surface for flaws. Instead, he found a machined perfection.

"The rocket launchers have been modified to fire the cannisters," Vorto explained. "They don't need to be as accurate as rockets."

"What's in it?" asked Enli. He picked up a cannister and gave it a gentle shake. Inside, something liquid sloshed about. He cocked his head to listen, unsure what he was hearing, then very slowly put the container down, horrified by the thought. When he lifted his eyes to Vorto he saw the general grinning.

"Goth," said the duke breathlessly. "Don't tell me—"

"Formula B," said Vorto. "Perfected, no thanks to Minister Bovadin. Just the thing to deal with your brother's flying pests."

"No!" railed Enli. "You can't let this poison loose in Dragon's Beak. I won't allow it!"

"You won't?" laughed Vorto. "Enli, it's not your choice. This is my army. *My* war to wage."

"It's my country, you idiot! I won't let you turn it into a wasteland just to wipe out some birds."

Vorto smoldered at the insult. "It's the north fork we're fighting for, not your territory. And I'll do what I must to take it. The Renaissance, Enli. That's what this is about. I'm going to eradicate it in Dragon's Beak just as I did in Goth. And if you get squeamish on me . . ." His three-fingered hand snatched Enli's lapel. "I will throw you to your brother's birds and watch them peck your liver out."

Very slowly, Duke Enli took hold of Vorto's hand and removed it. But he did not back away from the wild-eyed general. Instead he matched his steely gaze. "I won't let you murder my country, Vorto. You're coming with me to quell the rebellion. And that is all. When you're in Dragon's Beak, you're under *my* dominion."

It felt good just to say it. The general didn't bother stepping back, but Enli sensed the surprise in him nonetheless.

"It is there if we need it," said Vorto. "And if we need it, I will use it."

"If we need it, then we will all be dead, General." Enli noted the size of the cannister. "If you launch that poison in a stiff wind, there won't be anywhere for us to hide."

"God guides me," replied Vorto with confidence. "If it is His will to use the formula, He will protect us."

Enli turned away, his argument lost. Vorto was Herrith's puppet, and if Herrith had told him to bring the formula, then bring it he would. And he would launch at the first raindrop or thunder clap or falling leaf—whatever he saw as a sign from God. The duke poked at one of the cannisters with his foot, testing its veracity. He hadn't imagined Herrith would dare use the formula against Dragon's Beak. Bleakly he wondered if Biagio had miscalculated the bishop's mettle.

General Vorto, his pride clearly wounded, sauntered over to Enli and spun him around by the shoulder. "I thought you would be pleased," he said bitterly. "Look at all I've done for you." He made a sweeping gesture with his hand, indicating the mass of men. "Are you going to get weak-kneed on me? Like Colonel Kye or some woman? This was your idea, remember."

"This is fine," said Enli. "All but the poison." He walked past Vorto heading back to the coach. "Be ready to leave on the morrow."

"The Black Renaissance," Vorto called after him. "We're going to eradicate a cancer!"

Enli flashed a hidden smile as he walked away. *So long as you believe that, madman.*

NINETEEN

The Jackal's Daughter

As the sun descended, Simon Darquis stalked through the halls of Falindar, closing the distance to Dyana's chamber. It was dinner time for the Jackal's wife, who ate with the other women of the citadel in the main kitchen on the ground floor when her husband was away. Simon moved with practiced deftness, keeping to the shadows and to the lamp light equally. His head pounded and his hands trembled. He had ended his struggle with his conscience and had put it on a shelf, someplace in the trained recesses of his brain where it wouldn't nag at him.

Tonight, he was Dark-Heart.

The Vantrans' chambers were at the end of a corridor, unguarded, surrounded by other modest rooms like it. The doors in the hall stood half-open, some vacant, some issuing unsuspecting voices. At evening mealtime, the people of the citadel always gathered together downstairs, far away from the Vantran rooms. Simon had copiously observed their rhythms. He knew with the perfection of a time-piece when Dyana was with Shani—and when she was not. He had hardly spoken to her since Richius had left for Liss, for she was distant now. All of Falindar was buzzing with talk of the Jackal—how he had left his wife and child behind, how his blood-lust couldn't be slaked.

Today, Simon had analyzed Dyana's every movement. From the shadows he had stalked her, ghostlike and invisible. He had watched her walk with Shani in the garden, watched her dissolve into tears and walk back again, and he had done it all with remarkable detachment. Too distraught to feel his eyes on her, Dyana had gone on about her daily business, oblivious to the Roshann agent breathing in her perfume. And now she had left Shani with Tresh to dine with the others.

With easy nonchalance, Simon crossed the corridor to Dyana's chamber. He paused outside the door to listen and heard the shuffling of light footsteps. Inside the room, a door opened, then closed again. The sound of ruffling clothing, the unknown din of something scraping. Simon devoured the sounds and filtered them through his quick mind. One person, light enough to be the Triin nurse. The baby was asleep, perhaps. He took a breath, steadied himself, and knocked on the door with a painted smile.

The light footfalls approached the door and opened it. The Triin woman called Tresh stood in the threshold. Her eyes widened when she sighted Simon.

"Simon?" she asked through her thick accent. They barely knew each other, and the proper name startled Simon. "What is it?"

"Dyana," said Simon. He opened his hands. "Shani. Dyana wants Shani, downstairs." He pretended to struggle with the words. "Downstairs, yes? Do you understand?"

"I speak your language," said the woman. Her eyes narrowed. "Is Dyana all right?"

"She's fine. I was just down with her, supping." Simon gave a shrug. "She misses the child. This thing with Richius, I suppose. She was going to come up for her herself, but I told her I'd bring her. Would you come downstairs with us?"

Tresh grimaced. "Shani sleeps now. Dyana knows this. That girl . . ." She shook her head, exasperated. "Her mind is mud these days."

Simon sighed knowingly. "Richius."

"Yes, that husband of hers." Tresh wagged a finger in Simon's face. "You are his friend. You should have stopped him. Now Dyana is mad at you."

"I know," lied Simon. "It's my fault. I tried to stop him, but Richius wouldn't listen. Stubborn, you know?" With one eye he looked over Tresh's shoulder into the room. Shani was nowhere in sight. "Should I tell Dyana the girl's asleep?" he asked. "She'll understand, I suppose."

"No, no," Tresh grumbled. "I will wake her and take her down with you. It will be good for Dyana. She needs the baby close these days." The nurse turned her back on Simon and walked into the room. Simon followed cautiously behind. His stomach gave a sickening lurch. Very slowly he put his hand behind his back and gave the door a gentle nudge, just enough to close it without making a sound. His hand then drifted to his belt and withdrew a stiletto.

"Dyana will be happy to see the baby," Tresh was saying. "She is so sad now. Shani—"

Tresh's voice constricted the moment the blade severed her spine. Simon's free hand shot up and covered her mouth as he drove the stiletto deeper. The woman shuddered, her knees buckling. Blood sluiced from the incision onto Simon's hand. The sensation made him retch but he held fast, deepening the gash until Tresh's shaking ceased and a feeble death rattle trickled through his fingers.

"Good people go to Heaven," Simon whispered. Her eyes widened at the observation, horror-struck. Gently, Simon laid her down, withdrawing the blade but keeping his hand over her mouth. "Forgive me, woman," he begged. "Go with God. Curse me when you see Him."

The dying nurse tried and failed to move her paralyzed arms. What looked like a tear fell from her eyes. She gasped once, twice, trying to suck in air. A soundless scream climbed out of her mouth. . . .

And then she died.

Simon knelt over the dead woman. For a very long moment he forgot the direness of his mission. A wave of self-loathing drowned him. Carefully he reached out his bloodied hand and closed the woman's sightless eyes. He dragged the dead woman out of the center of the room, pulling her into one of the bedchambers. The scent told him at once it was Dyana's room, the one she shared with Richius. Simon cleaned his hands on Tresh's dress, composing himself. He didn't want the child to see him looking frightened.

Easy! he scolded himself. *Be still.*

At his command his heartbeat slowed. His breathing tranquilized. A serene smile crossed his face, as if the corpse at his feet existed only in a dream. Trancelike, he walked from the bedroom into the main chamber, quickly spotting the door to Shani's room. The hinges squeaked as he pushed it open and peered inside. At once he sighted the Jackal's daughter, asleep upon a tiny bed of wood and white sheets. The room was dark but for the last rays of sunlight splashing through the window. Shani's face glowed pink, unmindful of the murder of her nurse. Without waking her, Simon crept over to the bed and knelt down beside it, studying the child. She had her father's round eyes and her mother's milky skin. A strand of fawn hair fell across her forehead. At one year old, she could only toddle. Getting her out of the citadel would be difficult. But Simon was determined not to hurt her. He had considered gagging her, even stuffing her in a sack, but had quickly dismissed the idea. So instead he would try a different approach, one that might, with Heaven's grace, seem plausible.

He would just walk out with her.

Most of the folk of the citadel trusted him now, and if they saw him with the child walking toward the kitchen they probably wouldn't question him. Simon very gently reached out and touched the child, brushing the wayward hair from her face.

"Shani," he whispered cheerfully. "Wake up. I have to take you to your mother."

Shani's eyes opened at the sound of the strange voice. They focused on Simon in confusion, but were unafraid.

"Hello," he crooned. He gave the girl an encouraging smile while he continued stroking her hair. "Don't be afraid. I'm not going to hurt you. Mother wants you. *Mother.*"

Shani frowned, then let out a frustrated grunt. Simon slowly slipped the covers down and took her hand. It was impossibly small. Soft too, like a rose petal. Instinctively the fragile fingers wrapped around his.

"My name is Simon," he said. "I . . ."

He stopped, unable to complete the lie. A vision of Eris flashed through his mind, and then Biagio, waiting with the Mind Bender for the child. Even as he fought to still himself, he began to shake.

"Shani," he whispered desperately. "I know you can't understand me, but listen. I'm an evil man. But I love a woman, and I can't let her die. I'm taking you someplace, and I'll do my best to protect you there. I swear it."

Surprisingly, Shani smiled at him, not pulling her hand away. Simon guided her gently out of the bed. N'Dek and the *Intimidator* would be offshore, waiting for him in a few short hours.

He hadn't expected the babe to be so compliant. But Shani stood on her own, albeit shakily, her bare feet padding with him to a closet stuffed with clothing. Simon undressed her and hurriedly pulled some day clothes over her head. Shani squirmed and giggled, enjoying the attention. Simon rolled stockings and a pair of tiny shoes onto her feet, then took her hand again. Outside, not far from the entry to the citadel, he had hidden a coat to keep her warm on the long trek to the tower. An hour ago, he had stolen one of Falindar's precious horses. The missing horse, he knew, would be noticed quickly.

"We're going to go for a ride," he told Shani. "Be a good girl for me. Please."

Dyana left the kitchen after her meal, ignoring the appeals from her friends to stay with them and talk. She skirted the Triin warriors in the great hall of Falindar and made her way to the rear of the citadel where the heart tree grew and the cliff dove down to the ocean below. It was very cold, and she had no coat, but the moon was coming up and the shiver through her skin heightened her melancholy. The heart tree, that lone and legendary symbol of the Gods, erupted out of the rocky earth, blocking the moonbeams. Dyana stared at it, and before she could stop them, the tears came.

Without Richius, she was alone here. Her companions were nothing like her. She was more Naren than Triin, they said, more interested in being a man than a woman. Her independent streak had earned her a reputation in Falindar, and now, with her husband off on a foolish crusade, Dyana felt the crush of loneliness. She cowled her arms around her shoulders to stave off the breeze.

In the end, she hadn't begged Richius to stay. She had refused to shed tears for him. Now she wept openly, and wished he was here to comfort her. But men were foolish, even good men like Richius. And they were all too easily swayed by revenge. Dyana brushed her tears away angrily. Shani needed her. She would not be the weak-as-water woman the others expected her to be.

Dyana returned to the citadel, climbing the spiral staircase leading to the level of her bedchamber. It was very quiet in the corridor. Across the dim hallway, she found the door to her chambers an inch ajar. Without a thought she pushed open the door.

"I am here, Tresh," she said in Triin. "Shani? Are you awake?"

No answer. No sound, either. Dyana hastened to her daughter's room and gasped at the disheveled state of her closet. All of Shani's clothes, the little Triin skirts and shoulder wraps, were strewn about the floor. The bed was unmade but empty. Dyana's heart leapt with panic. She dashed into her own bedroom . . .

. . . and saw Tresh twisted on the floor.

Dyana froze. She stared at the dead woman, mute and breathless. Tresh lay in a waste of crimson, her eyes shut, her limbs stiff and impossibly bent. The color of life had drained from her flesh to stain the floor. Dyana backed away, slowly at first, then in a frenzy.

"Shani!" she screamed, racing from her bedroom. "Someone help me!"

Out in the hall, doors flung open. Startled Triin faces peered out from their chambers, roused by Dyana's screams. One by one she asked the onlookers if they had seen Shani, but each of them shook their heads in confusion, unaware of the dead woman down the hall. Dyana didn't bother to explain. She flew down the stairs, taking them three at a time. All she could think about was Simon.

"You bastard!" she muttered, already certain of her quarry. "You did it, you monster. . . ."

She found herself cursing Simon and Richius both—the Naren for taking Shani, her husband for abandoning her. The unendurable thought that Shani might be—

"No!" she spat, refusing to believe it. "You will not take my baby!"

Biagio . . .

The name rang in her head like a bell. At the bottom of the stairs she collided with Deemis. Seeing her distress, the warrior took hold of her.

"What is it, woman?" he demanded.

Dyana grabbed his shirt with both fists. "My daughter; have you seen her? Have you seen Shani?"

Deemis frowned, clearly perplexed. "I have not. What is it?"

"What about Simon? Have you seen him?"

"Dyana, no. I—"

"Deemis, help me! He has taken her, I know he has. Tresh is dead in my chambers! He killed her and took Shani. I have to find her."

She tried to tear away from the man but he held her fast. "Stop now!" he ordered roughly. "Where is Tresh? What has happened?"

Dyana hurriedly explained how she had gone upstairs and found Tresh murdered in her rooms. Her daughter was gone, she explained, and only Simon would have taken her.

"Richius was right, Deemis," she insisted. "He has taken her. We have to find him. Lorris and Pris, help me!"

"You will go to the kitchens and wait there with the women," Deemis ordered. He took her by the shoulders, forcing her to listen. "Stay with them. We will find your daughter and this snake," he snarled. "We will, Dyana. Now go."

"Deemis—"

"Go!" he barked, shoving her away. He didn't wait to see her leave, but instead turned his back and started bellowing for help and horses. The sound brought warriors running. At their master's order they scrambled for the gates, spreading out in a wave. Dyana fell backward against the wall and closed her eyes, and all the loss she had ever felt in her life was nothing compared to the void swallowing her now.

The horse Simon had stolen from the stables was fast and black and perfectly invisible in the moonlight. With the Jackal's daughter wrapped in a coat in front of him, he sank low in the saddle and rode hard, following the trails through the grassy valleys and woodlands, past the eyes of owls and far, far away from the towers of Falindar. For the first hour of the journey Shani hardly made a sound, but well into their second hour of riding she began to fret. Simon tried to cheer her, but he dared not slow his pace. Every rough jolt made the child more uncomfortable and vocal. By the third hour, Shani was crying hysterically.

"Easy, child. Easy," Simon pleaded. They were in a thick forest with only the moon to guide them, and Simon worried that the horse would break a leg. Shani wailed. It was very late, and the time of his rendezvous was fast approaching. He had made extraordinary time, but he wondered if the impatient N'Dek would wait past midnight for him to arrive. The recently departed Lissen schooners might have frightened the captain off, or he might decide that his passenger had been found out. Simon tried not to think of it, and found a distraction in Shani's knifelike cries.

"Not much farther, girl," he said, trying to soothe her. "I know it's cold. I'm sorry."

He *was* sorry. Remarkably, he regretted every step. But then he remembered Eris and the mind-sick Biagio, and was able to subdue his regrets. With one hand on the reins he wrapped the other around the child, holding her fast, imparting what comfort he could. Shani seemed to nestle in his embrace. The human need for warmth overcame her, and she buried herself in Simon's coat. She was light like her mother. Simon held her carefully, as if he were cradling an egg.

By now Dyana had discovered them gone. Doubtless, she was frantic. Simon knew he had ruined her, maybe in a way worse than he'd murdered Tresh. At least the nurse's pain was over. Dyana's would be endless.

"Your mother loves you very much," he said absently as they raced beneath a canopy of fruit trees. "You'll see her again, if I can help it. I'll do it if I can. God help me to try."

If God wasn't deaf to the prayers of assassins, if He cared at all for innocent children, He would help Simon find the way. Simon grit his teeth at the thought. Suddenly he wanted God to damn him, to drag him to Hell for all the countless sins and burn him eternally. With all the self-loathing in the world he made a silent promise to Heaven, that he would gladly burn forever to save both Eris and the Vantran baby.

They rode in darkness for another hour, burying the distance between Falindar and their hidden destination. What had taken Simon a day to walk, they were traversing in mere hours, and when at last Simon heard the shore again he knew they were near the tower.

Simon Darquis felt his stomach knot with dread.

He slowed his horse just a bit and cocked his head to listen. Even Shani stopped her crying, pacified by the distant sound of surf. Simon took a sniff and smelled the brine of the ocean. He sharpened his eyes on the horizon, peering through the moonlight, and with his trained vision glimpsed the dark outline of the tower. His vigor renewed, he kicked his heels into the horse's sides, propelling it on faster. The way was narrow and treacherous, but time was short and so was Simon's patience, and when the horse hesitated he struck it again, harder this time, all his guilt and frustration cracking against the animal's ribs. But when at last they neared the tower clearing, Simon drew back on the reins and slowed the horse to a cautious trot, finally bringing it to a full halt when the shadow of the structure fell upon them. In his arms Shani kicked and gave a gurgle of protest. Simon smiled bleakly down at her.

"You're right to fear, girl," he admitted.

The tower seemed deserted, but through the moonlight Simon saw two black specks floating on the ocean. He stared at the horizon, dumbfounded. Two ships? What was N'Dek doing? Not caring if the horse ran off without him, Simon dismounted, then helped down his little parcel. He did not let the child's feet touch the ground, though. Instead he held her in his arms as he abandoned the exhausted steed and headed cautiously toward the tower. The open archway beckoned with blackness. Simon held his breath. Shani, sensing his trepidation, did the same. Inside the dark recesses he heard a scraping sound, the sound of boots on stone. When he heard it a second time, he paused.

"Who's in there?" he called.

A long silence ensued. Finally a shadow appeared in the archway, man-sized and silent. Another one followed, and then two more. Simon could tell from the hue of their flesh that they weren't Triin. He addressed the shadows loudly.

"It's Simon Darquis. Come out here and show yourselves!"

The silhouettes came forward, giving Shani a start. Four men, two in uniforms of the fleet, the others clothed ordinarily, stepped out into the moonlight and peered questioningly at Simon. One of them, a tall man with a scarred, clean-shaven face, took the lead.

"Darquis," said the sailor with a wave. "Is that the child?"

"It is," Simon declared. "Those other two, who are they?"

All four men walked toward Simon, eyeing the confused child in his arms. The sailor who had spoken first laughed when he saw the girl.

"Captain N'Dek was right about you," he chuckled. "He said you'd make it, and with the child."

"We thought the gogs had found you out," added another, one of the men who wasn't a sailor. Simon fixed iron eyes on him.

"Who the hell are you?" he asked. "Not a sailor."

The stranger took no offense at Simon's tone. Instead he offered out his hand, saying, "We share the same master, Simon Darquis. We know of you. And we know of your work here."

Simon bristled. "Biagio sent you?" he growled. "Why?"

"We're to watch the Jackal for the Master while you bring his daughter to our lord," the man answered. He had the same lilting voice as many Roshann agents, the same inscrutable expression. "The Master is awaiting you back on Crote, but he doesn't want to be without eyes here."

Son of a bitch, hissed Simon silently. Biagio trusted no one these days.

"Is that why there are two vessels offshore?" he berated the sailor.

"You fools. There are Lissen schooners about! If they see your goddamn ships we're finished."

"We saw no schooners," stammered the sailor. "And this is Biagio's will." He seemed shocked by Simon's rebellion, almost in awe. "The other came to deliver these two. That's all I know."

"It has to be off the coast by daybreak," Simon snarled, turning again on the Roshann agents. He started to tell them about Richius being gone, but then, remarkably, stopped himself. "Do you hear me?" he stalled. "Before the dawn that ship must be gone!"

"The *Revenge* arrived two days ago," explained the other Roshann agent. This one was smaller and darker than his brother, with black eyes and sharp white teeth that reflected the moon. "She brought us here and we're establishing our base in the tower. When we are done, when we need nothing more from her, she will depart."

"We're to take you aboard *Intimidator*," said the sailor. He tried to look brave in the face of Simon's ire. "Whenever you're ready."

"Captain N'Dek is waiting for you," said the small one. He reached out and stroked Shani's cheek. "Go quickly. The Master is waiting for his prize."

Simon yanked Shani away. "Keep back," he threatened. "And don't presume to tell me what to do, Roshann. I am Dark-Heart."

The name had enough weight to erase the agent's grin. "And you've done well, as well as the Master expected. Now go and bring him the child. Go home, Dark-Heart. Rest in Crote."

The warm body in his arms gave Simon the smallest pause. He looked down at the creature he had kidnapped. Shani looked up at him, her expression confused, her face flush from the cold. A little trail of mucus ran from her nose. He bunched up his coat sleeve and wiped the trail away.

"The boat's waiting for you," said the sailor. He pointed toward the rocky shore. "That way."

Because they were all watching him, because he had done this evil thing and could never turn back, Simon walked in silence toward the shore and the rowboat that would take him to the *Intimidator*.

At midnight, when the moon had set and Falindar had fallen into silence, Dyana Vantran sat alone in the bedchamber of her abducted daughter. Deemis and the other warriors had found no trace of Shani, and though they were still hard at the search, hopelessness grew by the minute. Simon Darquis, if that was his name, had disappeared, and the coincidence of it convinced Dyana of her daughter's fate. As she stared at the moon through an open window, her husband's words came to her on the breeze.

The Roshann is everywhere.

She hadn't believed him. Neither had Lucyler. The golden demon Biagio who stalked Richius' dreams was very real, Dyana knew now, and obviously as evil as Richius had claimed. Tresh was dead. Deemis' men had taken her body away and had scrubbed clean most of the blood on the floor. Dyana didn't want to be with her women friends tonight. She insisted on being alone—in Shani's room. Dyana stared blindly out of the window, wondering bleakly what Richius would think of her. He had only been gone for a day and a half, and already she had lost their daughter. She was alone again, like she had been before meeting Richius, and the familiar feeling angered her.

"Where are you, Simon?" she whispered. She could hear the ocean and could see the moon on the waves, and these things calmed her and cleared her mind. "Roshann," she chanted. "Where are you?"

He had come to Lucel-Lor by ship, no doubt. There was simply no way he could have come so far on foot or horseback. Falindar was on the northern fringes of Lucel-Lor, and far away from the Saccenne Run, the only route linking the Triin to the Empire. Dyana focused on the ocean, recalling everything she could about the Naren. He was tall and thin and strangely quiet, especially lately. No doubt he had been planning his kidnapping. Dyana remembered her talk with him in the hall outside the meeting chamber, when Prakna had come for Richius. He had actually seemed to care about her. And she had stupidly believed him. It was like Richius had said—the Roshann were devils. Like shape-shifters.

"My fault," she hissed.

How, she wondered, had he come to them looking so ragged? Another Naren trick? Had he starved himself and laid in the sun? He had claimed he had wandered since the end of the Naren invasion. According to Richius, Simon had subsisted on the provisions of the land, stealing sometimes, gathering what he could, and generally keeping to himself. There were hundreds of villages in Tatterak alone.

But there were no towers.

Dyana inched away from the window, almost stumbling.

Towers.

Simon had said he'd seen towers. But there were no towers in the south. The only abandoned towers were . . .

She bolted from Shani's bedroom to her own, riffling through her closets for warm clothes and boots. Hurriedly she dressed, pulling on her clothing and lacing up her footwear, her mind exploding with hope.

"Towers," she gasped. "One tower!"

The one far away, past the valley on the sea. It was abandoned and had been for years. Lucyler had shown it to them once, when they had all ridden from Falindar to picnic on a summer day. It was tall and wretched and perfect for a hideout, and if Simon had known of it he had surely lied to them about coming from the south.

"He is there," she said. "He must be. . . ."

If he was trying to escape, then there would be a ship waiting for him.

There were few men left in the castle to help Dyana, and she knew they wouldn't let her go anyway. She was a woman, and in old-fashioned Falindar that meant very little.

She darted out the door and dashed down the stairs.

She would need a mount. She wasn't an accomplished rider like her husband, but she could handle a horse and knew that in the stables there was one already waiting for her, the one steed in Falindar that no Triin warrior dared to touch, not even Lucyler.

Lightning.

Richius' horse was fast, and Dyana knew that the gelding would be waiting there for her, unattended as the other men of the citadel rode off in search of Shani. At the bottom of the stairs she took a breath to quiet herself. The lateness of the hour had sent most everyone to bed, but Dyana risked no chances. If Deemis or one of his warriors sighted her, they would drag her back to her chambers. And time was running out. Carefully, she stalked through the silent hallways of Falindar and reached the double gates that would take her to the stables.

Cold night wrapped around her as she stepped outside. Her breath drew from her lungs in white vapor. Quickly she scanned the flat field, but there was no one around. Relieved, she walked across the trampled ground to the stable. It was an elaborate building, too grand for animals, built to the excesses of Falindar's former, royal rulers. The large wooden door, carved with ornate figures of horse heads, hung half open on its hinges. Dyana peeked inside. As she suspected, Deemis and his warriors had taken all the horses to hunt for Simon.

All but one.

Lightning stood in his stall at the far end of the stable. Dyana's mood jumped when she saw him. His brown eyes turned on her questioningly.

"Easy, boy," she whispered. She put out her hand and lightly patted his nose. "I am not going to hurt you. You know me, yes? I am Dyana."

The horse sniffed at her.

"Yes," urged Dyana. "It is me. Please, Lightning. Please let me ride you."

She had only ridden the gelding once before, and then only with Richius. But he was a good-natured beast, and Dyana hurried to fit him with a blanket and bridle, all the things she had seen her husband do countless times before. Finally she opened wide the gate to his stall and approached him.

"I need you to take me to my daughter," she told the horse. "Will you help me?"

Very gently she fit her foot into a stirrup. Lightning snorted. Dyana rubbed him, cooed to him, then threw herself up and onto his back. The steed shuddered. Dyana held tightly to his neck and kept up her encouragement, her voice as soft as a lullaby.

"It is all right," she said. "I will not hurt you. But we have to go quickly. My baby—your master's baby—she needs us. . . ."

The steed moved toward the gate. Dyana gave an encouraging cheer. She grabbed hold of the reins, remembered all she could about riding, and steered the horse out of the stall. From there they trotted through the stables, and finally out into the night. Once in the moonlight, Lightning stopped, awaiting her commands.

"Thank you," sighed Dyana. "Lorris and Pris, thank you. Come now, Lightning—give me some of your famous speed."

The *Intimidator*, still at anchor off the coast of Lucel-Lor, pitched in the moonlight. Though he had been on board for less than an hour, Simon was already seasick. He stood on deck, trying to regain his sea legs and staring at the other warship anchored beside them. The *Revenge* was bigger than the *Intimidator*, easier to detect from shore. Simon wondered whether either ship would make it back to Crote without the Lissens sighting it. If Prakna and his vessels were still in Triin waters, they would certainly be discovered.

On shore, Simon saw the outline of the abandoned tower, barely visible in the haze. The two Roshann agents Biagio had sent to spy on Vantran were still inside the filthy place, unaware that the Jackal had already fled Lucel-Lor. Simon puzzled over his intentional omission. Something was wrong with him, something he was losing control of. It occurred to him that they might go after Dyana now, and that frightened him, but they were dangerously vulnerable and wouldn't find out too soon that Richius was gone.

"I'll bring you the baby," Simon muttered. "For Eris. But nothing more."

Biagio would have to get Richius on his own. Simon would help no more. He would deliver the child to his master and then steal away with Eris. He would ruin the Vantrans, but Richius would be free to stalk Biagio and, later, him. Someday, if the Gods existed at all, Biagio would be accountable. Oddly, Simon had already mapped out the rest of his life. After marrying Eris he would flee Crote and Biagio, he would take Eris to a place hidden from the Roshann, if such a place existed, and they would spend the rest of their lives together. Eris would be happy. And Simon would be fearful. Every other thought would be of Biagio and his schemes, and every time he heard a branch snap he would jump. And he would worry about Richius, too, and how the Jackal of Nar's life had become a quest to find the man who killed his daughter. A great, relentless guilt fell atop Simon.

"Where's the child?" came a familiar voice. Captain N'Dek, commander of the *Intimidator*, strode up to Simon. A ridiculous smile squirmed on his face. "What have you done with her, spy? You didn't drop her overboard, did you?"

"She's in my quarters," Simon replied. "She was tired from the ride."

"We have food and some milk for her," said N'Dek. "Not much, but it should get us to a safe port. Then we can gather whatever you might need for her."

"Me? I'm no woman, N'Dek. Someone else will have to care for her."

"Last I looked my teats were too small. You should have kidnapped a nursemaid, spy."

I would have, but I had to kill her, thought Simon angrily.

"I'll keep her with me," Simon agreed. "I don't want anything happening to her."

"Good thinking," laughed N'Dek. "Biagio wouldn't be too happy with a dead little girl." He paused and looked out over the water. "He's after Vantran next. You saw the other agents?"

Simon nodded.

"Your master is a schemer, Darquis. I admire that. But he spends too much time on revenge, and not enough on winning the Iron Throne. I'll ferry you and the girl back to Crote, but after that I want to see some progress. I'm not a messenger boy."

"Biagio knows what he's doing," said Simon. "He'll move against Herrith when he's ready. Not before."

"I think he already has made his move," revealed the captain. "I've heard that Admiral Nicabar and a small armada have broken away from Crote. They're going to Dragon's Beak to help Duke Enli."

"Why? What's in Dragon's Beak?"

"That's the mystery," said N'Dek. "You see? We are all in the dark because of your master. And we don't like it."

Simon smiled mirthlessly. "Neither do I, Captain N'Dek." He turned to head back to his quarters. "When do we set sail?"

"Now," replied N'Dek. "We're pulling up anchor."

Simon departed quickly, determined never to see Lucel-Lor again.

What seemed like a hundred miles passed to Dyana in a fugue.

Richius' horse Lightning, accustomed to hard riding, had galloped like a surefooted blur in the moonlight. Time raced by as they ran through the valley and the woodlands and the rocky crags of the shoreline. Lightning had lathered up to the point of exhaustion, but the stout-hearted horse never faltered. Dyana, exhausted herself, fought to focus on the narrow roads and forest paths. Falindar was far away and she felt the uncertain fear of being lost, but she was sure she knew the way to the tower. Her eyes blurred. Her hands had gone raw with cold. Lightning's hot body warmed her legs and she leaned down into him as she rode, trying to shield her wind-lashed face.

And then at last, when she felt she would fall from the saddle, she saw the first hint of the tower. Dawn was very near. The sun began its first stirrings, swatting back the night. Dyana slowed the horse, drawing him down to a circumspect trot. The tower emerged in her vision, murky and foreboding. Just past the tower, barely visible on the ocean, was a ship. Hope rose in her. Simon was still here. He would be at the tower, she surmised, waiting for the light.

"There is not much time," she told the horse. She urged Lightning closer to the tower, keeping to the shadows. With eagle eyes she spied the clearing for movement, but all she saw were tumbling leaves. The dawn would bring light, and the light would expose her, and the realization quickened her pace. Lightning seemed to sense her caution. He picked his way along quietly, bearing her toward the tower like a hunting jaguar. When they reached the thinning trees bordering the clearing, Dyana brought the horse to a stop.

"Here," she whispered. "No farther."

She would have to go alone, and leave the exhausted horse to rest. She spied the tower entrance, black and vacant. Inside the structure a pinpoint of light flickered. Dyana bit her lip, sure that Simon had lit the flame. Sliding off Lightning's back, she gave the weary creature a thankful pat. He would wait for her, like he always waited for Richius. If she returned. If Simon didn't kill her. If Shani was still alive.

Enough!

Dyana made a fist. It hadn't occurred to her to bring a weapon, but now she wished she had. A dagger or an axe, anything to put in Simon's back. If Shani was harmed, she would use her fingernails to scratch out Simon's heart. He would pay.

She moved through the clearing to the tower arch, reaching it swiftly. There at the entrance she paused by the crumbling wall and peered inside. The little flame she had seen before was now clearly visible, glowing on the far side of the circular chamber. Simon wasn't inside. No one was, or so it appeared. It was a large room with a thousand black places. Dyana listened, and a startling sound reached her ears—the shuffling of footsteps. Her eyes darted to a spiral stairway leading up into nothingness. Someone was coming. Dyana steeled herself and stepped into the chamber.

"Simon!" she called. "Come down here!"

There was a blur of movement at her side. A figure darted from the blackness, startled by her shout. Down the stairs raced another man, shocked at the sight of her. The one behind her wrapped strong arms around her torso, pinning her arms. Dyana cursed and writhed to get free, but she was too weak and exhausted to break the hold. She felt hot breath on her neck, the unpleasant smell of sour spirits. The dark-haired man at the staircase came forward to stare at her.

"Who the hell are you?" he growled, pulling a dagger from his belt. Dyana kicked at him like a wildcat. He came at her again, carefully this time, and put the tip of the dagger to her chin. "Answer me, girl. Who are you?"

"Where is Simon?" Dyana hissed. "Where is my baby?"

The man holding her squeezed tighter, driving the air from her lungs. Dyana howled in anger, managing to spit at the one with the dagger. He reared back, laughing insanely.

"Your baby?" he chirped. "Are you the mother of the whelp? The Jackal's wife?"

"Where is she? Monster! Where is my daughter?"

The dark-haired man stared incredulously. "Donhedris, I think we've gotten ourselves a prize! This little beauty is Vantran's wife!"

Donhedris lifted her off the floor. "Well!" he declared, booming in her ear. "So you're the biddy Vantran betrayed the Empire for! Oooh, a pretty thing." His tongue darted out and licked her neck. The grotesque sensation made Dyana scream.

"Bastards!" She was frantic, roiling with dread. "God, where is she? Where . . . ?"

"Your daughter is gone," said the man with the dagger. He twirled the weapon between his fingers. "So is Dark-Heart, the one you call Simon. He has taken her away."

"No!"

"He has, and there's nothing to be done about it." The man's face wrinkled with thought. "The question now is what to do with you. Does your husband know you're here, woman?"

"Richius is gone!" Dyana spat. "He has gone to Liss to—"

In her anger she had spit it out, but now she clamped her mouth closed, cursing her stupidity. The dark one drifted up to her.

"Now that was interesting," he said. He brought a hand to Dyana's jaw and squeezed tightly. "Keep talking, or I will pull out your teeth."

Dyana shut her eyes against the viselike grip. "I will not tell you," she rasped.

"There are thirty-two teeth in a human mouth. How many in a Triin's, I wonder?"

"Don't," cautioned Donhedris. "Biagio wouldn't want her harmed. We should take her back to Crote for the Mind Bender."

"Yes!" declared the man, brightening. He released Dyana's jaw.

"There's nothing here for us with the Jackal gone, and the Master would welcome this additional prize. We've done very well, Donhedris." He took the flat of his dagger and brushed it across Dyana's cheek. "You'll get to see that whelp of yours," he taunted. "And there's someone else who'd love to meet you. Someone far better at making people talk than I am."

TWENTY

Awakenings

Lorla Lon, fully immersed in her new identity, had spent the day wandering the halls and chapels of the great cathedral, marveling at the ingenuity of human engineers. Goth had stunned her, Dragon's Beak had captivated her, but the soaring Cathedral of the Martyrs had burned itself into her soul. The Holy Father Herrith, who she simply called "Father" now, had been good to her, buying her trinkets and expensive clothing, and giving her full run of his splendid home. Except for a few sacred areas, Lorla was able to go wherever she wished, touch whatever artifact seized her fancy, and she explored all the cathedral's mysteries with a child's curiosity. She didn't miss Enli or Dragon's Beak anymore. She missed Nina a little, because Nina was a girl and there were no young women in the cathedral. There were nuns, but Lorla didn't like them because they were old and sour-tempered and always looked at her disapprovingly. But no one dared scold Lorla. She was the Holy Father's favorite, and she exploited her newfound status to the fullest. Each night she ate a sumptuous meal with Herrith, sometimes in the company of priests, sometimes alone to talk and laugh together. And each day was a new adventure. She would watch the pilgrims come to the cathedral, the white-skinned Dorians and the amber Crotans, the poor and the wealthy, and the beggars imploring handouts. There were ceremonies and posh, elaborate prayer meetings, where Herrith himself would summon God to touch the assembly and they would faint from the power of His invisible finger. On Seventh Day, the holiest day of the week, the main chapel of the cathedral swelled with Naren nobles and the grounds were packed with curious lay-folk. Too common to get a seat inside, they would wait in the rain for Herrith to appear on his balcony and dispense the word of Heaven. It was a spectacle, this great cathedral, a circus of pageantry and pomp, and Lorla adored it.

But of all the things the cathedral offered, Lorla liked weddings the best. Each day, a parade of Naren ladies came to the cathedral, their white gowns flowing and meticulous, theirs eyes wide and wet with tears. They were beautiful to Lorla, and their handsome husbands, all decked out in royal finery, made her wistful. They reminded Lorla of her true age, not the stunted midget she appeared to be, and they called up something carnal in her, something yearning to be loosed. Father Herrith rarely performed the ceremonies, usually leaving it to underlings, but sometimes, when it was a particularly influential couple or when he was simply in a giving mood, he graced the chapel himself and joined the two together, and when he did the congregation cheered and wept and threw golden coins onto the altar. They were gifts to God, Herrith had explained, and that was why the priests scooped them up.

Since coming to the cathedral, Lorla had only seen the orphanage from a carriage window. She had no need of friends, and she was afraid of what she might find there. Herrith had offered to take her to the orphanage so that she might meet some children her own age, but Lorla had steadfastly refused, playing on the bishop's weaknesses and telling him that she needed only him. His weird blue eyes had melted at that news, and Lorla knew she already had Herrith in her control. It was just as Duke Enli had predicted—he had not been able to resist her. But it wasn't for the reasons Enli claimed. It was because Herrith was sad and lonely and troubled by big things. He wasn't the lecherous demon Lorla had feared. He had been kind to her. And he had given her things without want of reward, simply out of the generosity of his heart. It pained Lorla to think of him sometimes, because she knew unflinchingly what she must do. He was, despite outward appearances, the Master's enemy, and that meant she would destroy him.

The afternoon of her ninth day in the cathedral was just like any other, uneventful but full of things to discover. At Herrith's suggestion, Lorla had avoided the great hall where the artist Darago was toiling, but today she felt particularly rebellious, and so skirted downstairs after the mid-day meal to see what astonishing work the legendary painter was producing. She had never seen Darago, but Herrith had warned her that he was a stern man who hated disturbances. Determined not to be detected, Lorla crept toward the great hall, wincing as her shoes squeaked on the marble floor. She could see the hall in front of her, well lit with a dozen torches and natural light pouring in through a stained-glass window. The sound of assistants hard at work echoed forth. There were voices too, mostly young, but one abrasive bellow that pulverized the rest.

"God-damn it, no!" cursed the voice. "I said dry, you fool. Not wet!"

Lorla froze, but the smell of paint was too tempting. She advanced, unable to contain her curiosity. Leading to the hall was a gentle bend in the corridor. She reached the bend, stopped at the rounded corner, and peered inside. The ceiling was fully exposed now, divested of the canvas covers that had hidden most of it before. Though unfinished, the fresco was nonetheless breathtaking. Lorla simply stared at it, forgetting her stealth. Fat cherubs and red-winged demons stared down at her, while saints and crucified martyrs battled serpents. As she looked she recalled the stories that Herrith had told her, about Keven the Baptizer and about the golden grail that had fed the Mother of God. It was all up there, he had claimed, the whole story of creation. Lorla felt wonderfully insignificant, as if nothing mattered but the roof above her. She would have climbed up to touch it if she could, just to feel its awesome power.

"Who is *that*?" rasped the truculent voice.

Lorla snapped out of her daydream and stared into the hall. In the center of a scaffold forty feet off the ground was a wild-eyed man with a painter's knife in his hand, splattered with color and plaster, his black hair falling like water around his stocky shoulders. He was on his way down from the scaffold, but when he saw Lorla he stopped, dumbfounded and choleric.

"You there!" he called. The young assistants around him jumped at his shout. But they breathed a universal sigh when they saw whom he was addressing. "Yes, you! What are you doing here?"

"Just looking," said Lorla as innocently as she could. She wasn't sure that her little girl act would work on the artist, but she tried it anyway. "I meant no harm, sir. I just wanted to see."

"There's nothing to see! Get out of here!"

"Are you Darago?" Lorla asked. "Yes, you must be. Right?"

The artist sputtered in disbelief. "Of course I am Darago! Who else would paint this masterpiece?" He waved his knife at her irately. "You are a very stupid little girl, not to know who I am. Shoo, now. I have work to do."

"Can I watch?" asked Lorla, daring a step closer. "I won't bother anyone, I promise. I just want to see you work."

"This is not a circus," boomed Darago. "And I'm not an acrobat. Go somewhere else to see clowns, little girl. I am an artist."

Lorla surveyed the ceiling with a shrug. "I don't understand half of what's going on up there. You're not so great."

Darago's round face reddened. Each of his assistants lowered their tools, their eyes darting between the girl and their enraged mentor.

"What?" hissed Darago. He dropped his knife, sending it clanging down the scaffold to hit the floor, splattering red paint along the cloth-covered marble. As he spoke his body shook. "You little waterhead, how dare you judge me? What do you know of art or the great Darago? I am without peer!"

"What's that?" asked Lorla, pointing toward one of the ceiling's panels. "They look like elves. Are they supposed to be elves?"

"They are the angels of Forio," said Darago. He slid down the scaffold, almost tumbling, and crossed the hallway to Lorla where he towered over her, glaring down. "Don't you know anything? They are the spirits that ferried Forio the Divine to Heaven."

Lorla blinked.

"From the book of Gallion!"

"Oh."

Darago's eyes bulged. "Open your eyes, for God's sake! It's all up there."

"Yes," Lorla relented. She enjoyed teasing Darago. He was very vain. "It's pretty."

"It's more than pretty. It's—"

Darago looked over at his assistants. They were all staring at him.

"Get back to work!" he snarled. Instantly they returned to their paints and brushes, pretending not to be listening. Darago frowned at Lorla. "You're a very stupid little girl not to know the story of Forio."

"I'm not from around here."

"Then where are you from? The moon? Everyone knows the story of Forio. It's the first of the holy books!"

"I suppose."

This infuriated the artist. "Who are you? And why are you disturbing me? The hall is not for public eyes, not until I am finished and satisfied."

"I'm Lorla Lon, the bishop's ward," Lorla explained. "And I was just curious, Master Darago. I meant no insult to your ceiling. It's very beautiful." She gave the man her finest smile. "Really."

Darago's countenance softened. "Really?"

"Oh yes," Lorla said. "It's the most beautiful thing I've ever seen. Archbishop Herrith showed me some of it when I first came here. Most of it was covered, though. But I could see that panel and that one." She laughed as she pointed at the ceiling. "Beautiful!"

"Yes," Darago agreed, folding his arms over his chest. "I have spent the last five years working on it. Emperor Arkus was alive then, but he never saw what I was doing. He was very feeble. The bishop has an eye for art, though."

"And you will be done soon," added Lorla. "That's what Father Herrith told me."

"Father Herrith?"

Lorla blanched, embarrassed. "That's what I call him. He takes care of me now. I'm an orphan."

The painter's eyebrows went up. "An orphan! Then you must know the story of Elioes."

"Elioes? No, I don't think so."

Darago directed her eyes upward. "There," he said, pointing to an unfinished panel in the eastern corner of the great hall. "That's Elioes. The crippled orphan that our Lord healed. She was lame from birth, until God's miracle."

Lorla stared at the ceiling. Captured in dry plaster was the figure of a girl, dressed in rags, her legs bent uselessly, her hair a mess of blond strings. But on her face was the most serene expression, and in her eyes glowed the light of Heaven. There was aura about her, painted in gold and fire, and a single, ethereal hand reaching out translucent fingers to transform her. She was beautiful. Like all of Darago's masterpiece, she bespoke something more than paint and plaster. When Lorla looked at Elioes, she thought she was seeing God.

"She looks like me," Lorla observed. "Look. She's got blond hair. And she's as tall as me, too. How old was she, Master Darago?"

Darago shrugged. "I confess, I don't know. Ten, perhaps? How old are you, little Lorla Lon?"

Lorla hated the idea of lying to the man, but she answered, "Eight. I'll be nine very soon. In just a few days, really."

"Ah, then you will share your birthday with the ceiling," said Darago. "I have only a month or so to finish her. Herrith wants to unveil my creation at the end of Kren."

"Kren?"

Darago gave her a disapproving scowl. "You don't know about Kren, either? Are you sure you're the bishop's ward?"

"I'm an orphan," said Lorla again, as if it explained away everything. "What's Kren?"

"High holy month," said Darago. "It begins in three days." He rose to his feet and took Lorla's hand, leading her to the scaffold. "Kren is the month of penance. We fast and beg God to forgive our sins." He frowned at Lorla. "You know what sin is, yes?"

Lorla nodded. "Bad things."

"Things against the word and will of Heaven. Bad things, yes. In Kren we prepare for the feast of Eestrii. That's thirty-three days from now. I must have my ceiling done for the great unveiling. Herrith has made promises to the city. They clamor to see my work. And with good reason."

The scaffold was on wheels. He let go of Lorla and started pushing the metal monster toward the eastern corner of the hall, where the unfinished panel of Elioes stared down at them. An assistant hurried over to help the Master, but Darago shooed him away.

"Can you climb?" Darago asked Lorla.

Lorla nodded eagerly. "That's what I do best." Not waiting for Darago, she began shimmying up the squeaking silver ladder. Darago followed, and when they were fifty feet in the air, they stood atop the scaffold's platform, face-to-face with the orphan. Lorla felt exhilarated by the height and the blazing colors. She stretched out her hand, knowing she couldn't reach the roof overhead, and sighed.

"I wish I could touch her," she said sadly. "She's so beautiful."

Without a thought, Darago wrapped his arms around her waist and hoisted her into the air, until she was nose-to-nose with Elioes. Lorla squealed with delight. Far below, the Master's assistants were staring up in disbelief.

"She is dry," said Darago. "Touch her."

Very gently, Lorla put her fingers to the ceiling. Elioes seemed to smile at her touch. Lorla dragged her fingertips along the girl's neck, barely brushing it, and down the perfectly realized fabric of her collar. Her flesh was pink and vital. She looked alive, as though Darago had encased a real girl in plaster.

"Ohhh . . . It's wonderful."

"She is my pride," Darago whispered. "I think she came alive more than any other figure I've done here. When she is revealed to Nar, she will melt this city's heart."

"Has Father Herrith seen her?"

"No. Not yet."

"He will love her. More than any picture on the ceiling, this will be his favorite. I know it." Lorla looked away from the image. "Put me down now. Please."

Darago complied, setting her down gently on the platform. "You like my painted daughter, yes?"

"Yes," said Lorla. "I want to know more about her. Tell me all you know about Elioes."

"I know only what I painted here," confessed Darago, laughing. "She is a girl. I bring her back from the dead. She was touched by God and now God touches me to give her life again. It is that way for me." He held out his hands for Lorla to inspect. They were callused and rough, caked with dried pigments. "These are the hands of God. When I paint or sculpt, they do not belong to me. Heaven possesses me. I am the instrument of angels."

Lorla nodded as if she understood. "Did God tell you to paint Elioes?"

"In His way, yes. None of this is me alone, Lorla Lon." He made a sweeping gesture at the ceiling, and all the angels seemed to listen. "Those trolls you see down there, the ones assisting me, they are nothing. They are like ants to God. Maybe someday they will do something great on their own, but not until God moves them. Like He moves me."

"I like Elioes," sighed Lorla. She looked back at the orphan's tranquil face, so peaceful now that God was healing her. "I want to know more about her. Tell me, Master Darago, please."

"You are asking the wrong man. Ask me about paints and stone. Ask the Holy Father about the child."

"Yes," Lorla agreed. "Yes, I will." She leaned over and surprised Darago with a kiss. "Thank you, Master Darago. Thank you very much."

Without waiting for the artist she began descending the scaffold, shaking it in her eagerness to get down. That old desire for knowledge was on her again. She hurried from the great hall, passing the tiny confession booths where cowled acolytes listened to Naren atrocities, and finally to the wide and magnificent stairway that would lead her up to the chambers of Father Herrith. She hadn't seen Herrith since breakfast, and it occurred to her that she rarely saw him in the middle of the day. Lorla would surprise him, she decided. He would be pleased to see her. He was always pleased to see her. Her mind raced with questions about the orphan, Elioes. Had she really been as beautiful as Darago had depicted? Was she really an orphan? And if she was a saint, then Lorla knew she had found her patron.

The Saint of Orphans, thought Lorla with a smile.

When she reached the hall to Herrith's chambers, Lorla slowed. The imperial-sized corridor swallowed her whole. The statues and portraits glared at her, but the hall was otherwise empty. Herrith had no need for guards, and his priests were always busy elsewhere. Even Father Todos was nowhere to be found. Lorla was glad for that. She liked Todos but she wanted to be alone with Herrith for a while and pick his brain without being disturbed. Herrith's chambers were at the end of the hall, barricaded by a pair of tall doors with bronze hinges and gargoyle reliefs. Lorla approached slowly, tiptoeing so not to be heard. She put her ear up to the doors and listened. Inside, she heard breathing, labored and unsteady.

For a moment she stood outside his door, wondering what to do. Finally curiosity overcame her and she gave the doorknob a slow, silent turn. It was unlocked and opened easily. The brass hinges moved smoothly, letting her crack the door open. With one eye she peered inside. The opulent living chamber spread out before her, dark in a shade-drawn room. The volume of the weird breathing grew. Lorla nervously widened the crack, trying to see inside. She noticed Herrith's ceremonial shoulder wrap strewn carelessly on the floor. Next to that was his white collar. And next to that was Herrith.

The Archbishop of Nar knelt on the floor, his shoulders slumped, his head bowed and sunken in his chest. He was clothed but for a single arm that was naked, the sleeve rolled up to his armpit. He held the arm fast against his chest, groaning as he rocked slowly back and forth. A tiny silver needle sprouted from his wrist, feeding him blue liquid from a tube. As he breathed he hummed a little, moaning tune, a hymn of sorts broken by erratic breathing.

Lorla stopped at the sight of him.

Cautiously she opened the door, then less cautiously as she realized he wasn't listening. She shut the door behind her. Herrith continued rocking, and it looked to Lorla as if he were crying.

"Father Herrith?"

The sound of her voice made Herrith turn. His mouth dropped open in shock.

"Lorla!" he rasped.

"What is this?" asked Lorla, not daring to go near him. "What's wrong with you?"

The needle in Herrith's arm caught the light and flashed. Lorla felt a rush of sickness, the hammer-blow of an unwanted memory. She stumbled backward, falling against the door, unable to take her eyes off the apparatus feeding Herrith's arm. The bishop reached out a clawlike hand.

"No," he groaned. "I'm all right. Don't be afraid."

But Lorla was afraid. An unknown terror had seized her. The sight of the needle and the potion had stirred her stomach and bowels, making her want to retch. She closed her eyes to banish the nausea, letting the wall support her as her knees turned to water.

"What is this?" she shrieked. "What are you doing to yourself?"

"Lorla, please," insisted Herrith. "Don't be afraid. This is just me. I'm taking care of myself. I'm helping myself."

"How?"

"Open your eyes and look at me!" the bishop demanded.

Lorla did as ordered. She saw Herrith still kneeling on the floor with the needle in his arm. His face was wide with worry and slick with sweat. His outstretched arm begged her to come closer.

"It's me, little one," he whispered. "It's only me. Don't be afraid. Nothing will hurt you."

Unable to move, Lorla stood her ground. Something once-forgotten flashed through her brain, a memory of pain and droning voices. She was cold suddenly, surrounded in a room without windows. Hands grabbed for her little body, holding her down. And she was screaming.

Her mouth opened to wail but no sound emerged. Herrith watched her, horrified.

"Lorla!" he called. She heard his voice as if from a great distance. "What is it, child?"

"I don't know," Lorla sobbed. "I don't know! What are you doing? What is this thing?"

She staggered over to Herrith and rattled the apparatus holding the tubes. Herrith's free arm seized hold of her, pulling her away.

"Don't!" he hissed.

His touch was ice on fire. Lorla leapt back, astonished by the sensation. Still he held her fast, drawing her close, down to her knees before him. He was weeping and laughing as the blue liquid dripped into his veins.

"Be not afraid, girl," he bade. "I am the Herrith you know."

"You're not," said Lorla. "You're different!"

"Not different. The same and getting better. Believe me, child. Believe me."

There was so much pain in his voice Lorla couldn't help but relent. She leaned in closer, inspecting his grooved face. The lines ran deep like red welts and his eyes burned a brilliant sapphire. It all reminded Lorla of something very long ago, a thing forgotten and buried, never meant to resurface. She tried to summon up the frightening memory but couldn't. All she felt was rage and pain.

"Father Herrith, I'm afraid."

"Oh, Lorla." He was fighting to control himself, to even form the words. "What are you doing here?"

It took a moment for Lorla to remember. "I came to talk to you," she said. "To ask you questions about the ceiling."

"And now you've found me," said Herrith. "And found me out." He shook his head regretfully. "God save me for showing you this horror."

"Father . . ."

"I look wretched, I know. But this is . . . a treatment, Lorla. It's something I need to do. Please, come sit with me. I need you. You can help me."

Lorla did as the bishop asked, sitting cross-legged on the floor in front of him. He put his head back and took a deep breath, then tried a crooked smile on her.

"It hurts, sometimes, this thing I do. This drug is very strong. But I need it, Lorla. I would die without it, and I wouldn't be strong. These days I need my strength. There is wise work to do. Can you understand that?"

Lorla nodded. "But what is it? Where does it come from?"

"That's not something I can tell you. It's a very special drug, very precious, and that's all I can say. But I don't have a lot of it, and I can't waste it. That's why I grabbed you when you reached for it." He looked at her sheepishly. "I didn't mean to harm you. Forgive me."

"Holy Father—"

"Father," he corrected.

"Yes. Father. What is it doing to you? Why are you so . . ." She struggled with the words, scanning him up and down. "Weak?"

Herrith reached out his hand and brushed her cheek. "Dear Lorla, there is too much to explain to you. You must trust me, that is all. And trust in God. I have asked Heaven for guidance, and the angels have told me to be strong. They have delivered this drug to me. I thought at first it had come from a demon, but now I know the truth. God gave it to me, because He needs to ready me for a final battle."

"Against Biagio?" Lorla queried. She had heard the bishop speak of the Master often.

"Yes. Biagio and his whole Black Renaissance." Herrith struggled to catch his breath. "They are a cancer, Lorla. They will ruin the Empire, drag us back into Hell. I alone can stop them. I *will* stop them, by Heaven. I will."

Lorla hid her feelings behind a placid mask. Every time Herrith mentioned her master, she gave him an encouraging smile. "You are strong," she said. "No one can stop you."

"No one can stop God," said Herrith. "I am guided by His mighty hand."

"Like Darago," Lorla said brightly. "He is like that, too."

"Yes," agreed Herrith. "How do you know this?"

"I have been to see the ceiling. I know I shouldn't have, but don't be angry. I've spoken to Darago. He's shown me things."

Herrith laughed. "Darago has spoken to you? A little girl? I can't believe it."

"It's true," Lorla insisted. "He took me up on his ladder to show me the ceiling. I touched it, Father!"

Herrith seemed to forget his pain. "Remarkable," he whispered. "You have touched the ceiling? That is a holy thing, little one. You are truly blessed."

"I saw the picture of Elioes," Lorla went on. "Darago said she was an orphan, like me. Is that true?"

"It is."

Herrith glanced at the tube in his arm. It was empty now. He shut his eyes in relief and popped the needle out. Lorla swallowed a recurring nausea.

"Tell me about her," Lorla pressed. "I want to know all about Elioes."

"Another time," declined Herrith. He put out his arm. "Help me up, please, child. These treatments weaken me."

Lorla offered her hand and helped with all her might to pull the portly bishop to his feet. He wobbled unsteadily for a moment, then quickly gained his balance.

"Yes," he breathed. "Yes, I'll be all right now. Thank you, child. Now . . ." He puzzled over her. "What is it you're asking me?"

"About *Elioes*. Darago said you could tell me about her."

"I can," said Herrith. He walked out of the chamber and into a room with an extravagant bed. The shades were open wide, sending sunlight streaming in. The bishop collapsed onto the thick mattress. After he caught his breath he patted the bed for Lorla to sit beside him. Lorla did so, sitting close to him, and gave him her full attention.

"I will teach you all about Elioes, and everything else I know about the holy book. You will learn and grow strong, little one. But first, tell me about the ceiling. You have seen it all?"

"It was uncovered," said Lorla. "Darago and the others were working on it. Yes, I saw all of it."

"Was it very beautiful? Is it almost done?"

"Very beautiful," melted Lorla. "More beautiful than anything. And yes, I think it's almost done. Darago says he must unveil it for you soon. For your holiday. Kren?"

"Eestrii. Kren is the month of penance. But yes, you are almost right." He frowned. "You know of Kren, don't you, Lorla? Or have I been so neglectful?"

"I have seen the priests decorating the cathedral. But no, I don't know about Kren. I'm sorry."

"Do not be. I've been remiss for not explaining these things to you. I forget how isolated you were in Dragon's Beak." Already he was stronger. With each breath his skin cooled and the lines in his face seemed to evaporate. Herrith put an arm around her shoulders. "Before Kren begins, there's a big festival called Sethkin. All the Black City will celebrate to prepare themselves for the month of deprivation. There will be music and dancers, food and acrobats." He laughed, full of delight. "I will take you myself! The streets will be beautiful. Would you like that?"

"Yes," said Lorla, excited by the prospect. "It will be one big birthday party for me!"

"Birthday?" asked the bishop. "Lorla, is your birthday coming up?"

Pretending she had let something slip, Lorla looked away. "Yes, Father. I'm sorry. I shouldn't have told you that."

"But why? This is joyous, little one. I'm so pleased. Now we can celebrate Eestrii and your birthday together. How wonderful!"

That old guilt started gnawing at Lorla again. Each day she deceived the bishop, she hated herself a little more. "It's nothing special, Father. I want to see the celebration. That's all."

"You will, dear child, you will." Herrith flashed her an adoring smile. "We will celebrate Eestrii and your birthday together, and I will treat you like a princess that day. There will be vendors in the streets and beautiful things to buy. And the shops will all have their doors open." He leaned over and gave her a kiss on the head. "Think hard on this. You must choose a gift for yourself. Something very special!"

Lorla smiled back at him. She already had the perfect present in mind.

TWENTY-ONE

The Ghosts of Gray Tower

Nina trotted her horse through a field of bodies, astonished at the carnage her father had wrought.

It was another frozen day on the north fork of Dragon's Beak—Eneas' fork. A terrible wind tore at Nina's cloak, slicing through it like fangs. Snow blanketed the roadway and the abandoned buildings, all shuttered closed, and the rigored bodies in the avenues stared in endless horror, their eyes turned to ice by the cold. Somewhere up in a fog of clouds, the afternoon sun fought to warm the earth. Slicks of frozen blood in the roadway reflected the light and snow. Nina's horse moved without purpose through the town, as aimless as its stunned rider, its vacant footfalls the only sound breaking the dreadful day. Ahead loomed Gray Tower, tall and shadowy, its hundred windows vacant of life. The home of Duke Eneas cast a pall on the ruined town, a gloomy headstone for all the icy dead.

Duke Enli's vengeance was awful and deep. Just how deep, Nina had never known—until today. All the rage that he'd suppressed, all the hatred for his brother, had gushed out of him in a violent torrent, a tidal wave without mercy. Nina looked about her, and realized with horrible certainty that she knew *nothing* about the man she called Father.

"My God, Grath," she whispered above the wind. "Did you do all this?"

Grath of Doria trotted up beside her with his entourage, a dozen mercenaries from his homeland.

"I had my orders, girl," he said without flinching. Nothing seemed to bother Grath—not the ferocious cold, and not the terrible deed he'd done.

"Whose orders?" Nina asked. "My father's?"

"Yes. And my employer's," replied the mercenary. All around him, his men nodded, as though such a claim could absolve them of the genocide. "Biagio was very specific," Grath went on. "I did what I was paid to do."

Nina couldn't look at him anymore, so she turned her eyes back to the remnants of men and women—even children. Crushed helmets encased the faceless skulls of raven soldiers, guardians of Duke Eneas. Their slaughtered remains were everywhere, stiff with cold, their clutching fingers reaching heavenward in death. This was the north fork's largest village, surrounded by farms and once populated by hardy peasants. It had been wiped clean. Other villages had been spared the ravages of Grath and his mercenaries, but not Westwind. The battle had taken place here, at the foot of Gray Tower. Eneas' troops had defended the memory of their duke, and had paid with their lives. Without their army of the air to protect them, the raven troops were slaughtered. The strange count from Crote had purchased a fortune in mercenaries to overwhelm the north fork, for Grath commanded a force of nearly three hundred. Nina wasn't an expert on military affairs, but she had heard her father, Duke Enli, speak of it often, for he was war-minded and constantly preoccupied with his brother across the channel. Now, it seemed, his obsession had erupted—with disastrous consequences.

Nina closed her eyes in disgust. These were her own people. To see them slaughtered made her wonder about her father's sanity.

"Good God, he left nothing," said Nina shakily. The sight overwhelmed her. "How could you, Father? How?"

There was no answer to such a question. Never had she imagined him capable of such an atrocity. Nina looked at the abandoned tower in the distance, now occupied only by corpses and angry ghosts. More than a decade had passed since she'd been there. In those days, she had run freely through her uncle's keep, happy to be with him and his ravens. Happy, as they all were, to live in a land of peace.

Times had changed remarkably.

"Grath, you are a monster. You and all your men."

Grath blinked without emotion. "I told you what you would see here, Nina. But you're as stubborn as your father." He started to rein his horse around. "Come. Let's be gone. If this were summer, the stink would kill us."

"Stay," Nina ordered. "I'm not done."

There was enough iron in her voice to keep the Dorian from going. It was true that he had warned her, begged her in fact not to come to this place. But Nina had been too long in the confines of Red Tower, wondering what had gone on in the frozen world outside. Since her father had gone to Nar City with Lorla, Grath and his mercenaries had been hard at work. It hadn't been difficult for Nina to guess at their activities, but she hadn't imagined anything so ghastly. She had even held out the vain hope that her uncle might still be alive.

Grath had explained things to her.

Upon returning from his black crusade, the Dorian had told her everything. About her father. About the murder of her uncle. And the news had shattered Nina. Like a sheltered child she had hidden herself, walled up in Red Tower, denying that her father could be launching a war against his brother even as it raged across the channel. She had even told Lorla that everything would be all right. Nina cursed herself now, hating her timidity. If she had stood up to her father, she might have convinced him to stop. She was the one thing he still cared about, and she knew it. She was his last link to Angel.

I should have tried, she thought.

Could she have reached into his mind and soothed the insanity there? God, was this her fault? Nina shook her head, banishing the idea.

No! Don't even think it.

"There's nothing else to see here," growled Grath. As the minutes ticked by, he grew more impatient. And maybe a bit fearful. No one had challenged them during the ride through the north fork, but that didn't mean no one *would*, and Grath kept a watchful eye on the vacant homes and dead bodies, half expecting them to come alive. His men seemed to share their leader's nervousness, wary of their gloomy surroundings. They had followed Grath this far because Nina had demanded it, but a mercenary's loyalty was only so good. Nina gave a mirthless grin. Her father had taught her that as well.

You got your wish, Father, she thought. *All of Dragon's Beak is yours now.*

Enli even had the ravens, his brother's vaunted "army of the air." Cackle, her pet, sat perched on her shoulder, clicking at the cold. Before he had gone to Nar City with Lorla, her father had warned her not to let the raven out of her sight.

"He is lead raven now," Enli had said.

Nina knew what the term meant. Cackle wore the gold chain around his neck now, symbol of lead raven. Nina remembered the story. Eneas had been very proud of his ravens, and had happily bragged to her about them. She knew all about lead raven status. No doubt Eneas' own lead raven was as dead as its master. Nina turned toward the bird on her shoulder, grateful he was with her. As far as any of them knew, the army of the air was still around Gray Tower, waiting for Eneas to return. Without a lead raven to follow, they had simply let Grath and his mercenaries slaughter the tower's defenders.

"Stay with me, Cackle," said Nina. "I might need you."

She didn't know what to expect when she reached Gray Tower. She hadn't even told Grath that the tower was her true destination. She wondered what his reaction would be. Though she was the duke's daughter and he was paid to protect her, he might easily abandon her. He had only come this far at Nina's insistence. She had needed to see the carnage for herself, to understand the depth of her father's madness.

Now Gray Tower beckoned in a way she hadn't expected. Memories rushed over her, long forgotten. She stared at the tower and felt its pull, and wondered if her life would change if she went there.

Or end.

"We go on," she said softly. Her voice was hardly audible over the wind.

"Go on?" said Grath. "Go where?"

"To the tower."

"No. Forget it."

Nina was resolute. "I'm going. Come with me if you want. Or stay, if you're afraid. I'll return to Red Tower on my own."

There was a grumbling from the mercenaries. Grath brought his horse in close to Nina's, leaning into her so his men wouldn't hear.

"Listen, you little wench," he whispered. "I've brought you this far, but that's enough. There's nothing in the tower worth seeing. Don't make me drag you back to the south fork like some child."

"I want to see it for myself," Nina said.

"There's nothing to see, you stupid girl! Just bodies. You want to see bodies? Take your fill of them here!"

Cackle ruffled his feathers, but Nina was adamant. "I'm going, Grath. With or without you."

The Dorian's face reddened. "You do, and so help me I'll—"

"What, Grath? Haul me back to Red Tower like a sack of grain? I don't think so." Nina sharpened hard eyes on him. "If you touch me, I'll tell my father you mistreated me. Raped me, even. He'll tell Biagio, and you won't get paid."

The menace in her voice made Grath hesitate. He knew Enli worshipped his daughter, and without Enli's goodwill, Biagio's purse just might not open. In the end, Grath relented.

"There's nothing to see," he warned again. "Nothing but those godcursed birds. If they attack us—"

"They won't," Nina assured him. "Cackle will protect us. Stay close to me and nothing will happen."

They were bold words, and Nina could tell the mercenaries questioned them. She herself questioned them. Though she had been but a child of five when last she'd seen Gray Tower, she remembered Eneas' ravens like a terrible nightmare. The memory of a thousand black eyes blazed in her mind. But only for a moment. Gray Tower awaited, and maybe some answers with it. Her father's treachery had left a vacancy in her soul. For the first time in her life, she doubted about him. Or maybe it was simply the first time she had courage. She didn't really know. But her sheltered life had come to a ruinous end, and she wanted someone to blame.

"Let's go," she ordered, spurring her horse up the road toward the keep. It was a long way off, through a narrow lane dense with trees. The wind picked up as she advanced. Grath and his Dorians grumbled but followed, and soon they had left the town behind, wandering into a thicket of trees canopying a winding road. Nina's horse snorted unhappily. On her shoulder, Cackle let out a long, low whistle, a habit he'd picked up from Duke Enli. Nina cupped her hood around her face to stave off the cold. It had been many hours since they'd left the south fork, and her hands ached beneath her gloves.

Grath rode up beside. "You're a fool, girl," he sneered. "You're chasing ghosts. I tell you again, there's nothing there."

"Then what are you afraid of?"

Grath answered with a grimace. "I fear nothing. But we're wasting our time, and it's god-damn cold out here. Maybe dangerous, too. For you."

"That's why I brought you; to protect me. Now stop talking. Your breath makes me sick."

They rode awhile longer. The lane was black with pines and rough with swales, and the branches knitting overhead bore heavy loads of fallen snow that sometimes gave way onto their heads. Here, they were nearing the tip of the Dragon's Beak. Nina could sense the faint tang of salt in the air, and the sound of distant surf whispered in her ears. She spurred her horse to a quicker pace, eager to be out of the cold.

At last, the corridor of branches opened, spilling them out into Gray Tower's shadow. The keep rose up high above them, abandoned, desolate, and bearing the scars of a thousand storms. Nina stared at it, shocked and amazed, drowning in a flood of reborn memories. Emotion choked her, and were it not for the arrogant Grath watching her, she knew she would have wept.

"Father," she whispered. "What have you done?"

Gray Tower responded with an empty silence. Across the uneven meadow leading to the keep, Nina could see the remnants of battle, the broken bodies of the castle's defenders fallen in the snow and the weapons left to rust on the ground, useless. The meadow itself was churned by horses' hooves, eaten away by rushing beasts and strewn with great clods of earth. Beneath the snow, dead men lay against each other, misshapen mounds of white bent in impossible angles. When the winter ended and the warm weather came, there would be disease here, maybe even enough poison to reach across the channel. Her father would be horrified, she was certain. Grath had done a very poor job of cleaning up. She scanned the castle grounds, hoping for a sign of life, any small, surviving thing, but saw nothing moving across the field.

Except for the ravens.

They were everywhere. Huge and black, they toddled along the bodies and stone fences, oblivious to the cold, pecking at the corpses and peeling off long strips of flesh. Their shining plumage caught the sunlight like a big, sable ocean. Some of the birds noticed the intruders and turned their corvine eyes eastward, spying Nina and her troops. A fearful tremor moved through the mercenaries. Nina swallowed hard. The sight of so many of the frightful things made her heart flutter. They were monsters, freaks of Eneas' careful breeding. Every alcove was covered with them, every fence post swathed in black. One by one they picked up the signals from their brothers, turning to regard Nina and the Dorians.

"Good God," murmured Grath. "Look at them all. Just waiting."

"We should go," insisted one of the mercenaries, a notion echoed by his comrades. Grath silenced them with a sharp look.

"Quiet, you idiots," he rumbled. Then he turned to Nina, saying, "They're right. Let's go, girl, before they eat our eyes out."

Nina stroked Cackle's plumage. "I'm not afraid. You can stay behind if you wish. All of you can. But I want to see what's in the castle."

"Why?" asked Grath, exasperated. "There's nothing there!"

"There is," Nina replied. "I have memories here." She smirked, realizing how stupid that must have sounded. "Go if you want, Grath. I'll be safe. And I don't want to startle them with so many riders. Take your men and go back into the woods. I'll be out for you soon."

"No," refused the soldier. "I'll go with you, though God curse me for it. I'm supposed to protect you." He sighed, miserable with the duty. "You're sure that bird will protect us?" he asked, pointing at Cackle.

"I'm sure," said Nina. She wasn't really, but saying it made her feel better. Cackle was lead raven now. And the army of the air did nothing without the lead raven's order. "Don't do anything stupid," she warned the bird. Cackle bobbed on her shoulder, understanding.

Nina gave her horse its head and began moving toward the tower. Grath kept well behind her, making certain the ravens in the yard could see the bird on her shoulder. There was some fluttering of wings and staccato caws. Nina fought to quell her growing fear. Beneath her, she could feel the trepidation of her horse as it, too, watched the rapacious birds. She heard Grath's desperate whisper behind her.

"God, look at them all."

"Quiet," she snapped. Any small sound might disturb them, sending them to flight. But Cackle was on her shoulder, perched proud and commandingly, and the ravens in the yard noticed the lead bird and the golden chain around his neck, and soon settled into a uniform disinterest. Nina's racing heartbeat slowed a bit, relieved. Up ahead, she could see the tower's door, blown open wide and buried with snow in its threshold. There was a dead man in a heap barring the way inside. An enormous raven stood on his head, comically oblivious to its gruesome perch. Nina steered her horse through the courtyard, careful to avoid the thickest patches of ravens. The way was choked with bodies. Eneas' men had numbered maybe two hundred at best, and Biagio's mercenary force had obliterated them. Now, amidst his bloody handiwork, Grath was stoic. Like one of the dead, he seemed not to notice anything. Or to care.

The ravens around them broke ranks, letting them pass. Nina drew a sigh of relief as she reached the tower. In the doorway, the last raven stared at them from atop the dead man's helmet, cocking its head inquisitively. A sudden, angry bark from Cackle sent it flying off. Nina smiled at her pet.

She and Grath trotted past the dead soldier and through the gate. Once inside, Grath dismounted and closed the castle doors, sealing them off from the birds. The hall went dark with shadows. Nina slowly slid off her horse. More than ten years had passed since she'd seen this great home, and the sense of it now was overwhelming. The sound of herself laughing as a child echoed in her mind. Exposure to the weather had ruined the carpet and pulled things from the wall, but it was still her uncle's house, even after so many years.

"Uncle," she said meekly, hoping his ghost was home. "It's me."

Unsure where to go, Nina stood there for a long moment. She pulled the hood off of her head and shook the dampness from her hair. She clapped her boots on the floor to dislodge the snow. She did all these things as a ritual of homecoming, a vain attempt to make some sense of the destruction and fractured bits of her past. Down the hall, light flooded in through broken windows. Like its twin, the Gray Tower had a simple layout. There wasn't much to the place, just a tall spire ringed with rooms. Across the hall was the library, and her uncle's study. Past that was the kitchen and dining hall, a big and jolly chamber where she had once sat with her father and uncle and listened to them laugh together over pints of beer. She remembered that now with an ache.

"I want to find my uncle's rooms," she said softly.

"This is madness. What's your point, girl?"

Nina shrugged. "Maybe nothing."

It was impossible to explain to Grath. No one could understand the hollowness her life had become, the mystery of not knowing. Only Lorla had come close to understanding, and she was gone now, part of her father's impenetrable schemes.

"Stay here, Grath. Look after the horses. I won't be long."

Grath balled up a fist. "No, Nina! Now this is enough. You're not going anywhere."

"Don't open the door," Nina warned, ignoring him. "You might not be safe without Cackle."

"Damn it, Nina . . ."

"Stay," she ordered, then drifted down the damp corridor. To her relief, Grath didn't follow. A thousand thoughts came at her at once, glad and mournful memories she had thought buried a decade ago. There were more bodies in the hall, servants that Grath had slaughtered, even an old woman Nina thought she recognized. She paused over the lifeless body, unable to recall the name but sure she had worked in the kitchen. Once she had served Nina carrot soup. Now she was dead. An enormous puddle of dried blood framed her face, gluing her hair to the floor. Nina forced herself to look away.

"Uncle," she called out, sure no one would answer. No one did.

She had to find his rooms. She rounded a corner and found herself near the stairway for the spire. The granite treads rang with echoes of her steps. As she ascended, Nina ran her hands along the curved wall, tracing it with her fingertips and pulling in more memories of a child who had once loved to play here. Finally, she came to the place where Eneas' rooms had been. She remembered them vividly. He had gargoyles on his balcony. The stone creatures had been gifts from Arkus of Nar himself, made by the great artist Darago. Nina stepped into the hallway and laughed. Her uncle had hated those gargoyles.

"We're very close," she said to Cackle. "I can feel it."

Cackle dug his talons deeper into Nina's coat. The bird seemed uneasy, understandable in this place of corpses. But here, on Eneas' floor, there were no corpses. No broken windows, either. Doors had been kicked in and the place had been searched, but it seemed to Nina that most of Gray Tower's inhabitants had rushed downstairs to defend their home—and meet their deaths. She drifted silently across the corridor, studying the burned out sconces and narrow windows, and remembered the place where Eneas' bedchamber waited, around the corner near a bookcase filled with musty manuscripts. As she rounded the bend she saw the bookcase with its carelessly stocked shelves, and the sight of it made her want to weep. There was her uncle's bedchamber, its door flung wide. A collection of things spilled over its threshold, the remnants of Grath's search for hidden survivors. Nina approached the room with dread, fearful of what she might find.

Eneas' ghost was not present to greet her. There was only more destruction—an overturned bed that might have hid a frightened child, some papers sprawled on the floor by the wind from open balcony doors, and the sight of Dragon's Beak beyond the balcony, lying like a white wasteland. Nina stepped into the chamber, holding back a rush of tears. The girl she had been had grown to a woman without her uncle, and she grieved for the lost years.

"Father," she whispered. "You are unholy."

Only a devil could do such a thing. Her father had sold his soul for revenge. Now he would return to a Dragon's Beak ruined by his own hand, and the peaceful place that it had been would be a mournful hell-hole, ruled by a tyrant and Biagio's iron fist. At last the tears came, rolling down Nina's cheeks. She wanted to hate her father, but couldn't. She wanted to save her uncle, but couldn't. Helpless, she crumpled to her knees amidst the blowing papers and the wind, and buried her face in her hands.

Lost in her sorrow, she didn't know how long she cried. Time was crawling here, or moving backward. But when she opened her eyes again the tears had stopped. They were pointless, she told herself. Tears didn't bring back the dead. Nina was about to rise when she glimpsed a piece of paper stuck to her boot. She picked it up and inspected it, recognizing her father's familiar handwriting.

Dear Father, it read.

Please help. I am outside the castle near the main road. Your brother is pursuing me. I know who I am now. Please come.

Nina.

Nina's hand shook, her jaw tightening with rage at the deception She thought back to that night, weeks ago now, when her father had left to do his filthy business against his brother. Nina had wondered just how he had gotten Eneas out of Gray Tower.

Now she knew.

"Father," she moaned. Then, uncontrollably, "Father!"

Suddenly she was in a rage, shaking and murderous. He had used her, made her a tool to murder a man she had once cared about. And . . .

Nina's heart stopped, seized by an impossible notion.

"Oh, God, no," she groaned. It couldn't be true. She read the note again, over and over, until slowly a picture of a possibility formed in her mind.

Father?

"Who am I?" she asked desperately. "Who?"

"Home!" Cackle exclaimed. He began hopping insistently on her shoulder. "Home! Home!"

Nina flashed the note in front of him. "Did you know about this, you wretched beast? Who am I, Cackle?"

The raven stared at her. "Home! Home!"

"I'm not going home! For all I know this is my home!"

Cackle cawed and dug his talons into her shoulder, piercing the coat and the skin beneath. "Home," he repeated. He gestured toward the window with his beak. "Angel."

"No," spat Nina, shaking her head. "We're not leaving, Cackle."

The bird screamed with anger, then flew from her shoulder. He paused before the open window, threatening her.

"Go if you want to," said Nina bitterly. "I'm staying here."

Cackle blinked at her sadly. And then, to Nina's surprise, he spread his wings and dashed out the window, abandoning her. She watched him go, and felt an icy shudder of loneliness. Enli had worked his magic on the bird.

Enli. Her father? She didn't know anymore. She had come to Gray Tower seeking answers and had gained a thousand questions for her troubles.

"Nina?" Nina's eyes snapped open. Grath called for her again, and when she answered he appeared in the doorway.

"What the hell's taking you so long?" he railed. "I want to get out of here."

"I'm not going, Grath," she said. "You go. I'm staying."

Grath laughed. "Right. Enough joking. Let's move it, all right?"

Nina glared at him hatefully. "I'm not joking, you pig. I'm staying. *This* is where I belong. And you can't make me leave."

"I can," rumbled the mercenary. He took a threatening step closer to her. "Stop acting stupid. Your father wouldn't want you staying here."

Nina laughed bitterly. "My father? You tell that madman I'm not going back to Red Tower. Not ever. If he wants to see me, he can come and get me himself."

"You idiot, how—" Grath stopped himself suddenly, looking around the room. "Where's the bird?"

"Get out," Nina ordered.

"Where's the god-damn bird, you bitch?"

"Gone," said Nina. "Looks like you're on your own now, Grath."

Grath catapulted across the room, taking her by the wrists and shaking her. "You ass! Why did you let it go?"

Nina wrenched free and pushed him away. "Don't you touch me!" she hissed. "Don't you ever! I swear, I'll make Duke Enli cut your heart out if you touch me again. Now go! Leave me."

"Go?" Grath barked. "How? You've killed us, you fool! Those ravens will tear us to pieces!"

"They won't," Nina assured him, not caring if it was a lie. "You saw how docile they were. They won't hurt you. They're lost without Eneas."

"But the bird—"

"The bird's gone," Nina snapped. She turned toward the balcony and stared out into the desolation. "Nothing to be done about it. But you won't need him. Just don't disturb them. Walk quietly and they'll let you pass."

Behind her, she heard Grath's nervous lingering. He wasn't at all sure if she was right, and the thought of a thousand ravens pecking out his liver obviously had him afraid. His sword would be very little use against the ravenous birds. If they *were* ravenous. Nina didn't know if they were or not.

"I'll tell your father where you are," said the mercenary at last. Then he added with a sneer, "He'll come and drag you out of here, no doubt."

"He can try," said Nina.

She heard his footfalls leave the room and disappear down the hallway. Stepping out onto the balcony, she saw the ravens down below and wondered absently what would happen to Grath and his men.

Grath was furious as he left the room, furious and a little daunted at the prospect of having to walk through the ravens unescorted. The whole day had been wasted with that spoiled bitch, and now he had to explain this, somehow, to her father. He swore that he wouldn't be swindled by the old man. If Enli tried to hold back payment, he would cut his heart out.

"Bitch," he spat as he descended the stairs. Hot-headed. Like her father. Let her stay here and rot with the corpses.

When Grath reached the hall leading to the doors he paused, considering things. He stroked his chin nervously. He pulled his sword halfway from its scabbard. What to do? The weapon might frighten the bloody beasts. It wasn't wise to entice them. Grath let the sword slip back down.

"Damn it!" he cursed, unsure of himself. They had let him pass once, when he'd fought at the castle, but things had been different then. Now he was horribly outnumbered. He wondered how his men in the woods were faring.

"You won't beat me, girl," he vowed, going to the doors and slowly pulling them open. Wind rushed in and struck his face. He licked his lips and peered outside. The ravens were there, just as he'd left them, studding the fences and perched in the trees. Across the yard, Grath could see his men looking worried. He took a small step outside, gingerly avoiding the dead man in the threshold, and waved to them. The signal caught their attention and they waved in return, eager to be on their way.

Grath took a breath to steady himself. The ravens looked at him without interest. Feeling confident, Grath moved out among them. They parted like a tide as he strode through.

"You're not so tough, eh?" he whispered to the birds. "Black bastards."

A raven at his feet ruffled its feathers, and that was all. Grath wanted to kick it. They were disgusting creatures, the product of a warped mind. Grath didn't wonder why Enli wanted his brother dead. He must have been a sick man indeed to conceive of such nightmares. The mercenary scanned the yard as he walked. There were so many of them, yet they hardly seemed a threat at all. He began to wonder if all the tales he'd heard were only stories told by Eneas to frighten people.

Halfway to his men, Grath noticed a particular bird gnawing on the finger of a dead soldier. His hand was sprawled open on the ground and the raven stood inside the palm, pecking wildly at a ring around the man's finger. A giant ruby caught the light, and Grath's attention. The raven was trying to free the ring. It had worked most of the flesh loose and was chewing intensely at the bone, anxious for the shiny bauble. Slowly, Grath approached the bird. He remembered something his father had told him once, about how ravens and crows sometimes collected shiny things and brought them to their nests. Grath didn't know why, but nothing was shinier than the ruby ring. It was worth a fortune, no doubt.

Carefully, so carefully that the snow didn't crunch beneath his boots, Grath made his way to the dead man and the raven pecking furiously at his finger. He stopped breathing as he drifted over the bird, letting his shadow fall lightly across it. Still the bird ignored him. It kept up at the impossible task of breaking the bone, taking the finger in its beak and trying to crack it like a nutshell. Grath flicked his hands at the bird, hoping to frighten it just enough to move it away.

"Shoo," he said softly. "Go. Go!"

The raven looked up at him, annoyed, its eyes blazing with black intelligence. The gaze infuriated Grath, who flicked at the thing forcefully.

"Away!" he growled. "Move!"

Finally angry, he dislodged the bird from the corpse with his boot, nudging it away. The bird bit at his foot, and when Grath tried to take the ring, the beast came forward, snapping at his hand. Without thinking, Grath's fist snapped out and batted the bird away. Quickly he freed the ring, then stood up and admired it in the dim light.

"My God," he said, turning it so every facet gleamed. "Beautiful."

A sudden explosion of feathers filled his vision. Grath screamed with an awful pain. The raven had flown up into his face, driving its talons into his cheeks and nose and tearing open the skin. Grath's arms flailed, trying to dislodge the bird, but its claws only dug deeper. With both hands he clamped down on the raven, pulling it free even as its talons sliced open his nostrils.

"Bitch!" screamed Grath. Blood gushed from his nose. The raven flew from his grasp, attacking anew. Grath put up his arms to protect himself, running blindly through the maze of birds, which suddenly rose up in a chorus of cries.

In a moment, they were all on him.

A thousand frenzied avians dug their talons deep, dragging him backward even as he tried to run for cover. He heard his garments tear, saw his men look on in horror as a flock of ravens came for them, too. Grath's world disappeared in a cloak of sable, as bit by bit the flesh was torn from his bones.

Up on her balcony, Nina watched in horror as the birds engulfed Grath and his men. There was an eruption of sound, a shrieking frenzy that tore open the sky. Over it, almost buried in raven sounds, were the gurgling cries of Grath, being dragged backward by a hundred insane ravens. The horses bolted, stranding the men. Grath's mercenaries began to scream. Nina stood frozen, watching it all in disbelief, and then at last had the good sense to run from the balcony, locking the doors.

Then she dashed down the stairs as fast as she could and began shuttering every window in the palace.

TWENTY-TWO

The Toymaker

High Street was one of the Black City's busiest thoroughfares. It was wide and tall and in the best section of the old city, near the apartments of the princely lords and just across the river from the Cathedral of the Martyrs. On summer evenings, when the sun threw long shadows across the city, High Street teemed with vendors and merchants; caterwauling slave traders peddling their captured flesh, travelling hunters with trussed-up game birds, beggars and thieves and harlots and prostitutes, and, amazingly, the occasional toy shop. There was money in this part of Nar, looted from a thousand successful campaigns, and the well-heeled of the city liked to spoil their greedy offspring. Naren women walked along High Street with their broods of arrogant children trailing out behind them, peering into the dressed-up windows of the shops. The bakery was most popular. It stood in the center of High Street near a money-changing shop, and was frequented by the Archbishop of Nar himself, a connoisseur of confections. The bakery's aroma was one of High Street's great treats, a welcome respite from the choking gases of the war labs. Children came just to stare in the bakery's window and coax a few cookies from the proprietor and his wife, and when they left, full of fresh-baked treats, they always noticed the other attraction of the street—the Piper's toy shop.

Besides the bakery, the toy shop was the real wonder of High Street. It had been in business for nearly forty years, and very few of the city's lords could recall a time without it. They were grown now, but each could still remember a special toy from the Piper's factory, some special doll they had dragged around until frayed, or perhaps a mechanical boat that skimmed across the water when wound. Made with typical Naren ingenuity, the toys in the Piper's shop were something unique, something worth making a long trip to see and purchase. The Piper was renowned in the Empire, a master toymaker who had studied with the craftsmen of Vosk before coming south and setting up his shop. He was legendary and beloved in the Black City, and his toy shop, a meager-looking storefront sandwiched between a candlemaker and a blacksmith, was frequently crowded with children and curious adults seeking guilty pleasures. But it was the toy shop's window that drew the most accolades.

Made of tall rectangles of glass, the window showed off the best of the Piper's creations. Here was a circus that could be viewed from the street, free of charge. There were toy soldiers with silver guns and brass cannons, and dolls with luxurious hair and exquisite dresses, their feet capped with meticulously made shoes, so tiny one wondered if human hands had crafted them. There were stuffed animals with real fur; stringed instruments of polished wood; and fabric-covered flying machines that actually glided through the air, suspended from the ceiling by translucent wire. Grand vessels floated in basins of water, and ships in bottles vexed young minds with the impossibility of their construction. A three-foot wooden model of an elf played on a flute, its animated fingers clicking with mechanical perfection as it blew out its endless tune. The elf's name was Darvin, and every child in the city knew his name. Darvin and his pipes were the symbol of the Piper's toy shop, as much a fixture of the city as the Black Palace or the Cathedral of the Martyrs. Each morning, when the Piper opened his toy shop, Darvin played the opening song, a long and complicated melody that had taken the toymaker nearly a year to set into the doll's clockworks. Like all the Piper's creations, Darvin had astonished the citizens of Nar, a difficult accomplishment for a city that had birthed the war labs.

But although the Piper was famous for his mechanical wonders, there was one particular skill that brought eager girls to his toy shop. He was, without question, the Empire's peerless maker of dollhouses. He could build anything, no matter how complex, no matter how big or small, and delight the most jaded Naren child. His replicas of the Black Palace were celebrated, and his skill at minutiae was unmatched by any scientist or engineer. Because he was so proud of his ability with dollhouses, the Piper had placed several in his shop window. Among them was an exquisite white home with a dozen gables and a thousand real wood shingles, each one lovingly carved from maple and stained with a glowing pink varnish. The house had three levels, working doors on golden hinges, and shiny glass windows that opened onto terraced balconies.

The house was named Belinda, after the Piper's long dead wife, and she was captivating, like all the toys in the toymaker's window. The Piper knew this, and so he was proud of his work. He didn't build toys, he used to say. He built smiles.

The Piper was nearly sixty now. His hands ached with arthritis when it rained, but he still rose early every morning and toiled in his workshop until late into the evening. His real name was Redric Bobs, but few people ever called him that. In his early days, before he'd discovered his love for toymaking, he had discovered an affinity for music, and was always found with a flute to his lips. An unaccomplished musician, the name had nevertheless stuck with him, and Redric Bobs had never really broken his musical habit. He still played the flute—but only on very rare occasions, and never for the pleasure of others. He had played for his wife Belinda, but she was dead now. The Piper was alone.

He had no children, and he had no family to speak of, for he had left them all behind years ago to come to the Black City and ply his new trade. His wife, Belinda, had died of a cancer fifteen years past, her womb barren, her dreams of a family unfulfilled. But she had loved her husband dearly and they had been happy, mostly, except for the emptiness of their home atop the toy shop, the one that Redric Bobs had built himself in anticipation of a brood of babies. Belinda Bobs and her husband had tried for years to conceive a child, had prayed mightily to Heaven for the great gift of life, but God had decided to ignore them. After ten years of trying, they had finally gone to the orphanage of the great cathedral, sure that the priests would not turn down so loving a couple. But just as God in Heaven was against them, so were his minions on earth.

"Too poor," they had told them. This was in the earlier days before the Piper's prowess was acknowledged. And later, when they had the money to care for children, the priests of the orphanage had slammed the doors with a different chant.

"Too old."

Belinda Bobs had been heartbroken. Redric Bobs' heart had hardened. A year later, Belinda battled cancer for the first time. It was the start of a hellish decade for the couple, one that eventually ate her alive. It was why the Piper rarely smiled now, why he shut himself off in his toy shop, hidden even from the eyes of eager children. It was why he was hard at work this very evening.

Alone in his shuttered workshop at the back of his store, Redric Bobs expertly balanced a bead of glue onto the needle-thin strut of a wooden tower. The tiny component was just one of a thousand like it, part of a complex myriad of criss-crossing joints making up the steeple of his giant model. The Cathedral of the Martyrs had presented the toymaker with some interesting challenges, not the least of which was its enormous tower of copper and iron. It needed to be perfect, sturdy, and built exactly to scale—and though Redric Bobs had no formal education in engineering, he supposed he shared some empathy with the humans who had designed the cathedral so many years ago. With a steady hand, the Piper dropped the strut into place and gave it a gentle press. Glue oozed slowly out. With his other hand he worked a piece of cloth, wiping the excess away. Satisfied, he stepped back to view his handiwork.

The steeple was half done, at last. Another week of work and it would be complete. Then he would start on the main structure. He grimaced, unsure if he would meet the count's aggressive schedule. Work like his required patience and time above all else, and Biagio wasn't giving him either. Worse, the Feast of Eestrii was only weeks away. The Piper clasped his hands together and studied his meticulous model. It was beautiful; it seemed a shame to destroy it.

"Almost time, Belinda, my love," he whispered. He was sure that Belinda watched over him still. She had promised on her deathbed never to leave him.

All the materials he needed were laid out before him. Great slabs of wood, tiny metal fasteners and bolts, golden wire and spools of thread, colored glass and a hundred pigments of paint, all strewn along his sawdust-covered floor. His tools hung from hooks along the walls, some as big as his arm, others so small they were difficult to see. His miniature work often required miniature tools, and these he kept in a box on his workbench and guarded jealously, for they were very rare and had come with him from Vosk decades ago. He had screwdrivers and little hammers, pliers and pins and sharp needles that could make an undetectable hole. They were no more than scraps of iron, but to the Piper they were precious. They gave his life meaning and dimension. And the thing he was constructing now, perhaps the greatest challenge of his career, would make him famous forever.

Or infamous, thought Redric Bobs with a frown. He really wasn't sure yet.

The workshop was cold. Piper felt his fingers tingle, rebelling against the chill. He went to his black iron stove and picked a few nuggets of coal from the bucket, depositing them into the fire box with a pair of long tongs. Shutting the stove door, he put his hands up to the hot metal to warm them. Winter was coming, and he never liked the winter. It was one of the reasons he had moved south. The Black City, with its tall spires and taller tales, had drawn him across the continent. That had been over forty-five years ago. When he had arrived, he had seen the Black Palace on its monolithic perch, beckoning travellers from miles away. The sight of it had forever changed him, as had all the city's marvels. But nothing was more beautiful than the Cathedral of the Martyrs.

Though the Black Palace was taller and more garish, the cathedral was the city's true jewel, the only thing in Nar that could still bring a tear to the old man's eyes. Over the years, he had tried many times to capture the cathedral's beauty in a model, but he had always failed. She was too complicated, too ornate. But time and hatred had sharpened the toymaker's skills, and he was ready at last to construct his masterpiece. As he warmed his frozen fingers his eyes flicked toward the miniature cathedral. The Piper smiled.

A bell jingled insistently in the distance. Piper pulled back his hands, wondering who would disturb him so late. Cautiously he crossed his workroom and stood in the threshold of his toy shop, clinging to the shadows as he spied the door. Shades were drawn over the door's glass, but Redric Bobs could see a silhouette against the fabric, cast there by the gas street lights. The figure was very small, no taller than a child.

A beggar, the Piper supposed. They were always bothering him to play with the toys in his window. He started toward the door, then heard a horse whinny. The sound startled him. The doorbell jangled again as the figure impatiently yanked the chain. Past Darvin and the other toys in his window, Redric Bobs saw a big brown wagon in the street outside his shop. Four stout men leaned against it, waiting for him to answer. The tiny figure at his threshold rang the bell one more time, then started pounding on the door.

"Piper Bobs," came an unknown voice. "Open up."

The voice was small and high, like a child's voice, but stronger. Piper puzzled over it, unsure what to do. He was expecting Biagio's agents, but hadn't guessed they would come so late at night or in such force. A fearful tremor made his steady hands shake.

"I'm coming," he called, rushing to the door. Quickly he undid the bolts, then cracked the door open. Night rushed in on a cold breeze. Out on his stoop, a tiny figure dressed in black looked up at him with preternatural eyes. From the lines on his face he looked like a man, but he was far shorter, almost dwarf-sized. There was no smile on his face, only an insistent look that blazed in his blue, hypnotic stare.

"Minister Bovadin! You?"

"Open the door, Bobs," said the midget tersely. "We have something for you."

Piper opened the door and stuck his head outside to better see the wagon. On its bed was a giant wooden crate. The men leaning against the conveyance looked over at him without regard, their expressions unreadable. Piper groaned at the size of the delivery.

"Is that it?" he asked incredulously.

The midget nodded. "That's it."

"All of that? I mean, it's so big!"

Nar's Minister of Science squeezed past the toymaker's legs and into the shop. "Don't worry. Most of it is wooden supports to keep the device stable. The thing itself isn't much bigger than me." His weird eyes surveyed the store. "We have to get it inside quickly. Where can we put it?"

"In my workshop," the Piper replied. "In the back. Will you help me unpack it?"

"Of course. I can't just leave it with you, now can I?"

Bovadin walked off toward the back of the store, disappearing for a few moments in the workshop. When he returned he nodded approvingly. "Good enough," he said, then went back outside and waved the men inside. His signal snapped the men into action. Each one climbed onto the wagon and grabbed hold of a corner of the crate. As they worked to unload the dangerous parcel, Bovadin opened the door as wide as it would go. The scientist gave an annoyed curse when he discovered the narrowness of the doorway.

"This won't do," he told the Piper. "It won't fit through the door."

"There are double doors in the back," said the toymaker. "Take it around there. I'll open up for you."

Bovadin groaned and returned to the cart, ordering his men to start taking down the crate. Redric Bobs dashed to the back of his workshop and undid the locks on the twin metal doors. He was always getting shipments that were too large for the front door, and it was better that the strange crate come in through the alley anyway. Soon Bovadin reappeared with his men. The bigger men grunted as they walked with an ungainly wobble, maneuvering the big box through the open doors. Piper directed the sweating men to a clear area of his workroom. Bovadin sat down cross-legged on the workbench. He clapped his hands excitedly as his men set down the crate.

"Gently," he said. "Yes, right there."

The crate eased down to the floor. Bovadin hopped down from the workbench. He struggled to reach a crowbar dangling from the wall, just out of reach of his stubby fingers. Piper rolled his eyes back and plucked the tool from its hook, handing it to the midget. Bovadin tossed the crowbar to one of his men.

"Open it," he ordered.

The man wedged the tool's clawed head beneath the sealed lid and gave a muscular pull. Slowly the nails crept outward, screeching free of the wood. The other men joined in, pulling the lid free of the crate and setting it aside. Then, very carefully, each men grabbed a corner of the crate and began peeling it apart like an orange. Piper stared wide-eyed at the contents, trying to see past the wooden supports. He caught a glimpse of silver metal and a ganglia of snakelike hoses, all held together with ropes and leather straps. Whatever it was, Bovadin wasn't taking any chances. Once the walls of the crate were down, the men stepped aside, letting the toymaker see.

Bovadin laughed, gladdened with himself. "Take a good look, toymaker. You won't see anything like this again." He walked into the center of the crate and stroked the metal tubes lovingly. "Beautiful, isn't it?"

The Piper wasn't sure how to answer. It was amazing, certainly. But beautiful? It was unrecognizable, like some metal monster from the ocean. Without precisely knowing what it was, Redric Bobs couldn't reply.

"I will say that it is interesting," he conceded. "More than that, I really don't know."

"That's because you don't understand it," Bovadin grumbled. Again he caressed his strange device. "No one does. Only me."

"Explain it to me," said Piper. "This is supposed to fit in my dollhouse, yes?"

"Yes," said the minister. He gave his men a scowl, the only gesture needed to send them scurrying out of the room. When he was sure they couldn't hear him, Bovadin continued, "According to the plans I sent to you. You've built the model big enough, I can tell."

"It's not done yet," said Piper. "But it should be big enough, yes."

"I've taken care of the clockworks myself," said Bovadin. He pointed out a little lever at the top of the metal cylinder. "The angel over the gates must be attached to this lever. It has to be movable, but only side to side." He jiggled the lever back and forth to demonstrate. The Piper blanched at the show. "It's not armed yet," explained Bovadin, grinning. "But when it is, there will only be an hour before the device starts up. You can build the angel, can't you?"

Piper nodded. "I've already made him."

He went to his workbench and slid open a hidden drawer. Inside was an unpainted figure of an angel, an archangel with a trumpet to his lips. It was perfectly detailed in every facet, just like the real one above the cathedral's gates. Gingerly he handed the figurine over to Bovadin, who cooed when he felt it in his small hands.

"It's lovely," the minister complimented. "You are a true craftsman, Piper Bobs." His little fingers brushed the angel's face and wings. "It's so detailed. So real."

"Of course," bragged the toymaker. "It's supposed to be real. That's what I do, Minister. I make dreams real."

Bovadin smirked at him. "That's an odd way to describe what we're about to do, don't you think?"

"You may think of it any way you wish, Minister Bovadin. I will keep thinking of it as a dream."

For Redric Bobs, it was a dream years in the making. He had put all his soul and skill into the model of the cathedral, had vested it with his finest effort. It was not merely for the purpose of revenge. Rather, it was to right an atrocious wrong. Cautiously he walked over to the device in the crate, studying its intricate design. It was astonishing, more so even than any of his prized toys.

"Tell me more about this thing," he said. "How does it work?"

"You don't need to know that," said Bovadin. "I want you focused on your work."

Piper scowled, insulted. "I may not be a scientist, but I'm sure I can understand it."

"I'm sure you can. But I don't want you understanding it. The little girl pulls the angel down. That starts the device. That's all you need to know."

"What are the hoses for?" Piper pressed. "The fuel, right? They keep it cool, don't they? And the fuel is under pressure, too. That's why it's made of metal. And that's why you're doing it in the winter." He smiled at Bovadin. "I'm right, aren't I?"

"You're smarter than you look, admittedly. But do your job, toymaker. Don't ask too many questions."

"I'm only trying to figure this out," Piper snapped back. "This is my home, my livelihood. I want to know what you've brought into it."

The scientist padded up to Piper and glared at him. "If we're going to work together, you'll have to do what I say. No questions. Understand?"

"No," said Piper. He folded his arms over his chest. "That's not my idea of working together. I want details about this thing. I want to know how it works."

Bovadin laughed. "And what else do you want? I wonder. I see a plan in your eyes, toy man. Do you think you won't be compensated for your work here? Let me put your mind at ease. Everyone who assists Biagio will be rewarded."

"What?" spat Piper. The insult was like having cold water tossed in his face. "Do you think that's why I'm doing this, little man?" He jabbed his finger at Bovadin's nose. "You are wrong. I don't care about Biagio or his Black Renaissance. I have bigger reasons for doing this."

The midget shrugged, unimpressed. "Nevertheless, you will be rewarded. *If* you follow my instructions. I've set the timer to start the device an hour after the lever is moved. It's up to you to do the rest."

"Don't worry," said Piper. "It will be flawless. But what about the girl? She hasn't come for the dollhouse yet."

"She will, during the festival for the start of Kren. She'll see your dollhouses in the window and she'll ask the bishop to buy her one. Herrith will say yes. You will tell him you will build it."

Piper nodded. "I understand. Just so she gets here on time."

"Have faith," said Bovadin. He turned his back on the toymaker and started out of the workshop. "All is going according to Biagio's plan. Soon enough you'll have whatever satisfaction you're seeking."

The four men who had come with Bovadin stood at attention when their master entered the storefront. Bovadin shooed them out the door. But before he followed them into the night, he gave Piper a final warning.

"Be swift with your work, toy man. Eestrii isn't far away."

"I'll be ready," Piper promised.

"I'll be back before then, to help you get the device into the dollhouse. Don't try to do it without me."

"What? You're not leaving the city?" Piper asked, surprised. Like Biagio, Bovadin was an outcast now.

"I have some friends who will hide me until Eestrii," said Bovadin. "No one will know I'm in Nar. And you won't tell anyone, will you, Piper?"

Bovadin didn't wait for an answer, just shuffled off into the night. Piper watched the strange group pile into the wagon and the wagon disappear into the shadows of High Street. For a long time Piper stood in his doorway, shivering. He didn't like Bovadin. He didn't like Biagio, either. But the pair had given him something he hadn't been able to acquire himself—the chance to strike at the church of Nar. Piper didn't care about idealogy or revolutions. The man who sat on the Iron Throne was of no interest to him. This crusade he had joined held no rewards for him save vengeance.

TWENTY-THREE

The Hundred Isles of Liss

Richius Vantran stood in the crow's nest of the *Prince of Liss*, marveling at the view. With his hands wrapped tightly around the rail, he tilted his face into the wind and let the cold sun caress him. A ferocious breeze tore at the rigging and the collar of his thick naval coat, and his hair streamed back, snapping like a flag. Before him stretched the endless ocean, as vast as the sky, and in the distance a pod of whales breached and glistened in the sunlight, sending up watery geysers. Richius watched the spouts fire into the air, and for the first time since leaving Falindar let all the guilt of his actions melt away. Feeling daring, he let go of the railing and raised his hands into the air triumphantly, letting out a gleeful cry.

He felt bodiless on the crow's nest, and the wind seemed to bear him up like a feather, until he could no longer feel the platform beneath his feet. He laughed joyously, and for a time forgot about the life and family he had left behind.

"Easy, boy!" Marus called from the deck far below. The first officer, who had coached Richius up the rigging, now stared up at his protégé with mild worry. "Put your hands on the rail, like I told you!"

Richius ignored the Lissen. He closed his eyes and let the sunlight twinkle on his eyelids, imagining himself a bird. Was this what life at sea was like? He wondered now why he had feared the long journey, and why he had wasted so much of it in his cramped cabin. Nearly two weeks out of Lucel-Lor, the call of the sea had finally seized him.

"Marus, look at me!" he shouted. "I'm the great Commander Prakna!"

"All right, that's enough!" called Marus.

Richius heard the annoyance in his voice and put his hands back on the rail. Thirty feet down, he knew Marus was scowling at him.

"Don't worry," he called. "I'm fine. This is amazing!"

Marus laughed. During the time they had shared a cabin, he had tried repeatedly to get Richius above deck. The crow's nest, he had assured Richius, would change his opinion about the sea forever. Richius acknowledged his change in attitude by returning the Lissen's grin. He was very cold but hardly felt it. All he knew was the roar of the wind and the vastness of the world. It had taken him long minutes to climb the rigging and master the sway of the ship, and he had thought more than once about backing down. But the reward of his climb was indisputable now. There was no land anywhere in sight, and no birds to hint at any. They were alone on the earth, in the company of giant whales, and though the Lissen flagship was mighty, she was like a piece of flotsam on the ocean. Her great sails groaned with wind, and her tall, wooden masts swayed, rocking the crow's nest. Just above Richius' head, the sea-serpent flag of the Hundred Isles snapped in the wind. The tails of his heavy coat twisted in the breeze, billowing through the railing. Richius drew the garment tighter around his body, checking the brass buttons with his fingers. With his unshaven beard and deep blue coat, he looked almost like one of the crew. He was beginning to feel like a crewman, too, and the sensation heartened him. There was work waiting for him in Liss. He wouldn't be an outcast.

The *Prince of Liss* pitched starboard as a wave crashed into her side. Richius held fast to the railing and watched the earth tilt sideways. He laughed, loving the ride. It was like breaking a wild mustang. It was like he was home again, in Aramoor, where only small things mattered. He reveled in the moment, knowing it wouldn't last.

"Richius," Marus cried. "That's enough. Come down now!"

Richius waved to the man and started out of the crow's nest, carefully shimmying down the stout rope ladder. The wind buffeted him, making him hold on tightly and move with sureness. He glanced down at the far below deck. Marus was pantomiming his climb like a worried father.

"I'm all right," Richius assured him.

A crowd of sailors had gathered around Marus and were cheering Richius down. They laughed and applauded when he finally reached the deck. Marus let loose a relieved sigh and slapped Richius' shoulder hard.

"Good boy!" he declared heartily. "You've lost your virginity!"

The sailors all laughed and assailed Richius with good-natured punches. Tomroy and Pips, the two other officers Richius shared his cabin with, bent in mock bows. They were lieutenants, and younger than Marus. No older than himself, Richius guessed. But they were good company and gracious about sharing their meager living space. Like Marus, they had welcomed him. And, like Marus, they had bombarded him with questions about Nar and Lucel-Lor and his battles against the Empire. Richius had been pleased to regale them. It was the only payment he could offer in return for their hospitality.

"I wish Prakna had seen you," Tomroy remarked. "He would have been amazed."

"He would have had a heart-attack and dropped dead," countered Pips. "We're supposed to be taking care of him."

"Aye," Marus added with a grin. "Prakna would have been angry. Ah, but it did the boy good, I can tell." The sailor reached out and pinched Richius' cheek. "Look at that face. Nice and ruddy, like the rest of us!"

More laughter from the crew. Richius smoothed down his windblown coat, then buried his hands in his pockets to warm them. The coat had been one of Marus' own, a necessity in so cold a climate. Though they were heading south, winter was still very real in Liss.

"That was wonderful," Richius said, shaking his head in disbelief. "I could see for miles! It was like being in a Naren tower, only better. No smoke, no buildings blocking the view. Lord, it was like I was a gull."

"Yes," said Marus dryly. "I thought for a moment you might indeed take flight. Don't ever take your hands off the railing again, Richius. That was very stupid."

"Leave the man alone," Tomroy said. "It was his first time. I think he did well. Maybe we'll make you a lookout, Richius. What do you say?"

"I say no," replied Richius. "Too damn cold."

"But you won't hide in the cabin anymore, will you?" asked Pips.

"The sea's part of you more than it is me," Richius observed. "But yes, it was great."

The officers all gave each other "I told you so" looks, proud that they had gotten Richius into the masts. It was true what Richius said—the sea really was part of them. He was learning that quickly. The sea was as much a part of a Lissen as tall pine trees or horses were to a man from Aramoor. They respected the sea and in return the sea respected them, and in some odd way they had a magic over the ocean, could almost bend it to their will. They were a strange and fierce race, and their mettle made him yearn to see their homeland.

"I want to go below, warm up a bit," Richius told them. There was a chorus of groans, to which he quickly replied, "Stop now, just stop. I want to get something warm to drink. Anyone coming?"

"Aye, boy, I'll come with you," said Marus. "Let these other rats get back to work. Tomroy, check the stunsails. The third looks loose to me."

"Yes, sir," said Tomroy, returning to protocol. He and the others dispersed to their stations with practiced speed. Marus put an arm around Richius and steered him to a gangway.

"Let's get to the galley before your nose starts leaking icicles," he said, taking the lead.

Richius followed him through the gangway and below deck, then down one more level until they reached the deck where the galley was situated in the rear of the ship. It was dark and narrow in the hall, and the walls wailed with the blows of the waves. The oiled wood glowed in the meager light from the thin, vertical portholes. Richius wobbled as he moved, still too green to walk with confidence. He had already banged his head a dozen times, and the welts were starting to show. When they reached the galley, he grabbed hold of the round doorway and pulled himself inside.

The galley was empty, a blessing since the room was so small. Spartan benches lined the walls, their wood worn smooth by a thousand backsides, and long, flat tables filled most of the space, their tops stained and pitted. In the corner of the galley was a small work area, dominated by an iron stove lined with rocks and a few battered pots and pans. Some copper tableware sat in a crate beside the stove, the only utensils available to the crew. There was, however, a kettle of steaming liquid bolted to the stove. The lid of the kettle was held securely by wire fasteners, and holes had been drilled into it to let the steam escape. Anyone with an appetite could come down and take a dip of the soup. It was the only food the crew could eat as much as they cared to, for it wasn't rationed like the bread and meat. Bowen, the ship's cook, always kept a kettle of it at the ready. It was thin and mostly flavorless, but the smell of it enticed Richius across the room anyway. He rattled through the tableware for two bowls and spoons while Marus undid the kettle's lid and with the community dipper drew out two hot bowls-full. After gingerly replacing the lid, the two men slid onto a bench and savored their meal. Richius rubbed his hands together over the steam. The smell of the soup and the warmth of the coal stove immediately drained the chill from his body. Marus, however, made no pretense at patience. He dug his spoon into the soup, fished out the biggest hunk of potato, and jammed it into his mouth.

"You did a good job topside," he said as he slurped. "I'm proud of you. We'll make a sailor of you yet, Richius."

"Don't bet on it," Richius cautioned. "It was great fun, but I'm no seaman."

Marus shrugged. "That's just as well. Prakna's not bringing you to Liss to start a navy. We already have one of those."

Richius eyed Marus over his spoon, waiting for the Lissen to start with his questions. Whenever they were alone, Marus always had questions.

"Aramoor doesn't have a navy at all, does it?" the first officer asked.

"Nope. Not a single ship. At least not while I was living there. No telling what the Gayles have done to Aramoor."

"I can't imagine fighting a war without ships," Marus remarked. "We'd be lost without our schooners."

"Aramoor isn't like Liss," said Richius. "It's just land. No canals; nothing like that." He lowered his spoon and decided to change the course of the conversation. "Tell me more about the canals, Marus. They're everywhere?"

"Everywhere," said Marus. "We get everywhere by boat. All the land is built on, and everything is tall. We make use of what little land we have."

"Amazing," said Richius. "It's very different from Nar, isn't it?"

The Lissen's eyes flicked up toward Richius. "*Very* different."

"I meant no offense, friend. Just an observation. I'm looking forward to seeing the Hundred Isles. I've never even known anyone who's seen Liss, besides all you. Prakna was the first Lissen I'd ever met." Richius leaned back, gauging Marus' mood. "He's a strange one, isn't he?"

"Who? Prakna?"

"Yes. He's very distant. Very . . ." Richius struggled with the word. "Moody."

"Prakna has a lot on his mind."

"I know. But I've hardly seen him since coming aboard. Lord, he spends more time in his cabin than I do. What's wrong with him, Marus?"

"Richius," cautioned Marus. "You're asking too many questions."

Richius smiled. "I think I have that right, don't you?"

"Maybe." Marus lowered his gaze evasively. "But Prakna's a complex man. He's seen a lot, done a lot. I'm not going to be able to explain him to you over a bowl of soup."

"You've known him a long time, though, haven't you? I can tell. You're friends. You've probably been through some tough times together, what with the war and all." Richius sipped slowly at his soup. "Prakna told me he's married."

Marus nodded.

"What about his children?"

The question made Marus freeze. "What about them?"

"Prakna told me he lost two boys in the war against Nar. Is that true?"

Very slowly Marus dropped his spoon into the bowl, then shoved the half-eaten soup aside to stare at Richius. Richius knew by the look in his eyes that he'd crossed an invisible line.

"Richius, let me give you a warning. Don't ever ask anyone onboard about Prakna again. Don't ask about his wife, and don't *ever* ask about his children. Do you understand me?"

"Marus, I understand." Richius shoved his own bowl aside. "But this vengeance of Prakna's is making him wild."

Marus' sad expression deepened. "There were bad times in Liss, Richius. For ten years. You know all about the war, but I don't think you know how devastated the isles were. Still are, really. There were a lot of men killed in the war with Nar. Young men, like you. It's true about Prakna. He lost two boys in the war. And I . . ." His voice crumbled, forcing him to look away. "I lost one boy. My only son."

The awful revelation struck Richius. He slid his hand across the table and touched the Lissen's fingertips, trying to apologize.

"I'm sorry," he said. "I'm a fool for asking. I should have known."

Embarrassed, Marus waved the remark away. "No," he said. "Look at me, crying like some woman! It was a long time ago. For both of us. But I don't know. Perhaps I've dealt with it a little better than Prakna. It's destroyed a part of him."

"I'm sure it has," said Richius. He remembered Sabrina, his first wife, and the indescribable horror of finding her head in a box. That one moment had set his life on fire, had etched itself forever in his brain. Men weren't supposed to forget such loss, not if they had hearts. "It was rude of me to ask you this," he said finally. "I didn't know. If I had, well . . ."

"They were good boys," recalled Marus. "They all served together on the *Fire Bird*, just as soon as they were old enough. Prakna didn't want both his sons serving on the same vessel. Turns out he was right about that. The *Fire Bird* went down in minutes."

"How?" Richius asked.

"The *Fearless*," replied Marus. "You know that ship?"

"God, yes. That's Nicabar's ship." Richius shook his head. "I've got unhappy memories about that fellow, let me tell you. I met him once in Nar City."

Marus' eyes widened. "Really? What was he like?"

"Big as a house and hard as rock. I'll never forget his face as long as I live, or what he said to me."

"Why? What did he say?"

Richius reconsidered the conversation. "Marus, I shouldn't tell you. It would only make you mad."

"Tell me," Marus insisted. "I want to know."

"All right. This was almost two years ago, when Nar was still attacking Liss, trying to make the isles surrender. Nicabar had some new ships the war labs had designed for him. He was eager to try them out against Liss. I think he was embarrassed that he hadn't been able to conquer you yet."

"Damn right," sneered Marus. "He tried for a decade, but we never lost. What else did he say?"

"He said he was going back to Liss for the last time, that you were ready to fall."

"And?"

"That he was going to feed every Lissen child to the sharks in your canals. He said he was going to turn Liss' canals red with blood. And he said he was going to drown your sailors. He thought that was very funny."

There was a stony silence between the men. Richius forced himself to look at Marus. A pall settled across Marus' face as all the memories of his past flooded in. They were on the same violent path now, the Lissens and Richius. All of their lives had been damaged by the Empire, warped into an all-consuming vendetta. Dyana was wrong, Richius decided suddenly. He *did* belong with these people.

"Admiral Danar Nicabar is a monster without peer," said Marus at last. "That's why Prakna has changed. That's why we must fight against Nar."

Richius gave his friend a bleak smile. "You must be a very strong people to endure the things you have, Marus. It will be my honor to lead your army. I'll do my best for you, I promise."

"I know you will, boy," said Marus. "Now eat. And rest up. We'll be in Liss in just a few days. You'll need your strength for the work ahead."

They returned their attention to their food, eating in contemplative silence. As Richius sipped at his soup he thought about Liss and its brave people, a race that had been audacious enough to stand against Nar and declare itself free. He *would* help these people, he determined. With all his might he would make an army of them, and someday he would return to Falindar triumphant and prove to Dyana that his trust in Prakna hadn't been misplaced.

On a morning light with snowfall and speckled with silver clouds, the crew of the *Prince* sighted the Hundred Isles of Liss. It was a long-craved homecoming, and across the flagship's deck the emotions were palpable as men and boys hung from the rigging, forgetting their work, and stared in silence at their magnificent islands. Fleet Commander

Prakna stood on the *Prince*'s forecastle, his long coat stirring in the breeze, his face set with a melancholy smile. To his left stood Marus. To his right stood Richius, who leaned out over the railing as far as he could, desperate for his first sight of Liss.

There were, he realized quickly, *at least* a hundred isles. Some were tiny, some seemed to rival Aramoor in size, and he could see the wide canals winding through them, full of sails and paddle vessels. In the distance were towers and spiraling structures of brass and stone, and wooden aqueducts that meandered high above the ground. Liss was white and serene in the snow, but she was also vast and troubled-looking, and Richius could see the damaged harbors on her shores, the jagged scars of a decade-long war. For every intact building there was another in decay, missing a top or balancing precariously on a cracked foundation. The hull of a giant vessel reached out from the depths, its pitted keel black and broken, its cracked masts peeking through the surface like the fingers of a drowning man.

But the Hundred Isles were more than their tattered shores, and past the harbors where the ruins stood, Richius saw cities on the horizon, great untouched arches and free-standing stonework, the beautiful labor of patient artisans. Liss looked ancient, as if it predated Nar and mankind itself, and the vision of so many lovely things screamed her history across the ocean, beckoning her sons home.

Fleet Commander Prakna clasped his hands and lowered his head in silent prayer, and Marus and the others joined him. For a brief time, the *Prince of Liss* fell silent save for the endless rush of the wind and water. Richius dropped his eyes in deference to the prayer. He was not a religious man, not after the things he'd seen, but he had respect for these men, and so he maintained his silence. When Prakna was done with his meditation, he turned to Richius and pointed at his homeland.

"Liss," he said softly. "My home. Now yours, Richius. At least for a while."

"It's beautiful," Richius acknowledged. "I never thought it would be so big."

"Oh, you're only seeing a bit of it. We're too far off yet. Wait, my friend. Just wait."

As patiently as he could, Richius waited as the Lissen flagship chewed up the waves, eager as her crew to get home. Signalmen along the deck flashed their colored flags toward the islands, summoning a small armada of single-masted boats to come out and greet them. Groups of children were gathering on the shores, waving across the sea to their heroes, and the men of the *Prince* waved back and shouted happily at the throngs, while Prakna folded his arms over his chest and let a smile conquer his face. Richius let Marus point all these things out to him. The first officer was buoyant, jubilant to be home, and all his knowledge about Liss and its sights spilled out of him in a jumble of facts and folklore. As they drifted closer and the great ship slowed, Richius could see the beautiful ruins marring the harbors and the dead ship rising from the murky bottom. In the far-off towers he saw colors he never knew existed, a rainbow of light glowing from a million panes of mirrored glass. Magnificent docks with gargantuan mooring posts stood along the shores, conspicuously empty of schooners, while overhead giant sea birds drifted, great gulls with impossible wing spans and bright orange bills. Behind the islands, the sun was breaking through the snowy morning, setting Liss aflame, and the flakes from the sky twinkled as they fell, blanketing the world in virgin white.

"See the cat boats?" Marus asked. "They'll escort us in."

"Cat boats?" asked Richius. He saw the boats, but not the meaning.

"That's what they're called, because of their rigging. A cat-rigged boat has one mast, put far forward in the hull. We use the cat boats to get around the islands. Usually we don't use the sails, though. They don't work in the canals."

Richius watched as the small fleet of boats began circling the *Prince*. Sailors in the boats waved at the comrades aboard the flagship, blowing boatswain pipes and ringing bells. Liss loomed ever larger as they neared a docking port, obviously built to accommodate ships like the *Prince*. As they drew closer to land, Prakna began giving orders to his crew to prepare for docking. The men set to the task, drawing ropes and trimming sails and steering the flagship toward port. The cat boats gave the *Prince* a wide berth as they paralleled her. On shore, the children and women who had gathered to greet them chatted amongst themselves, their faces glowing. There were very few men in the crowd. Richius squinted to study the assembly, counting only a handful of old men among them.

War, he reasoned bitterly. *What will this place be like?*

And what sort of army could he make of old men? His eyes shifted back to the ruins around him, the broken shipyards and falling walls, and he remembered how Nar had bombarded these people for ten years, trying and failing to drown them. He looked at the children and the pretty women, most of them thin and slightly built, and he wondered how they had endured so much. His own father had handed Aramoor over to Nar years ago, fearing such a plight. Since then Aramoor had flourished, without the destruction of war. But Aramoor wasn't free. It wasn't even ruled by the Vantran bloodline anymore. Despite the ruins around him, Richius was sure Liss had made the truly courageous choice—to fight.

The *Prince* eased toward the dock, slow and smooth, and the cat boats drifted alongside. A handful of sailors on the dock readied mooring lines as Prakna and Marus guided the flagship to a gentle docking. Chains rattled and pulleys unspooled as the crew hurried to secure the *Prince*. Men jumped from the deck onto the dock to catch the ropes and pull the *Prince* into place. Inch by groaning inch the *Prince* lurched forward, until at last it ground against the dock and jolted to an abrupt halt. Prakna and Marus exchanged congratulatory grins.

"Welcome to Liss, Richius Vantran," said the fleet commander boldly. "These people are all here to see you, too, you know."

A gangplank descended. Prakna led Marus and Richius off the ship, into the waiting throng. Richius felt the unusual sensation of steady earth beneath him and nearly toppled over, but Marus' arm was there to catch him.

"You'll get used to it," the officer whispered.

Richius wasn't so sure. He held on to Marus as he descended. All at once a wave of children pressed around him, their golden heads bobbing at his waist. They looked up at him with astonishment, tugging at his coat and grabbing for his hands. Prakna and Marus were swarmed too, but the sight of the Naren had the crowd entranced. The women on the docks, too proper to crowd around him, pointed at Richius with a mixture of fascination and fear. A little girl grabbed his fingers and squeezed, trying to pull him down to her. Richius stooped to smile at her. She was lovely, and when he looked at her she jumped back with a delighted laugh.

"Hello there," he said.

"Naren," she declared knowingly. "You're the Jackal."

"No," corrected Richius mildly. "Richius." He pointed to himself to stress the name. "Call me Richius."

"The Jackal!" said another child in the crowd. "The Jackal of Nar!"

Richius bristled. "All right," he grumbled. "The Jackal." He gave the girl's hair another tousle and walked off, shaking his head. Marus was next to him, chuckling.

"Get used to it, Richius," he advised. "That's how they know you here."

"Oh, really? And whose fault is that?"

"It's just the stories people tell, that's all," said Marus. "It's not meant as an insult. Just like the Triin calling you Kalak."

"Yes, well, that's not such a great name, either."

Prakna led them to another vessel, one of the boats that were everywhere in the ubiquitous canal, this one green and gold with a striking figure of a two-headed fish. A collection of oars jutted from the sides of the vessel, centipede-like. Waiting for them on the dock were a pair of regally attired sailors. Their long coats also bore the same unusual crest, stitched over their breasts. Prakna approached the men, who bowed to him and smiled.

"Fleet Commander Prakna," said one of them reverently. "Welcome home, sir."

"Good to be home," said Prakna. The commander was resplendent even in his threadbare uniform. "Permission to come aboard?"

The sailor stood aside. "Gladly granted, sir."

"Where are we going?" Richius asked Marus.

"Those are the queen's own," said Marus. "They'll take us to the palace, on Haran Island."

"The queen?" blurted Richius. He looked down at his own filthy clothes. "I'm supposed to meet a queen like this?"

"Just like the rest of us. Look around, Richius. Trust me, the queen won't be offended by your clothes."

In the ruins of the shoreline the statement seemed plausible, but Richius tried to smooth down his wrinkled coat anyway. Prakna was notoriously tight-lipped, and hadn't mentioned anything about meeting the Lissen ruler. He had thought they would rest awhile, maybe start to work in the morning. Obviously their mission was more desperate than he'd thought. And having already met Arkus of Nar, an audience with the Queen of Liss only made him a little nervous. He followed Prakna and Marus onto the boat, careful not to slip on the snowy planks, and gave a final wave to the people on the dock. They were all staring at him, still. Being a hero was rather pleasant, he decided. If only Dyana and Shani could see him now.

Once they were on board, the little boat shoved off under the power of the oarsmen and bore them through the wide canal cutting through the island. On either side the old structures of Liss rose up over them, threatening to topple onto their heads. Richius noticed the unmistakable scars of blast marks, the telltale signs of flame cannons. Many of the buildings bore gaps in their masonry where the guns of dreadnoughts had drilled fiery holes. Rubble littered the ground, and everywhere the canal streets were polluted with debris that had tumbled into the water. While Prakna and Marus talked with the sailors, Richius went to the prow of the boat for a better view. Before him, all of Liss was leisurely unfolding. The spiraling towers in the distance beckoned with an inaudible voice, and the snowflakes on the waterways brought a hush to the world. Abandoned buildings rose over him, but in the canal were other boats like their own, ferrying people and goods between the structures. Teenaged boys and girls toiled in the rubble, busy with the back-breaking work of reconstruction, pausing just long enough to notice the royal boat and offer it a weary wave.

"This isn't all of it," said Marus suddenly. He had come up behind Richius and put a hand on his shoulder. "It gets better, don't worry."

"There's so much destruction," said Richius. "I've never seen anything like it. You're a very brave people, Marus, to endure so much."

"These have been our islands since the beginning of time. We'll never give them up." The Lissen pointed to a wide inlet in the distance, now surrounded by blown-up buildings. "See that harbor? The *Fearless* was there. She opened fire with her guns before any schooners could get near enough to stop her. Over a thousand men and women attacked her, in boats just like this. It was hand-to-hand at times." Marus' expression dimmed. "Bloody as hell. The canal really did run red that day. That's where all this rubble came from. After the *Fearless* stopped firing, the whole place was in flames. It's taken a year just to rebuild this much."

"What about inland?" asked Richius. "Not so much damage?"

"No, thank God. Most of the canals are too narrow for dreadnoughts. And there's a whole system of locks and dams. Nicabar tried landing troops to invade, but they didn't know their way and were always slaughtered. We don't have any avenues to move heavy equipment, so none of the usual Naren tactics worked."

"So they just kept bombarding you," sighed Richius. "Amazing."

"For ten years," Marus echoed. He shut his eyes in remembrance of the bloody days. "It's over now, though. It's time for Nar to pay for what they've done."

"Tell me about Haran Island," said Richius. "What's that mean, Haran? Is that a Lissen word?"

"Sort of," said Marus. He pointed to the boat's figurehead, the remarkable, two-headed fish. "That's a haran."

"That? A fish?"

"Not just a fish," said Marus. "A haran. The word means divine one, or something like that. Lissens used to believe the harans were Gods, because they were so intelligent. There are still some of them, but only a few. All of them live in the waters around the queen's palace."

"They're incredible looking," remarked Richius. "Are they big?"

"Sometimes. No bigger than a man, usually."

"What?" Richius stepped back from the railing. "That big?"

"You'll see them when you get to the palace, Richius. The queen has some in her water garden. I'm sure she'll show them to you, if you ask."

"Tell me about your queen. What's she like?"

Marus beamed. "That's a treat I'll leave for you to imagine, my friend. Just trust me when I say that Queen Jelena is very special. You will be in awe of her, I know it."

Richius returned his gaze to the snowy horizon. "I have no doubt."

For nearly an hour the boat kept its slow pace through the canal, the oarsmen rowing with gentle ease. The waterway had narrowed some, branching off in places to link with other similar avenues, and all around them rose the weird structures of Liss. Overhead great bridges spanned, ancient constructs of sculpted stone, filled with folk going about their daily chores. They had left the ruins behind and were in the heart of Liss, where even the long-range guns of Naren dreadnoughts could not reach. The destruction had given way to marvelous architecture. Richius relaxed as they cruised leisurely along, astonished at the sights. The light snow fell in his hair and eyelashes, reminding him of Aramoor, and he thought of Dyana and Shani again, and how wonderful they too would find this place. Someday, he would bring them here and show them the marvels. When the world was at peace, there would be time for such pleasures.

Fleet Commander Prakna and Marus lingered in the back of the boat with the sailors, leaving Richius alone on the bow. Richius supposed it was their way of getting him acclimated to his new home, and he appreciated the privacy. Just days before, he had considered forming the Lissen army as something of a dream, but now he was here in Liss. What he had told Prakna in Falindar still haunted him—he wasn't really sure he was up to the task. But the people who waved to him from the bridges and balconies seemed to have no such doubts. Would they be disappointed?

At last the narrowness of the canal opened into a vast lake of crystal green water. Across the lake was a single island, detached from the others, without even a bridge connecting it. Green and gold sloops circled the island, and great hills rolled across it, studded with trees. At the center of the island was a simple structure of white limestone, a castle with three towers, the center spire taller than the others, and ringed with a river of sparkling water. Richius stood up and peered across the lake. The palace was lovely, perfect in its simplicity. Unlike the other buildings of Liss, this one seemed timeless, untouched by weather or war, gleaming in a thin sheen of snow. The river around it danced with sunlight and moved with life as flocks of gray waterfowl floated and flew across its surface. Beyond the river, near the central tower, was a gateway of cascading water, a giant waterfall that sprouted up from nowhere and fell against the rocks, feeding the river. Beneath the waterfall was a half-moon arch parting the cascade like a curtain and bidding visitors entrance. The arch was unimaginably tall, and the water that flanked it seemed to rise up as if by magic. Richius stared at it, amazed. He had already seen Nar with its stellar cathedral and foreboding Black Palace, and he had lived the last year in Falindar, a citadel whose beauty he had thought matchless. But the palace of Queen Jelena wasn't like any of these. It was effortless, a designer's inspired dream. If God had a home on earth, it would have been like this incomparable palace.

"I love this," said Richius softly. He wasn't quite out of earshot and didn't care who heard him. The palace had stirred something in him, something that made him yearn for his own home and steeled his conviction to fight against Nar. Prakna, hearing his statement, crossed the deck and stood beside him, sharing his admiration.

"That's Haran Island," said the commander. "Where the queen lives."

"It's magnificent," said Richius. "Truly. I'm not sure if I've ever seen anything so beautiful. How does the water rise like that?"

"Underground springs. The builders who made the palace wanted to make use of them, so they built the water gate." The fleet commander sighed. "Every time I see this place, I feel like weeping. To a Lissen, this island is what we fight for. It's the true heart of our homeland."

"Marus won't tell me about Queen Jelena," said Richius. "Will you?"

Prakna shook his head.

"I thought Liss had a king. What happened?"

"King Tyri died. I'll let the queen explain it to you."

"What does she want me for?" Richius pressed. "Do you know?"

"I think I do," replied Prakna, but didn't elaborate. He glanced up at the silver clouds and let the snowflakes speckle his beard. "She's an extraordinary woman. You should be honored."

"I am," said Richius. "I just want to know what to expect."

"Enough, Vantran, please. I'm sure Jelena has her reasons for wanting to meet you. Why should I guess at them when you'll find out soon enough? I've spoken to her guardians onboard. They will take you to her, alone. I am not even to be there when she greets you."

"What? Why not?"

"Because it is her will, that's why," said the commander. "Now, no more questions. Enjoy the moment. In the morning things will be different. We will set to work, you and I. But today is yours. This moment is yours. Today you are a hero, Richius Vantran."

The words were so final Richius couldn't reply. The royal boat drifted closer to the island. It took long minutes for the little vessel to reach its destination, and when it did the guardians of Queen Jelena who had piloted the boat took care of all the dock work. Neither Prakna nor Marus offered assistance. True to their high stations, they simply watched the others work, and when the vessel was secured to the dock Prakna gestured to Richius to disembark first.

"She wants to see you, not me," said the commander. "Go ahead."

Richius puzzled over his next move. "You're not coming at all?"

"I'll see the queen later," said Prakna. "For now, her business is with the Jackal of Nar. Don't worry. These men will take you to her." Prakna gave him an encouraging wink. "Go on, boy. She's waiting."

"I'll see you later, then," said Richius to his friends, and stepped off the rocking boat onto the snow-covered dock. The palace of the queen gleamed in front of him. He could hear the roar of the amazing waterfall, feel the spray of it on his face. Guardians like the ones that had ferried him here studded the grounds. Two of them came forward and bowed.

"King Vantran," said one of them. "My lady, Queen Jelena, begs an audience with you. She has already been told of your arrival and awaits you. Would you come with us, please?"

"Lead on," directed Richius.

It was a long walk to the palace, along an avenue of smooth cobblestones laid carefully in golden mortar. There were no children here, just the handful of young men guarding their queen. None of them appeared older than Richius, and so many youthful faces made him feel oddly ancient. When they reached the water gate, Richius paused to marvel at it, looking up at the great arch and letting the roar of water surround him. His guides made no attempt to rush him, allowing him time to ponder the fantastic gate. After a minute, though, Richius was satisfied, and crossed the threshold to enter the palace.

All at once the palace enveloped him in a near soundless chamber. The waterfall outside was only feet away, but the thick walls of stone swallowed the noise. Inside, the simplicity of the exterior had been carried over into the interior design. The walls were bare but for beautiful tapestries that hung loosely from the mouths of gilded haran heads, the same compelling creature Richius had seen on the figurehead. He studied the tapestries, noticing strange depictions in the embroidery, pictures of heroic sailing ships and ancient, godlike fish-men rising from the sea. Naked mermaids played on some, while hateful, armored Narens strode on others, their black weapons reflecting their wild faces. All of Liss' bloody history appeared on the tapestries, and there were dozens of them in the chamber, draping across the plain white walls, a gallery of sad and astonishing portraits. Richius let out an amazed whistle, which promptly echoed through the vaulted ceiling.

"We're to take you to the water garden," said the guardian. "Queen Jelena will meet you there."

The water garden lay just outside the grand room of tapestries, at the end of a domed corridor that terminated in a pair of wrought-iron doors. The doors were flung open wide. Both guides stood aside for Richius to pass and shooed him through the portal. Richius stepped out of the palace and into a vast plain of falling water and gentle hills, encircled by a curved row of tall, white columns. Tiny streams and rivulets wound through the garden, and rose vines climbed up the columns, dormant from winter. Snowflakes fell onto the heads of statues—young, nude women with serene expressions or mischievous smiles. At the left of the garden was a sloping hill with a stairway of slate that disappeared into a thickness of bushes. But most remarkable of all was a giant glass enclosure rising up out of a lake, filled with green water that splashed out over its rim. Gigantic in circumference, the enclosure anchored the garden, drawing Richius inexorably toward it. Behind him, the royal guardians closed the iron doors, sealing him off, but Richius hardly noticed at all, so taken was he by the enclosure and its unusual contents.

Haran.

Half a dozen of them stared back at him through the glass, their eyes full of sentience. Two heads each, like the heads of serpents, twisted on prehensile necks while their scaly bodies drifted through the water. Some were small, like trout. Others were as big as sharks. Like the palace they called home, the creatures were divine, even beautiful. Richius put his palm up to the glass and held it there. Seeing his gesture, a haran came up close and put a single mouth to his hand, as if to taste it though the glass. Its other head watched Richius, opening its mouth and blowing out a stream of bubbles. Awe-struck, Richius put his other hand to the glass for the second head, which like its twin now nudged at the barrier between them. Other haran gathered to watch, swishing their spiky tails, amused by the stranger in their midst. Richius laughed with delight. The creatures seemed to sense his joy and bobbed their heads, blowing rhythmic bubbles through their snouts. In pictures these things might have seemed demons, but to Richius they were godlike, just as Marus had claimed. He no longer wondered why the Lissens had worshipped them. As they laughed with him and slashed their fins, he knew why.

"Yes," called a voice from above. "They are special, aren't they?"

Startled, Richius removed his hands from the glass and stepped back from the enclosure. The haran all looked left. Richius followed their lead and gazed up to the top of the hill. There on the stairs stood a woman, a girl really, with long golden hair that fell to her knees and a shift of red and sea-green. Her shoulders were wrapped with silk, and the trailing skirt she wore over her long legs blanketed the ground behind her. Her eyes were emerald and fiery, and her teeth lit her face with a dazzling alabaster glow. She had red lips highly painted and soft cheeks gently rouged, and two hoops of gold dangled from her ears, clinking when she moved. On her feet were a pair of soft slippers that barely repelled the snow, but she stood as if impervious to cold, her hair wet with melted snowflakes. Richius gazed up at her.

Sabrina, he whispered to himself. *She looks like Sabrina.*

"You're the Jackal of Nar," said the young woman. She began descending the stairs, hardly disturbing the snow.

"I'm Richius Vantran," said Richius. "Who are you?"

She waited until she had reached the bottom of the stairs before answering. "My name is Jelena," she said gently. "I am queen here."

"Queen? Oh, but that's impossible. You're so . . ."

"Young?" guessed the woman. She went and stood before him, flashing him a lovely smile. "Yes, I am young. I am also queen, Richius Vantran." She took his hand in hers, then, remarkably, dropped to her knees before him, lowering her gaze to the ground and soaking her skirt in the wet earth. "I am your servant, Richius Vantran. Liss is yours."

"No, don't," begged Richius. "Rise, please," He tried to urge her up but she would not come.

"Liss is yours," she repeated adamantly. "We have very little for you to take, but whatever you see, whatever you desire, is yours. This is our thanks for your coming to us."

"My lady, please rise. That is all I ask of you."

She did not rise but she did at last look up at him. "Richius Vantran, Jackal of Nar, you have come to help us. You must understand our gratitude. Do not shun what little we can offer you."

As gently as he could, Richius pulled his hand away. "Queen Jelena, Prakna is already giving me all that I could want. I am here for less than noble purposes. You must already know that."

"You're here for revenge," said the girl. "I know about you, Richius Vantran. You are not so different from us. That is why you've agreed to help us."

"You've heard fairy tales, my lady. Too many of them, I think." Richius stooped a little, took her hand again, and drew her to her feet. "You mustn't bow to me. You're a queen. And I'm not worth it."

She was so perfect, like her palace, and her hand was soft and flawless like her face. When he pulled her up she made a sad grimace.

"I'm not sure I can do the things Prakna's asked of me," Richius continued. "Maybe everything you've heard about me is wrong. I will try, though. I'll do my best. But you should know I do this thing for selfish reasons."

The young queen looked away, turning her attention to the aquarium. "And you should know that we've brought you here for selfish reasons, too. As I said, we're not so different from each other."

Richius studied her. She was waiting for something. Why, he wondered, had she brought him here? Very softly he padded closer and pretended to watch the miraculous fish, waiting for her to speak. When she did her voice was low, rife with sadness.

"I want to thank you for coming to us, Richius Vantran. I can make you no promises, but I tell you again what I told you before. Anything you want while you are here on my soil, I will grant you willingly." Her eyes shifted from the enclosure, and she realized suddenly that he was staring at her. She smiled. "What is it? Do you see something?"

"Forgive me," said Richius. "You remind me of someone, that's all."

"Someone special?"

Richius nodded. "Oh, yes. Tell me, Queen Jelena, why did you bring me here? I don't mean to sound rude, but is there anything I should know?"

Jelena's face reddened. "Am I that obvious? It is nothing, really. Call it curiosity."

"I would call it that if I thought that's all it was." Richius stepped a little closer and dared to touch her hand again. "Anything?"

His gesture made her tremble, and she looked for all the world like a little girl. "King Vantran, I needed to see you. I've waited for months to know what you were like. I couldn't wait any longer, not another day. They speak of you in high tones here. Prakna says you are a great leader. My mother and father called you a hero. I had to see you for myself."

"I don't understand," said Richius. "Your mother and father? Who are they?"

She laughed prettily. "You said I was young, didn't you? How long do you think I've been queen? My mother and father ruled here before me, King Vantran. They were the true King and Queen of Liss." She reached out and touched his face. "You were twenty-five years old when your father died. That's when you became king of Aramoor. I am seventeen. Barely a woman. And I am lost and need your help."

Suddenly Richius grasped the sadness in the young queen's eyes. It was that same vacant look that he had seen reflected back at him from mirrors two years ago, when he had ascended the throne of Aramoor. Hardly more than a boy, he had been forced past manhood directly to kingship, and the shock had left him reeling. As it had, no doubt, this girl.

"Queen Jelena, I'm sorry for you," he offered. "Truly, I am. Your pain must be great."

"And my confusion," said Jelena. "King Vantran, I need to know what to do, and there is no one on Liss who can tell me. Just as there is no one here to lead an army for me. Prakna is a hero, but he is not king.

The people look to me to lead. And I'm just a child." She grimaced. "As you so rightly observed."

"No," Richius corrected. "I was wrong to say that. Do you know what Prakna and the others call you, Queen Jelena? They call you extraordinary. They say you are remarkable. And they are right. Anyone who can step onto a throne at so young an age, even survive it, must be remarkable."

A blush colored Jelena's cheeks. "You are kind, King Vantran. But I'll need more than words, even pretty ones. I need guidance. When you make this army, when you work it into a thing you think will succeed, will you also come to me? I'm asking for a tutor, King Vantran. Can you do this, too?"

It was such a sad, misguided question, Richius couldn't help but smile. "Queen Jelena—"

"Just Jelena," she interrupted. "I don't want to be called queen by you."

"Nor I king. And I am not a king anymore, anyway. But my lady, I fear you've misjudged me. Maybe Prakna, too. Maybe all of Liss, even. I am just a man. And just a vengeful one at that. Maybe I have some knowledge of tactics Prakna doesn't. I hope so. But I swear to you, if you think I can teach you anything about governing, you are wrong." A great, grieving guilt dropped over him. "Aramoor isn't mine anymore, because I am the world's worst king. I lost my father's homeland because I can't govern." He scoffed at himself bitterly. "You want a tutor? You've chosen the wrong hero, my lady."

Queen Jelena put her hand on his shoulder and spun him around to face her. "I brought you to me because I needed to see the king a boy can be. Tell me there is a queen inside this girl."

"I'm sure there is," said Richius. "These men follow you because they see the queen you already are. They are loyal to you, and that's all you will ever need. All the other decisions come from inside you." He pointed his finger into her chest. "Listen to your heart, Queen Jelena. Not me."

"My heart tells me to trust you," said Jelena. "Just as it told me to bring you here. Prakna speaks very highly of you. He says that you alone can form the army to invade Crote. He says that you are a military genius."

Richius laughed. "Yes, I've heard that one before. A good joke. My lady, I'm nothing more than the men I commanded. Just like Prakna and Marus and all the others make *you* strong. Your father must have known that about being king. He should have taught you that before he died."

Jelena's face tightened. "Maybe you're right. But my father and mother didn't plan on dying. It wasn't some long illness that killed them. It was Narens."

"Narens? Forgive me for asking, but how did that happen? This island seems so safe."

"It was a long war with Nar, King Vantran."

"Richius."

Jelena glowed. "All right. Richius. The war lasted for ten years. And by the end, Liss needed everyone to defend her. Even my parents. When my father was younger, he was a schooner captain, like Prakna. He took to a ship against the Naren armada. My mother went with him. So did everyone else in the palace. I was left alone here with just a few women to look after me. All of Liss fought off Nar, Richius. And almost everyone died. Like my parents."

"Good God," groaned Richius. "See? I told you I was a fool, Jelena. Your father sounds like a great man. And your mother a great woman."

"They were great," the girl agreed. "And now I will avenge them."

They stared at each other, and again that mirrored reflection stared back at Richius from across the years. He saw himself in the girl; the sum of all the hatred he had ever felt.

"Jelena," he began carefully. "This isn't right, what you're saying. It's fine to mourn your parents, but I think you should leave vendettas to others."

"Why?" asked the girl, plainly surprised. "It's a queen's duty to protect her people. And it's a daughter's duty to avenge her parents. At least that's the way we think in Liss."

"Then you're right," said Richius. "We're not so different, you and I. But you should think on what I've lost, what I've given up and left behind. I have a wife and child back in Lucel-Lor. I left them to come here, and if I don't return they won't have me anymore. They'll be all alone." He took her chin in his hand to make her listen. "That's what revenge does to a person, Jelena. Guard against it. You're too young to know such hatred."

"I'm seventeen," she said defensively. "Old enough to know right from wrong. Wrong is what Nar did to Liss. Right is what we're going to do to them now."

"Then don't ask me for advice," Richius growled. "Not if you won't listen to it."

"I need your advice on how to rule, Richius." Jelena was pleading with him, confused by his anger. "I know you can help me. Just like you'll help our army."

"Army? What will you give me, Jelena? Children? I didn't cross an ocean to lead a bunch of kids into a slaughterhouse. If that's what you have in mind, forget it."

"You will have the best Liss has to offer," said Jelena. She grabbed his hand, squeezing it with adoration. "I told you—anything you wish in Liss is yours to take. Ask me for anything and I'll see you get it. The sons and daughters of Liss are yours to command."

"Daughters? Oh, no, Jelena. No women. Not in any army I lead."

The young queen was indignant. "In Liss, women fight," she said. "In Nar they might be baubles, but not here. We defended our homeland for ten years. Now we will avenge it."

"Then do it without me! God, you ask the impossible of me, girl. I won't let women be massacred. I've got enough on my conscience to last a lifetime. I don't need that, too."

He turned his back on her and stared into the aquarium. A haran looked at him through the glass, its twin heads bobbing curiously. He felt Jelena at his back, felt her hands on his shoulders. His eyes dropped down to watch her jeweled fingers caressing him.

"Richius," she whispered sadly. "This can't work without you. Young men and women, maybe some older folk—that's all we have to offer you. But you can make an army out of them. I know you can."

"And if I don't?"

"If you don't, then Liss will never be avenged. My parents will have been murdered without recourse, and Nar will go on as it always has, taking whatever it wants from countries like Aramoor."

Richius shut his eyes. "Aramoor . . ."

"Yes. And Biagio will go free. He'll never be punished for his crimes, or for killing your first wife."

"What?" gasped Richius, turning on her.

"Yes, I know all about Sabrina. Is that who I look like, Richius? Do I remind you of her?"

Jelena's questions were calculating and brutal. She was already more of a ruler than she knew.

"Yes," admitted Richius. "Yes, you do."

"I'm glad. So when you look at me, remember her. Remember her head in a box, and then tell me you won't lead our army. Do you think you can do that?"

Richius said nothing. His silence was enough to bring a satisfied nod from the queen.

"You'll do it," Jelena said. "Prakna knew you would, and I know it, too." She went to him and put her head against his chest, giving him an affectionate squeeze. The gesture made Richius uncomfortable. "Thank you," she breathed. "Thank you, Jackal, for helping us."

Richius brought up his hand, let it hover uncertainly over her head, then lightly stroked her golden hair. It was too late to scold her. She was already ruined. Revenge had devoured her, as it had Prakna and Marus and all the others of this ancient nation. Richius knew there was nothing he could do to save her from herself. Without knowing why, he kissed her head.

"I'll do my best for you," he said gently. "I promise you that."

The young queen rested against his chest. "I know you will. You're the hero Prakna told me about."

TWENTY-FOUR

Homecoming

The snow had slackened into flurries when Prakna finally reached his home village of Chaldris. It was late in the day and the sun was low. Shadows darkened the water avenues and the spaces between buildings, and Prakna's little conveyance drifted across Balaro Canal, bearing him home. As was customary, he stood in the jarl, ignoring the bench seat while the driver poled his way through the canal. The seats were for children and old women. Men always stood in the jarl. And Balaro Canal was always choked with jarls. The little boats were everywhere, moored to docking rings and bobbing on the current. Chaldris was an ancient part of Liss, densely populated and well travelled. Prakna had been born here. It was where he had spent his life, when he wasn't on the ocean, and every time he saw his village it brought a pensive smile to his face.

Like all of Liss, Chaldris was a thousand tiny islands, threaded together by canals and a network of stone bridges spanning overhead. One had to be very careful in the jarl. There were always bridges built too low, and tall men like Prakna often had to duck to avoid a broken skull. Other bridges, like the one they were approaching now, were so high only a bird could bang into them. Prakna gazed upward as the little boat slid toward his apartments. The bridge to his home was covered with lichens and vines, all overgrown and carelessly left untrimmed. J'lari had been a fine gardener once, but now she barely ever lifted a finger. Behind the bridge, the sun was shrouded in a swathe of clouds. Tiny snowflakes drifted down onto Prakna's face. Along the narrow avenues and bridges, familiar people went about their business, occasionally waving to the returning hero, but Prakna hardly heard them. He returned their greetings perfunctorily, mostly out of duty, yet his eyes were locked on his apartments high above the village. By now J'lari would have heard the news. She would be expecting him. Prakna sucked his lower lip. It had been so long since he had seen her.

"Too damn long," he whispered.

The jarl driver heard his words and turned puzzled eyes toward him. "Sir?"

"Nothing," Prakna said. The man shrugged and returned to poling through the water. Prakna sighed heavily. In the pocket of his coat were all the letters he had written J'lari while on patrol in Nar. He had never sent them, hoping to one day return and deliver them himself. When she read them she would be happy, briefly, and they would rejoice in his homecoming until the grief overcame her and she drifted back into her ghostly fugue. Once, J'lari had been a strong woman. Proud. Life had taken its toll.

He had already visited the cenotaph on the way home. The huge monument, erected to honor the dead of the Naren war, wasn't far from Prakna's apartments. The cenotaph had an island all to itself, and when it snowed, like it had today, the hush was remarkable. Even the youngest children seemed to sense the sanctity of the place. Prakna had purchased two small flowers and laid them down next to the granite monolith, along with all the others that had been dropped there this day, to honor Liss' fallen. They didn't harvest bodies in Liss. There was too little land to waste on graves. When a man or woman died, they were thrown into the ocean. That's why the cenotaph had so much meaning. It was the only place for Lissens to grieve. Some had wanted to write all the names of all the men and women that had died on the monument, but then the monument would have been colossal. Ten years was a long time to fight. And too many of the dead were nameless. So the statue was nothing but a tall, granite rectangle, something like a giant headstone, carved with Lissen prayers and ornamented with flowers. The cenotaph was strangely beautiful in the snow. Prakna worshipped it. Besides the mementos his wife kept of their sons, it was the only thing Prakna had to remember them by.

Prakna had one more flower in his hand, a hearty, red dahlia he had purchased for J'lari. It had been very expensive, but the fleet commander's face had earned him a discount, leaving enough in his pockets to pay the pilot of the jarl. Prakna shielded the flower from the cold, hiding it beneath his open coat. He was sure it would brighten J'lari's day. When they reached the dock of Prakna's apartments, the pilot expertly guided his little boat to a stop, barely grazing the pier. He retracted his long, muddy pole and smiled at Prakna.

"Here you are, sir," he said cheerily. "Welcome home."

"Thanks," said Prakna. He dug into his pocket for his last few coins, but the driver held up his hands in protest.

"No, sir," he insisted. "No money. This was my pleasure."

Prakna didn't argue. He paid his fare with a handshake and departed the vessel, stepping onto the dock of his home for the first time in months. Up near the bridge he saw a single candle burning in the window. The tiny lights served as beacons for returning sailors. During the war, the whole village had glowed. And on those horrible days when a soldier didn't return, when he died or was simply missing, the candle was extinguished, replaced by a black star. Prakna looked around at the windows of the apartments. A galaxy of faded, black stars winked back at him.

The jarl slowly slipped away from the dock, leaving Prakna alone in the lightly falling snow. He heard a chorus of voices in the buildings above him, smelled the familiar scents of good, home cooking, and his mind skipped backward to a time when those voices were of his family, and those aromas came from J'lari's kitchen. Saddened, he pulled the dahlia out of his coat and looked at it. It was beautiful, the biggest the merchant had for sale, but a meager gift to a woman who'd lost two sons. Prakna loved J'lari very much. It pained him how little he could do to ease her loss. But he was just a man, and often he was gone, leaving her alone in the old, vacant home.

Ahead of him was a narrow stairway of quarried stone, zig-zagging up to his apartments. Prakna looked at it, suddenly afraid. When he had last seen his wife, she was pale like the snow.

"Time to be a man," he reminded himself.

He stuck his nose into the flower, took a whiff for strength, and quickly galloped up the stairs. Determined to look happy, he plastered a smile onto his face. Whenever he returned, the fleet commander always got a rousing welcome, but today his friends knew enough to spare his privacy. When at last Prakna reached the bridge leading to his home, he noticed that the door across the span was slightly open. He paused in the middle of the bridge. The door opened wider. Prakna steeled himself.

"J'lari," he called softly. "Come out, love. It's me."

There was a trembling sigh before the door opened fully. J'lari stood in the threshold, her eyes wet and opened wide, her cheeks flushed. In her hair was a bronze braid, pulling back her golden locks, and a fine, lacy dress clung to her body, stirring in the breeze. The dahlia dropped to his side as Prakna stood on the bridge, unable to move. When J'lari tilted her head and smiled at him, it was as if the sun had come again and burned off all the haze.

"Prakna," she choked. Her hand went to her mouth. Her shoulders shook. "Oh, Prakna . . ."

Prakna flew across the bridge and swept his wife up in a strong embrace. Staccato sobs overcame her and she melted in his arms, small and insubstantial. He put his nose in her hair and it was sweet; her breasts were warm against him. Fleet Commander Prakna closed his eyes and stroked J'lari's hair, thanking God he was home again.

"I've missed you," she whispered in his ear. "I was so afraid."

"I'm home now," he replied. "I told you I'd be back." He pulled himself free, then presented his gift. "For you."

J'lari blushed like a child at the offering. She was over forty now, but when she smiled she looked like a woman half her age. She reached for the flower, twirling it. A cold breeze blew on the bridge, but she seemed not to notice it at all, so taken was she by the dahlia.

"It's lovely," she said, her voice breaking. "Very beautiful." Her hand brushed his cheek. "Like you, Prakna."

Prakna took her hand and kissed it, holding it to his lips for a very long time. J'lari broke into sobbing laughter.

"Prakna . . ."

"Inside, J'lari," he said with a smile. He gestured to the windows good-naturedly. "There are eyes out here."

J'lari nodded and giggled. "Yes, you're right."

The curious eyes belonged to neighbors and friends, but neither wanted the moment spoiled. J'lari, her prize flower proudly in hand, led her husband into their home, the home he hadn't seen for months. Prakna followed willingly. He had dreamt of this reunion, had pined for it and the touch of his wife, and though she still seemed a ghost to him, she was substantial and warm and he craved her greatly. Tonight, if seaman's luck were with him, he would take her to his bed and love her.

Hours passed. Prakna reveled in his homecoming as J'lari moved about the house, making him comfortable. She was flawless, chatty like she was before the terrible occurrence, and Prakna wondered if his absence had given her time to recuperate, and to appreciate what she had left in life. They lingered over a perfect meal, drank good wine she had purchased for the occasion, and took the candle from the window to light their dinner table. The dahlia Prakna had brought for his wife was never far from her reach, and as they talked J'lari clung to it, admiring it constantly as she listened to him speak. Prakna had many things to tell her. And J'lari listened raptly, watching her husband as he cleaned his plate with a crust of bread and enjoyed his wine with a starving man's pleasure. Prakna ate until his stomach was stuffed and his belt groaned, and while J'lari cleared the table he spoke to her more, telling her about Nar and their plans for the Empire, and about Richius Vantran and his devouring revenge. And as Prakna talked to her he watched his wife, attuned to any signs of sadness. To his great relief, J'lari never broke into sobs. She misted a little when he gave her his letters, but those were good tears and Prakna brushed them away lovingly. J'lari sat and read them for a time. The candle had burned down to a nub, so Prakna got another and put it in the dish so she could read. Embarrassed, he laughed when she read aloud the most personal parts. But he was also a little drunk and tired, and though his stomach was full there was still a hunger in him. He watched her in the candlelight, wanting her.

It was very late when at last they retired. Prakna had deliberately avoided their bedchamber, but when she led him into it he saw that she had prepared it for them. The bed was fitted with their best lace coverings. There was a scent of perfume on the sheets and in the air, and the window shades were open wide, letting moonlight spill inside. Prakna shuddered when he saw the room. Since the deaths of their boys, they had made love only once, a disgusting episode that had been more like rape. J'lari couldn't bear the act anymore. But the look of the room seemed to herald a change in her, and Prakna fought hard to still his thundering passion. She was fragile, still, he reminded himself. And marriage was more than just the bedroom.

"Prakna," she said softly, leading him into the room. "Welcome home."

Prakna said nothing. He didn't want to talk, or hear anything that wasn't her breath. Outside the window, the snow had stopped. Purple moonlight lit the town, giving the canals a romantic twinkle. J'lari slipped off her shoes, then padded to the bedroom door and silently shut it. Prakna drifted to the bed. He sat down on the mattress and watched his wife, who stood before him, her lace dress clinging to her inviting curves. With her smooth shoulders and white skin, she looked like an angel, pure and breakable, too innocent for a cruel world. Prakna's eyes narrowed, drinking her in. He counted up the months since he had laid with a woman and found a giant deficit.

"My love," he whispered. "You're so beautiful."

The compliment made J'lari smile. Yet she didn't dare to speak, to spoil the perfect silence. Prakna saw the faint fever of worry in her eyes, but only for a moment. Her hand went up and pulled the braid from her hair, sending it tumbling around her shoulders. She drifted across the floor to her husband. Prakna held his breath. Their eyes met before the hunger overcame him, and he put his head to her belly, feeling her heat through the silk of her dress. He pressed his lips against her, kissing her and pulling her near, and J'lari's head fell back with a shuddering sigh.

Down he drew her, closer until she was on her knees before the bed. His fingers rummaged under her shoulder strap and pulled it down, and when he kissed her neck she trembled. She was a confection, sweet and irresistible, and the taste of her skin roiled through him, lighting him on fire. His mouth opened to suckle her nape and his hand cupped her head, holding it to him. J'lari's body shook. Prakna ignored the tremors. Both hands were on her shoulders now, stripping down her dress, exposing her to him. He opened his eyes to watch himself work, saw her naked back reflect the moonlight.

Slowly. Slowly . . .

She was almost nude now. Beneath his palms he felt her fear. She was a child again, a fearful virgin. He tried to catch himself but couldn't, and when his hand slipped over her breast he heard the most appalling cry. J'lari froze. Prakna stopped his skating hands, holding his breath. In his ear rang a whispered prayer, barely audible.

"Oh, God, help me. Please . . ."

Prakna held his wife against him.

On and on she cried, as if he weren't there at all, as if she were in a church on her knees before God. He didn't dare look at her. He didn't need to see her face. The wetness of her tears already stained his shirt. J'lari's shaking voice was all he heard, drowning all his pleasure. The lust that had seized him vanished in a flash, and all he felt was pity for the woman on her knees. Across the bedroom stood a mirror. He could see her nakedness reflected there, and the wretched astonishment of his own expression. He looked old. J'lari shivered. Prakna stooped and scooped his wife up in his arms, easily lifting her feather-weight, and placed her gently on the bed. She wouldn't look at him.

"I'm sorry," she said weakly. She wrapped her arms around her breasts to hide them. "Prakna, forgive me. . . ."

"Hush," cooed Prakna. Carefully he pulled up the sheets and covered her. Afraid to touch her, he hovered over the bed. "Rest now, J'lari. Just rest. I'm home."

J'lari quickly nodded. "Yes, home. You're with me. You'll stay with me." Still she wouldn't open her eyes. She brought the sheets up around her face, ashamed of herself, burying her painted mouth beneath the lace. "Don't go."

"I won't," said Prakna easily. "I'll sit with you. We'll just sit, all right?"

"Don't leave me. Not now or ever."

"Never is a long time, my love."

"The Jackal is here now. He'll deal with Nar for you. We can be together. Finally."

Prakna looked away, not wanting J'lari to see him. It had all been over too quickly—her buoyant mood, the perfect meal, the perfume. All too soon the wife he'd left behind had re-emerged. He loved her for her valiant effort, but inwardly he cursed her and her wounded heart. It wasn't grief anymore. It was more like dementia, and Prakna knew his wife could never be the woman he'd married.

"Don't talk, love," he said. "It's been a long day for us both. You just sleep. I'll watch over you. We'll talk more in the morning, if you like. I'll take you for a walk."

J'lari opened her eyes, and in a moment of clarity smiled at him. "I'm sorry," she offered. "Truly. I'm not a woman fit for you."

"You have always been more than enough woman for me," said Prakna. "It's what makes me return to you always. You draw me from across the world, J'lari."

His wife laughed lightly. "You always do come back. Sometimes I wonder why."

"Don't wonder," he said gently. He took the risk of touching her hand. "I'll always come back for you."

"You needn't go anymore. The Jackal can do the work for you." Her tone was earnest and imploring. "Let the young men do the fighting now, husband. Let's just stay together. Would that be so impossible?"

Prakna couldn't find his voice. "J'lari . . ."

"The Jackal has enough hate for all of us," she reminded him. "You told me so yourself. He doesn't need you, Prakna. Not like I do."

"The memory of our sons needs me," said Prakna. "I can't let a stranger avenge them. That's *my* duty. And my honor."

J'lari nodded. It was an impossible argument and she knew it. "I love you," she said simply. "You're all that I have."

Prakna grimaced. It was true for both of them. J'lari truly was his better half. The other half was rigid and dead, animated only by revenge. He didn't want to leave her, not precisely. He wanted to return to Liss with Naren heads on his belt, and spend the rest of his life with her, satisfied that he had done his best. Liss called him a hero, but in his mind there was still much to prove. His sons demanded action.

"Close your eyes," he bade his wife. "I'll see you in the morning."

"Will you stay with me?" asked J'lari.

"If you like."

J'lari nodded, then closed her eyes. Prakna sat down beside her on the bed, watching her in the moonlight. Her breath was short at first, but soon it steadied and grew placid, and the muscles in her face relaxed, making her beautiful again. In a few short minutes she was asleep, gone into some troubled dream-land. Prakna slowly lifted himself from the bed. She stirred at his movements but did not awaken, so he padded to the door and opened it. On the table in their living area was the dahlia he had brought her. He picked it up, admired it for a moment, then returned silently to the bedchamber. J'lari's head was turned away from him. He stared at her, then put the fragrant gift beside her on the pillow. When he did, the familiar chant of the cenotaph entered his mind. It was a bleak chant, a prayer that was always spoken whenever placing offerings at the monument. Somehow it seemed fitting when he looked at his wife.

"Flowers for the dead," he whispered, then turned and left the room.

TWENTY-FIVE

The *Intimidator*

Like her mother and father, Shani Vantran was an independent thinker. She didn't eat when Simon gave her food, she didn't sleep when it got dark. The constant rocking of the ship didn't make her sick, but she vomited whenever Simon tried to feed her. Not only did she have Richius' round eyes, she shared his moody temperament as well. She was, in Simon's opinion, a demonic one-year-old, and more of a handful than he had ever imagined.

Since leaving Falindar, Shani had shared Simon's cramped cabin, and the two had become less than genial to each other. Simon had done his best to make the child happy, but she was homesick and in shock over the loss of her parents, and the Naren warship frightened her and made her irritable. She ate sparingly, pushing most of her food onto the floor, and drank only enough to keep her little body from withering. Her color was good but her mood was irascible, and Simon knew she resented him. In that strange way children have of reading minds, she seemed to know Simon's crimes, and held him accountable.

Simon himself was no less choleric. The guilt that he wanted to leave behind in Lucel-Lor had followed him across the sea, sometimes waking him at night, and always suppressing his appetite. He ate even less than Shani did, and had spent a good deal of the voyage with his head in a bucket or hanging over the rails above deck. Rough seas had turned his legs to water and made his bowels diarrhetic. After two weeks at sea, he no longer dreamed of women or fresh food. Now his dreams were nightmares, populated with sea monsters and Biagio's golden face, taunting him. He dreamed of solid land that melted into quicksand and great gales that dragged the *Intimidator* beneath the waves, and he often awoke in his own sweat, stinking of the sea.

Three days ago, they had passed Liss, swinging wide around the Hundred Isles so that none of the schooners would sight them. They were in deep, dangerous waters, far from land and approaching the Cape of Casarhoon. Another week, maybe more, and they would be in Crote. Biagio would have his prize. And Simon would have Eris, a thought that gave him little solace. He thought of Eris often during the long hours of the journey, but they were always fractured memories, tainted by the evil thing he was doing.

Tonight, like every night, Simon sat in his chamber, preparing a bowl of food for Shani. The single porthole in his chamber let in a ribbon of light, faltering as the sun dipped beneath the waves. It was dark and cramped, with only a little candle burning in a dish for illumination. Shani sat on the floor, banging away with a toy he had given her—a curious-looking ship's ornament he had snapped off the deck when no one was looking. This one was the carved figure of a mermaid. Once the wooden toy had embellished the forecastle, but not anymore. Now it helped to preoccupy the little girl, who chewed on the mermaid's finned tail and rolled it across the floor in an effort to ease her boredom. Simon watched Shani bang the toy against the floor as he mixed her a porridge of bread and raisins, sweetened with a little sugar. Sugar was the only thing he could get her to eat, but they were nearing the end of their voyage and were running low on everything, so this time he sprinkled only a pinch into the mush and hoped she wouldn't notice. He stuck his finger into the bowl to test the porridge, wincing at its awfulness. If Shani were only a little older, he would have tried more solid food on her. But she still had a one-year-old's teeth, so the ship's dried meats and bread were out of the question. Everything she ate needed to be soaked in fresh water, all but the milk, and even that made her turn her nose up.

"You're a spoiled little brat," he said to her with a smile. She looked up at him and scowled. "Yes," he laughed. "You know you are, don't you?"

She had a beautiful face, like her mother, and fine, fawn hair that fell loosely over her eyes. A brilliant smile that rarely appeared made her look like an angel. No wonder she had been the light of her parents' life. Simon looked back into the bowl of porridge, stirring it absently. With luck, she would eat some of it and let him get some rest tonight. He himself would skip dinner. It hardly mattered, since everything he ate eventually came sluicing back out. He had lost weight again, dropping all the pounds he had gained in Falindar. He missed the good cooking of the Triin and the citadel's abundance. He missed fresh fruit and spring water and having a room that didn't sway.

"Tell you what, Shani," Simon said as he worked. "You don't keep me up all night crying, and I'll see what I can do about getting you another toy. I think N'Dek has another mermaid somewhere on this ship. What do you say?"

Shani gave him a blank expression.

"Mmm, looks good, huh?" he asked. He lifted the spoon and let a ribbon of mush dribble back into the bowl. "Simon loves this. Good stuff."

More awkward silence from the child. Simon brought her food over to her, sitting down with her on the cold floor. He pretended to taste the bread porridge.

"Oh, that's good," he said brightly. "You want some?"

As usual, Shani took a sniff at the spoon and made a disgusted face. Her hand came up and pushed the spoon away, spilling some of the mush onto Simon's lap. Simon grimaced, shaking his head. The little girl was exasperating. How the hell did Dyana deal with her?

"It's all we've got, girl," he told her. "If you don't eat you'll just go hungry."

Shani looked at him blankly.

"You don't care? All right, but don't come crying to me when you're stomach is empty. It's still a good distance to Crote, and days before either of us gets anything decent to eat."

The statement only depressed Simon more. Days from solid land and edible food. N'Dek and his crew were bottomless pits, able to scoff down any scraps they could get their hands on, but Simon had lived too long in Crote. He was used to Biagio's kitchens and abundant pantries. Surrendering, he dropped the spoon into the bowl and shoved the porridge aside, staring at Shani. Already she had returned her attention to her mermaid, oblivious to him. At first she had clung to him for protection, but she had quickly learned that no one else on board would hurt her, and so she risked alienating her only friend.

"I'm not happy about this, you know," he whispered. "I wouldn't be doing this if I had a choice."

She wasn't listening. Suddenly angry, Simon snatched her toy away. The action brought a chorus of cries from the girl, who grasped awkwardly for the mermaid while Simon held it just out of reach.

"No, listen to me," he scolded. "Listen or I won't give it back. I'm trying to tell you something, damn it."

More insistent cries. Simon shook his head, taunting her, dangling her toy in front of her.

"Be good, or I won't let you have it."

Shani stopped grabbing for it, frowned at Simon, then turned her back on him. Simon laughed in spite of himself.

"All right," he chuckled. "Here, I give up." He slid the wooden mermaid across the floor to her. Greedily she snatched it up, and in return for his gesture gave him her attention.

"Oh, so you'll listen to me now, huh? That's fine. Thanks so much."

He clasped his hands onto his lap and leaned back, trying to get comfortable. Shani watched him curiously, as if waiting for a bedtime story.

"Look, girl, I just want you to believe me. I'm a bad man, I admit that. But I wouldn't be doing this if I thought I had a choice. I don't. If I don't bring you to Biagio, he'll kill my woman, and I can't allow that. Can you understand what I'm saying? It's just the way life is. I don't know or care about you, but I care about Eris, so you lose. Right?"

Shani stared at him.

"Your father made a tough choice too, you know. Just like me. He could have stayed with you and your mother, but there was something eating him alive, something he *couldn't* ignore. It's like that for me, too. I love Eris. And if anything happened to her, I'd . . ."

Simon stopped himself. He was thinking of Dyana, and the loss he had inflicted on her.

"Well, it doesn't matter," he said softly. He reached out for Shani's soft hair, loving the feel of it between his fingers. As occasionally happened, Shani leaned into him, wanting more. Simon smiled sadly at her.

"What a bastard I am," he whispered.

He was no better than Biagio now. Or Bovadin. Even the Mind Bender with his knives and filthy mind was his twin. What were they but evil, demanding men? What was he but their shadows? In Crote, in his early days, he had been a man of high ideals. He had been very young, and he had thought the world a place he could bend to his will. But it wasn't.

"I hope you get through this," Simon said. "If you survive it, and I don't think you will, I hope you go back to your parents and have a long, safe life in Lucel-Lor. Stay away from Nar, girl. It will only devour you."

The little wooden mermaid dropped out of Shani's hand as she crawled over to him. The cabin was frightfully cold, too cold for a child, so Simon wrapped his arms around her and held her close, cooing in her ear. She put her head against him, resting in his warmth, breathing slowly.

"Remember my promise?" he asked her. "If I can help you, I will. I'll do whatever I can for you."

It wouldn't be enough, though. Simon closed his eyes, hating himself.

His promise was a lie. He had ruined Shani's chances the moment he'd stolen her. Once they got to Crote, there would be no escape.

Simon leaned back with the child in his arms, feeling the pinch of his belted dagger against his ribs. He always wore the dagger, and the minor pain made him think of it now. It might be better for them both if he simply slit their throats. Outside, the sun had vanished. The dark light through the porthole bathed the little chamber in shadows. Reaching into his belt, he pulled out his shiny dagger, careful not to let the girl see it. The sight of the blade made him thoughtful. Committing suicide was for idealistic men. It required a certain self-honesty.

Simon just wasn't the type.

Captain N'Dek sat across the table from Simon, staring at the cards with unnecessary scrutiny. He wore a grave and easily readable expression, the one he always used when he tried to cover up a winning hand. Simon looked away, feigning indifference. N'Dek was a very bad card player who thought he was good. Simon wasn't very good either, but his talent for reading body language gave him a distinct advantage over the pompous captain, and he had let N'Dek win a few hands, just to put the man at ease. The light of the single candle lit their faces over the cards, giving them both a ghostly pall. Little Shani slept in Simon's bunk, oblivious to the gaming being quietly conducted just feet away.

As predicted, Captain N'Dek had jumped at the chance to play cards with Simon. It was, Simon recalled, one of N'Dek's favorite pastimes, and because he was a captain of the Black Fleet he never fraternized with his crew, giving him little chance to exercise his passion for the game. Simon reached for his mug of flat ale. He took a gingerly sip, not wanting to upset his stomach, and stared at N'Dek over the rim. After three mugs, N'Dek was slowing down. His eyelids drooped and the ubiquitous tightness around his jaw had slackened some. Simon took another measured sip.

"The little brat's sleeping sound enough," N'Dek observed, not taking his eyes from his cards. "You complain too much, Darquis. She's no trouble at all."

"Except at mealtimes and my bedtime," countered Simon. Both men kept their voices low, not wanting to disturb the sleeping child. Simon stole a glance at Shani, amazed that she slept. Perhaps she had read his mind again. "Thank God we'll be in Crote soon," he said. "I can't bear another week with this whelp."

"You'll have to," said N'Dek. "We're at least a week away, and seas are rough. They're cutting down our speed."

"As long as you get me home in one piece, N'Dek."

"I'd better. And your little darling there, or Biagio will slit me open like a roast pig." The captain pulled one of his cards from his hand and discarded it, trading it for another. His face brightened almost imperceptibly, a signal he quickly buried in a scowl. "We're low on everything now. Hopefully we'll make Crote before we run out of fresh water."

"If you hadn't been so afraid of the Lissens, we'd have been there by now," goaded Simon.

The insult was enough to make N'Dek look up from his cards. "For a smart fellow you're remarkably stupid, Darquis. I had to maneuver around Liss. If I hadn't, we'd be served up as the main course in a Lissen feeding frenzy. That's what they do to prisoners, you know. Feed them to sharks."

"That's nonsense," scoffed Simon. "I never heard that."

"You're not in the navy. I know these things because I fought against those devils. They're demons, the whole damn bunch of them. But someday I'm going back there. Nicabar, too. We've talked about it."

"Oh?" asked Simon half-heartedly. He was studying his own cards, realizing what a poor hand he'd dealt himself. "What do you intend to do? Talk them to death?"

"I intend to finish what we started," replied N'Dek. "Those Lissen bastards, thinking they can attack Nar. They think the Black Fleet is finished? God damn them, we'll show them who's finished!"

"Shhh!" scolded Simon. "Keep your voice down. You'll wake her."

N'Dek shrank back a bit. "All right. All I'm saying is that we're not done with Liss, that's all. When Biagio takes control of Nar, he'll have to reward the men that helped him. And I already know what Nicabar will ask for."

"Really? What?"

"Liss, you idiot. Haven't you been listening? That's why Nicabar is helping your master. He wants a chance at Liss again, and that bastard Prakna." N'Dek lowered his cards. "Ten bloody years he went after that devil. And all for nothing. They never even battled each other, not once. Can you believe it? Ah, but that's all going to change. And I'm going to be there for it."

"That's nice," said Simon dryly. "A man should have dreams."

"It's not just my dream, Darquis. It's Nicabar's and everyone else's in the fleet. It should be your dream, too."

"Mine?" Simon laughed. "What do I care if Liss stands or falls? It's not my problem, N'Dek."

"See? That's what's wrong with you, Roshann. Nothing is your problem. You're a man without a conscience. You don't care about anything but yourself. If you did, you'd see the glory in going back to Liss."

Simon looked at N'Dek over his cards, barely smiling. "Another card?"

"One more," said N'Dek. This time he didn't discard any of his hand, but slipped the card Simon dealt him into the pack. Simon took a card also. His own hand was very bad, and the card he drew did nothing to improve it. N'Dek would certainly win this round.

"I don't bother getting involved in things that don't concern me, N'Dek," said Simon. "If you want to go and fight in Liss, that's your business. I won't stop you. But why should I care? Forgive me, great Captain, but I don't see the glory in it."

"What about the Renaissance? Don't you see the glory in that?"

Simon had to think hard about that one. There once was a time when he'd shared Biagio's vision of the future, but that was gone, too. "I think the Black Renaissance is unstoppable, because it has Biagio behind it. That's all that matters. What I think of it personally makes no difference. It's coming back to Nar. Herrith can't stop it, and neither can his God."

"Damn right," rumbled N'Dek. There was a bright glint in his eyes that told Simon he knew he'd won. The captain leaned back in his chair. "Last card," he said. "Time to see what you've got, spy."

"You know, you're right," Simon remarked. "I don't really care about much, N'Dek. It's a shame. Maybe someday I can be more like you."

"I doubt it. Come on, show me your cards."

Simon always held his cards in one hand, fanning them in his fingers. His other hand had spent the evening at his side, occasionally lifting the mug to his mouth, but almost always out of sight. Now it very slowly drifted to his belt and pulled out his silver dagger.

"You know, I don't think it really matters what a man does for his whole life. But in the end, when it's all over, he has to have done the right thing. I mean, if I spend the rest of my life killing and murdering, I think I can get away with it all, just as long as I do something good at the end. Just once, you know?"

N'Dek found the notion deliciously funny. "Oh, yes," he laughed. "If you're wrong about God you'll recant on your deathbed?"

"Something like that," said Simon. He watched N'Dek carefully, the fingers of his right hand closing around the dagger as his left fanned the cards out on the table. "Here's what I've got," he said. "How did I do?"

The captain's smile broadened when he saw Simon's cards. "You're the loser, Darquis," he said gleefully. "Again."

N'Dek moved to put his cards on the table. Time slowed down as Simon's hand shot out to seize N'Dek's, holding it firmly on the table. Simon's right hand flashed and brought the dagger up and down, slamming it through N'Dek's palm and pinning it to the tabletop. The captain screamed, jumping from his chair. Simon held the dagger fast and firm. Blood spurted from N'Dek's hand. Immobilized, he stared at

Simon in horror. With his free hand Simon reached across the table and grabbed hold of the seaman's lapel.

"Quiet!" he growled. "Shut up or I'll cut you're bloody throat!"

N'Dek was bawling like a baby, shrieking in pain as he tried to pull his hand free. But the dagger kept him fastened to the table. Quickly the cards soaked with blood. Shani jolted up in her bunk, awakened by the captain's screams. Simon put his hand over N'Dek's mouth.

"I'm not kidding, N'Dek," he hissed. "Shut your big mouth or I'll slit you open from ear to ear. Do you understand me?"

N'Dek could hardly respond. He closed his eyes against the pain and nodded vigorously.

"Good boy," crooned Simon. "We're all friends here. And you know what you're going to do for me, friend? You're going to turn this tub around. We're heading back to Liss."

A muffled protest burst from N'Dek's covered mouth. He pulled away from Simon and spat at him.

"Liss! Why?"

Simon ground the dagger deeper to make the man obey. N'Dek howled in pain, begging Simon to stop. He was near tears, crying for mercy.

"Are you going to listen to me, you ugly squid?" Simon asked.

"Why Liss?" N'Dek stammered. With his good hand over his punctured one, he tried to stop the sluicing blood. "What for?"

Thinking fast, Simon said the only thing that came to him. "Because that's what Biagio wants," he lied. "I'm taking the girl there."

"What the hell for?"

Another jerk of the dagger made N'Dek scream. "No questions!" Simon commanded. "I am Roshann. And you will obey me, N'Dek. You and all your crew. Or so help me God, when we get back to Crote, Biagio will indeed cut you open."

"Darquis, I can't take the ship to Liss! Biagio must be mad. I—"

Simon's hand shot out again and covered the captain's mouth. "I'm only going to tell you this once more, N'Dek. This ship is now under the command of the Roshann, by my authority. You will do exactly as I say. Because if you don't, this tub of yours is going to take you back to Crote for your execution. Now, I'll need you to give the order. We're going to turn the ship around. We're heading back to Liss. Tonight!"

Too frightened and in too much pain to argue, N'Dek nodded. "All right," he groaned. "All right, you crazy bastard. I'll do it."

Simon smiled. "That would be best, friend. For all your sakes. And I'm afraid I can't let you leave this cabin, either."

In another lightning move, Simon pulled the dagger from the table and put it to N'Dek's throat. The table crashed aside as Simon grabbed hold of N'Dek's hair, dragging him to the ground. With N'Dek on his stomach, the blade to his neck, Simon shoved his knee forcefully into the captain's spine. N'Dek wailed in agony.

"What the hell are you doing?"

"Making sure you don't go anywhere, Captain N'Dek. I'll need to keep an eye on you."

There were ropes beneath the table where Simon had hidden them. He worked quickly, binding N'Dek's bloodied hands behind his back. The captain whimpered and fought, but Simon was too strong for him, and in a moment N'Dek was helpless, trussed up like a prize turkey. He lay on the cabin floor, unable to rise, his hand oozing blood, and stared up hatefully at his captor.

"Biagio will pay for this!" he railed. "When Nicabar finds out about this, you'll all pay!"

"Oh, now don't be like that," said Simon. "I need your help, N'Dek. We're all one big happy family, right? And this family is going to do exactly what I say, because I'm the Roshann. And we all know what that means, don't we?"

N'Dek looked away defiantly.

"Don't we?" Simon roared, kicking N'Dek in the ribs. The captain hacked in pain, gasping for air. Simon knelt down beside him and put his lips against N'Dek's ear. "I know you understand me, Captain. I know you'll do exactly what I say. And if any of your crew try to mutiny or take this ship away from Liss, I'll cut you into tiny pieces."

N'Dek let out a little moan. Across the cabin, Shani was staring at them. Sure that N'Dek couldn't see him, Simon gave the child an encouraging smile.

Don't worry, girl, he thought boldly, hoping Shani would understand him. *You'll see your father soon enough.*

TWENTY-SIX

Island of Madness

Dyana awoke in perfect darkness.

It was as if she hadn't opened her eyes at all, as if the sun had disappeared from the earth. She didn't stir or bother to roll over. She didn't draw the useless blanket closer to her body. The smell of rotting grain and sour spices assailed her, but she was used to it now and didn't gag. She merely lay there in the blackness, trying to focus her mind.

Time had lost all meaning to her. She might have been asleep for days or merely minutes. Her ears rang with the drone of the ocean just outside the wall of her chamber, a filthy storage hold in the bowels of the Naren warship. Other than the constant darkness, the rapping of the sea against the hull was her only companion, save for the spiders and rats that crawled across her as she slept. Human contact was sparse and unwelcome, and the food slid under her nose, when it was given at all, was hopelessly wretched. So Dyana didn't eat. In time, perhaps another week, she might be dead from lack of food. But it wasn't food she craved. It was light.

Since leaving Falindar, so long ago now she could scarcely recall, she had only seen light briefly, whenever her captors brought her food or decided to empty her chamber bucket. Or worse, when they came to taunt her. The big one, called Donhedris, loved to run his hands over her. It hadn't gone any further than that yet, but Dyana knew it was only a matter of time. She had heard the stories of seamen, how they hungered for months without women. The dread of rape was only one more horror she endured. Her clothes were in tatters now, and her hair hung in stringy ropes from her head. The atrocious smell of the cargo hold had permeated her skin, making it reek, and her forearms bore the scars of rat bites. The curious creatures always tested her while she slept, nipping at her flesh until she awoke to bat them away. As with Donhedris, Dyana knew she would eventually lose against the rats, too.

The ship *Revenge* had been at sea for many days. Of that, Dyana was sure. Of other things, her mind was vacant. The cargo hold was freezing, and her coat and thin blanket barely beat back the frost. Spilled grain rubbed against her, chaffing her skin, and the spiders dwelling in the rafters made midnight excursions on their silken ropes, dropping down to bite her face and limbs.

Is it late? she wondered. It might have been noon or midnight. The darkness was always the same. And her meals, such as they were, came to her erratically, giving her no chance to gauge the passage of time. So Dyana dreamed of small things, trying to occupy herself with memories of better days, and fought to hold her mind together. She recalled with clarity the stories Lucyler had told her of his imprisonment in Falindar, when her first husband Tharn had locked him in the catacombs to teach him what torture was like. It had all been a lesson but Lucyler hadn't known it at the time, and so he had endured the bleak place with only his wits to keep him sane.

Wits, Dyana reminded herself. *You still have those. Hold on to them.*

Dyana was determined not to let insanity rule her. She needed to be strong for Shani, to face Biagio on his island and somehow wrest her daughter from him. For that she would need all her wits. Biagio was a clever devil. A peerless tactician, Richius had claimed. If she were going to match intellects with him, she needed to be whole. She grabbed hold of her blanket, bunching it up in her fists, and concentrated on Richius' face. Amazingly, it was starting to fade in her memory. So had Shani's, and that frightened her.

Think, Dyana commanded herself. *Do not let it confuse you. Think of a way out.*

She was on a ship bound for Crote. Even if she managed to escape her prison, there was nothing but the open sea. And if she tried to escape they might punish her. Donhedris was the lecherous one, but Malthrak, the little dark one, was more cruel. Sometimes when he brought her food he would smile sardonically, loving her fear. That's what the Roshann were, after all. Richius had been right. They were all dogs. Like Simon. When she found him, she would rip his heart out.

The thumping of footfalls echoed outside her room. Dyana sat up, dreading the intrusion. She heard the lock on the cargo hold jingle and the rattling of chains. Instinctively she shielded her eyes from the painful light she knew would come. The door opened with a squeal. Two silhouettes blocked a flood of stabbing sunlight. Dyana winced and looked away, already recognizing the pair. As always, Malthrak stepped into the room first, Donhedris on his heels.

"Ah, what a lovely stench," snickered Malthrak. He had left the door open and stood in its light, looming over Dyana. "Girl? Look at me, girl. I'm talking to you."

Dyana tried to look through her fingers, her eyes watering with the light. She had thought it nighttime, but the sunlight through the portholes told her it was morning. Or afternoon, maybe. She really didn't know. Malthrak was smiling at her, his sharp teeth glimmering. Donhedris had his mouth open as he breathed. Dyana sneered at them.

"What do you want now?" she spat.

"Get up," snapped Malthrak. "It's time to go."

"Go? Go where?"

"You'll see."

Malthrak stepped aside and let Donhedris enter the room. Dyana scooted away, backing against the wall, but Donhedris' arms encircled her, scooping her from the floor. A rush of dizziness sloshed over her brain, threatening to black her out. She was too weak to fight him, but she dug her nails into his forearms anyway, raking through the exposed skin. Donhedris grunted with annoyance and gave her a shake. The bone-breaking grip knocked the wind from her.

"Where are you taking me?" she demanded. "Tell me, you bastards!"

"God, what a mouth on this one," Malthrak remarked. He turned his back and left the cargo hold, gesturing for Donhedris to follow. Donhedris tossed Dyana over his shoulder and followed his comrade out of the hold. Orange light stung Dyana's eyes, releasing a flood of tears. She wiped at them furiously, trying to see where they were taking her. She heard Malthrak's quick feet climb a stairway, then felt Donhedris duck under a beam. He put his meaty hand onto her head and pushed it down, keeping her skull from collision.

Up they went, first one level, then another. Dyana heard voices and the clear sound of the sea. The air was fresh and smelled of salt. She could almost see now, but just barely. Donhedris' broad back was her first clear sight. His arms encircled her waist like a python, pushing out the air. One more level up, and a cold rush of wind ripped through her clothes. Sunlight poured down on her, warm and painful.

"Put her down," she heard Malthrak order.

Donhedris stooped and loosened his grip. Dyana tumbled onto the deck. She sat there shaking her head, squinting. There were men around her, sailors like she'd seen when they'd brought her aboard. Their dark outlines crowded and loomed over her. Unsteadily, she rose to her knees, then to her feet, wobbling with the movement of the ship. Malthrak grabbed a tuft of her hair and pulled her head back.

"Look," he ordered.

He pointed over the rail. As Dyana's eyes adjusted to the sun, she saw a growing landmass in the distance, an island floating in a vast blue sea. Around the island she saw ships, great black vessels with towering masts full of satiny sails.

"Crote," Malthrak declared. "Your new home."

Count Renato Biagio sat in his parlor, brooding over a snifter of brandy. Bright sunlight from a wall of windows flooded the room, and he could see the *Revenge* anchored on the horizon, just beyond his rose garden. A roaring fire blazed in the hearth, throwing off its scalding heat, and the leather of his thronelike chair groaned when he shifted, unable to get comfortable. Matters of great weight occupied his mind. The *Revenge* had returned too soon. And the *Intimidator* hadn't shown up at all. Already his servants were telling him that Simon wasn't onboard the incoming vessel. Biagio swirled the brandy in his glass, sniffing at it absently. He hadn't even tasted it yet, so angry was he over the turn of events. And something more than anger, something the Count of Crote hated to admit.

Worry.

Simon was a very poor sailor, but N'Dek was a master seaman. There was little chance they had blown off course or wrecked themselves, but either was always a possibility, especially on so long a voyage. That the *Revenge* should return so soon was unthinkable. Where the hell was Simon? Biagio closed his eyes, swallowing his nervousness. It wouldn't do for Malthrak and Donhedris to see him fret.

"They'd better have an explanation," said Savros. The Mind Bender had been waiting in the parlor with Biagio, eager to hear the news from the Roshann agents. Biagio had let him stay. The sight of Savros always had a peculiar effect on people, and Biagio wanted his agents afraid. Savros paced around the room, his blue eyes blazing with curiosity, his spidery arms crossed over his chest. He was precariously thin, and the shadow he threw on the floor was reedy. Biagio watched him stride the floor, noting the soundlessness of his footfalls.

"Don't speak," the count warned. "I'll do the talking when they get here."

"Renato, if they don't have the child—"

Biagio raised a silencing hand. The gesture quieted Savros at once. At times like this, most people knew better than to task the count. But Savros was like a parakeet, always chirping. Admonished, the torturer went to the writing desk and poured himself another brandy. He held the flask out for Biagio, who silently declined. Biagio wasn't in the mood for drink. The only thing he wanted was answers.

Before long, the mahogany door of the parlor rang with a cautious knocking. Savros glared questioningly at Biagio, who knew he needn't reply. The door swung slowly open, and Malthrak of Isgar stuck his head inside. Behind him was his brother, the giant Donhedris. Malthrak chanced a step into the parlor.

"My Master?" he said. "May we come in?"

"Of course," replied the count flatly. "I've been waiting."

"We've both been waiting," adding Savros with a smile. As predicted, the sight of the Mind Bender drained the color from Malthrak's face. The Roshann agents entered the room, closed the door behind them, and fell to their knees in homage.

"Forgive this intrusion, Master," said Malthrak. "But we have news for you. A gift."

Biagio's mood brightened. "A gift? You've brought the child, then?"

"No, sir, not the child," stuttered Malthrak. "Simon Darquis has the child."

"Look at me, Malthrak."

Malthrak dreadfully raised his eyes to Biagio. "My lord?"

"Simon Darquis isn't here," seethed the count. "The *Intimidator* never arrived. Why is this, my friend?"

"Honestly, I don't know, Master." The smaller man licked his lips nervously. "I saw Darquis when he left Lucel-Lor. They set sail a day before us." He shrugged apologetically. "I really don't know where he is."

"Donhedris?" pressed Biagio. "Is this so?"

"It is so, Master," agreed Donhedris. Unlike his brother, he kept his head bowed while he spoke. "The *Intimidator* left the day before us. I remember perfectly. Simon Darquis went on board. He had the Vantran child with him."

Count Biagio closed his eyes, letting a small, annoyed sigh dribble from his lips. Malthrak and his brother weren't liars. They had been loyal for years and were very skilled; everything they had ever told the count had been the truth, or at least the truth as they understood it. Biagio reasoned they had no reason to lie now, either, and that meant Simon had vanished.

"Explain this to me," said Biagio. "Where could the *Intimidator* be?"

"Honestly, my lord, I don't know," said Malthrak. "Darquis warned us of Lissen schooners in the area. He told us he had seen them. Perhaps the Lissens found them."

"Lissens?" boiled Biagio. "In Lucel-Lor? Why?"

Malthrak blanched. "I don't know."

"You know very little, Malthrak," said Biagio, his tone rising dangerously. "I want some answers, not some feeble gibberish. Speculate for me. Did you see any Lissens?"

"No, Master. None."

"And the weather? What was that like?"

"Nothing dangerous," said Malthrak. "Certainly not enough to take the *Intimidator* off course. She should have been here by now, my lord."

Biagio leaned forward in his chair. "That much I know already. Get up, both of you."

Malthrak and his brother stood. Savros walked over to stand beside Biagio's chair. The Mind Bender cocked his head at the pair, as if sizing them up for something unpleasant.

"My last question," Biagio said calmly. "Why have you returned?"

"My lord, we have special news," said Malthrak excitedly. He tried to smile but it came out askance. "And we've brought you something. A gift, you might say."

"Biagio is listening," said Savros. "Go on."

Malthrak came a little closer. "Master, Richius Vantran is no longer in Falindar. He has left Lucel-Lor and gone to Liss."

"What?" Biagio erupted, springing from his chair. "How do you know this?"

"His wife," Malthrak explained quickly. "We have her. We caught her, trying to find Darquis. We brought her back with us."

The news made Biagio drop back into his chair. He looked at Savros for support, but the Mind Bender was equally astounded. Malthrak nodded, pleased with himself.

"It's true, my lord. We captured the woman at the tower, where we rendezvoused with Darquis. Somehow she'd guessed he had gone there. She came looking for him, but he was already gone."

"So you kidnapped her instead?" asked Biagio. "Was she alone?"

"She was," answered Donhedris. "We are certain of that, Master."

"This is amazing," Biagio whispered, more to himself than any of his henchmen. He stroked his chin contemplatively, riffling through all the permutations. Simon was gone, but now he had the woman. That was almost as good as having the child, wasn't it? More pressing, though, was Vantran's journey to Liss. That had never been part of the grand design. If the Lissens had turned to Vantran for help, they might indeed be planning their attack.

"This woman," Biagio said softly. "Tell me about her. She is well?"

"Well enough," said Malthrak. "She hasn't eaten very much, and the voyage has sickened her. But she is well enough to talk, yes."

"Has she told you anything?" asked Biagio. "Why has Vantran gone to Liss?"

Malthrak shook his head. "She wouldn't say, my lord. And I thought it best not to try and make her tell us. I thought you should question her yourself."

Savros clasped his hands together. "Oh, smart fellows," he said. "That was very wise of you."

"So you know nothing more?" Biagio asked.

"No, Master. But the woman can surely tell you more. And since you don't have the child, now you can use her against Vantran." He looked down at his shoes, dejected. "We thought you'd be pleased."

Biagio graced them with a sunny smile. "Dear Malthrak, I *am* pleased. With you, too, Donhedris. You've both done very well. But now I want to see this woman. Is she ashore?"

"Yes, Master. She's ashore, and not too happy about it."

"Good," Biagio declared. "Bring her to me."

"Now, my lord?"

"Yes," said Biagio. "Right now."

The two brothers bowed and left the room, leaving the door slightly open. When they had departed, Biagio looked at Savros and saw the most grotesque hunger in his eyes, something like lust but far less normal. It was the same aura executioners showed, before they lowered the axe or pulled the lever. The Mind Bender happily knitted his thin fingers together.

"I've heard Vantran's wife is very beautiful," he said. "Oh, this is going to be wonderful."

"Easy, my friend," Biagio cautioned.

Savros wasn't listening. "Renato, I can make her talk. I'll get her to tell you everything about Vantran's trip to Liss. Please, let me. Please . . ."

"Patience, Savros. Let's see what the woman is willing to tell us, first."

"Renato . . ."

Another gesture from Biagio closed the torturer's mouth. Biagio hated hearing him whine. Sometimes he regretted bringing Savros with him to Crote. There just wasn't enough work for him here. He was growing agitated, less stable by the day. And the thought of giving him the Jackal's wife didn't inspire Biagio with confidence. Savros might bring her down into the dungeon and come up with nothing more than a flayed skin. And her husk wouldn't make a very useful bargaining chip.

A moment later, Biagio heard the ruckus of approaching feet outside his parlor. Donhedris' heavy boots pushed the door open and he barreled inside, dumping a woman onto the carpeted floor. Her hands were tied behind her back, but still she writhed violently to her feet. When she noticed Biagio, she made to lunge for him, but Donhedris' hand grabbed a fistful of her white hair and pulled her backward.

"Let me go!" she growled, kicking his tree-trunk shins. Donhedris ignored the assaults as if they were insect bites. The woman turned her wild eyes on the count and hissed, "Biagio!"

Count Renato Biagio smirked, amused at the trinket given him. She was very beautiful, even covered in her own filth. He could imagine her washed and perfumed and sharing his bed. The mere sight of the pretty woman made Savros weak in the knees. The Mind Bender started toward her then stopped himself, barely able to keep his desires chained. Malthrak entered the room with a smile on his face.

"Dyana Vantran," he said theatrically. "For you, Master."

Dyana kicked and cursed, spitting like a wildcat. Donhedris kept hold of her, jerking her head back painfully. And Biagio watched, enthralled by her fire and beauty. This was the creature Vantran had abandoned Nar for, the one that had worked her magic on him and made him murder Arkus by proxy.

"Where is she?" Dyana Vantran railed. "Where is my baby?"

Incredibly, she broke free of Donhedris and rushed at Biagio. "Tell me!" she screamed.

Donhedris was on her again in a second, dragging her away and wrapping stout arms around her. She was hysterical, like some insane Naren beggar. Biagio hardly flexed a face muscle.

"Dyana Vantran," he said softly. "You are more and less than I expected. Welcome to Crote, wild child. My home. And yours now."

The woman's face collapsed. "Let me see her," she pleaded. "Let me see Shani!"

"Oh, she's beautiful," groaned Savros. "Renato, let me have her."

"Be still," snapped Biagio. He was studying Dyana, examining her closely, and hated the constant interruptions. Realizing she was bound securely, he rose from his chair and towered over her, dropping his shadow across her face. Unable to stop himself, he reached out a frigid hand and brushed it across her perfect cheek. Dyana howled at his touch and Biagio shuddered, staggered by her warmth.

"Let go of her, Donhedris," he ordered.

"Master?"

"Do it."

Reluctantly, Donhedris complied. Dyana Vantran seethed but did not lunge at the count. Instead she stood there, her eyes silently pleading.

"Go. All of you," said Biagio. "Leave me with the woman."

"Renato!"

"Master?"

Biagio turned on them with a roar. "Go!" he bellowed. "Now!"

It took a moment for his underlings to understand. Savros was the last to go. His eyes lingered hungrily on Dyana before he, too, slipped reluctantly away, shutting the door behind him. Dyana stood motionless in the center of the room, engulfed in silence and drowning in Biagio's gaze. The count made no attempt to touch her again. His face was expressionless. Finally he moved away from her, settling back into his chair.

"Go to the fire if you're cold," he said.

"Where is Shani?" Dyana demanded. "Lorris and Pris, tell me!" The next word seemed to choke her. "Please . . ."

How much should he tell her? Biagio wondered. She was desperate for her child. Obviously she didn't know Simon hadn't returned. It seemed deliciously cruel to make her wait, but it was also pointless. Biagio picked up his brandy and considered the amber liquid.

"Your daughter isn't here, woman," he said simply. "I don't know where she is."

"Liar!" the woman flared. "You have her!"

"I don't. But I must say, I wish I did. Things haven't worked out quite the way I intended. You, for instance, shouldn't be here at all." The count set his glass down again and looked at her. There was incredulity on her face, and a kind of wretched fear. She believed him, almost. "It's not a lie, Dyana Vantran," he assured her. "If I had your child I would tell you so. This is my island. I'm lord and master here. I have nothing to gain by hiding her from you."

"Oh, God, no," she groaned. Her knees buckled and she crumpled to the carpet, exhausted and overwhelmed. "Where?" she gasped. "Where is she?"

"Lost at sea, maybe. The ship that was supposed to bring her here hasn't arrived yet. It may still come, but that remains to be seen." Biagio sighed theatrically. "Poor girl. This must be very hard for you, I know."

"What do you know?" she spat. "Monster! You have taken my daughter and now she's—"

Unable to finish, Dyana Vantran lowered her head and swallowed back sobs. The sound of her anguish stoked something primal in Biagio, a great loss he had hoped buried. He remembered Arkus' death and the awful vacancy in the aftermath, burying him. To his great surprise he actually felt sorry for his captive. Supposedly, losing a child was unimaginably painful. He wondered if it were anything like losing an emperor. With his long cape dragging on the floor, he rose from his chair again and went to her, staring down at her. She was a proud thing, too strong to resort to tears. Already he respected her.

"Woman, this need not be a horror for you," he said, trying to be gentle. "You will not be set free. Not ever. But you can make this easier on yourself."

"Burn in Hell, Biagio," she rumbled.

"I might yet if certain people have their way." The count crossed his arms over his chest. "Look at me, woman," he demanded. "I won't speak to a pile of rags."

"Speak or do not speak," said Dyana. "I do not care."

Enraged, Biagio grabbed her up in both fists and lifted her effortlessly off the ground.

"Yes!" he growled. "I'm stronger than I look, don't you think?" He gave her a vigorous shake. "You will listen to me, bitch-girl, or you'll be sorry."

A wad of saliva shot from her mouth, catching him in the eye. Biagio cursed and threw her back to the floor.

"Do not task me!" he roared. "I have questions for you, woman. Answer them, or I will give you to the Mind Bender and he will pull the answers from you!"

A horrified understanding dawned in her Triin eyes. Biagio grinned.

"Yes, you understand me, don't you? Make this easy on yourself, woman. Answer my questions and I will spare you from Savros. Otherwise he will sharpen his blades on you."

"What do you want from me?" asked the woman. "I know nothing."

"Oh, that's untrue. You know where your husband is." The count stooped a little closer. "He's in Liss. Why?"

She laughed resentfully. "Why would I tell you anything? You can burn, Biagio."

"You hate me very much, don't you?" asked Biagio playfully. "I understand. But there is the matter of Savros to consider. The Mind Bender has been very agitated lately, and you've made him hungry. Savros isn't like most men. Most men see a beautiful woman like you and want to take her to bed. Savros wants to peel her skin off."

Dyana Vantran turned an unnatural shade of white. Her mouth dropped open as if to speak, then abruptly closed again behind clenched teeth.

"Torture me, then," she said. "I will tell you nothing."

"I wonder," Biagio remarked. He circled her like a buzzard, looking down at her. "Savros could make you talk, but I don't care to subject you to that. You're no good to me dead, after all. I had planned on taking your little girl back to Nar with me when I reclaim the throne. I wanted to make your husband come there for her, surrender to me. I'll use you for that now, if you prefer."

The woman looked up desperately. "What?"

"Your daughter might still be on her way to me, Dyana Vantran. Simon Darquis is only a day late. When he comes, if he comes, he'll have the child with him. I don't need both of you." Biagio stopped circling and dropped down in front of her. He took her hand in his chin and forced their eyes together. "Why is your husband in Liss?"

Dyana trembled in his grasp. "What are you giving me?" she asked hopefully. "My daughter?"

"Will you answer me honestly?" he pressed.

"What about my daughter?"

"Tell me what I want to know, and I will spare the child. I'll take you to Nar with me instead. And I'll save you from my ignoble torturer." Biagio loosened his grip on her chin and gently brushed her cheek, fascinated by her. "Really, I give so much and ask so little. I think I'm being more than fair, don't you?"

She pulled away from his caresses. "Your word," she demanded. "For what it is worth, swear it to me. You will let my daughter go free?"

"I will send her back to Lucel-Lor in one piece, or I will send her back decapitated," said Biagio. "The choice is yours. Tell me what I want to know."

"That is your word?" Dyana scoffed. "How can I trust that?"

Biagio reached into his cape and withdrew his Roshann dagger, the only weapon he ever carried. The sight of it widened Dyana's eyes. With drama he twirled it in the light, making sure she saw it perfectly. Then, without another word, he circled around behind her and quickly cut the ropes binding her wrists. When he was done he stood up, returned the dagger to his belt, and casually walked over to his chair.

"I'm growing tired of asking you this," he complained as he sat down. "Why has the Jackal gone to Liss?"

The woman at his feet rubbed her rope-burned wrists, dumbfounded. For a moment the count thought she might lunge at him, but he saw no murder in her eyes, only the glint of confusion.

"Say it again," she demanded. "Tell me you will spare my daughter. Tell me you will send her back to Lucel-Lor safely, and then I will tell you the truth of what I know. Swear it, Biagio. Or I will tell you nothing."

"As you have said, so do I swear," promised the count. "If Simon Darquis brings your daughter here, I will see to it that she's returned safely to Lucel-Lor. She will not be harmed. Now . . ." He scowled at her. "Tell me what I want to know."

Her eyes dropped to the carpet in confession. "Richius has gone to Liss to help them fight against you," she said softly. "He is to form an army for them. They are going to invade your island."

To Biagio, the admission was like music. A little smile broke out on his perfect face. "When?"

"I do not know," she replied. "A Lissen captain came and took him away, not long before I was captured. His name was Prakna. He told my husband they were planning an invasion of Crote, but needed his help to do it." She looked away, sick with herself. "Your promise, Biagio. Remember it!"

"I have a memory like an iron box, woman. Go on."

"That is all," Dyana said miserably. "That is all I know."

"That can't be all," insisted the count. "How many men? And when? I need dates."

"I have no dates!" she flared. "I swear, I have told you the truth. Richius and the Lissens are going to invade Crote. They want to use it as a base, to strike at Nar City. But I do not know when. And I do not know how. Soon, I think. That is all."

Soon. Biagio's smile widened. He picked up his glass of brandy and hid behind it, unable to tame his glee. His Roshann agents had done very well for him. So had Nicabar and the others. Prakna was probably very proud of his tight-lipped bunch, but there were always leaks in any big scheme, and something like an invasion was impossible to keep secret, especially from the Roshann. Biagio gave himself a silent congratulations. Everything he had planned had come true flawlessly. Almost.

"You have been honest," he declared. "And for that I will honor my promise to you. I believe you have told me everything."

"I have," said Dyana desperately. "I swear it."

"Have no fear for your daughter, woman. Do not fear the Mind Bender, either. I will deal with him myself." Biagio looked her over, examining her filthy clothes. "You look atrocious. I'll have someone bathe you and find fresh clothing for you. My home is very comfortable, Dyana Vantran. I see no need for you to suffer here. It's not you that concerns me."

"No," said Dyana bitterly. "It is Richius. This is all just your way of getting back at him, is it not?"

"Your husband took something very precious from me," said Biagio. "I'm just exacting payment."

Dyana shook her head. "I know this story. You are wrong, Biagio. You blame Richius for killing your emperor, but he had nothing to do with it."

"He had everything to do with it!" exploded Biagio. Again he rose from his chair, stalking Dyana across the room. "Your wretched lover killed Arkus. He left Aramoor because of you, and sided with the Triin against Nar. And Arkus died because of it. Vantran was supposed to go to Lucel-Lor to save him!"

"No," Dyana insisted. "You are wrong. There was never any magic in Lucel-Lor to save Arkus. Richius could not have helped him."

The count felt the rage rise up in him. "Don't you dare defend him," he hissed. "Not to me! I know the truth about the Jackal. I know what he did to Arkus. And I will make him pay for what he's done to me!"

With a whirl of his cape he reclaimed his brandy and drained the glass, fighting the urge to strike the woman. She was despicable, entranced by the Jackal's magic like so many other fools. The brandy burned its way down his throat, scalding him and making him cough. When the glass was empty he tossed it against the hearth, sending it shattering to bits.

"Don't ever speak well of him in my presence again," the count warned. "I will cut your tongue out if you do."

"Just do not break your promise to me," said Dyana. "Or you might find a knife in your back someday."

He looked at her, impressed by the threat. "I'm sure you mean that," he said. "I will watch my back very carefully, never fear. Now go. Wash yourself. Get some food."

Confused, Dyana looked around the chamber, unsure what to do. "That is all?"

"For now. If I want you, I'll send for you. Go. Malthrak is surely waiting for you outside. Tell him to take you to my serving women. They'll find a room for you and bathe you." Biagio waved her away distastefully. "Hurry, please."

Still in a daze, Dyana Vantran walked from the chamber. Biagio heard her voice outside, directing Malthrak to take her to the servants. When he was sure she had found her way, he went to the door and closed it, not wanting Savros or the others to disturb him. The bottle of brandy on his antique desk beckoned him. He retrieved it, taking a draw. Good brandy was hard to get now in Crote. Supplies of everything were running low, including patience. Biagio brooded over the bottle. He should have been pleased with the news about Liss, but all he could think of was Simon.

Simon, his adored friend. Where was he now? On his way to Crote? Or perhaps at the bottom of the sea, surrounded by sharks? Count Biagio quickly drained his glass and poured himself another. He wasn't the type to jump to conclusions—except when emotions were involved. He closed his eyes and saw Simon's face, then quickly tried to squash the image. There was work to be done. No time to brood over a potential lover. His grand design was almost complete. Just a few more pieces remained.

Dyana sat in an enormous, sterling bathtub, her eyes closed, and let Count Biagio's servant pour wonderfully hot water over her head. The room the woman had taken her to was far from Biagio's parlor, in a part of the sprawling mansion peopled mostly by slaves like the one who serviced her now. Yet despite the lowly status of the wing's inhabitants, the bath chamber was ridiculously elaborate. The claw-footed tub stood in the center of the chamber, surrounded by mosaic tiles and beautiful, flowering vines climbing the tapestried walls. Fragile vessels of porcelain rested alongside satiny pillows, and gold-trimmed robes hung on brass hooks. The smell of lavender wafted in the steamy air, competing with an ivory orchid blooming from a golden vase on a sculpted pedestal of marble. There were glass bottles of colored bath oils on shelves and ornate displays of soaps, cut into whimsical shapes and piled high in woven baskets. Yet all Dyana could think about was Shani.

It seemed impossible to her that Simon hadn't returned to Crote, yet she believed Biagio. She could think of no reason for the count to lie to her, although lying was his speciality. But if he was telling the truth, that meant Shani was in danger. Or worse. Dyana groaned as the slave massaged her hair with oil, working out the filth. She had come all this way, endured the unspeakable voyage and the lecherous hands of her captors, and only Shani's bright face had kept her sane. The thought of finally seeing her daughter had forced her to be strong, but now she wilted in the bathtub. The deliciously warm water trickled down her face and breasts, and she was without shame in front of the stranger, lost in a melancholy fugue.

"You're very pretty," said the slave, a dark-haired girl with a brainless smile. Did she even realize she was a slave? Dyana wondered. What kind of place was this island? All the servants seemed sickeningly cheerful, as if the collars around their necks were little more than jewelry. The slave had told Dyana her name, but Dyana hadn't really listened. Was it Kyla?

"We'll get you clean again, don't worry," said the woman. She shook her head sympathetically. "It must have been wretched for you on that ship. Sometimes I bathe the sailors, when they come ashore. They're even filthier than you!"

Dyana let out a disinterested sigh. Small talk was just an annoyance to her, and this one loved to chatter. She had hardly stopped since bringing Dyana to the bath. The slave dipped her hands into the bubbly water and drew out a cupful, then dribbled it over Dyana's face to clear it of soap.

"I've never seen a Triin," said the woman. "Your skin is so white. Like a dove." She ran a soft hand over Dyana's shoulders to test the alien flesh. "Soft."

"What will happen to me here?" Dyana asked pointedly. "What will Biagio do to me?"

The woman laughed. "Nothing will happen to you, Dyana Vantran. I've been told to take care of you. After I bathe you I will take you to your chambers. Others are preparing them for you now."

"Chambers?" scoffed Dyana. "You mean prison, yes?"

"No," the woman corrected mildly. "You're not a prisoner here. Well, you are, I suppose, but you won't be treated like one. The Master is very kind to all his guests, except those that displease him. If you do as the Master says, you will be cared for."

"Master," spat Dyana. "Do you all call him that? I think it is disgraceful."

"You can call him Count Biagio," the girl whispered.

"I have no intention of speaking to that monster. He can imprison me on this island, but my mind is my own and I will speak to whomever I wish."

The woman smiled. "You'll feel different in time."

"I will not!" flared Dyana. She sat bolt upright in the tub, sending water sloshing over the rim. "And I can wash myself," she snapped. "Please. Just go now, will you?"

Her outburst stunned the woman, who shrank bank with a wounded expression. "As you wish, Lady Vantran." She got to her feet. "You must be very tired. I'll wait outside for you. Call me when you want to get out and I'll dry you."

"I can dry myself, too," said Dyana. She pointed toward the door. "Good-bye."

When the slave left the room, Dyana sank back down in the warm water, submerged to her chin. The insistent scent of flowers filled her nostrils, so much better than the awful smells of the cargo hold. Sensation was coming back into her limbs, beating back the cold, and the dirt she had shed like a second skin had all washed away, making her feel lighter. Biagio had made an exquisite prison for her. And if he kept his word, if he spared Shani as he'd promised, she would keep her vow to him, as well. Whatever plans he had for her, however vulgar his designs, it would all be worth it if Shani was safe.

"You will not take my baby," she whispered defiantly. "Or my husband. I will beat you, devil."

She started plotting an impossible plan when the door to the bath chamber opened again. Peeking through the threshold was another young woman, one Dyana hadn't seen yet, a remarkable beauty with raven hair and eyes that smiled shyly when she noticed Dyana. Around her neck was the typical collar of a slave, but her clothes weren't a slave's clothes. They were elegant and expensive, made of flowing fabric that clung perfectly to her body. The girl took a cautious step into the room.

"Am I disturbing you?" she asked carefully.

"Yes," said Dyana.

The girl frowned, but refused to leave. Instead she stepped inside and closed the door lightly behind her. She moved like a ghost, soundlessly and with purpose. Suddenly embarrassed, Dyana sank a little deeper into the tub and crossed her arms over her breasts.

"Who are you?" she asked.

The girl crossed the expanse of tile and paused at the side of the tub. She appeared nervous, unsure of herself. Her expression shifted between excitement and fear.

"My name is Eris," she said at last. "I wanted to see you."

"You are getting a good look. What is it you expect to see?"

Eris shook off her nervousness. "I'm not making any sense. I'm sorry, but I had to talk to you. You're Dyana Vantran, aren't you?"

"Yes, I am. And you are Eris. Hello, Eris."

The girl beamed. "Hello, Lady Vantran. I know I'm disturbing you. I'm sorry about that. But I had to see you, speak to you. It's very important."

Dyana smiled. The earnest girl was lovely, impossible to turn away. Dyana steered more bubbles over herself, saying, "Important? Well, then, you should tell me. Sit."

There was a stool at the side of the tub. Eris pulled it a respectful distance away from Dyana and sat down, crossing her legs awkwardly.

Her anxiousness intrigued Dyana. "What is it, Eris?" she asked gently. "How do you know who I am?"

"Everyone in the mansion knows who you are, Dyana Vantran. You're the Jackal's wife. Everyone is talking about it. When I heard you were here I knew I had to come. I have questions, if I may."

"Why is everyone so curious? Am I the first Triin in Crote?"

"Oh, my questions aren't about you, Lady. They're about someone else."

"Who else?"

Eris leaned closer, checked over her shoulders for eavesdroppers, then whispered, "Simon."

The name crushed Dyana's pleasant mood. "Simon?" she said indignantly. "What about that beast?"

Eris faltered. "Simon," she said again. "You know him, yes?"

"I know him," growled Dyana. "How do you know him?"

"He's my . . ." The girl lowered her voice again, almost blushing. "He's my lover."

Dyana blinked. She stared at the girl, unsure how to react, shocked that such a delicate thing could belong to such a horrid man. Eris stared back at her with bewilderment.

"Lady Vantran, you've seen Simon, haven't you? I'm worried about him. He was supposed to be home by now, but he isn't. Do you know where he is?"

"Oh, child," sighed Dyana sadly. "I cannot help you. Really, I think you should go now."

"Why?" asked Eris desperately. "Please tell me. What do you know of him? Is he all right?"

"Eris, stop," begged Dyana. She couldn't bear the pain in the girl's voice, or her innocence. "I do not know where Simon is. If I did, I would tell you. I . . ." She looked away. "Please. I do not know."

Very perceptively, Eris shook her head. "You're lying," she said flatly. "You're hiding something from me. I know you are. I won't leave until you tell me what it is." She got up from the stool and knelt down by the tub. "My lady, I know Simon went to spy on you for the Master. I know you must hate him very much. All I'm asking is for you to tell me you've seen him, that he's safe. Won't you do that for me?"

"Is that what you think?" said Dyana. "That Simon went to Falindar to spy? Child, you are a fool. Your lover went to steal my daughter. He has her somewhere, even now."

"Oh, no. That's impossible. Simon went to spy on your husband. He told me so!"

"He lied to you," Dyana insisted. "He murdered my little girl's nurse and stole her from me. He did. And if you do not believe me, ask Biagio. He has already admitted it."

The light in Eris's green eyes flickered and went out. Her jaw dropped open in shock, but no sound escaped, only a long, dreadful breath.

"It is true, Eris," Dyana continued. "That is why I am here. I went looking for Simon and my daughter and was captured by other men sent with Simon. I do not know where Simon is. I do not know where my baby is. But when I find him, I am going to kill him. I swear it."

"No," said Eris, shaking her head wildly. "It's impossible. Simon would never do that! I know he wouldn't!"

"You are wrong," said Dyana mercilessly. "He did it. He is a very charming man, your lover. He fooled all of us. He got us to care about him and made us think he cared about us. Then he took our little girl. Maybe he has fooled you, too."

"No!" Eris cried. She put her hands to her face, unwilling to listen. "You're lying. You hate Simon because of Biagio. But he's not like that. He's kind."

"Kind to you, maybe," said Dyana. "But to us he was unspeakably cruel." She reached out a dripping arm and beckoned Eris closer. "It is the truth, Eris. You can think what you want about Simon, but I am not lying to you. He stole Shani. And now they are both missing. If you have lost your man, then I have lost my daughter."

"Oh, God," Eris groaned. "It's Biagio. He made Simon do this. We were to be married! Biagio forced him to go, I know it!"

Eris dissolved into angry tears. Dyana kept her hand on the girl's arm, trying to comfort her and not really knowing why. She was innocent, certainly, duped like the rest of them by a cunning agent of Biagio. In the last few minutes an unlikely kinship had sprung up between them.

"He might be alive, still," Dyana suggested. "Maybe Shani, too. We cannot be like this, girl, falling apart. We have to have hope."

"But you'll kill him," sniffed Eris. "You won't be able to, but you'll try. Oh, please, Lady, please try to understand. He did this for *me*. It's the only thing that would have made him take your baby. Believe me, I know Simon better than anyone. He's not a monster."

"Eris . . ."

"He's not," Eris insisted. "I want you to believe that."

"I cannot," said Dyana. She tried to withdraw her hand but Eris grabbed hold of it.

"Lady Vantran, I don't think Simon hates you. Or your husband. He does what the Master tells him to do, that's all. If he does have your baby, I'm sure she's safe."

Dyana had to swallow hard to keep from crying. The thought of Shani in Simon's dangerous hands was too much for her, and she desperately wanted to believe the girl. She remembered her brief times with Simon in Falindar, how impenetrable he'd been, and she wondered if there was anything human under his mask, anything at all that would make him care whether Shani lived or died. Eris seemed to think so. Dyana hoped so, too.

"What is wrong with your master?" Dyana asked. "He is insane. I could tell when I met him. And his eyes! They are like blue diamonds. Why?"

Eris nodded dreadfully. "It's the drug." She explained how Biagio was addicted to the potion that kept him alive, and how she and Simon both believed it had eaten away part of his brain, made him demented. Dyana had known of the drug from Richius, but hearing about it from the girl and seeing Biagio's alien eyes had struck at her heart. Eris whispered when she talked, afraid she might be overheard. "He wasn't always this way," she continued. "When he was younger he was normal. But now the drug rules him. And he hasn't been the same since Arkus died."

"Arkus," Dyana groaned. "That is a name I know too well. Your master blames my husband for his death. I tried to tell him he is wrong, but he would not listen."

"He will listen to no one about that," Eris agreed. "He still grieves for the emperor. The old man was like a father to him. Simon says it's destroyed him. He has so little, you see. No family. Only the Iron Circle."

"Iron Circle?"

"His henchmen, the ones that sided with him against Herrith." Eris smiled. "There's a lot for you to learn, Dyana Vantran. A lot about Biagio you don't understand."

Dyana nodded. "Then you will teach me, Eris. I need to know these things if I am to survive here. Biagio means to take me to Nar. I want you to tell me everything you know."

A wicked smile crossed the girl's face. "I know a lot," she whispered, then proceeded to tell all she knew about Biagio and his unrequited love for Simon.

TWENTY-SEVEN

To Dragon's Beak

Admiral Danar Nicabar, full from a meal of beer and fish, drew his woolen collar close around his neck and stared out into the night, toward the two vessels trailing his flagship through the cold ocean. *Black City* and *Intruder*, his two escorts, were barely visible in the murkiness. A storm from the south was chasing them northward, racing them to Dragon's Beak. Nicabar could see the electric flashes of lightning on the horizon, briefly yellowing the sky. A fierce wind ripped at the deck, pulling at his coat and hair, but the admiral stood firm, hardly feeling it at all. Years of service had toughened his skin to leather. He had heard about the vaunted winters of Dragon's Beak and laughed. Nothing on land was as harsh as the sea.

Certainly not General Vorto.

Three dreadnoughts. And one of them was the *Fearless*. Nicabar grinned, satisfied. Biagio had wondered if three would be enough, but Nicabar had confidence in his guns. Vorto might go to Dragon's Beak with an entire legion, and still they would be too few to stand against a bombardment. If Enli had done his job and secured his brother's ravens, and if the mercenaries purchased by Biagio had already taken the north fork as planned, three dreadnoughts would be enough.

Nicabar's smile shifted to a frown. It suddenly seemed like a lot of ifs. But Duke Enli was a clever man. And Vorto was not. Biagio, of course, was the most clever by far, and since his grand design had succeeded up to now, Nicabar had few doubts about its ultimate outcome.

It was a complicated and precarious scheme, and sometimes even Nicabar wondered about its veracity, but Biagio was a master puppeteer. When he pulled the strings, the whole world danced.

A jagged blade of lightning sliced the southern sky, leaving its impression in Nicabar's vision. The admiral waited for the inevitable thunder. Then he heard it, louder than God, rumbling from Heaven. It would be like that in Dragon's Beak, he thought. When the *Fearless* opened up her cannons, the earth would tremble. Nicabar pulled off a glove, then reached out to caress a nearby mast. The wood felt stout and invincible against his fingers. Nothing Liss had ever built could compare to the *Fearless*. She was without peer, perfect, and Nicabar's greatest love. Some men longed for women; others, like Biagio, for the hearts of men. But Admiral Danar Nicabar had been born and bred to command mighty vessels. He knew this as certainly as anything. God on His throne had reached down and chosen him, saying, "Here is the man to command the seas. I give him dominion."

Nicabar's chest swelled with pride. It wasn't the fate of Liss to rule the waves. That was his destiny alone. The Lissens were pretenders. They thought their island gave them claim to the world's waters. They were wrong. So was Prakna. The thought of his nemesis made the admiral grin. Prakna was a sad, pathetic man. A good sailor, to be sure, but outclassed. Someday, Nicabar determined, he would prove that. Biagio would owe him for so much loyalty, and Nicabar wanted only one thing in payment.

Liss.

"Ah, but that must wait," whispered Nicabar. He gave his ship an affectionate pat, then pulled on his glove, blowing into his hand to warm it. His first duty was to deal with Vorto in Dragon's Beak.

Not an unpleasant task at all.

TWENTY-EIGHT

The Festival of Sethkin

On a day bright with sunlight, the great festival of Sethkin began in the center of Nar City near the Cathedral of the Martyrs. As was customary, Archbishop Herrith opened the festival with a rousing speech. It was the one day of the year when the Holy Father walked amongst his flock unguarded, as though he were one of them and was concerned with their lives. Colorful banners and long, flowing streamers capped the streets, and religious icons brooded over the avenues, tall and baleful. Musicians played and street vendors loudly hawked their wares. The air was filled with foreign smells, while animals and magicians entertained the crowds. Along the sidewalks, Naren noblemen sat with their families, enjoying the procession and the clean air, for it was at the bishop's holy order that the foundries were closed today, so that their belching smokestacks didn't ruin the festivities.

Throughout High Street, regal princes from around the Empire shouldered up to unwed maids, bragging about their wealth, and deep-pocketed merchants lavished their mistresses with dresses and trinkets from the shops, all of which were open and greedy for the tide of money washing through the city. Sethkin was more than just a religious day. It was Nar's great holiday from itself, when the nobles came down from their towers and mingled with the poor, and no one was excluded from the festivities.

On Herrith's decree, the doors to his orphanage had been flung wide. High Street was choked with parentless children, their faces glowing with excitement. The cathedral's many acolytes moved through the crowds, keeping a watchful eye on the brood and doing their best to remind the citizenry of the day's holy meaning. Kren was a time for fasting and reflection, a stretch of penance that culminated in Eestrii, the highest holy day of the Naren church. For the next month, believers were expected to be prayerful, to attend services regularly and to give their most generous offerings to the church. Most importantly, they were to beg God for His infinite mercy, and to forgive them for their sins. Herrith knew Nar had many sinners. He wasn't among them, but even he needed to be humble in the sight of Heaven. Heaven's vision was particularly keen during Kren.

Tomorrow they would all begin their spartan march toward Eestrii, but today they were free to frolic in the good things God had given them, and the Black City had turned out in force. Menageries from Doria had taken center stage in High Street, an awe-inspiring assortment of animals that left both children and adults slack-jawed. There were tusked elephants and tawny lions, dogs that danced and monkeys that laughed. Trainers and keepers spoke to the crowd, explaining about their strange pets and offering the children rides on the elephants. And while they directed their magnificent beasts, minstrel music played and merchants showed off their finery, and High Street wasn't commonplace anymore. Its yearly transformation had occurred, turning it from a busy, jaded thoroughfare into a little glimpse of paradise.

Archbishop Herrith walked happily through the crowd, giving out smiles to the curious Narens begging to touch the hem of his garment. Lorla Lon was with him, holding his right hand. With her left hand she held a frozen confection, a lump of fruit-flavored sugar on a stick that Herrith had purchased for her. She licked at it covetously, slurping with enjoyment, and the sight of the Dorian menagerie had captivated her. Herrith had already stuffed himself with pastries from the bake shop. Now his stomach was stretched, satisfied. Since taking Biagio's drug, his appetite had come roaring back. It wasn't a problem for him to inhale a dozen of the bakery's best.

Herrith led Lorla to a bench on the sidewalk. A man and his family had been sitting there, but when they saw the Holy Father they quickly vacated so the bishop and his ward could sit. A pair of acolytes who'd been trailing Herrith took up positions on either side of the bench. On this day, Herrith wasn't supposed to be guarded, but his cowled priests never took such chances. These two had long dirks beneath their robes. Lorla sat down on the bench first, her little legs dangling over the edge. Impatiently she craned her neck to see the parade of animals. Garbed in the blue dress Herrith had brought her for the occasion, she looked like an angel or one of Nar's beautiful, privileged young women. Herrith sat down beside her, tucking his long robes beneath his knees. The crowds, noticing the Holy Father, parted a little so he could see better.

"Enjoying yourself, child?" Herrith asked over the tumult.

Lorla nodded. "Oh, yes, Father. It's wonderful!"

It *was* wonderful. For Herrith, it was the culmination of a dream. As God's servant, he had never married or taken a woman since his vows. A family, and children like Lorla, had been long forbidden him. But now he had a sense of that normalcy he craved. He had God and a child to adore, and he was happy. Lorla had taken to him, more than he'd dared to hope. She didn't just call him "Father." Since coming to live in the cathedral, she had truly come to be a daughter. There was a blessed bond between them, and Herrith didn't care who noticed it or snickered behind his back. There was always gossip, even among priests. Some were saying unwholesome things about him. But Herrith knew his heart was pure. When he looked at Lorla, he saw nothing but a life he wished was his, and all the potential of youth. God loved children. God bade humankind to love children. What he was doing, Herrith was sure, was according to Heaven's law.

He took Lorla's hand again, pointing out the different animals, and surprising her with his knowledge. He had been through countless festivals, and every year the Dorians came with their menageries. Herrith knew all their routines. But his familiarity with the animal tricks didn't dampen his enthusiasm, and when the elephants stood on their hind legs and raised their trunks in a raucous trumpeting, Herrith laughed like the rest of them and covered his ears.

"Ohhh!" cried Lorla happily. "Loud!"

So loud she almost dropped her treat, but she was quick enough to rescue it before it tumbled onto her dress. Deciding her mouth was the safest place for it, she began to suck on the frozen sugar again, happily bobbing to the music. And as she ate, Herrith watched her peripherally, glad to be with her. In a few more days it would be her birthday. She would be nine years old, and he wanted to make it special. At that age, every year was a milestone for a child. Herrith wanted Lorla to have no doubts about his affection for her. It was why he had given her full run of the cathedral, why he allowed her to bother Darago periodically and marvel at his ceiling, even when he himself was kept from it. Lorla had already endured too much for so tender an age. The Black Renaissance had made her life a wasteland, stripping her of her parents and identity. But now she had a new life in the cathedral, and Herrith had one more little reason for crushing Biagio and his cancerous crusade.

"Lorla, look there," said Herrith, directing her eyes toward a group of clowns across the avenue. There were three of them, up high on stilts, their faces smeared with white paint and malevolent, ruby smiles. Each wore a long, brightly colored gown, festooned with ribbons and broad, rainbow stripes, and their long wigs of green hair bounced around their shoulders.

Lorla frowned. "They're scary," she decided quickly. "I don't like them."

"Do you know what they are?" he asked, sure that she didn't. With their white faces and terrible smiles, they looked more like demons than clowns. "Those are the Clowns of Eestrii. They're the symbols of sin. One is Pride, one is Lust, and the other is Hatred. Those are the things we're supposed to guard against during Kren."

Lorla pulled the ice treat from her mouth with a popping sound. "Clowns of Eestrii? I never heard of them. Why do they look so mean?"

"To remind us that they're always with us. Every year the Clowns of Eestrii walk among the crowd. They try to scare the children into remembering their faces. That's how the children learn." Herrith chuckled. "Some of the adults, too."

"They're ugly," said Lorla emphatically. "I don't think they belong here."

"Oh, but they do," Herrith corrected. "They're to remind us to beware them at all times, even at good times like this."

"Which is which?"

Herrith laughed. "I don't know. Which do you think?"

"What are their names again?"

"Lust, Hatred and Pride," Herrith told her. "Nar's three greatest vices. There, I think that one is Lust." He pointed at the smallest one of the bunch, whose stilts weren't as tall as the rest. This clown had a particular leer in his eyes that reminded Herrith of something impure. "What do you think?"

Lorla lowered her voice. "That one's Hatred," she said with certainty.

"Really?" Herrith looked at her, unnerved by her seriousness. "How can you tell?"

"I've seen him before." The girl turned her eyes from the clowns, looking down at the sidewalk. "I recognize him."

"Where have you seen him before, Lorla?" asked Herrith gently. He knew he was treading unstable ground, but couldn't resist. Lorla was an inscrutable little girl, a great puzzle with many mysteries in her head—mysteries Herrith was determined to unlock. "You can tell me," he cajoled. "I won't tell anyone else. Promise."

Lorla considered his offer with care. Finally she looked up, saying, "That's the face Duke Enli makes, when he thinks of his brother. That's what he looks like now."

The frightening revelation made Herrith slip his hand from Lorla's. She was cold suddenly, frozen in some other place. Her remarkable eyes, not so unlike his own, blazed with secret fury. Herrith at once regretted his question. Whatever she had seen, whatever had gone on in Dragon's Beak, had changed her. She wasn't just a little girl anymore.

"Duke Enli is going to be all right, Lorla," he assured her. "All of Dragon's Beak will be safe once General Vorto wins the day. And he will win, I promise." He smiled awkwardly. "You believe me, don't you?"

"I guess so."

"Have no doubt, little one. Vorto has taken all the troops he needs to win Dragon's Beak back for God. Duke Enli will be fine. Soon he'll rule all of Dragon's Beak. And maybe you'll see him again someday, when Dragon's Beak is safe. I can arrange that, if you like. Not yet, of course. But someday."

"I don't want to go back to Dragon's Beak," said Lorla. "Not ever. That's not my home anymore . . . Father."

Herrith smiled. "Then you will live here forever, in the cathedral, just like Elioes."

The mention of the orphan girl brightened Lorla's troubled face. "Tell me more about her. One more story."

"Lorla . . ."

"One more," she implored. "Any story."

Herrith's mind was blank. He had already told Lorla all he knew about the orphan. And Lorla had devoured his tales rapaciously. She had found a patron saint in the crippled child, and she wasn't satisfied with Darago's painting. She wanted more. Just like the child she was, she always wanted *more.*

"I've already told you all I know," said Herrith. "There's really not a lot about her in the holy books. Just what I've told you already."

"Then tell me again," said Lorla dreamily. "Tell me how she was an orphan, and how she met our Lord and He healed her. That's a good story. I like that one."

Actually, it was the only story about Elioes, but Herrith told it again. And as he spoke Lorla seemed to forget the festival around her, ignoring the menagerie and calls of hawkers. While he spoke, Herrith watched her eyes, and every time he said the word *orphan*, he saw a light flicker behind her emerald veil. She adored the simple story of Elioes, a tale meant to comfort children and convince them of God's holy powers. But Lorla heard more than just a simple fable. She heard truth.

"God saw something very special in Elioes," said Herrith finally. "Just as He sees something special in all of us. Even you and I."

"What does He see special in you?" asked Lorla. She licked at her treat, waiting for an answer.

Herrith stumbled through his collection of clichés, but then decided to tell her what he really believed. "I'm His servant," he declared proudly. "He knows I'll do His will without question. This is why He burdens me. He has set me to a great task."

"To destroy Biagio."

"That's right. He's the devil's own. I'm to destroy him, and all his evil works. That's what Heaven demands of me. No matter what the cost." Herrith glanced away, frightened by the challenge. A terrible feeling of old age made his shoulders slump. "Lorla, I've done things I'm not proud of. Horrible things. And I have to continue to do horrible things, because that's what God wants of me. It's why He called me to the church, maybe the very reason I was born. I am Nar's only hope. I'm its savior."

The little girl smiled crookedly. Herrith couldn't tell if she believed him, but the warmth in her eyes was comforting.

"Is that why there's war in Dragon's Beak?" she asked. "Because God wants it?"

"God wants His kingdom on earth," replied Herrith. "If we must battle for it, if we must sacrifice and die, so be it. God has been very clear to me on this, little one. It's why He killed Emperor Arkus, and why He's delivered me the weapons needed to fulfill His plan. Now . . ." Herrith forced a sunny smile. "No more talk of this. We have a whole month to reflect. Today is for fun."

No sooner had he said that than a monkey scooted across the street, landing in Lorla's lap. Lorla shrieked at the intrusion, dropping her treat to the pavement and putting up her hands, afraid to touch the curious creature. Herrith's bellow brought the monkey's trainer running.

"Bobo!" cried the man, a young Dorian dressed in festival clothes. The trainer bowed apologetically to the bishop, while Herrith's shadowy acolytes crept imperceptibly closer. The little monkey bounced up and down on Lorla's lap. Like its master, the creature wore a bright green tunic and a red hat on its fuzzy head shaped like a bell. Its yellow teeth flashed as it cried out, but it didn't threaten the girl at all. It seemed more interested in the ruined treat at her feet.

"It's all right," said Herrith quickly, putting Lorla and the trainer at ease. He gave a quick glance to his priests, who took a cautious step back. "Don't be afraid, Lorla. It won't hurt you."

"Bobo wouldn't hurt anyone, Holy Father," the young Dorian assured them. He smiled and laughed, seeing Lorla's sudden delight. "Don't worry, girl. He's just saying hello."

"Hello, Bobo," said Lorla, staring down at the mischievous monkey. Bobo bounced when he heard his name, then reached out a hand to explore Lorla's face. She giggled as his tiny fingers tickled her lips. "Can I touch him?" she asked. "He won't bite me, will he?"

"Go ahead," urged the trainer. "Rub his head. He likes that."

Lorla reached out and lightly stroked the monkey's head. When she did, the smile on her face stretched wide.

"He's so soft!" she declared.

"Bobo's from Casarhoon," the trainer explained. "He's come all the way up here just to say hello to you and the Holy Father. You like him?"

"Very much," Lorla cooed. She ran her hands over the creature's head repeatedly, a gesture that calmed Bobo and made his simian eyes droop. "He's very sweet."

"And smart," said the Dorian. "He can count to ten. And he knows his name better than some people. Bobo even helps me with the other animals. The elephants are afraid of him!"

Herrith watched Lorla and the monkey, and the spark of an idea occurred to him. It didn't do for her to be so alone in the cathedral. Without other children, she had no companionship save for the priests. A child needed pets. He took hold of the trainer's sleeve and pulled him closer.

"How much for the monkey?" he asked.

The Dorian blinked. "Holy Father?"

"I want to buy it, for the child. How much?"

"Really, Father?" asked Lorla elatedly. "For my own?"

"For your birthday," Herrith explained. He loved the explosion of joy on her face. "Something special for you. Would you like that?"

"Holy Father, Bobo's not for sale," said the Dorian. "I'm sorry, but he's mine."

There was enough trepidity in the young man's voice for Herrith to know he could be persuaded. The bishop smiled at him serenely, leaning back on the bench.

"Come now, my son. It's just an animal. How important can it be? I will pay you double what you paid for it yourself. Now that's more than fair."

"Uh, Father . . . ?" said Lorla shyly.

Herrith ignored her. "Double, my son," he said again, holding up two fingers. "Name your price."

"I'm sorry, Your Grace, it's not the money. Bobo's not just an animal. He's more like a friend. I could never sell him."

"Father, I don't want the monkey," said Lorla sharply, pulling at his robes. Herrith looked at her, startled.

"You don't?" he asked. "Why not?"

She shrugged. "I don't know. I just don't. Not for my birthday gift. I want something else."

"What else?"

"Just something else," she said simply, then frowned down at the monkey. "He's a very pretty monkey, though." Still stroking Bobo, she glanced at his relieved trainer. "You're lucky. I bet he's a good friend."

The trainer offered a smile of thanks. "Yes, he is," he said, then lifted Bobo off Lorla's lap. The monkey quickly scurried up its master's shoulder, perching there like a bird and waving at Lorla and the bishop. "Say good-bye, Bobo," the man instructed. Bobo squawked an incomprehensible farewell. Lorla returned the wave as the two disappeared back into the crowd. Her eyes lingered on the monkey until it was gone.

"I thought you would like a companion of your own," said Herrith. "That creature would have made a fine gift for your birthday. Now I'll have to think of something else. Still . . ." He stood, taking her hand and lifting her from the bench. "I think I know a place to get you something good."

"What place?" asked Lorla.

"You'll see."

Herrith led her by the hand along the sidewalk, past the performing animals, and past a street magician with a long cape and a handful of cards he kept making disappear. The bishop ignored the noise and the well-wishers crowding around him. What he wanted, what he knew Lorla could never resist, was on the corner of High Street, between a candlemaker and a blacksmith's shop. Halfway down the avenue, Herrith spotted his destination.

Piper's toy shop.

Crowded around the shop's window was a throng of children, all pressing their noses to the glass to get a glimpse of the marvels inside. Already Herrith could hear the faint music of the mechanical flute player in the window, even above the din of the street. He directed Lorla's view toward the shop.

"There," he said. "That's where we're going."

Lorla squinted. "What is it?"

"A toy shop. The most amazing shop you've ever seen, little one. Believe me, you'll find something special there for your birthday."

"Yes," cheered Lorla, squeezing Herrith's hand. "Yes, I'm sure I will."

Now it was she who led him through the street, practically dragging him in her excitement to reach the toy shop. When at last they reached the window, Lorla let go of him and dove into the mass of children, elbowing her way to the window. Herrith paused on the sidewalk, happily watching her. With a press of little bodies on both sides of her, she put her palms to the glass and peered inside. Herrith didn't have to see her face to know the awe splashed across it.

Lorla lingered at the window, staring into the toy shop. The other children around her shouted and laughed, but she was silent as stone, mesmerized by the mechanical piper and all the miraculous dollhouses. Inside the shop, Herrith could see Redric Bobs, the shop's proprietor. Their eyes met for a fleeting instant before the toymaker looked away to deal with his customers. Predictably, the Piper's shop was packed with patrons. Naren nobles and their spoiled offspring crowded every inch of the store, grabbing greedily at the beautiful things the toymaker had built. Herrith shrugged off the idea of fighting the crowd. He was the Archbishop of Nar. He wouldn't need to wait for service. As Lorla stared at the toys, Herrith stared at the toymaker. A sad man, really. A great artist in his own way, but a recluse since his wife died. No children. Herrith closed his eyes and mouthed a little prayer for Redric Bobs. He was probably very lonely.

"Father," Lorla called loudly. She didn't turn her attention from the window, or pull her hands from the glass. "Father, come look!"

Herrith gently pushed himself through the crowd of children and parents. The assembly parted a little as he moved through them, allowing him to pass. As always, the bishop's acolytes shadowed him. When Herrith reached the window, filled with toys and moving, mechanical marvels, he smiled down at his adopted ward.

"See? I told you. Isn't it fabulous?"

"Fabulous," Lorla echoed. Her eyes were fixed on a beautiful dollhouse in the window, a giant, meticulously detailed model with real wood shingles and varnished a flaming, feminine pink. It was grander than all the other grand houses in the window, more stunning even than the wooden piper and his songs. "Look at that dollhouse," she whispered. "The big pink one. Isn't it lovely?"

"Beautiful," Herrith agreed. "The man who makes them is called the Piper. Like the flute player in the window. See?"

He tried to show her the wooden man, but Lorla wasn't interested, so enthralled was she by the dollhouse. Her little lips twisted with a sad grimace.

"It's so pretty," she remarked. "I've never had anything like that."

"Would you like one?"

Lorla finally tore her eyes away from the window and looked at the bishop. "You mean it?"

"A gift, from me to you. Something special for your birthday."

"Oh, yes," sighed Lorla. "Yes, I would like that very much. And I want a big one! Like that pink one."

"I don't think the Piper will sell us that pink one," said Herrith. "From what I understand, he builds them one by one. That pink one is his own. It's been in his window forever."

"Then I want one for my own," said Lorla happily. "One that's just for me! He'll do that for me, won't he? He can build whatever I want!"

"Come," said Herrith, taking her hand again. "Let's ask him."

Like Lorla, Herrith was on a cloud when he walked into the toy shop, overwhelmed at the girl's exuberance. The strong smell of paint and sawdust greeted them in the shop, filling the air, and the Piper's many handmade gadgets whirred and spun and whizzed by on wires overhead. Lorla giggled at the sight, enchanted, and Herrith, who had only seen the toys from the window, laughed with her. Redric Bobs' shop was a wonderland. But as soon as the toymaker noticed his holy guest, Redric Bobs went white, ignoring his current customer, a Naren nobleman with a big stomach and, obviously, an equally large purse. The nobleman scowled at Redric Bobs insistently, then stepped back in shame when he noticed Archbishop Herrith.

"Your Grace," said the Piper shakily. He was a lanky man with thin fingers like the dolls he made, and when he spoke the sawdust in his hair fell like dandruff to the floor. "I wasn't expecting you." He bowed suddenly, as if he'd forgotten all protocol. "Welcome to my toy shop."

"Rise, Redric Bobs," commanded Herrith. "This is festival day. No need for all the pomp. I came here like all these other good folks, to do business with you."

The Piper came a little closer. He looked enthralled, just as Lorla had when she'd seen the dollhouse, but it wasn't awe of Herrith that brought the strange expression to his face. It was Lorla. The toymaker stared at her, sizing her up, as if she reminded him of someone or something long lost. Thoughtfully, he dropped to one knee in front of her. A crowd had gathered in a circle to watch them, but Redric Bobs hardly noticed them.

"You've brought this child here for something special, haven't you, Holiness?" he said, never taking his eyes off Lorla.

"Yes," said Herrith. "For her birthday."

"Birthday," trilled the Piper. "How nice."

"I'll be nine," Lorla explained.

"Nine," Redric Bobs parroted. He was being nonsensical, and it disturbed Herrith.

"Yes, man, nine years old," said Herrith sharply. "And she wants one of your dollhouses."

Lorla pointed back toward the window. "I saw the pink one. It's very beautiful."

"Ah, Belinda," said the toymaker proudly. "Yes, that's my favorite, too." He reached out and playfully messed up her hair. "Belinda always brings little girls like you into my shop. But she's not for sale, I'm afraid. She was built for my wife."

Herrith maneuvered himself between Lorla and the toymaker. "We don't want to buy that one. We want something special. One of your custom-made houses. You can do that for her, can't you?"

The Piper rose from his knees, and Herrith glimpsed the smallest resentment in his eyes. "Of course I can," said Redric Bobs. "That's what I do, after all. I can make a dollhouse for the girl. Anything she wants." He looked around at the shoppers staring at him. "But let's go somewhere and talk about it, away from everyone else, all right? I have an office where we can talk." He gestured invitingly toward the side of his store. "Holiness?"

"Very well," agreed Herrith, pushing Lorla along and guiding her toward the office. Piper cheerfully told his patrons to browse, then followed them through a doorway into a tiny room with a handmade desk. A collection of tiny toys sat on the desktop, waiting for a curious playmate. There was a chair next to the desk, and Lorla quickly claimed it. Redric Bobs closed the door to his office, shutting away the outside noise.

"I'm sorry, I don't have anything in here to offer you, Holiness," he apologized. "I don't get many visitors from the church in my toy shop."

"I'm already full of pastries and drink," said Herrith. "And I don't care to stay long." He sauntered over to stand beside Lorla. "Now, tell us what you can do for us, toy man."

The Piper smiled. "You're looking well, Your Grace," he remarked, ignoring Herrith's question. "I saw you in your carriage some months ago. You've gained some weight back. If I may say so, you look quite fit. Your color is better, too."

Herrith grimaced. Was that meant to be a compliment? Redric Bobs was a strange character in Nar City. Perhaps he'd been breathing too much paint vapor.

"I'm well," said Herrith. "Now . . ."

"Some of us didn't expect such a remarkable recovery from you," Bobs continued. "We all prayed for you mightily, Your Grace. God must have heard us."

God delivered a little blue bottle to me, thought Herrith bitterly. Since taking the drug, he had been a whole man again. But Redric Bobs knew nothing of the drug, nothing but the rumors that constantly floated through the Empire. Herrith narrowed his eyes on the Piper, trying to penetrate his cryptic facade. He didn't like being reminded of his addiction, especially not by a peasant toymaker. And the drug Biagio had sent him was running perilously low. Soon, Herrith knew, he would have to strike a bargain with Biagio to obtain more of the stuff. But that was in the future, not today. Today was a good day, and Redric Bobs was ruining it. When at last Herrith addressed the Piper again, his voice was low, almost threatening.

"Why don't you tell us what kind of dollhouse you can build for Lorla?" he said. "We'd like to get back to the festival before it's over."

"I want a big one," said Lorla, stretching out her arms for emphasis. "Like the ones in the window."

"I can build whatever you'd like, child," said Redric Bobs. "Any style or color. As big as you like, too. Do you know what you'd like, Lorla?"

"Any style?" asked Lorla.

The toymaker nodded. "That's right."

"No matter what?"

"No matter what."

Lorla smiled. "Then I know what I want you to build for me, sir." She turned to Herrith and smiled at him secretively. "I want you to build me something very special. The best thing you've ever built! And I want you to build it for both of us, me and Father Herrith."

"What?" blurted Herrith. "Lorla . . ."

Lorla looked at the toymaker again in earnest. "Sir, I want you to build me a dollhouse of the Cathedral of the Martyrs."

Herrith was astonished. He faltered back against the workbench, staring dumbfounded at Lorla. "Child, what are you saying? The cathedral? Why?"

"Because it's my home," said Lorla softly. "My new home. The only home I'll ever have now." She reached over and grabbed Herrith's fingers. "It's special to us both, Father. And it will be something everyone can enjoy. Like Darago's ceiling! We can even keep it in the great hall, under the painting. People can see both of them, two beautiful things."

"But, Lorla, that's not a gift for a little girl. I want you to have a dollhouse like the pretty ones in the window. Something pink and sweet-looking. Something to enjoy."

"But I will enjoy it, Father," said Lorla. Her smile was bright, imploring. "It's what I want. More than a monkey or just some toy. I want something special."

It was all too perfect. She was such a remarkable child, this orphan Enli had given him. At that moment, he realized she was truly a gift from Heaven.

"Well, Redric Bobs?" he asked over his shoulder. "Can you make this for us?"

There was a pause while the toymaker considered the request. "It's very complicated," he said, stroking his chin. "The cathedral has many details. It will take a lot of work. And time. When do you want it?"

"In time for Eestrii," said Herrith. "I want it to be on display for all the Black City to see when we show off Darago's masterpiece."

"Eestrii," muttered the toymaker. "That's not much time. Less than a month. I'll have to work hard to get it done so quickly."

"Work as hard as you need to," said Herrith. "From dawn to dusk, I don't care. I'll pay whatever it costs. But do a good job, Redric Bobs. This is a very special gift you're making. I want it to be perfect."

"Everything I do is perfect," said the toymaker defensively. "Your

Holiness will be astounded by what I build for the child, I promise that."

"Then send me your bill, toymaker," said Herrith. "I will gladly pay it." He lifted Lorla out of the chair, set her down gently on the floor, then led her out of the office. "Good day to you, Redric Bobs. Enjoy the festival. And remember—by Eestrii."

The toymaker bowed as they left, but Herrith hardly noticed. The drug and Lorla's love had invigorated him, making him feel truly immortal. They still had the whole afternoon before them, and Herrith was determined not to let it slip away. Today he was happy. Tomorrow or the next day he would hear bad news, learn about deaths in Dragon's Beak or some other far-off place, but today was the great festival of Sethkin. With a smile on his face, he walked out of the toymaker's fanciful shop, back into the revelry of High Street with his adopted, perfect daughter.

TWENTY-NINE

Lord Jackal

The nights in Liss were heavy and still. Haran Island echoed with the sound of water and winter breezes and the occasional stirrings of birds, but very few voices or footsteps marred the silence. Jelena's palace took on the bleakness of a tomb at night. It was a lonely, almost desolate place, too big for its young occupant. With its high ceilings and empty corridors, the palace was a constant reminder of everything Liss had lost in its long war with Nar. There weren't men and women talking noisily, or little children of the royal family scrambling through its halls. There was only the cold quiet of duty, and the stone-faced guardians of Queen Jelena rarely cracked a smile or uttered an unsolicited word. In the light of day the palace was a wonder, but at night, when the world was asleep, shadows ruled.

Richius had only been in the palace for three days, but already he knew its habits. Like the rising and setting of the sun, life on Jelena's island was predictable. Her guardians and servants saw to her every need. Catboats and jarls constantly navigated the island's lake front and canals, delivering supplies, and the enormous water gate continued to make Richius marvel. Other than that, life in the palace was a hellish bore, and Richius longed to be gone from it.

Since his coming to Liss, Queen Jelena had treated him like royalty. She had given him rooms not far from her own, a palatial spread on the ground floor of her palace with a view of her prized water garden and haran fish. There was always food and a warm fire for him, and a staff of eager servants to cater to his needs. Clean Lissen clothes had been put in his closets, a blessed relief from the sea-stinking garb he'd arrived in, and he was provided all the quiet he needed to think and plan his strategy against Crote. It was a marvelous arrangement for Richius, perfectly conducive to thought. Except for one problem.

He had no idea where to begin.

For three days he had been isolated on Haran Island, with only Jelena for company. Prakna had disappeared—to be with his wife, Jelena claimed—and the crew of the *Prince* hadn't returned to visit him. And there was no army yet, either, only the promise of one. Tomorrow, Jelena had assured him, Prakna would return to Haran Island and bring him to his waiting soldiers, but to Richius that promise rang hollow. Worse, he feared it might actually be true. Despite the finery of his surroundings, the things he really needed were denied him. He needed maps of Crote, of which there were none. He needed experienced fighters to explain the terrain to him, and weapons for his men. He needed timetables and lieutenants, predictions about Crote's abilities and ideas on their weaknesses. There were plans to be made and scenarios to draw up, attack strategies and failure contingencies. There was absolutely everything to win or lose, and Richius was alone, a general without an army and horribly afraid. This time his arrogance had ruined him. He had finally taken on an impossible challenge.

"Dyana was right," he muttered. He shouldn't have come to Liss.

The night was wistful. Richius had wandered from his rooms and found himself on the mooring docks just outside the palace, watching the catboats slip in and out. It had snowed erratically for the past three days, but tonight was clear and bright with clouds. The wind had stilled to a gentle breeze that blew his hair haphazardly over his eyes. His hair was getting longer, becoming more unkempt by the day. He hadn't shaved recently, either. But his clothes were fresh and clean, and he still wore the navy coat Marus had given him. He liked the feel of it, the way it kept his legs warm. And he liked the reflection he cut with it in mirrors. When he wore it, he felt very far away, on some great, nameless adventure that didn't include his troubled past. Richius leaned against a stout mooring post fitted with rusty chains and looked up into the sky. A blanket of stars swept to the horizon.

"Hero," he scoffed. "Jackal of Nar."

That's what they called him here. Even Jelena. She didn't seem to care that it was an insult. It was simply how she knew him. In Liss, the Jackal of Nar was some sort of saint, a great warrior who had beaten back the Black Empire and saved the Triin homeland. To some, it was a great story. To Richius it was a distorted joke. But it followed him everywhere now, and no matter how hard he fought it, no matter how many times he corrected people, they always called him Jackal or Kalak, and they always expected something grand from him.

"Can I do this thing?" he wondered aloud. Now and then he still talked to the sky, just as Karlaz had taught him. He was still waiting for it to answer. "They want so much from me. And I have nothing. Where's my army?"

Silence. The sky twinkled, ignoring him, and Richius looked away with a wry smile. He gazed across the great lake separating Haran Island from the rest of Liss. On the other side, he saw canals reflecting starlight and high, spanning bridges. Tall buildings reached heavenward, their windows blinking with candlelight. Silhouettes moved across the horizon, men in boats and women with golden hair. They were a beautiful race, these Lissens. And they were all enigmas to Richius, no more comprehensible to him than the Triin he had struggled so long to understand. Especially Jelena.

The thought of the queen made Richius close his eyes. She was very lovely. Like Sabrina. And her loneliness was palpable. It was a dark aura around her, a pall that never waned. She had lost her parents and identity, and had grown a vendetta to replace them, but still she was just a child. To Richius, she seemed a little girl playing in her mother's wardrobe; dressing like a queen, sometimes acting like a queen, but always through a thin veneer of adolescence. He liked Jelena. But just like Prakna and all the rest of them, she expected something impossible from him. She wanted a hero. She wanted a dragon-slayer from Naren mythology. Alone on the dock, weaponless and without an army, Richius felt barely able to defend himself, much less a nation.

As he always did when he felt alone, he thought of Dyana. It was very late. She would have put Shani to bed by now, and if he were there with her she would be in his arms, loving him. Prakna was with his wife. Marus might be with his wife, too. What the hell was he doing here, halfway across the world? But then the answer came to him like a hammer-blow.

"Biagio."

He said the name so loudly, it echoed down the dock. Behind him, the two guards that had been shadowing him cocked curious eyebrows at his outburst. Richius waved at them.

"Just talking to myself," he quipped. "Crazy men do that."

"And so do sane men," came a voice from the darkness. Startled, Richius whirled to see an hourglass silhouette walking toward him. Jelena lit the dock with a smile. She wore a long stole of white fur around her shoulders and a braid of sparkling silver in her hair that caught the starlight. As she approached him he drew back a little, annoyed at the intrusion.

"Jelena, what are you doing out here?"

"I've been looking for you," she said. She slid up to him on the dock until they were face-to-face. "When I didn't find you in your rooms I got concerned."

"Well, you found me. What do you want?"

Jelena frowned. "Richius, what's bothering you?"

"Nothing," Richius lied. "I just wanted to be alone, that's all. Why were you looking for me?"

"I wanted to see how you were, that's all. Tomorrow is an important day for you. I know you have a lot on your mind." The queen shrugged demurely. "I thought you might want to talk."

"Not particularly," said Richius. He leaned back against the mooring post, trying not to look at her. Sometimes seeing her was unbearable. The resemblance to Sabrina was uncanny. "You can go back inside now. I'm fine."

Jelena maneuvered herself in front of him, forcing him to look at her. "I'm very good at telling when a man is lying. If you were fine, you would be asleep, resting for tomorrow. But you are not fine, so you are out in the cold, staring like a dog at the moon." She looked at him demandingly. "Tell me what's wrong."

"Why don't I tell you what *isn't* wrong?" he snapped. "That would be a much shorter list."

"All right, then. What isn't wrong?"

"Nothing. Everything is wrong, Jelena. My being here is wrong."

Jelena sighed. "Richius, you're just afraid about tomorrow. You're nervous. But I tell you, everything will be all right."

"You're not listening to me, Jelena." Richius took her by the shoulders. "I'm very, very angry. Understand? And you're not helping me any. I need you to stop telling me how great I am and start giving me the things I need."

The queen stared at him, stunned. Her guardians, who had been lingering in the shadows, now rushed onto the dock. Richius saw them but didn't release her. Instead he stared back at her, eyes blazing.

"I need an army," he said flatly. "I need maps and men. And I need them now, Jelena. No more waiting. I need to know what I'm getting into."

"Richius," said Jelena softly. "Let go of me."

"Are you listening to me?"

The girl nodded. "I'm listening. So are my guards. If you don't release me quickly, they'll cut your head off." She tried to calm him with a smile. "Please . . ."

Reluctantly, Richius released her. His gesture kept the guardians at bay. At their queen's insistence, they moved back into the shadows, out of earshot. Jelena shook her head at Richius, clearly troubled.

"What is wrong with you tonight? I've never seen you this way, Jackal."

"Don't call me that!" Richius snapped. "My name isn't Jackal. It's Richius Vantran. Can't any of you get that through your thick heads? *Richius.*"

Jelena gave another, infuriating smile. "To us you are the Jackal. And I've told you, it's no insult."

"No? Well, I hate it. If you call me that again I just won't answer you."

"You must get used to it, Richius," said the queen. She slid her hand onto his shoulder. "You must understand what you are to us."

Richius rolled his eyes back. "I already know. I'm a hero."

"Yes. Is that so bad?"

"Jelena, I can't be your hero. If you keep calling me that, you're all just going to be disappointed. Let me do what I came here for. That's all I want. Please."

"That's all any of us want," she assured him. "Be at ease. We have more faith in you than you have in yourself. We know you can do this thing and be victorious."

"Don't be so sure. I haven't even started to put a battle plan together. And why? Because I can't! I need maps, Jelena. I need to know what the hell I'm doing!"

"Lower your voice," she directed. "Please. Don't make me tell you again."

Richius wanted to scream. Were they all mad on this island? No one was listening to him. And no one of consequence could even hear him. Only Jelena, and she was too enamored with a myth to see the truth.

"God, Jelena, please listen to me," he said. He kept his eyes closed as he spoke, talking softly, hoping she might hear a whisper better than his shouts. "Just listen to me, all right? I want to tell you the truth of things."

"I'm listening," said the queen.

Richius opened his eyes. She was indeed listening. He took her hand and pulled her down onto the dock, so they were both sitting with their legs dangling over the water. Jelena didn't protest the odd arrangement. In fact, she seemed to enjoy the intimacy.

"Talk to me," she begged. "Tell me what troubles you."

"First a promise. Will you listen to everything I say? I mean, will you truly hear me?"

The queen nodded. "Of course."

"Good." Richius sighed, arranging his thoughts. There was so much in his head, a fractured mirror of ideas and anxieties. Finally, he folded his arms over his chest, saying, "I'm no hero, Jelena. I can't lead an army this way. You think I'm a hero because you don't know the truth of things, and because Prakna and the others won't listen to the truth."

"So what is the truth?"

"The truth is ugly. The truth is I'm just a man who's been obscenely lucky. I've seen a lot of death."

"So have I."

Richius held up a finger in warning. "It's my turn, remember?"

"I remember," said the queen sheepishly.

Richius continued. "War isn't the glorious thing you think it is. War is ugly. I know, because I've lived through it. And it's only been by Heaven's grace that I'm even here to talk about it, because I don't deserve to be. Good people died just so I can be sitting here with you now, staring at the stars. I've lost a lot of friends and family." He looked up into the sky. "I'm afraid, Jelena."

There was an awkward silence after his confession. He glanced at Jelena, and found to his surprise that she was grinning at him.

"What is it? Why are you smiling?"

"Is that all you wanted to tell me? That you're afraid? We are all afraid, Richius. Every day I fear for my life and soul. I don't think any less of you for being like me. No one expects you to be more than human. Not me, and not your army."

"Army," Richius scoffed. "Right."

There was immediate offense in the girl's expression. "There is an army, Richius. Have no doubt." She stared at him, and when he wouldn't answer, she poked him with a finger. "You don't believe me?"

Her question made Richius shrug. "I think you're hiding them from me," he told her. "I think you're not at all proud of the rag-tag group you've assembled, and you're trying to whip them into something presentable before I see them. That's what I think. That's what I'm afraid of."

"You are wrong," she said with iron. "There *is* an army waiting for you. A proud group. On the morrow you will see them."

"On the morrow. Always on the morrow. I've been in Liss for three days, Jelena. Why can't I see them now? Why can't I get to work?"

"Because they've been assembling for you, Richius. There's much to do. On the morrow—"

"Yes, yes," snapped Richius with a wave.

The insult brought Jelena to her feet. "You really don't believe me, do you?" she asked, glowering at him.

"I've told you what I believe."

The queen grabbed hold of his collar, angrily pulling him to his feet. "Then come," she demanded. She turned from him and stormed down the dock, waving at him to follow. "Come on!"

"What? Where are you going?"

"*We* are going to see your army, Jackal. Right now."

"Now? Jelena . . ."

"Follow me," the queen commanded. She snapped her fingers at her guards, shouting orders that brought more of them running. Richius hurried up to her, confused and surprised at her vehemence. Suddenly there was nothing of the little girl in her. That adolescent veneer had vanished, unveiling a confident ruler. Jelena demanded a boat and men, and she wanted them quickly. To be precise, she wanted them right now.

"A boat? Now?" Richius asked, flabbergasted. "But it's so late. So dark."

"You wanted to see your army, yes?" she shot back. "Then that's where we're going. Since you don't trust me enough to wait 'til morning, we'll go now."

"I never said that I don't trust you," Richius tried to explain. But Jelena would hear nothing. Her face was granite as her guards went to work, arranging passage for their mistress. The docks sprang quickly to life as her sailors emerged from the darkness with lanterns and gear, shouting across the grounds in preparation for a journey. For the first time in days, there was actually real activity around the palace, a sight both heartening and confusing. Where the hell were they going?

Queen Jelena continued to ignore Richius as her men led them both to a waiting catboat at the other end of the pier. This one was like the boat that had brought Richius to the royal island, a splendid, single-masted vessel bearing the figurehead of the haran and outfitted with a polished brass sternpost. The sail had been furled, and a team of rowers climbed aboard, taking positions on the rowing benches and grabbing up the long, tapering oars. They were remarkably efficient and had readied themselves in an instant at their queen's request. A man in a royal uniform hurried up to the boat, still pulling on his coat as Richius and Jelena arrived. He greeted the queen with a bow and a smile, a gesture which Jelena perfunctorily returned.

"Timrin," the queen addressed him. "I want to go to Karalon. Right now."

The sailor Timrin blanched at the order. He was very dark and hidden in the shadows. "My queen, it's dangerous. Let me take the Jackal there himself. I think it would be best if you stayed behind. The lagoons around Karalon are, well, treacherous."

"The Jackal of Nar insists on seeing his army tonight," said Jelena. "I must escort him, to prove a point. No arguments, Timrin, please."

"As you wish," said the sailor reluctantly. He stood aside so that his monarch could step on board. Jelena didn't wait for the astonished Richius to accompany her up the gang-walk. But when she got on board and saw he wasn't following, she gave him an irritated scowl.

"Are you coming or not?" she barked at him.

Richius planted his feet resolutely in the dirt. "Not until you tell me where we're going. What's Karalon?"

"Karalon is where your army is stationed. And that's all I'll say to you. I can be as stubborn as you, Richius. Get aboard."

Against his better judgment, Richius walked up onto the waiting boat. Behind their oars, the rowers stared at him through the darkness while other sailors fitted the vessel with lanterns to pierce the darkness. One by one the lanterns were lit, until the boat glowed with yellow light. Timrin, the apparent captain of the vessel, was the last aboard. He pulled up the narrow plank, checked the darkness with a worried eye, then settled in to the bow, not far from where his queen was sitting. Richius stood, staring questioningly at Jelena. The queen ignored him.

"This show isn't necessary," he said softly. "I never said I didn't trust you."

"Sit down, Richius. You might hurt yourself."

"Jelena—"

"Just sit." She gestured to the place on the bench beside her. "You'll see where we're going soon enough."

So Richius sat beside her on the cold, hard bench, while the oarsmen waited for Timrin's command to shove off. A few straggling sailors on the dock undid the mooring lines, letting the boat drift away. In the distance, the palace glowed in the light of braziers and torches. Richius suddenly regretted his harsh words to the queen. Her palace, the only home he had right now, seemed painfully inviting. But the vessel floated away from it, and soon the rowers set to work with their oars, pulling them far from Haran Island and across the vast, black lake. Darkness swallowed them, and the pinpoints of lantern light shined insignificantly, barely brightening the few feet in front of them. To their left, the towns and villages of Liss glowed with distant light, but their heading was taking them away from those sights. They were plunging deeper into the darkness, toward a lightless meadow of still water stretching far off and away from Haran Island. Richius peered into the invisible distance, hoping to catch a glimmer of something solid, but there was nothing but endless water and murkiness. That feeling of isolation he had been battling now came roaring over him like a tidal wave.

"Is this right?" he asked incredulously. "Can Timrin see anything?"

Jelena looked away, pretending not to hear him.

"Don't ignore me, girl," Richius warned. "Tell me where we're going."

"I've already told you," said Jelena wearily. "To Karalon."

"Right. And what exactly is Karalon?"

"You'll see."

"Is it far?"

"Not very."

"What is it?"

Jelena turned away from him and said no more. The narrow boat slipped farther into the unknown, slowly skimming the water as the oarsmen dipped and pulled them forward. On the bow, Timrin worked the lanterns with an eagle-eye, trying to penetrate the darkness. The lanterns pitched their cold light forward, skidding across the water. Richius watched Timrin work, amazed at the concentration locked on his face.

Part fish, thought Richius. *All Lissens are part fish.*

As Marus had told him, they were part of the sea. Its salty water ran through their veins like blood. But Timrin was far from happy with this mission. Nothing distracted him or broke his concentration, but there was real worry on his face. Whatever Karalon was, it wasn't a place to be visited at night.

For nearly an hour they rowed without ceasing. Jelena kept up her stony silence, not sparing a word. The towns that had bid them good-bye were gone now, and the lake had finally narrowed into a winding, sluggish river. A stiff breeze blew, making Richius shiver. In the darkness, he heard the splash of night-things moving on the banks and the alien croaking of reptiles. His ears buzzed with the insistent drone of insects. To starboard and port, he could see boggy landmasses, misshapen blobs of earth striped with rivulets. The tendrils of water were everywhere, some as wide as Lissen canals, others barely big enough for a toy boat to maneuver. Timrin periodically held up his hand, slowing their vessel and making the oarsmen steer through unseen treacheries. Around them, the river narrowed still more. Up ahead was a sharp bend in the waterway.

"Easy here," Timrin coached. The oarsmen slackened their pace, letting the boat glide. Beneath them, Richius heard the sound of sand scraping the hull. The boat pitched suddenly to port, spilling Jelena into his arms. Timrin cursed and wrapped himself around the sternpost, ordering his men to push off. The sailors on the port side scrambled, grabbing long poles and pushing the boat off whatever had snared them. There were more jarring noises, more lurching as the vessel slowly freed itself. Sure that the boat would tear itself apart, Richius held tight to Jelena. If they spilled into the freezing water, they would surely die.

"I've got you!" he assured the queen. Jelena stayed in his arms, grateful for the security as she dug her fingers into the bench to keep from sliding off. Oarsmen and sailors grunted with exertion. Timrin shouted at them to heave, and at last the boat freed itself with a great groan. It splashed back into the water, righting itself and revealing a black outcropping of muddy rocks. As they drifted away from the dangerous peak, Timrin shook his head, shaken and angry. He rushed to check on his queen, but Jelena quickly signaled her safety.

"I'm all right," she proclaimed. "Go on, Timrin. Watch the course."

"You're sure you're all right?" Richius asked her. He still had his arms around her waist. Flustered, Jelena removed herself from his embrace.

"I'm fine," she said. "Thank you."

A little ashamed, Richius drew back.

"Tell me now," he said. "Where are we? Is this Karalon?"

Jelena nodded. "Yes. Or part of it. We're very near now."

"This bog? This is where my army is?"

"There's an island at the center of the bog," the queen explained. "Much bigger than these other islands. That's where your army is, Richius. They've been waiting for you, bringing in supplies and getting ready. But it's been hard to get them all here. That's what's taken so much time."

Richius looked around, astonished by the bleak landscape. He could hardly believe this boggy, desolated place hid his army. "Here?" he blurted. "I don't understand. Why?"

"Because it's the safest place for them," said Jelena. There was an agitation in her tone, a sadness Richius couldn't fathom. She didn't look out into the night as Richius did, she didn't crane her neck to see or show the slightest fear of her surroundings. She merely sat there, mute. Richius took her hand, imploring her to speak.

"Explain it to me," he said gently. "What is this all about?"

Jelena sighed. "Karalon is very remote. There is only one wide waterway here, and no way to reach the main island on foot. Anyone who goes to Karalon must take a boat like this one. And they must know the way, like Timrin does. It's a very dangerous route. And secret."

"That much is obvious. But why?"

"Because they're all we have," said Jelena angrily. She pulled her hand away from him. "They're our only hope, Richius. The only fighters we have to give you. We protect them here because we can't afford to fight Nar again, not on our own soil."

Suddenly Richius understood. If Nar were to come back as Queen Jelena feared, there was no way they could reach her precious army, not here in remote Karalon. Even the big guns of dreadnoughts would be useless in this rugged terrain of rivers and lagoons. They were probably far from any Lissen city or major waterway, deep inside the folds of the Hundred Isles, where no Naren could ever hope to find them or destroy their last hope for revenge. Richius gave the queen a sympathetic smile, conveying his understanding. They were indeed a beautiful race, these Lissens. And desperate beyond imagining.

"So you keep the men here to protect them," he said.

"Not just men. Women, too. Anyone old enough and willing to serve. This is where we house them. This is where you will train them, make an army out of them. We've brought them here for you, Jackal."

Richius shook his head. "God, the lengths you've gone to, Jelena! First you bring me across the world. And now . . ." He shrugged, unable to find words. "All this. I don't know what to say."

"Say that you were wrong," said Jelena. "Say that we do indeed have an army for you, and that I would never lie to you."

"I'm sorry," Richius offered. "I've been harsh with you. But I was afraid. And now I don't know what to think! This is all so astonishing. All of Liss. It's been so strange for me."

"Stranger than you imagined, I would think," agreed Jelena. "But now there is work to do. And if we're to succeed against our enemies, we must trust each other." Her gaze bore into him. "Can you do that, Richius?"

"I can try," said Richius. "I've already promised I would do my best for you, Jelena. Do not doubt me on that. Now . . ." He looked around. "Where is this army of mine?"

"It's a bad way," Timrin answered unexpectedly. "We have to go slow or we'll bottom out."

"We're not far, Richius," counseled Jelena. "Be patient."

Patience was a virtue Richius had never possessed, but he settled down as best he could, scanning the watery horizon. Around him, he could see only obscure shapes in the darkness, the vague outlines of thin rivers and blowing batches of water grasses. The rowers had stowed their oars and now were propelling the boat through the narrow lane with long, muck-covered poles. The steady sucking sound of mud and water filled the night. Up ahead, barely lit by lantern light, was the growing outline of an island. It was tall and sturdy-looking, with a beach of jagged rocks infested with cattails and sand dunes.

"Is that where we're going?" Richius asked, dreading the answer.

"That is Karalon," replied the queen.

Richius' heart sank. What kind of army could possibly be hidden here? But despite his dismay, the boat continued toward the island. Timrin leaned out over the prow, his arm wrapped around the sternpost, and guided them in. The expert sailors of Liss bested the treacherous shore, slowly piloting in the craft. Beneath them, the hull screeched and groaned as rocks and sand dunes scraped the boat's bottom. Men on both sides of the vessel fought off the encroaching dangers with their poles, snaking their queen safely through. At last the boat came to stop, beaching itself with a lurch. The world fell eerily quiet.

"What now?" asked Richius. "Do we get out?"

Jelena's expression was wicked. "Welcome to Karalon, my hero."

Richius stood up, then helped Jelena to her feet. Timrin and his men shuffled along the deck, spilling out onto the marshy beach and lowering the gangplank for the queen. Other sailors grabbed lanterns from the boat, preparing for the trek in the darkness. Timrin grabbed one, too, and went to his queen.

"My queen, stay close to me," he advised. He was older than she by far, and there was real concern in his voice. For the first time Richius noticed an unhealthy-looking scar across his face, and, remarkably, only one ear. "I don't want anything happening to you," he continued. He put a hand out for his queen. "The way is rocky, so watch your step."

The three departed the vessel, Timrin and Jelena leading the way, Richius following close behind. The air was thick and brackish. Tall patches of cattails tore at them as they walked, hindered by the unstable ground and the constant, gnawing cold. Timrin's lantern shined out a path, guiding them up and over the dune. And when at last he reached the top, he and Jelena paused, looking out over the island. Richius moved to stand with them at the peak. A flat meadow greeted him, dotted with tents and ramshackle structures and burning bright with torches. In the center of the meadow stood a flagstaff, a tall, slightly bowed tower bearing at its zenith the proud, sea-serpent standard of Liss. A giant barracks with a scissor-trussed ceiling stretched in a line toward the horizon, while on the other side of the field was a training ground, flattened to pulpy earth by a thousand booted feet.

Richius stood on the dune, letting the wind lash him, amazed at the encampment.

"This is incredible," he whispered. "This is . . ."

"Your army, Lord Jackal," answered Jelena.

Richius took a deep breath of the brackish air. He saw figures moving through the encampment, men in Lissen garb and women with helmets and long hair. Mostly the fields were deserted, but there was stirring in the camp, faces looking toward them. A buzz was growing. People were pointing toward the hill.

"I want to see them," said Richius. "Right now."

He didn't wait for Timrin or Jelena to lead. He was drawn inexorably down the hillside, stumbling toward the torchlight. The ground sucked at his boots, but he fought the soft earth, part running, part stumbling down the hill. Jelena and Timrin hurried after him. Jelena called out to Richius, bidding him to slow down, but it was as if he were in a tunnel and could not hear her, so spellbound was he by the encampment. Only when he reached the bottom of the giant dune did he finally pause. A figure was coming toward him. A woman. Dressed in a long, ragged coat, she wore no covering over her head, and her hair fell loosely around her shoulders. She was tall and sturdy-looking, with muscled arms and a lean face that stared back at Richius across the night, awed and bewildered. Her wild eyes jumped between Richius and the queen, and then finally came to rest on Richius again, wide with shock. She stopped walking toward him, tried to speak and couldn't, then dropped to her knees in the dirt, bowing deeply.

"It is you," she said over the wind. "Lord Jackal."

Richius stood motionless. Jelena had made it down the slope and was standing next to him, but the strange woman seemed to pay her sovereign no homage at all. The devotion, Richius knew, was all for him. As she knelt before him, she didn't raise her head or risk insulting him with eye contact. When she spoke her voice was thin, almost shaking.

"I prayed you would come, Lord Jackal. I prayed to almighty God you would lead us."

"Lord Jackal?" Richius whispered.

Jelena leaned closer to him, saying in his ear, "That is what they call you here. It's your title. Don't make them change it, I beg you."

The young woman stayed on the ground, keeping her face hidden. She was barely twenty, but her demeanor bespoke something older. Richius studied her uncertainly, unsure how to address her. Behind her, milling around the field, were others like her, young men and women both, all pointing and staring at Richius and their queen. The grounds were quickly swelling with noisy interest.

"Rise, girl," Richius ordered. He went and stood before her, staring down at her. The girl-woman looked up hesitantly. She had the oceanic green eyes of her race and that same, troubled look as Jelena. She was pretty like Jelena, too. Rougher, less coddled-looking than the queen, but attractive nonetheless. "Who are you?" Richius asked. "Tell me your name."

The girl licked her wind-dried lips nervously. "My name is Shii, Lord Jackal. Now leader of Karalon."

"Leader?"

"Forgive me, Lord Jackal," she stammered. "I correct myself. You are leader here. I'm just . . ." She struggled for the right word. "Someone who looks after the others."

"On your feet, Shii of Karalon. No more bowing to me."

The girl looked at him uncertainly. Richius gave her a smile, then offered his hand.

"Take it," he insisted.

She did, and her callused hands were like sand in his fist. This wasn't the pampered touch of a queen anymore. Shii had farmer's hands, the kind of hands that had worked hard. Richius could read her rough history in the leanness of her face. But she rose to her feet with pride and stood before him. Others like her were gathering in the distance. Too shy to step forward, they kept back a good pace, watching their "leader" greet their arriving lord. Some bowed to Richius, some to the queen, but all were amazed at the unexpected visitation. One by one lanterns and candles blinked awake in the buildings. There were dozens of them, then hundreds, all of them young and looking at him with wonder.

"They're so young," Richius remarked softly. "Jelena, why?"

"They are the children of Liss, Richius," said the queen. She didn't come forward to share the adoration, and when she spoke she spoke retiringly, letting him enjoy the moment. "They're here for you, to serve and follow you. Today you are Lord Jackal."

"How many?"

When Jelena didn't reply, Richius turned to Shii. "How many are you?"

"Nine hundred," answered Shii proudly. "Maybe more."

Richius blinked at the number. "That many? Here? On Karalon?"

"Some are still arriving, but yes, Lord Jackal." Shii smiled, pleased at his pleasure. "We've come to follow you. To avenge Liss."

"Oh, but you're children," sighed Richius. He turned and looked at her bright face, so earnest and full of broken promises. "Shii, you're but a girl. You're not over twenty, I can tell."

"I'm almost seventeen," said Shii defensively. "Not such a child, Lord Jackal. And I can fight. I'm not afraid."

"I'm sure you're not," replied Richius. None of them were afraid. Ten years of siege had stripped from them anything remotely like fear. They were bloodthirsty now, carelessly vengeful. "Seventeen," he chuckled. "Like your queen. But where are the older people? I expected grown men here."

Shii looked hurt. "The men who are older serve in the navy. We are what is left to form your army, Lord Jackal. But we are not children. We're grown. We volunteered for this."

"Some of them could have joined Prakna," said Jelena. "There are young men here old enough for that duty. But they chose to fight with you, Richius. They do you honor."

Richius smiled sadly. "They do indeed. Shii, I am honored by you. I am honored by you all." He looked at her with iron eyes. "And I'll do my best for you."

"We need to hear that, Lord Jackal," said Shii. "We have waited so long to greet you. Please don't turn us away."

He put his hand on her shoulder, like he had so many comrades in the past. "You have my promise. And you'll help me keep my vow. I'll need you, Shii. If you're the leader here, there's a lot of work for you to do. I'll need things. And I'll need them fast."

"Tell me anything," said Shii. "I'm yours to command."

"All of them are yours," echoed Jelena. "Look at them, Richius."

Richius looked. He stared past Shii with her eager face, toward all the others like her, gathering quickly in the cold night to glimpse the stranger from Nar. And all Richius could think of was their youth, and all he could feel was their awe. In their eyes was the passion for vengeance that had left them hollow of anything but anger. Like Jelena. Like Prakna. The great disease of all Lissens.

Without waiting for Jelena or the others, Richius walked toward the encampment. He moved into the midst of his waiting army, unsure what to say. As he approached, the gathered fell to their knees. And all at once the night filled with the wondrous sound of a thousand young voices chanting his name.

THIRTY

The Battle of Dragon's Beak

High in a tree, Cackle the raven waited, watching the goings-on below. He had left his mistress Nina long days ago, and had come to this perch to await the duke, his true master, and to do the duke's bidding. It had been a long and arduous siege, but Cackle had been trained from a hatchling to obey, and he moved from branch to branch only to find food for himself, and never to indulge in the normal things a raven might, like breeding. His brain, small though it was, was fixed on a single purpose.

Nina was, the raven supposed, still alone where he had left her. Part of his mind wondered about her. In his many cold hours of idleness, Cackle had flashes of her face, and in that way animals have of worrying, he considered going back for her, to see if she was all right or if the other ravens had harmed her. But his mission was more important. Duke Enli would return, and would be expecting to find him. So Cackle waited, perched not far from where the jaw of the Dragon's Beak split and became two forks, for this he knew was where his master would return from, and Cackle was very dutiful about seeing the duke arrive. For days he had sat atop the tallest tree he could find, enduring the lashing wind and snow, until at last his sharp eyes saw something, large and black, moving toward him and shaking the forest. But the bird still didn't move, not yet. He was still unsure until he saw their fires, which were big and bright. Part of Cackle's primitive brain told him that this was the duke coming home, and he took wing to investigate.

Now that it was nighttime, Cackle had found a new perch. Unobtrusively, he had alighted in a fir tree over the camp of soldiers. They were so numerous, they covered the forest floor like ants, and they had brought machine-things with them, strange and frightening. The other birds and animals had sensed the danger and had fled. Cackle had watched them go. He was not in Dragon's Beak anymore, but rather right on the border, and the river that fed the homeland of his duke was wide here and clear, a gathering place for elk. Men usually avoided this thick part of the woods, but these metal men were without fear. Cackle's eyes narrowed, searching until he found his red-haired master. And when he did, the bird felt satisfaction.

Duke Enli was near one of the great blazes, putting his hands up to the flame. Great puffs of steam drifted from his mouth in the cold. He was eating. There were other men around him, the metal men with their shiny skin. Cackle was right above them now. The raven never took his eyes from his master. And then at last it happened—Duke Enli acknowledged him.

It was only for a moment, but it was enough for the bird to know he had been noticed. Something like a smile crossed the master's lips. And Cackle, cold and satisfied, settled down with a ruffle of his feathers and patiently waited for the duke's summons.

Duke Enli sat by the fire, warming his frozen hands and doing his best not to gaze upward and betray his raven. When he saw Cackle, he smiled to himself. The bird was close by, low enough in the trees to be easily seen. It was late now, and the day of riding had exhausted Enli. All around him, Vorto's legionnaires went through the usual rituals, tending fires and making food, and rolling out beds for the night. The column of soldiers stretched far down the road, disappearing into the dark. Campfires burned all along the roadside. Horses and greegans drank from the river, sating their enormous thirst, and animal tenders covered the steeds with blankets and oiled the leathery hides of the greegans to stave off the skin-cracking cold. On the other side of the road, Enli could see war wagons burdened down with rocket and acid launchers. And the wagon of the poison—the stuff Vorto called Formula B—was positioned safely away from the fires, under heavy guard, patrolled by teams of sword-bearing legionnaires. Without wanting to, Enli's eyes flicked up at Cackle, acknowledging his pet with a blink. Now that the bird was here, Enli could finally relax. Things were going perfectly.

He picked up his plate full of beans and bits of meat and started eating. He was famished from the day's ride and the dreary food was delicious to him. Around him, Faren and the other men ate, too, oblivious to the bird in the trees and listening with disinterest to General Vorto. Vorto had already eaten and was now shaving his head with a straight-razor, dipping the blade periodically into a helmet full of river water. His gleaming scalp froze over with ice crystals in the ungodly wind, but Vorto ignored what should have been painful, carefully cutting down every hair as he spoke.

"... by afternoon," he bragged. "And then on to Gray Tower."

Enli sighed as he ate, barely hearing the general. For weeks now he had endured the same arrogant predictions every night, of how they would first roll into the north fork, taking down Eneas' troops before storming the tower. Vorto was supremely confident of victory, and now, on the eve of battle, he was jubilant. His head shaving, he had explained, was a ceremony.

"I always shave my head before battle," he explained. "It makes me look bigger."

Bigger was one thing the general didn't need to worry about, but he kept up with his ritualistic shave, slowly drawing the razor over his head until it was completely bald and gleamed in the moonlight. As he ate, Enli snickered at Vorto. Over the past month he had grown to hate the general, and was looking forward to killing him. If all went well, Vorto would be dead by this time tomorrow. Enli would be back in Red Tower, and all of Dragon's Beak would be his to rule. Biagio's grand design was coming together flawlessly.

"So, Enli," barked Vorto as he rinsed his head with icy water. "Why so glum? I thought you'd be the most talkative of us all tonight."

The duke swallowed his mouthful of food, trying to think of something to say. He didn't like talking to Vorto. Just looking at him was effort enough. "I think we should be very careful about getting cocky," he said at last. "We're still not in Dragon's Beak yet, General. Who knows what we'll find over the border?"

"Bah," Vorto scoffed. "You worry like an old fishwife, Enli. You should be happy to be home."

The general dried his head with a towel handed to him by his aide, the stoic Colonel Kye. Throughout the journey, Kye had said almost nothing. Of all the legionnaires, Enli liked Kye best. There was something contemplative about the colonel, something genuine. And he wasn't at all like his superior, always spouting holy writ. Kye stood dutifully beside Vorto, waiting for the towel to be handed back. He never ate until the general did. And never did he have a cross word or say anything to hint at his feelings. He was an enigma, this Naren colonel, impossible to read. Still, Enli thought he looked troubled.

"When we're done and I've returned to Nar," the general continued,

"I'm going to sit myself down in a bath full of hot water. And I'm not going to get out of it for days. God, the weather here! You must have skin like a greegan, Enli, to endure such misery."

"It's in the blood, General," Faren piped in. Always eager to defend Dragon's Beak, the soldier never let an insult of his homeland pass unchallenged. "We grow hardy men up here. Not like your legionnaires, too accustomed to the sun all year."

Vorto laughed. "Hardy? Hardy like a maggot, I say. I look forward to wasting Eneas' rabble and being done with it."

"We shall see," said Enli warily. "Tomorrow will tell much. They'll be ready for us, though. We should be prepared. Eneas' men have surely seen us by now."

"No doubt," agreed Vorto. "But it hardly matters. Look around, Enli. We have enough men here to easily best your brother's troops. They'll know that as soon as they look at us. There may be no fight at all." The notion made Vorto frown. "I'd prefer a fight, to be honest. But it's likely we've come this way for nothing. You'll be sitting on your brother's throne by nightfall."

Enli couldn't take it anymore. "You forget the army of the air, Vorto," he said sharply.

"I have not," the general retorted. "I simply have no fear of them. They are birds, and only a fool would be afraid of birds."

The duke smiled. "And you're not a fool, are you, Vorto?"

"No, I am not," declared Vorto proudly. "But I am hungry. Kye, get us some food. I need my strength for the coming day. Meat! Meeeat!"

Kye nodded wordlessly and stalked off to get them both some food. While he was gone, General Vorto sat down with Enli and his men, putting his hands to the fire and grinning like a madman. His enormous shadow fell across Enli's face like an eclipse. Enli watched him in the firelight, eager for the morrow when his ravens would peck out his eyes and send all his legion with him to hell. They were his one, great chance, the ravens. Without them, Enli knew his plan would fail. He hadn't the force needed to defeat Vorto's soldiers, but the army of the air, he knew, could destroy them.

"I'll ride out in the morning and rally my men," said Enli. "Whatever is left of my army, I'll bring to join your legions here."

Vorto shook his head. "No. Ride out and gather your men if you wish, Enli, but I won't wait. I have force enough to show Eneas. And I'm eager to move against him. We don't need your troops to back us up. I doubt that there are many of them left, anyway."

Enli raised his eyebrows, hoping what he heard was true. "You'll push on to Gray Tower, then? Without me?"

"You and what's left of your army can catch up with us. But yes, I intend to drive straight on to Eneas. He will see us from Gray Tower and surrender, I'm sure. And if not . . ." Vorto sighed with pleasure. "So much the better. I will kill him, and all his wretched birds." Then he crossed himself and closed his eyes. "For God," he added. "We do it for God."

Colonel Kye returned with two plates of food. One plate, heaped high with beans and meat, he handed to the general as he sat down. Vorto took up his spoon and began shoveling the hot stew down his throat with remarkable speed, hardly pausing to breathe. After a minute of non-stop eating, he let out an enormous belch. Enli grimaced, disgusted with the company. Not all these Narens were like Vorto, but Enli could still see killing them. Without remorse, he thought of his lead raven in the trees above, and how on the morrow Dragon's Beak would be his. If Grath and the other mercenaries were waiting for him as planned, and if Nicabar had managed to get his dreadnoughts into position, then the day would be interesting indeed.

Drive to Gray Tower, Vorto, thought Enli happily. *Nicabar will see you there.*

Vorto was such a perfect fool.

The next morning, at the first hint of dawn, Enli gathered Faren and the others and made ready for the trip across the border. They would ride just beyond the woods to the village of Larn, where, hopefully, Grath and the mercenaries would be waiting for them. Enli shook off his nervousness as he mounted his horse, desperate to be gone from the camp. The next time he saw the general, he would be a corpse.

"Don't wait for us," Enli told Vorto as he settled into his saddle. "Take your men and head for Gray Tower. We'll catch up. There may not be many of us, but we'll be there."

"Come when you can," Vorto agreed. "We'll try to save something for you."

For a brief second Enli stared into Vorto's eyes, searching for one reason not to kill the man. He found nothing. Vorto stared back at him with a kind of confusion.

"You look afraid, Enli," he observed. "Do not be. We will win your land for you."

The duke smirked. "Yes," he said softly. "Thank you, General."

Enli reined his horse around and rode off, his fellows of Dragon's Beak following. They plunged into the still-dark morning, taking the road toward their homeland and heading toward the south fork, Enli's own fork, where Grath and the Dorians would be waiting for them. None of them spoke as they rode, but Enli could feel the glee of his men, all of them eager to be away from the Narens and to join with their hired brothers. Enli wanted to laugh, but he let only an unseen smile creep beneath his red beard, and when they had ridden for long minutes and were deep in the forest, Enli brought his horse to a sudden stop. Faren and the others did the same. Enli looked over his shoulder and saw nothing but dark forest behind him. Listening, he heard nothing. Satisfied, he gazed heavenward, putting two fingers in his mouth and whistling.

"Cackle!" he cried. "Come to me, my friend. It's safe now!"

His eyes scanned the dark canopy of branches and the spots of sky peeking through. Long seconds passed. His men began to murmur. But Enli was confident, and in a moment a black speck wheeled overhead, becoming ever larger as it spiraled down. Duke Enli thrust out his arm, summoning the creature. Cackle swooped down in a graceful arc, alighting on his master. When he saw Enli's red-bearded grin, the raven laughed.

"Master," it cawed. "Home!"

"Home indeed, my friend," declared the duke. With his free hand he took up the raven and brought it to his face, gazing into its onyx eyes. "You've done well, my beautiful bird," he crooned. "Tell me the others are ready for me. What of my army of the air?"

The raven bobbed its head, its awkward signal for "yes."

"Then we ride," Enli declared. He put the bird on his shoulder and turned to his men. "For Larn, lads. And be quick, like the wind."

Quick they were, riding hard in the growing light, racing down the narrow forest road toward the south fork. There were farms and villages nearby, but Larn was the closest, and as they thundered through the dawn Enli's heart raced, hoping that Grath had indeed bested the troops of his brother and cleared the way for Vorto's run to Gray Tower.

We will drive him to the ocean, thought Enli. *We will drive him there and destroy him!*

Nicabar's dreadnoughts would do the rest. Trapped between the naval guns and the army of the air, Vorto's battalion would be decimated.

"Ride, lads," urged the duke. "We race against time."

The sun was fully up when at last the riders reached the village of Larn. It was a tiny community of farmers and smiths, all nested together in small stone houses. At this time of year, with the cold and snow, Larn was a sleepy bump in the road, barely alive in the choking winter. Enli knew it was the perfect place to hide his army. Being so close to the border, they could strike at the north fork in an hour. As they rode into Larn, Enli called out for his mercenaries.

"Grath!" he shouted. "We are here. We are here!"

He saw his hired soldiers, waiting impatiently on horseback in the center of the village. The people of Larn had shuttered themselves in their homes, giving the warriors full run of their village. There were at least three hundred of them, milling around aimlessly. They were a cruel-looking lot, and in their eclectic armor they seemed like a fractured mosaic of colors and metal, a sea of unruly barbarians. Long spears glinted in the new morning sun and unshaven faces laughed, and when they saw the approaching duke, the mercenaries hardly stirred to attention. Enli raced up to them, looking around for their leader.

"Where's Grath?" he barked. "Tell me!"

Some of the duke's own men, who were mixing within the throng, trotted over quickly to greet him. Yarlyle, a dragon soldier of Red Tower, led the procession. He looked gaunt and worried. Enli glared at him.

"What is it, Yarlyle?" he growled. "What's wrong?"

"My Duke, I'm sorry," the soldier stammered. "Grath isn't here. He is . . ." Yarlyle frowned. "Dead, sir."

"Dead?" blurted Enli. "How?"

"Killed in the fighting?" asked Faren.

"No, sir," said Yarlyle. He addressed Faren directly, who was his superior. "Not in the fighting. He was killed by the beasts, we think. The ravens."

Enli fell back in his saddle with a groan. "Explain it all to me," he ordered. "Quickly, man. I want answers!"

Yarlyle explained how the mercenaries had subdued the north fork. As per Enli's orders, the town of Westwind and all of Eneas' troops had been slaughtered.

"So?" said Enli. "This is good news. What happened to Grath?"

Yarlyle grimaced. "My Duke, I'm sorry, but . . ."

"What?"

"Your daughter," said the man shakily. "Nina. Grath and some others took her to Gray Tower. They did not return."

It took a moment for the words to sink in, and when they did Enli's jaw fell open with a moan. "Nina?" he gasped. "My Nina?"

"Sir . . ."

"Nina! Oh, God, God!" groaned Enli, balling up a fist. It was unthinkable. Faren and the others were speaking, trying to comfort him, but he heard their words as if through a fog.

"You're sure?" he managed. "You have seen her dead?"

"I have not," said Yarlyle. "But truly, it is impossible for her to have lived. The ravens—"

"No!" Enli railed. "They would not have harmed her if Cackle was with her!" He turned angrily toward the bird. "Tell me," he demanded. "Where is Nina, Cackle? Does she live?"

The mention of Nina's name made the raven dance excitedly. "Nina!" he cawed. "Alive! Alive!"

Enli held his breath. Alive! Cackle would know, surely. And if she were alive, there was only one place she could be.

"Good Lord," Duke Enli cried. "Gray Tower."

General Vorto rode at the front of his thousand-man column, resplendent in his armor and newly shaved head. On his back rested his giant war-axe, and in his heart was the need for blood. Colonel Kye rode in silence next to him, brooding over the cold, and beside the colonel trotted a standard-bearer, a proud young man bearing aloft the Light of God, high and white so everyone could see. The sound of snorting horses and clanking armor filled the air, and Vorto could hear the reassuring, grinding din of the war wagons as they rolled forward on their metal tracks. They had set out an hour ago and were making steady progress, having already crossed the border into Dragon's Beak. A peculiar calm lay before them, making the general uneasy. This was the one real road into the north fork. He was sure the inhabitants had spotted them by now. They hadn't reached a homestead yet, but their numbers were too big to conceal, and General Vorto frowned a little in the biting wind.

"We should ride ahead," suggested Kye. "Find out what's waiting for us. Or else wait for Enli to return. He knows the terrain better."

"Look around, Kye," said Vorto. "There's nothing here to threaten us. We go on."

"General, I think—"

"I don't care what you think, Kye. Really, I don't." Vorto didn't like being questioned, especially by Kye, who lately was less loyal than he should be. The general was beginning to think his aide a coward. "We don't need Enli and his dregs. And it looks to me like the fighting's stopped on its own, damn it all to hell."

Kye wasn't convinced. "It's winter," he reminded his superior. "Wars like this aren't fought in the winter. Perhaps they've called a truce until spring. Or perhaps they've seen us, and are laying a trap."

"A trap? With what? Eneas has maybe two hundred men. Probably half that now from the fighting. You worry too much, Colonel. We ride on."

Colonel Kye looked over his shoulder. Their numbers were vast indeed, enough to easily crush Eneas' troops. Yet there was real fear in Kye's expression, and it soured Vorto to see it. The general sighed bitterly, turning on his aide.

"Tell me, Colonel," he said. "What worries you? The ravens?"

"Yes," Kye replied. "And the quiet."

"We carry the Light of God into battle, Kye. Have faith. God will protect us."

"I prefer the protection of my sword, General."

Vorto laughed. "I wear no helmet because I fear nothing, Colonel Kye. I am protected by Heaven. You should have that kind of faith."

"I have instinct," Kye argued. "That serves me well enough, sir."

"Faith, Kye," repeated Vorto. "Faith."

They rode on in silence, and the column behind them ground forward. A snow began to fall, adding to their misery. Slowly at first, it soon quickened into a white fog that whipped at their faces and speckled the road. The horses snorted and greegans honked, but Vorto's legion didn't grumble or complain. The general stuck his face into the wind, smiling.

They are the best, he reminded himself proudly. *They will do as expected.*

But when the snow began to thicken, Vorto himself grumbled. His head was burning from the cold, and Kye was periodically blowing into his hands, trying to warm them. They would need shelter if the storm kept up. Should they stop and make camp? the general wondered. He bit down hard on the notion. No. There was work to do, and do it they would, and so they continued to ride, though the road became slick, and soon they were in a clearing rolling with hills and dotted on the horizon by shabby homesteads and farms. Again Vorto thought to stop, but a happy exclamation from Kye changed his mind.

"There, sir," said the colonel. "Look."

Vorto peered through the wind-blown snow. Across the hills, far off in the distance, stood what looked like a village. From his vantage the place looked decrepit and old, but it was shelter from the storm, and the sight of the village lightened Vorto's mood. He brought up his hand and ordered his column forward.

"Ride with me, Colonel," the general ordered, then spurred his horse on faster, eager to learn what the village could teach him. Colonel Kye snapped his reins and chased after his leader, and soon the pair were far ahead of the others, dashing through the storm toward the collection of broken homes and storefronts. Vorto knew that the people of the village had seen them by now. He expected to find peasants waiting for him when he reached the village, gawking at him in the middle of the avenues. But when he and Colonel Kye rode into the outskirts of the village, he saw no one. Not a single soul was there to greet him, and all the windows of all the shops were tightly shuttered. Vorto suddenly pulled in his reins, abruptly halting his charger. Something in the streets disturbed him.

"What is it?" Kye asked, bringing his own steed to a stop beside Vorto's.

The general stared very hard at the village and its avenues of dirt and gravel, scanning it all with a practiced eye. The snow hadn't been falling very long and still left uncovered patches of earth beneath his feet. There were hundreds of hoof marks in the dirt all around him, the telltale marks of hard riding. And the eerie quiet of the homes spoke to him loudly, reminding him of Goth. He looked around, studying the buildings. There were people inside them, watching him, fearing him.

"They've seen us," he told Kye. "Even now they watch us."

Kye spied the buildings, confused. "It's cold and storming. Maybe—"

"No, Kye. Look at the ground. Horses have been here. Lots of them. Recently, too."

Kye nodded, understanding. "A battle?"

"Maybe. Or maybe they just rode on."

"But where are the soldiers?" Kye asked. "Where are Eneas' men?"

Vorto chewed on the question for a long time. Defeated, maybe? Had Enli's men been that good? Had they already won? The general looked around suspiciously, unsure what to think or say. He listened to the snow falling, listened to the wind. He needed answers but the town wasn't talking.

Angry, he rode deeper into the village and drove his horse right up to the door of a storefront. Kye followed, confused. The general dismounted and unstrapped the battle axe from his back. Without asking why, Kye drew his own weapon, a thin sword of polished steel. Vorto didn't wait for anyone to answer the door. He didn't even knock. Instead he lifted up a heavy boot and slammed it into the door, kicking it open in an explosion of splinters. There was a scream from inside and the cry of a child. Vorto clasped his hands firmly around his axe and stepped inside the darkened home.

"In the name of Archbishop Herrith, come out!" he bellowed. "I order it!"

There was more worried gibbering from the shadows. Vorto's eyes adjusted to the light.

"I am General Vorto of Nar!" he roared. "Come out now, or face my judgment!"

At last there was movement from a darkened corner. A cowering figure appeared in a doorway, followed by two more. It was a man, a farmer from the looks of him, and his wife and daughter. All of them looked at Vorto fearfully. The child, barely past toddling, clutched at her mother's dress.

"Come here," Vorto ordered, trying to sound mild. He lowered his axe just enough to encourage them. "All of you."

The man led his little family out of their hiding place and into the center of the room. He averted his eyes, looking down at his feet. Vorto studied them all quickly, and, realizing they were no threat, took a step closer. The girl with the wild eyes cried when she saw his face, bursting into tears. Frantically her mother tried to calm her.

"Be easy," Vorto told them. "You'll not be harmed. I am General Vorto, supreme commander of the legions of Nar."

The farmer grimaced. "Yes, sir," he said meekly. "We've done nothing wrong, sir. I swear it. We were just afraid. All of us in the village. Just afraid."

"Afraid of what?" Vorto asked. "Enli's men?"

"Yes, sir," said the man. He finally looked up at Vorto, brightening. "You've come to help us against them? Enli's mercenaries?"

Vorto blinked. Unsure how to answer, he simply said nothing. He gave a questioning look to Kye, who returned it with equal confusion. A terrible feeling of dread quickly swept over the general.

"What mercenaries?" he asked. "What are you talking about?"

"Dorians," said the man nervously. He patted his daughter's head to quiet her. "Fighting alongside Enli's dragon troops from Red Tower. Hundreds of them."

Colonel Kye groaned. "My God . . ."

"Tell me everything," Vorto insisted. "What happened here?"

Suddenly the farmer seemed as confused as they were, but he explained how Duke Enli's men had invaded, killing Duke Eneas, and how the north fork had been ruined. The mercenaries, he said, had slaughtered Westwind, a town just outside of Gray Tower.

"There's nothing left of Duke Eneas' army," said the man. "Maybe the ravens still live, I don't know. But we've been afraid to leave our homes. There's no one to defend us now. And if the mercenaries come back . . ."

Vorto put up a hand to silence him. He needed to think, to decipher this puzzle Enli had laid at his feet. He felt warm suddenly, flush with fear.

"Clever beast," he whispered.

Enli had lured nearly a thousand legionnaires away from Nar City. Now they were trapped on this peninsula, miles from home, with winter bearing down on them. Dorian mercenaries, too. The general ran a hand over his bald scalp nervously.

"Kye," he said simply. "We're in trouble."

"We should hold up here," said the colonel quickly. "Make a stand against them."

It was a good idea, but not good enough.

"No," said Vorto. "We need a better place to fight from." Quickly he turned again to the farmer, demanding, "Gray Tower. Is it undefended?"

"I don't know," stammered the man. "I think so."

"That's it, then," said the general. He grabbed hold of Kye's shoulder, spinning him toward the door. "Quickly, Kye. We have to move."

• • •

Duke Enli rode like a madman through the gathering storm, loudly exhorting his men to follow. Three hundred strong, they galloped along the slick road, through the howling wind and driving snow, to the north fork of Dragon's Beak and the waiting forces of Nar. Faren rode beside him, and Cackle the raven wheeled above, leading them deeper into the unknown. Enli's beard was stiff with snow and frozen spittle. At his side his long sword slapped, eager for blood. The hot flesh of his horse steamed in the cold, run to a lather in the duke's zeal. They had long ago crossed the border and had already galloped through the first village. As Faren had predicted, it was shut up tight, and they hadn't bothered to stop for rest or information. Enli had known from the newly disturbed snow that Vorto had already passed through the village. He could see the wide tracks the war wagons had cut through the ice and the obvious prints of galloping horses. Vorto's men had moved quickly.

He has discovered me, thought Enli nervously. *He knows we have trapped him.*

Now he would go to Gray Tower to make his stand. Enli cursed himself, hating his arrogance. If Nina was still alive, she would certainly be there waiting for him. Vorto would discover her and . . .

Unable to bear the thought, he banished it from his mind. With ferocious single-mindedness he grit his teeth, refusing to accept defeat. If Nina still lived, he would rescue her. He would, and no one—not even Vorto—would stop him.

They were in a meadow now, wide and white with snow. The trail they were following was almost invisible, blanketed in ice, and the winds howling off the hills tore through their garments and dug at their skin, eating it alive. Enli's face burned with pain. If he could have seen his nose, he knew it would be black with frostbite. Great gushing tears poured from his eyes to stave off the wind, and his fingers bled beneath his gloves. Worse, his Dorians and dragon troops were faring no better. They rode with him because they knew they must, and because Vorto would turn on them all if their trap failed. But they were weary now from riding, hungry and unbearably cold. And Enli didn't know what they would be facing. He knew only that his daughter, whom he still called a daughter despite all evidence, was in desperate trouble, and that the love he had for her could make him endure any cold.

What seemed like an eternity passed in the storm. And then through the gales Enli saw the moving horde of Vorto's troops. He raised his hand, bringing his column to a halt. The Light of God flew above the legion. A dozen war wagons pulled by giant greegans trudged along, and the horses drove on, undaunted, toward Gray Tower. They were very close to the tower now. Enli could see the first inklings of it from his place atop a hill. But the ocean beyond was hidden, and he could not tell if Nicabar and his dreadnoughts were positioned there as promised.

The duke rubbed his hands together, desperate for a plan. They were woefully outnumbered. And if Vorto saw them first, they would be slaughtered. To Enli's mind, there was only one hope.

"Call the ravens," said Faren desperately, as if reading the duke's mind. "Do it now, before they see us."

"Aye," agreed Enli. It would only take a moment for Vorto's legion to discover them, and time was their enemy now. He stretched out his arm toward the sky, shouting, "Cackle! To me!"

The bird, who had been circling overhead, now swooped down to rest on Enli's arm. Enli looked at the raven desperately.

"I need you now, my friend," he said. "Call your brothers. Bring them here and attack our enemies. Kill, Cackle! Kill!"

He snapped his arm and sent Cackle winging skyward. The bird hurried into the storm, sailing toward the western horizon and Gray Tower. Enli watched him go, licking his lips with worry. A thousand yards away, he saw Vorto's legion coming to an unexpected stop.

"There they are!" seethed Vorto, pointing eastward. "There they are!"

Through the gauzy snowfall he had sighted them, waiting on an eastern hillside. There were three hundred, he supposed. Maybe more. And Dorians, just as the farmer had claimed. Vorto could tell by their haphazard colors that they were indeed mercenaries. Among them was a sprinkling of Enli's dragon troops, dressed in spiky armor and bearing the reptilian helmets of their ilk. One by one, the heads of Vorto's legion turned eastward to see their enemy. The column came to an abrupt halt.

"We have them now," Vorto laughed delightedly. He shook his fist in the air, hoping Enli could see him. "I have you, you traitorous dog! You're no match for us!"

He was glad he had brought so many men with him, glad he had war wagons and acid launchers for the fight. Enli had miscalculated the force he would bring, and it would be the duke's undoing.

"Stupid, stupid man," said Vorto. "Today you die."

Vorto looked around quickly, studying the terrain. They were in a snow-covered valley between the hills, wide out in the open with plenty of room to maneuver. That, along with their sheer numbers, gave them the advantage.

"This will be our battlefield, Kye," he said. "We will fight here!"

"Sir, they won't attack us," said the colonel. "When the mercs realize how many we are, they will retreat."

"Then we will run them down, Colonel Kye! For God and country, we shall destroy them! Make your men ready. This is why we've come so far!"

Without wasting another word, General Vorto thundered eastward, toward the hill where his enemies waited, and shook his giant fist again and cursed all manner of creatures in the name of God. He was possessed now, frozen to the bone and full of violence. And when he had separated himself from his legion, standing apart so he was easily seen, he spun his horse around and addressed them.

"We have been deceived, my men!" he cried. "But our true enemy shows himself! There, on yonder hill! Duke Enli!"

The legion of Nar let out a battle cry, pushing back the storm with their fury. General Vorto unstrapped the gleaming battle axe from his belt and brandished it.

"We have come to fight!" he shouted. "Are you ready?"

Another cheer, bold and bloody, rose up from the ranks. Swords leapt from scabbards and banged against shields in an anxious drumbeat. Greegans honked, filling the air with a prehistoric noise, and battle-ready horses pranced, eager to take their riders to the fight. Colonel Kye rode through the soldiers, shouting orders and positioning his battalions. War wagons circled around to flank the men, readying their acid launchers. Formula B, that noxious stuff that could kill them all, was in the center of the crowd, still heavily guarded by a troop of brawny soldiers. Vorto smiled, proud of his men. They wouldn't need the formula today. Today it would be old-fashioned steel.

He turned back to the hillside. Enli and his men were still there. Surprised they hadn't run yet, Vorto waved at them.

"Can you see me, Enli?" he shouted. "I'm going to kill you!"

There was a speck on the hill that looked vaguely like the duke. Vorto could just make out the hint of a red beard. As he shouted, the speck stared back at him, resolute, unmoving. Vorto took it as an insult.

"Brave bastard, aren't you?" he muttered. "We shall see about that."

"Good God!" someone cried.

Vorto whirled. He looked out over his men, confused, then noticed they were all staring westward. The general's eyes narrowed on the horizon. Something gigantic was moving toward them, a storm cloud maybe, big and black. Over the wind he heard a high-pitched tremor, like a thousand squeaky hinges opening. The thing that approached was moving quickly, too animated to be a storm, and far too loud to be a thunderhead. All at once Vorto's soldiers pointed skyward, gibbering and terrified. The general himself sat upon his horse, dumbfounded by what he was seeing. If the ocean were black and could fly, the thing would be a tidal wave.

"Mother of God," he whispered. "What in hell is that?"

But he knew what it was, and the revelation made him wither. The army of the air was winging toward him, filling the world with its horrible noise, bearing down on them with sharpened talons. Vorto crossed himself, begging God for strength. Never in all his imaginings had he considered anything like this. He rode back to his men, flailing his arms to get their attention.

"Be easy!" he ordered, hoping to steady them. "They are only birds! We will fight them! And we will win!"

Yet even as he made his claim, Vorto doubted its likeliness. The rapidly approaching beasts were like something from Hell, huge in the extreme and winged like demons. The air throbbed with their cries.

Determined not to die like a coward, General Vorto wrapped his fists around his axe handle and waited for his enemies to descend.

From his place atop the hill, Duke Enli watched the ravens fill the sky and fall upon the unprotected Narens. It was a horror to behold, and of such great pleasure to Enli that he could not help but grin. The ravens, he knew, would decimate the brigade, no matter how many or how well armed. They were in the open, easy prey for the flying monsters despite their metal armor, and would be driven one by one to their knees until the beasts pulled their helmets off and ate their eyeballs out. Duke Enli put his hands to his frostbitten nose. It had gone numb.

"My God," whispered Faren. The soldier's face was drawn with shock. "God help those poor wretches."

"What?" joked Enli. "God is on their side, remember? Surely He will help them."

"Should we attack?" asked one of the mercenaries. "Drive them to the tower?"

"No need," said Enli. "We'll let the ravens pick them clean first. Then we will go to the tower—alone."

And find Nina, he hoped. Vorto was the only thing blocking him from his daughter. Duke Enli grit his teeth, worried about the girl. He loved her truly, and to think of her gone was untenable. So instead he focused on the melee at his feet, pushing the ghastly image of a dead daughter from his mind, and hoped against hope that she still lived, and that these ravenous birds hadn't gotten her.

"Please God," he whispered. "Let her be all right."

Or maybe it was as Vorto claimed, that God only heard the prayers of the faithful. If God was truly Vorto's God, Enli knew his daughter was doomed.

Colonel Kye was in a panic. The sky had turned black and the earth was shaking, and all he could feel was the scrape of talons against his body and the insistent hammering of knifelike beaks. He was still on his horse, though only barely, and the thickness of feathers had blinded him so that he couldn't tell where Vorto was or even if the general still lived. All around him, men were shouting and swinging swords uselessly, and the ground was littered with fallen horses, their bellies picked apart by beaks. Kye had dropped his own sword and was using his hands to shield his helmeted head. As he rode through the insanity he felt the nutcracker jaws of the ravens chewing at his fingers, trying to pry them loose. He wanted to scream but could not, for there was precious little breath in him to waste.

Kye's horse stumbled through the snow, unsure where to go. The colonel tried to steer it westward, toward the distant tower and, maybe, to safety. But the ground was choked and slick with ice. His horse faltered. Ravens screamed everywhere, and as he moved amidst the battle, Kye heard the cries of tortured men as the birds somehow managed to pull off helmets and feast on the flesh beneath.

Fighting was useless; Kye knew that now. He had to call retreat, try and make it to Gray Tower. And then another thought occurred to him, a dark thought that made his insides curdle. The formula. If its cannisters were damaged . . .

"General!" Kye screamed. "Where are you?"

He swatted his way through the ravens, searching for Vorto. At last he found the general, near the wagons with the cannisters, desperately trying to retrieve a discarded helmet from the ground. Kye caught a glimpse of Vorto's bare head, now scarred horribly and bleeding. The colonel steered his frenzied horse up to the general.

"General!" he cried, offering his hand. "It's Kye! Take my hand. We have to retreat!"

Vorto was in a daze. His bloodshot eyes blinked at Kye through the slits in the helmet. On wobbly legs he moved forward, grabbing the colonel's hand and letting him pull him up onto the horse. Kye's charger whinnied under the weight but didn't stumble or throw them.

"To the tower," Vorto seethed. "We have to get to the tower."

"Sir, the formula. We can't—"

"I've already told the others to guard it," wheezed Vorto. "Once we reach the tower, we can launch the poison against the beasts. God, Kye, call retreat. Hurry!"

Seeing Vorto's weakened state, Colonel Kye took up command, waving his hands and crying out to his men. "Retreat!" he bellowed. "To the tower!"

Admiral Danar Nicabar was weary.

For five days now, he and his small fleet of dreadnoughts had been anchored off the coast of Nar, taking up positions within range of Gray Tower. It was tedious, boring work, and Nicabar felt useless, as if the entire world was somewhere else, living its life while he was stuck in this frozen wasteland. An arctic wind blew across the deck of the *Fearless*, biting through the admiral's long coat. Snow had been falling for over an hour, cutting down his visibility, but he kept an eye glued to his spyglass, hoping vainly to see something interesting. On the deck beneath him, the big cannons of his flagship were trained on the tower, primed and ready to fire. *Black City* and *Intruder* were also in position, to the flagship's bow and stern. They had the ancient tower in their sights, in an inescapable cross fire that would bring it crumbling down, and Nicabar was anxious to give the order. But so far, Vorto hadn't shown.

"Don't cheat me, General," said Nicabar to himself. "I've come a long way for this, you big bastard."

He had endured the cold and the long voyage, lived through the tedium without losing his mind, and all for the simple pleasure of blasting Vorto to Hell. As he stared through his spyglass, he wondered what might have happened to the Naren. Maybe Enli's schemes had been discovered. But Nicabar had seen the ravens take flight an hour ago. Surely they were on their way. Gray Tower was the only cover for Vorto's men. He *would* order them there. Nicabar was sure of it.

"Call down to the gun deck," he said to a boatswain. "Have them check the azimuths on the cannons. I don't want any mistakes."

"Sir, they've been checked," said the sailor. "Just a moment ago."

"Well, check them again!" Nicabar growled, sending the young man off in a scurry. The admiral lowered the spyglass and collapsed it with a curse. No one knew the pressure he was under, the enormous strain of their mission. If it worked, Vorto would be dead, along with a goodly chunk of his army. What was the matter with all these fools, not to see the importance of it? Nicabar shook his head. He had already had so many disappointments in his career, had seen the loss of the Empire to Herrith and lost a ten-year battle against Liss. Now, on the eve of Vorto's destruction, he couldn't bear the thought of failing again. All he needed was a little luck, and for Vorto to have the common sense to come in out of the rain.

A sudden shout from the rigging grabbed the admiral's attention. He snapped his spyglass open again and peered through the whiteout engulfing Gray Tower. For a moment he saw nothing and swore at the lookout in the masts, but then his vision cleared and something came to his eyes, something big and moving ponderously. Something black and armored.

"Vorto," Nicabar hissed triumphantly. "Welcome to Gray Tower."

He turned to his sailors, who were awaiting his commands. "Make ready," he said happily. "Tell the gunnery deck to prepare to fire. Signal *Black City* and *Intruder*. And no one fires till I give the order. This one is all mine."

. . .

Vorto and his men reached Gray Tower through a haze of shock and blood, kicking open the gates of the keep and barreling inside. They had lost many men, so many Vorto couldn't count. All that he knew was that he'd left behind a trail of lacerated bodies stretching from the battlefield to the tower. They had abandoned the greegans in the frenzy, leaving the war wagons and acid launchers to Duke Enli, a tactical blunder which might well come back to haunt them. But they had managed to save the Formula B. The wagon containing the super-poison was intact, along with a single, modified launcher. Now, as his men piled into the keep, Vorto ordered his soldiers to unload the cannisters of Formula B, even as the monstrous birds continued their endless assault. They were crashing against the windows now, breaking the glass and tearing at the shutters. The entry hall of Gray Tower echoed with their cries. Vorto and Colonel Kye hurried the men inside, urging those unloading the poison to hurry.

"Quickly now!" Vorto roared through the open door. He had picked up a sword and was swatting at the beasts buzzing around him like giant wasps. Kye was tending to the wounded, fretting over their dwindling numbers. The casualties had been unbelievably high. Even now, just outside the courtyard, Vorto could see some of his men being dragged off, pulled into the storm by the impossibly strong birds. Knowing they had to shut the doors quickly, he dashed outside to help unload the formula. The wagon was covered with squawking ravens, violently biting and scratching at his men, denting helmets with their iron beaks. Vorto threw himself onto the wagon, crushing a raven beneath his boots and grinding it to pulp. There were only two of the cannisters left to unload, so the general wrapped his arms around one of them and lifted it with a grunt, ignoring the ravens covering him and clawing at his helmet. Blood from his previous wounds spilled into his eyes, blinding him. He could hear Kye's voice, encouraging him forward. Next to him, two others were manhandling the last cannister into the keep. A raven seized on his helmet just as he staggered into the keep. The doors shut loudly behind him and Vorto dropped the cannister, then reached up with his bare hands, pulling the bird from his shoulders and strangling it with a scream, snapping its neck.

"Damn you!" he roared, tossing the carcass against the wall. "Damn you to Hell!"

Vorto collapsed to the floor, his whole body battered. He tore off the pitted helmet and tossed it aside, then ran his hands over his scalp to feel his hundred wounds. All around him men were groaning, wide-eyed with shock. Quickly Vorto counted up their numbers. There were at least a hundred of them in the hall.

A hundred. He closed his eyes in grief. So few. So many more lay dead outside, a feast for the demon-birds. They were trapped here now, with no hope of escape save for the formula, and Duke Enli and his mercenaries would soon be circling outside, making demands. Vorto balled up a fist and slammed it against the floor.

"We're not done yet," he hissed. "Kye, have some of the men search this place, anyone who can walk. I want all the windows closed and shuttered. Doors, too. Barricade them fast. And find any weapons you can." He looked around the bleak chamber, realizing only now that not all the bodies in the hall were Naren. There had been a slaughter here, just like he had seen in Westwind, the little town below the tower. "God condemn your soul to Hell, Enli," he said, examining the ruined hall. "Hurry now, Kye. We don't have much time."

"General, sir?" came a voice from across the hall. "Look at this!"

Vorto looked up, blinking the blood from his eyes. He saw a man at the end of the hall, one of his soldiers, with another figure next to him. Vorto blinked again, unsure what he was seeing. A woman?

"What the hell . . . ?"

The soldier dragged the woman forward, shoving her toward Vorto. She was hissing like a snake. The general got unsteadily to his feet and studied her. Kye did the same, and soon all the men in the hall had their eyes on the woman.

"Who are you?" Vorto demanded.

"Be damned!" the woman spat.

Vorto's hand shot out and slapped her across the face, sending her tumbling backward. Vorto stalked after her, taking her jaw in his hand and squeezing until she screamed.

"I am in no mood for games, wench. Tell me who you are, or I will throw you out a window for those birds to eat."

"Nina," she choked. "My name's Nina. I'm—"

"Enli's daughter!" Vorto released her at once. "What are you doing here, girl? Are you alone?"

She grit her teeth in defiance, but a threatening, raised hand from Vorto loosened her tongue. "Yes," she said. "I'm alone. I came here looking for something and got trapped here."

Vorto stepped back with a malicious grin, his mind racing with an idea. "Kye, I think we have a weapon here."

Duke Enli and his band of mercenaries had chased the Narens into Gray Tower, a contingency that now had the duke frantic. Just outside the courtyard, his men began to circle the tower, milling around on its eastern face where the gates were and where the ravens now rested, full of blood and waiting for their prey to re-emerge. Enli fretted as he galloped through the group, unsure what to do. Gray Tower was locked up tight, and though Vorto's ranks had been decimated, they suddenly had the advantage of the fortress. They also had the formula, a secret weapon the duke had not told his men about. But he was too desperate to call retreat now. Especially if Nina was inside.

Through the storm, he could see Nicabar's dreadnoughts floating threateningly on the horizon. He wondered if Vorto had noticed them yet. He wondered also if he needed to signal the admiral, or if Nicabar would simply open fire. Enli cursed, wringing his frostbitten hands. His mercenaries wanted to fall back, to let the *Fearless* and her sisters finish what they'd started. There was a murmur of dissent from the men as they milled about the courtyard. Duke Enli ignored it, trying to focus on saving his daughter. If she was alive, then Vorto had probably discovered her by now. The general would have terms, surely.

"Son of a bitch," muttered Enli, watching the tower's windows for a sign. "What are you waiting for, Vorto?"

Faren, slick with snow and mud, rode up to his master and gave him a disapproving scowl. "We must go, Duke Enli," he insisted. "If the ships open fire, we're done for!"

"We stay," growled the duke. "I won't leave Nina."

"You don't even know if she's alive," said Faren. "Please, listen to me. Let the ravens guard the tower. Vorto won't dare try to escape. And we can't do anything to signal Nicabar. We have to go!"

"No!" roared Enli, turning fiercely on his man. "We stay until I know she's not in there! I won't—"

"Enli, you hellspawn!"

The duke looked skyward, amazed to hear his name. Up on one of the balconies a door had opened, revealing a fist-shaking figure.

Vorto.

The general's head was pitted with cuts and bleeding badly, and he had a woman in his arms. Enli gasped when he saw her.

"Oh, God," he groaned. "Nina . . ."

At Nicabar's orders, the signalmen on the deck of the *Fearless* waved their flags at *Black City* and *Intruder*, giving the go-ahead to fire. All along the flagship, sailors braced themselves for the coming concussions, stuffing balled-up fabric in their ears and holding tight to rigging and rails. Admiral Nicabar lowered his spyglass confidently, sure that all of Vorto's soldiers were trapped inside the tower by now. He would give one warning shot to let Enli's men get clear—then he would pulverize Gray Tower.

"I have waited a long time for this," he said to his lieutenant, a young man who had spent the last hour standing next to him. "One shot to start, high across the tower. Let's make Vorto know we're here. Give the order, please, Lieutenant."

The young man shouted the order down the line. Nicabar folded his arms across his chest, waiting for the fireworks to start.

"What do you want?" Enli called up to Vorto. He was desperate to deal, certain he was running out of time. "Tell me and I will consider it!"

"First, call those beasts away!" demanded Vorto. He had Nina in a headlock, one massive arm wrapped around her neck. She struggled to free herself from the unbreakable grip. "Then we'll talk! Not before, traitor! You know I have the formula. Meet my demands, or I'll use it, I swear!"

Enli considered the ultimatum. He wasn't at all sure if Vorto was bluffing, but he knew the risks the formula posed to them all, even the general. Trapped within the tower, the poison might easily kill them, too. The duke cringed, knowing he had no choice, but before he could speak he saw a gigantic flash of light from far off behind the tower . . .

. . . and then heard the thunderous report.

Overhead, a funnel of flame blasted by, scorching the top of the tower and burning back the storm. The sky opened in a world-shaking boom. Enli's horse reared up in a panic, sending the duke tumbling to the ground, and all around him the steeds broke out in a frenzy, snorting and whinnying uncontrollably. The men began to shout. Faren was looking around, astonished. Enli gazed up to the balcony. Vorto, completely in shock, was craning his neck to peer at the horizon. Even in the snow the general looked white with terror.

"The dreadnoughts!" Faren called to Enli. "They're firing! Sir, we must leave! Now!"

Enli was in a fugue. "Nina," he said blankly. "My God, I have to save her."

Faren grabbed the duke's sleeve, trying desperately to pull him to safety. "No, sir!" he shouted. "There's nothing to be done for her! Come on!"

"Go, Faren!" cried Enli, snapping free of the man's grasp. "Go and get to safety. All of you! I have to find Nina!"

There was another blast, shattering the sky, and this one was close enough to feel. Enli's nose now burned with a sudden heat as the plume from the flame cannon smashed against a tower wall, wrapping around it like a hand. Two more detonations followed directly. Enli's head rang with their roars. He grabbed Faren's shoulders and shook his friend, demanding his attention.

"Hurry, Faren," he insisted. "Take the others and get back to Red Tower."

Faren's face collapsed with grief. "My Duke . . ."

"Do it!" screamed Enli. With all his strength he pushed Faren toward the woods, then turned and ran toward the barred gates of Gray Tower.

Inside the hall, Colonel Kye could hardly believe his bleeding ears. The place had become a chamber of echoes, so loud and painful Kye thought his teeth would rattle from his jaw. His already wounded men were beginning to vomit from the pressure, hardly able to get to their feet as the barrage hammered their haven and made the walls shake. Vorto hadn't returned from the top of the tower, and Kye wondered if he would at all. He recognized the sound of naval guns and knew they were in a cross fire. Weakly, his head swimming with pain, he put his hands over his ears and got to his feet.

"We have to get out of here!" he shouted, hoping his men could hear him. He gestured to the doors they had barricaded. There was a desperate thumping from the other side. Unbelievably, someone was trying to get *in*. A pair of legionnaires stumbled forward and began removing the piled furniture from the doorway. Two more blasts rocked the tower. Kye went to join them, to help free them all from their deathtrap, then noticed the teetering cannisters of poison. With each cannon shot the cannisters shivered a little more, threatening to pop their seals. Kye stared at them, not knowing if he should touch them or not. The ceiling overhead began to crumble, shaking down gritty dust and pieces of plaster. The pressure in the hall continued to grow with each blast, louder and louder, until the colonel felt himself blacking out with pain.

Shaking off the agony, he threw himself toward the doors, digging his fingernails into the cracks to open them. His men were grunting and cursing, pulling away the heavy barricades and lowering the wooden bar stretched across the threshold. The banging at the doors continued. Kye heard a desperate voice outside, begging them to open up. When the last of the locks was unbolted, he threw open the doors and was almost barreled over by Enli.

"My daughter!" cried the duke. "Where is she?"

"Get out, you fool!" Kye hissed.

Outside, he could see the deserted courtyard in flames. The horsemen had fled and the ravens had scattered to the winds. The air glowed orange as the naval guns bombarded them, tossing scalding streams of molten fire into the yard and making the granite foundation quake.

Duke Enli heard nothing of Kye's warning. He pushed past the colonel, stumbling through the hall and the crowds of wounded men, now dragging themselves to safety outside.

"Get out, all of you!" Kye clamored. He helped his men to their feet, pushing them toward the door, keeping one eye on the unstable cannisters as he worked. They were metal, he reminded himself. Surely they would hold. But the unbelievable noise had done something to them. Each bombardment made them resonate, loud and louder, until they now sounded like a nest of angry bees. As the tower rocked, so did the cannisters.

Colonel Kye worked like one possessed, desperately helping his wounded men to safety.

High up in the shaking tower, General Vorto stumbled down the stairs, the girl still in his arms. She was biting and kicking but his choke hold was weakening her, and he was determined not to let his only chance at survival slip away. The endless blasts from Nicabar's dreadnoughts had blown off the roof of the tower, and half the stairway stood exposed to the sky, letting wind rush in with the heat from the cannon blasts. A red flash blew by overhead, making him duck. The stairway shook, jarring his knees. Through the ruined wall he could see the *Fearless* in the distance and knew that Nicabar had come to kill him.

"Let me go!" the girl screamed, wheezing in his hold. She drove her booted feet into his armored shins to free herself. Vorto flexed his biceps to still her, almost snapping her neck.

"You little bitch," he sneered. "I'm going to make your father pay for you!"

His head swam and his face burned from cannon blasts, and the stone risers beneath his feet buckled, threatening to give way. He had barely taken three more steps when he noticed Enli rushing up to greet him.

"Vorto!" cried the duke. "Put her down!"

"Not another step, Enli!" warned Vorto. "Or God help me, I'll snap her like a twig."

"There's no time for this, you idiot. Let her go and we'll both escape. The dreadnoughts—"

"You ordered the dreadnoughts here, you treacherous dog! I came here to help you and this is what you've done! You've ruined us!"

"We can live," argued Enli. "Just put my daughter down."

Vorto shook his head, but before he could speak the girl in his arms slammed an elbow into his jaw, making him stagger. She tumbled out of his arms and down the stairs toward Enli. A cannon blast detonated against the tower, enveloping Vorto in a dazzling heat. When he could see again, he realized suddenly that his armor was smoking. A great pain seized him, a searing of skin and eyeballs. Enli and the girl were looking at him in shock. Vorto screamed in agony as his whole body exploded with fire, covered with the burning fuel from a flame cannon. He staggered down toward Enli, cursing.

"God damn you!" he roared.

Another blast cut off his words. It skimmed the top of Vorto's bald head, blowing out his brains.

"Daughter!" Enli cried. He was blinded by the blast, unable to see her through the orange haze. "Where are you?"

"Father?" came a thin reply. Nina's voice reached him out of the confusion, weak and unsteady. "Father, where are you? I can't see you."

Enli groped along the shaking staircase, blinking against tears and smoke. His own skin was horribly burned. He could feel it through his icy numbness, like acid eating up his flesh. Each step was an agony, but he moved swiftly, dreading what he would find when the smoke cleared.

"I'm here, daughter," he gasped. "I'm coming for you."

The stairway was in flames. Vorto's decapitated body slid down past him. As the smoke and fire cleared, Enli found his daughter. He let out a sigh of relief and scooped her into his arms.

"I've got you!" he told her. "Don't be afraid."

Nina's blond head bobbed. Her eyes opened for a brief moment; she was feather-light in his arms.

"Father," she moaned. "Am I hurt?"

Enli looked at Nina and discovered with horror that her legs were gone, blown off at the thighs and gushing blood. Enli's knees buckled. He fell to the ground with his daughter in his arms.

"You're my daughter," he cried. "*My* daughter. Mine!"

Nina shuddered. "Is it the truth?"

Duke Enli stared at the girl he had called his daughter, the beautiful young thing so much like the woman he had loved. She was very much like her. And his brother.

"Yes," he lied to her. "You are my daughter. Mine alone, Nina."

"Father?" Nina whispered. "I'm still alive. I'm . . ."

Dead.

Enli screamed. All of Dragon's Beak would have heard his cry, but a jagged bolt of orange lightning slammed into the tower, silencing him forever.

Colonel Kye had almost evacuated all his men when the ceiling collapsed.

He lay beneath a bone-crushing slab of granite, his legs shattered, his vision blurred, and watched through angry tears as the cannisters of Formula B shuddered and hissed, ready to breach. The vibrating containers filled the chamber with a high-pitched drone, glistening with dew as the poison inside them heated and stirred, becoming ever more unstable. Outside, his men were hurrying to escape the relentless bombardment. He heard their screams as they cooked in their armor and clawed their way desperately across the yard. But Colonel Kye knew that he was a dead man. The cannisters were just out of reach, and even if he could touch them he didn't know how to stop the reaction setting them off. He cursed, hating life in that instant, hating everything he had ever done for Nar and its indulgent rulers. His life had been a waste.

"Dear God," he prayed. "I am a sinner. If you exist at all, forgive me."

And then the cannisters lost their tenuous cohesion, springing leaks one by one and spewing forth a pestilent vapor.

Colonel Kye shut his eyes, happy to die.

After nearly half an hour of bombardment, Nicabar finally gave the order to stop firing. His signalmen along the *Fearless* passed the order to the other dreadnoughts, and the world fell eerily silent. Nicabar pulled the tiny balls of fabric from his ears as the smoke cleared. The snow had stopped but the wind was still fierce. A long gale brushed away the last remnants of smoke, until at last Nicabar could see the damage he had wrought.

Gray Tower was a smoking skeleton. Nothing living moved along its courtyard, not even the ravens. Nicabar's first feeling was pride. But then it turned to puzzlement. Surely he couldn't have destroyed *everything*? And everyone? He snapped open his spyglass and peered toward the tower. Truly, it was demolished. Great fissures gutted the place and the walls were crumbling and smudged with blast marks. But in the courtyard lay an astonishing number of corpses. Ravens rested among the dead, unmoving, littering the white snow, and men that should have made it easily to safety sat frozen on the ground, stiff with death. The bodies of fallen horses dotted the courtyard, not blown to bits by the cannons or pulled to pieces by the birds. To Nicabar's eye, they looked strangely intact.

But when he saw a wisp of green fog, he understood.

"Holy Mother," he whispered. Then, exploding into action, he screamed, "Hoist anchor! Get us out of here! Right god-damn now!"

The bombardment had released the formula. Vorto had actually been fool enough to bring it here! Nicabar ran across his deck, shouting for his men to hurry and hoping the wind wouldn't carry the gas to them. Across the flagship sailors snapped into action, making ready to get the behemoth moving. They had to hurry, Nicabar knew, before any of the poison could reach across the ocean.

But he would be back. He would give the gas time to dissipate, a week maybe, but he would return to the ruined Gray Tower. He had to. He had promised Biagio he would deliver a very special message to Herrith.

As he listened to the rattling chains of the rising anchor, Admiral Nicabar wondered how much would be left of Vorto's body. He only needed a piece.

THIRTY-ONE

Reunion

From his tiny cabin window onboard the *Intimidator*, Simon watched the Hundred Isles of Liss come magnificently into view. He held Shani's face up to the glass, and together they stared at the islands, not exactly sure what they were seeing. Simon had never been to Liss, but he'd heard the stories from sailors like N'Dek. It was rumored to be an incomparable place, with ancient bridges and spires, and waterways instead of streets. Anxious for a better look, he wiped the obscuring mist from the window. The sun was coming up behind the islands, making them glisten. A far-off copper tower caught the light and reflected it. Shani cooed in Simon's ear, entertained by the sight and laughing a good child's laugh. Simon held her closer. She would see her father soon. He had done it. And he was remarkably proud of himself.

"Land ho, N'Dek," he mocked. "I told you we'd make it."

Captain N'Dek, still in ropes, sat on the side of the cabin's bunk, looking drawn and exhausted. For days he had been trapped in the room with his captor and the child, having Simon feed and clean him, reduced to shouting orders through the door at his worried crew, who were all sure they were sailing into disaster but who knew better than to challenge the authority of the Roshann. Even in this time of imperial strife, the Roshann had sway. Enough, Simon had noted with relief, to convince *Intimidator*'s crew to sail to Liss. They had spotted the islands an hour ago and were coming dangerously close now. But N'Dek didn't bother going to the window to see. He was full of hate for Simon and shame for himself, and had barely uttered a word throughout his captivity.

"Once they see us they'll send ships," said N'Dek bitterly. "Are you ready to die, Darquis?"

"They won't sink us," said Simon. "We're only one ship. They'll want to talk to us first. I'll have them escort us in to talk to their leaders."

N'Dek laughed. "What? Just like that? What is this mission of Biagio's?"

"Just keep your mouth shut," snapped Simon. He hadn't explained any of his plan to the captain. He didn't really have a plan. He hoped only that Richius had made it to Liss safely, and that having his daughter aboard would buy all of their lives. "I'll do the talking when the ships come," said Simon over his shoulder. "Remember that, N'Dek. I'm still in command of this vessel."

"Do you know what I'm going to do if I get back to Crote, Darquis?" said the captain. Behind his back he fidgeted with his hand, the bandaged one Simon had driven a dagger through.

"Tell me, please," drawled Simon.

"I'm going to tell Nicabar what you've done. I'm going to tell him that it was all on orders of that man-loving freak Biagio. And when he finds out, he's going to cut both of you into chum and feed you to sharks."

"That's nice."

"I'm a captain of the Black Fleet, for God's sake!"

"Quiet down, N'Dek," advised Simon. "You're making an ass of yourself."

N'Dek seethed. Simon could almost taste his fear. Fear was a contagious thing, and Simon felt a tremor of it, too. But he tried not to pass any of it onto Shani, whose mood had improved perceptibly at the sight of land. No doubt she was as eager as any of them to leave this stinking chamber. So together they stared out through the octagonal glass, watching Liss loom ever larger, until eventually four ships appeared, heading fast for them. They were big ships, all of them, with white sails and sea-serpent flags and gleaming rams on their prows. Shani laughed when she saw them, pointing through the glass.

"That's it, child," said Simon. He leaned into her ear, whispering, "They're going to take you to your father."

"What is it?" N'Dek asked. "What's out there?"

"Four ships," said Simon. "Coming toward us."

The captain contorted to his feet, ignoring his bound hands. "Coming fast? What positions?"

"I don't think they mean to ram us, N'Dek," said Simon.

"What the hell do you know? Get out of the way!"

N'Dek shouldered past them, pushing them away from the porthole and looking outside. There was a sudden banging on the cabin door.

"Captain, sir!" came a crewman's voice. "Four ships approaching. Fast!"

"I see them," N'Dek shouted back. He turned on Simon. "All right, smart fellow. Let's see you work your magic on these devils. They're coming up quick and they'll want some god-damn answers. I sure hope you have some."

Simon drew his dagger from his belt, the one he had used to cripple N'Dek's hand. "You did a very good job of paying attention to me, Captain," he said, putting the point of the blade beneath N'Dek's chin. "Don't disappoint me now. We're going to go above deck. You're going to tell your men to surrender. No swords, no weapons of any kind. I'm going to talk to these Lissens, make them understand me. Right?"

"Fool," N'Dek sneered. "They won't listen to you."

Simon pushed him roughly toward the door. "We'll see."

He hoisted Shani up in his arms. The little girl wrapped herself around his neck.

"Open the door!" he yelled. The command brought the door swinging open. Two sailors stood outside the cabin, waiting, a little wild around the eyes. They had seen their trussed-up captain before, but now the knife at his back seemed to make them more wary.

"We're going above," snapped Simon. "You two lead. And I swear to God, if there's any trap waiting for me on deck, the captain gets it first, and then you two. I'm fast with this knife so don't doubt it. Now move!"

The bold threat had the sailors jumping. Even burdened with a child in his arms, Simon could still make men fear him, and the revelation brought a smile to his face, giving him confidence. All he needed to do was convince the Lissens he had Vantran's baby. They wouldn't dare harm them then. If possible, he would have them spare the crew. N'Dek was a bastard, but a loyal one. Simon didn't want any of their blood on his conscience.

With N'Dek stumbling in front of him, Simon followed the sailors up the gangway to the decks above. When they hit the frosty air, it was like a hammer-blow. None of them were dressed for the weather, and Shani shivered in Simon's arms, huddling closer for warmth. A dozen sailors milled around them, watching but keeping their distance. Simon looked around quickly. He saw the four ships closing in on them from the east. With his dagger he maneuvered N'Dek toward a rail, then kept his back to the ocean and the blade at N'Dek's neck as he spoke.

"Lower the flag. I don't want to do anything to instigate them. And get a blanket for the child. It's bloody freezing up here!"

The sailors stared at Simon dumbly, unsure what to do.

"Move your tails!" flared N'Dek. The order sent his men scurrying. The Black Flag squeaked down from its high mast as the ropes were pulled, stripping the ship of its proud colors. Simon wondered if the Lissens aboard the schooners could see their goodwill action. They were getting closer now, close enough to make out striking details on their odd-looking ships. The lead vessel was larger than the rest, grander too. When he noticed it, Captain N'Dek let out a groan.

"Oh, God, that's the *Prince.*"

"Prince?" asked Simon. "What Prince?"

"The *Prince of Liss,*" said N'Dek, bristling. "That's Prakna's vessel. The lord high Lissen himself."

"Prakna?" Simon squinted harder, then recognized the schooner he had seen when Prakna came to Lucel-Lor. They were getting a royal welcome. Or a grand execution.

"You'll need to talk fast to make this one listen. Prakna's a bloody butcher, and he won't take kindly to us being here. I hope you've rehearsed your lines well, Darquis. Or we're all dead. Including you."

The *Prince of Liss* and her three escorts slowed as they approached. Simon saw Lissen men on deck, blond-headed sailors with milky skin that reminded him of the Triin. They lined the decks of the schooners and looked resolute, like they had no qualms at all about sinking the stranger that had entered their midst. But Simon was sure they wouldn't, not without asking questions. He readied himself and waited for the flagship to come closer. The *Prince* was a marvelous-looking ship, long and curved like some creature of the depths, with a toothy ram that dazzled him with sunlight. As she approached, Simon could see the men on her deck. Prakna was one of them. Tall and hard-faced, he stared at the *Intimidator*. He stood with his arms folded, letting his sailors guide his flagship closer, close enough so that they could see each other.

"That's Prakna," decided Simon quickly. "Tell your men to surrender. Unconditionally. Do it now."

N'Dek grumbled for a moment, then gave the order to one of his lieutenants.

"Get rid of any weapons you have!" shouted Simon. "Throw them overboard!"

All around him the sailors discarded their rapiers and daggers, tossing them into the sea in an obvious show of surrender. Prakna watched through narrowed eyes, obviously suspicious. N'Dek's lieutenant called over the rail, waving his hands and shouting the word *surrender*. Prakna hardly blinked.

"Prakna!" shouted Simon anxiously. "We surrender! Surrender!"

The *Prince of Liss* came closer, trimming her sails to keep from drifting too near. Simon continued waving at Prakna, but the Lissen commander never let a spark of interest light his face. He was granite, made so by ten years of war, and Simon suddenly worried that his plan might fail. Maybe N'Dek was right. Maybe they were all doomed.

"Prakna, it's me!" he shouted. "Simon Darquis! From Lucel-Lor."

Finally, Prakna's face thawed. His eyebrows went up and he turned to the man beside him on the deck, as if verifying what he had just heard. The fleet commander moved closer to the railing and squinted through the sunlight.

"It's Simon Darquis!" said Simon again. "Vantran's friend! I have to talk with him! It's important!"

The mention of Vantran made the captive N'Dek whirl around. "Vantran?" he hissed. "What?"

"Not now, N'Dek."

"His friend?" cried the captain. "What the hell are you talking about?"

"Shut up and let me get us out of this," hissed Simon. He tried to smile at the Lissens, to look unthreatening. Prakna's face was set with a scowl. Simon lifted Shani higher in his arms. "I have Vantran's child here!" he shouted. "I need to see him. Quickly!"

"What are you doing here?" bellowed Prakna. "What business have you in our waters?"

"Let me come aboard and explain it to you," Simon shouted back at him. "Please. It's very urgent."

The strangeness of everything had Prakna confused. He turned back to the man next to him, talking and gesturing and generally wondering what to do. Simon watched him, trying to read his lips, hoping he had convinced the Lissen to listen. He had Vantran's child, after all. There was no way Prakna would risk her.

At least he hoped not.

"Prakna, please!" Simon urged. "I swear, we're no danger to you. We've disarmed and we surrender!"

Fleet Commander Prakna put his hands on the railing and leaned over. "If this is a trick, Naren, you will die."

Simon put up his free hand, as if to promise to Heaven. "It's no trick, I swear it. Let me come aboard and bring you the child. I have news for Vantran. Important news, for all of you. There's no time to confer, Prakna. Just do it. Please!"

"All right," growled the Lissen. "We'll send over a boat. Just you and the child are allowed aboard. And listen to me carefully, you Naren pig—if anything goes wrong, anything at all, I will drown every last one of you with my bare hands."

After his threat, Prakna turned away in disgust. But Simon was satisfied. He turned to N'Dek, who was staring at him in astonishment.

"What is this, Darquis?" asked N'Dek. "What have you done to us?"

Simon swallowed hard. "I can't explain it to you, N'Dek. It's—"

"You've betrayed us, haven't you? This isn't a Roshann mission. My God, Darquis. You're a traitor!"

Simon didn't move. He knew he was safe from the Naren crew now. The Lissens would protect him, for a time. But N'Dek's accusation rang in his mind over and again. Traitor.

"Nothing's going to happen to you," he said. "I'll make sure of it. They'll let you go free."

N'Dek grit his teeth. "You're wrong. You've destroyed us, Darquis. You've murdered us all." The captain stared at him. "Why?"

The only answer Simon could give was to cut the captain's ropes away with his dagger. He half expected N'Dek to strangle him when he was finally free, but the Naren only glared at him, rubbing his rope-burned wrists, his eyes full of confusion. Simon walked through the sailors toward a rope ladder dangling off the side of the *Intimidator* and waited for the little boat from Prakna's ship to fetch him. The fleet commander had dispatched the boat as promised, and now the little vessel was splashing toward him, rowed by two sailors and holding four more, who each kept a short sword in their hands. When they reached the side of the *Intimidator*, one of them called up to Simon.

"Hurry down."

"I have the child," said Simon. "Look out for her."

The boat was positioned directly beneath him. Simon held Shani firmly and stepped out over the side of the ship. But before he placed his foot on the first rope-rung, he looked at the girl in his arms.

"Shani, you've got to hold on tight to me, all right? Don't let go."

Shani coiled her arms around Simon's neck, readying for the descent. Simon slowly shimmied down the ladder, carefully holding the girl as he navigated the rungs. It was a tedious trip, but finally he stepped into the shaking boat and gratefully felt the solid feel of wood beneath his feet. The sailor that had ordered him aboard tried to take Shani from him, but Simon guarded her jealously.

"Just take me to Prakna," he snapped at the man. "And keep your hands off the girl."

The Lissen smirked but said nothing, and soon the little boat shoved away from the *Intimidator*, rowing toward the waiting *Prince of Liss*.

Within a few short days of coming to Karalon, Richius had learned a terrible truth about the young Lissens he was training—none of them had escaped the Naren war without scars. It was, he was beginning to understand, a disease that afflicted all the people of the Hundred Isles. And in a sense, these Lissens were all just different versions of Queen Jelena. Like their ruler, all of them had lost someone dear to them. It might have been a father or brother, or maybe a mother taken off and raped. Or, in the case of Shii, an infant son, ripped from her hands and drowned by Naren sailors. They were an inscrutable bunch, Richius had learned, eager to please but close-mouthed about their violent pasts. They trained hard and rose early in the morning, and they followed orders without question, because he was Lord Jackal and a hero, and because they simply had nowhere else to go. They were on a great and violent mission, these children of Liss, and nothing could stop them or ease their burning scars.

Just as Shii had claimed, his army was nine hundred strong now—enough, he was sure, to swarm over Crote and seize it from Biagio. They were like zealots, these Lissens. Unquenchable, they longed for Naren blood. And Richius had taken that thirst and tried to focus it, to channel it into something useful. He had seen the loss in Shii's eyes, in all their eyes really, and knew the fire in them could easily rage out of control. He wanted an army, not a band of berserkers. So he had set to work quickly, talking to them in small groups, telling them that they had worth and value beyond their need for revenge, and trying his best to tame the beasts within them. It wasn't an easy job, and Richius wasn't at all sure he would succeed. Shii, the one he depended on most, was a fiery woman, hate-filled and driven, and like Queen Jelena she was convinced of the rightness of their mission.

"An army isn't built on revenge," he had told his young assistant. "If we're to be an army, we must have honor and discipline."

The words had resonated in Shii. Day by day, she was becoming less the wildcat and more the soldier, inclined to think before reacting. Because he was Lord Jackal, Shii listened to Richius. And he got down in the mud with them all. Refusing to direct the training from a comfortable chair, he was with his army every day, getting filthy and insect-bitten, staying up late and rising early. He showed them how to move like an army, the way he had in his war against the Triin, how to slink through the brush with your sword at your side, how to side-wind through mud and cover your face with it. Prakna's raid on Nar had won them a bounty of swords, and Richius instructed them in the art of close combat, recalling his early days in Aramoor at his father's knee, and how the older Vantran had been relentless in his teachings—insisting that his son learn—because he had the foresight to know that war was inevitable.

Inevitable. For Richius, it was a sad truth, and he thought about it often as he taught his army. He wasn't an expert in any of these things. There were swordsmen and tacticians far better than he, but he had experience and memories, and the young Lissens of Karalon respected him.

Of all the things Richius tried to teach them, the most important was how to listen. They were supposed to be an army, after all. With Shii's help, he had organized them into platoons, each led by a capable young man or woman, so that he could confer with the platoon leaders and talk over certain troubles or concerns. He was open with them, always willing to lend an ear. After only a few days as their general, Richius was, he supposed, having an effect on them. And he was proud of himself.

In mid-afternoon of his fifth day on Karalon, Richius worked in a tent just outside the parade field where his platoons were drilling. He was leaning back in an uncomfortable chair, fretting over a map he was drawing. Despite his appeal to Jelena, he still had no maps of Crote, only vague charts put together by Prakna and other sailors. Lissen intelligence about their target was spotty at best, and their chances of a successful invasion would be vastly slimmer without more information. Richius knew only what he had heard throughout his years in Nar—that Biagio lived in a great villa near the sea, and was protected by a contingent of personal bodyguards, all of them Crotans, who watched over their master day and night and who, presumably, had learned some tricks from their Roshann teacher. Whether or not there were actual Roshann agents on Crote was another thing entirely. Richius supposed there were some, at least—especially since there were members of the Iron Circle who had fled to Crote with Biagio. And they all might have their own bodyguards, another factor Richius had to consider. It wasn't actually the numbers that frightened him, though. He had nine hundred crazy Lissens on his side. What concerned him was the imprecision. Unless Biagio's villa shined like a beacon, they might not even find it. They might be stranded on the Crotan beaches with no sense of where to go, and that troubled him greatly. He could teach these people how to use a sword, but not how to sniff out Biagio.

As he studied his charts and papers, Richius ran a worried hand through his hair. He hadn't been sleeping lately, and his eyelids drooped as he tried to read his scratchy penmanship. A draft from the tent flap stirred the papers on the table and crept over his skin, making him shiver. He poured himself another cup of hot tea and wrapped his hands about it for warmth, then saw Shii in the doorway, watching him. She was a bold woman normally, but shy when around her new lord. She didn't smile when he noticed her, but instead offered an apologetic grimace.

"Shii?" Richius asked. "You need me?"

Shii wavered in the door. "I'm sorry, Lord Jackal," she said. "There is someone to see you."

"Who?"

"Fleet Commander Prakna," said the woman. "He's just arrived. He says he needs to speak with you urgently."

"Prakna?" Richius sprang to his feet. He hadn't seen the commander since coming to Liss. "Here?"

"Yes, Lord," said Shii. "But he's not alone. He's brought someone."

"Shii," said Richius mildly. "I don't understand. Who's with Prakna?"

"Lord Jackal, I think it's a Naren," Shii replied. "I saw him from Prakna's boat."

Richius drifted slowly over to Shii, making very sure he understood her. "A Naren is here with Prakna?"

Shii shrugged. "He looks like a Naren, dark like you. I saw him from a distance. Prakna was landing his catboat. He called across to us, saying it was urgent he see you. I think you should come."

"I think you're right." Richius buttoned up his coat and pushed back his hair, eager to see Prakna again but worried about who—or what—the commander had brought with him. Maybe a prisoner, caught in one of the Lissen raids. Or a spy, perhaps. Whoever he was, Prakna wouldn't have brought him to Karalon without the best of reasons.

Richius followed Shii out of the tent and onto the field where teams of Lissens worked with spears, training with them just as he'd shown them, burying the blunt ends in the ground to deflect a charging horse. Richius frowned a little. He didn't even know if Crote had horses! He might have been training them for nothing. He followed Shii toward the dunes. Prakna was already coming toward them in the distance. Three well-armed Lissen sailors were with him, surrounding a fourth man with a bundle in his arms that looked like a child. Richius squinted to see better. The man was tall and lean, dark like a Naren. When he saw the man's face, Richius had an odd flash of familiarity. It looked like . . .

He paused. "Son of a bitch!"

Shii turned on him, worried. "Lord Jackal? What is it?"

It was impossible. Richius knew it was, and yet there he stood, walking with Prakna.

"Simon," he whispered dreadfully. "What the hell . . . ?"

"Simon? You know that man?"

Richius wasn't listening. Prakna was coming closer, his face rigid. Neither he nor Simon waved at Richius when they noticed him. Richius couldn't move. That was Simon, wasn't it? What was he carrying? The men and women on the field stopped what they were doing. They had noticed the commander and his odd companion, and looked as shocked as Richius at the intrusion. But as they drew closer Richius lost all doubt about what he was seeing. Simon's face was perfectly clear. And the child in his arms was no less a mystery. When he realized it was Shani, Richius bolted forward in terror.

"Shani!" he cried, racing toward them. "My God, what's wrong? What happened?"

Prakna put up his hands quickly. "Easy, boy," the commander urged. "There's nothing wrong. Your daughter's safe. I looked her over myself."

Richius caught up to them and ripped his daughter out of Simon's arms. Shani squealed with delight when she saw him. Richius put his hands to her face, holding her close, thrilled and horrified to see her.

"My God, what are you doing here?" he roared at Simon. "What happened? Where's Dyana? Is she safe?"

"Richius," Simon sputtered. "I swear to God, Dyana's safe. I swear to God."

Richius stepped up to him. "What is this, Simon?" he hissed. "Answer me! What are you doing here? Why do you have Shani?"

"He came here on a Naren ship," Prakna answered. "We intercepted her on her way here to Liss. She was coming here for you, Richius. This Naren said he had your daughter. I brought him here as soon as I could."

Richius looked at Simon. "What's going on?"

Simon went white, chewing his lip with consideration. He glanced at Prakna, then at all the Lissens in the field, staring at him. "It's . . . difficult," he said. "I don't really know where to start."

Prakna exploded, bringing up a flashing boot and kicking Simon in the back. The blow sent Simon sprawling to his hands and knees in the dirt before Richius.

"You'd better talk, you Naren pig," Prakna threatened. "Or I'll cut your heart out and eat it."

"Simon," began Richius gravely. "I think you'd better give me an explanation."

Simon didn't get to his feet. He merely knelt in the dirt with his head bowed, sighing miserably. "I took your daughter," he said. "I'm not who you think I am." He raised his face to Richius. "You were right about me the first time, Richius. I'm Roshann."

Roshann. The word hung in the air. Richius stared down at Simon, a man he had come to call friend, and all the world came crashing down on his shoulders, suffocating him. He glared at Simon in disbelief, not believing, or not wanting to believe.

"It's true," said Simon. "I'm sorry. I took your daughter away from Dyana. My mission was to bring her back to Crote for—"

"No!" roared Richius. "Do not say it!"

Simon closed his eyes. "I'm sorry, Richius. It's true."

Richius hugged Shani closer, looking her over with worry. She seemed fine, albeit pale, and she laughed happily, running her fingers over her father's face. A knot of emotion swelled in Richius' throat. He wanted to weep, or to run from them all with his daughter, to dash across the ocean to Dyana and hide them both away. But something else grew in him, too. Without thinking he handed his daughter to Shii, then lunged at Simon.

"Bastard!" cried Richius. He was straddling Simon and wringing his neck. "How could you do this?"

"Had to . . ." Simon gasped. "Had to!"

A crowd was gathering, but Richius hardly saw. His vision had gone red.

"You tell me what that devil Biagio wants!" he roared. "You tell me or I'll kill you!"

Simon could barely breathe. His face purpled as he tried to speak. "Shani," he managed awkwardly. "Your daughter . . ."

"Why?" Richius lifted Simon's head, then banged it hard against the ground. "What for?"

The Naren stared at him sadly, uttering a remarkable word. *"You."*

Suddenly, Richius stopped. He sat on Simon's chest, reflecting. Biagio was still on the hunt. Even after all this time.

"Did he send you?" Richius asked. He was breathing hard and shaking with rage. "Did Biagio send you to take my daughter?"

Simon looked away in shame. "Yes. He wanted me to take her back to Crote. I think he wanted to lure you there."

"Where's Dyana?" asked Richius. He took up fistfuls of Simon's clothes and gave him a violent shake. "If you've hurt her . . ."

"I didn't, I swear," said Simon. "She's safe. She's still in Falindar."

Richius sat back, closing his eyes. Dyana must be in agony, he knew, and the thought of his wife in so much pain was staggering. Losing control, he made a fist and slammed it against Simon's face. Simon winced at the blow but did not cry out. He only stared back at Richius as blood gushed out of his nose.

"Richius, I—"

"Don't talk to me," hissed Richius. "Don't you ever. You may have killed my wife without knowing it, you bastard. I should have known when I met you what filth you are."

"My God, we will kill him," spat Prakna. "Let me take him away, Richius. Give me the honor of gutting this pig, please!"

Still Simon said nothing. He seemed lost, almost like a child.

"Is that what you want, Simon?" Richius barked. "Should I have Prakna cut your liver out?"

"It's what he deserves!" Prakna flared. "Jackal, please!"

"Say something, Simon. Please say something to keep me from killing you."

Still Simon wouldn't answer. He closed his eyes, blocking out the world.

"Simon, look at me," Richius ordered. "Open your eyes and look at me."

Simon looked. His eyes were deep, rich with pain.

"Why did you bring her back to me?" Richius asked softly. "There's something, I know there is. Tell me."

The Naren's lips began to tremble. "Because I love a woman."

"Rubbish! Don't listen to him, Richius!"

Richius put a hand up to quiet Prakna. "What do you mean?" he asked Simon. "What woman? A wife?"

"Not a wife. Not yet." Simon turned his bleeding face away. His nose was on fire, just like the first time Richius had broken it. "She's trapped on Crote. I had to do this, Richius. I *had to*. Or Biagio would have kept her from me." He put his hands to his face. Richius thought he might be weeping. "Now he'll kill her. He will, if we don't stop him. That's why I brought your girl back to you. God, Richius, help me. . . ."

"What? Help you how?"

Simon swallowed his choking emotions, summoning enough steadiness to look at Richius directly. "I can help you with your invasion of Crote. I know Crote better than anyone. If you'll let me, I can get Eris out of there! You can—"

"Lies!" Prakna roared. "Don't listen to him, Jackal!"

"I'm not lying!" Simon cried. He was desperate now, near hysteria. "Please, Richius, listen to me. I can help you. If you'll let me go with you I can lead you straight to Biagio. Then I can rescue Eris and you can take the island. It's true, every word of it!"

Richius shook his head sadly. "You swore to me once before, Simon. Remember? You swore you'd never harm Shani or Dyana. How am I supposed to believe you now, after what you've done?"

"I can help you," Simon said again. "I'm not lying. If I was lying I wouldn't have brought Shani back to you."

It was sound enough logic, Richius supposed. He glanced at Shani, who had her little arms wrapped around Shii's neck and was looking down at him, confused by the whole situation. Richius rose and went to his daughter, taking her from Shii. Prakna reached down and lifted Simon roughly to his feet. The fleet commander held the Naren by the collar as he waited for Richius' answer. They were all waiting—Prakna's men, Simon, Shii and all the Lissens—staring at him as if he had some great wisdom to impart. But Richius ignored them. He smiled at Shani, cooing at her and rubbing his nose against hers, and all he wanted was to be away from here, back in Falindar with Dyana. He would have to get word to her. Somehow, Prakna would have to send a ship back to Falindar, to let Dyana know their daughter was safe.

"Oh, Shani," he sighed. "Your mother must be so worried about you."

"Richius," Prakna interrupted. "What should I do with this piece of filth?"

"I'm not lying, Richius," said Simon desperately. "You have to believe me. I'm not asking this for myself, but for Eris. We were to be married when I returned to Crote with Shani. But if I don't return, Biagio will kill her. He will, and that won't be my fault. It will be yours if you turn me away."

"Don't you dare blame me for any of this," flared Richius. "And if this Eris is anything like you, I say let her die."

Simon shook his head. "You don't mean that. I know you don't. Eris isn't like me at all. I may be evil, but she's not. She's innocent." He tried to shake off Prakna's grip, but the fleet commander didn't let go, so Simon stood there imploringly. He looked exhausted, as if he was about to collapse. "Richius, please. I can help you. I know Crote. And you don't, do you?"

"Very perceptive, Roshann," spat Richius. But he knew Simon was right. Without at least a map of Crote, they might all be cut to pieces. In typical Roshann fashion, Simon had maneuvered them into a corner. Richius wondered if he had any choice at all. Yet even with so much logic, Richius couldn't bring himself to answer Simon. At that moment, he couldn't even look at him.

"I'm going to my quarters," he said. "And I don't want to be bothered. Not by any of you."

He turned away. Simon called after him desperately, but he ignored the Naren's pleas. Only when Prakna called did he bother to answer.

"Jackal?" asked Prakna. "What should I do with him?"

"Nothing," replied Richius bitterly, then walked away.

That night, sleep didn't come to Richius. Too restless from the day's events, he spent hours alone in his private quarters, a little room attached to one of the barracks and warmed only by a small stone hearth the Lissens had built for him in the center of the room, far enough from the close wooden walls to keep the place from catching fire. The floor was dirt and the hearth was dug deep, with poorly cut slate tiles laid on the ground to lend a semblance of finish. Richius had given Shani his bed. A carefully preserved fire glowed in the chamber, turning her sleeping face orange above a pile of blankets. It was very late now and Shani was exhausted, not only from the trip but also from the hours of attention

Richius had lavished on her. Seeing his daughter again had done something to him. He couldn't take his eyes off her. He *wouldn't*.

A cloud of insects droned somewhere off in the dunes. Richius sat back in his creaky chair, listening to them while he watched Shani sleep. Because it had been built so quickly, there were no windows in the room, but the distant noises seeped through the boarded walls. There was probably a moon outside, and stars. Richius thought about waking Shani to show them to her. The stars were very clear here. But she was so perfectly asleep he didn't want to disturb her. In the morning he would have to send her back to Dyana. Somehow, he would have to convince Prakna to spare a ship for her. Richius wasn't sure the fleet commander would do the favor for him, and hoped he wouldn't have to get Queen Jelena involved.

And then there was the question of Simon.

"What should I do?" Richius whispered. Simon had come a long way just to give Shani back to him. The Naren had even risked his life. Richius wanted to think that signaled some change in him, but Simon was a Roshann agent and that they were all master manipulators, not to be trusted. Like Biagio.

Biagio. Richius remembered how he had told Dyana that Biagio would never forgive him or forsake his vengeance, and how Dyana and Lucyler had both thought him paranoid. But they were Triin. They didn't know the truth about Biagio, and couldn't possibly understand his insanity—not like Richius could. He had only met the count a few times, but he still remembered his blazing eyes and golden skin, all the foppish mannerisms belying the iron beneath. Biagio was frightful, both beautiful and terrible to behold, and a demon without peer. Of all the dead emperor's henchmen, Biagio was the worst.

There was a knock at the door, startling Richius from his musings. He looked at Shani, still asleep, then got out of his chair.

"I asked not to be disturbed," he said crossly as he pulled open the door. He didn't expect to see Simon staring back at him. Prakna was with him, holding him by the arm.

"What is this?" asked Richius.

"He wouldn't shut up until I brought him here, Jackal," said the Lissen. "He says he has important things to talk to you about."

"And it couldn't wait 'til tomorrow?"

"No, Richius, it couldn't," said Simon. He had lost his earlier deference and now was his old, arrogant self again. "It's important you listen to me. I told you once before, I won't be your prisoner."

Richius scowled at Simon. "There's nowhere for you to go, Simon. I could let you loose right now and you'd die of exposure in a day. You *are* my prisoner, Roshann. Like it or not."

"Don't be a stubborn fool, Richius," Simon advised. "I can help you. You know I can."

"But I don't know that you *will*," Richius corrected. "You're a liar. You've already proven that."

Simon's face hardened. "I'm not lying. You have my word on that."

The claim made both Richius and Prakna laugh. Simon shook off the Lissen's grip and glared at Richius.

"Don't send me away," he warned. "You'll be sorry if you do. I know what your mission is, remember? And I know Crote, better than any one of you. Right?"

"You're a Naren pig," jeered Prakna.

"Right, Richius?" pressed Simon.

Richius wanted to close the door on him, but couldn't. They just looked at each other, Simon imperious, Richius trying to retain his hatred. But eventually his expression softened just a little. Simon seized on it.

"I can help you," he said with earnest. "Please, for Eris."

"I don't even know Eris."

Simon smiled. "But you'd like her if you did."

Richius shook his head in exasperation. "Prakna, do me a favor. Please leave us alone. I'll look after him for now."

The fleet commander's eyes rolled in disgust. "Richius . . ."

"No, it's fine. Really. I just want to listen to his offer. Please, Prakna. Trust me on this."

"Whatever," the commander rumbled, then stalked off into the night, leaving Simon alone with Richius.

An awkward silence engulfed them. Richius shut the door so as not to disturb his daughter. Simon stared down at his feet, embarrassed. Then he shrugged.

"You broke my nose again," he said.

"I think you deserve that, don't you?"

"I suppose."

Richius looked at Simon in the starlight. The bleeding had stopped but his nose had indeed swollen into a purple mass. It looked like it hurt badly. Richius was happy to see it. But Simon didn't seem happy about anything. He seemed dejected, sick of himself and weary of his life. He couldn't even bring himself to lift his head.

"Look at me, Simon," Richius directed. He wanted to see into those eyes, to try and gauge the truth in them. Simon looked up reluctantly.

"I'm sorry," he said. "Believe it or not, I am sorry."

"I don't know what to believe," said Richius. "I thought you were a friend, Simon. Do you know what a colossal fool I feel like now?"

Simon didn't look away, though it was clearly a struggle for him. "I don't blame you for hating me. You have that right. And you have the right to turn me down. But if you do, you'll only be hurting your own chances. I know what you want, Richius."

"Oh, really? And what would that be?"

"Biagio."

Richius grimaced. "Good guess."

"I can help you get him," Simon continued. "I know everything about him, all his habits and strengths. I can serve him up to you on a silver platter."

"And why would you do that?" asked Richius. "Isn't he your *master*?" He spat out the word in disgust.

"I'm doing this for Eris," Simon insisted. "That's the only reason."

"Nonsense. You're a Roshann agent. I know what that means. You're supposed to serve Biagio until you die. That's the deal, isn't it? Death before dishonor? What you're saying is treason." Richius poked at Simon. "Why?"

Simon sighed, leaning against the wooden wall and staring up at the stars. "My life is complicated, Richius. I'm not what I used to be. And neither is Biagio. He's insane now. He takes a drug to make him immortal."

"I know about the drug," said Richius. "Go on."

"It's made him mad, I think. I know he would kill Eris if he found out I betrayed him. And he will find out. If I don't get her away from him, she'll die."

"And why should I care about that? Any woman who loves you must be as mad as Biagio."

Simon gave Richius a sad smile. "I know you better than that, Richius Vantran. Eris is innocent. And you can't stand to see innocent people die."

"So?"

"If you don't let me help you, Eris is going to die. And probably a whole lot of these *children* you're planning on leading against Crote."

"They're soldiers," corrected Richius icily. "They don't kill because they're getting paid for it, Roshann. They have honor."

"All right," Simon conceded. "But maybe I have honor, too. Maybe just a scrap of it, something the years haven't buried yet." His eyes flicked back to the stars. "I guess that's what I'm trying to tell you."

There was something so genuine in Simon's tone that Richius wanted desperately to believe him.

"Can I ask you something, Richius?" asked Simon quietly.

"Go ahead."

"What are you trying to accomplish here? I mean, besides killing Biagio?"

The odd question made Richius bristle. "Simon, I don't understand."

"I looked around. I saw these so-called soldiers of yours. They're just kids."

Richius chuckled. "You have a lot to learn about these people. Once I thought as you do, but not anymore. There's more heart on this little island than in all the nations of Nar combined." He looked out over the darkened camp, proud of himself. "I'm not just leading an army. I'm championing a cause."

"Is that right?" Simon quipped. "And what cause would that be?"

"One word," said Richius. "Justice."

"Justice," scoffed Simon. "Looks more like revenge to me."

"Call it whatever you like. But these men and women have something you'll never have. They have heart. You say you're going back for a woman. You think that gives you heart? Maybe it's just lust, did you ever think of that?"

Simon regarded Richius. "You know, I remember another story about a man who turned his back on his country for a woman. Lots of people thought he was insane, caught up by a pretty face. But he did what he thought was right. At least that's what he claims. I never argued with *him*, or questioned *his* heart."

"That's different," Richius snapped. "I never kidnapped anyone."

"I brought her back, Richius. I did because it was the right thing to do. Please, at least try to believe that." Simon put his hand on Richius' shoulder. "Don't make me beg for this. Not to save the woman I love."

Richius didn't shrug off the Naren's hand. He knew he should have, knew that Prakna would be appalled to see their camaraderie, but he liked the touch and the sincerity in it. He closed his eyes, considering things for a long moment.

"You know, Prakna might kill me for this," he said finally. "Are you sure you can help me?"

"Yes," said Simon. "Very sure."

When Richius opened his eyes, the Naren was looking at him brightly, his face aglow with new hope. He stuck out his hand for Simon, who took it and gave it a hard, promising squeeze.

"Don't make me regret this, Simon."

"I won't," said Simon softly. "If I have a soul, I pledge it to you now."

Richius nodded, giving Simon his tepid approval. Then he turned his back on the Naren and returned to the chamber where his daughter slept, closing the door gently behind him. He knelt down beside the bed, resting his head on the mattress and lightly playing with Shani's fine hair.

"Forgive me, Shani," he whispered. "But I have to trust him. I need his help."

Just then, Shani opened her eyes. She yawned, confused, and looked at her father through a sleepy haze.

"I love you," Richius told her. "Please don't hate me for what I'm about to do."

His soft voice made Shani smile.

THIRTY-TWO

Prakna Defiant

A black sea greeted Prakna as he stood on deck. Silent and sure, his *Prince of Liss* cut a swathe through the ocean, racing toward the three schooners anchored in the harbor and the Naren dreadnought they were guarding, the one called the *Intimidator*. The Naren vessel had been their prisoner since coming to Liss, not daring to make a run from the faster schooners, and Prakna knew that her crew was waiting onboard, fretting over their fate. He stood on the *Prince*'s prow, letting the wind pull back his hair, and wondered what would happen if he listened to Vantran.

The Jackal had left Prakna with clear orders. He was to take the Naren sailors ashore as prisoners, and bring their ship back to dock. After the invasion of Crote, the prisoners could be returned to the Empire. Not until then, Vantran had said, because they might compromise the mission. Prakna steamed as he thought about his orders. Apparently, the Jackal still had a soft spot for his own kind.

On the deck next to Prakna, Marus directed the flagship toward the waiting schooners. There were lights flickering on the other Lissen ships, signaling them closer. The *Prince* slowed on Marus' order as she drew near. Prakna squinted through the blackness. The *Intimidator* was still in the center of the ring, as ugly as ever. Men in Naren naval coats stood on the deck, talking among themselves nervously. Prakna was nervous, too. He tried not to show it, but he knew Marus could tell.

"Bring us about," he told his first officer.

Marus called the order down the line. The flagship bent in the wind, leaning starboard toward the other ships.

"How close do you want to get?" Marus asked his captain.

"Close enough to talk," Prakna replied. "I want to see this Captain N'Dek."

"He won't believe you, you know."

The fleet commander shrugged. "He doesn't have to."

A rushing wind blew over their conversation. The *Prince* skirted closer, until at last she slipped between two of the Lissen schooners and approached the *Intimidator*. Marus called his orders, bringing them up along the dreadnought's port side. All along the Naren's deck, the men turned their heads expectantly and fretted over the coming schooner. Prakna stepped off the prow and went to the side of his ship, which was coming perilously close now to scraping the dreadnought. But Marus' masterful piloting brought them up alongside with room to spare, and the *Prince* paused there, bobbing on the ocean as her crew worked to still her.

The fleet commander put on his harshest scowl. He stared out over the thunderstruck Narens, their dirty faces sickening him. It was like looking at a bunch of rats.

"Where's your captain?" Prakna shouted. "I want to speak to him."

A figure emerged out of the crowd, a man with a beaklike nose and sharp eyes. His uniform was torn and filthy and he favored his right hand as he came forward, playing with the bandages wrapped around it.

"I'm Captain N'Dek," he said without flinching. "You're Prakna, right?"

"*Fleet Commander* Prakna," replied Prakna icily. "I'm your master and your better, pig. Remember that."

N'Dek glowered. He had that same awful arrogance as all Narens, the same ridiculous confidence. "What's your business?" he asked tersely.

Prakna cleared his throat, quickly going over the lines as he'd rehearsed them. "You're free," he said. "On the orders of Richius Vantran and Simon Darquis, you're being released."

"What?" N'Dek blurted. "You're letting us go?"

"Get the seaweed out of your ears," rumbled Prakna. "You heard me. Your ship's being released."

The proclamation sent a ripple through the Naren crew. N'Dek put up a hand to quiet them. "Why?" he asked suspiciously. "Why are you letting us go?"

"Don't ask me," said Prakna. "It's not my decision. It's Vantran's."

"Same question," said N'Dek. "Why?"

"Would you rather be taken prisoner?" snapped Prakna. "Because if so, I'd love to arrange that for you."

The Naren captain looked around, surveying the three schooners encircling his ship. He seemed pensive, not at all sure of himself. Prakna struggled to keep up his facade. If the Naren suspected anything, they might not set sail.

"Get under way," Prakna ordered. "I want you out of Lissen waters within the hour. And if you don't sail straight and true, I'll come after you myself and sink the lot of you."

N'Dek flashed an arrogant grin. "I know what you look like now, Fleet Commander Prakna. This has been an honor for me. Shall I send Admiral Nicabar your regards?"

Marus exploded forward. "You lice-covered—!"

"Enough," Prakna demanded, putting his hand on his officer's shoulder. There would be time enough to avenge the insult. "Get under way, Naren," he commanded. "I'm going to escort you out of Lissen waters myself. Make your heading due east. You deviate, you die."

The captain gave him a sarcastic bow. "As you say, Fleet Commander."

He turned and began barking orders to his startled crew. Prakna stood at his ship's edge, watching. The Narens jumped at their captain's orders, readying their vessel for sail. Marus shouldered up to Prakna and nudged his friend.

"Well played, Prakna," he observed.

Fleet Commander Prakna spared a modest grin. "Move us off, Marus. Let's give our pigeon room to fly."

An hour after leaving the Lissen coast, the *Prince of Liss* broke off its escort of the *Intimidator*. Captain N'Dek stood on deck and watched the schooner turn back into the night, happy to see it go. He had escaped with his life and the lives of his crew, and, most remarkably, his ship. In war terms, that was a victory. N'Dek closed his eyes for a moment and let out a tremendous sigh. His hand ached and his stomach growled for food, but most of all he was tired. All he wanted was to disappear into his cabin and sleep.

"Sleep." He chanted the word like a prayer. For the last several days, the only sleep he'd gotten was when Simon Darquis had let him, sprawled out on the cold floor of his cabin. N'Dek grit his teeth, remembering the Roshann agent. He recalled his promise to Darquis, that he would return to Crote and tell Nicabar what had happened. Nicabar would be outraged.

Good, thought N'Dek bitterly. Maybe then he'd do something about Biagio.

The only thing that vexed N'Dek now was the mystery of his survival. Vantran was on Liss? That had been a surprise. And for some reason, the Jackal had let them go. N'Dek shook his head, baffled by the turn of events. Perhaps Vantran was part of Biagio's grand design. Or maybe Simon had convinced the Lissens to spare their lives. The captain shrugged, knowing he would never have his answers.

Be happy you're alive, he told himself, then headed for his cabin.

The *Prince of Liss* headed west for two nautical miles before Prakna gave the order to turn. They were almost in sight of their sister ships when the order came. Dawn would be breaking soon, and Prakna wanted the cover of darkness for his attack. He remained above deck as his flagship began its arc, turning eastward again in pursuit of the fleeing dreadnought.

Captain N'Dek would never get his chance to send regards to Nicabar. That much Prakna had promised himself. He didn't care about Vantran's orders, and couldn't stomach the thought of sparing the Narens. They had entered Lissen waters. They were Naren. That made them prey.

"Marus," he called to his waiting officer. "Take us in fast, before the sun breaks. I don't want them to see us coming."

Marus nodded. Like Prakna, neither he nor any of the *Prince*'s loyal sailors cared about Vantran's orders. Here on the sea, Prakna's word was law. When he got back to Liss, he would explain to Richius how the dreadnought had tried to break away, how the crew had resisted being taken prisoner. He had been given no choice but to pursue them, Prakna would say. He wasn't sure Vantran would believe him, but then he didn't really care, either. None of them cared. Prakna knew his Lissen sailors would never betray the truth.

The *Prince of Liss* devoured the waves. Soon the *Intimidator* would be in sight. Prakna drew his heavy collar close around his neck, settling in for the brief wait. He was looking forward to sinking the dreadnought. It had been too long since he'd sent Narens to the bottom. This one he would sink for J'lari.

Alone in his tiny cabin, N'Dek finished a simple meal of cold soup and beer, then blew out the candle and settled in to the sheets. The soft embrace of his mattress was like the touch of a woman to his aching body, and he moaned as he got comfortable. His cabin had one porthole, a window of octagonal glass that let in starlight. He had already given the command to head straight for Crote, and was confident that he would have no more troubles. In a little more than a week, he would be safely back in the waters of the Empire.

Captain N'Dek closed his eyes and began fantasizing about a prostitute he had met once in Casarhoon, when a distant shout reached him. His eyes opened slowly and he cursed, angry at the disruption. Then he heard the shout again, loud and desperate. N'Dek blinked, unsure what he was hearing, and swung his legs over the side of his bunk.

"Lissens!" came the shout again. "Off the port side!"

N'Dek's stomach somersaulted. He went to his little porthole and looked outside. It was dark and the glass was covered with sea spray, but he could just make out a hint of something monstrous and shining.

N'Dek realized a Lissen ram was racing toward him. In the next second he was dead, cut cleanly in half by the all-devouring blade.

Prakna and his crew howled like madmen as the *Prince of Liss* slammed into the unsuspecting dreadnought. They had come flying out of the darkness, catching the *Intimidator* amidships and landing a fatal blow. Water poured into the gash in the dreadnought's hull, flooding her lower decks as the *Prince* bobbed up, pulling free its fanged ram and ripping off a mouthful of timbers. A tide of freezing ocean blasted across the dreadnought, sweeping away its sailors and pushing her down like a giant hand. Exhilarated, Prakna shook his fist, shouting above the beautiful noise.

"Give my regards to Nicabar!" he crowed.

All across the sinking vessel, sailors clung vainly to rigging as their ship listed to port. The ocean gushed in, drowning their screams. Prakna hoped his victims were married and would leave behind widows. With cold detachment, he folded his arms over his chest and watched the Naren warship sink, enjoying the show.

THIRTY-THREE

The Swift

Captain Kelara of the Black Fleet vessel *Swift* stood on the prow of his ship as it swooped out of the rising sun. A full wind filled the sails of his fleet-footed ship, speeding her along like a dolphin. For three weeks the *Swift* had been on patrol in Lissen waters, carrying out Biagio's orders. They were to wait until the Lissens set sail for Crote. Then they were to fly home with all the speed of Heaven to warn the count of the coming invasion. It was a task for which the scout ship was well suited, for she was of the Leopard class, the only vessels in the Black Fleet capable of pacing Lissen warships. She had a keel like a knife and seven wide sails slung low on her masts, and with a complement of only twenty seamen, she wasn't fat amidships. She had no armaments or cannons to slow her, no extraneous weight at all. Built for speed, she had but one purpose—to be as fast as her Lissen enemies.

Captain Kelara admired Renato Biagio. Because he believed the Crotan count to be a peerless tactician, he had taken this perilous commission with pride. Through careful planning and well-placed lures, Biagio had managed to lull the Lissens into a sense of superiority. Soon, Biagio had promised, the Lissens would launch their attack on Crote. And Crote needed to be ready for it. Most importantly, they needed forewarning. That was Kelara's mission. And with the *Swift* at his command, he was sure he would succeed.

But Captain Kelara hadn't counted on the *Intimidator*, and when he'd seen it heading recklessly toward Liss, all the bravado had left him. He had tracked the dreadnought from a distance, careful to stay hidden in the sun's glare. And when the warship had gotten too close to Liss and disappeared, he had not pursued it. That had been nearly fifteen hours ago.

Then she had reemerged.

And she wasn't alone.

Kelara had watched through his spyglass as the *Prince of Liss* rammed the unsuspecting *Intimidator*. He had been about to give the order to rendezvous with the dreadnought when he'd seen the schooner. Too late to warn his doomed comrades, he had witnessed the dreadnought's quick destruction. The *Prince* had remained in the dark waters for nearly an hour, watching the *Intimidator* go down. Only when the Lissens had gone did Kelara finally order the *Swift* forward.

Now, with lookouts posted high in the masts, the Naren scout ship raced to the place where the dreadnought had been, scanning the sea for survivors and the horizon for the *Prince*. Thankfully, Kelara saw no Lissen ships. He barked orders to his crew, telling them all to look sharp. He didn't like approaching Liss in the daylight, and after seeing the bloody murder of the *Intimidator*, he was taking no chances. As they approached the area where the dreadnought had gone down, bits of flotsam and buoyant wood floated up to greet them. Kelara ordered the vessel to slow, scanning the dark waters. The impact of the Lissen ram had been enormous, shattering *Intimidator*'s hull. She had cracked like an egg.

Not far off, he began to see the bodies. They were stiff in the freezing water, bobbing slowly on the waves among the remnants of their ship. Each of the corpses had turned an icy blue.

"Seven hells," cursed Kelara, shaking his head. He was too late. If there had been survivors, they had already frozen to death. The captain smashed a fist into an open palm, infuriated with himself. The *Swift* was a fine vessel, but without guns she could do nothing against a schooner. A feeling of impotence engulfed Kelara. Someday, the Black Fleet would return to Liss. And when they did . . .

"Captain, look!"

The cry came from the masts above. Kelara looked to the crow's nest, then to the place in the ocean where the sailor was pointing. At first he saw nothing but empty water. Then his vision focused, revealing a bobbing speck far off starboard. Instantly the captain snapped open his spyglass and located the object—a living man, waving at them.

"Holy Heaven!" Kelara exclaimed. "Lieutenant Nan, bring us about. There's a survivor!"

At the captain's orders, the *Swift* pitched starboard toward the flailing man. Kelara's heart leapt with new hope. If there was one, there might be others. Quickly he scanned the area, looking for survivors and finding none. The man was surrounded by bloated, blue corpses.

"All right," said Kelara. "Just the one. I was quick enough for him, at least." He whirled back to Lieutenant Nan, who was carefully guiding the ship toward the man. "Faster!" the captain bellowed angrily. "Get him aboard before he freezes to death!"

THIRTY-FOUR

Dyana's Discovery

To Dyana, who had known both privilege and poverty, Count Biagio's mansion was a marvel.

Since coming to Crote, she had lived like a pampered pet, hardly a prisoner at all, with all of the count's splendid surroundings about her. She admired his private beaches, ate his exotic foods, and dressed herself in silk, the softest she had ever felt. Biagio spared no expense for her comfort. He had no argument with her, he had explained, only her husband, and had left orders with his vast staff of slaves that she was to be well treated. He had even given her a splendid room, a rambling chamber with antique furnishings and glass doors leading to a garden. At night she heard the ocean as she slept, and she roused each morning to a delectable breakfast laid out for her by Kyla, the young slave that had greeted her on her first day in Crote. Dyana didn't know how long her captivity would last, or when Biagio would take her to Nar as promised, but he had obviously decided to make the last days of her life exceedingly comfortable.

With nothing to occupy her, she spent most of her days wandering the mansion's manicured grounds, admiring the gardens and extraordinary topiaries, and reading books from the count's impressive libraries. She avoided the other Narens, who Eris had explained were exiles like Biagio. They weren't at all like Richius. They were pale-skinned and oily, and even the men painted their lips. Eris said they were Naren lords. Dyana wondered exactly what that meant. In Aramoor, Richius had been a king. But he had never been girl-pretty like Biagio or the others. She feared going to Nar City as Biagio had threatened. Of all the tales Richius had told her of that place, only now was she beginning to believe them.

Among the Narens there was one that Dyana feared the most, the lanky one named Savros. He had been watching her. Sometimes, when she was alone in the gardens or reading, she suddenly felt his eyes on her back. Eris had warned Dyana to stay clear of Savros. She had said that he was a torturer, one of Biagio's close confidants, and that he was called the Mind Bender. He killed for pleasure, Eris had told her, and the claim made Dyana shudder. There was murder in his eyes. Dyana had seen it, along with a kind of childish adoration. He was a volatile creature, and Dyana did her best to avoid him.

She hardly saw Biagio, either. The count had spoken to her only once since her arrival on Crote, and only then to make small talk, to see if she was comfortable in her rooms. Dyana thought him a braggart. He had shown her the marvelous gardens and then walked away with a regal smile, his sapphire eyes burning brightly. After finally meeting the Count of Crote, Dyana still didn't know what to make of him. Eris claimed he was insane, but that he hadn't always been so. He could be kind and gentle, she had told Dyana, and Dyana had actually seen some of that, two virtues she would never have expected of Biagio. Still, he had a remarkable cruel streak. He still used her as a lure, and would probably kill her when his game was done.

Of all the people in the mansion, only Eris was a friend. She and Dyana spent long hours together, took their meals together, and gossiped over the goings-on in the Empire across the sea. Dyana told Eris all about Richius and Shani, whom she missed beyond words, and Eris danced her beloved ballets for Dyana, taking Dyana's mind off the constant horrors plaguing her. When Dyana watched her perform, perfect and without music, she would stare with wonder and forget her troubles for a time, marveling at the way a trained body could move. Dancing was the girl's life. She loved it more than anything—even more than she loved Simon—and she seemed not to mind her slave status at all. Biagio had made her a great dancer, she told Dyana. He had trained and shaped her, for he had an ear for music and an eye for greatness. Back in Nar, his vast fortune had paid for the finest tutelage. As much as she feared her patron, Eris also loved him. And she truly believed he loved her, too.

It was the love a collector feels for gems, Dyana knew, but she didn't tell that to Eris. That truth would have broken the girl's heart, and

Dyana had no wish to shatter Eris' illusions. So she let Eris believe as she wished, listening to her stories and watching her dance, grateful to have a friend.

On a night like every other, Dyana awoke to the strains of the distant sea. The shades were open over her glass doors and she could see the island beyond her rooms. Swaying grasses in the garden tossed shadows on the walls, and Dyana sat up in the grip of fright, recalling a nightmare with awful clarity. She had been on a ship with Richius and Shani. A storm had come and sunk their vessel, and she alone had swum ashore. Dyana put a trembling hand to her forehead. Richius and Shani *were* gone. Somewhere. And suddenly, it was all too much for her. She wanted to weep but found herself empty of tears. Instead, she sank back against her pillows and stared out the glass doors. Shani might still be on her way to Crote, but that seemed unlikely now. And Richius was lost, too, gone off on some fool's vendetta. Dyana was alone. Again.

Unable to sleep, she rose from the bed, feeling the urgent need to move. She dressed in a fog, putting on some of the expensive clothes Biagio had supplied, and slipping her feet into a pair of leather shoes with soft soles that wouldn't make noise when she walked. A quick check in the mirror revealed a face lined with exhaustion, but she ignored the frightening visage, going for the door and stepping out into the echoing hallway. The marble corridor stretched out on either side of her, decorated with sculptures and scalloped woodwork. It was immensely quiet this late at night. Dyana closed the door behind her, quickly deciding on a direction.

Count Biagio was a very private man. Though he had given her full run of his palace, he had his own private wing that was forbidden to all, even his Naren henchmen. Dyana was resolute about seeing it. He meant to kill her anyway, she reasoned. She might as well see what he was hiding. She moved swiftly through the corridor, and passed the place where the slaves were quartered, far from her own rooms but no less elegant. Even Biagio's servants were coddled. Past the servants' area, she came to an enormous, circular chamber with white columns and decorated with portraits of Biagio's family, all lean and golden like the count. Dyana paused to regard the paintings. She caught Biagio's likeness in most of them, but none had his blue eyes or girlish beauty. Biagio was far more striking than any of his kin.

Dyana left the chamber and soon found herself near the count's private wing. An archway of baby-smooth plaster separated the place from the rest of the villa. Festoons of flowers hung on the walls, perfuming the air, and a small fountain babbled in the corridor. From the mouth of a naked nymph, water cascaded over smooth, white rocks. Dyana listened, loving its sound, then heard something else in the distance down the hall. Music? She cocked her head to listen closer.

What sounded like a piano rang in the distance. It was very late, and the sound drowned the melody of the fountain. The music was harsh and thunderous. But it drew Dyana forward. She moved toward it, following its strains through bends in the halls, until at last she was deep in Biagio's private wing, outside a pair of slightly open doors. Behind the portals she could hear the fractious music and the determined slamming of fingers on a keyboard. Dyana slid closer to the doors, peeking inside. The music was atrociously loud. Inside, she saw a room of pink marble and thick, wine-red rugs, decorated with porcelain busts and furious-looking portraits. At the edge of her vision she saw the end of a white piano, but she couldn't see who was playing. Feeling bold, she pushed the door open a little more, and saw to her astonishment a crazed Biagio.

He was hunched over the instrument, violently hammering the keys as sweat dripped from his face and drenched his flying, golden hair. The music he made screamed from the piano, shaking the room and its fragile decorations. He was lost in it, pounding it out like a madman as he swayed to the fierce rhythms. He was dressed in his usual silks, but the sleeve of one arm had been torn from his shirt, revealing golden skin and a flashing needle. A tube ran from the needle to a vial on the piano. The vial jumped along the piano with each pound of the keyboard. Biagio's face was set, his eyes gushing tears, his jaw tight. He looked to be in enormous pain, but he didn't cry out, nor even utter the smallest moan.

Dyana stared at him, dumbfounded by the sight. She inched the door open a fraction. A blue residue stained the vial on the piano. The last of the stuff swam through the line into Biagio's arm. The count continued his thunderous playing, unaware of her intrusion. He was breathing hard and perspiring in torrents. He looked on the verge of collapse. The luster of his golden skin had turned pallid, the color of sickness, and his hair hung in strings around his neck and face. Dyana didn't know whether to help him or flee. She knew that this was the drug treatment, just as Richius had described it. But she had no idea it was such a violent, rapelike act. Biagio looked weak, destroyed and void of his usual strength. With his tears and tired eyes, he looked like a little boy.

And then suddenly his playing stopped. His breathing raced in the silence, and he raised his head with an agonized groan. That's when he saw Dyana, frozen in the doorway. He erupted at the sight of her, springing from the piano bench.

"What are you doing here?"

Dyana staggered back. She wanted to run but knew it was too late.

"Get in here!" the count commanded. "Now!"

Dyana held her breath and pushed the doors open wide. She walked into the room and stood before the shaking count. He was inhuman-looking, about to teeter from exhaustion. But his rage kept him upright, and his chest heaved with angry gulps of air. He balled his hands into fists and shook them at his sides, pulling the empty vial from the piano and sending it smashing to the ground.

"This is *my* place," he hissed. "Mine! What are you doing here?"

"I am sorry," Dyana stammered. "I meant no harm. I heard the music and came to find out what it was."

"It's my music!" he screamed. "You have no business here!"

"Sorry," said Dyana again. She backed toward the door. "Forgive me, Count. I will leave."

"Don't you dare!" he roared, racing forward and seizing her arm. His grip was iron and painfully cold, and when he clamped his fingers around her wrist, Dyana cried out.

"You are hurting me," she said, trying to stay calm. "Please . . ."

"You want to hear music?" he asked indignantly. "Or did you come to stare at the freak?"

"I did not!" Dyana protested. "I just heard your music. I did not know you were in here." She grimaced at the strength of his grasp, then looked up at him, pleading. "Let go," she said softly. "Please."

Biagio's face softened. Slowly his fingers uncoiled from her wrist, letting her loose. Dyana's first instinct was to bolt, but she curbed the urge. Biagio was watching. He stumbled backward and fell upon his bench, sitting there with his hands trembling and his skin dripping sweat.

Dyana said nothing. Biagio closed his eyes and sighed, then used his dainty fingers to dig out the needle, popping it from his flesh. He tossed it nonchalantly to the floor, among the broken glass of the shattered vial. With painful slowness, his breathing normalized and a healthy color gradually returned to his skin. When at last he opened his eyes again, they were the old iridescent blue.

"Music is the only thing that helps me," he rasped. "Otherwise the treatments would be unbearable. Arkus used to listen to a harpist when he took his treatments. He said the music took away the pain."

"Are you all right?" Dyana asked. She chanced a step closer, afraid he might erupt again, yet somehow compelled to remain.

"I will be," he said. "The drug is very strong. It takes time."

"I know this drug," said Dyana. "It makes you young, yes?"

Biagio nodded. "Something like that." He looked up at her. "You shouldn't have come. I don't like being seen this way."

"You are right," said Dyana sheepishly. "I am sorry."

She turned and made it halfway to the door before he stopped her.

"Why aren't you sleeping?" he asked.

Dyana hovered in the doorway. She should have hated Biagio, but in that moment he seemed too frail to loathe. "I had a dream," she answered. "It woke me."

"I have dreams," said Biagio. He ran his hands over his damp hair. "You can't imagine the nightmares I have."

"I think I can," Dyana replied. "I have lost my child and my husband both."

The count scoffed. "That's nothing compared to losing an empire."

"If you say so." Dyana went for the door again. "Good-night, Count."

"Wait," Biagio called. "You might yet be wrong. Your child might still be alive."

"If she is . . ."

"Yes, yes," said Biagio with an annoyed wave. "I remember my promise, woman. You needn't remind me every time you see me." He ran his fingers over the keys distractedly, hitting a string of discordant notes. His shoulders slumped and a vacant expression crossed his face. Dyana knew he was thinking about Simon. Once again she approached him.

"You need not do this, you know," she said carefully. "I am no threat to you. And neither is my husband."

Biagio's eyes flared, insulted. "Believe me, I know that. Your husband and his wretched Lissens are of no concern to me. They're insects."

"Then why hurt us?" Dyana knew it was a lost cause, but she had to try. "If you let me go, I can tell Richius that you know about his plans. I can get him to call off his invasion of Crote."

The count smiled. "Now why would I want that? Your husband is the perfect sheep. He's part of my grand design, you see."

"What do you mean?"

He waved her away. "You ask too many questions."

"But you know I am right," Dyana pressed. "Why do you not let me go free? Richius never meant you any harm. And he did not kill your emperor. I am sorry for your loss, but—"

"What do you know about my loss?" spat Biagio. "Save your pity, woman. You know nothing of what you speak."

"You are wrong," Dyana countered. She got even closer to him, close enough to feel his remarkable cold, then fell to one knee beside the bench. "I know you loved Arkus. Richius told me so. I know the emperor was very dear to you. And you to him."

Biagio's face twitched. "Yes," he whispered. "That is true. I loved him dearly." He fingered more notes on the keys, his mind skipping back over memories. "But you may not be so right about his love for me. He had the chance to give me Nar. He knew he was dying, yet couldn't admit it. He wanted to live forever."

"And there was no magic in Lucel-Lor to save him. The mission you gave Richius was impossible."

"There *was* magic," Biagio insisted. "I know there was."

"There was a man," Dyana corrected. "My first husband, Tharn. He was touched by the Gods. But even he could not have saved your emperor. Even if he had wanted to, he could not. You have to believe that, Count Biagio. Richius did nothing to you."

Biagio was silent. Dyana sighed.

"Look at you," she said. "This drug will kill you someday. It is not natural."

The count gave a black laugh. "Not natural? Ah, then it's perfect for me. For I'm not natural and never have been. Archbishop Herrith could tell you that." He turned and sneered at her. "Don't you know what I am, woman? Or is that why you feel so safe with me? Because you know I'll never take you to my bed?"

"I know what you are," said Dyana. "And I am not afraid of you."

"Well, you should be. I'm a monster."

He turned his back on her, resting his elbows on the keyboard and burying his face in his hands. Dyana didn't know if it was a signal to leave, but she remained in the chamber, waiting for Biagio's gloomy mood to pass. Eris was right. The drugs *had* made him insane. Yet Dyana didn't fear him. Something inside her told her to stay, to try and coax enough humanity out of the count to make him see his mistakes. And maybe, to save Richius' life.

"It does not have to be this way," she said softly. "I have heard things about you. And not just from my husband. I can even see it myself."

"See what?" Biagio growled.

"The drugs, what they have done to you. People say you were not always this way. They say you were different when you were younger."

Biagio lifted his head and stared at her. "Eris has been very naughty, hasn't she?"

"Do not blame Eris," said Dyana. "She only told me what I asked. And it is obvious, anyway."

"What is?"

"That you are insane. Like Arkus."

"How dare you!"

"It is the drug," Dyana insisted. "It has made you mad. Anyone can see that just by looking at you."

"Fool," scoffed Biagio. "You're only seeing the treatment. I'm not always like I am tonight. The drug keeps my body young. I am better than I ever was. Stronger and smarter." He made a dismissive gesture with his slack wrist. "Don't believe everything you hear, woman. If you were a Roshann agent, you would know better."

"I know what I know," said Dyana. She knelt down beside him. "All of this, everything you have done—it is all for revenge. But if you let me go, if you send me to Liss on a ship, I will tell Richius not to invade. He will listen to me, and then you can both end this madness."

"I don't want to end it. Haven't you been listening? I *want* Liss to invade!"

"Why?"

Biagio slammed a fist down on the keys. "You think I'm going to tell you that? Suffice it to say, I have my reasons."

"Madness," said Dyana softly. "That is all this is. And you are so insane you cannot even see it. The drug—"

"The drug keeps me alive," spat the count. "It keeps me beautiful." He took her wrist again, forcing her to look into his hypnotic eyes, holding her and not letting go. "Look at me. Am I not beautiful?"

Dyana was afraid to answer. He was beautiful, but he was also inhuman, and in those lovely, blazing eyes she saw madness. "Yes," she replied. "You are beautiful. But not beautiful enough." She pulled free of him. "I still see you as a monster. And not because of the way you look." Carefully she reached out a finger and tapped his chest. "It is what is inside you that is diseased."

"You are wrong, Lady Vantran. The drug makes me strong. I would not be able to tame the Empire without it."

"And that is all that matters? You arrogant man. Maybe Arkus was right about not giving you the Empire. Maybe he saw how mad you were. He never—"

Biagio's hand shot out, slapping Dyana hard across the face. She fell back, startled by the blow. Biagio towered over her, his face twisting.

"Don't you ever speak his name to me again," he seethed. "You wretched bitch. Arkus loved me! I was like a son to him."

Dyana put a hand to her cheek. "Mad," she said again. "That is what you are."

She turned and left the chamber. Biagio called after her but she darted down the hall, desperate to be away from him. Her face stung but that was hardly a concern. What hurt far worse was her pride. Like a fool she had tried to reason with him. And for a moment, she had even thought it was working.

Stupid, stupid woman, she chastised herself as she hurried from the count's wing. Her soft shoes echoed with her eagerness, but she didn't care who heard her now. She was irate, not only with Biagio but with herself. If Richius had seen her beg, he would have been appalled.

She made her way past the slave quarters toward her own rooms far removed from Biagio. Only when she saw her chambers did she breathe a little easier. But her relief was short when she noticed her door slightly ajar. She took a careful step forward and listened at the door. Hearing nothing, she pushed the portal open and peered into her rooms. All seemed just as she'd left it. The chamber was dark, but a paralyzing moonlight froze the furniture in its rays. Without a sound she took a cautious step inside, then, emboldened, took another. She heard the wind outside but nothing else. Shadows danced on the walls, reflecting the moonlight. Dyana frowned, sure that her imagination was getting the better of her. No doubt she had forgotten to close the door on her way out.

"I need sleep," she said softly. Sleep would take her mind off things.

She went to her bedchamber and found it dark. The shades were drawn over the glass doors. Dyana stared at the doors uncertainly. And then she felt afraid.

"I left those open," she whispered to herself. "I know I—"

From out of the darkness a hand shot over her mouth. Arms wrapped themselves around her, enormously strong.

"Don't be afraid," came a voice. Its tone was high, like a hissing snake. Not Biagio. Worse. Dyana tried to scream but the cold hand muffled her sounds. She tasted chemicals on the flesh. Savros the Mind Bender leaned forward and put his cheek against hers. "Pretty thing," he cooed. "Pretty, pretty thing."

He was breathing fast and lustily. Dyana fought to break free. She kicked and twisted against his lanky arms, amazed at his iron grip. Savros giggled at her struggles.

"Oooh, please, save your strength," he whispered. "Don't fight me so. Save your vigor for the chains."

No! Again Dyana tried to scream and heard only a feeble gurgle. Savros tightened his coiling arms. She could see him smile from the corner of her eyes.

"I've watched you so long," he moaned. "You're so beautiful. Your skin, like a flower. I have to take you, pretty Dyana."

He parted his lips and let his ruby tongue dart out, lapping at her cheek. Dyana hit a wall of nausea. She drove an elbow into his ribs, but Savros' reedy body was made of stone, and he absorbed the blows too easily for a normal man. His arm came up in retaliation, snaking around her neck and tightening until she thought she'd black out.

"I have a place," he said. "Downstairs. I've prepared it just for you. Yes, yes, just for you."

He was gibbering, overcome with perverted lust. Dyana could feel the unnatural heat pouring off his cold skin. He began dragging her backward toward the door. Still she fought against the pain and blackness, but her acrobatics only delighted Savros the more.

"Yes, yes!" he chimed. "Dance for me, pretty thing. You will dance for me."

He pulled her out of the bedroom and into the main chamber. Dyana could barely breathe now. She was exhausting quickly, but knew she had to break away before he got her down into his dungeon. Fear exploded in her brain, an awful mix of pain and bloody visions. Amazingly, Eris' voice came to her out of the fog, telling her to watch out for Savros.

The Mind Bender hadn't even broken a sweat. Like it had to Biagio, the drug had given him preternatural strength. He forced her out into the hallway, pushing open the door with his shoulders as he kept a hand over her mouth and a steel arm around her neck. Dyana was about to suffocate when another figure cast a shadow across the corridor. Savros stopped, and his solid arms weakened to water. Down the hallway stood Biagio, pausing in mid-step when he saw them.

"Savros," he exclaimed. "What is this?"

The Mind Bender's hands fell away. Dyana tore free of him, darting toward Biagio. But Biagio was already racing forward, his two hands reaching our for Savros. He blazed past Dyana and fixed his hands around the torturer's throat.

"How dare you defy me!" he cried as his fingers tightened. Savros was gasping, taking great gulps of air and begging for mercy.

"Master, please . . . !"

Biagio heard none of it. He was in a rage, lifting Savros off the floor and pinning him against the wall. "You little beast! I'll kill you!"

"No, Master!" pleaded Savros, his voice barely a rasp. He fought like a wildcat, trying to pry loose Biagio's determined fingers. His feet kicked at the air. Dyana fell back against the wall, horrified. Her own breath was returning and she tried to steady herself, shocked at what she was seeing. Savros' face turned a ruddy purple. His blue eyes bulged, threatening to burst. And still Biagio kept up his throttling, banging the Naren's head against the wall and cracking the plaster.

"Die, you wretched pig! Die!"

There was the rattling of breath and the popping of bone. Savros' gangly body trembled in the air, hanging there in a moment of rigidity. Biagio's hands tightened still more, until the neck between them cracked. The Mind Bender's body suddenly went limp. Biagio held it for a second, then flung it to the floor in disgust.

"I warned you," he spat at the corpse. "Don't tell me I didn't!"

Then he turned on Dyana, stalking toward her. She could see the struggle on his face for control.

"Are you hurt?" he asked.

Dyana shook her head, unable to speak. The count went to her and gave her a swift inspection. He took her hand with a reassuring squeeze.

"This is an outrage," he said. "I am sorry."

Finally, Dyana found her voice. "I am all right," she said. "I think . . ."

"You look uninjured," observed Biagio. "I was coming to speak to you. To . . ." He shrugged, looking away. Amazingly, he seemed to have forgotten the corpse on the floor.

"What?" Dyana probed. She kept hold of his frozen hand, hoping vainly to thaw it.

"I should not have struck you as I did," the count managed. "I apologize. I do not want us to be enemies, Dyana Vantran. That's not what you're here for. And this . . ." He gestured to the dead Savros. "This brutalization wasn't what I wanted for you."

He was such a contradiction, Dyana couldn't fathom him. In mere seconds he had gone from a madman to something almost human. She closed her eyes, suddenly overcome. The night had overwhelmed her and her knees began to buckle. Only Biagio's hand kept her upright.

"You are *not* all right," he insisted. "Come, you need rest."

"I need air," said Dyana. She still felt Savros' arm around her throat, choking her. And the blow across the face Biagio had given her wasn't helping. "Please, just let me sit."

Without a word he swept her up in his arms and took her back into her chambers, ignoring the dead Savros. He went straight to her bedchamber, then laid her down on the mattress. Dyana's head was swimming. The bruise he had given her was starting to swell, and the struggle with Savros had taken all her strength. Biagio hovered over her bed, watching her. He looked strange in the moonlight, glowing with an amber aura.

"I'll fetch Kyla for you," he said. "And get rid of that disgusting thing outside your door."

Dyana nodded. "Thank you."

"Do not thank me, woman. It was my stupidity that caused all this. Savros would not have attacked you if I had been more vigilant. It won't happen again."

"No," Dyana agreed. "I suppose not."

They stared at each other in awkward silence. Biagio's expression was pained.

"I am not mad," he said softly. "You are wrong about me."

Dyana tried to smile. "Perhaps," she said gently. "And perhaps you are wrong about Richius."

Biagio grimaced. "Unlikely." He left her bedside and went to the door. But he paused there for a moment before crossing the threshold. "Though I suppose anything is possible."

And with that remarkable admission, he left her alone in the dark. Dyana stared at the place where he had been, hardly believing her ears.

THIRTY-FIVE

Gifts

Two days before the great holy day of Eestrii, Nar City waited beneath a blanket of penance. The streets far below the Cathedral of the Martyrs had been swept clean of acrobats and menageries, and pilgrims had begun pouring into the city, ready to bend their knees to God and beg His forgiveness. In all the city, hardly a hint of the festival of Sethkin remained. On Eestrii, the vast square outside the cathedral would swell with people, a great mass of the faithful, ready to receive the word of God through His servant, Herrith. It was a time of reflection, the day when the lords of the Empire looked inward and decided if their souls were clean or unclean. They would listen to Herrith, and he would tell them what the year would bring, and if the angels in Heaven were pleased with what they saw below. And after his speech, Herrith would go down among the people and perform the sacrament of Absolution. He would spend the rest of the day touching foreheads and doling out forgiveness, and all for the good of Nar's rotten soul.

In the days of Arkus, Eestrii was always a time for pride. But now the archbishop ruled Nar, and no one knew for certain how this had changed Heaven's view of things.

For years, Herrith had made the same annual trip to his balcony, raising his hands to the masses and imparting his wisdom. It was a perilously brief moment, and Herrith always tried his hardest to come up with something special for the day. Usually, he locked himself in his chambers for days before the event, carefully writing a speech and praying for divine inspiration.

Usually.

But not this year.

This year, Archbishop Herrith had other matters occupying him, and though he still locked himself in his chambers, so alone that not even Lorla came to see him, he was not busy with a speech or prayer. He was in the early throes of a violent withdrawal, and not even God could save him this time.

The shades of his window were pulled wide open, letting in a stream of sunlight. Herrith sat at his ornate desk, his hands trembling as he stared at the tiny vial. A blue residue barely coated the interior of the vial. It was the last of the drug Biagio had given him, hardly enough to blend into a potion. Every few days, he had been mixing a few drops of the potent stuff with water, making the elixir that kept him ageless. Just as Nicabar had claimed, Bovadin had made this batch powerfully strong—strong enough to have lasted Herrith for weeks. But now it was gone. Only the faint blue residue remained.

Herrith let out a whimper. His bones ached and his eyes burned. The withdrawal had seized him two days ago, squeezing the life out of him like a constrictor, and since then he had puzzled over his nearly empty bottle, mourning its loss and trying to devise the best way to ingest what little of the life-giving drug remained. He knew the dangers of mixing so little with water. To do so might kill him. And he worried that he might mix the solution so weakly as to have no effect on him at all. That was unthinkable, because that meant enduring more withdrawal and, quite possibly, madness. He set the vial down and ran his hands over his head. He had already gone through the hellish withdrawal once. He couldn't face it again.

"Merciful Heaven," he whispered. "What shall I do?"

He needed more of the drug, enough to sustain him just a little while longer, just long enough to think of a way out. Bovadin couldn't wait forever on Biagio's island. Herrith was certain the midget would someday return to Nar, but Herrith had been unable to think of a way to coax him back. He had even hoped himself free of the drug, a theory Biagio's gift had plainly proven wrong. Worse, Vorto had tried to warn him. The bishop grit his teeth against the pain, the thought of the general assailing him.

Vorto. He had always been the strongest. Herrith knew the general had more faith than anyone, even himself. He hadn't even flinched when he'd seen Biagio's gift.

I should have listened to him. I should have resisted the urge. Now look at me.

Herrith slammed his fist down on the table. "Enough! No more whining." He picked up the vial with his shaking hands. "I will take you," he said softly. "And if you kill me, you will simply send me to God."

There was a pitcher of water on the desk beside him. Herrith picked it up, spilling some, and poured the liquid into the drug vial, filling it halfway. Then he put down the pitcher and stopped-up the vial with his thumb, giving it a shake to wash all the precious blue liquid from its sides. He looked at his concoction in the sunlight. A hint of azure tinged the water. Herrith felt a dreadful quiver in his stomach. He thought of just swallowing it down, but that would be suicide. For reasons no one really knew, the drug needed to be introduced directly into the bloodstream, or it would not work at all. The bishop stared at the vial uncertainly. He was a faithless fool. He realized that now. But he was tired, so very tired. And the drug meant strength and vigor. It owned him. Herrith surrendered to it.

"I fear you're the one power greater than Heaven," he said. "We should both be damned forever."

So he went to the place where he kept his apparatus, and blithely administered the last of the drug.

He awoke with his head on the floor, realizing that hours had passed.

His tear-stained eyes opened warily to the stabbing sunlight. He had vague memories of sickness. In his guts moved a strange burning. Herrith took a breath to test the life in him. Except for a cramping in his bowels, he felt strangely satisfied, without the marrow-chewing pain of earlier.

"Dear God," he whispered, lifting his head and examining himself. "It's worked. I'm all right again."

He clasped his hands before him and gave Heaven its proper thanks, unspeakably relieved. This had purchased him at least another day, a whole bagful of clear-headed hours to plan his bargain with Biagio. Somehow, he needed more of the drug. And quickly, too, before the pains seized him again.

Now that he was strong enough to walk, he stood and went to the window. Outside, all of repentant Nar was at his feet. Soon they would be looking upward toward him, waiting for his words. The realization startled him. Eestrii was only two days away, and he had no idea what he would say.

"God will inspire me," he reasoned. "I will pray for it."

And I will pray for forgiveness for my own sins, he added silently, *and hope that Heaven still has a place for me.*

He had been so sure of himself when he'd conquered the drug that first time. Now he was weak, and his vague reflection in the window sickened him. Had he been so wrong about things? Did God really speak to him at all?

"I am still a man of God," he told the reflection. "Do not doubt it."

There were signs enough to convince him. He still had Nar. Even now he towered over it. And Vorto would be returning soon, with a subdued Dragon's Beak to his credit. Surely God would not allow a heretic to rule an empire so vast. It was why He had killed the immortal Arkus. Herrith put a hand to his head. Sleepiness tugged at him, bidding him back to his chair. But the aches of his body had subsided a little. He smiled to himself.

"I'm still alive, Biagio," he said softly. "You'll have to do better."

From across the vast chamber he heard a knock on his door. Before he could reply, Father Todos pushed the door open. He looked troubled.

"Holiness?"

"Yes?" replied Herrith tersely. "What is it?"

Todos stepped into the room and eyed his superior. Herrith had hardly seen the Father since taking to his chambers, and Todos had prowled outside the bishop's domain like a worried mother. Now the priest's face brightened at seeing his master robust again.

"It's good to see you up and around," Todos remarked. "I was concerned."

"Thank you."

Todos eyed the empty vial on the desk. Suddenly the cheer left his expression. "Is that all of it?"

"The last drop."

"Holiness . . ."

"Don't lecture me, please, Todos," said Herrith gravely. "I know what I'm doing."

"Do you? I wonder sometimes." Father Todos came closer, inspecting the bishop. "You look terrible; your color. And you haven't been eating again."

"I have," said Herrith indignantly.

"No, you haven't. I've been keeping a close eye on what's been coming in and out of here, Herrith. Your trays are almost as full when they leave as when the women bring them. It's that God-cursed drug. You're withdrawing again."

Herrith turned toward the window. "It will pass," he said. "I'm in control."

"But now you're done with it. What will happen now?"

I don't know, thought Herrith bleakly.

"I'll think of something," he said.

Todos stepped around him, blocking his view. "And if you can't?" he asked. "What then?"

"Have faith, old friend," Herrith said gently. "Biagio wants Nar. He gave me that drug as a bribe. And yes, I fell for it. But that won't be the end of it. We will hear from the count soon enough. When we do, I will secure more of the drug for myself." He looked at his friend seriously. "There's still much work to do, Todos. Nar is diseased. I need to be strong. An old man can't do what's necessary."

"Herrith, please . . ."

"Enough," bid the bishop. "Believe in me. I am guided by Heaven." He smiled warmly, forgetting the pain swimming through his head. "Now, what is it you came here for?"

Father Todos brightened again. "Yes, I almost forgot. That toymaker is here. He's brought the gift for Lorla."

Herrith looked up excitedly. "Has he? That *is* good news. It's almost Lorla's birthday. She'll be pleased."

"He's brought men with him, too, Holiness. The dollhouse you had him build is enormous! It takes four men to lift it."

"You've seen it?"

"No, Holiness. It's still crated. But he wanted to deliver it to you personally. Shall I have him wait?"

"By all means," said Herrith. "I must see this thing he's built." He rubbed his cold hands together gleefully. "I'm sure it's a marvel. Lorla will be thrilled."

"Shall I go and find her?" asked Todos.

"No, not yet. I want to see it for myself first. And Redric Bobs would likely take all the credit. He'll be paid, of course, but I want to see Lorla's face. That reward will be mine alone." He looked down at his wrinkled clothes, frowning. "I must wash and dress. Go and tell the toymaker to wait for me. And have him move his dollhouse into the great hall. Make sure Darago isn't in there. If he is, have him leave."

Todos grimaced at the order. "Holiness, I don't think Darago would care for that."

"I don't care what that pompous painter wants," said Herrith. "He's done with his work now. He shouldn't be spending so much time in the hall."

Todos laughed. "He's very proud of his work."

"As he should be, no doubt. But this dollhouse of the Piper's is a work of art, too. I want to unveil it with the ceiling on Eestrii. Lorla's birthday must be special. Go now, Todos, please. Do as I say. I'll meet you in the hall presently."

With a reluctant bow, Todos left the chamber so that Herrith could dress. The bishop hurried to his wash basin and splashed his face with cool water. The mirror above the basin revealed a weary, weathered face, not young at all. His eyes were still blue but noticeably dimmer. Herrith fretted over the visage, frightened by what it might mean. It was like a ghost staring back at him, or one of those vampires from Dorian folklore. He put up his hand and shielded himself from the reflection, then turned away and went to his dressing chamber where he found himself a robe and cassock and quickly slipped everything on. He was eager to see the thing the Piper had made. Four men! How elaborate it must be, how beautiful. Lorla would be ecstatic. And she'd been such a good girl, and such a fine daughter. To please her, he would have done anything.

When he finished dressing, he took a drink of water to steady himself, then headed downstairs. He passed the confession booths filled with silence and was soon in the great hall, that part of the cathedral that had stood empty for so long, closed to the public while Darago and his assistants worked their magic on the ceiling. Herrith sighted Redric Bobs in the center of the gigantic chamber, staring up at the ceiling. The panels of the painting were each covered with sheets, all carefully layered over the masterwork to hide it from curious eyes. But the Piper craned his neck anyway.

Beside him was a giant crate with three of its sides still erect. The fourth side had been torn away to reveal the glimmering contents. Herrith licked his lips in anticipation. Redric Bobs was alone in the room. Blessedly, Darago was nowhere to be seen. The bishop's footfalls echoed as he walked, catching Bobs' attention. For a brief second, Herrith thought he saw a flash of disdain in the toymaker's eyes.

"You've brought it, Redric Bobs," said Herrith. "How wonderful."

"As promised, Holiness," said the toymaker. He inclined his head slightly in deference. "The girl's birthday is only days away, yes?"

"Two days," said Herrith. "On Eestrii. You've been timely, Redric Bobs. I thank you."

"And would your Holiness care to see what he's bought?" Bobs asked. There was a distinct ring of pride in his voice.

"I'm as curious as a little boy," replied Herrith. "Let me see this jewel!"

The Piper stepped aside so that Herrith could see inside the crate. What the bishop saw in the wooden box took his breath away. Redric Bobs had built a masterpiece, a perfect likeness of the great cathedral, meticulously detailed and lovingly ornamented, replete with tiny angels and gargoyles, and bearing a steeple of iron and copper. Over the cathedral's miniature gates flew an archangel, a winged-man with a trumpet to his lips, a flawless rendition of the real one. It was a stunning representation, true in every detail, and Herrith was awed by it. He stared at the model, basking in its tall shadow, and could not imagine anything more lovely.

"It's priceless," he whispered. "Absolutely priceless."

"Well, actually no," quipped Redric Bobs. "In fact, it's quite expensive."

"Oh, Piper Bobs," sighed Herrith. "Compared to this fantastic thing, money is nothing. You have no idea the joy you've brought me. And Lorla."

"I'm pleased to oblige," muttered the toymaker.

Herrith turned and regarded him questioningly. "What ails you, Piper Bobs? You've created a masterpiece. You should be pleased with yourself. If it's payment you're worried about . . ."

"No, Holiness, I'm not worried about money. Your Father Todos has gone to fetch me some of my payment. He says the rest will be delivered to me soon."

"So then? Why the long face?"

The Piper shrugged. "Nothing," he said evasively. "I am glad you approve, that's all."

"I do," said Herrith with a smile. He didn't know if it was the drug or merely the sight of the magnificent model, but he felt invigorated, better than he had in days. He stepped closer to the dollhouse. The fine details required eyes sharper than his own, but he could see all the care and time that was lavished on the thing, the tiny components glued expertly together, the bits of precious metals and woods, and all the carvings running along its sides, so perfectly mimicking the runes that decorated the real cathedral's walls. But most amazing of all was the angel in the middle. Herrith reached out for it.

"No," cried Bobs suddenly. "Don't touch it."

"What? Why not?"

"It's very fragile. You might break it. Please, it's really not meant to be handled."

Herrith's expression soured. "It's a dollhouse, Piper Bobs—for a little girl."

"It's also a work of art, Holiness," said the toymaker defensively. "If she plays too roughly with it, it might break. Especially the archangel. I say again—please don't touch it."

"Very well," sighed Herrith, stepping away from the model. Fragile or not, it was a marvel. "Thank you for bringing it," he said. "And for finishing it on time."

The toymaker nodded. "You're welcome, Holiness. I hope it gives you and the child much pleasure."

"It will give all of Nar City pleasure, be assured. We will leave it here for all the faithful to see, so that they may admire it with Darago's great ceiling."

"Yes, the ceiling," remarked Bobs. "When will this be unveiled? On Eestrii?"

"Indeed. You should come to the unveiling, toymaker. It will be a fabulous day. It's my gift to Nar, you see. I want all the faithful to admire it."

Redric Bobs flushed a little. He wasn't "faithful," and they both knew it.

"Perhaps," replied the toymaker mildly. "If I can get away."

The arrival of Father Todos ended the awkward moment. In his hand was a small sack of coins.

"For you, Redric Bobs," said Todos. "With our thanks. You will have the rest soon."

Redric Bobs smiled. "No hurry. Just seeing your faces is payment enough."

"Nevertheless," Herrith interrupted. "You will be paid handsomely for your work. Thank you, Redric Bobs. You're a true craftsman."

The toymaker bowed, then backed out of the chamber, sensing the dismissal in Herrith's tone. The bishop was pleased to see him go. Redric Bobs was such an inscrutable man, and not a friend to the church. But he was a genius, and his rendering of the cathedral was without peer.

"Find Lorla for me, Todos," said Herrith. "Tell her that her birthday gift is waiting."

Lorla was in the chapel when Todos found her, watching a wedding between a baron's son and a young redheaded woman from Goss. She was on the landing, crouched behind a statue of Saint Gowdon, doing her best not to disturb the fascinating ritual. It was a small wedding by Naren standards, maybe three hundred people in all, and the duke's son was a handsome fellow with jet hair. Very soon it would be her birthday. The ticking clock had set her to thinking.

Father Todos let out an exasperated sigh when he found her, loud enough to echo in the chamber and stir the crowd below. Lorla cringed when she saw him. She spent a lot of time in the chapel watching the priests work, and none of them seemed to mind her presence. Only Father Todos treated her like a nuisance. She supposed he was jealous of the attention Herrith gave her.

"Lorla," he whispered loudly, beckoning from across the landing. "Come over here."

"Shhh," Lorla scolded. She pointed down to the floor below. "I'm watching the wedding."

"Now," said Todos sternly.

Whenever he took that tone with her, Lorla knew she had to obey, so she carefully backed away from the landing's edge, scooting out of Saint

Gowdon's shadow. "What's wrong?" she asked. "I wasn't doing anything. Father Herrith always lets me watch the weddings."

"It's not that," said Todos. "Archbishop Herrith wants to see you. Your birthday gift has arrived."

The words struck Lorla like a fist. Birthday gift? Already? She wasn't sure that she wanted her gift to arrive anymore. Ever.

"Really?" she chirped, feigning a smile. "Where is it?"

"In the great hall. His Holiness is waiting there for you."

"Yes. Yes, all right," said Lorla. "That's wonderful."

"It *is* wonderful, child. You won't believe your eyes! Father Herrith spared no expense for you. I hope you realize that."

"I know," said Lorla sharply. She didn't like Todos' constant reminders about Herrith's good nature. She already knew the bishop was kind-hearted, not at all like she had been taught to believe. "We can go now to see it?" she asked.

Todos shook his head. "You know the way, child. I think Father Herrith wants to share this gift with you alone."

The priest flashed her an insincere grin before departing. Lorla watched him go, afraid of him. Sometimes she wondered what Todos thought of her. He alone seemed to sense the difference in her. When he was near, Lorla felt suspicion. Still, none of that mattered. Herrith loved her, and that was all she had ever hoped to accomplish. She spared a glance over her shoulder, looking forlornly at the wedding below, then hurried off toward the great hall and her waiting gift.

As she moved through the quiet corridors, she heard voices in her head—again. Lorla slowed, cocking her head to listen. The voices had been getting louder recently. They didn't frighten her, though. They were like hearing music. And she couldn't make out what they were saying. Sometimes she thought it was Master Biagio's voice, gently cooing to her like a father. The sound of it comforted her. Lately she had been wondering about her place in the world. When she did, the voices always came to calm her. Master Biagio still had a plan for her, and hearing his voice, if it *was* his voice, made her feel less alone. Herrith seemed like a decent man and she cared for him greatly now. But he was the Master's enemy.

That was all that mattered.

Lorla quickened her pace, driven on by the murky voices. She left the wedding far behind, then descended a set of stairs leading to the lower levels. Cowled acolytes passed her by, prevented from greeting her by their vows of silence. But other priests gave her gentle nods, and scholarly monks who had come to the cathedral on pilgrimages flashed her curious smiles, obviously amazed to see a little girl wandering the sanctified halls. Lorla reveled in the attention. She loved the cathedral and all its odd denizens. She loved its soaring ceilings and the way her feet could fill a room with echoes.

When she reached the great hall, she slowed. She caught a glimpse of Herrith alone in the chamber, looking up at the covered ceiling. He looked weak and white-faced. Lorla hadn't seen him for days, and his appearance troubled her. Beside him was a wooden box, far bigger than himself. One of its sides had been torn away, but from her angle Lorla couldn't see what was inside it. And suddenly she no longer cared.

"Father?" she called down the corridor.

Herrith looked up at the sound of his name. A smile lit his gaunt face. "Lorla! Come here, little one. I have something for you."

Lorla hurried up to him, scanning him with a worried eye. "Are you all right?" she asked.

"Fine, fine," said Herrith, waving off her concern. "Your gift has arrived, Lorla. It's magnificent." He stepped aside so she could see within the crate. "Look!"

Lorla looked, and what she saw was mesmerizing. The whole Cathedral of the Martyrs was there in miniature, magically shrunk and put in the box.

"Oh," she sighed. "It's beautiful."

It was more than beautiful, but there were no words good enough to describe it. Its metal steeple, its rune-carved walls, its tiny gargoyles with lolling tongues—all of it bespoke perfection and the hand of God. Lorla was entranced by it. And when she saw the archangel flying over its gates . . .

A bracing shock seized her. She stared at the angel, her eyes wide, and the voices that had whispered in her brain now exploded, screaming at her.

"The angel!" they cried. "The angel!"

Lorla swallowed hard, almost staggering backward. She felt hot, like scalding water were falling on her head. Herrith was staring at her, frowning. She fought to steady herself, to beat back the insistent voices and regain her possessed mind.

"I love it," she said breathlessly. "Oh, yes, it's very nice."

"Nice?" asked Herrith. He came closer to her, looking down at her with concern. "Lorla? Are you all right?"

I don't know! thought Lorla. *What's wrong with me?*

"Yes," she lied. "Fine."

"You don't look fine."

Stop yelling at me! she demanded, but the voices didn't obey. They kept after her, crying "angel" over and over. Lorla forced a twisted smile.

"I love it, Father," she said. "Thank you so much."

Herrith seemed disappointed in her reaction. Lorla hurried to salvage the moment.

"It's sooo lovely," she said, falling down to her knees before it. "And so real-looking! Was the toymaker here? Did he bring it himself?"

"Yes," said Herrith. He got down on one knee next to her, and together they admired the impossibly beautiful dollhouse. The voices inside Lorla subsided a little. But still she stared at the angel, somehow knowing what needed to be done.

"Will you unveil it on Eestrii?" she asked softly. "With the ceiling?"

"That's up to you," replied the bishop. "It's your birthday present, Lorla. If you want to put it somewhere else, you may."

"No," said Lorla quickly. "No, I want to leave it here. I want everyone to see it on Eestrii. With Darago's ceiling."

Lorla tilted her eyes upward. Far above them, the ceiling was covered with lengths of cloth to hide Darago's masterpiece. The scaffolds had been pulled away too, so that now the great hall was empty except for the huge crate and the marvelous, meticulous dollhouse. Lorla's gaze drifted toward the panel where she knew the little orphan girl, Elioes, was hidden behind the cloth. Elioes had been touched by God. She was one of Heaven's favored, someone very special. The thought saddened Lorla. Wasn't she special, too? That's what everyone had always told her. Soon it would be Eestrii, her birthday. She would have to prove her worthiness to the Master. And now she didn't want to. Slowly, she slipped her hand into Herrith's. The bishop looked down at her and smiled.

"Father?" she asked in a whisper. "Does God love everyone?"

Herrith grinned. "Of course, little one."

"Does He forgive our sins, no matter what they are?"

"Yes. But you needn't worry about that, Lorla." He squeezed her hand tightly. "You're pure. You're without sin."

Lorla grimaced. *For now.*

"Holiness!" came a sudden voice from across the chamber. Both Lorla and the bishop looked up to see Father Todos hurrying toward them. The priest looked distressed, his face drawn with worry. He was clearly out of breath, and by the time he reached them was gasping. Herrith rose to his feet.

"Todos, what is it?"

Father Todos clasped his hands out in front of him. "God in Heaven, he's back," he said quickly. "He's delivered something for you. A message."

"Make sense, man," rumbled Herrith. "What message? What are you talking about?"

"Nicabar! His ships have returned to the harbor!"

Lorla blinked at the name. *Nicabar?*

Herrith blanched. "Merciful God," he droned. "What's that devil want now?"

"He's left a message for you, Herrith," said Todos. "A box and a note. He had some of his sailors bring it ashore. It's waiting for you in your study."

"A box?" parroted Herrith.

"And the note," added Todos. "Please, Herrith, come quickly. Nicabar's ships might open fire on us! And without Vorto to protect us . . ."

"Be easy, Todos," bade the bishop. "I'll see what the devil has brought us this time." He turned to Lorla apologetically. "I'm sorry, little one," he said gently. "I have business to attend. We'll sup together tonight, all right?"

Lorla nodded. "Yes, Father," she replied, then watched him leave the great hall with Todos.

An awesome silence filled the chamber. Lorla looked back at the cathedral model. The angel was speaking to her.

Herrith hurried toward his study, his mind racing. Another delivery from Nicabar could only mean one thing: Biagio had delivered more of the drug. He would have known that the small dosage he'd first given would have run out by now. Herrith wrung his hands as he walked, full of hope. Behind him walked Father Todos. The priest's worried chattering hadn't ceased since he'd come to the hall.

"I don't know what it is," he repeated. "And our defenses are weaker without Vorto here. There are three dreadnoughts, I think. Or four. I don't know why the admiral didn't come ashore. Afraid, I suppose."

Todos was babbling; Herrith hardly heard him anymore. He didn't care why Nicabar hadn't come ashore. Really, the reason was obvious. Without an escort sent to protect him, the legionnaires in the city would tear him to pieces. Herrith wondered if Nicabar's note would explain things. Perhaps he wanted to come ashore and was waiting for safe passage to the cathedral. No matter. They would know soon enough.

The door to Herrith's study stood open. Inside, a pair of priests loomed over his desk, their expressions bleak. On the desk sat a wooden chest. Next to the chest rested an envelope. Herrith eyed the chest greedily as he entered his study. A box so large could hold a gallon of the drug!

"You haven't opened it, have you?" he asked his priests. Each of them shook their head.

"Holiness, it's for you," explained Todos. "We wouldn't dare."

"Fine, fine," said Herrith absently. He hovered over his desk, inspecting the chest. A little latch kept the lid closed. Herrith ran his hand over it, feeling the leather, afraid to open it. Biagio was a devil. If the chest did contain the narcotic, the count would be bargaining for it. Herrith held his breath as he fingered the latch. It sprung open with a metallic click. The three priests watched, mesmerized. Herrith slowly opened the lid and peered inside.

Something rotten and dead stared back at him. Herrith's heart froze. He stared at the thing, and realized at last that it was a head, and that the head was Vorto's.

"Mother of God!"

Todos screamed. The two priests crossed themselves, horrified at the sight. A stench rose up, striking Herrith squarely. Vorto's head was like a shattered melon, bald and burned almost beyond recognition. Herrith put his hands to his mouth and backed away from the desk.

"God have mercy on you, Biagio," he whispered.

"What happened?" Todos cried.

Herrith took a deep breath, then slowly closed the chest. A trancelike mood fell over him. He was fighting the devil himself, he realized suddenly. Biagio was more of a monster than he'd feared.

"Vorto," he said softly. "Rest, my friend. You were a loyal soldier."

"My God!" exclaimed Todos. "How can this be?"

"Todos . . ."

"Herrith, Biagio's killed him! We have no general anymore!"

"Shut up, Todos," snapped Herrith, turning on his friend. "Let me think." He collapsed into his chair in front of the desk, brooding over the chest and the terrible circumstances Biagio had delivered him. Todos was right. Without Vorto, they had no commander. They had soldiers still, but they would be demoralized by this. Biagio was very slowly turning the tide.

Then Herrith noticed the envelope again.

With an unsteady hand he reached across the desk and retrieved the note. Todos started to say something, but Herrith silenced him with a glare.

"Todos, you stay," he said. "Jevic and Merill, please leave us."

The two lesser priests bowed and left the room, shutting the door behind them. Todos hovered over Herrith.

"They're demands," he prophesied. "Biagio means for us to surrender."

Herrith opened the envelope and pulled out a piece of paper. The penmanship was Biagio's. But he didn't read the letter aloud. Instead he studied it, holding it close so that Todos couldn't see.

Dearest Herrith,

It is sad indeed that things have come to this. But you see now that I intend to get your attention, and will not be ignored. Your champion is dead, as are the soldiers who went with him. There has been much bloodshed, for which I am truly regretful.

I ask you again to come to Crote with all the Naren lords loyal to you. I cannot come to the Black City myself, as you well know. Now that I have slain their general, the legions would not have me on Naren soil. But I sorely want peace, and beg you to treat with me.

There is also the matter of the drug. It is here, waiting for you. You have my word that I will not withhold it if you do as I ask. Nicabar and his ships will remain in the harbor until you decide to join me. Do not try and send him away, because he will not leave until you change your mind.

And you will change your mind.

Your friend,
Count Renato Biagio

Herrith tossed the letter onto the desk before him. "You're certain of that, are you, Biagio?" he seethed.

Todos snatched up the letter and began to read.

"He thinks I'll change my mind!" Herrith thundered. "He thinks he is stronger than me and God!" He smashed a fist down onto the desk, sending the gory chest jumping. "Well, he is not!"

Todos shook his head, worried. "He taunts you with the drug, Holiness. If you don't talk peace with him—"

"Not on his own island, I won't," snapped Herrith. "Let Nicabar wait in the harbor 'til he grows spiderwebs. I will never set foot on Crote."

He laid his hands on the chest containing Vorto's head, praying to God for strength. It was all unraveling now, faster than a hurricane. Only Heaven could save them.

"Send a message back to Nicabar," the bishop directed. "Tell him I will not speak peace with Biagio, and that neither I nor any Naren lord will be going to Crote. Tell him also that we are still strong. Biagio may have killed a handful of our army, but we are not doomed yet. Go, Todos. Make haste with my message."

Todos departed, leaving Herrith alone to brood. The bishop got out of his chair and walked weakly toward the wall of glass displaying all of sprawling Nar. In the harbor he could see the *Fearless* and her sister dreadnoughts bobbing on the ocean. They were a formidable trio. Like Biagio, Nicabar, and Bovadin. At his worst,

Herrith had never dreamed Biagio would go this far. Or accomplish so much.

"It's slipping away," he said mournfully.

A year ago, he had thought himself invincible. Now he just wondered what the morning would bring.

THIRTY-SIX

Betrayal

Count Renato Biagio felt wonderful. One day remained before Eestrii.

The count was in a lazy mood. He was world-weary and profoundly satisfied with himself, for his grand design had almost been achieved after a long year of planning. Tomorrow, if all the pieces of his vast puzzle fell into place, Nar would understand the power of its true master.

Biagio leaned back in his giant leather chair, sipping at a glass of sherry and admiring the view through his window. Crote was very beautiful. He would miss it sorely. But great victories always came at a price. Someday, when Nar was his, he would retake the island of his ancestors. He wondered how it might change in that time. What would the Lissens do to his precious homeland? The thought made him take another sip, deep and contemplative. Every building they burned, every statue they defaced, would be paid back in magnitudes. He would see to it. And so would Nicabar.

But that was the future, and Biagio didn't care to think so far ahead. He was basking in the moment, and in the moments soon to come, and as he drank his fine sherry he smiled to himself, imagining Bovadin in the streets below the cathedral, watching his device go off. The midget had worked exceedingly hard. He was a loyal servant, and Biagio was proud of him. Just as he was proud of Nicabar and, to a lesser extent, the little girl named Lorla.

Lorla.

Biagio mulled the name over in his mind. It suited her. He had named her himself. The count smiled. She had been the perfect candidate for his mission, and Bovadin had worked his miracles on her. Lorla was like a clock ticking toward midnight. Outside his window, Biagio noted the position of the sun. It would be dark soon. Not too much longer.

"And so I will win, Herrith," he said to himself. "And you will come to Crote because you are weak and because you underestimated me."

They had all underestimated him. Even Arkus. His beloved emperor hadn't had the foresight to leave him the Empire. It wasn't vanity or self-promotion. He was simply the logical choice, and Arkus had forsaken him. A full year later, Biagio still didn't know how to forgive the man who'd been like a father to him.

The one bright spot in his days was the Vantran woman. Dyana was a marvel he hadn't expected, and after almost two weeks, he no longer minded having her around. She had the brains not to contemplate escape, and on those rare occasions when they spoke she always tried to convince him of her husband's innocence. She was a good and loyal woman. And faithful to her husband. Biagio's own wife Elliann had never been like that. But then, neither had he.

He would find Elliann, he decided. When he returned to the Black City, she would crawl back to him like the bitch she was, smelling wealth and power, and he would turn her away for the simple pleasure of seeing her scowl.

Biagio put down his glass. On his desk sat some loose leaves of paper, a journal of sorts that he had been keeping of recent events. He had chronicled everything meticulously, sometimes transcribing whole conversations, for he wanted a record of his grand design not only as a souvenir but also as a guideline of sorts for his Roshann agents. They were still scattered throughout the Empire, awaiting his return. He would have much to tell them.

But sometimes his journal wasn't about his reforms at all. Sometimes his notes were just the offerings of a cool, reflective mind. Biagio picked up his pen and began to write.

The Jackal's wife is nothing like I imagined, he wrote. *She sees my secrets with the eyes of a jaguar, and yet she seems not to care. Nor does she have fear of me. When I tell her my plans to take her to Nar, she hardly flinches. And she calls me mad. Clearly, my mastery of her means nothing.*

Still, she has set my mind to thinking.

Biagio put the end of the pen into his mouth, chewing on it pensively. Thinking about what? His own mortality? Yes, that and so much more. He didn't like having his sanity questioned, especially not by the Jackal's wife. There were plenty in the Empire who thought Richius Vantran insane, yet that didn't seem to bother Dyana. She was blinded by him, dazzled by his strange glamour. Just like everyone else.

And Biagio still hated him. Despite Dyana's appeals, the count's fury knew no satiety. His one wish was that he could be here on Crote when Vantran invaded. He would have liked to see his old nemesis again.

"Patience," he counseled himself. "You have the woman."

Dyana could lure Richius Vantran to the ends of the earth. She had proven that once already. Biagio leaned back, putting his hands behind his head and resting his feet on his handmade desk. Today, life was good. Tomorrow, it would be even better. He closed his eyes and started to daydream, but was quickly interrupted by a knock at his door. The count's eyes snapped open with a growl.

"Leraio, if that's you . . ."

"Master, please," came his house slave's voice. "It's urgent."

"Come in, then, damn it."

Leraio opened the door and stepped meekly inside. He knew his master hated disturbances, so he got right to the point.

"A ship just arrived, Master," said the slave. "One of the fleet."

Biagio quickly pulled his feet off the desk and got out of his chair. "The *Swift*?"

"Yes, Master," replied the slave. He had a worried smile on his face that made Biagio wonder.

"What else?" probed the count. "I can tell by that stupid grin you're not telling me everything."

"Captain Kelara has already come ashore, Master. He says he has to meet with you urgently."

Biagio tossed up his hands. "Well? Bring him in here!"

"I'm sorry, Master, I just thought—"

"What, Leraio? What did you think? I told you I wanted to see Kelara the moment he arrived. So why are you wasting my time with this nonsense? Just bring him to me."

"But, Master," the slave implored. "It's not what you think. Captain Kelara isn't alone. He's brought someone ashore with him. Another sailor."

Biagio grimaced. Why were there so many surprises lately? "What sailor?"

"Master, Kelara says he's from the *Intimidator*."

The count fell back into his chair with a groan. "Oh, no . . ."

It wasn't just interesting news. It was terrible news. Biagio tried to tame his emotions, but they were suddenly overwhelming. This unpredicted arrival could only mean one thing.

Simon was dead.

"Bring them in," whispered Biagio. "Both of them."

Leraio backed away with a bow. Biagio picked up his sherry and quickly finished the glass, ignoring the pleasant sting it gave his throat. He wanted to run away suddenly, to hide where no one could find him. And he cursed himself for his foolishness, sure that the mission he had thrust on Simon had killed him. He set down the glass and stared at the threshold, waiting for his guests to arrive and bracing himself for dreadful news.

Captain Kelara appeared in the doorway first. He was dressed in a clean uniform, and readied himself for the audience by taking off his hat and giving Biagio a deferential bow.

"Count Biagio?" he asked. "A word, please?"

"More than a word, I hope," replied the count. He beckoned him closer with a finger. "Come in, Kelara."

Kelara stepped aside to reveal another man, a much younger sailor with fair hair and an eager look about him. He was thin and pale like many of Nicabar's ilk, and when he saw Biagio he gave a quick, awkward bow, mimicking Kelara.

"What's your name, sailor?" asked the count.

"Boatswain Dars, sir," replied the young man nervously.

"Boatswain Dars of the *Intimidator*, is that right?"

"Yes, sir."

"How is that possible?"

The boatswain grimaced, shifting his eyes toward Kelara for support. Kelara took a step forward. His expression grew grave.

"We rescued him, Count Biagio. I'm sorry to say, the *Intimidator* was lost. Dars here was the only survivor."

"Lost," echoed Biagio. "How?"

"We were rammed by a Lissen schooner," the young man interjected. "She came out of the dark and struck us amidships. We didn't even see her coming. Captain N'Dek and the rest of the crew went down with her." His eyes hit the floor guiltily. "I'm all that's left."

Biagio felt his insides twist. No other survivors. Not Simon. And not the Vantran child. He let out a heavy groan.

"There's something I'm not understanding," he said. "The *Intimidator* was struck by a Lissen schooner. And then, what . . . ?" The count shrugged. "You swam to Liss?"

"No sir."

"Then how did the *Swift* find you?" pressed Biagio, losing patience. "Where the hell was the *Intimidator*?"

"Uh, Count Biagio, I think I should explain," said Kelara.

"Yes, Captain, that would be very nice."

"Count, the *Intimidator* wasn't en route to Crote as planned. She was in Lissen waters when she went down. That was her heading . . . on the orders of Simon Darquis."

"What?" hissed Biagio. His eyes darted between Kelara and Dars. "What are you saying, man? Explain yourself."

"It's true," said Dars. "Simon Darquis was aboard. He had the Jackal's daughter with him. He ordered us to Liss."

"Darquis took Captain N'Dek hostage in his cabin," added Kelara. "He ordered the *Intimidator* to Liss on authority of the Roshann. *Your* authority, Count Biagio. N'Dek did as he was told, and they dropped Simon off on the islands. According to Dars, here, Richius Vantran was on Liss, too. Darquis stayed with him."

"Darquis said it was all part of your plan," said Dars. "We didn't understand it, but when they let us go we didn't care. Only they didn't let us go. We thought we were free, but then the *Prince* came."

"The prince?" probed Biagio.

"The *Prince of Liss*," Kelara explained. "Prakna's flagship. And he didn't really let them go. When they thought they were safely away, the *Prince* came after them in the night. Sunk 'em." The captain shook his head ruefully. "I saw the whole thing, but I was too far away to do anything. And the *Swift* doesn't have any cannons. All that I could do was rescue poor Dars here."

Biagio listened, appalled at the tale. He didn't care that the *Intimidator* had been sunk, or that a whole crew was dead. What fixed his mind—what screamed at him—was that Simon was on Liss. It was unthinkable, and yet the word that best described it rang unceasingly in his mind.

Betrayal.

"This is impossible," he gasped. "What business had Simon in Liss? I gave no such orders!"

"I swear, it's true," insisted Boatswain Dars. "Every word of it. Simon Darquis took control of our vessel and sailed us to Liss. That's where we left him." The young man sneered. "That lice-ridden dog. He betrayed us, and on your orders, sir. He did, and I'll go to my grave saying so."

"I'm sorry, Count Biagio," added Kelara. "But it's all the truth. We picked up Dars and then sailed for Crote. I thought you'd want to hear this news quickly."

Biagio was silent. Kelara looked at him questioningly.

"My lord?"

"Yes, yes," whispered Biagio. "You did the right thing, of course, Captain."

Kelara and Dars exchanged puzzled glances. Biagio saw them only peripherally. He was lost in a fog, crushed by the news and unable to lift himself from the chair. Simon had betrayed him. The thought of it was agonizing. It had been painful to think him dead. But this new revelation was crippling.

"Thank you, Captain Kelara," he said finally. "But you must return to your patrols."

"Yes, my lord, just as soon as we're ready. We'll take on some supplies and head back. I thought maybe we could rest a day, maybe take on some fresh crewmen from the other ships."

"Whatever you wish," replied Biagio absently.

Boatswain Dars stepped forward. "Sir," he asked. "I'd like to go back with the *Swift*. I'd like to take my revenge on those Lissen pigs in any way I can. With your permission . . ."

Count Biagio glanced up. "Revenge?" he said bitterly. "Certainly. Why not? If Kelara can find a place for you, you have my permission to go with him. Take all the revenge you want, crewman. Gorge yourself on it."

The two sailors bowed politely and left the chamber. Biagio listened sadly to the closing of the door. A powerful feeling of aloneness settled over him. He glanced at his sherry glass and found it empty. He looked absently out of the window and saw no one in his garden. Past the glass doors, there was only silence, not even the distant call of a bird. Winter was coming to Crote, walling them up.

"Why?" Biagio whispered. "Oh, my dear friend. Why did you do this?"

There were no answers. He had given Simon everything—including Eris. He had lavished his favorite friend with gifts and freedom, opulent clothing and jewelry galore, yet still Simon had betrayed him. Like so many fools before him, he had fallen for the spell of Richius Vantran. Biagio swatted the wine glass from his desk, sending it shattering against a wall, then rose from his chair, shoving it violently backward.

"How dare you do this to me!" he roared. "I am Count Renato Biagio!"

Near his bookcase he found the sherry bottle. In a rage he tipped it to his lips, swallowing down great gulps and spilling it over his satin shirt. He didn't care about being genteel anymore. He didn't care how he looked or what others thought of him. That game had been played-out long ago. Now he drank like one of Nicabar's sailors, ceaselessly and without a breath until almost all the bottle was drained. Then he threw the bottle against the wall, too, striking a priceless painting and splattering it with glass and wine stains.

"Oh, I'm not done with you, Simon," he rumbled. "I loved you. And you spurned me!"

His eyes darted around the room for something to smash. An ivory bust of Arkus was the nearest item. He stalked toward it, suddenly hating his old mentor, and with a grunt hefted the statue off its pedestal and tossed it through his garden doors. The glass shattered.

"Damn you, Arkus. You and Simon both!"

He was out of control and he knew it, and the sherry was burning a hole in his guts, snaking up toward his brain. It was a delicious madness, and the count did nothing to stop it. He was possessed with loathing and the sting of unrequited love. But the smashing and the screaming did nothing to ebb his growing pain. His mind flashed with pictures—of Elliann, the wife who had left him, and Arkus, the emperor who had died on him. But most of all he thought of Simon, and the image of the man burned him and tore at his heart. The great wall Biagio had erected around himself began to crumble, and with it went all his self-control.

"Hurt me?" he growled. "No, Simon. I will hurt *you*."

He raced from the room in a blind rage, and the servants in the halls gave him a wide berth as he thundered past them, shoving aside any who got in his way. Simon didn't have very much in Crote. He had possessions, of course, but they were meaningless because he was a Roshann agent and accustomed to being away from home. Biagio had thought of burning his clothes, of throwing all his trinkets into the ocean and forbidding his name ever to be spoken. But what harm would that do his treacherous friend? None at all, and Biagio wanted to do harm. He was in that nether-world between normality and madness, clear-headed enough to think but powerless to stop himself.

Abruptly he found himself outside his music room, its doors shut tightly closed. But he didn't stop. With a great howl he kicked open the doors. As expected, Eris was inside, stretching against the warmup bar. She jumped at his intrusion, frightened. Biagio saw her through a red veil.

"Master?" she asked. "What's wrong?"

Biagio stalked toward her. "You took him from me. You turned him against me!"

Eris backed up against the wall, terrified. The count's tall shadow fell over her face.

"Master, please!" she stammered. "What's happened to you?"

He seized her, clamping a hand around her windpipe. Eris screeched in fear and struggled against his icy fingers. Biagio's voice trembled.

"He was dear to me, girl," he hissed. From beneath his cape he produced his Roshann dagger. "Now I will take what is dear to *you*!"

Twenty slaves heard Eris scream. Not one of them dared to help her.

• • •

Dyana had spent most of the afternoon in her private chambers, far removed from the slave quarters. It was a quiet area of the mansion, and since she had already eaten her mid-day meal, she sat undisturbed as she read through volumes from Biagio's library, practicing the Naren language. She could speak it almost flawlessly now. But she still had trouble reading the Naren tongue and making the strange symbols on paper, and as she read she studied everything with careful clarity, sometimes reading aloud to be sure her interpretations were correct.

Because she had very few acquaintances on Crote, Dyana kept mainly to her chambers. Since the incident with Savros, she took great pains to avoid the other Narens. Except for Eris, she hardly spoke to anyone, and Eris had a daily ritual of practice that kept her busy. Today, Dyana had decided not to disturb her friend. They would be returning to Nar soon, Eris had said, and she needed to practice diligently to perform at her peak. She would be the toast of the Black City. Biagio had told her so. Dyana looked up from her book, grinning at the thought. She and Eris weren't so far apart in age, but the dancer had an innocence that made her seem vastly younger. No matter what Biagio did, she refused to see him as anything but her master.

A glance out the window told Dyana it was getting late. She realized suddenly that she was hungry again. The mid-day meal had passed hours ago, and soon it would be time to sup. Since she always took her supper with Eris, she decided to go find her friend. At this time of day, Eris would still be in the music room, endlessly practicing to make herself perfect.

Dyana set her book aside and left her chambers, going down the soundless hallways toward the more populated parts of the mansion. The first thing she noticed were the long faces of the servants she passed. Each of them avoided her eyes and had a vacant look about them. Dyana spied them suspiciously. Biagio's home was full of unintended surprises. But when at last she approached the music room, she noticed that a crowd had gathered near the doors. Among them was Kyla, Dyana's bodyservant. Dyana paused before going any closer, studying the mournful throng. A few of the women were crying.

"Kyla?" Dyana called. "What is wrong?"

"Oh, Dyana," sighed Kyla, hurrying up to her mistress. "It's Eris. The Master has hurt her."

The words were jolting. "What happened?" asked Dyana desperately. She looked over Kyla's shoulder toward the milling servants. "Where is Eris? Is she all right?"

"No, Lady Dyana, she's not. She's hurt. Master Biagio . . ." The girl broke down into sobs. Dyana grabbed hold of her shoulders.

"Kyla, tell me what is wrong!" she demanded. She was in a panic and needed answers. "Where is Eris? What has happened to her?"

"She's in her rooms," replied Kyla. She was shaking, almost incoherent. "The others took her there, bandaged her. God, there was so much blood."

Dyana didn't wait another second. She flew from the hall, heading straight for Eris' rooms. Her mind raced with black possibilities. Had Biagio raped her? Beaten her? He was a taskmaster when it came to his teachings. Dyana grit her teeth as she ran. If he had hurt her . . .

Outside Eris' room, Dyana found another crowd of women. They were silent, as if holding a vigil. The door to the dancer's chamber was closed. Dyana shouldered her way through the crowd.

"What happened?" she asked. "Is she all right?"

An older woman with blood on her clothes shook her head ruefully. Her name was Bethia. "The Master took a knife to her," she said. "She's in great pain. I've given her something to help her sleep, but—"

"A knife?" blurted Dyana. "My God, he stabbed her?"

Bethia put a calming hand on Dyana's shoulder. "He cut her," she said gently. "Her foot."

Dyana blinked. "I do not understand," she stammered. "Why did he do that?"

"To punish her," replied the woman. She went on to explain how Biagio had gotten news from Liss, and how Simon Darquis had betrayed the count. He was with Dyana's husband, the woman explained, helping the Lissens.

Dyana couldn't believe her ears.

"Simon is alive?" she asked. "What about—"

"Your child is with him," said Bethia. There was a wide, sad smile on her face. "Shani's alive, Dyana."

Dyana wept. Without shame, she let the tears run down her face. Shani was alive! And safe with Richius. There could be no happier news. Except . . .

"What happened to Eris? Why did he hurt her?"

The woman shrugged. "I don't know, child. He meant to punish her, I suppose, for what Simon has done. But it's cruelly unfair. He's killed her, that's what he's done. He's taken off half her foot."

"Oh, no," Dyana moaned. "Oh, Eris."

She had to go to her. None of the servants protested as she moved toward the door. Dyana mustered up her courage and pushed the door open without knocking. A dark room with drawn shades enveloped her.

"Eris?" she called lightly. "It is Dyana."

"Dyana, go away," came Eris' pleading voice. "God, don't look at me like this."

Dyana saw her through the darkness, lying across a bed on the far side of the room. There were blankets over most of her body, but her wounded foot stuck out of the coverings, swathed in bandages. Hot tears outlined her red eyes, and when she saw Dyana she turned away. Dyana ignored Eris' pleas for her to go. She slipped into the room, shutting the door behind her. The darkness grew with the door's closing. Carefully, she picked her way through the blackness, approaching the bed as her eyes gradually grew accustomed to the dark.

"Eris, do not send me away," she said gently. "I want to help you."

"No one can help me. Look what he did to me, Dyana. Look what he did. . . ."

Dyana could barely see the ruined appendage in the darkness. But she knew what Bethia had meant. In a sense, Biagio *had* killed Eris.

"Why did he do it?" sobbed Eris. "I never harmed him."

"Oh, Eris," sighed Dyana. "I am so sorry."

"I'll never dance again. Never. He's taken that from me. Why?"

There was no answer for the agonizing question. Biagio was mad. It was the only suitable excuse. Dyana knelt down at Eris' bedside, reaching under the blankets to grab her hand. The fingers were lifeless. Two eyes stared at her blindly.

"Eris, be strong," Dyana begged. "Please. For me. I need you here with me. You are all I have."

"I can't, Dyana," whispered Eris. "I'm lost. He's taken my life away. There's nothing else for me. I'll die."

"You will not die," insisted Dyana. "I will not let you. And there is more than dancing to live for. Simon is alive, Eris."

The girl nodded. "I know. That's why the Master did this to me." She turned her face away. "And Simon couldn't love me now. I'm a cripple, a freak."

"Eris . . ."

"Go, Dyana, please," cried Eris. "Please just leave me alone."

Dyana rose and hovered over the bed. She wanted to comfort Eris, but there were no words to soothe the pain, or ease the enormous loss. Eris was a dancer, body and soul. Now she was nothing, and it was like a wraith had come to replace her.

"I will look in on you later," said Dyana. "Rest now."

Eris didn't reply. She merely lay there in the bed, unmoving. Dyana bent down and kissed her forehead, then turned and left the chamber.

This time, though, she wasn't going back to her own rooms.

"Where is Biagio?" she barked at the slaves. They milled like sheep, afraid to answer. "Tell me!" said Dyana. She whirled on the old woman who had greeted her. "Bethia, where is he? Do you know?"

"Dyana, don't go to him. He'll only get more angry."

"Do not protect that monster," rumbled Dyana. "Just tell me where he is."

"I don't know," said Bethia.

"I know," a small voice interjected. A servant girl stepped forward. "I saw him go out the southern gates, toward the beach."

Dyana didn't thank the girl. She just stormed off toward the south side of the mansion. Bethia called after her, but Dyana ignored the old woman's pleas. She was enraged, and wanted to face Biagio while she still had the courage.

There were two guardians near the southern gate. Dyana braced herself for a confrontation, but was surprised to see them step aside. Sunlight struck her face as she exited the mansion. Down the beach, she sighted Biagio sitting in the sand, staring blankly at the warships on the horizon. He looked remote and contemplative, far worse than he had that night she had seen him taking his drugs. Dyana quelled her trepidation and strode toward him. The wind had picked up and the surf smashed against the shore, spraying Biagio where he sat. It was frightfully cold. Without a coat, Dyana shivered.

I'm not afraid, she told herself.

"Biagio!" she called across the beach.

When he heard her voice, he merely shook his head. Dyana came up to him, staring down at him. His hair was wind-blown and damp with sea spray, and wine stains splattered his shirt. When he finally looked up at her, she saw how red his eyes were, inflamed from weeping. His face was an insane mask.

"I knew you'd come," he sneered, half laughing. "Will you scold me now?"

"You bastard," Dyana boiled. "How could you do it?"

"Count Biagio does what he wants, woman. He doesn't ask permission."

Without thinking, she reached out and slapped his arrogant face. A stunned silence rose up between them. Dyana took a step back, sure she had doomed herself. But Biagio didn't fly into one of his rages. Instead he put a hand to his bruised cheek and, remarkably, looked chastened.

"Talk," Dyana demanded. "Do not ignore me. I am not one of your slaves. And I am not afraid of you."

"Then you are like your husband, woman. Afraid of nothing." The count paused. "Do you know what has happened?"

"I think I do. Simon is alive."

"He's on Liss."

"That is no reason to savage Eris. My God, you butchered her."

"He betrayed me!" Biagio flared. "After I gave him everything. He's on those cursed islands with your husband, even now. I merely took from him what he took from me."

"You had no right—"

"I had every right!" he cried. He was shaking, sick with rage. "I am Count Renato Biagio! Eris is mine to do with as I wish. Everything on this island is mine!" Then he looked away again and began babbling to himself. "Soon the whole Empire will belong to me. Things will be like they should have been. I'll sit on the Iron Throne. I'll bring back the Black Renaissance. My grand design will work!"

He was almost beyond coherence. Dyana didn't know whether to stay or go. But Biagio's guards had let her pass for a reason. She knew the madman wanted her here.

"You are not telling me everything," said Dyana. "Your guards let me pass. Why?"

Biagio shrugged. "You already heard the news."

"What news?"

"About Simon. And your child."

"Shani? What about her?"

Biagio shook his head in exasperation. "Why are you so dense? Your child is alive. I thought you should know. That's all."

The incredible admission left Dyana speechless. "You wanted to tell me that?" she asked softly. "That is why you let me come out to you?"

"Yes," said Biagio flatly. "Now you may go. Good-bye."

"I am not leaving," said Dyana. "Not yet." She sank down into the sand next to him, close enough to feel his breath. He was horrible-looking. All the golden beauty had left him in a flood of tears. But when she came close to him he flinched, turning his face away.

"I don't want you here," he said. "Go away."

Dyana tried to smile. Progress with this madman was painfully slow, but she was sure she was making some. "You destroyed her," she said. "Do you not know how terrible that is?"

"What I did to Eris was my right," he seethed. "I own her, woman. And I own you, whether you know it or not."

"No one owns me," said Dyana. "I am a free woman."

Biagio gave a wicked chuckle. "You're my prisoner. Unless you can swim back to Lucel-Lor, I own you. And do not think me so gentle, woman. Today has given me more reason than ever to hate you and your husband. If you don't fear me, you're a fool."

Dyana was resolute. "I do not fear you. Not anymore. Look at you, weeping for someone you love. I had never thought that possible before, but now I see what you really are. Oh, you can say that you are something special, but you are not. You are just a man."

"I am *not* just a man," said Biagio, insulted. "Soon I will be the emperor. And then you'll treat me with the respect I deserve, and you won't presume to speak to me like this." He leered at her. "I am taking you back with me to the Black City, Dyana Vantran. Do not doubt that for a moment."

Dyana shook her head. "No matter how I try, you will not listen, will you? You are so full of hate."

"With good reason. Your husband keeps taking from me. Taking, taking, taking! First Arkus. And the Empire. Now . . ." Biagio stopped himself. "Well, I will take from him this time. You will be my lure. And when he comes to rescue you, I will have him. I'll make him linger, I promise."

"You are insane," said Dyana. She rose from the sand, realizing all her efforts were wasted. "And you are right. I am a fool. I thought I could convince you how wrong you are. I thought I could get through all your madness, make you hear me. But I cannot. No one can." She sighed miserably. "If you're going to take me to Nar, then go ahead and do it. But I will not live in fear of you, Biagio. You will never own me."

Biagio smiled. "I'm still sane enough to remember our bargain, Dyana Vantran. And I will never seek out your child again. I don't have to with you here. Remember that."

Dyana stared at the count in bemusement. It was like looking at two different people, two sides of a broken mirror. He had gone to the ends of the earth to steal her daughter, and now was promising her safety. At last, unable to decipher him, Dyana merely shrugged, resigned to his mystery.

"Do not expect me to come to you anymore," she said. "I will not speak to you again."

Then she turned and left the brooding count, heading back to the mansion.

Eris lay awake in her bed, caught in a narcotic embrace. The simples Bethia had given her had done a surprising job of deadening the pain in her butchered foot, but they did nothing to ease her loss. She had trained all her life to perform; it had given her meaning and dimension. She wasn't just a slave; she was a performer, sought after and respected.

Now she was nothing.

She didn't understand why the Master had done this to her. She knew only that it *had been* done, and that she would never walk again like a normal person, much less grace a dance floor or perform in the Black City to crowds of adoring nobles. Those girlhood dreams were gone. Now she was looking forward into an endless void of obscurity.

I am nothing now, she told herself. Her voice was loud and rang in her head, amplified by the feeling of drunkenness. *And I don't want to be here.*

Eris climbed painfully out of her bed and pulled off one of the sheets.

This she coiled into a long rope, tying one end of it around a sturdy sconce high on the wall. She kept the shades drawn as she worked. With great effort she pushed a chair against the wall, climbed onto it unsteadily, and tied the other end of the sheet around her neck.

No one knew she had killed herself until later that night—when Dyana discovered her.

THIRTY-SEVEN

Eestrii

Lorla stared up at Darago's masterpiece. For more than an hour, the faithful of Nar City had been streaming into the cathedral's great hall to be awestruck by Darago's ceiling, which the painter himself had unveiled in a storm of fanfare. Dorians and Highlanders, pilgrims from Casarhoon and families from far-north Criisia, had all come to see the result of the artist's long toil. They filled the cathedral and the grounds outside by the thousands. Priests and bodyguards moved through the crowds, keeping order, and wailing children stopped their cries when they looked up, baffled by the beautiful thing above them. The hall was swelled to capacity. A long line queued up just beyond the chamber, snaking through the cathedral and spilling out onto its grounds, where thousands more milled in the cold sunlight, patiently awaiting their turn to see the ceiling of the great Darago, the gift Archbishop Herrith had bestowed on them.

Lorla waited in the great hall, admiring the artwork with the other spectators. Today was Eestrii, the highest of the Naren holy days. It was also her birthday. Or was it the day Master Biagio simply called her birthday? She wasn't sure anymore. All that she knew for certain was her mission.

The angel had told it to her.

It spoke to her with a disembodied voice, something that came from inside her own brain. Every time she saw the angel it reminded her of her duty. Her memories were clearer now. She recalled the war labs and the strange potions they had given her, and the shiny needles and cold rooms. All those fractured faces that for so long had been gray ghosts were now evident. She saw Biagio. He had a golden face and a compelling smile. And she saw a midget, too, but she didn't know his name. Lorla felt like a different person. And it frightened her.

Not far away, Darago was standing on the side of the crowds, calling to them as they admired his masterpiece. He wore a proud smile on his face. Occasionally he would turn to Lorla and wink. His assistants were gone now, and only Darago remained to show off his accomplishment. The crowds adored him. They loved what he had done for them, and the most faithful among them wept when they saw his vision of the holy books, stretched out in a marvelous fresco overhead. All the characters Darago had shown Lorla were fully alive now in vibrant colors. The orphan girl Elioes received her touch from God. Adan was betrayed and thrown out of Heaven, while on another panel his children slew each other. Lorla saw the great battles and the creation of souls, and laughed like the rest of them at the comical rendition of Judik, the saint who had betrayed God. Father Herrith had explained these things to Lorla. He had set her on a path to righteousness and unfolded the mysteries of the holy books. As she stared up at the painting of Elioes, she didn't feel like an orphan anymore. She felt loved.

But Herrith was the Master's enemy. She didn't know why, but it was so. And the Master was her true father. He had rescued her from some horrible life with her terrible parents, and had chosen her for this because she was special. Even the angel told her she was special. She glanced at it now from across the hall. The fantastic model had been put on display as well, and it drew almost as many raves as Darago's ceiling, a fact that made the Crotan painter simmer. Like his masterwork, the cathedral model was meticulous, and all who saw it commented on its perfection and design, and the obvious love that went into its construction. All except Lorla. When she saw the model, she hated it. It was beautiful and perfect and devilishly clever, and though she didn't know its exact purpose, she knew that something bad lurked within its walls.

Bad? she corrected herself. No, that couldn't be right. It was the Master's will, and the Master always had a purpose. Angrily she shook her head, hating the voices inside her. She had been arguing with them and they had been scolding her, and part of her knew that they were right to be angry.

"Master Biagio has given you life," they would tell her. "Why would you betray him?"

Guiltily, Lorla always acquiesced to the voices. Biagio was her master. He had given her life. Hadn't he? But Herrith had given her love. She cared for the old man now, and didn't want to hurt him. She had come to his cathedral expecting a devil, and had found a gentle, troubled patron instead. More, he had not seen past her ruse. To him, she was just a perfect little girl of eight.

I'm a freak, she told herself bitterly. *Not a woman or a child.*

Duke Lokken and Kareena, Duke Enli and Nina; they had all tried to tell her what she was, but not Herrith. He had merely accepted her. He alone had let her be what God would have made if the labs hadn't interrupted Him.

"Master Biagio," she whispered desperately. "Don't make me do this. I don't want to."

The voices screamed back at her. Lorla began to cry. A man with his family, who had been admiring the ceiling, saw her tears and turned to comfort her.

"Child?" he asked. "What's wrong?"

Lorla looked up at him. He was very tall, and she realized suddenly how unnaturally short she was. His clothes were plain, not rich like a nobleman's, and his family was big and plain-looking too, with a girl and a boy and a weary-faced wife, all staring up and marveling dumbly. Lorla glanced down at her expensive dress, suddenly ashamed of herself.

"I'm all right," she said. "It's the ceiling. It's very pretty."

The lies came too easily to her.

"Yes, it is," said the man. "Today we see what God has made for us. It's so beautiful. He wants the whole world to be beautiful. But since it can't be perfect, He sends us men like Darago to show us Heaven."

Lorla blinked, fascinated by the bit of wisdom. "Really? Do you believe that?"

"Oh, yes," the man declared. "There is so much evil in the world. But sometimes we get to see a glimpse of Heaven." He looked back up at the towering ceiling and melted with awe. "God has a plan bigger than the plans of man, child. No man can stand against God or nature. Not even a great man like Herrith."

"No?" asked Lorla.

"No," said the man serenely. "There is an order to things. God has set them. It's not the place of any man to undo those things."

With those remarkable words hanging in the air, he left Lorla alone to ponder. She watched him return to his family and shuffle out of sight, getting lost in the crowd. Once more she glanced at the cathedral model across the hall. A crowd of children had gathered around it, giddy with astonishment.

Lorla trembled when she saw them. Soon Father Herrith would give his address to the faithful. When he was done, he would leave the cathedral to perform the rite of Absolution.

Time was running out.

On a little balcony room overlooking Martyr's Square, Archbishop Herrith sat with his forehead in his hands. Father Todos and a handful of other priests stood close by, staring out the glass doors to the thousands of people below, the throngs of faithful that had come to hear the bishop's yearly address. Herrith heard their collective din, like the sound of the ocean. He knew they expected much of him this year.

But he had nothing for them.

This Eestrii, for the first time in decades, the bishop had no plans for his speech. He had spent the last two days brooding over Vorto's death and the slippage of his own body, deeper every day into the clutches of withdrawal. He had not even attended the unveiling of his beloved ceiling, an event he had anticipated for years. It was an awful day and Herrith was profoundly troubled.

Suspicions were already spreading through the Black City. Nicabar's dreadnoughts waited on the horizon, visible by all in the streets. People were afraid. They wondered where Vorto was and why Herrith hadn't sent the Black Fleet away. They looked to the Cathedral of the Martyrs for guidance, and their needs were heavy on Herrith's shoulders. The bishop closed his eyes and prayed.

"Dear Father in Heaven, help me. Help me tame this demon inside me, just for today. I have sinned. I am weak. Forgive me."

It was Absolution day, the day Herrith was to go among the people and grant them God's forgiveness. He laughed at the notion. How could he, a sinner without peer, grant absolution to anyone?

"There is so much blood on my hands, Father," he continued. "So many wrongs. But I did it all for you. I . . ."

He paused, unable to go on. The Black Renaissance was a cancer. Biagio was a devil. And God had a plan for Nar. Weren't all these things true? Herrith simply didn't know anymore.

"Herrith?" nudged Todos gently. "It's almost time. They're waiting for you."

Herrith opened his eyes and looked at his associate. The priest seemed nervous. Do I look so bad? Herrith wondered. By nightfall, he would be in the cold grip of withdrawal again, sick with fever and barely able to care for himself. Food would make him vomit and music would make him scream. But Herrith didn't care about that now. He wanted only to get through the day. And if he died in bed tonight, then he would go to God and answer for his sins, and God would judge him good or evil, and reward or punish him.

"Waiting? Yes, I suppose they are," he said, managing a crooked smile.

Todos offered a hand. "Can you stand?"

"I'm strong enough," said Herrith, declining the aid. "For now." He got to his feet and faced the balcony. Through the glass he could see an ocean of people in Martyr's Square, waiting patiently for their spiritual leader. Some said Narens had no God but themselves, but they were wrong, Herrith knew. They feared for the future like all men, and looked to the sky for answers. And to Herrith.

The bishop braced himself with a deep breath, then gave a nod to his waiting priests, who opened the doors. With a final, silent prayer for strength, Herrith stepped out onto the balcony to the cacophonous cheers of ten thousand Narens.

Amid the crowds in Martyr's Square, Redric Bobs stood with his back to the sea and his eyes lifted to the balcony above. Around him milled a vast assortment of people, loyal Narens all, who had come to this place to hear the words of their leader, Herrith, and to gain wisdom from him. A thrill of anticipation moved through the toymaker. He had arrived at the square early and waited patiently for the bishop to appear. Cheers rose up all around him as the venerable Herrith stepped out onto the balcony. But the Piper didn't cheer. When he saw Herrith, he gasped.

"My God," he exclaimed. "He looks terrible."

The small, shadowy figure at his side looked up. Minister Bovadin peeked at the balcony from beneath the thick folds of his hood and gave a twisted laugh.

"The drug," he whispered over the noise. "It's eating at him."

The Piper nodded as if he understood. Bovadin was a furtive man with only his blue eyes to betray his secrets. But like most in Nar City, Redric Bobs knew something about the life-sustaining drugs of the high nobility. The sight of the bishop above made him wince. Herrith looked horrid. And Bobs, who hated the bishop and his church, took a small measure of glee in his misery.

Around him the cheers went on as Herrith lifted a shaking hand to try and still the crowd. The toymaker smirked, folding his arms across his chest.

"Listen to these fools," he remarked acidly.

Next to him, Bovadin's hidden head shook. "Herrith is a persuasive speaker, Redric Bobs. He knows much about the ways of Heaven."

"I'm not interested," the toymaker scoffed. "I'm only here to watch the . . . festivities."

"Not too much longer," counseled Bovadin. "And believe me, you'll be dazzled."

There was real pride in the scientist's voice. But Redric Bobs felt no such pride. He wasn't really glad he had built the dollhouse, or that he had gotten it into the cathedral so clandestinely. These were mere necessities. What he was doing today, he did for his own good reasons. He knew that with certainty. Yet he felt no pride.

"So?" he whispered, bending down so Bovadin could hear him. "When will it happen?"

"Not until the girl sets the device," replied the midget. "And that won't happen until Herrith is done with his address. During Absolution, however, I'd advise you to stand back."

Absolution. Piper Bobs bit his lip. He was still a devout man, despite all. No one knew that, of course, because he hadn't attended a service in years, but he kept the holy days in his own way, and as the clock ticked toward its fateful hour and Herrith kept his arms outstretched, the toymaker wondered about his place in the scheme of things, and about his place in Heaven.

"It has to be done, you know," he said absently. "Really, there's no choice."

Bovadin smiled. "You don't have to convince me."

"No, really," insisted the toy-smith. "He's an evil man. He doesn't know it, but he is. He's hurt a lot of people. He hurt me and my wife."

Bovadin turned to look at him. "Steady, Bobs," he warned. "Don't get weak on me."

"I'm not," snapped Bobs. "I know exactly what I'm doing. And what I've done. Now be quiet, he's talking."

Up on the balcony, hovering over the adoring crowd, Archbishop Herrith began to speak. His voice was weak and shaky. Redric Bobs could hardly hear him. Frustrated, he snapped at the people around him to be silent, all of whom were only breathing but whose rasping breath annoyed the toymaker nonetheless.

"What's he saying?" Bobs asked peevishly.

"Shut up, you idiot," rumbled Bovadin.

Slowly, Herrith's voice grew in volume. Redric Bobs leaned closer, as though the few inches would help him hear. All around him, thousands did the same, staring up in confusion at the leader of their church. Bobs felt a sudden wave of nausea. Herrith looked about to collapse. And the blotches on his face—were they tears?

". . . forgiveness," said the bishop. He put his hands on the balcony to steady himself. "None of us here is without sin. Even my own soul is clouded."

Bobs jerked back, stunned by the admission. He stared at Herrith, thunderstruck, and watched as the feeble man grew in strength with the conviction of his words, until at last his voice rang through the square, like the voice of God Himself.

"And just as all of you ask God for Absolution today," Herrith roared, "so too do I bend my knee to Heaven, and ask the Lord for forgiveness of my sins. I have led the Empire down a terrible path. I have killed and maimed in the name of God. I thought it was His will. But I was wrong."

The bishop paused, and when he did there was an awesome silence. He had them all in the palm of his hand. Even Redric Bobs. The toymaker's hard heart softened with every unexpected word, and as the bishop wept, openly and without shame, Piper felt his own throat constrict with emotion.

"Oh, no," he whispered. "Don't do this to me, you bastard."

"You have seen the warships over our shoulders," Herrith proclaimed. "They would bring war back to our land. I have tried my best to give Nar peace. But I have murdered and maimed to earn that peace, and my soul is soaked in blood. I beg God to forgive me." Again he stretched out his arms. "I beg you all."

Another silence ensued, and then the silence ebbed with the first cry from the crowd, a cry of love that was picked up by another and then a hundred more, until at last all of the thousands in the square were roaring their approval. Redric Bobs felt the life drain out of him.

"What's he saying?" spat Bovadin. The scientist pulled his hood back, glaring up at Herrith. "What is this?"

Redric Bobs sighed heavily. "He's asking us to forgive him, midget."

"A ruse," snarled Bovadin. "Another of his tricks. Don't listen to him, any of you!"

But it didn't look like a trick, and Redric Bobs knew the truth of Herrith's tears, for no man could be such an actor. The toymaker shook his head ruefully. Too late. Everything was too late. They had all pushed the bishop over the edge, and now the weapon they had in their pockets was about to go off needlessly.

"God help me," he groaned. "Oh, my God . . ."

"Stop saying that, you fool," hissed Bovadin. "We've done nothing wrong."

Redric Bobs looked down at him. "We have," he said gravely. "And there's nothing we can do to stop it."

Lorla didn't join the others out in the square to hear Father Herrith's address. Instead she waited in the great hall and stared endlessly at the model of the cathedral. She was alone in the vast chamber, except for Darago. The painter still couldn't take his eyes off his masterpiece, and seemed to be in prayer as he admired it. High above Lorla, Elioes and the other paintings stared down, almost alive. Lorla wished that they could speak, to drown out the voices screaming in her head. There was a great weight pressing down on her chest. She wondered what they had done to her in the labs, and why the pain was so sudden and so strong.

Is this what it means to be special?

Time was ticking away, and the voices grew ever louder, compelling her to move the angel. The tiny figurine flew over the cathedral's gates, beckoning to her with its trumpet. She could almost hear its diabolical music. And whose voice was calling to her? Was it the Master's? Or was it the midget whose name she didn't know?

Time moved still faster. Lorla knew Father Herrith was finishing up his address. Soon he would go into the square and absolve sins. Lorla took a step forward.

"Do it," urged the voices. "The Master needs you."

Duke Enli needed her. And Nina. Lokken and Kareena, too. She reasoned that she was part of something bigger than herself, something vast and important.

"The Master loves me," she said, desperate to believe it. "He wouldn't hurt me. He needs me to be strong."

"Be strong and finish the mission," agreed the voice.

Darago wasn't looking. Carefully, her hand shaking, Lorla reached out and touched the angel.

"Side-to-side," the thing reminded her. "Move me side-to-side."

Lorla's hand was as still as stone. Whatever she did here today would change her world forever. Everyone had told her that her mission was good. And important. Now she wasn't sure. *Herrith* was good. He wasn't the beast she had been led to believe.

Was he?

I don't know!

Yet despite the battle within her, Lorla moved the angel from left to right. She moved it barely an inch, but it snapped into its new place with a mechanical click, startling her. She stepped back, staring at the thing, certain something dreadful would happen. Almost imperceptibly, she heard a purring drone.

"Lorla," called a voice from across the chamber. She jumped. On the other side of the great hall stood Father Todos. The priest had tears in his eyes and wore a huge, uncharacteristic smile. "Archbishop Herrith is done with his address," he said. "He's going into the square now, to perform Absolution. He wants you with him, Lorla."

Lorla stood frozen for a long moment, then stepped away from the dollhouse. A foggy pall settled over her brain. She had done what the Master had required her to do. It had all been over in an instant. Suddenly the voices in her brain fell silent, giving her peace for the first time in days. Exhausted and confused, she nodded at the priest.

"Coming," she said wearily, then followed him out of the chamber.

Inside the walls of Lorla's birthday gift, Bovadin's machine awoke. The hoses that had been dormant for so long now filled with rushing air, and the pressure within the silver cylinder gradually began to build. The combustible fuel within the housing swam through the mechanisms, chilled by scalelike cooling vanes.

The pressure would build for an hour more.

Out in Martyr's Square, Archbishop Herrith sat on a dais surrounded by priests, doling out forgiveness from his golden chair. The gigantic crowd that had listened to his address now lined up in the cold to receive the sacrament of Absolution. For nearly an hour the bishop worked ceaselessly, his face alight as the countless pilgrims from around the Empire knelt before him and asked for God's forgiveness. And the bishop met each request the same way—by touching the penitent's forehead and mouthing the same small prayer over and over.

"God forgive you, my child."

From her place near Herrith on the dais, Lorla watched the bishop work, enthralled by his patience and devotion. He still looked weak, but his eyes jumped with life. His smile was brighter than the sun. Lorla loved the bishop, she realized now. And as she waited with him on the dais she kept looking over her shoulder toward the cathedral, certain that something dreadful would soon happen.

Father Herrith had wanted her here. He had hugged her when he'd seen her, kissing her firmly on both cheeks and giving her a place of honor next to him on the dais, completely oblivious to the thing she had done to him.

As the minutes ticked by, Lorla grew more anxious. She fidgeted in her seat on the dais, not far from Father Todos. The priest kept a careful eye on Herrith, like a mother worried about a sick child. Herrith himself seemed not to notice his ailments. Lorla looked out over the crowd. Some of the same faces she had seen in the great hall were now waiting for their turn at Absolution. And then she saw another face, vaguely familiar. Lorla puzzled over him for a moment before realizing it was the toymaker.

Redric Bobs stood in the line, his face ashen. Next, it would be his turn to kneel before Herrith. The toymaker kept his head bowed, and he looked as if he'd been crying. Lorla studied him hard, terrified he might expose her. But the toymaker apparently had other things on his mind. Herrith dismissed the young woman he was absolving and looked up to see his next patron—Redric Bobs.

"Piper Bobs?" asked Herrith incredulously. "Is that you?"

The old man stepped onto the dais in front of ten thousand onlookers, kneeling before the bishop. He looked up at Herrith with his wild, pain-filled eyes. Lorla's breath caught in her throat.

"Holiness," rasped Redric Bobs. "Forgive me. Forgive me for what I've done."

Father Herrith smiled at him. Lorla's heart raced. Slowly the voices came back into her head.

"Be at ease, Piper," said Herrith, obviously confused. "This is a day of joy. Do not look so forlorn."

The Piper shook his head. "You don't understand," he said. "And I can't explain it to you. It's too late. Forgive me, Holiness." He reached out and grabbed Herrith's hand, then buried his face in it, sobbing.

Lorla got out of her chair. The voices commanded her to sit, but she ignored them. Seeing the toymaker's tears had fractured something deep inside her.

"Father Herrith," she blurted, unable to control herself. "I . . . I'm sorry!"

"What?" sputtered Herrith, looking between her and Bobs. He pulled his hand free of the toymaker. "Lorla, what's wrong? What's the matter?"

Lorla couldn't speak. She could hardly breathe. The voices clamored in her head.

"No!" she cried, putting her hands to her head. "Stop yelling at me!"

"Lorla," cried Herrith, getting to his feet. Piper Bobs looked at her, dumbfounded. From out of the crowd a midget was climbing onto the dais. Memories hammered into Lorla's mind. She backed away from the midget, sure he was coming for her, but noticed instead that he grabbed Redric Bobs.

"Bovadin!" shouted Herrith.

There was an uproar from the crowd. The midget pulled hard on Bobs' coat, trying to hurry him away. Herrith stared at them, stricken. The priests on the dais rose and drew daggers. The midget cursed and threw himself off the dais, vanishing into the crowd. Lorla watched it all in a blur. Time was ticking madly away.

She had to do something.

So she ran. She bolted from the dais, scrambling through the crowds and clawing her way back to the cathedral. Off in the distance she heard Herrith call after her, desperate and confused. It was bedlam suddenly and the crowds around the dais erupted with shouts. Lorla tried to ignore them all. She blocked out everything, focusing all her energies on reaching the great hall. Again she heard the Master's voice roaring at her angrily. Once more she squashed it. She hated the Master suddenly. Father Herrith had been good to her. And Redric Bobs knew that. He'd been crying and she'd seen it!

"Let me pass!" she cried, shouldering her way through the crowds. Somehow she would reach the cathedral and stop what she had done. A group of families waiting at the cathedral gates blocked her way. She threaded through them like a running dog, skirting past their legs and racing into the empty cathedral. Her little heart thumped madly as she moved.

Almost there . . .

The great hall loomed before her. Lorla hurried into it and found Darago there, admiring his amazing ceiling.

"Go, Master Darago!" Lorla shouted as she ran to the cathedral model. "Leave!"

"What?" sputtered Darago. "Why?"

"Just go!"

Lorla reached for the archangel and tried to move it. But the angel wouldn't budge. She heard the relentless drone of something inside the model.

"Move!" she screamed at the angel. "Please!"

"Lorla, what are you doing?" flared Darago, rushing up to her. Lorla burst into frustrated tears.

"Leave!" she cried. "I can't stop it!"

Darago grabbed hold of her, dragging her away from the model. Lorla fought him off with a furious scream.

"Stop!"

Breaking free, she lunged one more time toward her birthday gift. Then, barely an inch from the angel, she saw a dazzling light.

The force of the explosion roared through Martyr's Square, deafening the crowd. Herrith put his hands to his ears and watched a rolling fireball consume his cathedral. A sudden shockwave blew by with a vengeful wind, tearing at his garments. All around him priests and patrons screamed as bits of burning metal rained down around them. Fire poured from the cathedral's gates, and the great metal steeple groaned as its foundation weakened, threatening to topple. Giant plumes of inky smoke belched from the shattered stained glass. Martyr's Square filled with a chorus of screams.

Herrith collapsed to his knees. The hot light of the dying cathedral burned his blue eyes. He looked away, covering his face with his hands, and knew with dreadful certainty that Lorla was dead. And all that came to him was one word, a name that had haunted him for the past year. Defeated, Herrith sobbed his nemesis' name.

"Biagio . . ."

THIRTY-EIGHT

The Company of the Queen

The day before he was to set out for Crote, Queen Jelena summoned Richius back to Haran Island. Prakna was with him, as were Simon and Shii, too, for she was Richius' lieutenant now and would be an integral part of their invasion. Prakna piloted them to the queen's island aboard a catboat. It had been the first time Richius had left Karalon since his arrival, and stepping foot on Haran Island felt strange to him.

Since sending Shani back to Dyana aboard one of Prakna's vessels, Richius had felt profoundly alone. He had Simon and his work kept him busy, but he missed his daughter. And his wife. Part of him looked forward to Jelena's company. She was young, like Dyana, and she reminded him of his wife sometimes. As he walked quietly toward the queen's palace, Richius remembered what Marus had said to him weeks ago, that Jelena was a remarkable woman.

The queen wanted to know what her subjects had planned. Tomorrow, they would set sail on the long journey to Crote, and Prakna had told Richius that the queen was nervous. With good reason, Richius knew. His army had trained hard, but they were still unseasoned. Richius wasn't sure how they would perform in battle, though he wouldn't tell that to the queen. Nonetheless, and to his great surprise, Richius was looking forward to the campaign against Crote.

While he would have liked more time to plan the invasion, Prakna's raiders were getting tired. They needed a port close to the Empire from which to launch their attacks; Crote would serve that purpose. It was warm and very near the Black City. And it didn't have a large army; at least, not according to Simon. Richius glanced over at the Naren who was walking beside him. Simon held several rolled-up parchments in his hand, a collection of maps he had been working on for days. At Richius' insistence he had drawn up all that he knew about Crote's coast and waterways, as well as the layout of Biagio's mansion. Richius had been impressed with Simon's knowledge of the terrain. And the spy had been remarkably forthcoming with details, a fact that eased everyone's suspicions.

Everyone except Prakna. The fleet commander did nothing to hide his disdain for Simon. To Prakna, Simon was not only a Naren pig, but now he was also a traitor. The Lissen commander kept a close eye on Simon whenever he was near, and when they argued, which was often, Prakna was vocal. But Simon had the hide of a greegan; insults bounced off him like a summer rain. And Simon had changed. He had stopped apologizing for his colored past and looked toward the future with a single-minded purpose. Only one goal drove Simon now—to save Eris from Biagio.

As the foursome approached the palace, Simon slowed his pace, staring up at Jelena's home and marveling at the gate. The great, gushing arch greeted them like a warm smile. Behind the palace, the sun was beginning to dip. Its red rays made the water jump with color.

"That's beautiful," Simon said. "Like something from a dream."

"That's what you pigs have been trying to destroy," quipped Prakna. He breezed past Simon and headed toward the arch.

When the rest of them reached the spouting entrance, a pair of Jelena's guards came out to greet them. Prakna did the talking. The sentries gave them all polite bows and led them into a room Richius had never seen, a council chamber near the western gates. Queen Jelena was already there, sitting at the head of a long table. Goblets of wine had been set out for each of them, along with a few plates of food. A bank of windows offered a perfect view of the setting sun. The young queen rose when they entered.

"Hello, my friends," she said brightly, embracing Prakna first, then Richius, whom she favored with a warm kiss. Richius flushed at her affection, embarrassed but enjoying it.

"Jelena," he said, smiling. "I'm glad to see you again."

Her eyes flashed with poorly hidden affection. "And I you," she said. She waved to dismiss the sentries who'd led her guests inside. The pair left the council chamber and closed the doors behind them. Jelena took Richius' hand and led him to the table. "Sit, all of you, please," she told the group. She guided Richius to a chair beside her own; Prakna quickly grabbed the seat on her other side. Shii sat down dutifully beside the commander, but Simon remained standing.

"Queen Jelena," he said. "I'm Simon Darquis." He gave her a perfect bow. "I'm honored to meet you."

"Yes," said the queen. "The Naren spy. Welcome, Simon Darquis. I thank you, especially, for coming."

They regarded each other awkwardly. Richius felt the invisible wall between them. In her own way, Jelena hated Narens almost as much as Prakna. She did a far better job of hiding her contempt, however, and when she offered Simon her hand, he kissed it like a nobleman.

"Sit down, Darquis," grumbled Prakna. "We've business to discuss."

"That's why I'm here," said Simon. He ignored Prakna and spoke directly to the queen. "Thank you, my lady, for letting me help you."

Jelena blanched. "It is on the suggestion of Lord Jackal that I trust you, sir. When word of your arrival reached me, I confess I was troubled. But Richius speaks well of you." Her gaze narrowed. "Please don't make a fool out of him."

Simon took the implied threat genteelly. "I've given my word, and I will give it again to you now. I'm here to help." He laid his maps out on the table, spreading them wide for all to see. "I know Biagio's island better than almost anyone. I was born and raised on Crote, and I've spent time with him in his mansion. These maps contain all the details I know."

Jelena nodded. "Good," she said, taking her seat. She leaned back, regarding each of them in turn. To Richius she seemed like an ice sculpture, glistening with beauty yet hard and cold to the touch. She was every bit the queen, suddenly. At last Simon took a seat beside Richius, keeping his sharp eyes on the young ruler.

"You'll all be leaving tomorrow," said Jelena. "And it will be weeks before I see any of you again. I brought you here because I wanted to know what you're feeling, what you think of your chances against Crote. Karalon is remote, even for me. So, a simple question. Are you ready?"

"We are," Prakna declared. "The *Prince of Liss* is ready to sail, as are the other ships. We're taking four schooners with us. That will be enough to get the troops to Crote. I'd prefer more but the others are still engaged in Nar. I plan to send word to my armada as soon as Crote is secure. Other ships can rendezvous with us then."

Jelena's gaze flicked toward Richius. "And you, Lord Jackal? What do you think? Are your people ready?"

It was a difficult question, and Richius didn't really know how to answer. But across the table he noticed Shii straighten proudly in her seat, and knew that he could have only one reply.

"They're a good bunch," he said. "Shii has helped me work with them, and I know they won't disappoint us. They haven't had much time to prepare, but they've trained hard and they follow my orders. I think we're ready, Jelena."

"We *are* ready, my Queen," added Shii earnestly. "I know we are. Lord Jackal speaks truly. We have trained hard, and we're eager for this mission. We won't fail. I promise you that, on the soul of my son."

"Richius makes good choices, no doubt," said Jelena. "He must think highly of you to make you his second, Shii."

Shii looked down at the table modestly. "I will try my best."

"And lastly, you," said Jelena, staring pointedly at Simon. "Tell me, Naren. What do you think of our chances for success?"

"I think they're far better with my involvement," said Simon. He was never shy, and the queen's iciness didn't frighten him. "Without me, you'd be going in blind. Richius practically admitted that to me. But I've got everything you need right in here." He tapped his skull. "Don't worry, Queen Jelena. We'll take the island for you. And get Biagio in the bargain."

"You seem remarkably sure of that," quipped the queen. "Why?"

"Because Biagio's not a god," replied Simon, "no matter what he thinks. And his mansion isn't protected by many guards. He's got a handful, maybe forty in all, but Crote doesn't have an army. They've never needed one."

"They've always had the protection of the Empire," Richius added.

Simon nodded. "That's right. So nine hundred men and women armed with swords can overrun the mansion easily. And once that is taken, Crote will be ours."

"What about the populace?" argued Prakna. "Won't they fight us?"

"No," said Simon. "I'm Crotan, remember; I know what they're like. Without Biagio, they won't lift a finger against us, not if we secure the mansion and make our presence known. They'll see the Lissen ships in their waters, and they'll know they've been beaten. They won't fight back."

"What about other countries?" asked the queen. "Do you think they'll come to Crote's aid?"

"How can they?" asked Simon. "Other countries have armies, but the Black Fleet would have to take them to Crote, and the fleet isn't anywhere near Crote anymore." He glanced at Richius. "That's right, isn't it?"

"I think so. Prakna?"

"Darquis is correct," said the commander. "My schooners have them busy off the coasts of the Empire. By the time the Black Fleet does return to Crote, we'll have it secured. I intend to call my armada back to surround the island. Even the Black Fleet won't be able to break us. Not this time."

Richius loved the conviction in Prakna's voice. He knew why men followed him so willingly. Prakna was the lion of the ocean.

"Prakna," asked the queen. "Are you satisfied with the maps Simon Darquis has made?"

The fleet commander gave a grudging nod. "They seem adequate."

"They're better than that," snapped Simon. "They're as detailed as you'll need, Prakna. I know something of tactics, remember."

"Oh, we remember," sneered Prakna. "Perfectly."

Richius cleared his throat. "Fellows . . ."

"Don't patronize me, Lissen," said Simon hotly. "You should be glad I'm helping you."

"Glad? A traitorous Naren pig? If it wasn't for the Jackal—"

"Stop," flared Richius, slamming a fist down on the table that sent the wine goblets jumping. "I don't want this arguing. We've got a mission to perform. We have to work together. This bickering is pointless."

"I agree," said the queen mildly. "Remember where you are, please."

Prakna took a breath. "Forgive me, Jelena. You're right, of course."

Richius smiled. "You see? We're a happy family, Jelena."

"Yes," laughed the queen. "You've done a splendid job with them, Richius. If they don't kill themselves on the way to Crote, we might have a chance."

"We'll have more than a chance, my Queen," Shii interjected. "Simon Darquis is right. If Crote is unprotected, we'll have no problem taking the island from Biagio. I promise you, my Queen. I won't let us fail."

"None of us will," agreed Prakna. He kept his eyes on Simon as he spoke. "Isn't that right, Darquis?"

Simon chuckled darkly. "I have my own reasons for wanting this to succeed. It won't fail because of *me*, that's for certain."

"Good," said Prakna. "Then we understand each other."

Simon was about to reply, but Richius interrupted him.

"We won't fail, Jelena," he said quickly. "We've got good people and a solid plan."

"And we've got you to lead them," added Jelena with a smile. Richius saw that familiar fondness in her eyes again. Jelena was so beautiful. Like Sabrina. He supposed the resemblance had something to do with his need for victory. Maybe it was that part of him that still wanted to rescue Sabrina.

Too late, he reminded himself.

Sabrina was dead and there was no going back. This was something he was doing for *himself*. And when it was done, he would return to

Lucel-Lor and live there with Dyana and Shani, satisfied that he had killed Biagio. Maybe then Sabrina's ghost would stop haunting him.

"I want to be clear on something," he said, surprising himself. "After we take Crote, you're all on your own. Just like Simon, I'm in this for my own reasons. I want Biagio. That's all."

Jelena looked heartbroken. "We understand that, Richius," she said softly. "But there will always be a place for you here. And we may need you a little longer than that. Please don't talk about abandoning us. Not until your work is done, at least."

"Just so you know what my work *is*, Jelena. I want Biagio."

"We all want that, Jackal," said Prakna. "Believe me."

Richius nodded. "I do believe you. But it goes deeper for the rest of you. I just want the count."

"You'll get him," said Simon. He slipped a hand on Richius' shoulder. "He won't be able to escape us. Promise."

The odd pledge made Richius shudder. He didn't know whom to trust anymore. He wanted to believe Simon, but Simon was planning on murdering his master. He respected Prakna, but the doom-haunted commander had a wildness around the eyes, just like Shii. And Jelena? She was the greatest mystery of them all.

They spoke for nearly an hour more, going over Simon's maps and discussing timetables for the invasion. It would take them more than a week to reach Crote, Prakna predicted, so they needed fresh food and water for the voyage, all items that his crews were taking care of. Richius' troops would be divided into three main groups, each of which would be led by a separate commander reporting to Shii and to Richius himself. They would converge on the mansion from three sides, surrounding it and securing it with minimum casualties.

At least that was the plan.

Richius hoped Biagio would simply surrender when he saw himself trapped. Simon didn't hazard a guess either way. He said only that Biagio was proud and crafty, and that he might fight to the death before surrendering his homeland. He loved Crote almost as much as anything, Simon explained to them. Getting it from him wouldn't be easy. But Richius didn't care if Biagio died. That was the plan, after all. He wanted only to spare the others in the mansion, including Eris. For Simon's sake, he prayed the girl would be all right.

When they had concluded their business, they lingered a while over the wine and food trays. Finally, Jelena rose from her chair and smiled at them all wearily.

"I don't know what to say now," she confessed. "All that I can do is wish you luck, and hope you all come back to Liss safely." She grinned at Simon. "Even you, Simon Darquis. If you are truly what you say you are, you are welcome to bring your woman back here to hide from your Naren enemies."

Simon seemed moved by the offer. "Queen Jelena, that is generous," he said softly. "We will need a place to go. But I didn't think it would be Liss."

"If the Jackal leaves us, we might need a man of your skills and knowledge, Simon Darquis. It's something to consider."

"Yes," agreed Simon. "Yes, it is."

Prakna smoldered at the pleasantries. "I think you would be better off among your own kind, Darquis. Not all Lissens are as forgiving as the queen."

"Nevertheless," corrected Jelena sharply. "You're welcome here, Simon Darquis. *If* you do as you say."

"I will, Queen Jelena. Just give me the chance to prove it to you."

Jelena nodded. "Then good luck to you all. Come home safely."

All of them rose and began leaving the chamber. They would stay the night in the queen's palace, then set out in the morning. Always eager for a bed, Simon was the first through the doors. Shii followed him, and then Prakna, but Richius never made it.

"Richius," called Jelena softly. "Please wait. I want to talk with you."

Shii waited for her lord, pausing in the threshold. Richius gave her an encouraging nod.

"It's all right," he told her. "I'll catch up. You and Simon go rest. We'll talk later."

Shii politely shut the doors again as she left the chamber. Richius took a deep breath, smelling Jelena's perfume When he turned around she was right behind him, beaming a beautiful, forlorn smile.

"What is it?" he asked.

"I'm going to miss you, Jackal," she said. "More than you know. I wanted to spend some time alone with you, just to tell you that."

"Just that?"

Jelena blushed. "I think you know the rest."

Richius backed up a step. "Don't," he cautioned.

"But I want to," said the young woman. She looked up at him, and the sorrow in her eyes was so real Richius drowned in it. Jelena said, "There's so much I wanted to learn from you. Now I'll never get the chance. If you don't come back, I'll never see you again."

"Never is a very long time, my Queen. Let's not try and predict the future."

Jelena embraced him, putting her head against his chest. Suddenly she seemed like a brave little girl again. "It doesn't have to be this way, you know. Crote might just be the start for us. After that, we'll grow stronger. We can reach the Black City itself from there."

Richius sighed. "Perhaps."

"There will still be a place for you. There's still so much for you to show us. And me."

"Jelena . . ."

"Shhh," the queen bade. "Just listen to me. Just this one more time."

Richius closed his eyes. "All right."

"When you first came here, I expected something more," she whispered. "I thought you would be a hero, even though Prakna warned me you were just a man, and not much older than myself. Now I see that we were both right. You are just a man. But you're still a hero to me. I want so much for you to stay here, even just to have you near. I need you, Richius." She tightened her embrace. "I'm afraid."

"It's all right to be afraid," said Richius as gently as he could. "But you don't need me."

"Oh, but I do . . ."

"No," said Richius. "You've been a queen without me, and you'll be a queen when I leave. You've done a fine job. You just don't see it. And I can't give you that confidence. That has to come from inside you." Firmly, he broke the embrace. "Look at me, Jelena. I'm just a man."

She smiled sadly. "And what am I? Just a woman?"

"A woman and a queen. You should be proud of that."

It wasn't what Jelena wanted to hear, so she drifted away from him, going back to where her wine goblet rested. She took a long, slow sip. Richius watched her curiously, sure that she had something else on her mind.

"I'm going to worry about you, you know," said Jelena finally. "I'm glad you're confident, but I wonder about Simon Darquis. And about your troops."

Richius raised an eyebrow. "You were the one who gave me those troops, remember?"

"I know. But they're young and untested. Like me."

Richius laughed. "If they're as strong as you, Jelena, I should have nothing to worry about." He glided over to her, sitting himself down on the table beside her and grabbing his own goblet. "Don't be afraid," he urged. He touched his glass to hers. "This is a new beginning."

But Jelena didn't drink. "Do you believe that?"

"I do," said Richius. "I'm certain of it."

"I suppose," replied the queen dully. Then, more forcefully, "Yes. Yes, it is."

"Good," Richius beamed. "Because these children of Karalon are going to make you proud. You'll see."

"Richius," added the queen, looking up at him. "Just be careful."

He gave her a wink. "I will."

"I'm serious," said Jelena. "Watch out for yourself. And watch out for Prakna. He's a vengeful man, and I see the way he looks at Simon Darquis. He might be trouble."

"I can handle Prakna," said Richius. "We understand each other, I think."

"You know he sunk that Naren dreadnought, don't you?"

Richius nodded. He'd heard Prakna's explanation and was satisfied. "I don't think he had a choice. The ship tried to escape."

Jelena shrugged. "Still . . ."

"Jelena, please don't worry about these things. I've got a good group of people, thanks to you. And with Simon's help I know we'll succeed. You might not trust him, but I really believe him this time." Richius scoffed at himself. "Maybe I'm just a fool. After what he did to me, I don't know why I should trust him. It's just a feeling I get when I'm around him now. He's going to help us. I'm sure of it."

Queen Jelena put out her hand for him to take, and when he did she smiled warmly. "Thank you for everything," she said, her voice breaking. "Please don't forget us."

"I never will," promised Richius. He put her hand to his lips and kissed it. "Never."

Slowly her hand slipped from his fingers. Richius felt her eyes on him as he went to the door. Before leaving, he turned and gave her one last look.

"Good night, Queen of Liss."

Jelena lingered in her council chamber, waiting for Prakna to arrive. She had left orders with the sentries outside the chamber to summon the fleet commander when the Jackal was gone. It didn't take long for Prakna to respond to her order. The sailor appeared at the door, a little concerned that his queen wanted to see him.

"My Queen?" he probed, sticking his head inside the chamber. "You summoned me?"

Jelena put down the glass she'd been sipping at and bid Prakna forward. "Come in, please, Prakna," she said lightly. She was flush from the wine and her encounter with Richius, and her mood hovered somewhere between sour and profoundly sad. "Close the door."

Prakna did as his queen commanded, stepping into the chamber and shutting the doors behind him, sealing off the outside noise. The room had grown darker since he'd left, and Jelena could barely see him in the shadowy lamp-light.

"Sit near me," she said. "Talk with me."

"What about?" asked Prakna as he took a chair beside her. He looked genuinely concerned for her, a trait that made her love him. "My Queen, what troubles you?"

"Tomorrow you will set sail and I will not be there to control you, Prakna. You will take all that vengeance with you to Crote. That's what troubles me."

Prakna went ashen. "Jelena, I will do what must be done. No more or less."

"Like you did with the Naren ship?"

The commander nodded. "It was necessary. And the Jackal still knows nothing of it."

"You're right," said Jelena sadly. "He believes your story. We've deceived him perfectly, and that troubles me, too."

"I know," admitted Prakna. "He's a good man. I don't take pride in lying to him. But he will get what we promised him. He'll have his revenge on Biagio. That should satisfy him. You heard it yourself—that's all he wants."

Jelena grimaced. She hated herself for deceiving Richius, her beautiful new friend from across the ocean. He was nothing like other Narens. He was a hero. Certainly, he deserved better than lies.

"I don't want you to do any more than you must to take Crote," she said finally. "Richius wouldn't want that."

"I know," said Prakna.

"Do you? I've heard about your handiwork, Prakna."

The fleet commander leaned back, obviously offended. "Jelena, did it ever occur to you that the Naren pigs on that dreadnought might have been the same ones that slew your parents? Or Shii's child? Would you feel so bad for them then?"

"No," admitted Jelena. "I wouldn't."

"Of course you wouldn't. So let me do my job. Let me erase the memory of Liss the Raped. Let's make sure the Empire of Nar doesn't trifle with us again."

The speech stoked a fire deep within her. He was right, of course. Nar deserved every bit of derision. Jelena didn't care about Nar, but she did care about Richius Vantran, more deeply than she had ever thought possible.

"I want no harm to come to the Jackal," she said firmly. "Or I swear, Prakna, you will know my anger."

The fleet commander grinned. "I respect that boy as much as you do, my Queen. I swear to you, I won't let anything happen to him."

"And the other one. Simon Darquis. I see how you hate him, Prakna. Give me your word you will protect him, too."

The commander frowned. "Don't make me wet-nurse that pig, please."

"Your word, Prakna," she insisted. "You will treat him as an ally. Yes?"

After a long pause, Prakna reluctantly acquiesced. "I promise," he said bitterly. "But I don't approve."

"You don't have to like it," Jelena reminded him. "Just do as I say." She smiled to herself, remembering Richius' words. "After all, I am the queen."

THIRTY-NINE

Eleven Lords

Two days after the tragedy of Eestrii, Herrith and his loyal Naren lords set out for Biagio's island of Crote.

It had been a surprisingly easy decision for the bishop, because he knew he simply had no other choice, and the Naren lords agreed. Biagio could reach them, even from his island. With the orchestrated murder of Vorto and the destruction of the cathedral, Biagio had proven that he could not be safely ignored. And Herrith, distraught over the death of Lorla, didn't care about his own safety anymore. He hoped only to convince Biagio that the Black Renaissance was a godless heresy, and that the Empire had been better off since the old emperor's death. He was not planning on handing the Iron Throne over to Biagio. None of the Naren lords would agree to that, anyway. This journey was simply the opening of a dialogue. Where it would lead, no one wanted to guess.

Archbishop Herrith chose eleven Naren lords to accompany him to Crote, the most influential men in the Black City. Among them was Baron Ricter, master of the Tower of Truth; Claudi Vos, Arkus' former Lord Architect; Tepas Talshiir, the city's leading merchant, who lived in a royal-sized palace of his own; and Kivis Gago, Nar's Minister of Arms, representing the civilian interests of the Empire's military machine. Since Vorto's death, Kivis Gago had been very busy, rearranging the power structure of the legions and convincing the irate soldiers that he was capable of leading them. The military leadership had been calling for Biagio's head in retribution for Vorto's slaughter, and Kivis Gago's job was to convince them that this was essentially impossible, at least for now. Biagio was on an island, with the entire Black Fleet protecting him. It was this fact, more than any other, that convinced the eleven lords to accompany Herrith to Crote. Biagio had forced them into a corner.

It was a gray morning when Herrith and the noblemen, all accompanied by throngs of bodyguards, disembarked from the docks of Nar City. The *Fearless* and her two sister dreadnoughts waited far off in the harbor, and Nicabar had sent long rowboats to ferry his passengers over. Herrith was the only one who didn't bring guardians. Not even Father Todos accompanied the bishop on the dock. With the Cathedral of the Martyrs in ruins, every one of Herrith's priests and acolytes were needed in the Black City. There were deep spiritual wounds to tend, for the audacious attack had left the population stunned.

"It is now," Herrith had told Todos, "that we really do the work of God."

God might want him to speak to Biagio, or God might not. Herrith didn't know, because his prayers went unanswered. He was quickly becoming faithless. As he shivered in the cold, waiting for his own ferry boat, he wondered if God had abandoned him. Or if he had abandoned God. He saw the sunlight glint off the big guns of the *Fearless*. The warship had her cannons trained on the city. One slip-up, Nicabar had promised—one act of sabotage against his vessels—and he would open fire. He would pummel Nar City day and night in retaliation to any attack. That message had gone to Herrith and Kivis Gago both. Gago in turn relayed it to the legions, who impotently agreed. At least for a while, there would be a truce.

Time enough, Herrith hoped. He pulled up the collar of his coat, hating the wind. He was sick and weak, and the thought of the long sea voyage brought bile to his throat. The last effects of the drug had worn off and his entire body was in rebellion, hellishly craving more. He thought his bones might break in the breeze, and he had swallowed down pain-killing potions from his physicians, hoping to stem the unbearable pain. The remedies were useless. Herrith had been through the drug withdrawal before. He knew the ordeal facing him.

From across the harbor, another of the long rowboats approached. Herrith spied it warily. It bore the markings of the *Fearless*. He and Kivis Gago both would be travelling aboard Nicabar's flagship. Apparently, Nicabar hoped to prepare them for the coming peace talks. The other Naren lords, steadfastly refusing Nicabar's hospitality, would voyage on *Black City* and *Intruder*. Herrith braced himself as the boat approached the dock. Onboard were four sailors, all of them dressed in the dark uniform of the fleet. As the boat slid into a mooring, one of the sailors, obviously a man of some rank, jumped out and approached them. Kivis Gago's bodyguards coiled, ready to defend their master.

"Archbishop Herrith," said the seaman loudly. "My name is Lieutenant R'Jinn. I'm to take you aboard the *Fearless*, along with Minister Gago." He gave the minister a polite bow. "Admiral Nicabar requests that you be at ease. He promises no trickery, and that no harm will come to any of you aboard his vessel."

"That better be true," spat Gago. He was a tall man, prone to gaudy threats. "If anything happens to me, Nicabar will be the most hunted man in the world."

The seaman didn't flinch. "You may bring your bodyguards or any belongings you wish. Admiral Nicabar wants your voyage to be a pleasant one."

"I go nowhere without my bodyguards, pup," sneered Gago. "I don't need Nicabar's permission."

"And I don't have any bodyguards," said Herrith. "Just take us aboard."

The lieutenant frowned. He looked at the stooped bishop, and Herrith thought he saw pity in his eyes.

"Very well," said the sailor. "Let me help you."

Weak from sickness, Herrith didn't refuse the offer. Two more sailors climbed out of the rowboat to help him aboard. Every step was an agony. His head swam with nausea and his joints screamed with fire, and when he placed his foot into the boat, the rocking of the vessel made him groan. The lieutenant guided him into one of the benchlike seats. Herrith took a weary breath. He felt unconscionably old.

When Kivis Gago and half his bodyguards were aboard, the rowboat shoved off again. Another was passing them, approaching the dock. The second vessel would take the rest of the minister's entourage to the *Fearless*. Gago sat down next to Herrith, rocking the boat with his weight.

"Traitorous skunks," he scoffed, loud enough for the sailors to hear. Gago had always been a loudmouth, and Herrith wished one of the other lords had come with him instead. None of them were friends, precisely, but he cared for Gago the least. Like General Vorto, Gago didn't know when to keep quiet. Herrith looked out over the sea toward the waiting Naren flagship. He had never been aboard a dreadnought before, and wondered what it would be like. Nicabar had been among the best of the Iron Circle. Herrith wished the admiral had never sided with Biagio.

Biagio is a demon, he thought miserably. *A monster who lies with men and makes the best out of every vice.*

It wasn't supposed to be this way. When Arkus had died, Herrith had seized the Empire for good reasons. Now those reasons seemed specious. There had been far too much bloodshed for him to think it worth the struggle. He had ordered the deaths of thousands and wasn't sure anymore what God would think of that.

And then there was Lorla.

The memory of his precious adopted daughter brought a lump to his throat. Had she been part of Biagio's designs? Probably. She was just one more of Bovadin's wicked creations. The war labs had given Nar the acid launcher and the flame cannons and the heartless, world-eating Formula B. Herrith had no doubts that Bovadin could turn his foul imagination loose on a child. The midget had already proven his diabolical nature, a hundred times over. After walking through the rubble of his cathedral, Herrith had seen the twisted remnants of Bovadin's device. He still didn't really know what it was, but he knew that only Bovadin could have constructed it.

Herrith thought back to something that Lorla had told him once, that she was something very special. At the time he had merely grinned like a proud father, agreeing with her. But now he knew the dark truth of things. It was the only explanation that made sense. She had lured him to the toymaker, begging for the dollhouse. And she had gotten to him through Enli, whose treason was now infamous. But she had never feigned her love for him.

That was real, he told himself. Maybe it had started false, but in the end she had loved him. She had even tried to save him.

The *Fearless* loomed ever larger. The rowboat cut through the waves, anxious to reach its mother. Herrith and Gago stared up at the growing warship, mesmerized by it giantness. The dreadnought was behemoth, and its numerous cannons poked out of its gun deck like the thorns of a beautiful, dangerous rose. Lieutenant R'Jinn guided the rowboat to the side of the vessel. A long rope ladder dropped down to greet them. All along the deck, Herrith saw more sailors staring down at them. His holy presence broke their militant professionalism, and some of them pointed at him, surprised and maybe pleased to see him.

They're all your flock, Herrith reminded himself. *Even if they serve an evil master.*

"Archbishop," called the lieutenant. "Think you can climb that ladder?"

Herrith looked at the ladder sourly. "God is testing me," he muttered.

"I'll help you," said R'Jinn encouragingly. "I'll be right behind you."

"Very well," said Herrith. He waited until the rowboat came to a stop, then got shakily to his feet. Lieutenant R'Jinn and two other crewmen grabbed hold of his arms, guiding him out of the boat. The little platform pitched and rolled, making Herrith ill. He summoned all the strength he could, refusing to look weak, and took the ladder in his hands. With a powerful grunt he lifted himself onto the first rung. R'Jinn and the others helped by pushing. Kivis Gago gave a laugh, clapping.

"Well done, Herrith," he joked. "You can do it!"

The insult was all the prodding Herrith needed. He summoned his remaining strength, struggling up the ladder just to show the arrogant nobleman he was able. It was a long climb, but with R'Jinn beneath him for support he made it to the top without slipping. When two more sailors on the deck helped him aboard, he had a giant smile on his face. But the smile vanished quickly. Standing in front of him was Admiral Danar Nicabar.

"Welcome aboard, Herrith," said the commander. "This is an honor."

Surprisingly, there was no gloating in Nicabar's tone. His stony countenance held not a trace of arrogance. Herrith, breathing hard, nodded at the admiral.

"It seems you were right, Danar," he said. "Here I am."

"*Biagio* was right," Nicabar corrected. "Myself, I never thought you'd come aboard."

"Peace guides my actions, Danar, not personal gain. Peace is the only reason I've agreed to speak with your wicked master."

Nicabar smiled. "Very well, Herrith. As I said, I'm glad to have you aboard. We're going to try to make this as pleasant as possible for you. I have a cabin ready for you. It's one of the largest on board."

Herrith scoffed. "Not as big as yours, I'm sure."

"Big enough," said Nicabar. "You'll be well cared for, I promise."

"I'm not a pet, Admiral."

Nicabar sighed. "Do you want to see it? Or do you want to stand in the cold like a fool? Personally, I think you should rest. You look awful."

"Yes, well, I've been through a lot recently," jabbed Herrith. He stared at Nicabar hard. "But you already know that, don't you?"

"Casualties of war, Herrith," replied Nicabar. "And no worse than some of the things you've done."

It was true, so Herrith didn't argue. "Take me to my quarters," he said. "Let's get going as soon as we can. I—"

His words died in his mouth. Across the deck he saw the diminutive figure of Bovadin. The scientist was coming toward him.

"You!" Herrith roared, losing all control. "You little monster!"

Bovadin put up his hands. "Easy, Herrith . . ."

Herrith bolted forward and grabbed the midget's lapels, lifting him off the ground. Howling, he wrestled Bovadin to the edge of the deck, pinning him against the railing. All the strength of the drug flashed back into his muscles with a wrathful charge. The midget struggled to get free, gasping.

"Herrith, stop!" he cried. "Stop!"

Nicabar came rushing forward. He pulled Herrith away from the rail. Herrith held fast to Bovadin, shaking him.

"You murderous beast!" he seethed. "You killed her!"

"Herrith, stop!" Nicabar demanded. He pulled the bishop roughly off of Bovadin. Three crewmen rushed into the fight, stepping between them. Herrith roared at Bovadin even as the sailors dragged him away.

"We're not done, dwarf!" he swore. "Not at all. I'll see you burn in hell for what you did!"

"I'll meet you there, Herrith!" the midget shot back. Nicabar held him back with a single hand, but Bovadin fought scrappily against him, cursing at Herrith. "This is your war. You started it."

"Shut up, both of you!" thundered Nicabar. He tossed Bovadin aside like an insect. "Get away, Bovadin. I told you not to come up here."

"Danar . . ."

"Go!"

The scientist glared once more at Herrith, then strode away, shaking his head. Nicabar turned on the bishop.

"You're stronger than you look," he quipped. "But I won't have a spectacle like that again. This is my vessel. You want to kill Bovadin? Do it when you get to Crote."

"I just might," hissed Herrith. "And maybe you, too."

Admiral Nicabar growled, "Come with me. Let me lock you in your cabin!"

Exhausted from the melee, Herrith followed willingly. Nicabar led him through a narrow hatchway in the bridge, down a small flight of wooden stairs and into a claustrophobic, swaying corridor. At the end of the corridor the admiral paused at a door, opening it and gesturing inside.

"This is your cabin," he said sharply. "I think you'll find it has everything you need."

Herrith peered inside. It was ridiculously small, with only a cot built into the wall and a small table and chair. On the table was a letter, stamped with the familiar seal of Count Biagio. Herrith froze when he saw it. Holding the letter to the table was a paper weight—a small vial of blue liquid.

"Oh, no," whispered Herrith. "Please . . ."

"From Biagio," Nicabar explained. "He knew you'd need it by now. The apparatus for taking it is stored under the bunk." The admiral gave a victorious smile. "Feel better, Herrith," he said, then stepped aside to let Herrith enter the cabin. The bishop stumbled over to the table. He picked up the vial and stared at it, dreading the upcoming decision.

"You should have thrown it overboard," he said. "It's poison, Danar."

The admiral's blue eyes laughed. "Not for me."

"Oh, you're wrong," Herrith said. "You're very wrong."

"Rest," advised Nicabar. "It's a two-day voyage to Crote. I'll send a cabin boy to see to your needs after we get under way. If you need anything, ask me."

Nicabar was being very kind, making Herrith suspicious. "I don't want to be interrupted," he said. "When I need anything, I'll get it myself."

"Stop being a fool, Herrith. You don't know your way around the ship and my crew isn't yours to order around. Let the cabin boy help you. That's what he's here for."

Nicabar left the cabin, shutting the door behind him. Herrith slumped down in the small chair. He studied the vial, hating it and loving it, dying to pour it into his veins. His body screamed for its soothing power. He licked his lips, unsure what he should do, then noticed Biagio's letter. His hand trembling, he put down the vial and reached for the envelope, opening it.

My dear Herrith, the letter began.

I knew you would change your mind. Thank you.

It was signed very simply, *Count Biagio*.

Enraged, Herrith balled up the letter and tossed it aside. Biagio's arrogance was boundless. He had the obnoxious ability to see into the future, or to manipulate the present to get the tomorrow he wanted. Herrith felt the count's cold hands all over him. He was being worked like a lump of clay. And he felt powerless.

"But I am not powerless," he whispered. "This, at least, I can do."

Slowly, haltingly, his hand reached out and picked up the vial again. Then he unlid the lid and poured the contents on the floor.

FORTY

The Lissens

The Naren vessel *Swift* had been in Lissen waters for barely a day. Captain Kelara, weary from the recent voyages back and forth he had endured, spent most of his time above deck, scanning the horizons with his lookouts. For his mission to succeed, he needed to sight the Lissen invasion force well in advance, and to remain undetected himself.

Kelara did not expect to see his quarry so soon.

Out on the horizon, he caught a glimpse of a big schooner through his spyglass. Quickly he tabulated the speed and distances. From the size of her, she could easily be the *Prince*. A second later, a lookout in the crow's nest verified his sighting.

"Four ships!" came the cry. "Off starboard, ten degrees!"

Boatswain Dars, who had eagerly accompanied the small crew back to Liss, rushed up to Captain Kelara's side. The young man shielded his eyes with a hand, squinting out over the ocean.

"I can't see anything," he said, annoyed. "Where are they?"

Kelara didn't need his spyglass anymore, so he handed it to Dars. The boatswain hurriedly pointed the lens ten degrees off starboard, paused, then let out a venomous curse.

"That's the bastards!" He snapped the spyglass closed and turned to Kelara. "What now?"

The captain backed away from the railing, ready to give the order. "Now we head back to Crote, Boatswain," he said. "Here's where the fun begins."

FORTY-ONE

Secrets

Alone in the cabin he shared with Simon, Richius sat at the tiny table built into the wall, staring at his journal. Writing was an old habit he had neglected since the end of the Triin war, but the tedium of the sea voyage had reacquainted him with the task. It took his mind off the boredom and the questionable things to come. The *Prince* was four days out of Liss. Prakna's best estimates put them in Crote in three more days. The battle was joined, looming ever nearer, and Richius daydreamed as he sat in the flickering candlelight, contemplating the violent times ahead.

We are not far now, he wrote. *In three more days we will make landfall in Crote, and I do not know what we will find there. Perhaps Biagio's guardians will surrender peacefully. If not, they will have a massacre on their hands. These nine hundred orphans I bring with me are bloodthirsty. I have done my best to tame their anger, but they still seethe for vengeance. Seeing them reminds me a little of myself. They are all the things I'd hoped never to be.*

Richius stared at the line he'd just written. He was sorry for his feelings, but there they were, put down on paper, making them real. Long ago, his father had given him a valuable piece of advice; that a general must love the men he leads. If not, the men will know it and not fight for him. Richius sighed miserably. Did he love these Lissens? He didn't think so. He respected and admired them, but he didn't love them. What he felt was more like pity. The realization frightened Richius. He lowered his pen, unable to continue.

In Aramoor—if Aramoor still existed—he would have been a king. It was a title he never sought or craved. He never wanted to go against the emperor or fight in Lucel-Lor or earn the name Jackal, and suddenly he felt the years rush over him.

"I've changed," he whispered.

For the first time in his young life, Richius felt old. He was afraid of going to Crote, and of facing Biagio. Much as he wanted to cut the count's heart out, he also wanted to turn the ship around and sail back to Falindar to see Dyana's bright face. It wasn't his own mortality that worried him; his fears concerned his soul and his sanity. Sometimes, both seemed to be slipping away. He might live forever as a madman, like some hero in a Naren fairy tale who could not be harmed by any blade but whose mind slowly devoured itself.

"Enough," he chastised himself, throwing down the quill. He needed to focus.

Suddenly the cabin door opened and Simon staggered inside. It was very late and normally they both should have been asleep, but Simon's seasickness always kept him awake and above deck. The Naren's face was shadowed with an unhealthy pall. He closed the door and collapsed into his bunk with a groan. Richius noticed the stains of vomit on his coat.

"You look terrible," he remarked.

"You stayed up to tell me that?" snapped Simon.

"No." Richius closed his journal and pushed it aside. "Just thinking."

"My guts are on fire," Simon groaned. "You shouldn't have made me eat."

"Starving yourself won't help. You'll only waste away. And I want you strong when we reach Crote."

Simon rolled over and glared at him. His eyes were lusterless. "Staying up all night worrying won't help, either, you know. You can go over those plans a thousand times, but you'll never know what's going to happen until it happens. Words of wisdom, boy. Learned the hard way." Simon's vision narrowed on Richius' journal. "What are you writing in there, anyway?"

"Just things," said Richius evasively.

Simon smiled. "Come on, I can tell you want to talk. What is it? What's on that sharp mind of yours?"

Richius didn't answer right away. He listened to the gentle rocking of the ship and its endless creaking, and considered the man sharing his cabin. Still, after all that had happened, he liked Simon Darquis. Richius turned his chair toward his cabin-mate's bunk, deciding to trust him.

"Simon, don't you ever wonder about yourself?" he asked softly.

Simon chuckled. "What?"

"I saw you when you came to Liss," Richius pressed. "Do you remember how sorry you looked?"

Simon glanced away. They had never really talked about that, and Richius had thought it best to stay quiet. But he had seen such remarkable sorrow in Simon that day. It had made him wonder.

"I remember," replied Simon. "It's not something I enjoyed."

"It's a regret, though, isn't it?"

"Richius, you're not making any sense," said Simon, annoyed. "What are you asking me?"

Richius shrugged. "Maybe nothing. I'm just a little worried, that's all."

"About Crote?"

"And about myself," said Richius. He glanced away, unable to explain it. Dyana hadn't wanted him to go on this journey. She had warned him that revenge was folly, and seeing Jelena and all the rest of Liss' orphans made him reconsider his wife's advice.

"If you're worried that you're doing the wrong thing, don't be," Simon said. "I know what Biagio did to your lady. I heard about it when I was in the Empire. He's a beast, Richius."

Richius frowned. "He's your master."

"That doesn't mean anything. So I followed a beast. Maybe that makes me a beast, too." Simon closed his eyes. "Is that what you mean by regrets? If so, then you're right about me. I'm not proud of the things I've done."

"And what about all this?" asked Richius. "Will you be proud when we kill Biagio?"

"*If* we kill Biagio," corrected Simon. "And no, I won't be. You don't understand what it's like to be Roshann, Richius. Biagio gave me an identity. He gave me something to believe in."

"So why are you doing it? Just for Eris?"

"Mostly. But also because Biagio isn't the same. The drug has made him a wild man. Personally, I think he's insane. We might be doing him a favor by killing him."

"A favor?" barked Richius. "I'm not going to kill him for sentimental reasons, Simon. You can think whatever you want, but for me it's just plain old revenge."

"And he deserves it," agreed Simon. "I'm not arguing with that. Just don't expect me to be happy about it. Biagio will always mean something good to me. I don't think there's anything he could do to change that." He glanced over at Richius and gave him a knowing look. "If you knew Biagio ten years ago, you'd probably feel different about him."

"I doubt it," said Richius sourly. Biagio's impending death was the one thing he had no qualms about. "I don't know how you can say he's a good man after all the evil things he's done. Maybe I was wrong about you, Simon. Maybe you haven't changed a bit."

"Easy, boy," warned Simon. "I'm not so sick I can't stuff you through a porthole. And I never said he's a good man. All I meant was that he's not the man he used to be. People change, Richius. Sometimes for the better. Sometimes for the worse, like Biagio."

"People change," Richius echoed, nodding. "That's what I'm worried about." He leaned back in his chair, watching the candle flicker in its glass enclosure. "Before I left, Dyana warned me to be careful. I thought she meant she wanted me to watch out for myself, to not get killed. Now I think I know what she meant. She sees the change in me."

"What change?"

"Oh, it's hard to explain," sighed Richius. "It's what revenge does to a man. I wasn't always like I am now, either. I guess I've changed, too—just like Biagio."

"And me," Simon reminded him.

Richius smiled. "I suppose."

Simon sat up, putting his legs over the edge of the bunk. "Richius, listen to me. You're a good man. After you finish this business with Biagio, you can go back to your wife and child and start over. You'll be able to put all this dirty business behind you. With Biagio dead, you'll be forgotten in Nar. No one's going to come hunting for you again."

Richius closed his eyes. "Sounds wonderful."

"And your daughter can grow up strong and healthy, and you won't have to worry about war anymore or spies crawling through your window. It will be a whole new life for you. You can forget all about Biagio and Nar. Forget Aramoor—"

"What?" blurted Richius, his eyes snapping open. "Simon, I can never forget Aramoor."

"You must," said Simon relentlessly. "Or it will haunt you forever. It's not your kingdom anymore. Forget about it."

"I can't," Richius argued. "It's impossible."

"Do it," Simon urged. "You'd be a fool not to. Because Aramoor is never going to be yours again, Richius. Never."

The words hung in the air. Richius swallowed hard. Part of him had never dared acknowledge what Simon was telling him, that Aramoor was lost forever.

"Then what's all this for?" he asked softly. "Why am I even here?"

Simon grinned. "You know the answer to that one, friend."

Richius nodded.

"Strike a blow for Aramoor," said Simon. "Ease your conscience the best you can. Take out Biagio, then walk away."

"I don't know . . ."

"Don't know what?" thundered Simon. He leaned forward on his bunk. "You don't know if you want to live the rest of your life in peace? Or watch your daughter grow up? Let me tell you something, Richius. I think you're a fool for being here. The Lissens could have invaded Crote without your help. They're fools, too. But you're smarter than them. You should have had the brains to ignore Prakna when he came to Falindar. But you chose a vendetta over the love of a good woman. I think that's incredibly stupid."

Abruptly, Simon fell back into his bunk, turning his back on Richius. The cabin fell uneasily quiet. Richius stared at Simon.

"You don't understand," he said.

"Right," said Simon. "No one ever understands poor Richius. That's the story of your life."

"Simon, be fair. You're not a king. You don't know what it's like for me."

"Good night, Richius."

"You didn't betray a kingdom!"

"Blow out the candle, would you, please?

Seething, Richius blew the candle out, then sat quietly in the dark, staring at Simon's back. *Did* he like Simon? He wondered about that now. The Naren was crass and thoughtless.

But he was also remarkably perceptive.

After pulling off his boots, Richius climbed into his own bunk and drew the covers over himself. A light draft made him shiver. There would be no sleep tonight; his mind was too full.

"I'm not like the Lissens," he whispered.

"You're right. You're not. Go to sleep."

"I'm not! You heard what I told Jelena. I just want to get Biagio and then go home."

"I heard you."

"And you don't believe me?"

"That's right."

"Why not?"

Simon cursed. "God almighty, haven't you been listening? You could have been satisfied letting the Lissens go to Crote themselves. They would have killed Biagio for you, and you know it. But you weren't satisfied with that. And you won't be satisfied when you get back to Falindar, either. You'll always be whining about how you betrayed Aramoor. You should listen to Dyana, Richius. You're not a king anymore. The sooner you realize that, the sooner you'll start living again. Now, good night!"

Richius said nothing. Simon's outburst had left him speechless.

I'll just get Biagio, he told himself. *I will. Then I'll go home.*

The words echoed endlessly in his mind. Even as he heard them, he fretted over their truth.

On the other end of the sleepy schooner, Fleet Commander Prakna was also awake in his cabin. He was at his writing desk awaiting a visitor. An open flask of wine waited with him, accompanied by two mugs. It was very late, and Prakna was weary. He would have preferred to be sleeping, but he had business that could only be attended to when curious eyes were closed. Confident that Marus could pilot the *Prince* without him, Prakna had come below decks hours ago. He had whiled away the time writing a letter to J'Lari. In it he had told her how much he loved her, again, and how much he missed her. Again. The commander was sick of writing his heart-wrenching notes. Each one was an ordeal. They reminded him of how old he was, and how much he'd lost. They reminded him that J'Lari wasn't whole anymore.

In three more days, they would reach Crote. Soon, no one would dare call his homeland Liss the Raped.

"Never again," he mumbled darkly.

There was work to do. They would take Crote in a lightning attack, then look eastward toward the mainland. The Narens would tremble when they heard the news of Crote's seizure. Prakna smiled grimly. He liked the thought of Narens trembling. So many of his own men had trembled, brave as they were. It was time for some retribution.

Prakna poured himself a little of the wine just as the expected knock came at his cabin door. "Come in," he called softly, then poured wine into the second mug. The door opened to reveal Shii. The young woman stood in the threshold questioningly.

"Sir?" she asked. "You wanted to see me?"

"Step inside, Shii," said Prakna. "Close the door."

Shii did as Prakna bid, quickly and without question. The effect of his rank was obvious. She stood before him dutifully, waiting for him to speak. When he offered out the wine mug she declined.

"No, thank you," she said politely.

Prakna smiled. "You're nervous. Don't be. You're doing nothing wrong."

The young woman relaxed almost imperceptibly. "No, sir."

"You know that, don't you?"

"Yes, sir."

"Good." Prakna eased the mug into her hands. "Then drink with me." He got up and offered her the only chair in the cabin, seating himself on the edge of his bunk. Shii hovered over the chair before sitting, then took a sip of the wine, obviously trying to relax. Prakna watched her closely. She was a good soldier. Loyal, both to Liss and her Lord Jackal. He didn't like seeing her squirm.

"Shii, please be at ease," he said. "I just want to talk to you, that's all. There's no reason for you to be afraid."

"I'm not afraid," she said defensively. "It's just, well . . ." She paused, careful with her words. "You told me not to tell Lord Jackal about our meeting. I'm uncomfortable with that."

"I understand," said Prakna. "Vantran has done a fine job with you. All of you."

"He's made an army of us," declared Shii.

"And I appreciate that. You'll make him proud when we get to Crote, I know that. I just want to make sure you understand our mission."

Shii blanched. "Sir?"

"Our mission, Shii," Prakna repeated. He leaned closer, his tone growing grave. "Do you understand it?"

"Yes, of course I do," said Shii. "We're to take Crote."

"And?"

"And?" asked Shii. "That's it. We're taking the island and securing it for Liss. You're going to use it as a base for your fleet." She looked at him curiously. "Isn't that right?"

"Mostly," said Prakna. "But our mission is more than to just take Crote. We want to make a statement to the rest of the Empire. When we seize Biagio's island, we'll be saying to all of Nar that Liss isn't the Empire's plaything anymore. And we'll be striking a blow for all the people we've lost." He let that last part work on her. "Do you understand me, Shii?"

The young woman nodded. "I know about loss, Fleet Commander. That's why I volunteered to serve with Lord Jackal."

"An admirable decision, no doubt about it," said Prakna. "All of Liss is proud of you for that. But don't forget that you're a Lissen. You have an obligation to your people. Lord Jackal isn't one of us. He might not realize all that we need to accomplish."

Shii looked flustered. "I'm sorry, sir. I'm not understanding you. What do you mean?"

Tired, Prakna decided to be direct. "I mean to destroy Crote utterly, Shii," he said flatly. "I don't want there to be a living thing left in Biagio's mansion when we leave. When we get to Crote, our dead sons are going to be watching us. I don't want to disappoint them."

The young woman grimaced. "Sir, my orders come from the Jackal. He hasn't said anything about this to me. I know he wants to take the island with as few casualties as possible."

"The Jackal isn't Lissen," Prakna reminded her. "When it comes to the Hundred Isles, the Empire has a lot to answer for. I certainly don't want to disappoint my sons when they look down on me. What about you? Your infant son deserves vindication, doesn't he?"

Shii hesitated.

"Doesn't he?"

"Yes," cried Shii. She put down the mug and rose from her chair angrily. "Don't make me say it!"

"There's a thousand more like him, Shii," said Prakna. "All of them dead. Think about it. A thousand mothers who will never hold their babies. You think they have that problem in Nar? They take their children for walks, feed them, play with them. All the things you'll never get to do."

Shii turned away from him. It was working; Prakna knew it. He waited a moment before speaking again.

"It's justice," he said softly. "Some people call it revenge."

"I don't care what they call it," spat Shii. "I just want it."

Prakna smiled inwardly. "We all want it, girl," he said gently. "Even the Jackal. That's why he's here with us. Revenge. I know him. He plans on pulling Biagio's heart out for what the count did to his wife. And why shouldn't he? Don't you think Biagio deserves it?"

"Yes," gasped Shii. She was on the verge of angry tears.

"And do you think the Narens that slaughtered your son deserve to die?"

Unable to speak, Shii gave a strangled nod. Prakna walked over to her. He put his hands on her shoulders and his lips to her ear.

"So do I," he whispered. "*That's* why we're going to Crote."

Suddenly, the hard young woman seemed insubstantial in his hands. In a few minutes he had diminished her. Awful memories could do that to a person. Gently, he turned her around, making her face him. She looked up at him, her eyes full of pain.

"It's time," he said softly. "We are obligated to your son, and to my sons. To all our sons. You know that. Are you with me, Shii?"

Shii couldn't bring herself to look away. He was the Fleet Commander of Liss, more of a hero than the Jackal himself. Prakna knew the power he had over his people. He could see it reflected in Shii's impressionable eyes.

"I'm with you," said Shii finally.

"It's the right thing to do," Prakna promised her. "In three days, we become the servants of justice."

Without thinking, he placed a light kiss on her forehead. Shii melted. Prakna sighed. He hated making pawns of these fine men and women. Shii bent easily to his will, almost crying when she felt his loving kiss. Prakna held her close. She was desperate for the contact. It was what war had made of Liss' children; forlorn, touch-starved orphans. Like Jelena.

"Be easy, Shii," he whispered gently. "In three more days, we'll start to ease some of your pain."

"Will we?" asked Shii hopefully.

Prakna considered the question for a very long moment. Finally, he decided to lie. "Yes," he said softly. "It can't last forever."

FORTY-TWO

A Meeting of Monarchs

Barely two days after leaving Nar, the *Fearless* and her escorting dreadnoughts arrived in Crote. Biagio watched the warships from his beach, immensely satisfied with himself. Around him stood an entourage of bodyguards, a well-groomed group of peacock-colored Crotans with their sidearms still sheathed. The count didn't expect any trouble, but he wanted to make a show. He still didn't know how many of the Naren lords were aboard the ships. He hoped there were enough of them to have made it all worth his efforts. Still, Herrith was aboard—that much Biagio knew for certain. Nicabar had left Crote with clear orders not to return until the bishop was with him.

It was a clear day, and Biagio could see the rowboats coming toward him. Some still dropped from the sides of their mother ships, laden down with Naren nobles and their guards. Biagio's sharp eyes scanned the blue ocean. The lead boat came from the *Fearless*. At its prow stood Nicabar, guiding her in. With him was a white-haired man in priestly garb, barely visible behind the admiral's impressive bulk. Biagio licked his lips, anticipating Herrith's arrival. He had pulled a lot of strings to make this happen, made a lot of puppets dance. He even felt some remorse. Vorto was a fine general. His death would make ruling the Empire all the more difficult. The count sighed, shrugging off the consequences. He wanted his mind unburdened. No doubt Herrith would engage him in verbal fencing. Biagio closed his eyes for a moment, sharpening his foil.

Since learning of Simon's treason, Biagio had been unable to relax. He paced his mansion like an angry cat, stalking the halls at night and freezing in the gardens with only a cape to warm him. He felt friendless and profoundly misunderstood, and Dyana Vantran had kept her promise to shun him, refusing his polite smiles. She locked herself away in her rooms, desolate of human contact. Eris' suicide had struck her hard. Biagio's mood soured. If he had known his prize dancer was going to kill herself, he might not have been so drastic with her.

Control, he reminded himself. *Control.*

That was his biggest struggle now. Lately, his mind had been slipping into daydreams and flashes of rage. It was the stress, he knew, and the all-importance of his grand design, but that didn't excuse some of his actions. Biagio kicked distractedly at the sand beneath his boots. Dyana Vantran was on his mind often these days. She was a perceptive little gadfly, and she annoyed him. More, she had started him thinking about things he'd wanted to keep buried. Insanity came only to the feeble-minded; he had always been sure of that. And Arkus wasn't insane, was he? The drugs that kept them all vital did almost nothing to the brain.

Or so Biagio wanted to believe.

"She's a witch," he scoffed. "She's trying to distract me."

The count squared his shoulders. Nicabar's launch was approaching. He could see Herrith more clearly now, staring at him from across the water. The bishop's eyes were lusterless. Biagio frowned. Hadn't Herrith taken the drug? Nicabar had offered it to him, surely. The count tried to relax. Eventually he'd get the bishop hooked again. Herrith was so malleable.

When the rowboat approached, two sailors splashed out of the vessel. They dragged it onto the sand, bringing it to a halt. In the boat was another man, sitting beside Herrith, coming into view as Nicabar stepped out. Biagio's pleasure grew enormously.

Kivis Gago.

Nar's Minister of Arms had made it to Crote. It was a pleasure the count hadn't really expected. Like Herrith, Kivis Gago had always hated Biagio. Biagio tried not to let his grin overwhelm him. He cautioned his bodyguards to keep back as Gago's servants stepped out of the boat and shielded their master. Instantly they drew their swords in a net of steel. The tiresome show irked Biagio but he did nothing to stop it. He merely watched as Kivis Gago stepped out of the boat and waded through the water. Gago's face was set with ice. He looked different from when Biagio had last seen him. The blue of his eyes was gone, replaced with a natural, vastly less interesting brown. He had dropped weight, too, an obvious consequence of the withdrawal.

"Welcome to Crote, Gago," said Biagio. He offered his enemy a mannerly bow. "I would say it's good to see you, but that would be a lie."

Gago paused, stunned at the statement. Hatred bloomed on his face. "Still an impertinent little elf, eh, Biagio?" he said. "I had hoped your exile might have changed you for the better. But I see it has only made you more bitter."

Biagio wasn't listening. He was looking over Gago's shoulder toward Herrith. The old bishop was struggling out of the boat and coming ashore. Refusing Nicabar's help, Herrith walked alone, his head held high despite his weakened appearance. Behind him came Nicabar, his expression stoic.

"Who else has come?" Biagio asked absently.

"Claudi Vos, Tepas Talshiir, Deboko," replied Gago. "Eleven lords in all."

Biagio's heart leapt. "Good," he said evenly. "I'm glad. Maybe we can accomplish something."

"Don't be too sure of that, Biagio," warned Gago. "Some of us aren't in the mood to bargain."

But you came, didn't you? thought Biagio happily. *Stupid man.*

"Let's be open-minded," he said. Then he walked toward the approaching Herrith. Surprisingly, Biagio felt a little fluster of fear. Even after so much derision, there was still something awe-inspiring about Herrith. Biagio made sure to give his nemesis a respectful greeting, bowing low.

"Herrith," he said reverently. "You honor me by coming here. My thanks, old friend."

Herrith had the look of the heartbroken about him. He stared at Biagio vacantly. The count tried to coax him to speak with a smile.

"I want you to be comfortable here," he said. "Have no fear. We're here to talk, nothing more."

"The sight of you still sickens me," said Herrith finally. "Do not call me friend, Biagio. We are not friends and never will be. God curse you for what you've done. God burn you."

The curses stung Biagio's pride. He heard Kivis Gago's annoying snicker. The minister's bodyguards kept their swords drawn. Biagio mustered up his diplomacy.

"Still, I thank you for coming, and for bringing the others. Gago tells me Vos has come. That's good. What about Oridian?"

"He's aboard the *Black City*," Nicabar chimed in. "The skunk wouldn't stay aboard the *Fearless*."

"Never mind, Danar," said Biagio cheerily. "Old differences. We'll settle them soon."

"No," said Herrith icily. "We will *not*, Count. Not so easily. I agreed to come to put an end to the bloodshed. That's all."

Biagio nodded. Herrith had no idea about bloodshed. "As you say in your sermons, Herrith, peace is the way to Heaven. Let's begin right here, right now." He glanced at Gago. "No?"

Gago smirked. "We shall see, sinner."

Biagio leveled his eyes on Gago. "We are all sinners, Kivis," he said. "Make no mistake."

"Some are worse than others, Count," countered Gago. He put up his hand, and the gesture made his bodyguards sheathe their swords. "But you are right, at least partially. We will listen to you. Just don't waste our time."

"You see, Herrith?" said Biagio. "We can put our differences aside, for a while at least. We must talk. We must also listen."

The bishop scowled. "There are things I want to hear," he growled. "Explanations. That's first. And I make you no promises, devil. I am here. That is all."

The venom in Herrith's voice was appalling. Biagio had expected it, but not to feel its bite so keenly. He swallowed down a counterattack, gracing Herrith with a smile.

"Walk with me, Herrith," he said calmly. "Please."

The count stalked off down the beach a few paces. Then he paused, waiting for Herrith to follow. The bishop looked at him questioningly, but he soon relented, following Biagio down the beach. The bishop walked slowly and with effort. Biagio waited until they were well out of earshot before speaking. The constant sound of the surf helped to mask their words. He decided to start with an innocent question.

"How are you feeling?" he asked. "You do not look fit."

"I am withdrawing from your devil's brew," replied Herrith.

"Withdrawing? Why? Didn't Nicabar give you my last gift?"

"He did. You can suck it out of his floor boards if you like. That's where I poured it—right on the floor."

Biagio was aghast. "How could you? I mean, look at you! You need it, Herrith."

"I do not." Herrith straightened. "God gives me vigor, sinner. I will not surrender my soul to Bovadin's potion any longer."

"It keeps us alive, Herrith," said the count. "And there is more of it. I plan to spare you the agony of mortality, at least."

"Dying will send me to God," said Herrith. "Someone *you* will never see, believe me."

Biagio sighed. "We have much to discuss, you and I. It would be easier if you weren't so sarcastic."

Herrith stopped dead. His hand shot out and grabbed Biagio's sleeve, pulling him roughly around.

"Don't talk to me like a child, you sick little monster," he hissed. "I'm here because of what you and your midget did to my cathedral. And to my daughter!"

"Daughter?" Biagio grinned. "Oh, yes. I thought you'd like her."

Herrith's face purpled; Biagio thought the old man might strike him.

"God *will* curse you, Biagio," swore the bishop. "You can laugh in His face now, but there will come a judgment. You will answer for your sins and crimes, sodomite."

"Do not call me that," Biagio warned. He held up a finger. "That's the last time I will listen to that word from your lips. This is *my* island. You might still rule Nar, but on Crote I am the lord."

"Blasphemous snake," said Herrith. "Blind and stupid, too. All this murder. For what?" He looked at Biagio imploringly. "Why, Count?"

"For Nar," said Biagio with conviction. He pointed at himself with his thumb. "Because it's mine, and you took it from me."

"You're wrong. Nar belongs to no man. It is in the hands of God."

"It's an empire, Herrith," spat Biagio. "It's supposed to be ruled by an emperor. Arkus wanted me to have it."

"He never said so."

"He was afraid," argued Biagio. "Afraid of his own death. He was incapable of passing it on to me. But you know I'm right. You knew it even then, but you stole it from me. Now you see that I can't give it up so easily, though. That's why you're here. Now you're the one who is afraid."

The bishop's face was placid. "Biagio, I have more fears now than I ever thought possible," he said sadly. "You're just one in a giant collection. I'll listen to your rants. And I'll talk peace with you, if that's what it takes to stop your murdering. But I'll never agree to make you emperor."

"Say it, Herrith," Biagio insisted. "Say Arkus wanted me to rule Nar. You know it's true."

"I'll say it, if that's what pleases. Arkus *did* want you to have Nar. He loved you like a son. It changes nothing."

But for Biagio, the statement changed everything. He stared at Herrith, thunderstruck at the admission.

Loved me. Like a son.

Biagio's anger wilted into sadness. "Then why did you fight me, Herrith? Why did you start this acrimony?"

"For the same reason I'm going to continue fighting you, Count. Because you're a lunatic and a sinner. And because the Black Renaissance is a disease that enslaves men and degrades Heaven. You want to bring that back to Nar." Herrith shook his head. "I won't let you."

"You can't stop me, Herrith," warned Biagio. "None of you can. I can reach you anywhere you go. I've already proven that."

"Yes, you've done a fine job of terrifying us," admitted the old man bitterly. "But we're all aligned to stop you. You have too many enemies now, Biagio. You can't beat us all."

The threat made Biagio laugh. "I see there's much to talk about," he said. "Let's wait before we make such claims and say things we'll regret. Today and tomorrow you should rest, all of you. After that, we will begin our talks."

"I would rather get this over with," snapped the bishop. "I'm not anxious to stay on your island."

"Stay, Herrith, please. If you won't take the drug, then have some food and wine. We have plenty of both. I've spared no expense to make all of you comfortable. And I can tell the sea voyage has worn you out."

Herrith grimaced. "Very well. The day after tomorrow, then." He turned and walked back toward the beaching rowboats, leaving Biagio alone. The count watched his old enemy go, still astonished at his strength. To refuse the drug was unimaginable. Biagio had never thought Herrith capable of such resolve. Still, the count was pleased.

"The day after tomorrow," he whispered.

He had not told Herrith that the *Fearless* and her escorts weren't the only Naren vessels to come to Crote today. The *Swift* had arrived three hours earlier.

Dyana had spent the day in her chambers, blankly studying the walls. She had heard the buzzing of Kyla and the other servants, saying how eleven Naren lords had arrived on the island, and that Archbishop Herrith was among them. Yet despite the interesting news, Dyana didn't care. Biagio was simply casting out one more of his elaborate schemes. Sure that she would somehow get caught in his net, Dyana decided to wait, and let things take their course. She was powerless now. Eris was dead, and Biagio was lost to her, and she knew that the count meant his threats. He would take her to the Black City. She was his bait in the trap he was springing for Richius. She had hoped she might reach into his warped mind and fix the broken things she found there, but Biagio was far beyond the influence of such naive tampering.

Since Eris' death, Dyana hadn't spoken to Biagio at all. They had passed each other in a hallway once, and he had given her an awkward smile, but Dyana had happily snubbed him. She didn't want his pleasure or his pity, and she was determined not to give him the satisfaction of seeing her fear. Surprisingly, she didn't really hate Biagio, not even after the heinous thing he had done to Eris. Dyana saw him more as a pathetic child, petulantly screaming for some out-of-reach toy. He was a menace and a murderer, but the question of his evilness still vexed her. Richius had called him a devil. *The* devil, even. But Dyana was Triin, and Triin Gods were more complicated. None of them were purely evil. To Dyana, that notion seemed impossible.

But he is unreachable, she reminded herself. *So do not even try.*

It was well past midnight and the mansion was silent. Dyana lay awake in her bed, staring at the ceiling. An ornate plaster mural looked back at her, depicting something from Crotan history, but she didn't know what. Occasional footfalls passing her door disturbed her. The Naren nobles who had come were obviously keeping the servants busy. Dyana thought about Falindar, and how she had been pampered when she was Tharn's wife. Tharn had been a good man. He had never let her want for anything. Sometimes, she surprised herself by missing him. She wanted desperately to go home.

"Woman," said a sudden voice.

Dyana bolted up, frightened. She searched her dark bedroom and saw a golden figure in the threshold. Her pulse exploded.

"What do you want?" she asked. She pulled the sheets closer, hiding her body.

Count Biagio drifted toward her bed. His eyes glowed with incandescence. A rich cape of crimson trailed out behind him like a bride's train.

"Don't be afraid," he urged.

"How did you get in here?" she asked, realizing how stupid the question sounded. But she didn't care that he was master of the house. This was her bedroom!

"I didn't knock because I feared you wouldn't hear me," he explained. He was watching her with odd interest. Something like longing shone on his face. "I didn't mean to frighten you."

"Please get out," said Dyana. She felt herself shrink away from him. He was magnificent in the dark. "I do not want you here."

Biagio took another step toward her bed. "I will leave presently," he said softly, "but I want to make sure you understand what I'm going to tell you. Tomorrow night at this very time, you must be ready to leave Crote."

"Leave?" asked Dyana. "Why?"

He gave her the answer she dreaded. "We're going back to the Black City. When it's time, I'll send a slave for you. They'll take you to the beach. A boat will be waiting. You will get on it."

Dyana sat up. "Why now?" she asked. "Why so soon?"

Biagio grinned menacingly. "Your husband and his Lissen heroes are coming, woman. They mean to take my island from me."

"Richius?" Dyana gasped. "How do you know?"

The count's eyebrows went up. "So many questions. I thought you weren't going to talk to me anymore."

"Tell me," demanded Dyana. "Richius is coming? You know this truly?"

"I am the Roshann, woman," he reminded her. "I have my sources. Your worthless husband is on his way. No doubt he has a band of filthy Lissens with him. When they get here, it won't be safe for anyone. Not even you." The count folded his arms, mocking her with his glare. "I wouldn't want to lose you so quickly. I still have plans for you."

He enjoyed tormenting her, but Dyana saw through his motives. "Do not try to frighten me with your threats, Biagio," she scoffed. "It seems that you are the one who is afraid. You are running from the Lissens."

"Oh, woman, you are so shortsighted," he chuckled. "You truly don't know me at all, do you? Just be ready when I send for you. If you're not, I will drag you onto the *Fearless*. Naked, if I must."

From out of his pocket he pulled a key on a little silver chain. Dyana spied it suspiciously.

"What is that?"

"I'm afraid I can't let you out of these chambers until tomorrow night. I don't want any of my Naren guests knowing about you."

He turned to go, but Dyana called after him.

"You can lock me in, but I am still not your prisoner," she said hotly. "I am a free woman. You will never own me, Biagio."

The count paused. "Dyana Vantran, I could snuff you out like a candle anytime I wish. Is that what you call freedom?"

He didn't wait for her answer. The darkness enveloped him and she heard him leave her chambers, locking the door behind him. Dyana sat in bed, listening to the sounds of her captivity. But her fears weren't for herself.

"Richius," she whispered desperately. "Please be careful."

FORTY-THREE

The Day After Tomorrow

Richius Vantran waited in the cold hours before dawn, watching the island of Crote through a spyglass. Biagio's island was barely visible in the dark, and the *Prince of Liss* and her three escorts were reasonably far offshore, letting the night hide them from Crotan eyes. They had not seen any Naren dreadnoughts in the waters around the island and had moved in closer with confidence. The *Prince* stood at anchor, one nautical mile from Biagio's mansion. A wicked ocean wind tore through Richius' shirt. Like his troops, he wore no coat, only a thick woolen shirt topped with a chainmail chest-guard. A pair of deerskin dueling gauntlets kept the cold from his fingers.

He peered through the lens, trying to penetrate the darkness. The Crotan shore was smoother than the shores of Liss, with a long, white beach and cleanly cut grasses that were visible even in the pale starlight. Richius was very quiet as he surveyed the terrain. On the deck beside him stood Simon and Prakna. Shii and a dozen Lissen troops were piling into the first launch, a long rowboat dangling off the side of Prakna's flagship. A similar boat was filling up on the starboard side of the vessel, and on both sides of Prakna's three other schooners. Each carried as many fighters as possible.

It was at least two hours until dawn. Enough time, Richius hoped, to surround Biagio's mansion. He didn't want his troops cut down trying to get ashore, so he was having them beach away from the mansion, where Biagio's guards couldn't see them. Simon had chosen a safe landing spot, a place the Naren promised would be free of sentries. From there Richius would march a small force onto the mansion's grounds, taking out the sentries posted around the mansion. Here, too, Simon would be indispensable. Simon knew all the habits of the count's household. Or so he claimed. Richius grit his teeth and handed the spyglass back to Prakna. He glanced apprehensively at Simon.

"I can't see anything," he whispered. "I hope you're right about those sentries."

"I'm right," Simon assured him. "Biagio posts about a half dozen men around his grounds. I told you."

Richius nodded. Simon had told him, countless times. But Richius kept running over the numbers anyway. Half a dozen men, two at each entrance and two roaming, patrolling the grounds. Those latter would be the hardest to find and eliminate. And they had to be found quickly. That would be Simon's job. The Roshann agent had readied himself for the task, dressing in black like a lean and hungry panther. He wore a dagger and short scimitar at his side, both simple, and had cropped his hair around his skull. In the darkness he cut a frightening image. His malevolent look reminded Richius that the Roshann were still a hidden danger throughout the Empire.

"How long a march to the mansion, do you think?" Richius asked. "Less than an hour, right?"

"A little," said Simon. "We'll make better time than the rest of them, though, since I'll be leading."

"The others have the maps," Richius agreed. He was confident those groups would find their way to the mansion without a guide. And he wanted Simon to lead the first wave to Biagio's home quickly. A smaller number could go unnoticed more easily. Shii and the others in the boat would come with them. The other three leaders, Tomr, Loria and Delf, would take up positions on the north, west and east, respectively. Together they would form a noose, tight enough to force Biagio out of hiding. Prakna, it had been agreed, would stay aboard the *Prince* with Marus and the other sailors, none of whom were experienced fighters anyway. Nevertheless, they had curved Lissen scimitars ready if they were needed. Richius didn't plan on calling the sailors into combat, but Biagio might surprise them. He looked at Prakna in the starlight. The fleet commander's face was grave.

"Time to get aboard, my friend," he said, gesturing to the waiting launch. Then he stuck out a hand for Richius to shake. Richius took it warmly.

"Don't leave without us, Prakna," Richius joked. He felt the Lissen's grip tighten.

"Richius, no matter what happens, I want you to know I've always thought well of you. Liss thanks you for what you've done."

The peculiar sentiment flustered Richius. "Don't worry, Prakna," he said. "I plan on coming back."

"A good plan." Then Prakna turned to Simon, saying, "Naren, good luck to you as well."

It was an unaffectionate good-bye, but Simon grinned anyway. "Luck to you, Prakna. I hope no dreadnoughts show up."

"These waters are safe," said the commander. "Just worry about yourself."

"I always do," quipped Simon. He stared at Prakna. "Isn't that right?"

Prakna shrugged, not wanting to argue. "As you say, Simon Darquis. As you say."

"Let's get aboard," said Richius, taking Simon's shoulder and steering him toward the rowboat. Four sailors waited by the rail with ropes, ready to lower the launch into the water. Shii waited onboard, standing amongst her sitting troops. She looked resolute in the murky light, the perfect symbol of Lissen honor. Richius felt profoundly proud of her. He took the first step into the boat, squeezing past the other troops who looked up at him with earnest faces. He recognized Johr in the crowd and his sister Teeli, and the youngest one of the group, Griff, a boy of barely sixteen. Griff looked afraid, just as he had the night before, when Richius had told him he didn't have to go ashore. But Griff had been adamant about invading Crote. He gave Richius a nervous nod. Richius winked back at him, taking a seat beside Shii. Simon entered next, without a smile or greeting of any kind. He was still an outcast among the group and as such took a seat at the prow of the boat, away from them all. Four of Prakna's sailors would row them ashore, so not to tire out the troops before their march.

"Let us down," Richius ordered. On his command the pulleys began to squeal as the rope-men lowered the launch. Across the water, he saw other boats begin dropping from the sides of the escort vessels. Richius glanced up as the rowboat sank and saw Prakna staring at them. The fleet commander offered a little wave. Richius looked at him, perplexed. He had expected Prakna to be elated. The rowboat slipped down the *Prince*'s side and splashed into the water. The oarsmen quickly took to rowing, shoving them off from the side of the flagship and pointing them toward the dark coast of Crote. Simon guided them in. Other boats took their point, following them through the gloom. Richius drew a breath of salty air and tried to still his racing pulse. Beside him, Shii had gone white. He nudged her a little with his elbow.

"You all right?"

Shii only nodded.

"You sure?" he asked. "You don't look it."

"I'm fine," replied Shii distractedly. She licked her lips, betraying her fear.

Richius raised a hand to get his group's attention. "Listen to me, everyone," he whispered. "We're about to do this thing, and I know you're all afraid. But that's all right. I'm afraid, too."

"You're afraid?" asked Griff. Richius smiled at him, remembering other young men like him from Aramoor.

"It's normal to be afraid," he said. "But you've all trained hard and you know what to do. And if we're lucky, Biagio will simply surrender."

They all glanced away, looking sheepish.

"I know you don't believe me, but Biagio isn't impractical," Richius went on. "When he sees how many of us there are, he just might surrender."

"We're all right, Lord Jackal," said Shii imploringly. "Please . . ."

Richius said nothing more. He could tell that Shii was nervous, so he let her collect herself on the trip to shore. Simon sat in the prow, guiding the boat with hand signals. He had promised Richius that he knew a place on Biagio's vast property where the count's sentries couldn't see them land. Richius still feared it might be a trap. As much as he wanted to trust Simon, there remained a nagging suspicion. Perhaps even this was part of Biagio's elaborate scheme. Perhaps the count knew they were coming and that Simon was leading them.

"There," whispered Simon to the oarsmen. "Put in there."

A lagoonlike inlet appeared out of the darkness. The Lissens piloted the rowboat into it. It was wide enough to accommodate a dozen boats and was bordered on all sides by secretive, sandy hills. Richius smiled when he saw it. Simon had kept his word.

One by one the other boats followed them into the inlet. Delf's boat was first. He waved to Richius when he saw him. Richius looked over Delf's shoulder to the other incoming launches. The *Prince* and her sisters were barely visible on the horizon, but he could just make out the image of more departing rowboats. The boats would have to make multiple runs to get the nine hundred fighters ashore.

Quickly, Richius got out of the boat and splashed through the water. His troops followed. Soon the inlet was filled with bodies. Richius watched them carefully, sizing up their precision. They moved just as he had taught them—silent and swift, and without any wasted moves.

"All right then," he said to Shii. "Let's go." He turned to Simon, who would lead the first dozen to the mansion. "Ready?"

"Ready," said Simon, then turned and stalked off up the northern hillside. Richius followed him, ordering Shii and the rest of the platoon after him.

Very near dawn, Archbishop Herrith left his luxurious rooms in the mansion's west wing and went in search of Count Biagio. Like all who had been addicted to Bovadin's drug, Herrith was an early riser, sometimes going the entire night without sleep. Because he knew Biagio suffered from the same insomnia, Herrith was sure the count would also be awake. It was the day after Herrith's arrival, and the bishop was eager to begin his talks with the devil of Crote. His stay had so far been restful, and Herrith felt refreshed despite his gnawing cravings. A month's supply of the drug had been waiting for him in his rooms when he'd arrived. It was a well-appointed room, and Herrith had taken pleasure in dropping the blue liquid onto the carpet. Kivis Gago and the other Naren lords had been given similar apartments in the mansion's west wing. Herrith had been awed by Biagio's wealth. He had always known the count to be a man of expensive tastes, but there were Daragos in his home and works from other renowned artists, and everything seemed to be made of gold or silver, or upholstered in the finest leather, or sculpted from the best imported marble. All the hallways were gilded, and all the sheets were silk. And Herrith had hardly been able to concentrate from the parade of slaves offering him foods and services. He had spent the day before talking with the other Naren lords. All of them loved the lavish lifestyle, and all agreed that the talks with Biagio should take place on schedule. But none of them knew what that schedule was, because Biagio hadn't come to them, and neither had any of his aides. So Herrith had elected himself spokesperson for the group, and had decided not to wait for the sun to rise. He wanted to see Biagio. Now.

But now was very early, and as he moved through the empty corridors, the dearth of servants did not perplex him. Even slaves needed their rest, and the eleven lords and their numerous bodyguards had kept the count's staff ridiculously busy with petty requests. Herrith moved quietly through the halls, not wanting to disturb anyone who might be sleeping.

Herrith paused in the hallway for a moment, staring through a bank of body-length windows. The island was very dark and he could barely see the ocean for the lack of light. It was a peaceful moment, the kind he liked to think God created to make men thoughtful. Today, Herrith was very thoughtful. Lorla would have loved this view, and this magnificent place. But she wasn't alive anymore to share such things—if she ever really had been alive. She was a creation of the war labs—Biagio had practically admitted it. That made her something less than human. And, in a way, something more than human, too. Herrith still ached over her death, and he didn't care if she had been spawned for the sole purpose of seducing him. In the end, she had tried to trade her life for his, and that was all that mattered.

I'll make you pay, Biagio, thought Herrith relentlessly. He caught a glimpse of something moving in the distance outside, but in his rage ignored it. *We're not done, you and I. Not yet.*

He wanted to squeeze every bit of blood out of Biagio's body and feed it to rats. He wanted to peel off Biagio's golden skin and upholster a chair with it. Herrith realized how clouded his mind had become, but he could do nothing to stop it. His daughter, his beloved cathedral, even Darago's laborious masterwork; all gone in a blaze of madness. When Herrith shut his eyes, he saw his life in flames. He had so many regrets on his shoulders these days, he could barely stand. And not all of them were Biagio's fault.

When I get back to Nar I will do things differently, he swore. There would be no more Formula B. He would keep peace some other way, without murdering children. He had thought the Black Renaissance the greatest threat in the world, worthy of the most drastic means imaginable, but he had been wrong. All the while he had thought God was speaking to him, but now Herrith knew the voices were only in his mind.

Herrith opened his eyes and saw something peculiar outside the window, something quick and shadowy. He squinted to see better, but was quickly distracted by the call of his name from down the corridor.

"Archbishop Herrith," said the voice. "Good morning, Holiness."

It was Leraio, Biagio's manservant. Herrith had met him two days before, but it took a moment to recall the face. Leraio was coming toward him with a smile. Herrith recoiled, unsure why. Perhaps because Biagio had a penchant for having underlings deliver bad news—like Vorto's head.

"It's very early," Herrith observed. "What are you doing up and around?"

"Looking for you, Holiness," the slave answered. "Count Biagio wanted me to deliver a message to you. He told me you might be up very early, and that I should speak with you as soon as possible, as a matter of respect to you."

"Biagio? I was on my way to see him," said Herrith, baffled. "What's your message?"

Leraio reached into his silky vest and pulled out a letter, another of Biagio's dreaded envelopes. Herrith groaned when he saw it.

"What is this?" he asked. "I want to see Biagio."

Leraio shook his head, smiling implacably. "I'm sorry, Holiness. Count Biagio isn't on Crote any longer. He left last night, while you were sleeping."

The words were so strange Herrith hardly heard them. "Left? What do you mean?"

"I'm sorry to say, Count Biagio is gone," Leraio explained. "With

Admiral Nicabar. As I said, they left last night. I'm sorry, Holiness. I really don't know any more than that. That is my message. Perhaps the letter will explain it better."

"What are you talking about?" Herrith barked. "Biagio's gone?"

Leraio blanched. "Yes, Holiness," he replied meekly. "I'm very sorry."

"Gone?" Herrith roared. "Gone where?"

"To the Black City, Holiness. He wanted me to tell you when he was gone, and to give you that letter, with his respects."

Herrith was stunned. "Is he coming back?"

"I don't think so," said Leraio. "I'm very sorry, Holiness."

"Sorry doesn't help me, you fool!" Herrith spat. He fumbled with the envelope, trying to get it open. Leraio offered to help but Herrith angrily turned him away, tearing open the paper housing and unfolding the note. Again he saw Biagio's distinctive, mocking handwriting.

My dear Herrith,

Thank you again for bringing so many of my enemies with you. It was good to see them again, though I fear it will be for the last time. I have gone to the Black City with Nicabar, and we have taken all the ships with us. There is no way off the island.

I hope you enjoy the rest of the day. Please help yourself to whatever you like. If I'm correct, you have very little time.

Your friend,
Count Renato Biagio.

"My God," Herrith gasped. "What is the meaning of this?" He shook the letter in Leraio's face. "He's left us! Why?"

Leraio didn't bother to answer.

"He's abandoned us!" Herrith roared, tossing the letter to the floor. "What wicked plan is this?"

Outside the window, something flickered again past Herrith's vision. "What is that?" he growled, pressing his nose up to the glass. Dawn was slowly creeping awake, barely lighting the world. Herrith caught a glimpse of four ships on the horizon. For a moment he was heartened.

"Is this a joke? Look, the dreadnoughts are still—"

But they weren't dreadnoughts. They weren't of Naren design at all. Herrith backed away from the window.

"Oh, merciful Heaven," he moaned. "Liss . . ."

Simon worked with the speed of a leopard, darting through Biagio's yard and locating the two roving sentries. The first one was by a flower bed, urinating, when Simon slipped his dagger into his spine. The man went to the ground silently, paralyzed, and didn't know what had happened until he saw Simon staring down at him. A slice to the throat finished him. The second sentry had been harder to find, but Simon had kept to the shadows, waiting for him to come in search of his comrade. He remembered that the two used a circular pattern to walk the grounds, one coming clockwise, the other counterclockwise, around the perimeter. It took them about ten minutes to complete one circuit. Eight minutes after he'd killed the first one, Simon homed in on the second. It was still very dark but the man was by a window in the west wing, looking up stupidly at the stars. He saw Simon leap out of the trees—barely. The Roshann agent was on him in a second. Simon plunged his dagger into the sentry's windpipe and covered his screaming mouth in one perfect movement. The sentry dropped dead to the ground. Simon hurriedly dragged the body away from the window, hiding him in a small batch of fruit trees. The rush was on him now and he looked around wildly, his eyes wide, his muscles tingling with energy.

Two down, he thought quickly. *Four more.*

Richius had led his troops to the mansion in the cover of darkness, but dawn was breaking fast on the horizon. He needed to work quickly. Griff and the others had gone off to the north gate to deal with the two sentries there. Richius led Shii and the twins, Akal and Wyle. They were quickly creeping up to the south entrance, where Simon had promised they would find two more sentries. Richius and his team were on their bellies when they sighted their quarry. They had slithered through a group of topiaries trimmed to look like birds and were almost near the entrance. As Simon had warned, there was no cover for the next fifteen yards. Without speaking, Richius signaled his team to hold up, then pointed toward the gate. Shii nodded. Akal handed each of them a crossbow, already loaded with a bolt. Richius and Shii would take the first shots. If they missed, the second missiles from Akal and Wyle would have to silence the sentries. Richius waited until he was ready. The two sentries in their brilliant blue outfits were talking casually, oblivious to the assassins hunting them. Richius wished he could hear what they were saying.

I'm sorry, he thought. *You're innocent, I know.*

He rested his elbows into the dirt, putting the crossbow to his chin. Then again, no one on Crote was innocent. Not if they served Biagio.

I was trained as a horseman, he told himself. *Not a killer. Not like Simon.*

Richius closed one eye and focused on his target, the sentry on the left. Shii had already fixed her aim.

I have him, she signaled.

Richius signaled back, cuing the attack.

They both pulled the triggers and sent their silent missiles racing forward. Shii's caught its quarry through the eye, dropping him instantly. But Richius didn't match the amazing shot. His bolt hammered into the wall, inches away from the sentry's head. Richius grit his teeth, biting back a curse. Akal and Wyle fired. Akal missed. Wyle didn't. The sentry cried out as the bolt entered his skull. He let out a wailing scream.

"Damn it!" Richius hissed, leaping from his position and drawing his dagger. Amazingly, the sentry saw him coming and put up a defense. Richius barreled into him, driving his knee into the man's face and shattering his teeth. The dagger flashed and ripped through flesh, severing the man's throat. A hot stream of blood gushed out, catching Richius on the cheek. The man slumped against the wall. Shii raced forward and helped Richius drag the dying man aside. Richius felt the dizzying rush of fear. He looked around, trying to spot his troops on the hill in the distance, but couldn't see anything. They were still perfectly invisible. And more were coming. Soon Tomr and Delf would have their troops in position. Richius wondered if Simon had found the other sentries. Then, as if magically summoned, Simon appeared like a wraith out of the darkness.

"Fall back," he whispered. "I got them."

Richius signaled Shii and the others. "Fall back," he ordered. "That's it."

Now he had to get everyone into position. The noose was forming.

The eleven Naren lords had come quickly to Herrith's call, gathering in the west wing with their bodyguards. The mood was generally a panicked bedlam. Baron Ricter was still in his sleeping clothes. The master of the Tower of Truth held a gigantic mace in his meaty hands and was screaming incessantly at his red-caped servants, ordering them to protect him. The baron's booming voice rocked the hallway. The noblemen had gathered into a tight little circle, unsure what to do and gawking at Herrith for guidance. Kivis Gago was at Herrith's side, frantically trying to piece together what had happened. All that they knew for certain was that Biagio had abandoned them and that Lissen soldiers were swarming around the mansion. There was no way out, except through a bloody fight. Herrith quickly counted heads. Eleven lords, most capable of combat. Each had about a dozen bodyguards with them. That meant they had over a hundred men. Not a bad number, Herrith supposed. But he wasn't a military man. That's why he leaned so heavily on Gago.

"I don't know," said Gago desperately, shaking his head. "I don't know how many Lissens there are!"

"We will fight them," spat Oridian. The Naren Minister of the Treasury was as accomplished with a sword as he was with an abacus, and he held his serrated blade out before him, grinning like a madman. "Lissen pigs! We'll slaughter them all!"

"We don't know how many there are, you idiot," Claudi Vos reminded him harshly. Unlike Oridian, Vos was only an architect, and didn't seem to own a weapon. He stood wringing his womanly hands in the outskirts of the circle, sticking close to his bodyguards. "We should talk to them."

"They're not here to talk, fool," snapped Oridian.

"Biagio brought them here," Tepas Talshiir chimed in. "That devil has trapped us."

That much was obvious. Herrith rubbed his forehead nervously. They *were* trapped, maybe without escape. And he knew Biagio wouldn't have brought them here if he'd thought they'd make it out alive. The bishop forced the clutter from his mind, blocking out the arguing voices. Somehow, he needed to get control. He needed to find out what the Lissens wanted, if anything. Maybe they were looking for Biagio. If they found out the count wasn't here . . .

No, Herrith scolded himself. There were enough Narens in this hall to satisfy Lissen vengeance for a year. Biagio wasn't the only one Liss hated. Still, the only option that came to Herrith was talk. If they were to have any chance of surviving, they would have to try and reason with the invaders.

"Claudi Vos is right," he said finally. "We have to talk to them. Find out what they want."

"They want to kill us!" Oridian shrieked. "What do you think they want?"

"They haven't attacked yet," argued Gago. "Maybe they'll listen."

Baron Ricter, who had overheard the conversation, stopped yelling at his men and came forward. "I won't bargain with those animals," he boomed. "They're untrustworthy snakes, like Triin. You can't believe a word they say. We should fight them." He gestured around the room. "We have the strength."

An agreeing cheer went up from about half the noblemen. Herrith held up his hands, begging for silence. "We don't know how many Lissens are out there," he reminded them. "We might fight them only to get cut to pieces."

"We'll take our chances," said Oridian. The treasurer grit his teeth. "I say bring them on. Who's with me?"

"I am," said Tepas Talshiir. The merchant folded his arms over his chest, emboldened by his contingent of bodyguards, the most numerous of the group. "I pledge all my men to fight them. Claudi Vos, are you with us?"

The Lord Architect grimaced, contemplating their situation. He looked apologetically at Herrith. "What choice have we, Bishop?" he said at last. "We are many, after all."

"But perhaps not enough," replied Herrith. "Please. We came here to talk peace with Biagio. Can't we now talk peace with these Lissens?"

Oridian sighed. "You don't know them, Herrith. They're dogs. If we let down our defenses they'll cut us to shreds. We can't show them any weakness. Gago knows this." He turned to the minister. "Don't you, Gago?"

Kivis Gago looked away, shaking his head. "I don't know," he said gravely. "We are many. Enough perhaps." He glanced at Herrith. "Bishop, I just don't know. . . ."

"Fine," growled Herrith, his patience snapping. "Fight them, then. Win if you can. Die if you must. I want no part of this."

Herrith turned and walked away. They called out after him, but he ignored them all, even Kivis Gago, who hurried up to Herrith and tried to pull him back into the protective folds of the guards. Herrith shook off the nobleman's grip, practically shoving Gago aside. The minister, who had never been a friend to Herrith, looked shocked.

"Herrith," he cried desperately. "Come back!"

"I will not," Herrith replied. He was almost out of the hall.

"Where are you going?"

Herrith didn't answer. He headed out of the west wing and through the maze of corridors, doing his best to remember where the mansion's gates lay. Something told him none of Biagio's sentries would be around to stop him.

Richius waited on the south side of the mansion, at the head of his gathering troops. Shii was beside him, looking paler by the minute. The sun was rising, lighting the gardens and burning away their cover. Messages were coming in quickly. Tomr's forces were almost in place on the north side of the mansion, and Loria and Delf were close behind, walling in the west and east sides. Richius' own troops were already fully assembled. His army of orphans lurked in the bushes and bramble of the south side. Richius had his weapon drawn and was quietly giving orders to his troops, relaying them through Shii, who also kept a wary eye on the mansion. Things were eerily quiet. They had expected more of Biagio's sentries to come in search of their murdered brothers. Richius spied the rising sun nervously. They had been sighted by now, surely. So why the quiet?

"Simon, what's going on?" he asked. "Why hasn't Biagio made a move?"

Simon shook his head almost imperceptibly. He did not turn to look at Richius or take his eyes off the mansion. There was no movement in the windows.

"I don't know," Simon admitted. "It's early. Maybe no one's seen us."

"We shouldn't hide anymore," said Shii. "Let them see us. We're too many to hide."

"True enough," agreed Richius. They were many and quickly growing more numerous. Once the sun came up, there would be nowhere to hide their numbers. Richius stopped crouching and stood, urging his followers to do the same. One by one their heads popped out of hiding, until there was a sea of young Lissens visible in the yard. To the east, Delf's group did the same, materializing out of the haze. Richius turned to Shii.

"Send someone to Loria and Tomr. I want Biagio to see us. Let's make some noise."

Shii fired the order to another young woman, sending her scampering off to the west, where Loria and Tomr were getting their troops organized. Richius gripped his sword, readying for Biagio's response. He hoped the count might surrender, but he expected a fight.

"There are nine hundred of us," he reasoned aloud. "He must see that."

"Don't underestimate him, Richius," cautioned Simon. The Naren had sheathed his dagger and now favored a long, Lissen scimitar. The weapon gleamed in the burgeoning light, looking dangerous in Simon's skillful hands. It was no mistake that he was an assassin. With the glint in his eyes and the sharpness of his stance, he looked every bit the part. "When he sees us, he'll send word," Simon guessed. "He'll try to talk. That's the most dangerous time. Don't trust him, Richius."

"No talk," spat Shii angrily. "That's not what we're here for."

Richius regarded her icily. "We will listen," he said sharply. "I don't want anyone dying who doesn't have to."

"Lord Jackal, please . . ."

"Quiet, Shii," Richius snapped. "Just follow my orders."

Shii shrank back like a wounded child. Richius ignored her, focusing instead on the mansion. He didn't have time for an argument, and he didn't want his orders questioned. Not now, when so much was at stake.

"Simon," he whispered. "If Biagio sees you . . ."

Simon nodded. "I know. But I have to get her out of there, Richius. Somehow."

"Then go," urged Richius. "Try and find her. Bring her out if you can, before the fighting starts."

Simon looked at Richius. "You'll need me," he warned.

"Eris needs you," Richius replied. "Go." He gave Simon a sad smile. "I'll be here when you get back."

Simon didn't say another word. He slithered away through the graying darkness, shooting toward the south face of the mansion, ducking behind sculptures and huge urns of plants. He tested a window by peeking inside, broke it with his gloved fist, and quickly went through it, disappearing from view. It all passed in the space of seconds. Richius stared at the place where Simon had been, marveling at the man's speed. He turned to make a remark to Shii . . .

. . . and saw Prakna coming toward him.

The fleet commander was flanked by two of Richius' soldiers, a man and a woman he had assigned to Delf. They looked afraid, as if they had done something stupendously wrong. But Prakna's expression was resolute. He held a scimitar out before him as he walked, and Richius noticed that he had doffed his naval coat and wore fighting mail like the rest of them.

"What the hell . . . ?"

Prakna waved at Richius. "Don't be alarmed, Jackal; I've come to help." He stepped up to Richius and offered out a hand. When Richius didn't take it, the commander retracted it with a grin. "I know you're angry," he said. "I caution you, do not be."

"Prakna, what are you doing here?" asked Richius desperately. "Go back to the *Prince*. We don't need you!"

Prakna shook his head. "I can't do that," he said. "I'm sorry, but I'm here to make sure you do the right thing."

"What?" sputtered Richius. "What are you talking about? I'm trying to—"

"Lord Jackal," interrupted Shii. She stepped forward with an agonized expression. "Don't stop us. Please . . ."

"Shii, what the hell is going on here?" Richius demanded. "Do you know about this?"

"They all do," said Prakna. "And they'll do as I say. Don't stand in our way, Jackal." His jaw tightened. "Please."

"Is that a warning, Prakna?" asked Richius angrily. "After all I've done for you?"

Prakna sighed. "You don't understand."

"Yes, I do," spat Richius. "You're planning on massacring everyone inside. I didn't want that!"

"They deserve it!" roared Prakna. He towered over Richius, staring down at him irately. "You know they do. We're not going to stop you from butchering Biagio. So don't you try and stop us from taking our revenge!"

Richius whirled on Shii. "God damn it, Shii, how could you?"

Shii's face collapsed. "Lord Jackal, please," she gasped. "It's the way it must be."

"No!" Richius cried. He stepped out of Prakna's shadow so all the troops could see him, waving his sword to get their attention. "It doesn't have to be this way. You can be men and women of honor today. Fight them 'til they surrender. Don't butcher them, please!"

The troops looked away, unable to face him. Richius lowered his sword. They weren't listening. They were unreachable, full of the same poison that had polluted Shii and Prakna. Richius turned to growl at the commander.

"You're a bastard," he said. "You used me to make an army of murderers. Well, I won't lead them." He tossed his sword down into the dirt. "You want a massacre, Prakna? *You* lead them."

Prakna stooped and retrieved Richius' weapon, handing it back to him. "Biagio's in there, my friend," he said mildly. "Don't throw away this chance. You've come too far. And if you don't do it, I will."

Richius stared at his sword, then up at Prakna. There was no malice on the commander's face, just the vast emptiness of the driven. Richius knew he would never dissuade him. In a sense, it was something he'd known all along.

"Do what you must," he said finally. "I can't stop you." He turned to Shii sadly. "Shii, I expected more from you. You're not a murderer. You know you're not."

"Lord Jackal," Shii whispered. "There's no choice for me."

Richius shook his head. "You're wrong. You just can't see that yet."

"Lissens!" came a call from across the yard. They all turned toward the gate. In the morning light stood a figure dressed in robes, an old man with outstretched hands and a fearless look in his eyes. Richius gasped, vaguely recalling the face. Nearly two years ago, this very man had married him to Sabrina.

"Oh, my God," whispered Richius. "That's Herrith."

"Who?" asked Prakna, stunned at the interruption.

Richius was too flabbergasted to explain. Herrith waved at them, within plain shot of a crossbow, beckoning them to listen. The young army broke into a concerned murmur. Prakna swore as he finally realized who had appeared.

"Herrith!" he said breathlessly. "How?"

The impossible question went unanswered. Richius' first instinct was that they had blundered into a gigantic trap. But Biagio and Herrith were enemies. Weren't they?

"What is this?" he asked blankly. He took a step toward Herrith. Shii immediately jumped in front of him.

"No, Jackal," she cried. "Get back!"

Prakna grabbed Richius' shoulder, pulling him into the safety of the fold. "Easy, boy," he cautioned. "Shii's right. You stay back."

"Lissens, listen to me," cried Herrith. "Let me come forward. I want to talk."

"No talk, holy man!" Prakna roared. "Today we fight you!"

"No," Richius insisted, pressing past Shii and the others who had gathered to guard him. Akal and Wyle stood by with their crossbows, loading them quickly and beading on Herrith. Prakna held on to Richius' sleeve as he tried to struggle forward.

"Let me talk to him," Richius pleaded. "He knows me."

"I want to make arrangements," Herrith cried, oblivious to his danger. He held up his hands in a show of peace. "Let me come forward." He took one careful step toward the army.

"Not another move, butcher," Prakna warned. "One more step and you die."

"Herrith, it's me," Richius cried. "Richius Vantran!"

The bishop paused for a moment, clearly confused. "Vantran?" he called back. "King Vantran?"

"Don't move!" demanded Prakna. He let go of Richius and ripped the crossbow from Akal's hands, aiming it at Herrith. "Or I swear to Heaven, I'll kill you!"

"Stop, Prakna," Richius seethed. "Don't you dare fire!"

"I will, Richius," said Prakna evenly. "I'm warning you. . . ."

Richius reached out for Prakna's crossbow, grabbing at it desperately. Prakna howled in anger, bringing up a boot and slamming it into Richius' belly. The blow knocked the breath from Richius and sent him tumbling backward. He struggled to rise as Prakna took aim. Herrith held up his hands and took one more fateful step.

"No!" Richius bellowed.

Prakna shot the bow, putting the bolt into Herrith's heart. The bishop's white tunic exploded with crimson. He staggered back, looked down at his punctured chest, then collapsed in a heap. Richius got to his feet and stared at Herrith's body. He glanced at Prakna, who lowered his crossbow with a resolute nod.

"A trap," he said gravely. "It's a trap."

"You fool," Richius hissed. "You murdering fool!"

Prakna exploded. He grabbed Richius by the lapels and shook him, spittle spraying from his mouth. "*They* murder!" he hollered. "Not me!" He tossed Richius aside. Turning on his troops, he screamed at them to attack.

"Take them!" he cried. "Drag this god-damn mansion down to Hell!"

Richius watched, horror-stricken, as all the young men and women he had worked so hard to mold reverted instantly back to the mob he had first met on Karalon. The cry was picked up by the forces on the east and west sides, and all at once they started running toward the mansion, swarming toward the gates in a great, unstoppable torrent. Prakna led the charge to the south gate. He had his scimitar in his hand and he was howling with lust, his blond head shining terribly above the army as they rushed inward. Everyone followed the Lissen hero, leaving Richius standing alone in the garden.

Except for Shii.

The young woman had dropped her weapon and was weeping, her arms folded over her chest, her head slung helplessly low. She didn't dare look at Richius.

"Lord Jackal," she said desperately. "Forgive me."

The morning erupted in a melee of cries and shattering glass. The Lissens stormed through the gates and the broken windows, their weapons eager for the feast. Richius went to Shii. He wanted to strike her.

"Shii," he gasped, shaking. "I could kill you for this."

"Forgive me," she sobbed. "Forgive me. . . ."

"You knew," said Richius. "Why?"

At last Shii lifted her tear-stained face. She had the same unreachable madness in her eyes as Prakna. "Because I want to kill them," she said. Then she stooped, retrieved her weapon from the ground, and stalked off after her comrades.

Richius watched her go, utterly appalled. "Fool," he scolded himself. "This is my fault."

But he wasn't done. There was one criminal on the island, one man who truly deserved to die. Richius had come this far to find Biagio, and still couldn't let the count slip away. Like Shii, he picked up his weapon and went in search of his quarry.

Kivis Gago and the other Naren lords had looked out the windows of the west wing and had seen the Lissen army in the growing light. The numbers had stunned them. Gago quickly tabulated the figures and knew they were vastly outnumbered. He called his guardians to surround him and took a sword from one of the suits of armor in the hall. They would make a stand here, they had all decided, and would hold the wing as long as they could. Baron Ricter and his troop of red-caped soldiers lined the windows facing westward. Oridian's men barricaded one side of the hall, while Claudi Vos' men took the other, backed up by the troops of Tepas Talshiir. Gago's own men stayed in the center, readying to aid whoever needed it. And as he waited for the Lissens to descend on them, Kivis Gago's only thoughts were of Biagio, and how the count had bested them.

"If I live through this I will kill him," the minister muttered. "I will make it my life's work to punish him."

But Kivis Gago didn't expect to live, or even to last more than another hour. There were hundreds of Lissens waiting for him, all full of hate from the decade-long war his ministry had overseen. Kivis Gago resigned himself to die with a sword in his hand.

He didn't have a very long wait.

The windows along the western wall shattered in a violent implosion. Lissen soldiers swarmed inside. Ricter's men hacked at them, trying desperately to push them back. But the wave kept coming. Kivis Gago ordered his own men into the melee, sure that they'd be shredded.

Simon hurried through the familiar corridors with his sword in his hand, trying to reach Eris' quarters. He could hear the battle ringing through the halls and knew that Richius' efforts at peace had failed. That didn't give him much time. But Simon had expected more resistance. Instead he found the halls empty. Guessing that Biagio had ordered all his sentries against the Lissens, Simon started running. He was in a headlong dash now, very near Eris' chambers. She would be frightened by the fighting. She might even be hiding.

I'm coming, thought Simon desperately. *Hold on, my love.*

Near the slave quarters he saw his first group of familiar faces. A gang of servants were huddled together, peering around the corner. They pointed at him as he raced forward.

"Where's Eris?" he cried, coming up to them. "Tell me, quickly!"

The slaves were thunderstruck at his appearance.

"Simon Darquis!" they said. "You're back!"

"Tell me where Eris is!" Simon thundered. He recognized Kyla, one of Biagio's slaves. Simon grabbed her arm and shook her.

"Tell me," he demanded. "Where is she?"

Kyla shrieked, trying to pull free. "She's dead!" cried the girl. "Please, let me go!"

Simon's iron grip turned to water. He stood in horror, unable to move. "What?" he gasped. "What did you say?"

"They're close," cried one of the slaves. "I can hear them."

"Dead?" asked Simon. "That's impossible. Eris . . ."

"She's dead," cried Kyla desperately. She was about to run when Simon seized her again. The rest of the slaves scrambled, dashing for cover. Simon heard the din of fighting in the distance. He ignored it all, sick with dread.

"Tell me!" he demanded. "Tell me you're lying! Eris is alive!"

Kyla shrieked hysterically, breaking into sobs. "Please, let me go!"

"Tell me!"

"She's dead! She killed herself! Please . . ."

"You lie," Simon roared. His whole body began to shake. "Don't tell me that. Eris . . ."

Kyla finally tore free of him. She raced away, desperate to be gone. Simon's brain descended into a fog.

"Eris," he moaned. "Eris!"

He broke into a run, dashing through the corridors to Eris' rooms, screaming her name all the way.

Prakna prowled quickly through the corridors, searching for Richius. He had promised his queen he would protect the Jackal, and he knew that Richius had entered the mansion in search of Biagio. Prakna had left behind the protection of his army. Most of his soldiers were in the west wing, fighting their way through a barricade of Naren soldiers. There had been more guards on the island than they'd thought, but Prakna was confident his troops could best them.

"Richius!" he called, scanning every opulent crevice.

No one came out to challenge the commander. He had seen some slaves race around corners, but they hadn't threatened him. Suddenly, Prakna felt invincible. Liss the Raped was a quickly fading memory. Today, Liss the Glorious was reborn. They were unstoppable, just as he'd always known they'd be. But he had to find Vantran. Vantran was alone, questing for Biagio in this dangerous place. Prakna stumbled through the halls until at last he heard a weeping voice in a room up ahead. He cocked his head to listen.

"Eris," said the voice miserably. "My beautiful dancer . . ."

Prakna stopped, recognizing the voice. "Darquis."

Carefully, he inched forward, approaching the chamber. He peered inside and saw Simon Darquis huddled on the floor, weeping. The Naren held a pair of small shoes in his hands. The sight appalled Prakna. For one brief moment, his hate-filled heart softened. The Naren didn't hear him enter the chamber, so lost was he in grief. Prakna hefted up his sword.

"Darquis," said Prakna softly. "Look at me."

Simon looked up at Prakna. He noticed the sword in the Lissen's hand and the terrible expression on his face, full of madness. Simon didn't move. He couldn't move. He held Eris' dancing shoes against his chest.

"Eris is dead," he said weakly.

Prakna said nothing.

"I tried to save her," Simon choked. "I truly did. Damn me to Hell for failing."

He knew what Prakna intended. Surprisingly, he didn't care. He could have exploded up and saved himself, he could have wrestled the scimitar from Prakna's hand, but he did nothing but wait, weeping like a child while the Lissen hovered over him, blinded by his own enormous wrath. Simon smiled sadly, yearning to be dead.

Prakna held the scimitar, unable to strike. He stared down at the thing at his feet, and the only emotion that came to him was pity. He had never seen anything as broken as Simon Darquis. Not even his ghost-like J'lari seemed so frail.

"Do it," Simon whispered. "Kill me."

He wanted to die, and his longing frightened Prakna. The fleet commander lowered his weapon.

"I'll not be your executioner, dog."

"Oh, you god-damn coward," spat Simon. Tears ran down his face. Angrily he wiped his nose on his sleeve. "Kill me!"

Prakna sheathed his scimitar. All the hatred had gone out of him, replaced by a brooding sympathy. "Get up," he directed. "Get out of here."

Simon clutched the shoes closer to his breast. "Go where? I have nothing now."

"You have your life, Roshann. Be glad for it. Now hurry. Run now, or I will not be able to save you."

Darquis rose unsteadily to his feet. He looked confused, staring at the world through bleary eyes. The shoes in his hands caught his falling tears. He gave Prakna a vacant glance, wondering what to do.

"You are not safe here," said Prakna. "Go as quickly as you can. Find a boat and get off Crote. I will tell Vantran what has happened."

"Richius . . ."

"Go!"

The order shattered Simon's stupor. Still clutching the shoes, he darted out of the room.

Richius hadn't been able to stop the slaughter. He hadn't even tried. The west wing of the mansion clamored with battle as the army of Liss swarmed over the defenders barricaded inside. It would be a massacre. The Lissens certainly outnumbered the Narens. And Prakna had whipped his troops into a frenzy, filling them with blood-lust. It was just a matter of time before the melee was over and the mansion was reduced to rubble. Time was the enemy now, and Richius felt it slipping through his fingers.

He needed to find Biagio.

Instead he found himself in a magnificent hallway, facing down a curious little man with a retiring smile. The man was dressed in silk and gold, and he stood at the end of the hall, watching Richius approach. All around them the sounds of battle rang out, threatening to come nearer. But the man stood unwavering at his post, blocking Richius' path.

Richius pointed his sword out at him. "Stand aside," he warned. "I won't let you stop me."

"I recognize you, young Vantran," said the man. "From the Black City."

"You're one of Biagio's servants," guessed Richius. "Get out of the way. I mean to find your master."

"You won't find him," said the man. "He isn't here. But he left me behind to tell you that he's waiting for you."

"What?" spat Richius. "Where is that monster?"

"Gone," said the man. "I am Leraio, Count Biagio's manservant. The count has left for the Black City. You will not find him on Crote, King Vantran."

The news was staggering. Richius lowered his sword. "Son of a bitch," he muttered, not certain if he should believe the slave. "Why? Why has he left you here, then?"

Leraio frowned as he considered the question. "I suppose it suits his purposes. But I am not done with my message yet. There is more."

"Tell me," Richius demanded.

"Count Biagio wanted me to give you this." The slave reached into his vest and pulled out something white and unremarkable. Richius squinted to see it better.

"What is that?" he asked angrily.

Leraio came closer, dropping the item into Richius's hand. It was a lock of white hair, soft and short. Triin hair.

Richius puzzled over it for a moment. "Explain this," he said. "Whose hair is this?"

"Count Biagio has your wife, King Vantran. He has taken her back to Nar City. He requests that you—"

"No!" Richius grabbed the little man and pinned him against the wall. "That's impossible."

Leraio was remarkably calm, even with Richius strangling him. "It is true. She went searching for your child, the one called Shani. She was captured by Naren ships and brought here. I promise you, she is unharmed. For now."

Richius let go of the slave, staggering backward. "You're lying!" he spat.

"I am not," corrected Leraio.

The world around Richius swam with doubts. Was it possible? He rummaged over the floor, picking up the bits of hair where he'd dropped them. A quick run through his fingertips revealed the same silky softness as Dyana's hair. Hardly proof. But with Biagio, anything could have happened.

"He has her," Leraio promised. "He left last night aboard the *Fearless*. And he wants you to follow."

"My God," Richius groaned. As impossible as the tale sounded, Biagio was capable of anything. He turned and bolted out of the hall, screaming for help.

Prakna was racing back to the west wing when he heard Richius' cry. Vantran was in a panic, and when he saw Prakna the young man came to a skidding halt, hardly able to breathe. They were not far from the battle and the sounds were deafening. Prakna heard shattering glass and human screams, and the unmistakable din of metal on metal. He wondered desperately how his troops were faring.

"Richius!" Prakna shouted. "What's wrong?"

Richius was flushed with sweat. He took great panting breaths as he struggled to speak. "Dyana," he gasped. "He has her. . . ."

"Dyana?" blurted Prakna. "Your wife?"

"Biagio. He's taken her."

Prakna couldn't understand. "Take it easy, boy," he directed. "Breathe. And tell me what happened."

Richius struggled with every word, but Prakna managed to glean that Biagio had somehow taken Richius' wife to the Black City.

"God, Prakna, help me," begged Richius. "He'll kill her. I have to get to her."

Prakna listened to the fighting; he wanted to join the battle. "Richius, listen to me," he implored. "You go outside and stay safe. Hide yourself. When this is done, we'll find a way to get your wife."

"No!" Richius begged. "That's too late. We can catch them if we leave now. Biagio left aboard the *Fearless*, just last night."

Prakna felt himself turn white. The *Fearless*. Suddenly, all the noise in the world fell away. "How do you know that?" the Lissen asked. "Are you sure it's the *Fearless*?"

Richius nodded, still struggling to catch his breath. "Yes, I'm sure. Biagio's slave told me. They're not far, they couldn't be. Not yet. We can catch them, Prakna, aboard the *Prince*."

Prakna shook his head. "I can't. The others . . ."

"They can fight for themselves," roared Richius. "They don't need me or you. Please, Prakna, I'm begging you. Help me."

"Richius . . ."

"God-damn it, you owe me! You got me into this, you arrogant bastard! Now help me save my wife!"

"All right," said Prakna. "I'll take you."

Richius glanced around. "I want Simon," he said desperately. "Do you know where he is?"

"He's gone," said Prakna. "I'll explain later." He spun Richius around, facing him in the opposite direction of the murdered Naren. "Come on, we have to move."

Together they raced out of Biagio's embattled mansion, abandoning their bloodthirsty comrades and hurrying to reach the *Prince of Liss*. Prakna's heart soared. Finally, his chance had come to battle Nicabar. And as he ran, Prakna saw the faces of his two dead sons. Very soon, he would avenge them.

FORTY-FOUR

The Fearless

Ten nautical miles off the coast of Crote, Admiral Nicabar ordered the *Fearless* and her escorts to slow, beginning a long circling pattern that took them absolutely nowhere. They raised their sails halfway on the yards, catching less of the winter wind, and turned their rudders against the tide, tacking back and forth. A beautiful sun had risen on the watery horizon, painting the sea a glowing green. Biagio stood on the warship's forecastle, contemplating the dawn. To starboard and port, the *Black City* and the *Intruder* waited with the flagship, drifting aimlessly over the waves. The count liked the way the dreadnoughts looked in the morning sun. They were powerful, invincible. They would herald his return to the Empire. He kept his arms folded over his chest, huddling in his crimson cape. The wind was strong on deck and made his sensitive skin shiver. But he didn't want to go below. He wanted to see the *Prince* when she arrived.

It had taken Renato Biagio a long time to reach this moment. It had been a long and arduous climb, and it had taxed him dearly, requiring all his faculties. The strings he had pulled were long and treacherous. Not everything had gone perfectly. He had been betrayed by Simon and had resorted to the most violent methods to get Herrith to Crote, and his grand design had cost him his beloved homeland, at least for a while. He wouldn't be returning to Nar as a hero, either. He would have the politics of the army to deal with and assassinations to guard against.

And, of course, there was the Vantran woman. She was aboard, unwillingly, in her cabin below deck. Since she couldn't escape without going overboard, Biagio had left her unguarded. The count considered her for a moment, and the picture of her face brought a little smile to his face. She was very beautiful. He understood now why the Jackal had abandoned the Empire for her. Some women had that effect on men.

And some men, too.

Biagio's smile vanished. It made no sense that Simon had betrayed him. More, it pained him. At times he wanted to kill Simon—but he knew he never would. He wouldn't even hunt for him, or try to find out where he had gone. Perhaps Simon would go to Lucel-Lor with the Jackal. Or perhaps he would simply stay in the Empire, constantly looking over his shoulder. Roshann agents were good at hiding. Biagio sighed forlornly. If he'd had a flower, he would have thrown it into the ocean.

"Why the disappointment, Renato?" asked Nicabar suddenly. The admiral had appeared out of nowhere, shattering Biagio's mood. He had a smile splashed across his face, anticipating the coming battle.

"Just thinking, my friend," replied Biagio. "And waiting."

"Thinking about Herrith?"

Biagio smirked. "As little as possible."

"He beat the drug, you know," Nicabar observed. The admiral's brow furrowed. "He was stronger than I thought."

Stronger than me? Biagio wondered. For the first time, it seemed plausible. Originally, Biagio had thought the withdrawal would kill Herrith. Yet in the end, it seemed to have made him stronger. The fact that withdrawing was even possible intrigued the count.

"I do not want to speak of Herrith anymore," he said. "And we have the Lissens to deal with yet, don't forget."

Nicabar nodded, looking out in the direction of Crote. "They'll be here," he promised. "Prakna won't be able to resist."

"How soon?"

"Soon," said Nicabar. "The *Prince* is a fast ship." His smile widened. "But not fast enough. When she opens fire—"

"*If* she opens fire," Biagio interjected. "And not until she does. Control yourself, Danar. I want the Jackal on board first." Then, more mildly, he added, "Don't worry. The Lissens are too bloodthirsty to leave without a fight. You'll get your chance at Prakna. And after we return to Nar, I'll turn you loose on Liss."

Nicabar snorted. "I don't understand you anymore, Renato. You're not the man you used to be."

Biagio looked at his friend curiously. "No?" he asked. "Maybe not. Please do as I say, Danar. This one last time."

"I'll do it," promised Nicabar reluctantly. "I won't start anything until the Jackal is aboard." The admiral glanced across the deck. Then, "Renato," he said, pointing off toward the stern. "Look there."

Biagio followed Nicabar's finger and saw Dyana Vantran above deck, staring aimlessly over the ocean. A group of sailors milled around her, but Dyana seemed not to notice their glances. She merely watched the nothingness of the ocean, lost in a fugue. Biagio studied her. She was a curious creature, and he wasn't sure what he really thought of her. At first he had hated her, simply because she was the Jackal's wife. Now he sometimes surprised himself by liking her.

"Excuse me, Danar," said the count, then strode across the deck. The sailors parted like a curtain when they noticed him, scurrying back to their work. Biagio went to the railing beside Dyana. He saw her eyes flick toward him momentarily, then back out to sea, ignoring him. She wore a cape around her slight shoulders to stave off the cold, but Biagio could tell she was shivering.

"You should be below, out of the wind," he observed.

"Why have we stopped?"

Biagio thought before answering. "We're waiting."

Dyana nodded. "For Richius."

"Indeed."

She looked at him. "So this is how it ends, then? You will kill him here and now? No torture?"

The count smiled mildly, ignoring her insults. "Liss will send a schooner with him. We'll be here to greet it."

She glared at him, her gray eyes full of pain. "I hate you," she said. "I thought I could make you understand how wrong you are, but you are too insane to understand anything but revenge. And now . . ."

Her voice trailed off as she looked away. She pushed at him to leave her. "Go," she pleaded. "Leave me alone."

But Biagio wouldn't go. There was still a magic about her that enamored him, making him want to be near her. And it wasn't a lusty attraction, either. It was something else, maybe just her gentleness. Either way, Biagio couldn't leave her side.

"Nar will be mine soon," he said. "I will make changes in the Empire."

"Please . . ."

"Do not doubt me, Dyana Vantran," he warned. "Others have underestimated me before. Now they are dead."

"And you are proud of that?"

"My enemies deserved to die. They stole the Empire from me, when they knew it should have been mine. I am not a usurper. I am merely Nar's rightful heir. And when the Iron Throne is mine, there will be a change."

"Your Black Renaissance," spat Dyana. "Yes, I have heard of it. A madman's fantasy."

The count shook his head. "You understand so little, you and your husband both. The Black Renaissance brings peace to the Empire. There are no wars, no civil strife. I'll rule with an iron hand, because that is what an empire requires. You may think it cruel—"

"I think it is insane," Dyana argued. "Now go. Please. Leave me alone."

She turned from him and looked back at the horizon, refusing to acknowledge him, even as he stood there watching her. Finally, Biagio backed away.

"Make yourself ready. It won't be long," he said, then returned to the forecastle.

The *Prince of Liss* tore through the ocean in pursuit of the *Fearless*. She was three hours out of Crote with the sun high in front of her. Marus and the officers kept a tight leash on the men, trimming sails and spinning the wheel to make the most out of the wind. Great gusts filled the schooner's sails, speeding her along, and the cannoneers readied their weapons, preparing powder and shot. Richius stood with Prakna on the prow, spying the endless ocean before them. He was exhausted and full of dread, and the *Prince* simply couldn't go fast enough for him. His every thought was of Dyana, captured and at the mercy of Biagio. All sorts of wicked imaginings played in his mind. If he had hurt her . . .

"There!" cried Prakna, pointing northeast. Richius jumped at his shout. He tried to focus on a little speck bobbing on the horizon. A call came from the crow's nest, affirming the commander's call.

"It's them, Prakna," said Marus. The first officer had hurried up to his captain's side. "That's the *Fearless.*"

Prakna stared studiously through his spyglass. "Yes. And she's not alone. There are two other dreadnoughts with her." He paused, puzzling over the sight. "But they're hardly moving. *Fearless* has her sails pulled. What the hell is she up to?"

Richius understood instantly. "They're waiting for us," he said. "Biagio knew we'd come."

Prakna lowered his spyglass. His face was set in the most disquieting way. "The *Fearless*," he whispered. "Look at her, Marus."

"Aye, sir," the first officer replied. "She's a big bitch."

"Too much for us, do you think?"

Marus smiled. "Doesn't mean we shouldn't try."

"They won't make us fight them," said Richius. He was certain of Biagio's motives. "Biagio wants me. He's not going to open fire until he has me aboard. You can get away if I go to him."

Prakna shook his head. "Very brave, boy, but I'm not giving you up that easily. If Nicabar wants a fight, he'll get one."

"Prakna, please," Richius implored. "Don't open fire. You wouldn't stand a chance against them, and you know it. Just bring us in, and let's try to talk with them. Maybe I can get Dyana off the ship. Biagio might trade for her."

"You instead of your wife," said Marus darkly. "A sick trade."

Richius knew he had no choice. "If that's what it takes," he said. "I think Biagio might agree. It's me he wants, not Dyana."

"Very well, Jackal," said Prakna. "We'll get in closer. Let's see what the devil wants."

Dyana noticed the Lissen schooner just as the call came from the masts above. All along the deck of the warship, men made ready for the conflict. She heard the admiral barking orders and the strange creaking of metal monsters below her feet, where the gun deck held Nar's infamous flame cannons. Biagio flew to the ship's railing, pointing out the incoming ship.

"There she is!" he shouted. "The *Prince of Liss*." He shook his fist in victory. "I told you they'd come, Danar. I told you."

Admiral Nicabar wasn't listening. He was getting his ship into position, ordering it around to face the interloper. Dyana watched in confusion as sailors along the deck signaled the two other dreadnoughts with colored flags. The dreadnoughts signaled back, responding with shouts and movements of their own. Together the two ships broke their mindless pattern and slowly came into formation, flanking the flagship and turning their starboard guns toward the Lissen schooner. Dyana panicked.

"No!" she screeched, dashing along the deck toward Biagio. "Do not fire! Please!"

She grabbed a fistful of Biagio's cape and tugged wildly, fighting to make him listen. Biagio seized her wrist, almost lifting her off the ground.

"Let go, little beast!" he hissed. "I'm not going to fire unless I have to!"

He tossed her aside, sending her tumbling backward. She scrambled up again, refusing to be ignored.

"Listen to me," she begged. "Richius is no threat to you. You do not have to do this. Please!"

"Shut up, woman," Biagio snapped. "I can't hear myself think."

Dyana grabbed his hand, falling to her knees before him. "You want me to beg?" she asked angrily. "All right, then, I am begging. I am your prisoner. You have won. You have already beaten him." She stared up at him, hating herself for pleading. "Please, Biagio. Do not kill my husband."

Count Biagio looked down at her. For a moment she thought he would strike her, but there was no rage in his eyes. He took her hand, squeezing it with surprising gentleness.

"Do not beg me, Dyana Vantran," he insisted. "Rise."

He lifted her to her feet. Dyana trembled. Why didn't he *do* something?

"Count Biagio, please . . ."

"I'm going to call the Jackal aboard," he said. Then, without explanation, he turned his back on her and went to Admiral Nicabar.

Prakna piloted the *Prince* toward the waiting dreadnoughts, ordering her cannons moved to her port side. The starboard guns of the *Fearless* and her smaller sisters tracked the *Prince*'s movements as she slipped closer, still at full sail. They were barely a quarter mile away, and the three dreadnoughts grew in their vision, looking ominous. The Black Flag of Nar flew from their masts, stiff with wind. Richius waited on the *Prince*'s prow, cracking his knuckles nervously. A boat was descending off the side of the *Fearless*. In it were a handful of sailors. Richius couldn't tell exactly how many, but none of them looked like Dyana.

"What the hell's he doing?" wondered Prakna. "Sending over a launch?"

"It's for me," said Richius. "He wants me to come aboard."

"Well, you're not going," said Prakna. "Not just like that."

"Yes, I am. It's my decision, Prakna. Please don't try and stop me."

The fleet commander groaned. "All right. We'll have to get you closer, then."

He ordered his crew to slow them. The sailors responded with their usual precision, working the sails and yards until the schooner lost the wind and drifted toward the waiting dreadnoughts. But he made certain that his cannons were ready, ordering his gunners to stay alert.

Slowly the *Prince of Liss* approached the dreadnoughts, coming up alongside of them and matching their speed. Hardly a ship's length lay between them. The little launch struggled across the gap, rowed by four brawny seamen. Richius went amidships. Prakna and Marus followed like two older brothers. All the Lissen crewmen watched as Richius waited for the rowboat. He could feel their eyes boring through his back and wished suddenly that he had never left Lucel-Lor. Biagio had beaten him. Now, his only hope was that he could get Dyana free.

"Wait for my wife," he said to Prakna. "If Biagio lets her go, take her back to Lucel-Lor." He smiled awkwardly at the fleet commander. "Will you do that for me, Prakna?"

Prakna's hard face melted. "God, you honor me," he said sadly. "I am pleased to have known you, Richius Vantran."

"Will you, Prakna? Promise me. A real promise, this time."

"I can't make that promise, Jackal," said the Lissen. "Nicabar won't let me go. Even if your wife comes aboard, she would only die in the battle."

Richius knew Prakna was right. Nicabar's hatred of Prakna was legendary. And mutual. So he settled for shaking the commander's hand, and hoping that somehow, Biagio would let Dyana go.

"Good luck to you, Prakna," said Richius. The graveness of the moment seemed to erase the earlier events. Now they were just men again, rivals against Biagio. "Tell Jelena I'll be thinking about her."

"Richius," said Marus, gesturing over the rail. "The boat's here."

Richius looked down and saw that the rowboat had indeed reached the *Prince*. The four Naren sailors glanced up anxiously.

"Are you here for the Jackal?" Prakna called down to them angrily.

"We are," replied a sailor.

Marus gave the order to drop the rope ladder, then told the crew to slow the *Prince* to a standstill. Richius gazed down at the bobbing rowboat, so small and insignificant beside the grand schooner. A rush of fear overwhelmed him for a moment, but he subdued it quickly. In many ways, he had lived longer than he should have. Today, at last, his charm of protection had worn off.

With a final nod to his Lissen comrades, Richius straddled the rail and dropped over the side, catching the rope ladder and easing himself down toward the waiting Narens.

Biagio stood beside Nicabar, his heart thundering with anticipation. Across the gap between the *Fearless* and the *Prince*, the little rowboat they'd dispatched was returning with Richius Vantran. The Jackal sat up straight, scanning the deck for his wife. Dyana leaned over the railing, calling out to him with tears in her eyes.

"Richius!"

The Jackal saw his wife and smiled, holding out his hands as if to touch her. Biagio watched their reunion, astonished. Richius Vantran looked much as he had two years ago—dark and brash and far too young to have brought an empire to its knees. Seeing him made Biagio's jaw go slack. The count listened to Dyana's cries, wondering if he should silence her. But he did not. He let her call out to her husband.

The rowboat ground against the hull of the *Fearless*. Nicabar called down to his men, ordering them to get Vantran aboard. Dyana hurried over to him, shouldering Nicabar aside and reaching out to her distant husband.

Biagio stepped back, so as not to see their reunion. He heard the rope ladder fall and the sounds of his enemy climbing aboard. He was safe, certainly, and yet he feared the man coming toward him. Or rather, he feared seeing him. Richius Vantran was a potent reminder of all the things that had gone wrong in his life.

The first thing Richius saw when he looked up was Dyana's beautiful face. She was reaching down to him with tears in her eyes.

"Dyana!" Richius cried. He threw himself onto the warship's deck and into Dyana's waiting arms, ignoring all the sailors around him.

"Dyana," he moaned. Her smooth arms encircled him in a rapturous embrace, and he buried his nose in her hair, smelling its sweetness. She kissed him savagely, refusing to let go.

"Richius," she sighed, "I am all right. Do not worry. . . ."

He peeled her away and looked at her at arm's length, running his eyes over her perfect body and seeing that she was, indeed, all right.

"You're all right," he gasped. "You really are . . ."

Then he saw Biagio. The count had yet to step forward or say a word. Richius turned slowly toward his enemy, holding Dyana's hand. Biagio's golden face was lit with a strange fascination. He stared at Richius curiously, but remained remarkably hushed.

"I'm here," said Richius, trying to sound brave. He wondered if Biagio could see him trembling. "Now, let Dyana go."

Count Renato Biagio merely looked at Richius, his blue eyes sparkling with unnatural light, his amber skin beautiful. He was frightening to behold. Richius could barely stand the sight of him.

"Say something, you bastard," Richius demanded. "I'm here. Isn't that what you wanted?"

Biagio's eyes flicked toward Dyana for a brief second. Then he offered a dazzling smile. For the first time in years, Richius heard his treacly voice.

"Your wife says I have no quarrel with you, Jackal of Nar," said the count. "I wonder, what do you think?"

"Let her go, Biagio. You don't need her."

The count took a step closer, regarding Richius coldly, the way a scientist might stare at a specimen. "You haven't changed very much, Jackal. A bit older. Still the same arrogance, though. Perhaps that's what your wife loves so much."

The riddles enraged Richius. "Will you let her go or not?" he flared.

"I came aboard in an honorable exchange. Just for once, show the world you have some honor, too. Let Dyana go."

"First, answer my question," said the count. "What about our quarrel?"

"*Your* quarrel," replied Richius bitterly. "I never had one. All I wanted was to save Dyana. That's why I left Nar." He grit his teeth, trying to contain his rage. "And that's why you killed Sabrina. God, I hate you, monster."

Biagio laughed. "That is the second time today I've heard that," he mocked. "But continue, please. Have you no quarrel with me at all?"

"I would kill you if I could," said Richius, meaning every word. "But I give myself to you instead. Let Dyana go. I won't fight you."

"And if I let you both go free?" asked Biagio. "What then?"

Richius was stunned. So was Dyana. She let go of Richius, taking a step forward.

"What are you saying?" she asked. "Would you let us go?"

Count Biagio's face was impossibly serene. His expression brightened when he looked at her.

"You have given me much to think about, Dyana Vantran. Perhaps I owe you something in return."

"Don't play with us," Richius growled. He took a step toward the count, only to be halted by Nicabar's sailors, who grabbed at his coat and dragged him backward. But Biagio raised a hand to them, making them release Richius. Richius looked around, unsure what was happening.

"A trick," he sneered. "Dyana, don't believe him."

Biagio ignored him. "Lady Vantran, I offer you back your wretched husband. You're free to leave."

"What?" blurted Nicabar. "Renato, what are you doing?"

"Repaying a debt, Danar," replied the count lightly. He reached out and took Dyana's hand, then gave it a gentle kiss. Richius couldn't believe his eyes.

"Why?" he gasped. "I don't understand."

Count Biagio turned and went to him. "You have a remarkable wife," he said with soft anger. "This favor is for her, not you."

"Biagio, if this is a trick . . ."

"It is no trick, Vantran," said Biagio. "I have an empire to rule now. I cannot entertain myself with trifles like you any longer."

Richius was astounded. "That's it? You're letting us go? After all you've done?"

"Biagio," said Dyana, coming up to him. "Look at me."

The count obeyed. Dyana studied his face. After a moment, she slowly nodded.

"I believe you," she said. "But why?"

Biagio scoffed, straightening proudly. "Count Biagio does not explain himself," he said gruffly. "And Jackal, know this—our quarrel is done. Do not try to seek your revenge on me again. If you do, I will most certainly kill you."

Richius was speechless.

"Go in peace," Biagio added. "Keep your hands off of Nar, and I will keep mine off Lucel-Lor. Are we agreed?"

"Yes, but . . ."

"Good," smiled the count. "You are a cagey opponent, Richius Vantran. It has been interesting dueling with you. But I'm tired of it now. Please leave me alone."

"You do the same," said Richius. "Then we will have a bargain."

Biagio rubbed his hands together, grinned wickedly, then said to Dyana, "Farewell, Lady Vantran. We will not be seeing each other anymore. But you were a graceful guest. I will miss you."

Dyana put a hand to her mouth. "Thank you," she gasped. "Thank you."

"The boat will take you to the *Black City*. From there you'll be brought back to the Lissens on Crote."

"What?" flared Richius. "Take us back to the *Prince*!"

"I cannot," said Biagio. "It wouldn't be safe for you there." He glanced at his admiral. "Danar, *Black City* and *Intruder* can escort them back to the Lissens, can't they?"

"I suppose," replied Nicabar. "But, Renato, I don't understand. . . ."

Biagio smiled. "You will," he said lightly. Then, to Richius and Dyana, "Go now. And do not trouble me again, Jackal."

Astonished, Richius wondered what Biagio had planned for Prakna. But he realized also that he had just struck a remarkable bargain with the count, one that might evaporate without warning. So he took Dyana's hand and led her quickly off the *Fearless*, accompanied by a sailor who would explain Biagio's orders to the captain of the *Black City*. Before she descended the rope ladder, Dyana gave a last lingering look at the inscrutable man of gold. Then she followed Richius into the rowboat, as amazed as her husband to still be alive.

Prakna watched in mute fascination as the little boat left the *Fearless* with Richius and his wife aboard—then set off in the wrong direction. She was headed toward the lead dreadnought, the one just behind the *Fearless* on her port side. Prakna stared at the rowboat uncertainly. He could see Richius standing up in the boat, shouting and waving his arms wildly.

"What's he saying?" Prakna asked.

Beside him, Marus studied the goings-on through a spyglass. "He's waving us off," said the first officer. "I think he wants us to go."

"Go? Go where?"

Marus shrugged. "I don't know. Maybe Biagio set them free."

"And sent them to another dreadnought? What for?"

Even as he left the rowboat and climbed up the side of dreadnought, Richius continued shouting at them. With his free hand he went on waving, trying to signal them. Prakna let out a frustrated curse. What was Vantran saying?

"Shall we move off?" asked Marus. "They have him. If they're not letting him go, we won't be able to get him back."

Prakna considered the option. He waited a very long time before answering, long enough to see the two rear dreadnoughts unfurl their sails again and pick up the wind, pulling away from the *Fearless*. But the big flagship still made no moves. Prakna snatched the spyglass from Marus and scanned her deck. He saw Nicabar on board, scowling at them.

"That whoreson," Prakna rumbled. "He's waiting for us."

On the forecastle of his giant ship, Admiral Nicabar watched his nemesis across the narrow gap, impatiently hoping that she'd open fire. Even without the protection of *Black City* and *Intruder*, he knew the *Fearless* could devour the *Prince*. Biagio stood beside him, tapping his foot impatiently. The insipid noise did nothing to break the admiral's steely concentration.

"Ready, my friend?" asked the count.

Nicabar nodded. "Yes, thank you."

"It's nothing," quipped Biagio. "I just thought it was time I paid you back, as well. You've been very loyal, Danar. I appreciate that."

The admiral smiled. It had been a great gamble to side with Biagio against Herrith, but now his bet was paying off. He balled his hands into fists, anticipating the coming battle. If he knew Prakna as well as he thought, the fleet commander wouldn't run from the fight.

"He's baiting me," said Prakna. "He wants me to fight him."

The deck of the *Prince* had gone quiet. Sailors stood ready, awaiting their captain's orders. Marus leaned against the rail beside Prakna, both of them considering their options. Nicabar was giving them a chance to turn and run. Or a chance to land the first blow.

"We could leave," Marus suggested.

Prakna nodded. "Aye. We could."

They looked at each other. Two men who had served together for years, who had both lost sons to the devils of Nar, gazed deeply into each other's eyes and saw the same restless need for vengeance.

"Or we could fight," said Marus.

Prakna clasped his comrade's shoulder. A lot of people had died today. In the great scheme of things, a few more hardly seemed to matter. And for Prakna and his crew, it was the difference between living like sheep or dying like lions.

"Give me full sails, Marus," said Prakna. "I want speed."

When he saw the *Prince* unfurl her sails, Biagio frowned, surprised that he had been wrong. "They're moving off," he said incredulously. "They're not fighting."

"No," replied Nicabar, blackly jubilant. "They're just giving themselves some room to maneuver." The admiral turned to his waiting lieutenants, shouting orders down the line. "Full sails!" he cried. "Bring us five degrees starboard. Don't let them out of our sights. And tell the gun deck to stand by."

The warship sprang to life, lurching forward as the endless yards of silk sails ate up the wind. The *Fearless* banked gently starboard, still paralleling the *Prince*. Nicabar knew she had put all her mobile cannons on her port side. She wouldn't waste time trying to turn.

"Renato, you might want to go below," the admiral suggested. "It's about to get damn noisy up here."

Prakna stood amidships on the *Prince*, waiting near the cannons. His crew had primed the guns with grapeshot and had aimed them at the *Fearless*' masts, hoping to tear her sails. The *Prince* was picking up speed, trying to pull away from the dreadnought. Surprisingly, the other two dreadnoughts had kept back so not to join the fight. Prakna considered the move respectfully. Nicabar knew he already outgunned the schooner. Anything more than the *Fearless* would have been gratuitous, and not really worth bragging about.

"And so we go down," sang Prakna softly, remembering the lines to a sailors' poem. "To the bottom far, far below."

Prakna knew his vessel had no chance at all, but he didn't really care. He was prepared now to die. So was his crew. Today they had struck a blow for Lissen freedom. Today was a good day to go to the bottom. He hoped J'lari would understand.

Because her cannons didn't have the reach of the Naren guns, the *Prince* would have to fire early, hopefully damaging the *Fearless* and slowing her. But the *Fearless* had guns on both sides, while the *Prince*'s were already committed to port. The fleet commander wondered how much damage four good shots could do to the black behemoth.

He gave the order to fire.

The flash from the *Prince*'s deck caught Nicabar by surprise. He hadn't expected it to come so early. But he didn't bother to duck. He knew Prakna's targets were the sails. A great, fiery eruption exploded overhead as the grapeshot from the *Prince* burned the foremast, chewing at its sails. Nicabar surveyed the damage, impressed with the aim. He knew Prakna's crew were preparing another volley. A few more similar shots would slow the *Fearless* to a crawl. And the *Prince* was too quick to let go easily. A piece of burning silk fell down onto his shoulder, singeing his coat. Nicabar batted it away with a growl. Off the starboard bow, he saw the *Prince* pulling away as her crew worked diligently to cram another round of powder and shot into her guns.

"Lieutenant R'Jinn," shouted Nicabar. "Return fire."

R'Jinn cried the order. The command quickly ricocheted down to the gun deck. Nicabar felt the wood beneath his feet rumble. He stuck his fingers into his ears, waiting for the concussion.

Three long-barreled flame cannons opened up. Fire flew across the water, rocking the *Fearless* and blowing apart the morning. Nicabar waited for the smoke to clear, then saw the *Prince* enveloped in flames. She was still moving away from them, burning but intact.

Nicabar ordered continuous fire.

Prakna scrambled across the deck of the *Prince*, rallying his men. The first blast from the *Fearless* had torn away the stunsail and a big chunk of the prow. The *Prince*'s cannons opened up again, returning fire and catching the dreadnought amidships. More of the Naren's sails caught flame. Prakna ordered his ship hard about, steering her away to narrow her profile. But even the *Prince of Liss* couldn't outrun the Naren guns. They opened up in a non-stop volley, one by one hammering at her hull. The whole world turned orange. Prakna's breath burned in his lungs. He choked up a ball of blood, stumbling through the haze. Another shot crashed against the hull, blasting a hole in it. The *Prince* began listing to port as water flooded her holds.

It was over before it had really begun. Prakna searched the burning chaos for Marus, but couldn't find his friend. He craned his neck to see, forgetting the battle, wanting to die near his first officer.

One more shot from the *Fearless* blew him off the deck, scattering pieces of him over the ocean.

• • •

Richius and Dyana watched the carnage from the deck of the *Black City*, covering their ears to shut out the bombardment. Dyana huddled close to Richius, her head against his chest, blinking in disbelief as she witnessed the awesome firepower of the Empire. The *Prince of Liss* was quickly being incinerated. Constant volleys from the *Fearless* had tattered her sails to burning husks and excavated a giant hole in her hull. She limped over the waves, directionless, letting her giant rival pummel her. It was hopeless for Prakna and Marus and the rest of them. The ship that had been their home and greatest love was suddenly an inferno. The *Prince* sent up huge plumes of fiery smoke, opaquing the horizon. The *Fearless* hammered her ceaselessly. Somewhere on the dreadnought's deck, Richius knew, Nicabar was crowing, pleased with himself for finally vanquishing his old nemesis.

And Biagio was with him. Biagio the mystery, who had somehow puppeteered an entire empire into his palm. As Richius watched the *Prince of Liss* fade to ashes, he thought about the ruthless Count of Crote, and all the fears he had engendered. Biagio had reached across a continent and snatched a baby from its parents. He had somehow convinced his greatest enemy to come to Crote and be murdered. He was a great and powerful enigma, and Richius knew he would never fully understand him, or why he had let Dyana go free. Richius lowered a hand from his ear and stroked Dyana's hair, kissing her. She was a remarkable woman, his wife, extraordinary enough to make any man think twice—even Biagio.

The *Prince of Liss* slowly began to sink like a burning sun.

FORTY-FIVE

Outcast

Simon ran from Biagio's mansion, racing like the wind.

He ran until he thought his heart would burst, seeking cover where he could, and never looking back at the massacre taking place at his master's former home. And when Simon could not go on, when his muscles screamed with fatigue and all his body burned with pain, he stopped running. It was late morning. Biagio's mansion was far behind him, but the news of the Lissen invasion had already swept through Crote. Simon had made it to the town of Galamier, where he had grown up. The fishing village was aghast at the sight of Lissen schooners on their shores. Already fleets of scows were abandoning Crote, desperately fleeing to the mainland. And Simon, who still had his wits about him despite the shocking morning, found his way onto one of them.

The sun was overhead as the little vessel slipped away from Crote, going unnoticed by the Lissen invaders. She was smelly and packed with panicked people, and the owner of the boat urged them all to keep calm, shouting above the sea and the cries of children. But Simon didn't need to be yelled at. He was already perfectly calm. His Roshann-trained mind had focused on survival.

On the horizon he watched Crote float away. Something told him that Biagio had already fled. Richius wouldn't find him. Simon knew it instinctively. Biagio was already safe. Somewhere.

Simon forgot his seasickness. In his mind was a vision of Eris, dancing across her practice floor. The memory was flawless. Eris had been very beautiful. Simon pulled her dancing shoes out of his pocket. A girl standing next to him eyed the shoes curiously. Simon smiled to her, then tossed the shoes overboard. The girl blinked.

"You don't want them," he told her. "They're tainted."

Everything was tainted now. But it was no more than he deserved, Simon supposed. If the fishing boat made it to the mainland, Simon planned to flee to Doria. He would go underground, just as he had hoped to do with Eris. He was still Roshann. There were tricks he could use to avoid being discovered. Even Biagio wouldn't find him.

After a life of spying and assassinations, Simon wondered what it would be like to be a farmer. Perhaps he would work as a stable hand, or try to find employment in a coopery. Dorians often hired mercenaries, but Simon sniffed at the notion. He had already thrown his dagger overboard, too. Convinced that he had spent enough time killing, he decided to forgo such bloody employment. Simon Dark-Heart was dead.

"Hello," he said to the little girl next to him. "What's your name?"

"Numa," replied the child. "What's yours?"

Simon considered the question. "Simon," he told her. "Simon Jadiir."

In the tongue of Vosk, where his mother had been born, the name meant "barrel-maker."

FORTY-SIX

Emperor

After destroying the *Prince of Liss*, the *Fearless* waited before returning to the Black City. Because he wanted the protection of additional ships, Biagio arranged a rendezvous off the Naren coast, finally sailing into the city's harbor four days after leaving Crote. Accompanying the *Fearless* was a contingent of ships recalled from battling the Lissens, including the dreadnoughts *Shark* and *Intruder*, and the cruisers *Conqueror*, *Angel of Death* and *Furious*. Together they dominated the harbor, and all Naren eyes fell on them and wondered if the world was coming to an end.

Count Biagio knew he had many enemies in Nar. But he had already annihilated the bulk of them. Kivis Gago, Claudi Vos, and all the others who had so foolishly aligned themselves with Herrith were dead now, fallen under Lissen scimitars. The Naren Empire was leaderless, completely. And the people of Nar, who had never been able to function without a strong ruler, looked on the arriving Count of Crote with apprehension.

Biagio explained to them how Liss, their great enemy, had invaded his homeland during the peace talks, savagely murdering the other Naren noblemen. Because he had barely escaped with his life, there had been no way for him to save the others. And Liss was on the prowl, he told the citizens of Nar, and had sinister designs on the Empire. With the Lissens firmly on Crote, only the Black Fleet could protect Nar City now.

There would be politics and enemies still, Biagio knew—and maybe feeble attempts on his life, which would all certainly fail—but he was home again and immensely happy, and when he sat himself down on Arkus' Iron Throne, an unimaginable thrill went through him.

He was emperor.

He had struggled for the title, as Nar would struggle, still. Herrith had left him a land in strife. Like the rubble of the great cathedral, the Empire needed rebuilding. Goth was a wasteland, and Dragon's Beak was torn by civil war, as ambitious lords scrambled to fill the void left by the twin dukes. All across the fractured land, kings and princes questioned the authority of the capital, wondering what Biagio and his new Black Renaissance might bring. And rumblings out of Talistan were worrisome, too, as King Tassis Gayle made very clear his feelings about the foppish new emperor.

But Biagio had time. Time, at least, to rest. Tomorrow there might be war, but today he had won the Iron Throne. For him, that was enough.

After a week as emperor, Renato Biagio called a meeting of his Roshann agents, a secret gathering that took place in the highest tower of the Black Palace. A winter wind ripped through the walls, chilling the air and sending the great hearth into ripples. A giant, circular table rested in the center of the chamber, seating Roshann members from around the Black City and the outlying Empire, all of whom still adored their master and loudly reaffirmed their pledges to serve him until death. Emperor Biagio thanked them all with gold and kisses, and gave them lands for their loyalty and the beautiful slaves he had purchased with the remains of his private fortune.

After rewarding them, Biagio turned to business. He had only two remarkable orders for them. The Jackal of Nar was never to be hunted again. Neither was Simon Darquis. The peculiar command made the agents murmur, but none of them questioned the edict or looked disapprovingly at Biagio. He was their master; that was all that mattered.

After their meeting, Biagio returned to his quarters. He had set himself up in the old rooms Arkus had enjoyed, with a peerless view of the magnificent city and all the old emperor's clutter around him. The trinkets and baubles connected Biagio to Arkus, and he liked the memories they evoked. At last, his grief was fading.

And Biagio thought of Dyana Vantran often too, and the things she had said to him. Her scathing accusations had started the new emperor thinking. He wondered how true it was that the drug had warped his mind.

Biagio sat alone by his window, well past midnight, contemplating these things. The wind howled around the tall tower. There was much for him to do, and Nar needed him sound. It had been over a week since he had taken the drug, and his cravings were enormous. But he knew that Herrith and Vorto had both been able to endure the withdrawal, and he was determined not to be bested.

FORTY-SEVEN

The Jackal at Rest

The Naren dreadnought *Black City* had indeed returned Richius and Dyana to Crote, leaving them off where the Lissen schooners could not see them. From there they walked across the tiny island, astonished at the things they'd seen.

The Lissens had devoured Crote. It was theirs now, just as Prakna and Jelena had always wanted, the perfect base from which to continue their violent mission against the Empire. The slaughter had not stopped at the mansion, but rather had carried over to the surrounding farmlands and villages, until at last the army of orphans had come to their senses and began occupying Crote without killing it. Richius supposed Shii had something to do with their change of heart. He had seen her before leaving, aboard a Lissen schooner. She looked vacant and afraid and not at all young, and Richius knew she had murdered her youth during the campaign, trading it for vengeance.

A Lissen schooner with the dubious name *The Dolphin* took Richius and Dyana back to Lucel-Lor. It was an uncomfortable journey. The Lissen sailors mostly avoided Richius, embarrassed that they had betrayed him. Apparently, "Lord Jackal" no longer existed. He was merely Richius Vantran again—not a king, and certainly not a hero. And when at last he and Dyana arrived at Falindar, the world seemed a wholly different place.

Falindar smelled a little sweeter than it had. The winter was cold and the wine was strong, and Dyana and Shani were happy again. And

Lucyler had returned from Kes. The master of the citadel was no less preoccupied than when he'd left. There was still trouble brewing between the warlords Ishia and Praxtin-Tar, and Lucyler worried endlessly about the tenuous peace he had arranged. But Richius didn't think about those things. He thought only about being alive and about his miraculous luck, which continued to save him from death. He didn't want to be troubled any longer with talk of war. More than ever in his life, he craved peace. Even Aramoor seemed a distant memory. It was lost to him, that was certain, and he had no plans to break his bargain with Biagio. The Empire was Biagio's now. And Richius had all of Lucel-Lor to occupy him. He would make his life here, among the Triin.

Or die trying.

A week after returning to Falindar, Richius set off with Lucyler to hunt and came upon the place where he and Simon had felled the ancient oak. It was just a stump now. The grass around it was trampled and littered with snapped branches. Richius recalled the tree with melancholy. It had been remarkable. At the time, he had not understood Simon's hatred of it. He lowered his bow as he stared at the stump, wondering about Simon. Prakna had told him that Simon had fled the mansion. Apparently, Eris had been killed. Now no one knew where Simon was, or even if he was alive.

Richius sat down on the stump, forgetting the hunt, and invited Lucyler to sit beside him. His Triin friend relaxed gladly, weary from stalking through the woods. Neither spoke for a very long time. Lucyler had the gift of silence. He hadn't even asked Richius the obvious, impossible questions, like why he'd gone to Liss and abandoned his wife and child, and why he had been so profoundly unhappy in Falindar. And he wouldn't ask, either. Lucyler knew Richius' heart well enough.

Then, after several long minutes, Lucyler finally spoke.

"Cold," he remarked.

Richius nodded. "Yes." The cold felt good. It reminded him of Aramoor.

"Ishia worries," said Lucyler. "I do not know what I should do."

Another impossible question. Richius shrugged. "Is it really your concern?"

"I am Master of Falindar," replied Lucyler. "These things are expected of me." He sighed. The light caught his eyes, revealing sadness. "I am riding a wildcat, and I cannot control it. Praxtin-Tar is a madman."

Richius grimaced. He'd had his fill of madmen recently.

"The warlords need to fight, I think," Lucyler continued. "I am not sure I can stop them."

"If it's their nature to kill, you won't be able to stop them, Lucyler. Don't kill yourself in the process."

The Triin gave a black laugh. "Is that your wisdom now, my friend? Is that what you've learned? I could use more than silly prophecy."

"That's all I've got these days."

"I was thinking that perhaps you would come with me to speak with Praxtin-Tar," said Lucyler. "He remembers you from the Naren war. He knows that Tharn respected you. If you speak to him, he might listen."

"No," said Richius. "He will not listen."

"You are so sure? You should try, at least."

Richius shook his head. "Sorry."

"You will not do it?"

"Can't do it," said Richius absently.

The promise he had made to Biagio extended past the borders of Nar. It was a promise to himself, really. As Lucyler watched him questioningly, Richius studied the sky, enjoying its grace. Suddenly the sky seemed more important than anything.

ABOUT THE AUTHOR

JOHN MARCO lives on Long Island, New York, where he was born and raised. He is a fan of military history and a long-time reader of fantasy literature. Since the publication of his first novel, *The Jackal of Nar,* he has been writing fiction full time. He is currently at work on the next book in the Tyrants and Kings series.